*Everyman, I will go with thee,
and be thy guide*

THE EVERYMAN
LIBRARY

*The Everyman Library was founded by J. M. Dent
in 1906. He chose the name Everyman because he wanted
to make available the best books ever written in every
field to the greatest number of people at the cheapest possible
price. He began with Boswell's 'Life of Johnson';
his one-thousandth title was Aristotle's 'Metaphysics',
by which time sales exceeded 40 million.*

*Today Everyman paperbacks remain true to
J. M. Dent's aims and high standards, with a wide range
of titles at affordable prices in editions which address
the needs of today's readers. Each new text is reset to give
a clear, elegant page and to incorporate the latest thinking
and scholarship. Each book carries the pilgrim logo,
the character in 'Everyman', a medieval mystery play,
a proud link between Everyman
past and present.*

Harriet Beecher Stowe

UNCLE TOM'S CABIN

and

Frederick Douglass

NARRATIVE OF THE LIFE OF FREDERICK DOUGLASS, AN AMERICAN SLAVE

Edited by
CHRISTOPHER BIGSBY
University of East Anglia

EVERYMAN
J. M. DENT · LONDON
CHARLES E. TUTTLE
VERMONT

Introduction and other critical apparatus
© J. M. Dent 1993
First published in Everyman's Library in 1993

All rights reserved
Photoset by Cambridge Composing (UK) Ltd
Cambridge

Printed in Great Britain by
The Guernsey Press Co. Ltd Guernsey, C.I. for
J. M. Dent
Orion Publishing Group
Orion House
5 Upper St Martin's Lane, London WC2H 9EA
and
Charles E. Tuttle Co. Inc.
28 South Main Street,
Rutland, Vermont 05701, USA

ISBN 0 460 87139 0

CONTENTS

NOTE ON THE AUTHORS AND EDITOR

HARRIET ELIZABETH BEECHER STOWE, American author and reformer, was born in Litchfield, Connecticut, on 14 June 1811. She was one of nine children born to the Presbyterian clergyman and seminarian, Lyman Beecher (1775–1863), and his first wife Roxana Foote Beecher. Harriet, like her brothers and sisters, many of whom were to be noted preachers in their own right, was profoundly influenced by her father's orthodox (Calvinistic) theology which offered a formulaic approach to salvation. For Harriet the struggle for Salvation was intimately connected with her concurrent struggle to find her own identity in a family of dominant and strong personalities.

In 1832 she moved to Cincinnati to work as a teacher with her sister Catherine at the Western Female Institute. Four years later she married Professor Calvin Stowe. During the next sixteen or so years before the publication of *Uncle Tom's Cabin*, life was not easy for Harriet who was mentally and physically drained by being a 'homemaker', a freelance writer, and a mother to seven children. A collection of Harriet's short stories, *The Mayflower*, was published in 1843. The publication of *Uncle Tom's Cabin*, in 1852, marked a high point in her writing career and her life. Before the publication she had been known as a writer of temperance tales and sketches on Puritan life, but almost overnight she became a worldwide celebrity and her novel a cultural phenomenon which in popularity and influence has never been equalled. Her *Key to Uncle Tom's Cabin* (1853) was published as a response to criticisms that the novel was sentimental and lacked verisimilitude. Her next novel, *Dred: A Tale of the Great Dismal Swamp*, (1856) was an attempt to initiate reform in the South while also addressing the moral problems of abolition – the novel's weaknesses reflected Harriet's own uncertainty about slavery.

Harriet's aesthetic of ambivalence, which had developed and matured in the struggle to reconcile the New England tradition with the modern movements of suffragettism and emancipation, controlled the composition of her New England historical novels *The Minister's Wooing* (1859), *The Pearl of Orr's Island* (1862), *Oldtown Folks* (1869) and *Poganuc People* (1878). Her popularity suffered a blow after the publication of an article, *Lady Byron Vindicated*. She was again involved in public controversy in the 1870s when her brother Henry Ward Beecher, a prominent theologian, was accused of adultery involving Elizabeth Tilton.

Harriet died in 1896 after a long career as a professional writer and reformer, remembered not only as the author of *Uncle Tom's Cabin*, which had influenced so many people, but as a Christian feminist whose 'rebellion of the heart' had encouraged women to find Salvation in the home.

FREDERICK DOUGLASS was born, to the best of his knowledge, at Holm Hill Farm on Tuckahoe Creek, Talbot County, Maryland, on St Valentine's Day 1818, the son of a slavewoman and a white man. Over the years his life has become examplary not only for the Afro-American community (as a founding father), but for many Americans.

From very early on, Frederick Augustus Washington Bailey, as he was named by his mother, showed exceptional talents which set him apart from other slave children. After the death of his mother in 1825, Frederick was removed to Hugh Auld's family in Baltimore. There he was taught to read by his master's wife. The account of his life up until his escape in 1838 is covered in his first full-length publication, *Narrative of Frederick Douglass an American Slave*.

After his escape Douglass joined the Anti-Slavery movement, and within a very short time established himself as the leading black Abolitionist, drawing crowds wherever he lectured. With the publication of *The Narrative* in 1845, which became a bestseller, came greater fame. He sailed to Britain in the same year where he was lionised and his speeches reported in many newspapers. The laws of the United States meant that although he had escaped he was still legally a slave but this fact, together with his eloquence, won him the sympathy of the British who paid Hugh Auld £150 for Douglass's manumission in 1846.

Upon his return to the United States, now a free man, Douglass continued to crusade for the emancipation of blacks. In 1847 he started his own newspaper, the *North Star* (renamed

Frederick Douglass's Paper in 1851), in Rochester New York. He became a firm supporter of the Women's Movement after attending the Women's Rights Convention held in New York. A Christian, he converted in 1831, Douglass broke with William Lloyd Garrison over the latter's political and atheistic approach to the campaign. One year after the publication of *My Bondage and My Freedom* (1855), another autobiographical work, Douglass endorsed the Republican presidential candidate.

His later involvement with John Brown and the attack on Harper's Ferry meant he had to flee to Canada and from there he sailed to England again. Three years after returning to the United States he helped the North with their recruitment drive by encouraging blacks to enlist. In 1864 he endorsed Lincoln in his re-election campaign. Douglass bought the Washington-based *New Nation Era* in 1870. He held various posts under different administrations, was appointed United States Marshal and later recorder of deeds for the District of Columbia, minister resident and consul general to Haiti, and finally commissioner of the Haitian exhibit at the World Fair in Chicago. He published his third autobiography, *Life and Times of Frederick Douglass* in 1881.

Douglass died of a heart attack in Washington DC on 20 February 1895.

CHRISTOPHER BIGSBY, Professor of American Studies at the University of East Anglia, is the author of more than twenty books on aspects of American culture. He has written on the literary achievement of Afro-Americans (*The Black American Writer; The Second Black Renaissance*); on popular culture (*Superculture; Approaches to Popular Culture*); and on the American theatre (*Confrontation and Commitment; A Critical Introduction to 20th Century American Drama; American Drama: 1945–1990*). His books include studies of Edward Albee and David Mamet, an edition of the plays of Susan Glaspell and a collection of original essays by actors, directors, playwrights and critics called *Arthur Miller and Company*.

Christopher Bigsby is a regular broadcaster with BBC radio and television and is the author and co-author of several radio and television plays. In 1994 he published *Hester*, a prequel to *The Scarlet Letter*. He is also the Director of the Arthur Miller Centre for American Studies. He lives in Norwich, England.

CHRONOLOGY OF HARRIET BEECHER STOWE'S LIFE

Year	Age	Life
	1811	Harriet Elizabeth Beecher is born 14 June in Litchfield, Connecticut, the daughter of Lyman and Roxana Foote Beecher
1813	2	Henry Ward Beecher b.
1816	5	Death of Roxana Beecher
1818	7	Lyman Beecher marries Harriet Porter
1824–27	13–16	Attends Hartford Female Seminary, funded by her older sister Catherine
1825	14	Harriet experiences a religious conversion after hearing one of her father's sermons. Attends her first communion service
1827	16	Becomes full-time teacher at Hartford Female Seminary
1832	21	Moves to Cincinnati with the Beecher family; her father becomes president of Lane Theological Seminary and pastor of the second presbyterian church. Harriet teaches in the Western Female Institute which had been established by Catherine Beecher
1833	22	Co-author with Catherine Beecher of *A Primary Geography for Children*
1834	23	Writes short stories, some of which are published in Cincinatti's *Western Monthly Magazine*
1836	25	Marries Calvin Stowe, a Professor of Biblical Literature at Lane who had been the husband of Harriet's late friend, Eliza Tyler Stowe (d. 1835). Harriet gives birth to twin girls, Harriet and Eliza
1837	26	Harriet and Calvin help their Negro servant, a fugitive slave, to escape via the underground railroad
1838	27	Henry Ellis Stowe b.
1839	28	Publishes stories in various national periodicals, including *Godey's Lady Book*
1840	29	Frederick William Stowe b.

Year	Age	Life
1843	32	Georgiana May Stowe b. *The Mayflower; or, Sketches of Scenes and Characters among the Descendants of the Pilgrims* published
1845	34	Pro-Abolitionist Essay 'Immediate Emancipation' is published
1846	35	Takes the water-cure at a spa in Brattleboro, Vermont
1849	38	Samuel Charles Stowe b. but dies in a cholera epidemic. Harriet is deeply affected by his death. Calvin Stowe is appointed Professor of Natural and Revealed Religion at Bowdoin College, Brunswick, Maine. The family moves there in 1850
1850	39	Publishes stories in the *National Era*, an Abolitionist paper in Washington, DC. Charles Stowe b.
1851	40	*Uncle Tom's Cabin; or, Life among the Lowly,* published in installments in the *National Era*
1852	41	*Uncle Tom's Cabin* appears as a book, published by J. P. Jewett in Boston. Within the year 300,000 copies are sold. The Stowes move to Andover, Massachusetts, where Calvin becomes Professor of Sacred Literature at Andover Theological Seminary
1853	42	*A Key to Uncle Tom's Cabin,* a verification of the facts in the novel, published. The Stowes tour Europe
1854	43	*Sunny Memories of Foreign Lands* published
1856	45	*Dred: A Tale of the Great Dismal Swamp* published by Philips Sampson in Boston. Second trip abroad
1857	46	Henry Stowe, her son, drowns
1859	48	*The Minister's Wooing* published. Third European trip
1862	51	*The Pearl of Orr's Island* and *Agnes of Sorrento* published by Ticknor and Fields in Boston. Meets with President Lincoln
1863	52	The Stowes move to Hartford. Calvin Stowe retires. *A Reply to the Women of England in Behalf of the Women of America* published. Harriet's father, Lyman Beecher, dies
1865	54	*House and Home Papers* written under the pseudonym of Christopher Crowfield
1869	58	*Oldtown Folks* published by Fields, Osgood in Boston. Co-author with Catherine Beecher of *The American Woman's Home*
1870	59	*Lady Byron Vindicated* published
1871	60	Two domestic or social novels: *My Wife and I* and *Pink and White Tyranny* published

Year	Age	Life
1872	61	*Old Town Fireside Stories* published
1873	62	*Palmetto-Leaves* and *Women in Sacred History* published
1875	64	*We and Our Neighbors* (sequel to *My Wife and I*). Supports her brother Henry Ward Beecher when he is accused of adultery with a member of his congregation, Elizabeth Tilton
1878	67	*Poganuc People* (New York: Fords, Howard, & Hubert) published
1882	71	A reception is given by publishers, Houghton, Mifflin and Company of Boston, to celebrate Harriet's seventieth birthday
1884	73	*Our Famous Women* published
1886	75	Calvin Stowe dies
1896	85	Harriet dies on 1 July from a stroke

CHRONOLOY OF
FREDERICK DOUGLASS'S LIFE

Year	Age	Life
1818		b. Frederick Augustus Washington Bailey in February (Douglass assumed it was the 14th) at Holm Hill Farm on Tuckahoe Creek, Talbot County Maryland
1824	6	Moved to Lloyd Plantation, Wye River, the residence of Aaron Anthony
1825	7	His mother dies
1826	8	Serves as Hugh Auld's houseboy in Fells area of Baltimore. Death of Aaron Anthony, his first master and possible father
1827	9	Anthony's estate is divided among his heirs. Frederick is inherited by Thomas Auld. Frederick returns to Hugh Auld and is taught to read by his wife Sophia
1830		
1831	13	Experiences a religious conversion
1832	14	His sister Sarah is sold to Perry Cohee of Mississippi
1833	15	Lives with Thomas Auld
1834	16	Works as a field hand under the local 'slave breaker' Edward Covey
1835–6	17	Field hand to William Freeland. He attempts to escape but is jailed with others in Easton
1836	18	Returned to his old Master, Thomas Auld
1836–38	18–20	Works in the shipyards as an apprentice in the calking trade. He meets Anna Murray his future wife
1838	20	Succeeds in escaping to the North where he is joined by Anna. They marry in New York City on 15 September. They move to New Bedford, Massachusetts. Takes name of Frederick Douglass
1839	21	Addresses a gathering of New Bedford blacks; hears the white Abolitionists Garrison and Phillips
1840	22	Lewis Douglass b. 9 October
1841	23	Garrison hears Douglass address a predominantly white Abolitionist meeting at Nantucket, Mass. Douglass is contracted as an agent for the Massachusetts' Anti-Slavery Society

Year	Age	Life
1842	24	Frederick Douglass (son) is born on 3 March
1843	25	Attacked by pro-slavery mob at Pendleton
1844	26	Charles Redmond Douglass b.
1845	27	*Narrative of Frederick Douglass An American Slave*. Sails on the steamer Camria to Great Britain. He is segregated from the other passengers, and threatened by pro-slavery Americans. Lectures in Ireland
1846	28	Embarks on a lecture tour of Scotland and England which is a great success. He buys his freedom from Hugh Auld with support from British sympathisers
1847	29	Starts his newspaper *North Star* using the $2,175 raised in England. Settles in Rochester, NY
1848	30	Douglass attends the first Women's Rights Convention at Seneca Falls, New York. At a meeting in Cleveland he is chosen as the President of the Colored Convention Movement
1849	31	Daughter Annie b. 22 March
1851	33	*Frederick Douglass's Paper* is started with help from Gerrit Smith, a political opponent of Garrison and leader of the Liberty Party (an Abolitionist party)
1855	37	*My Bondage and My Freedom*, the second autobiography, is published
1856	38	Endorses John C. Fremont Smith, Republican candidate
1857		
1858	40	Meets John Brown
1859	41	John Brown and others attack Harper's Ferry. Douglass, who knew of the plan, flees (leaving his family behind) to Canada, and then on to England
1860	42	Douglass's daughter Annie dies. He returns to the US
1863	45	Urges blacks to join the Union army. His sons Lewis and Charles Redmond enlist. Visits Abraham Lincoln. Cessation of *Douglass's Monthly* (1860–3)
1864	46	Endorses Lincoln
1865–66	47–8	Supports extended enfranchisement in the South
1868	50	Campaigns for Ulysses S. Grant
1870	52	Works as editor and later buys the *New National Era*
1871	53	Appointed Assistant Secretary of the Commission of Inquiry to Santo Domingo
1872	54	Nominated by Equal Rights Party as their vice-presidential candidate but chooses instead to campaign for Grant's re-election
1874	56	*New National Era* folds due to collapse of Freedman's Bank (Douglass had been named its President)

Year	Age	Life
1877	59	President Hayes names Douglass United States Marshal for the District of Columbia, the first black person to ever hold this office
1881	63	Appointed Recorder of Deeds of Columbia : *Life and Times of Frederick Douglass* published
1882	64	Anna Douglass dies
1884	66	He marries a white woman : Helen Pitts. His former secretary
1885–87	67–8	The Douglasses tour Europe and the Near East
1889	71	Benjamin Harrison appoints Douglass Minister-Resident and Consul-General to Haiti and chargé d'affaires for the Dominican Republic
1891	73	He resigns his post over the US Department's plan to seek a naval lease at Mole St Nicolas
1892–93	74–5	Serves as commissioner of Haitian exhibit at World Fair in Chicago. Freedom Manufacturing Co., a project of Douglass's which would employ hundreds of blacks, is wrecked by fraudulent promoters
1894	76	'Lessons of the Hour', his last major speech
1895	77	Suffers a fatal heart attack in the evening of 20 February ; is buried in Mount Hope Cemetery, Rochester, NY

CHRONOLOGY OF THEIR TIMES

Year	Literary Context	Historical Events
1777		Vermont Constitution prohibits slavery
1780		Gradual aboliton of slavery in Pennsylvania. Blacks protest about taxation without representation, Dartmouth, Massachusetts
1783		Massachusetts and New Hampshire abolish slavery
1784		Connecticut and Rhode Island pass Gradual Emancipation laws. Thomas Jefferson, *Notes on Virginia*
1787		Prohibition of slavery in Northwest Territory. Free African Society organised in Philadelphia
1791		Slave revolt in Santo Domingo
1792		Anti-slavery societies organised in all states from Massachusetts to Virginia
1793		First Federal fugitive slave law passed
1799		Gradual abolition of slavery in New York
1800		Gabriel Plot, Virginia
1804		Abolition of slavery in New Jersey. Insurrection on the slave ship *Tryal*
1808		Federal law forbidding African slave trade goes into effect
1816		American Colonisation Society organised
1820	*Emancipator*, first Southern Abolitionist newspaper	Missouri Compromise
1821		Liberia founded

Year	Literary Context	Historical Events
1822		Denmark Vesey Conspiracy, South Carolina
1824	Elizabeth Heyrich, *Immediate, Not Gradual Abolition*	Abolition of slavery in Central America
1827	*Freedom's Journal*, first Afro-American newspaper	
1829		Walker's appeal. Abolition of slavery in Mexico
1830		First national Negro Convention
1831	Garrison's *Liberator* established. Gray, *Confessions of Nat Turner*	Nat Turner insurrection, Virginia. Virginia legislature debates emancipation. Abolition of slavery in Bolivia
1832		Organisation of New England Anti-Slavery Society. South Carolina passes Nullification Ordinance
1833		American Anti-Slavery Society organised. British government enacts bill abolishing slavery throughout Empire
1834		Lane Seminary debates 'Ought the people of the slave-holding states to abolish slavery immediately'
1835		Garrison mobbed in Boston. Anti-black, anti-Abolitionist riots in New York. Murrell Affair in Mississippi. Post Office sacked for anti-slavery mail in Charleston. Amos Dresser, Lane student, whipped in Nashville
1836	Paulding (pro-Slavery), *Slavery in the United States*. Hildreth, *Archy Moore*	Congress passes gag law against anti-slavery petition. Birney mobbed in Cincinnati
1837	Roper's *Narrative*	Elijah Lovejoy murdered at Alton, Illinois
1838	William's *Narrative*	
1839	Weld's *American Slavery As It Is*	Slave insurrection on the ship *Amistad*
1840	Hildreth, *Despotism in America*	American and Foreign Anti-Slavery Society formed in consequence of Abolitionist schism. Liberty Party organised

Year	Literary Context	Historical Events
1841		Slave insurrection the ship *Creole*
1842		Fugitive slave case: Latimer. Abolition of slavery in Uruguay Child, 'The Quadroons'
1843	Henry Highland Garnet, 'Address'	
1844		Garrison advances slogan, 'No union with slaveholders'. Slave plot, Cuba. Placido executed
1845	Clarke, *Narrative* (revised and republished, 1846)	
1847	*North Star* established by Douglass. William Wells Brown, *Narrative*	Liberia declared an independent republic
1848		Slave insurrection on the ship *Pearl*. Free Soil Party founded
1849	Josiah Henson, *Life*	
1850		Fugitive Slave Law and Compromise of 1850
1851		Fugitive slave case: Shadrach rescued. Fugitive slave case: Sims returned to slavery. Fugitive slave case: Christian Affair. Abolition of slavery in Columbia.
1852	Brown, *Three Years in Europe* (revised and retitled *American Fugitive*, 1855). Delaney, *The Condition, Emigration, and Destiny of the Colored People of the United States, Politically Considered*. Simms, *The Pro-Slavery Argument*. Simms, *The Sword and the Distaff* (retitled *Woodcraft*, 1854). Hildreth, *The White Slave*	
1853	Brown, *Clotel*	Abolition of slavery in Argentina
1854		Fugitive slave case: Burns returned to slavery. Garrison burns Constitution. Kansas-Nebraska Act. Republican Party formed. Abolition of slavery in Venezuela

Year	Literary Context	Historical Events
1855		Abolition of slavery in Peru
1856		Lawrence, Kansas sacked. Sumner caned on floor of Senate
1857		Dred Scott decision
1859	Delaney begins serialisation of *Blake*	*Clothilde*, last African slave ship, docks in Alabama
1860	Craft, *Running a Thousand Miles*. Brown, *Miraida* (revision of *Clotel*)	South Carolina secedes
1861	Delaney, *Official Report of the Niger Valley Exploring Party*	Inauguration of Lincoln. Fort Sumner fired upon
1862		Abolition of slavery in District of Columbia. Union Army accepts black troops
1863		Emancipation Proclamation
1865		The Thirteenth Amendment to the American Constitution
1869		Fifteenth Amendment

INTRODUCTION

Frederick Douglass was born, as far as he could discover, in 1818, in Tuckahoe, Maryland, the date of birth of a slave being regarded as hardly worthy of recall, except for reasons of accountancy. For his first seven years he lived at or near the plantation of Colonel Edward Lloyd. From there he was sent to Baltimore to serve Hugh Auld, whose wife began the young slave's instruction in the basics of literacy before being required to desist by her husband who recognised the danger of educating slaves beyond their status. Such education as he secured thereafter was a product of his own efforts. It was illicit and so of itself subversive.

Returned to the countryside he found himself for the first time required to perform as a field slave. To curb him of his city ways and to prepare him for his new work he was handed over to a 'nigger breaker' whose job it was to break the spirit of a slave, to make him wholly tractable. He nearly succeeded with Douglass who nonetheless resisted and finally escaped to the North rather than face a lifetime of servitude. Once there he was attracted to the abolitionist cause, testifying eloquently, at public meetings, to the nature of southern slavery. So effective was he that he was urged to write an account of his experiences.

Frederick Douglass wrote three autobiographies. It is not just that they expanded with his life but that the first, the *Narrative*, was more patently an argument with his society than those which followed. Beyond that, the details which he concealed in the *Narrative*, in order to protect those who helped him escape and to preserve an escape route still available to others, were slowly revealed. He had in fact taken a train from Baltimore to the Susquehenna River, using borrowed papers. From there he crossed to Wilmington, Delaware, and took a steamship to Philadelphia and thus, by means of another train, reached New York. Pausing only to marry, he travelled to New Bedford, the first of several moves. Escape from slavery was not merely a matter of following the North Star (later the name he took for the newspaper which he founded and edited). The passage from South to North required a difficult journey but the distance travelled was measured in far more than miles. It was a transformation which required and resulted in a change of name. His trip North was undertaken carrying false papers but in a sense all slaves carried such in that, denied identity, denied possession of their own experience, refused permission to be anything but that which their masters required, they presented a public face which concealed a private truth.

Douglass begins his *Narrative* by reminding the reader that his life, in common with that of his fellow slaves, lacks what other narratives require – a starting point. Few slaves knew their date of birth. It was as though they were to be wholly the invention of their owners. By the same token he was stripped of parentage, his mother and he being separated when he was a baby, his father being rumoured to be his master, who by that fact would deny him. On the rare occasions he saw his mother – hired by a nearby farmer – it was night. Such a relationship was kept in the shadows, as, more obviously, was his genetic link to his father, an inheritance which, like the naming of all slaves after present or former owners, was itself evidence of the total vulnerability of the slave. Yet if his very name was a token of his enslavement it was also a lesson in the power of language, a lesson which he learned quickly. Language, indeed, was the key to his rebirth. The moment a master forbade him lessons in reading for fear it would breed discontent he realised the power of words as resistance. To learn to write was to be able to receive and communicate ideas, it was to offer evidence of an intellectual achievement denied by the defenders of slavery. It enabled Douglass to forge passes which would facilitate escape, a practical device but one which can also stand as an image, as writing itself became a pass, a means of escape. For all his articulateness, however, he was also acutely aware of the limitations of language. 'I wish I could commit to paper the feelings with which I beheld it,' he says of his aunt's beating by a brutal owner. However eloquent he became he was aware that he could never hope to express the true nature of black suffering. To that extent the *Narrative* was bound to fall short of its objective. Yet if in some fundamental way it must be a failed enterprise, words never being commensurate to experience, it proved a powerful weapon in the hands of the abolitionists.

In a sense Douglass's was an archetypal American story. The voyage from South to North could be seen as merely another version of that prototypical journey, often itself involving a process of renaming, which brought, and was to bring, so many to America. Douglass's transformation from despised and marginal being to integral self was precisely that offered by a national experience in which change was both motive and consequence. To accommodate him to a norm in this way, however, is to miss the unique nature of the black experience of America which was precisely one which precluded access to American myths, values and rights. The drive towards a new identity, so much a theme of American writing as of American life, was consciously and deliberately blocked by an institution which denied identity, autonomy and freedom. The struggle to attain it, therefore, was not of a piece with the immigrant's dream nor was the escaped slave a Horatio Alger hero whose luck and pluck won access to a national bounty. Douglass was a self-made man, it is true, but his was an act of self-invention which challenged rather than endorsed the pragmatics of a culture which had come close to trading principle for profit.

Douglass's 'real' name was Bailey, but since no slave had a real name, Bailey, in his case, being the name of his enslaved mother and hence the badge of his servitude, his rebirth as Douglass (named for the hero of Sir Walter Scott's *The Lady of the Lake*), was a conscious statement, a celebration of his emancipation.

Douglass's personal life, after his escape, was largely untroubled. His first marriage lasted forty-four years and was followed by an inter-racial marriage which bothered others but not him. His, though, was essentially a public life. In publishing the *Narrative* he had consciously offered himself as exemplar. Events are chosen for the light they throw on the institution of slavery rather than merely for the truth they reveal about a developing self. The central figure becomes a construction, not in the sense that he lacks credibility but to the extent that he is designed to serve a didactic purpose. Frederick Douglass becomes, like Walt Whitman, a representative man.

The man who had struggled so hard to acquire written and verbal skills became one of the nineteenth century's greatest orators and a public symbol of resistance to an institution whose corruptions struck deep into the heart of the American ideal. Before the Civil War he spoke and wrote of the need for abolition; during the war he insisted that abolition should be its primary goal. Thereafter he became a politician, a black Republican, and a supporter of women's rights. He held a number of public positions, from Marshall of the District of Columbia to Minister of Haiti.

Powerfully influenced by the abolitionist William Lloyd Garrison (though they later quarrelled) he believed, despite experience to the contrary, in human perfectibility. He presented America with a series of moral demands. Ironically he found that the abolitionists preferred that he restrict himself to accounts of his slave experiences rather than expand on a larger theme. In other words, in some senses they, too, wished to impose the status of slave on him, afraid that his very articulateness would be the denial of that authenticity as escaped slave which they believed to be his chief value. Eventually he rebelled against this as he had against slavery itself.

African-Americans clearly had an ambiguous relationship with the language they spoke. It was an agent, an assertion of enslavement. When they first arrived in America their existing languages were burned away by English, which was to be the language of command and submission. The moment in which the slave first articulated his or her slave name became the moment when another history was denied, when a line was drawn across an experience which lay elsewhere. At that moment the self was colonised. To speak at all was to risk becoming confederate with those who enslaved them. Yet that language was also the only agent of protest. To become articulate in what, in another context, Amiri Baraka was to call the 'jargon of power' was to stake a claim for equal rights not only to that language but to the system of power and rights and presumptions which it represented. It became necessary to undertake a linguistic infiltration in order to storm the citadel. Yet that assault could never be undertaken without a sense of unease. In the 1960s James Baldwin was to be attacked by fellow black writers for assimilating too completely the language of the King James Bible and the rhetorical tropes of American prose and thereby the values which it expressed, language coming between himself and the experiences which that language was charged with communicating. Some likewise suspected Douglass of being altogether too fluent, too linguistically competent, for a man whose life had, by his own admission, been brutal and brutalising. They looked for something rougher and hence more authentic.

White America was equally ambivalent. The necessities of slavery required a common language yet there was a danger in permitting free entry to that language. To become fully articulate is to gain access to knowledge, to secure a means of communicating ideas, to achieving the means to ferment rebellion and to deny that very assertion of inferiority upon which slavery based its moral case. Thus while declaring the natural incompetence of slaves it became necessary to deny them the skills of written language, the acquisition of which would provide evidence to the contrary.

Frederick Douglass's *Narrative* was by no means the only such. Accounts by former slaves formed a key aspect of abolitionist strategy, though for obvious reasons few were written by their subjects. Their importance, however, went beyond their value as recorders of fact, as evidence presented before the bar of public opinion. The form itself was a statement, a claim to possession of one's own experience. It is an assertion not only of identity but of the coherence of the self. It is a statement of proprietary rights over one's past and present life and in that sense a denial of the very basis of slavery which would make that life the property of another. It is triumphal, in that whatever the nature of that life, of those experiences and of that identity, the act of writing implies a sense both of autonomy and transcendence. Not for nothing has the autobiographical essay and book proved the most significant form adopted by the black writer from the slave narratives, through the work of Booker T. Washington and W.E.B. Dubois to the key documents of the second half of the twentieth century (with works by Richard Wright, James Baldwin, George Jackson, Huey Newton, Bobby Seale, Malcolm X, Claude Brown, Angela Davis, Maya Angelou). It was a claim to be the possessor of one's own experience, master of one's own past, and hence the definer of one's own future. Douglass's *Narrative* is about mastery. In describing a slave owner he says that he was the best he had known 'till I became my own master'.

The problem facing Douglass as a writer was to communicate across precisely those barriers to understanding which slavery itself had a vested interest in sustaining. Describing slave songs he confesses that 'I was myself within the circle; so that I neither saw nor heard as those without might see and hear'. He expresses amazement that whites should read such songs as an expression of contentment when they are a cipher best decrypted in terms of pain, as a way of sustaining onself in the face of injustice and inhumanity. In the knowledge that 'one must needs experience it, or imagine himself in similar circumstance' to hope to understand, he nonetheless offers his own text as a means of bridging that gap of experience, as a mechanism for achieving what the imagination alone cannot accomplish. The *Narrative* addresses white America and Douglass offers himself in the role of interpreter, and though his account contains evidence of the failure of white southerners to understand the lives of those they enslave the book itself is predicated on the assumption that such understanding is possible.

When it first appeared *The Narrative of the Life of Frederick Douglass* had a preface by William Lloyd Garrison, a validation which might seem to vitiate its authority since its claim to authenticity lay precisely in the fact that it was not a story which had been mediated by others. Douglass's was not a life which required interpretation, justification, vindication. To enter the text by way of Garrison is, thus, to risk precisely that nod of approval, that patronage seen as celebration, which might lay the foundation for a more subtle form of subversion than that practised by slave masters. Douglass needed the sounding board of the abolitionists as they assuredly needed him. There was a compromise involved on both sides.

Yet there is certainly an ambiguity in Garrison's simultaneous desire to show that the black slave has survived servitude, and its depraving nature, intact, and his belief that slavery is inevitably brutalising. To substantiate this he offers an account of a white American sailor held in slavery in Africa for three years who is found thereafter to be 'imbruted' and speaking 'some savage gibberish'. For all his sensitivities, it seems, not merely was Garrison unsure as to which horse he was riding, he was also, and crucially, insensitive to the question of language and its use as an agent of enslavement, and unaware that he was displaying precisely the contempt for other cultures which in part underpinned slavery itself. His conclusion that 'the white slave can sink as low in the scale of humanity as the black one' is clearly offered as evidence of his concern for servitude over race, but it sits a little uneasily beside his argument for the slave's heroic resistance to corruption which he also wishes to assert.

The preface, while recognising the crucial importance of Douglass telling his own story, is also explicitly apologetic about the style of the narrative, excusing it in terms of the manifest disadvantages suffered by its author. It is an apology which says rather more about the abolitionists' fear than it does about the *Narrative* itself. In fact the book is written with considerable assurance and, if it seems at times to echo sentimental romances, this influence can be felt in a number of such narratives. Garrison's preface, by contrast, is overwritten and patronising but, then, he had a vested interest in emphasising Douglass's supposed disadvantages. The abolitionists required an honest and disingenuous reporter, not a man who might be suspected of being too sophisticated to have experienced the privations he described, and there were those who suspected precisely this. But the book's strength survives even Garrison's equivocal enthusiasm. A century and a half later its disturbing power is still evident.

The *Narrative* was an enormous success. Within five years thirty thousand copies had been sold. Its impact in Europe was equally great and it was an English couple who bought his freedom from Hugh Auld in 1846. The value of his freedom was set at seven hundred dollars. In subsequent years Douglass became a major publisher and editor, founding a number of journals, and a national leader of integrity and influence. He died on 20 February 1895. Nobody noted the date of his birth; few were unaware of the date of his death.

The essence of Frederick Douglass's claim was that he was the man, he suffered, he was there. Experience was not reshaped as art and therefore falsified, even if such falsification were no more than truth dressed up in its Sunday best. For if autobiography is plainly shaped by its author this is presumed to be no more than the discovery of form in a contingent life.

Harriet Beecher Stowe could make no such claim, though she had visited the South. She heard the story of a slave woman crossing the Ohio, on which she based the Eliza incident in *Uncle Tom's Cabin*, when on a trip to that state. It is true that her own brother had narrowly escaped death at the hands of a pro-slavery mob and that while Douglass was escaping she was teaching ex-slaves in the school founded by her older sister. Nonetheless, her knowledge had to be in large part second hand. Indeed a slave narrative – *The Life of Josiah Henson* – was one of the sources for her novel, as was Theodore Weld's volume, *American Slavery As It is: Testimony of a Thousand Witnesses*, while, in 1851, she wrote to Frederick Douglass, whose own narrative she had studied, asking for information on which she could base aspects of her book, then already being serialised in the *National Era* (its forty-one episodes were published over a period of nine months). However, when her facts were challenged she assembled evidence which detailed cases of violence and published it in *A Key to Uncle Tom's Cabin*, a volume which appeared a year after the novel.

Uncle Tom's Cabin appeared in book form in 1852 and by the following year had sold, it is thought, some two and a half million copies. It remains the most popular work of fiction ever published. Some one hundred and fifty editions have appeared in English with more than half that number in Germany alone. It is one of the most widely translated books in publishing history. President Lincoln once famously, if somewhat facetiously, credited it with provoking the Civil War. It is certainly true, however, that its impact was far greater than that of all the slave narratives combined. We are thus confronted with the fact that this white woman, the daughter of a Congregational minister, who lived all her life in the North, had a far greater influence on the anti-slavery movement than any black slave who had experienced the iniquities of slavery at first hand. Longfellow noted that the novel had shaken the world, Henry

James that it was a 'triumphant work'. Macaulay thought it the most valuable additon that America had made to English literature, while Heine could only invoke the Bible by way of comparison. The play version, not by Stowe, was one of the most successful in American theatrical history. *Uncle Tom's Cabin*, in other words, was a phenomenon.

Harriet Beecher Stowe was born in 1811 into a deeply religious family. She published her first story at the age of twenty-two and married two years later, in 1836. Her husband was a professor of Biblical Criticism. Her own sister, Catherine, published her *Essay on Slavery* in the following year. She was in fact surrounded by abolitionists with many of her family serving the cause. In 1843 she published her first book, a series of short stories entitled *The May Flower: or Sketches of Scenes and Characters among the Descendants of the Pilgrims*. Seven years later she began work on *Uncle Tom's Cabin*. From something close to genteel poverty she found herself both successful and rich, though capable of offering a modest account of herself in a letter to a friend. 'I am,' she confessed, 'a little bit of a woman, – somewhat more than forty, about as thin as a pinch of snuff; never very much to look at in my best days, and looking like a used-up article now.' The little bit of a woman had nonetheless written a book which made her a world figure.

William Lloyd Garrison praised Frederick Douglass for his pathos. The word was not meant pejoratively. It was a quality which Stowe had in unlimited supplies. Garrison evidently meant that Douglass had the ability to turn social and political fact into emotional reality, to convert suffering into affecting language, and that was certainly a skill possessed by his northern counterpart. Nor is there such a sharp distinction between the two writers. Both conjured up wicked overseers who whipped the flesh from women slaves. Both stressed the stoicism and the courage of those who lacked even the consolation of hope. But Stowe dived rather deeper into the waters of melodrama. There was, of course, melodrama enough in slavery as an institution. It hardly needed the skills of a sentimental novelist to point up the obvious reality of innocence corrupted, of families broken and lives destroyed, but where the rhetoric of the abolitionist appealed to principles of natural justice and advocated social and political change, Stowe infiltrated the imagination and the conscience by another route.

She said in later years that she was inspired to write her book by the passage of the Fugitive Slave Act, which required the return of escaped slaves to their masters, even if they should reach the supposed safe haven of the North. No longer, then, was it possible simply to see as a regional issue what now so clearly contaminated the whole nation. The object of her book, Stowe states in her preface, was 'to awaken sympathy and feeling for the African race'. She herself explained that the urgency of the subject was such that structure and style necessarily took second place, which makes Garrison's similar apology for Douglass look like something of a convention. Anticipating criticism she acknowledged that 'in the Northern States these representations may, perhaps, be thought caricatures' but insisted that 'in the Southern States are witnesses who know their fidelity'. What might seem aesthetic shortcomings, in other words, were a project less of literary inadequacy than of a culture which had already reduced the complexity of the black self by submitting that self to coercive institutions. Like Douglass, she reached for an authenticity of which art might seem a denial but hoped through art to open the way for true feeling. If Douglass knew and addressed the inner life of those required to live a double life, having experienced it himself, Stowe could of necessity read only the public drama; that she was aware that there was a shadow text and sought to give it substance, gave her novel something of its affecting force.

The novel's sentimentalities, the basis of much of its success in the nineteenth century, led to its marginalising in the twentieth, except as exemplary social text. More recently it has inspired deep suspicion on the part of some black critics for whom it can be seen as infringing on the cultural hegemony of those who suffered. Though never attacked in the same way or with the same virulence as William Styron's *The Confessions of Nat Turner*, a novel by a white southerner which was seen as taking a free ride on the back of black suffering, colonising the black experience, *Uncle Tom's Cabin* was seen by some critics as patronising in so far as it spoke for those who had had their own voices suppressed by slavery and now had to suffer the additional indignity of seeing their experience articulated. for them by a white woman.

The figure of Uncle Tom, in particular, has been seen as demeaning because submissive. In *The Way of the New World* Addison Gayle Jr dismissed Uncle Tom as a 'meek mannered, mild, brainless, man child'. Richard Wright entitled a book of short stories *Uncle Tom's Children* precisely to signify the end of such passivity. For James Baldwin, Stowe's book was 'a very bad novel', having in its self-righteous, virtuous sentimentality, much in common with *Little Women*, adding that:

> sentimentality, the ostentatious parading of excessive and spurious emotion, is the mark of dishonesty, the inability to feel; the wet eyes of the sentimentalist betray his aversion to experience, his fear of life, his arid heart; and it is always, therefore, the signal of secret and violent inhumanity, the mask of cruelty.

Nor were Gayle and Baldwin, different as they were in their approach, alone. Amidst the general air of celebration which marked the book's publication, there were already dissenting voices. Douglass may have welcomed it as a key document (Tolstoy, Dickens and Hugo, perhaps not altogether surprisingly, hailing it also as high art), but black abolitionists were not united in their praise. Uncle Tom's passivity, in particular, rankled with them as it was to do with later black writers. Nor did Stowe's decision to send one of her characters to Liberia go down well with those who were at that moment fighting the various colonisation schemes being offered as a solution to the problem of race in America.

It is possible partially to exonerate Harriet Beecher Stowe, and this by means of granting more than good intentions and acknowledging profound effects. She does struggle to invest lives, whose inner dynamics were denied to her, with something more than casual and impressionistic force. And if the leap of imagination was finally, perhaps, too great for her, the attempt was already a statement, a declaration, a commitment to possibility. She was not a condescending Lady Bountiful, offering her talents to the disadvantaged, but a woman who challenged those with the power to do more than denounce her from platform and pulpit.

On the other hand she was no unworldly moralist. She was a

professional writer who made her living by her pen. She earned a fortune out of *Uncle Tom's Cabin* and spent a fair amount of it buying land and property, as well as dispensing it to charities. She was a hard bargainer. When she was asked to write her husband's obituary she overcame her grief sufficiently to negotiate a rate for the job, playing off one publisher against another.

It is easy to project from the sentimentalities of *Uncle Tom's Cabin* an image of Stowe as a sensitive but impractical woman, deflecting into fiction a sense of outrage better directed towards political action; easy but wrong. Her sister, Catherine, did believe that it was wrong for women to act directly in the public world, preferring that they should exert an indirect and humane influence on those – men – who did. Stowe was equivocal in this regard, as is evident from *Uncle Tom's Cabin* itself which embodied the notion of a feminising force, essentially moral because essentially compassionate, but which was as public a statement as it was possible to make. To write, after all, is to act directly. Nor did she flinch from public controversy. She spoke out on behalf of women and in support of the working class of America and Europe and, incautiously, in later life, even came to the support of Lady Byron, revealing her husband's incestuous relationship wtih his sister in a book which became the cause of scandal.

It has been argued that not all the anger in *Uncle Tom's Cabin* is directed towards slavery and that its sentimentalities, far from being a weakness, are a deliberate assertion of women's values in a culture whose polarities are differently aligned. The very nature of slavery is seen as expressing an essentially male version of the world whereby dominance and subservience are the axes of a graph against which we may plot history. Sentiment thus becomes not an evasion, not, as Baldwin suspected, an averting of the gaze, still less a sign of the substitution of art for feeling, but an argument for the validity of spontaneous emotion as a key to moral sense. Seen thus, indeed, Christianity itself becomes a feminised religion, resisting coercion in the name of love. The woman novelist thus becomes the ideal figure to deal with such issues. It may be that there is something to this. It is certainly possible to find references in Mrs Stowe's letters to her own sense of domestic enslavement, as she felt herself confined within the role ascribed to her by a male society, while in her novel religion and sentiment do come into alignment as though they are indeed aspects of that same resistance to a system of power which has turned its back on humanity in the name of patriarchy.

Baldwin hints at a final question. It was clear that Mrs Stowe wished to liberate the slave, but to become what? He suspected to be re-enslaved to religion or a bland, but potentially lethal, American norm. There is perhaps evidence for the former, though she could never have seen as enslavement what she must regard as salvation. Of the latter it is harder to say. Her work for women suggests that she regarded the norm as wholly unacceptable. This was, internationally, the age of revolutions. Exiles from the 1848 rebellions had flooded into America. It is perhaps hard to see in this woman, who ended her days demented, leaping out of bushes to confront her unsuspecting neighbour, Mark Twain, as a radical. But she did have a radical spirit. If she has come to be regarded as a writer whose achievement was real but whose work was vitiated by its style and manner it is worth recalling the degree to which she transcended her age, rejecting its imperatives, its equivocations. She did have a vision of the future. The fact that her moral paradigm derived from the past, from the New Testament to be precise, does not deny her that vision any more than the conventionalities of her art deny her the integrity of that art. Others turned to the public platform. Douglass chose the autobiography. Harriet Beecher Stowe found in the novel a perfect instrument for her social concerns as well as for her artistic ambitions.

The novel, with its multiplicity of voices, its democracy of character, its fluidity of form, was altogether a fit place for her to inhabit. It might carry the force of social conscience reborn as narrative logic, but the novel is far more than that. It is already an assertion about the nature of experience. Its pluralism, which enables characters to co-habit within a single story who might otherwise be held apart, its resistance to singular readings, its assertion of the legitimacy of thought and imagination made it not merely an appropriate mechanism for the morally committed writer but itself an embodiment of the values which it invoked. For Harriet Beecher Stowe and the millions around the world who read her book it became a moral instrument. She may not have provoked the Civil War but *Uncle Tom's Cabin* is clearly one of those very few texts which can be said to have influenced the course of history while engaged in dramatising the impact of history on the lives of its individual characters.

CHRISTOPHER BIGSBY

AUTHOR'S PREFACE

THE scenes of this story, as its title indicates, lie among a race hitherto ignored by the associations of polite and refined society; an exotic race, whose ancestors, born beneath a tropic sun, brought with them, and perpetuated to their descendants, a character so essentially unlike the hard and dominant Anglo-Saxon race, as for many years to have won from it only misunderstanding and contempt.

But, another and better day is dawning; every influence of literature, of poetry and of art, in our times, is becoming more and more in unison with the great master chord of Christianity, 'good will to man.'

The poet, the painter, and the artist, now seek out and embellish the common and gentler humanities of life, and under the allurements of fiction, breathe a humanising and subduing influence, favourable to the development of the great principles of Christian brotherhood.

The hand of benevolence is everywhere stretched out, searching into abuses, righting wrongs, alleviating distresses, and bringing to the knowledge and sympathies of the world the lowly, the oppressed, and the forgotten.

In this general movement, unhappy Africa at last is remembered; Africa, who began the race of civilisation and human progress in the dim, grey dawn of early time, but who, for centuries, has lain bound and bleeding at the foot of civilised and Christianised humanity, imploring compassion in vain.

But the heart of the dominant race, who have been her conquerors, her hard masters, has at length been turned towards her in mercy; and it has been seen how far nobler it is in nations to protect the feeble than to oppress them. Thanks be to God, the world has at last outlived the slave-trade!

The object of these sketches is to awaken sympathy and feeling for the African race, as they exist among us; to show their wrongs and sorrows, under a system so necessarily cruel and unjust as to defeat and do away with the good effects of all that can be attempted for them, by their best friends, under it.

In doing this, the author can sincerely disclaim any invidious feeling towards those individuals who, often without any fault of their own, are involved in the trials and embarrassments of the legal relations of slavery.

Experience has shown her that some of the noblest of minds and hearts are often thus involved; and no one knows better than they do, that what may be gathered of the evils of slavery from sketches like these, is not the half that could be told, of the unspeakable whole.

In the northern states, these representations may, perhaps, be thought caricatures; in the southern states are witnesses who know their fidelity. What personal knowledge the author has had of the truth of incidents such as here are related, will appear in its time.

It is a comfort to hope, as so many of the world's sorrows and wrongs have, from age to age, been lived down, so a time shall come when sketches similar to these shall be valuable only as memorials of what has long ceased to be.

When an enlightened and Christianised community shall have, on the shores of Africa, laws, language, and literature, drawn from among us, may then the scenes of the house of bondage be to them like the remembrance of Egypt to the Israelite, – a motive of thankfulness to Him who hath redeemed them!

For, while politicians contend, and men are swerved this way and that by conflicting tides of interest and passion, the great cause of human liberty is in the hands of One, of whom it is said:

'He shall not fail nor be discouraged
Till He have set judgment in the earth.'

'He shall deliver the needy when he crieth,
The poor, and him that hath no helper.'

'He shall redeem their soul from deceit and violence,
And precious shall their blood be in His sight.'

UNCLE TOM'S
CABIN

INTRODUCTORY REMARKS

TO HENRY G. BOHN, Esq.

SIR, – For the copy of *Uncle Tom's Cabin*, which you have done me the honour to send for my acceptance, I beg to express my obligations. Its excellent typography, and almost unparalleled cheapness, place it above any edition which I have seen. I was about to wish it success; but I have since learned that the entire edition of 5000 copies was sold in a single day – a fact as extraordinary to me as the book itself. However, as the slave cannot, I beg on his behalf to thank you for the enterprise you have thrown into a mere speculation, and thereby have assisted to plead his cause. And now I have my pen in hand, I am tempted to write a few words about the book, and the subject of which it treats.

Uncle Tom's Cabin needs no panegyric from me. The public have done justice to its thrilling contents by purchasing and perusing many thousands of copies. By the verdict of the people of England and America it has taken its place as a standard work among the beauties of English literature. The genius which has strung together so many real incidents in slave life – the dramatic beauty with which the scenes are painted – the rich vein of humour which pervades almost every dialogue – the variety of characters introduced as well among slaveholders as slaves – and the genuine nature displayed in every page, render it as irresistibly attractive to the learned and unlearned as Bunyan's *Pilgrim's Progress* or De Foe's *Robinson Crusoe*. Youth and age are alike enchanted by its representations, and know not how to lay it down when its perusal has been commenced.

Besides all that is beautiful in the work as a composition, its truthfulness and piety are, in my estimation, its chief charms. To exquisite womanly tenderness it unites the most dignified and scriptural sentiments. It equally opens the flood-gates of the affections and enlightens and sanctifies the judgment. Not only is the imagination pleased with the graphic sketches, as the eye would be with the beauties of a landscape, but the mind becomes ennobled and strengthened by the doctrines advanced; as he who sits down to a sumptuous feast may admire the elegance and ornaments with which it is served, but rises refreshed and nourished by the healthful provision of which he has partaken.

Against this characteristic of the book, critics, favourable to the present state of slavery, have directed their chief objections. They tell us that the characters are overdrawn – that the cruelties are not so extreme, nor the slaves so pious, as the authoress has represented; that, with few exceptions, the slaveholders are a humane and indulgent race, and the slaves in general are as happy as our poor in England; that we must estimate Mrs Stowe's book as an exaggerated description of 'the domestic institution of slavery in America,' and make due allowance for the feminine weakness which has transgressed the bounds of simple truth. Happily for the cause of righteousness, the details of the work have received a confirmation as singular as it is valuable. The Earl of Carlisle, it is well known, a few years ago visited America. His lordship's position would gain him access to all their institutions; and we can conceive that only the best features of slavery were seen by him, and those which were repulsive were, as much as possible, kept out of his way. Notwithstanding this, upon a review of *Uncle Tom's Cabin* appearing in the *Leeds Mercury*, Lord Carlisle sent the following letter to Edward Baines, Esq., the intelligent editor of that paper:

'NAWORTH CASTLE, *Sept.* 6.

'MY DEAR MR BAINES, – I write a line to thank you, as privately or as publicly as you think fittest, for your admirable comment upon an admirable book, *Uncle Tom's Cabin*. It gave me the more special pleasure, from having been somewhat disheartened and disappointed in other quarters. There are, however, very few subjects, I will not say there are none, upon which I have not found that our sympathies flow in common. With respect to the work in question, its genius, its pathos, its humour, must sufficiently commend themselves to its nearly unparalleled number of readers: I feel that I have seen and known enough to convince my own mind equally of its general fairness, fidelity, and truth. – Very faithfully yours,

'CARLISLE.'

The testimony of a man who is no unreflecting enthusiast, but a statesman of large views and cool judgment, on the work before us, must be regarded as that of the most calm and enlightened of judges, and the most unexceptional of witnesses. His lordship has conferred a great boon on the slave by thus endorsing Mrs Stowe's book, while his opinion will give to English readers the very confidence they required.

It has been stated that books like the present are not the legitimate means to put down slavery. We might ask then very fairly, what are? Are we to wait till slaveholders propose the abolition of slaves? or till a pro-slavery legislature, which has just passed the Fugitive Slave Bill, and ruled America by slaveholders for above sixty years, voluntarily declare the slaves free? How, but by enlightening and influencing public opinion, can we expect the abomination to cease? Public opinion, guided by religious sentiment drawn from the Word of God, alone settled the question in England, and that, too, will effect it in America if she will listen; and, if *not*, it is by no means difficult to divine what must be the sad result. Slavery is an unmixed, unmitigated evil in any civilised country. Under the light of the Gospel it deprives man, not only guiltless, but unaccused of crime, of every civil and religious right; denies him legal compensation for any wrong however grievous; annihilates conjugal and parental relations; consigns him at pleasure to heathenism; withholds from him the Bible and education; and reduces him to the condition of brutes.

For making the Israelites slaves, and tyrannically inflicting cruelties on their persons and children, we justly condemn Pharaoh; the crime, even in a heathen, was in the sight of God very aggravated. In what light, then, must He view the sin of the professed ministers of his Son, who is 'the Saviour of all men,' or of the officers and members of His church, who are bound to 'love one another with pure hearts fervently,' when they hold as chattels their fellow-creatures, whose souls are as precious as their own, and redeemed with the same precious blood, deny them the knowledge of salvation, and forbid them the means of reading the only book which God has designed for all men? The following statistics may well amaze us: –

SLAVES HELD BY MINISTERS AND THE CHURCH

Denominations	Ministers	Members	No. of Slaves
Methodists	5080	1,178,637	219,563
Presbyterians, Old and New Schools	3264	333,458	77,000
Baptists	6598	812,921	125,000
Campbellites			101,000
Episcopalians	1404	67,550	88,000
Other denominations			50,000

Total number of slaves held by ministers of the gospel and
    members of the different Protestant Churches   660,563

The denominations above cited have under their control 89
colleges, with 5495 students; and 26 theological seminaries,
with about 700 students. Some of these colleges and seminaries
have been built and endowed partly by the sale of slaves, and all
are looking for slaveholding patronage. When we contemplate
the above facts, and consider the influence which the Church
and the ministry have in America, it is impossible not to think
of the truth contained in the memorable saying of the distinguished Albert Barnes: –

'THERE IS NO POWER OUT OF THE CHURCH THAT COULD
SUSTAIN
SLAVERY AN HOUR IF IT WERE NOT SUSTAINED IN IT.'

It must be remembered that, beside these ministers and church
members, who hold slaves and deal with them as property – sell
children from their parents and divide husband and wife –
lacerate their flesh and ruin their souls – a large number, if not
a majority, of the ministers of religion in America patronise the
system of slavery, though they hold no slaves themselves. Some
indeed profess in theory to abominate slavery, but they stand
aloof from all efforts to suppress it. You will never hear a
petition presented in public to either God or man from their lips
for the emancipation of the slave. Dr Gardener Spring, an
eminent Presbyterian clergyman of New York, well known in
this country by his religious publications, has declared that, 'if
by one prayer he could liberate every slave in the world, he
would not offer it.' The Rev. Dr Parker, of Philadelphia, affirms,
in a recent thanksgiving sermon that 'there are no evils in slavery
but such as are inseparable from any other relation in civil and

social life.' Professor Moses Stuart, the celebrated commentator, in reply to Rev. President Fisk, of the Wesleyan University, represents Paul as 'sending Onesimus back to Philemon to be a servant for life,' in direct contradiction of the Apostle's statement, '*not* now as a servant but *above* a servant, a brother beloved especially to me, but how much more to thee, both in the *flesh* and in the Lord.' And how does he send him back? He first preaches the Gospel to him, instrumentally converts him, writes a letter to his former master, sends it by the liberated man himself without officer to watch or chains to bind him! Will the conduct of those who attempt to carry out the Fugitive Slave Law bear any comparison with that of Paul?

I ask, therefore, what but public opinion will influence such teachers of 'good will to man?' If conscience is made by education, lessons of instruction must be given them by the press. Mrs Stowe delicately, but decidedly, refers once or twice in her book to this sad ministerial delinquency; but I should have expected at least a chapter devoted to scenes in ministers' houses, and to sermons delivered by them from the sacred desk. This strikes me as a great omission; for, however ministers may like to have their portrait exhibited in their robes, and adorning the drawing-rooms of their congregation, it creates another sensation to be represented in type, in the undress of life, admonishing a mother with a whip, because she pleads and weeps when that minister tears her child from her bosom, and sells it to a stranger.

And I cannot but hope that Mrs Stowe, whose rare and sanctified talents command the eye and ear of the multitude, will turn her attention to the ecclesiastical state of the question, and show to American ministers their sin and shame. It would confer a real blessing on them; for slavery is the bane of all the churches; it prevents divine influence from flowing among them, and is a barrier to the progress of those revivals for which so many of their churches have been eminent. Get the ministers to act and speak aright, and you gain the churches; get the churches to do their duty, and you move the legislature; for no enlightened legislature can long resist a deep religious sense of right to our fellow-men, when calmly, but firmly expressed – even by a minority.

Though deeply distressed for the present state of the injured and oppressed slave, there is hope for the future. His emancipation is certain – it is only a question of time. The tendencies of the age to improvement and progress are all in favour of abolition. Every step taken for the diffusion of light – the establishment of free institutions, and the reformation of ancient abuses – directly or indirectly tends to the downfall of slavery. The experiment which has been so successfully made in the West Indies, of the liberation of thousands without injury to life or property – the advancement of black men, once slaves, to honourable posts at the bar and in the senate – the acquisition of piety and learning by many slaves, in spite of the restrictions imposed upon them – have taught literary and theological objectors that they must seek for new arguments against emancipation. Such pleas as the dangers of freedom – the inferiority of the negro – the curse on Canaan – the contentment of the slave in slavery – the superior prudence of gradualism – which were so formidable twenty years ago, are seldom mentioned now except in derision. The little heroic band, who against public sentiment have sacrificed property, reputation and comfort, to defend the oppressed, and insist on the rights of their black brethren, have received large additions by the passing of the Fugitive Slave Bill – and, having truth on their side, must ere long succeed. Opposed – as they have been – by those who should have co-operated with them, and forsaken by some who made loud professions of attachment to the cause, they have never despaired of ultimate success. The work of Mrs Stowe has already given a blow to slavery from which it will never recover: it will create a new era in the cause of emancipation; it will enlist millions of sympathetic hearts, who never before properly understood the question; and it will produce a sober excitement among the thoughtful and religious in America against the accursed system. Besides, it has set an example of treating this subject, of which there will be many imitators, each, with varied talent, maintaining the great truth that all men are free, and pouring broadside after broadside on the citidel of slavery, until it falls. And if we add to this, that God is on the side of justice and mercy – that it is predicted, 'He shall judge the poor of the people, He shall save the children of the needy, and break in pieces the oppressor' – we must have confidence in our Leader and our cause.

Let every Christian abolitionist, then, take heart and hope.

Let them, with unsparing liberality, circulate such works as *Uncle Tom's Cabin*. Let them seek for stations in the Church or State where they can use a power favourable to emancipation. And, above all, let fervent prayer to Almighty God arise, that He may pour out an influence which can move the heart of ministers of religion, and senators on the floor of Washington, 'to break every yoke, and let the oppressed go free.'

> Men of thought! be up and stirring
>   Night and day;
> Sow the seed – withdraw the curtain,
>   Clear the way!
> Men of action, aid and cheer them,
>   As ye may!
> There's a fount about to stream,
> There's a light about to beam,
> There's a warmth about to glow,
> There's a flower about to blow;
> There's a midnight blackness changing
>   Into grey:
> Men of thought, and men of action
>   Clear the way!
>
> Once the welcome light has broken,
>   Who shall say
> What the unimagined glories
>   Of the day?
> What the evil that shall perish
>   In its ray?
> Aid the dawning, tongue and pen;
> Aid it, hopes of honest men;
> Aid it, paper – aid it, type –
> Aid it, for the hour is ripe,
> And our earnest must not slacken
>   Into play.
> Men of thought, and men of action,
>   Clear the way!

I am, Sir
Yours very truly,
JAMES SHERMAN

Uncle Tom's Cabin

Chapter 1

IN WHICH THE READER IS INTRODUCED TO
A MAN OF HUMANITY

LATE in the afternoon of a chilly day in February, two gentlemen were sitting alone over their wine, in a well-furnished dining-parlour in the town of P—, in Kentucky. There were no servants present, and the gentlemen, with chairs closely approaching, seemed to be discussing some subject with great earnestness.

For convenience sake we have said, hitherto, two *gentlemen*. One of the parties, however, when critically examined, did not seem, strictly speaking, to come under the species. He was a short, thick-set man, with coarse, commonplace features, and that swaggering air of pretension which marks a low man who is trying to elbow his way upward in the world. He was much over-dressed, in a gaudy vest of many colours, a blue neckerchief, bedropped gaily with yellow spots, and arranged with a flaunting tie, quite in keeping with the general air of the man. His hands, large and coarse, were plentifully bedecked with rings; and he wore a heavy gold watchchain, with a bundle of seals of portentous size, and a great variety of colours, attached to it, which, in the ardour of conversation, he was in the habit of flourishing and jingling with evident satisfaction. His conversation was in free and easy defiance of *Murray's Grammar*, and was garnished at convenient intervals with various profane expressions, which not even the desire to be graphic in our account shall induce us to transcribe.

His companion, Mr Shelby, had the appearance of a gentleman; and the arrangements of the house, and the general air of the housekeeping, indicated easy and even opulent circumstances. As we before stated, the two were in the midst of an earnest conversation.

'That is the way I should arrange the matter,' said Mr Shelby.

'I can't make trade that way – I positively can't, Mr Shelby,' said the other, holding up a glass of wine between his eye and the light.

'Why, the fact is, Haley, Tom is an uncommon fellow; he is certainly worth that sum anywhere – steady, honest, capable, manages my whole farm like a clock.'

'You mean honest, as niggers go,' said Haley, helping himself to a glass of brandy.

'No; I mean, really, Tom is a good steady, sensible, pious fellow. He got religion at a camp-meeting, four years ago; and I believe he really *did* get it. I've trusted him, since then, with everything I have, – money, house, horses, – and let him come and go round the country; and I always found him true and square in everything.'

'Some folks don't believe there is pious niggers, Shelby,' said Haley, with a candid flourish of his hand; 'but *I* do. I had a fellow, now, in this yer last lot I took to Orleans – 'twas as good as a meetin' now, really, to hear that critter pray, and he was quite gentle and quiet like. He fetched me a good sum, too; for I bought him cheap of a man that was 'bliged to sell out; so I realised six hundred on him. Yes, I consider religion a valeyable thing in a nigger, when it's the genuine article, and no mistake.'

'Well, Tom's got the real article, if ever a fellow had,' rejoined the other. 'Why, last fall, I let him go to Cincinnati alone, to do business for me, and bring home five hundred dollars. "Tom," says I to him, "I trust you, because I think you're a Christian – I know you wouldn't cheat." Tom comes back sure enough – I knew he would. Some low fellows, they say, said to him: "Tom, why don't you make tracks for Canada?" "Ah, master trusted me, and I couldn't!" They told me about it. I am sorry to part with Tom, I must say. You ought to let him cover the whole balance of the debt; and you would, Haley, if you had any conscience.'

'Well, I've got just as much conscience as any man in business can afford to keep, – just a little, you know, to swear by as 'twere,' said the trader, jocularly; 'and then I'm ready to do anything in reason, to 'blige friends; but this yer, you see, is a leetle too hard on a fellow – a leetle too hard.'

The trader sighed contemplatively, and poured out some more brandy.

'Well, then, Haley, how will you trade?' said Mr Shelby, after an uneasy interval of silence.

'Well, haven't you a boy or gal that you could throw in with Tom?'

'Hum! – none that I could well spare. To tell the truth, it's only hard necessity makes me willing to sell at all. I don't like parting with any of my hands, that's a fact.'

Here the door opened, and a small quadroon boy, between four and five years of age, entered the room. There was something in his appearance remarkably beautiful and engaging. His black hair, fine as floss silk, hung in glossy curls about his round, dimpled face, while a pair of large dark eyes, full of fire and softness, looked out from beneath the rich long lashes, as he peered curiously into the apartment. A gay robe of scarlet and yellow plaid, carefully made and neatly fitted, set off to advantage the dark and rich style of his beauty; and a certain comic air of assurance, blended with bashfulness, showed that he had been not unused to being petted and noticed by his master.

'Halloa, Jim Crow!' said Mr Shelby, whistling, and snapping a bunch of raisins towards him; 'pick that up, now!'

The child scampered, with all his little strength, after the prize, while his master laughed.

'Come here, Jim Crow,' said he.

The child came up, and the master patted the curly head and chucked him under the chin.

'Now, Jim, show this gentleman how you can dance and sing.'

The boy commenced one of those wild, grotesque songs common among the negroes, in a rich, clear voice, accompanying his singing with many comic evolutions of the hands, feet, and whole body, all in perfect time to the music.

'Bravo!' said Haley, throwing him a quarter of an orange.

'Now, Jim, walk like old Uncle Cudjoe when he has the rheumatism,' said his master.

Instantly the flexible limbs of the child assumed the appearance of deformity and distortion, as with his back humped up, and his master's stick in his hand, he hobbled about the room, his childish face drawn into a doleful pucker, and spitting from right to left, in imitation of an old man.

Both gentlemen laughed uproariously.

'Now, Jim,' said his master, 'show us how old Elder Robbins leads the psalm.'

The boy drew his chubby face down to a formidable length, and commenced toning a psalm-tune through his nose with imperturbable gravity.

'Hurrah! bravo! what a young 'un!' said Haley; 'that chap's a case, I'll promise. Tell you what,' said he, suddenly clapping his hand on Mr Shelby's shoulder, 'fling in that chap, and I'll settle the business – I will. Come, now, if that ain't doing the thing up about the rightest!'

At this moment the door was pushed gently open, and a young quadroon woman, apparently about twenty-five, entered the room.

There needed only a glance from the child to her, to identify her as its mother. There was the same rich, full, dark eye, with its long lashes; the same ripples of silky black hair. The brown of her complexion gave way on the cheek to a perceptible flush, which deepened as she saw the gaze of the strange man fixed upon her in bold and undisguised admiration. Her dress was of the neatest possible fit, and set off to advantage her finely-moulded shape. A delicately-formed hand, and a trim foot and ankle, were items of appearance that did not escape the quick eye of the trader, well used to run up at a glance the points of a fine female article.

'Well, Eliza?' said her master, as she stopped and looked hesitatingly at him.

'I was looking for Harry, please, sir;' and the boy bounded toward her, showing his spoils, which he had gathered in the skirt of his robe.

'Well, take him away, then,' said Mr Shelby; and hastily she withdrew, carrying the child on her arm.

'By Jupiter,' said the trader, turning to him in admiration; 'there's an article now! You might make your fortune on that ar gal in Orleans, any day. I've seen over a thousand, in my day, paid down for gals not a bit handsomer.'

'I don't want to make my fortune on her,' said Mr Shelby,

dryly; and seeking to turn the conversation, he uncorked a bottle of fresh wine, and asked his companion's opinion of it.

'Capital, sir – first chop!' said the trader; then turning, and slapping his hand familiarly on Shelby's shoulder, he added: 'Come, how will you trade about the girl? What shall I say for her? What'll you take?'

'Mr Haley, she is not to be sold,' said Shelby; 'my wife would not part with her for her weight in gold.'

'Ay, ay, women always say such things, 'cause they ha'nt no sort of calculation. Just show 'em how many watches, feathers, and trinkets one's weight in gold would buy, and that alters the case, I reckon.'

'I tell you, Haley, this must not be spoken of. I say no, and I mean no,' said Shelby, decidedly.

'Well, you'll let me have the boy, though?' said the trader; 'you must own I've come down pretty handsomely for him.'

'What on earth can you want with the child?' said Shelby.

'Why, I've got a friend that's going into this yer branch of the business – wants to buy up handsome boys to raise for the market. Fancy articles entirely – sell for waiters, and so on, to rich 'uns, that can pay for handsome 'uns. It sets off one of yer great places – a real handsome boy to open door, wait, and tend. They fetch a good sum; and this little devil is such a comical musical concern, he's just the article.'

'I would rather not sell him,' said Mr Shelby, thoughtfully; 'the fact is, sir, I'm a humane man, and I hate to take the boy from his mother, sir.'

'Oh, you do? – La! yes – something of that ar natur. I understand perfectly. It is mighty onpleasant gettin' on with women sometimes. I al'ays hates these yer screechin', screamin' times. They are *mighty* onpleasant; but, as I manages business, I generally avoids them, sir. Now, what if you get the girl off for a day, or a week, or so; then the thing's done quietly, – all over before she comes home. Your wife might get her some earrings, or a new gown, or some such truck, to make up with her.'

'I'm afraid not.'

'Lord bless ye, yes! These critters an't like white folks, you know; they get over things, only manage right. Now, they say,' said Haley, assuming a candid and confidential air, 'that this kind of trade is hardening to the feelings; but I never found it so. Fact is, I never could do things up the way some fellers manage the business. I've seen 'em as would pull a woman's child out of her arms, and set him up to sell, and she screechin' like mad all the time; — very bad policy — damages the article — makes 'em quite unfit for service sometimes. I knew a real handsome gal once, in Orleans, as was entirely ruined by this sort of handling. The fellow that was trading for her didn't want her baby; and she was one of your real high sort, when her blood was up. I tell you, she squeezed up her child in her arms, and talked, and went on real awful. It kinder makes my blood run cold to think on't: and when they carried off the child, and locked her up, she jest went ravin' mad and died in a week. Clear waste, sir, of a thousand dollars just for want of management, — there's where 'tis. It's always best to do the humane thing, sir; that's been *my* experience.'

And the trader leaned back in his chair, and folded his arm with an air of virtuous decision, apparently considering himself a second Wilberforce.

The subject appeared to interest the gentleman deeply; for while Mr Shelby was thoughtfully peeling an orange, Haley broke out afresh, with becoming diffidence, but as if actually driven by the force of truth to say a few words more.

'It don't look well, now, for a feller to be praisin' himself; but I say it jest because it's the truth. I believe I'm reckoned to bring in about the finest droves of niggers that is brought in — at least I've been told so; if I have once, I reckon I have a hundred times — all in good case — fat and likely, and I lose as few as any man in the business. And I lays it all to my management, sir; and humanity, sir, I may say, is the great pillar of *my* management.'

Mr Shelby did not know what to say, and so he said, 'Indeed!'

'Now, I've been laughed at for my notions, sir, and I've been talked to. They an't pop'lar and they an't common; but I stuck to 'em, sir; I've stuck to 'em and realised well on 'em; yes, sir, they have paid their passage, I may say;' and the trader laughed at his joke.

There was something so piquant and original in these elucidations of humanity, that Mr Shelby could not help laughing in company. Perhaps you laugh too, dear reader; but you know humanity comes out in a variety of strange forms nowadays, and there is no end to the odd things that humane people will say and do.

Mr Shelby's laugh encouraged the trader to proceed.

'It's strange now; but I never could beat this into people's heads. Now, there was Tom Loker, my old partner, down in Natchez; he was a clever fellow, Tom was, only the very devil with niggers – on principle 'twas, you see, for a better-hearted feller never broke bread; 'twas his *system*, sir. I used to talk to Tom. "Why, Tom," I used to say, "when your gals takes on and cry, what's the use o' crackin' on 'em over the head, and knockin' on 'em round? It's ridiculous," says I, "and don't do no sort o' good. Why, I don't see no harm in their cryin'," says I; "it's natur," says I, "and if natur can't blow off one way, it will another. Besides, Tom," says I, "it jest spiles your gals; they get sickly, and down in the mouth; and sometimes they gets ugly – particularly yallow gals do, and it's the devil and all gettin' on 'em broke in. Now," says I, "why can't you kinder coax 'em up and speak 'em fair? Depend on it, Tom, a little humanity, thrown in along, goes a heap further than all your jawin' and crackin'; and it pays better," said I, "depend on't." But Tom couldn't get the hang on't; and he spiled so many for me, that I had to break off with him, though he was a good-hearted fellow, and as fair a business hand as is goin'.'

'And do you find your ways of managing do the business better than Tom's?' said Mr Shelby.

'Why, yes, sir, I may so. You see, when I anyways can, I takes a leetle care about the onpleasant parts, like selling young uns and that – get the gals out of the way – out of sight, out of mind, you know: and when it's clean done, and can't be helped, they naturally get used to it. 'Tan't, you know, as if it was white folks, that's brought up in the way of 'spectin' to keep their children and wives, and all that. Niggers, you know, that's fetched up properly, ha'n't no kind of 'spectations of no kind: so all these things comes easier.'

'I'm afraid mine are not properly brought up, then,' said Mr Shelby.

'S'pose not. You Kentucky folks spile your niggers. You mean well by 'em, but 'tan't no real kindness, arter all. Now, a nigger, you see, what's got to be hacked and tumbled round the world, and sold to Tom, and Dick, and the Lord knows who, 'tan't no kindness to be givin' on him notions and expectations, and bringin' on him up too well, for the rough and tumble comes all the harder on him arter. Now, I venture to say, your niggers would be quite chop-fallen in a place where some of your plantation niggers would be singing and whooping like all possessed. Every man, you know, Mr Shelby, naturally thinks well of his own ways; and I think, I treat niggers just about as well as it's ever worth while to treat 'em.'

'It's a happy thing to be satisfied,' said Mr Shelby, with a slight shrug, and some perceptible feelings of a disagreeable nature.

'Well,' said Haley, after they had both silently picked their nuts for a season, 'what do you say?'

'I'll think the matter over, and talk with my wife,' said Mr Shelby. 'Meantime, Haley, if you want the matter carried on in the quiet way you speak of, you'd best not let your business in this neighbourhood be known. It will get out among my boys, and it will not be a particularly quiet business getting away any of my fellows, if they know it, I'll promise you.'

'Oh, certainly! by all means, mum! of course! But I'll tell you, I'm in a devil of a hurry, and shall want to know, as soon as possible, what I may depend on,' said he, rising and putting on his overcoat.

'Well, call up this evening, between six and seven, and you shall have my answer,' said Mr Shelby, and the trader bowed himself out of the apartment.

'I'd like to have been able to kick the fellow down the steps,' said he to himself, as he saw the door fairly closed, 'with his impudent assurance; but he knows how much he has me at advantage. If anybody had ever said to me that I should sell Tom down south to one of those rascally traders, I should have said, "Is thy servant a dog, that he should do this thing?" And now it must come, for aught I see. And Eliza's child, too! I know that I shall have some fuss with wife about that; and, for that matter, about Tom, too. So much for being in debt – heigho! The fellow sees his advantage, and means to push it.'

Perhaps the mildest form of the system of slavery is to be seen in the State of Kentucky. The general prevalence of agricultural pursuits of a quiet and gradual nature, not requiring those periodic seasons of hurry and pressure that are called for in the business of more southern districts, makes the task of the negro a more healthful and reasonable one; while the master, content with a more gradual style of acquisition, has not those temptations to hard-heartedness which always overcome frail human nature when the prospect of sudden and rapid gain is weighed in the balance, with no heavier counterpoise than the interests of the helpless and unprotected.

Whoever visits some estates there, and witnesses the good-humoured indulgence of some masters and mistresses, and the affectionate loyalty of some slaves, might be tempted to dream the oft-fabled poetic legend of a patriarchial institution, and all that; but over and above the scene there broods a portentous shadow – the shadow of *law*. So long as the law considers all these human beings, with beating hearts and living affections, only as so many *things* belonging to a master – so long as the failure, or misfortune, or imprudence, or death of the kindest owner, may cause them any day to exchange a life of kind protection and indulgence for one of hopeless misery and toil – so long it is impossible to make anything beautiful or desirable in the best-regulated administration of slavery.

Mr Shelby was a fair average kind of man, good-natured and kindly, and disposed to easy indulgence of those around him; and there had never been a lack of anything which might contribute to the physical comfort of the negroes on his estate. He had, however, speculated largely and quite loosely – had involved himself deeply, and his notes to a large amount had come into the hands of Haley; and this small piece of information is the key to the preceding conversation.

Now, it had so happened that, in approaching the door, Eliza had caught enough of the conversation to know that a trader was making offers to her master for somebody.

She would gladly have stopped at the door to listen, as she came out; but her mistress just then calling, she was obliged to hasten away.

Still she thought she heard the trader make an offer for her boy; – could she be mistaken? Her heart swelled and throbbed, and she involuntarily strained him so tight, that the little fellow looked up into her face in astonishment.

'Eliza, girl, what ails you to-day?' said her mistress, when Eliza had upset the wash-pitcher, knocked down the work-stand, and, finally, was abstractedly offering her mistress a long night-gown in place of the silk dress she had ordered her to bring from the wardrobe.

Eliza started. 'O, missis!' she said, raising her eyes; then, bursting into tears, she sat down in a chair and began sobbing.

'Why, Eliza, child! what ails you?' said her mistress.

'Oh, missis, missis!' said Eliza, 'there's been a trader talking with master in the parlour! I heard him.'

'Well, silly child, suppose there has.'

'Oh, missis, *do* you suppose mas'r would sell my Harry?' And the poor creature threw herself into a chair and sobbed convulsively.

'Sell him! No, you foolish girl! You know your master never deals with those southern traders, and never means to sell any of his servants as long as they behave well. Why, you silly child, who do you think would want to buy your Harry? Do you think all the world are set on him as you are, you goosie? Come, cheer up, and hook my dress. There now, put my back hair up in that pretty braid you learnt the other day, and don't go listening at doors any more.'

'Well, but, missis, *you* never would give your consent – to – to—'

'Nonsense, child! to be sure I shouldn't. What do you talk so for? I would as soon have one of my own children sold. But really, Eliza, you are getting altogether too proud of that little fellow. A man can't put his nose into the door, but you think he must be coming to buy him.'

Reassured by her mistress's confident tone, Eliza proceeded nimbly and adroitly with her toilet, laughing at her own fears as she proceeded.

Mrs Shelby was a woman of a high class, both intellectually and morally. To that natural magnanimity and generosity of mind which one often marks as characteristic of the women of Kentucky, she added high moral and religious sensibility and principle, carried out with great energy and ability into practical results. Her husband, who made no professions to any particular religious character, nevertheless reverenced and respected the consistency of hers, and stood, perhaps, a little in awe of her opinion. Certain it was, that he gave her unlimited scope in all her benevolent efforts for the comfort, instruction, and improvement of her servants, though he never took any decided part in them himself. In fact, if not exactly a believer in the doctrine of the efficiency of the extra good works of saints, he really seemed somehow or other to fancy that his wife had piety and benevolence enough for two – to indulge a shadowy expectation of getting into heaven through her superabundance of qualities to which he made no particular pretension.

The heaviest load on his mind, after his conversation with the trader, lay in the foreseen necessity of breaking to his wife the arrangement contemplated – meeting the importunities and opposition which he knew he should have reason to encounter.

Mrs Shelby, being entirely ignorant of her husband's embarrassments, and knowing only the general kindliness of his temper, had been quite sincere in the entire incredulity with which she had met Eliza's suspicions. In fact, she dismissed the matter from her mind without a second thought, and, being occupied in preparations for an evening visit, it passed out of her thoughts entirely.

Chapter 2

THE MOTHER

ELIZA had been brought up by her mistress, from girlhood, as a petted and indulged favourite.

The traveller in the south must often have remarked that peculiar air of refinement, that softness of voice and manner, which seems in many cases to be a particular gift to the quadroon and mulatto women. These natural graces in the quadroon are often united with beauty of the most dazzling kind, and in almost every case with a personal appearance prepossesing and agreeable. Eliza, such as we have described her, is not a fancy sketch, but taken from remembrance, as we saw her years ago in Kentucky. Safe under the protecting care of her mistress, Eliza had reached maturity without those temptations which make beauty so fatal an inheritance to a slave. She had been married to a bright and talented young mulatto man, who was a slave on a neighbouring estate, and bore the name of George Harris.

This young man had been hired out by his master to work in a bagging factory, where his adroitness and ingenuity caused him to be considered the first hand in the place. He had invented a machine for the cleaning of the hemp, which, considering the education and circumstances of the inventor, displayed quite as much mechanical genius as Whitney's cotton-gin.[1]

He was possessed of a handsome person and pleasing manners, and was a general favourite in the factory. Nevertheless as this young man was in the eye of the law not a man, but a thing, all these superior qualifications were subject to the control of a vulgar, narrow-minded, tyrannical master. The same gentleman, having heard of the fame of George's invention, took a ride over to the factory, to see what this intelligent chattel had been about. He was received with great enthusiasm by the employer, who congratulated him on possessing so valuable a slave.

He was waited upon over the factory, shown the machinery by George, who, in high spirits, talked so fluently, held himself so erect, look so handsome and manly, that his master began to feel an uneasy consciousness of inferiority. What business had his slave to be marching round the country, inventing machines, and holding up his head among gentlemen? He'd soon put a stop to it. He'd take him back, and put him to hoeing and digging, and 'see if he'd step about so smart.' Accordingly, the manufacturer and all hands concerned were astounded when he suddenly demanded George's wages and announced his intention of taking him home.

'But, Mr Harris,' remonstrated the manufacturer, 'isn't this rather sudden?'

'What if it is? Isn't the man *mine*?'

'We would be willing, sir, to increase the rate of compensation.'

'No object at all, sir. I don't need to hire any of my hands out, unless I've a mind to.'

---

[1] A machine of this description was really the invention of a young coloured man in Kentucky.

'But, sir, he seems peculiarly adapted to this business.'

'Dare say he may be; never was much adapted to anything that I set him about, I'll be bound.'

'But only think of his inventing this machine,' interposed one of the workmen, rather unluckily.

'Oh, yes! – a machine for saving work, is it? He'd invent that, I'll be bound; let a nigger alone for that, any time. They are all labour-saving machines themselves, every one of em. No, he shall tramp!'

George had stood like one transfixed, at hearing his doom thus suddenly pronounced by a power that he knew was irresistible. He folded his arms, tightly pressed in his lips, but a whole volcano of bitter feeling burned in his bosom, and sent streams of fire through his veins. He breathed short, and his large dark eyes flashed like live coals; and he might have broken out into some dangerous ebullition, had not the kindly manufacturer touched him on the arm, and said, in a low tone, –

'Give way, George; go with him for the present. We'll try to help you, yet.'

The tyrant observed the whisper, and conjectured its import, though he could not hear what was said; and he inwardly strengthened himself in his determination to keep the power he possessed over his victim.

George was taken home, and put to the meanest drudgery of the farm. He had been able to repress every disrespectful word; but the flashing eye, the gloomy and troubled brow, were part of a natural language, that could not be repressed – indubitable signs, which showed too plainly that the man could not become a thing.

It was during the happy period of his employment in the factory that George had seen and married his wife. During that period – being such trusted and favoured by his employer – he had free liberty to come and go at discretion. The marriage was highly approved of by Mrs Shelby, who, with a little womanly complacency in match-making, felt pleased to unite her handsome favourite with one of her own class who seemed in every way suited to her: and so they were married in her mistress's great parlour, and her mistress herself adorned the bride's beautiful hair with orange-blossoms, and threw over it the bridal veil, which certainly could scarce have rested on a fairer head;

and there was no lack of white gloves, and cake and wine – of admiring guests to praise the bride's beauty, and her mistress's indulgence and liberality. For a year or two Eliza saw her husband frequently, and there was nothing to interrupt their happiness, except the loss of two infant chilren, to whom she was passionately attached, and who she mourned with a grief so intense as to call for gentle remonstrance from her mistress, who sought, with maternal anxiety, to direct her naturally passionate feelings within the bounds of reason and religion.

After the birth of little Harry, however, she had gradually become tranquillised and settled; and every bleeding tie and throbbing nerve, once more entwined with that little life, seemed to become sound and healthful; and Eliza was a happy woman up to the time that her husband was rudely torn from his kind employer, and brought under the iron sway of his legal owner.

The manufacturer, true to his word, visited Mr Harris a week or two after George had been taken away, when, as he hoped, the heat of the occasion had passed away, and tried every possible inducement to lead him to restore him to his former employment.

'You needn't trouble yourself to talk any longer,' said he, doggedly; 'I know my own business, sir.'

'I did not presume to interfere with it, sir. I only thought that you might think it for your interest to let your man to us on the terms proposed.'

'Oh, I understand the matter well enough. I saw your winking and whispering, the day I took him out of the factory; but you don't come it over me that way. It's a free country, sir; the man's *mine*, and I do what I please with him – that's it!'

And so fell George's last hope; nothing before him but a life of toil and drudgery, rendered more bitter by every little smarting vexation and indignity which tyrannical ingenuity could devise. A very humane jurist once said, 'The worst use you can put a man to is to hang him.' No! there is another use that a man can be put to that is WORSE!

Chapter 3

THE HUSBAND AND FATHER

Mrs Shelby had gone on her visit, and Eliza stood in the verandah, rather dejectedly looking after the retreating carriage, when a hand was laid on her shoulder. She turned, and a bright smile lighted up her fine eyes.

'George, is it you? How you frightened me! Well; I am so glad you's come! Missis is gone to spend the afternoon; so come into my little room, and we'll have the time all to ourselves.'

Saying this, she drew him into a neat little apartment opening on the verandah, where she generally sat at her sewing, within call of her mistress.

'How glad I am! – why don't you smile? – and look at Harry – how he grows!' The boy stood shyly regarding his father through his curls, holding close to the skirts of his mother's dress. 'Isn't he beautiful?' said Eliza, lifting his long curls, and kissing him.

'I wish he'd never been born!' said George bitterly. 'I wish I'd never been born myself!'

Surprised and frightened, Eliza sat down, and leaned her head on her husband's shoulder, and burst into tears.

'There now, Eliza, it's too bad for me to make you feel so, poor girl!' said he, fondly, – 'it's too bad. Oh, how I wish you never had seen me – you might have been happy!'

'George! George! how can you talk so? What dreadful thing has happened, or is going to happen? I am sure we've been very happy till lately.'

'So we have, dear,' said George. Then drawing his child on his knees, he gazed intently on his glorious dark eyes, and passed his hands through his long curls.

'Just like you, Eliza; and you are the handsomest woman I

ever saw, and the best one I ever wish to see; but, oh, I wish I'd never seen you, nor you me!'

'Oh, George, how can you?'

'Yes, Eliza, it's all misery, misery, misery! My life is bitter as wormwood; the very life is burning out of me. I'm a poor, miserable, forlorn drudge; I shall only drag you down with me, that's all. What's the use of our trying to do anything, trying to know anything, trying to be anything? What's the use of living? I wish I was dead!'

'Oh, now, dear George, that is really wicked! I know how you feel about losing your place in the factory, and you have a hard master; but pray be patient, and perhaps something—'

'Patient!' said he interrupting her; 'haven't I been patient? Did I say a word when he came and took me away, for no earthly reason, from the place where everybody was kind to me? I'd paid him truly every cent of my earnings: and they all said I worked well.'

'Well, it *is* dreadful,' said Eliza, 'but, after all, he is your master, you know.'

'My master! and who made him my master? That's what I think of — what right has he to me? I'm a man as much as he is; I am a better man than he is; I know more about business than he does; I'm a better manager than he is; I can read better than he can; I can write a better hand; and I've learned it all myself, and no thanks to him — I've learned it in spite of him; and now what right has he to make a dray-horse of me? — to take me from things I can do, and do better than he can, and put me to work that any horse can do? He tries to do it; he says he'll bring me down and humble me, and he puts me to just the hardest, meanest, and dirtiest work, on purpose.'

'Oh, George — George — you frighten me! Why, I never heard you talk so: I'm afraid you'll do something dreadful. I don't wonder at your feelings at all; but oh, do be careful — do, do — for my sake — for Harry's!'

'I have been careful, and I have been patient; but it's growing worse and worse — flesh and blood can't bear it any longer. Every chance he can get to insult and torment me, he takes. I thought I could do my work well, and keep on quiet, and have some time to read and learn out of work-hours; but the more he sees I can do, the more he loads on. He says that though I don't say anything, he sees I've got the devil in me, and he means to bring it out; and one of these days it will come out in a way that he won't like, or I'm mistaken.'

'Oh, dear, what shall we do?' said Eliza mournfully.

'It was only yesterday,' said George, 'as I was busy loading stones into a cart, that young Mas'r Tom stood there, slashing his whip so near the horse, that the creature was frightened, I asked him to stop as pleasant as I could; he just kept right on. I begged him again, and then he turned on me, and began striking me. I held his hand, and then he screamed, and kicked, and ran to his father and told him that I was fighting him. He came in a rage, and said he'd teach me who was my master; and he tied me to a tree, and cut switches for young master, and told him that he might whip me till he was tired; and he did do it. If I don't make him remember it some time!'

And the brow of the young man grew dark, and his eyes burned with an expression that made his young wife tremble.

'Who made this man my master — that's what I want to know?' he said.

'Well,' said Eliza, mournfully, 'I always thought that I must obey my master and mistress, or I couldn't be a Christian!'

'There is some sense in it, in your case; they have brought you up like a child — fed you, clothed you, indulged you, and taught you, so that you have a good education, — that is some reason why they should claim you. But I have been kicked, and cuffed, and sworn at, and at the best only let alone; and what do I owe? I've paid for all my keeping a hundred times over. I *won't* bear it — no, I *won't!*' he said, clenching his hand with a fierce frown.

Eliza trembled and was silent. She had never seen her husband in this mood before; and her gentle system of ethics seemed to bend like a reed in the surges of such passions.

'You know poor little Carlo that you gave me?' added George; 'the creature has been about all the comfort that I've had. He has slept with me nights, and followed me around days, and kind o' looked at me as if he understood how I felt. Well, the other day I was just feeding him with a few old scraps I picked up by the kitchen-door and Mas'r came along, and said I was feeding him up at his expense, and that he couldn't afford to have every nigger keeping his dog, and ordered me to tie a stone to his neck, and throw him in the pond.'

'Oh, George, you didn't do it!'

'Do it! – not I; but he did. Mas'r and Tom pelted the poor drowning creature with stones. Poor thing! He looked at me so mournful, as if he wondered why I didn't save him. I had to take a flogging because I wouldn't do it myself. I don't care; Mas'r will find out that I am one that whipping won't tame. My day will come yet, if he don't look out.'

'What are you going to do? Oh, George, don't do anything wicked; if you only trust in God, and try to do right, he'll deliver you.'

'I an't a Christian like you, Eliza; my heart's full of bitterness; I can't trust in God. Why does He let things be so?'

'Oh, George, we must have faith! Mistress says that when all things go wrong to us, we must believe that God is doing the very best.'

'That's easy to say, for people that are sitting on their sofas and riding in their carriages; but let 'em be where I am, I guess it would come some harder. I wish I could be good; but my heart burns, and can't be reconciled anyhow. You couldn't in my place; you can't now, if I tell you all I've got to say. You don't know the whole yet.'

'What can be coming now?'

'Well, lately Mas'r has been saying, that he was a fool to let me marry off the place; that he hates Mr Shelby and all his tribe, because they are proud, and hold their heads up above him, and that I've got proud notions from you; and he says he won't let me come here any more, and that I shall take a wife and settle down on his place. At first he only scolded and grumbled these things: but yesterday he told me that I should take Mina for a wife, and settle down in a cabin with her, or he would sell me down river.'

'Why, but you were married to *me*, by the minister, as much as if you'd been a white man,' said Eliza simply.

'Don't you know a slave can't be married? There is no law in this country for that: I can't hold you for my wife, if he chooses to part us. That's why I wish I'd never seen you – why I wish I'd never been born; it would have been better for us both – it would have been better for this poor child if he had never been born. All this may happen to him yet !'

'Oh, but master is so kind !'

'Yes, but who knows ? he may die ; and then he may be sold to nobody knows who. What pleasure is it that he is handsome, and smart, and bright ? I tell you, Eliza, that a sword will pierce through your soul for every good and pleasant thing your child is or has – it will make him worth too much for you to keep.'

The words smote heavily on Eliza's heart ; the vision of the trader came before her eyes, and, as if some one had struck her a deadly blow, she turned pale and gasped for breath. She looked nervously out on the verandah, where the boy, tired of the grave conversation, had retired, and where he was riding triumphantly up and down on Mr Shelby's walking-stick. She would have spoke to tell her husband her fears, but checked herself.

'No, no, he has enough to bear, poor fellow !' she thought. 'No, I won't tell him ; besides, it an't true ; missis never deceives us.'

'So, Eliza, my girl,' said the husband, mournfully, 'bear up, now, and good bye ; for I'm going.'

'Going, George ! – going where ?'

'To Canada,' said he, straightening himself up ; 'and when I'm there, I'll buy you – that's all the hope that's left us. You have a kind master, that won't refuse to sell you. I'll buy you and the boy – God helping me, I will !'

'Oh, dreadful ! – if you should be taken !'

'I won't be taken, Eliza – I'll *die* first ! I'll be free, or I'll die !'

'You won't kill yourself ?'

'No need of that ; they will kill me fast enough ; they never will get me down the river alive.'

'Oh, George, for my sake, do be careful ! Don't do anything wicked ; don't lay hands on yourself, or anybody else. You are tempted too much – too much ; but don't – go you must – but go carefully, prudently ; pray God to help you.'

'Well, then, Eliza, hear my pain. Mas'r took it into his head to send me right by here, with a note to Mr Symmes, that lives a mile past. I believe he expected I should come here to tell you what I have. It would please him, if he thought it would aggravate "Shelby's folks," as he calls 'em. I'm going home quite resigned, you understand, as if all was over. I've got some preparations made, and there are those that will help me; and, in the course of a week or so, I shall be among the missing, some day. Pray for me, Eliza; perhaps the good Lord will hear *you*.'

'Oh, pray yourself, George, and go trusting in Him; then you won't do anything wicked.'

'Well, now, *good bye*,' said George, holding Eliza's hands and gazing into her eyes, without moving. They stood silent; then there were last words, and sobs, and bitter weeping – such parting as those may make whose hope to meet again is as the spider's web; and the husband and wife were parted.

Chapter 4

AN EVENING IN UNCLE TOM'S CABIN

THE cabin of Uncle Tom was a small log building, close adjoining to 'the house,' as the negro, *par excellence*, designates his master's dwelling. In front it had a neat garden-patch where, every summer, strawberries, raspberries, and a variety of fruits and vegetables, flourished under careful tending. The whole front of it was covered by a large scarlet bignonia and a native multiflora rose, which, entwisting and interlacing, left scarce a vestige of the rough logs to be seen. Here, also, in summer, various brilliant annuals, such as marigolds, petunias, four-o'clocks, found an indulgent corner in which to unfold their splendours, and were the delight and pride of Aunt Chloe's heart.

Let us enter the dwelling. The evening meal at the house is over, and Aunt Chloe, who presided over its preparation as head cook, has left to inferior officers in the kitchen the business of clearing away and washing dishes, and come out into her own snug territories, to 'get her old man's supper;' therefore, doubt not that it is her you see by the fire, presiding with anxious interest over certain frizzling items in a stewpan, and anon, with grave consideration, lifting the cover of a bake-kettle, from whence steam forth indubitable intimations of 'something good.' A round, black, shining face is hers, so glossy as to suggest the idea that she might have been washed over with white of eggs, like one of her own tea-rusks. Her whole plump countenance beams with satisfaction and contentment from under her well-starched checked turban, bearing on it, however, if we must confess it, a little of that tinge of self-consciousness which becomes the first cook of the neighbour-hood, as Aunt Chloe was universally held and acknowledged to be.

A cook she certainly was, in the very bone and centre of her soul. Not a chicken, or turkey, or duck in the barn-yard, but looked grave when they saw her approaching, and seemed evidently to be reflecting on their latter end; and certain it was that she was always meditating on trussing, stuffing, and roast-ing, to a degree that was calculated to inspire terror in any reflecting fowl living. Her corn-cake, in all its varieties of hoe-cake, dodgers, muffins, and other species too numerous to mention, was a sublime mystery to all less practised compound-ers; and she would shake her fat sides with honest pride and merriment as she would narrate the fruitless efforts that one and another of her compeers had made to attain to her elevation.

The arrival of company at the house, the arranging of dinners and suppers 'in style,' awoke all the energies of the soul; and no sight was more welcome to her than a pile of travelling trunks launched on the verandah, for then she foresaw fresh efforts and fresh triumphs.

Just at present, however, Aunt Chloe is looking into the bake-pan, in which congenial operation we shall leave her till we finish our picture of the cottage.

In one corner of it stood a bed, covered neatly with a snowy spread; and by the side of it was a piece of carpeting of some considerable size. On this piece of carpeting Aunt Chloe took her stand, as being decidedly in the upper walks of life; and it and the bed by which it lay, and the whole corner, in fact, were treated with distinguished consideration, and made, so far as possible, sacred from the marauding inroads and desecrations of little folks. In fact, that corner was the *drawing-room* of the establishment. In the other corner was a bed of much humbler pretensions, and evidently designed for *use*. The wall over the fireplace was adorned with some very brilliant Scriptural prints, and a portrait of General Washington, drawn and coloured in a manner which would certainly have astonished that hero, if ever he had happened to meet with its like.

On a rough bench in the corner, a couple of woolly-headed boys, with glistening black eyes and fat shining cheeks, were busy in superintending the first walking operations of the baby, which, as is usually the case, consisted in getting up on its feet, balancing a moment, and then tumbling down – each successive failure being violently cheered, as something decidedly clever.

A table, somewhat rheumatic in its limbs, was drawn out in front of the fire, and covered with a cloth, displaying cups and saucers of a decidedly brilliant pattern, with other symptoms of an approaching meal. At that table was seated Uncle Tom, Mr Shelby's best hand, who, as he is to be the hero of our story, we must daguerreotype for our readers. He was a large, broad-chested, powerfully-made man, of a full glossy black, and a face whose truly African features were characterised by an expression of grave and steady good sense, united with much kindliness and benevolence. There was something about his whole air self-respecting and dignified, yet united with a confiding and humble simplicity.

He was very busily intent at this moment on a slate lying before him, on which he was carefully and slowly endeavouring to accomplish a copy of some letters; in which operation he was overlooked by young Mas'r George, a smart, bright boy of thirteen, who appeared fully to realise the dignity of his position as instructor.

'Not that way, Uncle Tom – not that way,' said he briskly, as Uncle Tom laboriously brought up the tail of his g the wrong side out; 'that makes a q, you see.'

'La sakes, now, does it?' said Uncle Tom, looking with a respectful, admiring air, as his young teacher flourishingly scrawled q's and g's innumerable for his edification; and then, taking the pencil in his big, heavy fingers, he patiently recommenced.

'How easy white folks al'as does things!' said Aunt Chloe, pausing while she was greasing a griddle with a scrap of bacon on her fork, and regarding young Master George with pride. 'The way he can write, now! and read, too! and then to come out here evenings and read his lessons to us, – it's mighty interestin'!'

'But, Aunt Chloe, I'm getting mighty hungry,' said George. 'Isn't that cake in the skillet almost done?'

'Mose done, Mas'r George,' said Aunt Chloe, lifting the lid, and peeping in; 'browning beautiful – a real lovely brown. Ah, let me alone for dat! Missis let Sally try to make some cake t'other day, jes to *larn* her, she said. "Oh, go way, missis," says I; "it really hurts my feelins, now, to see good vittles spiled dat ar way! Cake ris all to one side – no shape at all, no more than my shoe – go way!"'

And with this final expression of contempt for Sally's greenness, Aunt Chloe whipped the cover off the bake-kettle, and disclosed to view a neatly-baked pound-cake, of which no city confectioner need to have been ashamed. This being evidently the central point of the entertainment, Aunt Chloe began now to bustle about earnestly in the supper department.

'Here you, Mose and Pete, get out de way, you niggers! Get away, Polly, honey: mammy'll give her baby somefin by-and-by. Now, Mas'r Gorge, you jest take off dem books, and set down now with my old man, and I'll take up de sausages, and have de first griddle full of cakes on your plates in less dan no time.'

'They wanted me to come to supper in the house,' said George, 'but I knew what was what too well for that, Aunt Chloe.'

'So you did – so you did, honey,' said Aunt Chloe, heaping the smoking batter-cakes on his plate: 'you know'd your old aunty'd keep the best for you. Oh, let you alone for dat – go way!'

And with that Aunty gave George a nudge with her finger, designed to be immensely facetious, and turned again to her griddle with great briskness.

'Now for the cake,' said Mas'r George, when the activity of the griddle department had somewhat subsided: and with that the youngster flourished a large knife over the article in question.

'La bless you, Mas'r George!' said Aunt Chloe, with earnestness, catching his arm; 'you wouldn't be for cuttin' it wid dat ar great heavy knife! Smash all down – spile all de pretty rise of it! Here, I've got a thin old knife I keeps sharp a purpose. Dar now, see – comes apart light as a feather! Now eat away – you won't get anything to beat dat ar!'

'Tom Lincoln says,' said George, speaking with his mouth full, 'that their Jinny is a better cook than you.'

'Dem Lincons an't much 'count no way!' said Aunt Chloe, contemptuously; 'I mean, set alongside *our* folks. They's 'spectable folks enough in a kinder plain way: but, as to gettin' up anything in style, they don't begin to have a notion on't. Set Mas'r Lincon, now, alongside Mas'r Shelby. Good Lor! and Missis Lincon – can she kinder sweep it into a room like my missis – so kinder splendid, yer know? Oh, go way! don't tell me nothin' of dem Lincons!' and Aunt Chloe tossed her head as one who hoped she did know something of the world.

'Well, though, I've heard you say,' said George, 'that Jinny was a pretty fair cook.'

'So I did,' said Aunt Chloe; 'I may say dat. Good, plain, common cookin', Jinny'll do; make a good pone o' bred – bile her taters *far* – her corn-cakes isn't extra, not extra, now Jinny's corn-cakes isn't, but then they's far. But, Lor, come to de higher branches, and what *can* she do? Why, she makes pies – sartin she does; but what kinder crust? Can she make your real flecky paste, as melts in your mouth, and lies all up like a puff? Now, I went over thar when Miss Mary was gwine to be married, and Jinny she jest showed me de weddin' pies. Jinny and I is good friends, ye know. I never said nothin': but go long Mas'r George! Why, I shouldn't sleep a wink for a week if I had a batch of pies like dem ar. Why, dey wa'n't no 'count 't al.'

'I suppose Jinny thought they were ever so nice,' said George.

'Thought so! – didn't she? Thar she was showing 'em as innocent! Ye see, it's jest here, Jinny *don't know*. Lor, the family an't nothing! She can't be 'spected to know! 'Tan't no fault o' hern. Ah, Mas'r George, you doesn't know half your privileges in yer family and bringin' up!' Here Aunt Chloe sighed, and rolled up her eyes with emotion.

'I'm sure, Aunt Chloe, I understand all my pie-and-pudding privileges,' said George. 'Ask Tom Lincoln if I don't crow over him every time I meet him.'

Aunt Chloe sat back in her chair, and indulged in a hearty guffaw of laughter at this witticism of young Mas'r's, laughing till the tears rolled down her black, shining cheeks, and varying the exercise with playfully slapping and poking Mas'r Georgey, and telling him to go way, and that he was a case – that he was fit to kill her, and that he sartin would kill her one of these days; and, between each of these sanguinary predictions, going off into a laugh, each longer and stronger than the other, till George really began to think that he was a very dangerously witty fellow, and that it became him to be careful how he talked 'as funny as he could.'

'And so ye telled Tom did ye? O Lor, what young uns will be up ter! Ye crowed over Tom? O Lor, Mas'r George, if ye wouldn't make a hornbug laugh!'

'Yes,' said George, 'I says to him, "Tom, you ought to see some of Aunt Chloe's pies; they're the right sort," says I.'

'Pity, now, Tom couldn't,' said Aunt Chloe, on whose benevolent heart the idea of Tom's benighted condition seemed to make a strong impression. 'Ye oughter just ask him here to dinner some o' these times, Mas'r George,' she added; 'it would look quite pretty of ye. Ye know, Mas'r George, ye oughtenter feel 'bove nobody on 'count yer privileges, 'cause all our privileges is gi'n to us; we ought al'ays to 'member that,' said Aunt Chloe, looking quite serious.

'Well, I mean to ask Tom here some day next week,' said George; 'and you do your prettiest, Aunt Chloe, and we'll make him stare. Won't we make him eat so he won't get over it for a fortnight?'

'Yes, yes – sartin,' said Aunt Chloe, delighted; 'you'll see, Lor! to think of some of our dinners! Yer mind dat ar great chicken-pie I made when we guv de dinner to General Knox? I and missis, we come pretty near quarrelling about dat ar crust. What does get into ladies sometimes I don't knows; but sometimes, when a body has de heaviest kind o' 'sponsibility on 'em, as ye may say, and is all kinder *seris* and taken up, dey takes dat ar time to be hangin' round and kinder interferin'! Now, missis, she wanted me to do dis way, and she wanted me to do dat way; and finally I got kinder sarcy, and says I, "Now, missis, do jist look at dem beautiful white hands o' yourn, with long fingers, and all a sparkling with rings, like my white lilies when de dew's on 'em; and look at my great black stumpin' hands. Now, don't ye think that de Lord must have meant *me* to make de pie-crust, and you to stay in de parlour?" Dar! I was jist so sarcy, Mas'r George.'

'And what did mother say?' said George.

'Say? – why, she kinder larfed in her eyes – dem great hand-some eyes o' hern; and says she, "Well, Aunt Chloe, I think you are about in the right on't," says she; and she went off in de parlour. She oughter cracked me over de head for bein' so sarcy; but dar's whar 'tis – I can't do nothin' with ladies in de kitchen.'

'Well, you made out well with that dinner – I remember everybody said so,' said George.

'Didn't I. And wan't I behind de dinin'-room door dat bery day? and didn't I see de Gineral pass his plate three times for some more dat bery pie? and, says he, "You must have an uncommon cook, Mrs Shelby." Lor! I was fit to split myself.'

'And the Gineral, he knows what cookin' is,' said Aunt Chloe, drawing herself up with an air. 'Bery nice man, de Gineral! He comes of one of de bery *fustest* families in Old Virginny! He knows what's what, now, as well as I do – de Gineral. Ye see, there's *pints* in all pies, Mas'r George; but tan't everybody knows what they is, or orter be. But the Gineral, he knows; I knew by his 'marks he made. Yes, he knows what de pints is!'

By this time Master George had arrived at that pass to which even a boy can come (under uncommon circumstances), when he really could not eat another morsel, and, therefore, he was at leisure to notice the pile of woolly heads and glistening eyes which were regarding their operations hungrily from the opposite corner.

'Here, you Mose, Pete,' he said, breaking off liberal bits, and throwing it at them; 'you want some, don't you? Come, Aunt Chloe, bake them some cakes.

And George and Tom moved to a comfortable seat in the chimney-corner, while Aunt Chloe, after baking a goodly pile of cakes, took her baby on her lap, and began alternately filling its mouth and her own, and distributing to Mose and Pete, who seemed rather to prefer eating theirs as they rolled about on the floor under the table, tickling each other, and occasionally pulling the baby's toes.

'Oh, go along, will ye?' said the mother, giving now and then a kick, in a kind of general way, under the table, when the movement became too obstreperous. 'Can't ye be decent when white folks come to se ye? Stop dat ar, now, will ye? Better mind yerselves, or I'll take ye down a button-hole lower, when Mas'r George is gone!'

What meaning was couched under this terrible threat it is difficult to say; but certain it is that its awful indistinctness seemed to produce very little impression on the young sinners addressed.

'La, now!' said Uncle Tom, 'they are so full of tickle all the while, they can't behave themselves.'

Here the boys emerged from under the table, and, with hand and faces well plastered with molasses, began a vigorous kissing of the baby.

'Get along wid ye!' said the mother, pushing away their woolly heads. 'Ye'll all stick together, and never get clar, if ye do dat fashion. Go long to de spring and wash yerselves!' she said, seconding her exhortations by a slap, which resounded very formidably, but which seemed only to knock out so much more laugh from the young ones, as they tumbled precipitately over each other out-of-doors, where they fairly screamed with merriment.

'Did ye ever see such aggravating young uns?' said Aunt Chloe, rather complacently, as, producing an old towel, kept for such emergencies, she poured a little water out of the cracked teapot on it, and began rubbing off the molasses from the baby's face and hands; and having polished her till she shone, she set her down in Tom's lap, while she busied herself in clearing away supper. The baby employed the intervals in pulling Tom's nose, scratching his face, and burying her fat hands in his woolly hair; which last operation seemed to afford her special content.

'Ain't she a peart young un?' said Tom, holding her from him to take a full-length view; then, getting up, he set her on his broad shoulder, and began capering and dancing with her, while Mas'r George snapped at her with his pocket-handkerchief, and Mose and Pete, now returned again, roared after her like bears, till Aunt Chloe declared that they 'fairly took her head off' with their noise. As, according to her own statement, this surgical operation was a matter of daily occurrence in the cabin, the declaration no whit abated the merriment, till every one had roared, and tumbled, and danced themselves down to a state of composure.

'Well, now, I hopes you're done,' said Aunt Chloe, who had been busy in pulling out a rude box of a trundle-bed; 'and now, you Mose and you Pete, get into thar; for we's going to have the meetin'.'

'Oh, mother, we don't wanter. We wants to sit up to meetin' – meetin's is so curis. We likes 'em.'

'La, Aunt Chloe, shove it under, and let 'em sit up,' said Mas'r George, decisively, giving a push to the rude machine.

Aunt Chloe, having thus saved appearances, seemed highly delighted to push the thing under, saying, as she did so, 'Well, nebbe 'twill do 'em some good.'

The house now resolved itself into a committee of the whole, to consider the accommodations and arrangements for the meeting.

'What we's to do for cheers, now, I declare I don't know,' said Aunt Chloe. As the meeting had been held at Uncle Tom's weekly, for an indefinite length of time, without any more 'cheers,' there seemed some encouragement to hope that a way would be discovered at present.

'Old Uncle Peter sung both de legs out of dat oldest cheer, last week,' suggested Mose.

'You go long! I'll boun' you pulled 'em out; some o' your shines,' said Aunt Chloe.

'Well, it'll stand, if it only keeps jam up agin de wall!' said Mose.

'Den Uncle Peter mus'n't sit in it, 'cause he al'ays hitches when he gets a singing. He hitched pretty nigh across de room t'other night,' said Pete.

'Good Lor! get him in it, then,' said Mose, 'and den he'd begin, "Come, saints and sinners, hear me tell," and den down he'd go.' And Mose imitated precisely the nasal tones of the old man, tumbling on the floor to illustrate the supposed catastrophe.

'Come, now, be decent, can't ye?' said Aunt Chloe; 'an't yer shamed?'

Mas'r George, however, joined the offender in the laugh, and declared decidedly that Mose was a 'buster.' So the maternal admonition seemed rather to fail of effect.

'Well, ole man,' said Aunt Chloe, 'you'll have to tote in them ar bar'ls.'

'Mother's bar'ls is like dat ar widder's Mas'r George was reading 'bout in de good book – dey never fails'; said Mose, aside to Pete.

'I'm sure one on 'em caved in last week,' said Pete, 'and let 'em all down in de middle of de singin'; dat ar was failin', warn't it?'

During this aside between Mose and Pete, two empty casks had been rolled into the cabin, and being secured from rolling by stones on each side, boards were laid across them, which arrangement, together with the turning down of certain tubs and pails, and the disposing of the rickety chairs, at last completed the preparation.

'Mas'r George is such a beautiful reader, now, I know he'll stay to read for us,' said Aunt Chloe; ''pears like 't will be much more interestin'.'

George very readily consented, for your boy is always ready for anything that makes him of importance.

The room was soon filled with a motley assemblage, from the old grey-headed patriarch of eighty to the young girl and lad of fifteen. A little harmless gossip ensued on various themes, such as where old Aunt Sally got her new red headkerchief, and how 'missis was a-going to give Lizzy that spotted muslin gown, when she'd got her new berage made up;' and how Mas'r Shelby was thinking of buying a new sorrel colt, that was going to prove an addition to the glories of the place. A few of the worshippers belonged to families hard by, who had got permission to attend, and who brought in various choice scraps of information, about the sayings and doings at the house and on the place, which circulated as freely as the same sort of small change does in higher cicles.

After awhile the singing commenced, to the evident delight of all present. Not even all the disadvantage of nasal intonation could prevent the effect of the naturally fine voices, in airs at once wild and spirited. The words were sometimes the well-known and common hymns sung in the churches about, and sometimes of a wilder, more indefinite character, picked up at camp-meetings.

The chorus to one of them, which ran as follows, was sung with great energy and unction:—

'Die on the field of battle,
Die on the field of battle,
Glory in my soul.'

Another special favourite had oft repeated the words—

'Oh, I'm going to glory – won't you come along with me?
Don't you see the angels beck'ning, and calling me away?
Don't you see the golden city and the everlasting day?'

There were others, which made incessant mention of 'Jordan's banks,' and 'Canaan's fields,' and the 'New Jerusalem;' for the negro mind, impassioned and imaginative, always attaches itself to hymns and expressions of a vivid and pictorial nature; and, as they sang, some laughed, and some cried, and some clapped hands, or shook hands rejoicingly with each other, as if they had fairly gained the other side of the river.

Various exhortations or relations of experience followed, and intermingled with the singing. One old grey-headed woman, long past work, but much revered as a sort of chronicle of the past, rose, and leaning on her staff, said:

'Well, chil'en! Well, I'm mighty glad to hear ye all and see ye all once more, 'cause I don't know when I'll be gone to glory; but I've done got ready, chil'en; 'pears like I'd got my little bundle all tied up, and my bonnet on, jest a waitin' for the stage to come along and take me home; sometimes, in the night, I think I hear the wheels a rattlin', and I'm looking out all the time: now, you jest be ready too, for I tell ye all, chil'en,' she said, striking her staff hard on the floor, 'dat ar *glory* is a mighty thing! It's a mighty thing, chil'en – you don'no nothing about it – it's *wonderful*.' And the old creature sat down, with streaming tears, as wholly overcome, while the whole circle struck up—

'Oh, Canaan, bright Canaan,
I'm bound for the land of Canaan.'

Mas'r George, by request, read the last chapters of Revelation, often interrupted by such exclamations as 'The *sakes* now!' 'Only hear that!' 'Jest think on't!' 'Is all that a comin' sure enough?'

George, who was a bright boy, and well trained in religious things by his mother, finding himself an object of general admiration, threw in expositions of his own, from time to time, with a commendable seriousness and gravity, for which he was admired by the young and blessed by the old; and it was agreed, on all hands, that a 'minister couldn't lay it off better than he did;' that "twas reely 'mazin!'

Uncle Tom was a sort of patriarch in religious matters in the neighbourhood. Having, naturally, an organisation in which the *morale* was strongly predominant, together with a greater breadth and cultivation of mind than obtained among his companions, he was looked up to with great respect, as a sort of minister among them; and the simple, hearty, sincere style of his exhortations, might have edified even better educated persons. But it was in prayer that he especially excelled. Nothing could exceed the touching simplicity, the childlike earnestness of his prayer, enriched with the language of Scripture, which seemed so entirely to have wrought itself into his being as to have become a part of himself, and to drop from his lips unconsciously; in the language of a pious old negro, he 'prayed right up.' And so much did his prayer always work on the devotional feeling of his audiences, that there seemed often a danger that it would be lost altogether in the abundance of the responses which broke out everywhere around him.

While this scene was passing in the cabin of the man, one quite otherwise passed in the halls of the master.

The trader and Mr Shelby were seated together in the dining-room afore-named, at a table covered with papers and writing utensils.

Mr Shelby was busy in counting some bundles of bills, which, as they were counted, he pushed over to the trader, who counted them likewise.

'All fair,' said the trader; 'and now for signing these yer.'

Mr Shelby hastily drew the bills of sale towards him, and signed them like a man that hurries over some disagreeable business, and then pushed them over with the money. Haley produced, from a well-worn valise, a parchment, which, after looking over it a moment, he handed to Mr Shelby, who took it with a gesture of suppressed eagerness.

'Wal, now, the thing's *done*!' said the trader, getting up.

'It's *done*!' said Mr Shelby, in a musing tone; and, fetching a long breath, he repeated, 'It's *done*!'

'Yer don't seem to feel much pleased with it, 'pears to me,' said the trader.

'Haley,' said Mr Shelby, 'I hope you'll remember that you promised, on your honour, you wouldn't sell Tom, without knowing what sort of hands he's going into.'

'Why, you've just done it, sir,' said the trader.

'Circumstances, you well know, *obliged* me,' said Shelby, haughtily.

'Wal, you know, they may 'blige *me*, too,' said the trader. 'Howsomever, I'll do the very best I can in gettin' Tom a good berth; as to my treating on him bad, you needn't be a grain afeard. If there's anything that I thank the Lord for, it is that I'm never noways cruel.'

After the expositions which the trader had previously given of his humane principles, Mr Shelby did not feel particularly reassured by these declarations; but as they were the best comfort the case admitted of, he allowed the trader to depart in silence, and betook himself to a solitary cigar.

Chapter 5

SHOWING THE FEELINGS OF LIVING PROPERTY ON CHANGING OWNERS

MR and Mrs Shelby had retired to their apartment for the night. He was lounging in a large easy chair, looking over some letters that had come in the afternoon mail, and she was standing before her mirror, brushing out the complicated braids and curls in which Eliza had arranged her hair; for, noticing her pale cheeks and haggard eyes, she had excused her attendance that night, and ordered her to bed. The employment, naturally enough, suggested her conversation with the girl in the morning; and, turning to her husband, she said, carelessly,—

'By the by, Arthur, who was that low-bred fellow that you lugged in to our dinner-table to-day?'

'Haley is his name,' said Shelby, turning himself rather uneasily in his chair, and continuing with his eyes fixed on a letter.

'Haley! Who is he, and what may be his business here, pray?'

'Well, he's a man that I transacted some business with last time I was at Natchez,' said Mr Shelby.

'And he presumed on it to make himself quite at home, and call and dine here, eh?'

'Why, I invited him; I had some account with him,' said Shelby.

'Is he a negro-trader?' said Mrs Shelby, noticing a certain embarrassment in her husband's manner.

'Why, my dear, what put that into your head?' said Shelby, looking up.

'Nothing – only Eliza came in here, after dinner, in a great worry, crying and taking on, and said you were talking with a trader, and that she heard him make an offer for her boy – the ridiculous little goose!'

'She did, eh?' said Mr Shelby, returning to his paper, which he seemed for a few moments quite intent upon, not perceiving that he was holding it bottom upwards.

'It will have to come out,' said he, mentally; 'as well now as ever.'

'I told Eliza,' said Mrs Shelby, as she continued brushing her hair, 'that she was a little fool for her pains, and that you never had anything to do with that sort of person. Of course, I knew you never meant to sell any of our people – least of all, to such a fellow.'

'Well, Emily,' said her husband, 'so I have always felt and said; but the fact is, that my business lies so that I cannot get on without. I shall have to sell some of my hands.'

'To that creature? Impossible! Mr Shelby, you cannot be serious.'

'I am sorry to say that I am,' said Mr Shelby. 'I've agreed to sell Tom.'

'What! our Tom? – that good, faithful creature! – been your faithful servant from a boy! Oh, Mr Shelby! – and you have promised him his freedom, too – you and I have spoken to him a hundred times of it. Well, I can believe anything now; I can believe *now* that you could sell little Harry, poor Eliza's only child!' said Mrs Shelby, in a tone between grief and indignation.

'Well, since you must know all, it is so. I have agreed to sell Tom and Harry both; and I don't know why I am to be rated as if I were a monster for doing what every one does every day.'

'But why, of all others, choose these?' said Mrs Shelby. 'Why sell them of all on the place, if you must sell at all?'

'Because they will bring the highest sum of any – that's why. I could choose another, if you say so. The fellow made me a high bid on Eliza, if that would suit you any better,' said Mr Shelby.

'The wretch!' said Mrs Shelby, vehemently.

'Well, I didn't listen to it a moment – out of regard to your feelings, I wouldn't; so give me some credit.'

'My dear,' said Mrs Shelby, recollecting herself, 'forgive me. I have been hasty. I was surprised, and entirely unprepared for this; but surely you will allow me to intercede for these poor creatures. Tom is a noble-hearted, faithful fellow, if he is black. I do believe, Mr Shelby, that if he were put to it, he would lay down his life for you.'

'I know it – I dare say; but what's the use of all this? I can't help myself.'

'Why not make a pecuniary sacrifice? I'm willing to bear my part of the inconvenience. Oh, Mr Shelby, I have tried – tried most faithfully, as a Christian woman should – to do my duty to these poor, simple, dependent creatures. I have cared for them, instructed them, watched over them, and known all their little cares and joys, for years; and how can I ever hold up my head again among them, if, for the sake of a little paltry gain, we sell such a faithful, excellent, confiding creature as poor Tom, and tear from him in a moment all we have taught him to love and value? I have taught them the duties of the family, of parent and child, and husband and wife; and how can I bear to have this open acknowledgment that we care for no tie, no duty, no relation, however sacred, compared with money? I have talked with Eliza about her boy – her duty to him as a Christian mother, to watch over him, pray for him, and bring him up in a Christian way; and now what can I say, if you tear him away, and sell him, soul and body, to a profane, unprincipled man, just to save a little money ? I have told her that one soul is worth more than all the money in the world; and how will she believe me when she sees us turn round and sell her child ? – sell him, perhaps, to certain ruin of body and soul!'

'I'm sorry you feel so about it, Emily – indeed I am,' said Mr Shelby; 'and I respect your feelings, too, though I don't pretend to share them to their full extent; but I tell you now, solemnly, it's of no use – I can't help myself. I didn't mean to tell you this, Emily; but, in plain words, there is no choice between selling these two and selling everything. Either they must go or *all* must. Haley has come into possession of a mortgage, which, if I don't clear off with him directly, will take everything before it. I've raked, and scraped, and borrowed, and all but begged, and the price of these two was needed to make up the balance, and I had to give them up. Haley fancied the child; he agreed to settle the matter that way, and no other. I was in his power, and *had* to do it. If you feel so to have them sold, would it be any better to have *all* sold ?'

Mrs Shelby stood like one stricken. Finally, turning to her toilet, she rested her face in her hands, and gave a sort of groan.

'This is God's curse on slavery! – a bitter, bitter, most accursed thing! – a curse to the master, and a curse to the slave! I was a fool to think I could make anything good out of such a deadly evil. It is a sin to hold a slave under laws like ours; I always felt it was – I always thought so when I was a girl – I thought so still more after I joined the church; but I thought I could gild it over. I thought by kindness, and care, and instruction, I could make the condition of mine better than freedom. Fool that I was!'

'Why, wife, you are getting to be an Abolitionist, quite.'

'Abolitionist! If they knew all I know about slavery, they *might* talk! We don't need them to tell us; you know I never thought that slavery was right – never felt willing to own slaves.'

'Well, therein you differ from many wise and pious men,' said Mr Shelby. 'You remember Mr B.'s sermon the other Sunday ?'

'I don't want to hear such sermons; I never wish to hear Mr B. in our church again. Ministers can't help the evil, perhaps – can't cure it, any more than we can – but defend it! It always went against my common sense. And I think you didn't think much of that sermon, either.'

'Well,' said Shelby, 'I must say these ministers sometimes carry matters further than we poor sinners would exactly dare to do. We men of the world must wink pretty hard at various things, and get used to a deal that isn't the exact thing. But we don't quite fancy when women and ministers come out broad and square, and go beyond us in matters of either modesty or morals, that's a fact. But now, my dear, I trust you see the necessity of the thing, and you see that I have done the very best that circumstances would allow !'

'Oh, yes, yes !' said Mrs Shelby, hurriedly and abstractedly fingering her gold watch. 'I haven't any jewllery of any amount,' she added, thoughtfully, 'but would not this watch do something ? – it was an expensive one when it was bought. If I could only at least save Eliza's child, I would sacrifice anything I have.'

'I'm sorry, very sorry, Emily,' said Mr Shelby, 'I'm sorry this takes hold of you so ; but it will do no good. The fact is, Emily, the thing's done ; the bills of sale are already signed and in Haley's hands ; and you must be thankful it is no worse. That man has had it in his power to ruin us all, and now he is fairly off. If you knew the man as I do, you'd think that we had had a narrow escape.'

'Is he so hard, then ?'

'Why, not a cruel man, exactly, but a man of leather – a man alive to nothing but trade and profit ; cool, and unhesitating, and unrelenting as death and the grave. He'd sell his own mother at a good percentage – not wishing the old woman any harm either.'

'And this wretch owns that good, faithful Tom, and Eliza's child ?'

'Well, my dear, the fact is, that this goes rather hard with me – it's a thing I hate to think of : Haley wants to drive matters, and take possession to-morrow. I'm going to get out my horse bright and early, and be off. I can't see Tom, that's a fact ; and you had better arrange a drive somewhere, and carry Eliza off. Let the thing be done when she is out of sight.'

'No, no,' said Mrs Shelby ; 'I'll be in no sense accomplice or help in this cruel business. I'll go and see poor old Tom, God help him in his distress ! They shall see, at any rate, that their mistress can feel for and with them. As to Eliza, I dare not think about it. The Lord forgive us! What have we done that this cruel necessity should come on us!'

There was one listener to this conversation whom Mr and Mrs Shelby little suspected.

Communicating with their apartment was a large closet, opening by a door into the outer passage. When Mrs Shelby had dismissed Eliza for the night, her feverish and excited mind had suggested the idea of this closet; and she had hidden herself there, and, with her ear pressed close against the crack of the door, had lost not a word of the conversation.

When the voices died into silence, she rose and crept stealthily away. Pale, shivering, with rigid features and compressed lips, she looked an entirely altered being from the soft and timid creature she had been hitherto. She moved cautiously along the entry, paused one moment at her mistress's door, and raised her hands in mute appeal to Heaven, and then turned and glided into her own room. It was a quiet, neat apartment, on the same floor with her mistress's. There was the pleasant, sunny window, where she had often sat singing at her sewing; there a little case of books, and various little fancy articles ranged by them, the gifts of Christmas holidays; there was her simple wardrobe in the closet and in the drawers; here was, in short, her home, and, on the whole, a happy one it had been to her. But there, on the bed, lay her slumbering boy, his long curls falling negligently around his unconscious face, his rosy mouth half open, his little fat hands thrown out over the bedclothes, and a smile spread like a sunbeam over his whole face.

'Poor boy! poor fellow!' said Eliza; 'they have sold you! but your mother will save you yet!'

No tear dropped over that pillow. In such straits as these the heart has no tears to give; it drops only blood, bleeding itself away in silence. She took a piece of paper and a pencil, and wrote hastily,—

'Oh, missis! dear missis! don't think me ungrateful – don't think hard of me, any way – I heard all you and master said to-night. I am going to try to save my boy – you will not blame me! God bless and reward you for all your kindness!'

Hastily folding and directing this, she went to a drawer and made up a little package of clothing for her boy, which she tied with a handkerchief firmly round her waist; and so fond is a mother's remembrance, that, even in the terrors of that hour, she did not forget to put in the little package one or two of his favourite toys, reserving a gaily-painted parrot to amuse him when she should be called on to awaken him. It was some trouble to arouse the little sleeper; but, after some effort, he sat up, and was playing with his bird, while his mother was putting on her bonnet and shawl.

'Where are you going, mother?' said he, as she drew near the bed with his little coat and cap.

His mother drew near, and looked so earnestly into his eyes, that he at once divined that something unusual was the matter.

'Hush, Harry,' she said; 'mustn't speak loud, or they will hear us. A wicked man was coming to take little Harry away from his mother, and carry him 'way off in the dark, but mother won't let him — she's going to put on her little boy's cap and coat, and run off with him, so the ugly man can't catch him.'

Saying these words, she had tied and buttoned on the child's simple outfit, and taking him in her arms, she whispered to him to be very still; and, opening a door in her room which led into the outer verandah, she glided noiselessly out.

It was a sparkling frosty, starlight night, and the mother wrapped the shawl close round her child, as, perfectly quiet with vague terror, he clung round her neck.

Old Bruno, a great Newfoundland, who slept at the end of the porch, rose, with a low growl, as she came near. She gently spoke his name, and the animal, an old pet and playmate of hers, instantly wagging his tail, prepared to follow her, though apparently revolving much in his simple dog's head what such an indiscreet midnight promenade might mean. Some dim ideas of imprudence or impropriety in the measure seemed to embarrass him considerably; for he often stopped, as Eliza glided forward, and looked wistfully, first at her and then at the house, and then, as if reassured by reflection, he pattered along after her again. A few minutes brought them to the window of Uncle Tom's cottage, and Eliza, stopping, tapped lightly on the window-pane.

The prayer meeting at Uncle Tom's had, in the order of hymn-singing, been protracted to a very late hour; and as Uncle Tom had indulged himself in a few lengthy solos afterwards, the consequence was, that, although it was now between twelve and one o'clock, he and his worthy helpmeet were not yet asleep.

'Good Lord! what's that?' said Aunt Chloe, starting up, and hastily drawing the curtain. 'My sakes alive, if it a'nt Lizzy! Get on your clothes, ole man, quick! there's ole Bruno, too, a-pawin' round – wat on airth! I'm gwine to open the door.'

And, suiting the action to the word, the door flew open, and the light of the tallow candle, which Tom had hastily lighted, fell on the haggard face and dark wild eyes of the fugitive.

'Lord bless you! I'm skeered to look at ye, Lizzy! Are ye tuck sick, or what's come over ye?'

'I'm running away, Uncle Tom and Aunt Chloe – carrying off my child. Master's sold him!'

'Sold him?' echoed both, lifting up their hands in dismay.

'Yes, sold him!' said Eliza, firmly; 'I crept into the closet by mistress's door to-night, and I heard master tell missis that he had sold my Harry and you, Uncle Tom, both to a trader, and that he was going off this morning on his horse, and that the man was to take possession to-day.'

Tom had stood during this speech with his hands raised, and his eyes dilated, like a man in a dream. Slowly and gradually, as its meaning came over him, he collapsed, rather than seated himself, on his old chair, and sunk his head down upon his knees.

'The good Lord have pity on us!' said Aunt Chloe. 'Oh, it don't seem as if it was true! What has he done that mas'r should sell *him*?'

'He hasn't done anything – it isn't for that. Master don't want to sell, and missis – she's always good – I heard her plead and beg for us; but he told her 'twas no use – that he was in this man's debt, and that this man had got the power over him – and that if he didn't pay him off clear, it would end in his having to sell the place and all the people, and move off. Yes, I heard him say there was no choice between selling these two and selling all, the man was driving them so hard. Master said he was sorry; but oh, missis! you ought to have heard her talk! If she an't a Christian and an angel, there never was one. I'm a wicked girl to leave her so; but then I can't help it. She said herself one soul was worth more than the world; and this boy has a soul, and if I let him be carried off, who knows what'll become of it? It must be right; but if it an't right, the Lord forgive me, for I can't help doing it!'

'Well, ole man!' said Aunt Chloe, 'why don't you go too? Will you wait to be toted down the river, where they kill niggers with hard work and starving? I'd a heap rather die than go there, any day! there's time for ye; be off with Lizzy – you've got a pass to come and go any time. Come, bustle up, and I'll get your things together.'

Tom slowly raised his head, and looked sorrowfully but quietly around, and said: –

'No, no; I an't going. Let Eliza go – it's her right. I wouldn't be the one to say no. 'Tan't in *natur* for her to stay; but you heard what she said! If I must be sold, or all the people on the place, and everything go to rack, why, let me be sold. I s'pose I can b'ar it as well as any on 'em,' he added, while something like a sob and a sigh shook his broad, rough chest convulsively. 'Mas'r always found me on the spot – he always will. I never have broke trust, nor used my pass noways contrary to my word, and I never will. It's better for me alone to go than to break up the place and sell all. Mas'r an't to blame, Chloe; and he'll take care of you and the poor—'

Here he turned to the rough trundle-bed full of little woolly heads, and broke fairly down. He leaned over the back of the chair, and covered his face with his large hands. Sobs, heavy, hoarse, and loud, shook the chair, and great tears fell through his fingers on the floor – just such tears, sir, as you dropped into the coffin where lay your first-born son; such tears, woman, as you shed when you heard the cries of your dying babe – for, sir, he was a man, and you are but another man. And, woman, though dressed in silks and jewels, you are but a woman, and, in life's great straits and mighty griefs, ye feel but one sorrow!

'And now,' said Eliza, as she stood in the door, 'I saw my husband only this afternoon, and I little knew then what was to come. They have pushed him to the very last standing-place, and he told me to-day that he was going to run away. Do try, if you can, to get word to him. Tell him how I went, and why I went; and tell him I'm going to try and find Canada. You must give my love to him, and tell him, if I never see him again,' she turned away, and stood with her back to them for a moment, and then added, in a husky voice, 'tell him to be as good as he can, and try and meet me in the kingdom of heaven.'

'Call Bruno in there,' she added. 'Shut the door on him, poor beast ! He mustn't go with me.'

A few last words and tears, a few simple adieus and blessings, and, clasping her wondering and affrighted child in her arms, she glided noiselessly away.

Chapter 6

DISCOVERY

Mr and Mrs Shelby, after their protracted discussion of the night before, did not readily sink to repose, and in consequence slept somewhat later than usual the ensuing morning.

'I wonder what keeps Eliza,' said Mrs Shelby, after giving her bell repeated pulls, to no purpose. Mr Shelby was standing before his dressing-glass, sharpening his razor ; and just then the door opened, and a coloured boy entered with his shaving-water.

'Andy,' said his mistress, 'step to Eliza's door, and tell her I have rung for her three times. Poor thing !' she added to herself, with a sigh.

Andy soon returned, with eyes very wide with astonishment.

'Lor, missis ! Lizzy's drawers is all open, and her things all lying every which way ; and I believe she's just done clared out !'

The truth flashed upon Mr Shelby and his wife at the same moment. He exclaimed,—

'Then she suspected it, and she's off !'

'The Lord be thanked !' said Mrs Shelby ; 'I trust she is.'

'Wife, you talk like a fool ! Really, it will be something pretty awkward for me if she is. Haley saw that I hesitated about selling this child, and he'll think I connived at it to get him out of the way. It touches my honour.' And Mr Shelby left the room hastily.

There was great running and ejaculating, and opening and

shutting of doors, and appearance of faces in all shades of colour in different place, for about a quarter of an hour. One person only, who might have shed some light on the matter, was entirely silent, and that was the head cook, Aunt Chloe. Silently, and with a heavy cloud settled down over her once joyous face, she proceeded making out her breakfast biscuits, as if she heard and saw nothing of the excitement around her.

Very soon about a dozen young imps were roosting, like so many crows, on the verandah railings, each one determined to be the first one to apprise the strange mas'r of his ill luck.

'He'll be real mad, I'll be bound,' said Andy.

'*Won't* he swar !' said little black Jake.

'Yes, for he *does* swar,' said woolly-headed Mandy. 'I hearn him yesterday, at dinner. I hearn all about it then, 'cause I got into the closet where missis keeps the great jugs, and I hearn every word.' And Mandy, who had never in her life thought of the meaning of a word she had heard, more than a black cat, now took airs of superior wisdom, and strutted about, forgetting to state that, though actually coiled up among the jugs at the time specified, she had been fast asleep all the time.

When at last Haley appeared, booted and spurred, he was saluted with the bad tidings on every hand. The young imps on the verandah were not disappointed in their hopes of hearing him 'swar,' which he did with a fluency and fervency which delighted them all amazingly, as they ducked and dodged hither and thither to be out of the reach of his riding-whip ; and all whooping off together, they tumbled in a pile of immeasurable giggle, on the withered turf under the verandah, where they kicked up their heels and shouted to their full satisfaction.

'If I had the little devils !' muttered Haley between his teeth.

'But you han't got 'em though !' said Andy, with a triumphant flourish, and making a string of indescribable mouths at the unfortunate trader's back, when he was fairly beyond hearing.

'I say now, Shelby, this yer's a most extro'rnary business !' said Haley, as he abruptly entered the parlour. 'It seems that gal's off, with her young un.'

'Mr Haley, Mrs Shelby is present,' said Mr Shelby.

'I beg pardon, ma'am,' said Haley, bowing slightly, with a still lowering brow ; 'but still I say, as I said before, this yer's a sing'lar report. Is it true, sir ?'

'Sir,' said Mr Shelby, 'if you wish to communicate with me, you must observe something of the decorum of a gentleman. Andy, take Mr Haley's hat and riding-whip. Take a seat, sir. Yes, sir; I regret to say that the young woman, excited by overhearing, or having reported to her, something of this business, has taken her child in the night, and made off.'

'I did expect fair dealing in this matter, I confess,' said Haley.

'Well, sir,' said Mr Shelby, turning sharply round upon him, 'what am I to understand by that remark? If any man calls my honour in question, I have but one answer for him.'

The trader cowered at this, and in a somewhat lower tone said that 'it was plaguy hard on a fellow, that had made a fair bargain to be gulled that way.'

'Mr Haley,' said Mr Shelby, 'if I did not think you had some cause for disappointment, I should not have borne from you the rude and unceremonious style of your entrance into my parlour this morning. I say thus much, however, since appearances call for it, that I shall allow of no insinuations cast upon me, as if I were at all partner to any unfairness in this matter. Moreover, I shall feel bound to give you every assistance, in the use of horses, servants, etc., in the recovery of your property. So, in short, Haley,' said he, suddenly dropping from the tone of dignified coolness to his ordinary one of easy frankness, 'the best way for you is to keep good-natured and eat some breakfast; and we will then see what is to be done.'

Mrs Shelby now rose, and said her engagements would prevent her being at the breakfast-table that morning; and, deputing a very respectable mulatto woman to attend to the gentlemen's coffee at the sideboard, she left the room.

'Old lady don't like your humble servant, over and above,' said Haley, with an uneasy effort to be very familiar.

'I am not accustomed to hear my wife spoken of with such freedom,' said Mr Shelby dryly.

'Beg pardon; of course, only a joke, you know,' said Haley, forcing a laugh.

'Some jokes are less agreeable than others,' rejoined Shelby.

'Devilish free, now I've signed those papers, cuss him!' muttered Haley to himself; 'quite grand, since yesterday!'

Never did fall of any prime minister at court occasion wider surges of sensation than the report of Tom's fate among his compeers on the place. It was the topic in every mouth, everywhere; and nothing was done in the house or in the field, but to discuss its probable results. Eliza's flight – an unprecedented event on the place – was also a great accessory in stimulating the general excitement.

Black Sam, as he was commonly called, from his being about three shades blacker than any other son of ebony on the place, was revolving the matter profoundly in all its phases and bearings, with a comprehensiveness of vision and a strict lookout to his own personal well-being that would have done credit to any white patriot in Washington.

'It's an ill wind dat blows nowhar – dat ar a fact,' said Sam sententiously, giving an additional hoist to his pantaloons, and adroitly substituting a long nail in place of a missing suspender-button, with which effort of mechanical genius he seemed highly delighted.

'Yes, it's an ill wind blows nowhar,' he repeated. 'Now, dar, Tom's down – wal, course der's room for some nigger to be up; and why not dis nigger? – dat's de idee. Tom, a ridin' round de country – boots blacked – pass in his pocket – all grand as Cuffee; who but he? Now, why shouldn't Sam? – dat's what I want to know.'

'Halloo, Sam – Oh Sam! Mas'r wants you to cotch Bill and Jerry,' said Andy, cutting short Sam's soliloquy.

'High! what's afoot now, young un?'

'Why, you don't know, I s'ppose, that Lizzy's cut stick, and clared out, with her young un?'

'You teach your granny!' said Sam, with infinite contempt; 'knowed it a heap sight sooner than you did. This nigger an't so green, now!'

'Well, anyhow, mas'r wants Bill and Jerry geared right up; and you and I's to go with Mas'r Haley, to look arter her.'

'Good, now! dat's de time o' day!' said Sam. 'It's Sam dat's called for in dese yer times. He's der nigger. See if I don't cotch her, now; mas'r'll see what Sam can do!'

'Ah! but, Sam,' said Andy, 'you'd better think twice; for missis don't want her cotched, and she'll be in your wool.'

'High!' said Sam, opening his eyes. 'How you know dat?'

'Heard her say so, my own self, dis blessed mornin', when I bring in mas'r's shaving water. She sent me to see why Lizzy didn't come to dress her; and when I telled her she was off, she jest riz up, and ses she, "The Lord be praised!" And mas'r he seemed real mad, and ses he, "Wife, you talk like a fool!" But, Lor! she'll bring him to! I knows well enough how that'll be – it's allers best to stand missis' side the fence, now I tell yer.'

Black Sam upon this scratched his woolly pate, which, if it did not contain very profound wisdom, still contained a great deal of a particular species much in demand among politicians of all complexions and countries, and vulgarly denominated 'knowing which side the bread is buttered;' so, stopping with grave consideration, he again gave a hitch to his pantaloons, which was his regularly organised method of assisting his mental perplexities.

'Der an't no sayin' – never – 'bout no kind o' thing in *dis* yer world,' he said, at last.

Sam spoke like a philosopher, emphasising *this* – as if he had had a large experience in different sorts of worlds, and therefore had come to his conclusions advisedly.

'Now, sartin I'd a said that missis would a scoured the varsal world after Lizzy,' added Sam thoughtfully.

'So she would,' said Andy; 'but can't ye see through a ladder, ye black nigger? Missis don't want dis yer Mas'r Haley to get Lizzy's boy; dat's de go.'

'High!' said Sam, with an indescribable intonation known only to those who have heard it among the negroes.

'And I'll tell yer more'n all,' said Andy; 'I specs you'd better be making tracks for dem hosses – mighty sudden, too – for I hearn missis 'quirin' arter yer; so you've stood foolin' long enough.'

Sam, upon this, began to bestir himself in real earnest; and after a while appeared, bearing down gloriously towards the house, with Bill and Jerry in a full canter, and adroitly throwing himself off before they had any idea of stopping, he brought them up alongside of the horse-post like a tornado. Haley's horse, which was a skittish young colt, winced and bounced, and pulled hard at his halter.

'Ho, ho!' said Sam, 'skeery, are ye?' and his black visage lighted up with a curious, mischievous gleam. 'I'll fix ye now,' said he.

There was a large beech-tree overshadowing the place, and

the small, sharp triangular beech-nuts lay scattered thickly on the ground. With one of these in his fingers, Sam approached the colt, stroked and petted, and seemed apparently busy in soothing his agitation. On pretence of adjusting the saddle, he adroitly slipped under it the sharp little nut, in such a manner that the least weight brought upon the saddle would annoy the nervous sensibilities of the animal, without leaving any perceptible graze or wound.

'Dar!' he said, rolling his eyes with an approving grin; 'me fix 'em!'

At this moment Mrs Shelby appeared on the balcony, beckoning to him. Sam approached with as good a determination to pay court as did ever suitor after a vacant place at St James's or Washington.

'Why have you been loitering so, Sam? I sent Andy to tell you to hurry.

'Lord bless you, missis!' said Sam, 'horses won't be cotched all in a minnit; they'd done clared out way down to the south pasture, and the Lord knows whar!'

'Sam, how often must I tell you not to say "Lord bless you, and the Lord knows," and such things? It's wicked.'

'O Lord, bless my soul! I done forget, missis! I won't say nothing of de sort no more.'

'Why, Sam, you just *have* said it again.'

'Did I? O Lord! I mean – I didn't go fur to say it.'

'You must be *careful*, Sam.'

'Just let me get my breath, missis, and I'll start fair. I'll be berry careful.'

'Well, Sam, you are to go with Mr Haley, to show him the road, and help him. Be careful of the horses, Sam; you know Jerry was a little lame last week; *don't ride them too fast.*'

Mrs Shelby spoke the last words with a low voice, and strong emphasis.

'Let dis child alone for dat!' said Sam, rolling up his eyes with a volume of meaning. 'Lord knows! High! Didn't say dat!' said he, suddenly catching his breath, with a ludicrous flourish of apprehension, which made his mistress laugh, spite of herself. 'Yes, missis, I'll look out for de hosses!'

'Now, Andy,' said Sam, returning to his stand under the beech-tree, 'you see I wouldn't be 't all surprised if dar ar gen'lman's crittur should gib a fling, by and by, when he comes to be a gettin' up. You know, Andy, critturs *will* do such things;' and therewith Sam poked Andy in the side, in a highly suggestive manner.

'High!' said Andy, with an air of instant appreciation.

'Yes, you see, Andy, missis wants to make time, – dat ar's clar to der most or'nary 'bserver. I jis make a little for her. Now, you see, get all dese yer hosses loose, caperin' permiscus round dis yer lot and down to de wood dar, and I spec mas'r won't be off in a hurry.'

Andy grinned.

'Yer see,' said Sam, 'yer see, Andy, if any such thing should happen as that Mas'r Haley's horse *should* begin to act contrary, and cut up, you and I jist let's go of our'n to help him, and *we'll help him* – oh yes! And Sam and Andy laid their heads back on their shoulders, and broke into a low immoderate laugh, snapping their fingers and flourishing their heels with exquisite delight.

At this instant Haley appeared on the verandah. Somewhat mollified by certain cups of very good coffee, he came out smiling and talking, in tolerably restored humour. Sam and Andy, clawing for certain fragmentary palm-leaves, which they were in the habit of consideration as hats, flew to the horse-posts, to be ready to 'help mas'r.'

Sam's palm-leaf had been ingeniously disentangled from all pretensions to braid, as respects its brim: and the slivers starting apart, and standing upright, gave it a blazing air of freedom and defiance, quite equal to that of any Fejee chief; while the whole brim of Andy's being departed bodily, he rapped the crown on his head with a dexterous thump, and looked about well pleased, as if to say, 'Who says I haven't got a hat?'

'Well, boys,' said Haley, 'look alive now; we must lose no time.'

'Not a bit of him, mas'r!' said Sam, putting Haley's rein in his hand, and holding his stirrup, while Andy was untying the other two horses.

The instant Haley touched the saddle, the mettlesome creature bounded from the earth with a sudden spring, that threw his master sprawling, some feet off, on the soft, dry turf. Sam with frantic ejaculations, made a dive at the reins, but only succeeded in brushing the blazing palm-leaf afore-named into the horses' eyes, which by no means tended to allay the confusion of his nerves. So, with great vehemence, he overturned Sam, and giving two or three contemptuous snorts, flourished his heels vigorously in the air, and was soon prancing away towards the lower end of the lawn, followed by Bill and Jerry, whom Andy had not failed to let loose, according to contract, speeding them off with various direful ejaculations. And now ensued a miscellaneous scene of confusion. Sam and Andy ran and shouted, – dogs barked here and there, – and Mike, Mose, Mandy, Fanny, and all the smaller specimens on the place, both male and female, raced, clapped hands, whooped and shouted, with outrageous officiousness and untiring zeal.

Haley's horse, which was a white one, and very fleet and spirited, appeared to enter into the spirit of the scene with great gusto: and having for his coursing ground a lawn of nearly half a mile in extent, gently sloping down on every side into indefinite woodland, he appeared to take infinite delight in seeing how near he could allow his pursuers to approach him, and then, when within a hand's breadth, whisk off with a start and a snort, like a mischievous beast as he was, and career far down into some alley of the wood-lot. Nothing was further from Sam's mind than to have any one of the troop taken until such season as should seem to him most befitting, – and the exertions that he made were certainly most heroic. Like the sword of Cœur de Lion, which always blazed in the front and thickest of the battle, Sam's palm-leaf was to be seen everywhere when there was the least danger that a horse could be caught; – there he would bear down full tilt, shouting, 'Now for it! cotch him! cotch him!' in a way that would set everything to indiscriminate rout in a moment.

Haley ran up and down, and cursed and swore and stamped miscellaneously. Mr Shelby in vain tried to shout directions from the balcony, and Mrs Shelby from her chamber window alternately laughed and wondered, – not without some inkling of what lay at the bottom of all this confusion.

At last, about twelve o'clock, Sam appeared triumphant, mounted on Jerry, with Haley's horse by his side, reeking with sweat, but with flashing eyes and dilated nostrils, showing that the spirit of freedom had not yet entirely subsided.

'He's cotched!' he exclaimed, triumphantly. 'If't hadn't been for me, they might a bust theirselves, all on 'em; but I cotched him!'

'You!' growled Haley, in no amiable mood. 'If it hadn't been for you, this never would have happened.'

'Lord bless us, mas'r,' said Sam, in a tone of the deepest concern, 'and me that has been racin' and chasin' till the sweat jest pours off me!'

'Well, well!' said Haley, 'you've lost me near three hours, with your cursed nonsense. Now let's be off, and have no more fooling.'

'Why, mas'r,' said Sam, in a deprecating tone, 'I believe you mean to kill us all clar, horses and all. Here we are all just ready to drop down, and the critters all in a reek of sweat. Why, mas'r won't think of startin' on now till arter dinner. Mas'r's hoss wants rubben down; see how he splashed hisself; and Jerry limps too: don't think missis would be willing to have us start dis yer way, no how. Lord bless you, mas'r, we can ketch up, if we do stop. Lizzy never was no great of a walker.'

Mrs Shelby, who, greatly to her amusement, had overheard this conversation from the verandah, now resolved to do her part. She came forward, and, courteously expressing her concern for Haley's accident, pressed him to stay to dinner, saying that the cook should bring it on the table immediately.

Thus, all things considered, Haley, with rather an equivocal grace, proceeded to the parlour, while Sam, rolling his eyes after him with unutterable meaning, proceeded gravely with the horses to the stable-yard.

'Did yer see him, Andy? – did yer see him?' said Sam, when he had got fairly beyond the shelter of the barn, and fastened the horse to a post. 'O Lor, if it warn't as good as a meetin' now to see him a dancin' and kickin' and swarin' at us. Didn't I hear him? Swar away, old fellow (says I to myself); will yer have yer hoss now, or wait till you cotch him? (says I). Lor, Andy, I think I can see him now.' And Sam and Andy leaned up against the barn, and laughed to their hearts' content.

'Yer oughter seen how mad he looked, when I brought the hoss up. Lord, he'd a killed me, if he durs' to; and there I was a standin' as innercent and as humble.'

'Lor, I seed you,' said Andy; 'an't you an old hoss, Sam?'

'Rather 'spects I am,' said Sam; 'did yer see missis upstairs at the winder? I seed her laughin'.'

'I'm sure, I was racin' so, I didn't see nothing,' said Andy.

'Well, yer see,' said Sam, proceeding gravely to wash down Haley's pony, 'I'se 'quired what yer may call a habit o' *bobservation*, Andy. It's a very 'portant habit, Andy; and I commend yer to be cultivatin' it, now yer young. Hist up that hind foot, Andy. Yer see, Andy, it's *bobservation* makes all de difference in niggers. Didn't I see which way the wind blew dis yer mornin'? Didn't I see what missis wanted, though she never let on? Dat ar's bobservation, Andy. I 'spects it's what you may call a faculty. Faculties is different in different peoples, but cultivation of 'em goes a great way.'

'I guess if I hadn't helped your bobservation dis mornin', yer wouldn't have seen your way so smart,' said Andy.

'Andy,' said Sam, 'you's a promisin' child, der an't no manner o' doubt. I thinks lots of yer, Andy; and I don't feel noways ashamed to take idees from you. We oughtenter overlook nobody, Andy, 'cause the smartest on us gets tripped up sometimes. And so, Andy, let's go up to the house now. I'll be boun' missis 'll give us an uncommon good bite dis yer time.'

Chapter 7

THE MOTHER'S STRUGGLE

IT is impossible to conceive of a human creature more wholly desolate and forlorn than Eliza when she turned her footsteps from Uncle Tom's cabin.

Her husband's suffering and dangers, and the danger of her child, all blended in her mind, with a confused and stunning sense of the risk she was running, in leaving the only home she had ever known, and cutting loose from the protection of a friend whom she loved and revered. Then there was the parting from every familiar object, – the place where she had grown up, the trees under which she had played, the groves where she had walked many an evening in happier days, by the side of her young husband, – everything as it lay in the clear, frosty starlight, seemed to speak reproachfully to her, and ask her whither could she go from a home like that?

But stronger than all was maternal love, wrought into a paroxysm of frenzy by the near approach of a fearful danger. Her boy was old enough to have walked by her side, and, in an indifferent case, she would only have led him by the hand; but now the bare thought of putting him out of her arms made her shudder, and she strained him to her bosom with a convulsive grasp, as she went rapidly forward.

The frosty ground creaked beneath her feet, and she trembled at the sound; every quaking leaf and fluttering shadow sent the blood backward to her heart, and quickened her footsteps. She wondered within herself at the strength that seemed to be come upon her; for she felt the weight of her boy as if it had been a feather, and every flutter of fear seemed to increase the supernatural power that bore her on, while from her pale lips burst forth, in frequent ejaculations, the prayer to a friend above, 'Lord, help; Lord, save me!'

If it were *your* Harry, mother, or your Willie, that were going to be torn from you by a brutal trader, to-morrow morning, – if you had seen the man, and heard that the papers were signed and delivered, and you had only from twelve o'clock till morning to make good your escape, – how fast could *you* walk? How many miles could you make in those few brief hours, with the darling at your bosom, – the little sleepy head on your shoulder, the small, soft arms trustingly holding on to your neck?

For the child slept. At first the novelty and alarm kept him waking; but his mother so hurriedly repressed every breath or sound, and so assured him that if he were only still she would certainly save him, that he clung quietly round her neck, only asking as he found himself sinking to sleep:

'Mother, I don't need to keep awake, do I?'

'No, my darling; sleep if you want to.'

'But, mother, if I do get a sleep, you won't let him get me?'

'No! so may God help me!' said his mother, with a paler cheek, and a brighter light in her large dark eyes.

'You're *sure*, an't you, mother?'

'Yes, *sure*!' said the mother, in a voice that startled herself; for it seemed to her to come from a spirit within, that was no part of her; and the boy dropped his little weary head on her shoulder, and was soon asleep. How the touch of those warm arms, the gentle breathings that came in her neck, seemed to add fire and spirit to her movements! It seemed to her as if strength poured into her in electric streams, from every gentle touch and movement of the sleeping, confiding child. Sublime is the dominion of the mind over the body, that, for a time, can make flesh and nerve impregnable, and string the sinews like steel, so that the weak becomes so mighty.

The boundaries of the farm, the grove, the wood-lot, passed by her dizzily, as she walked on; and still she went, leaving one familiar object after another, slacking not, pausing not, till reddening daylight found her many a long mile from all traces of any familiar objects upon the open highway.

She had often been with her mistress, to visit some connections, in the village of T—, not far from the Ohio river, and knew the road well. To go thither, to escape across the Ohio river, were the first hurried outlines of her plan of escape; beyond that she could only hope in God.

When horses and vehicles began to move along the highway, with that alert perception peculiar to a state of excitement, and which seems to be a sort of inspiration she became aware that her headlong pace and distracted air might bring on her remark and suspicion. She therefore put the boy on the ground, and, adjusting her dress and bonnet, she walked on at as rapid a pace as she thought consistent with the preservation of appearances. In her little bundle she had provided a store of cakes and apples, which she used as expedients for quickening the speed of the child, rolling the apple some yards before them, when the boy would run with all his might after it; and this ruse, often repeated, carried them over many a half-mile.

After a while, they came to a thick patch of woodland, through which murmured a clear brook. As the child complained of hunger and thirst, she climbed over the fence with him; and sitting down behind a large rock which concealed them from the road, she gave him a breakfast out of her little package. The boy wondered and grieved that she could not eat; and when, putting his arms round her neck, he tried to wedge some of his cake into her mouth, it seemed to her that the rising in her throat would choke her.

'No, no, Harry darling! mother can't eat till you are safe! We must go on – on – till we come to the river!' And she hurried again into the road, and again constrained herself to walk regularly and composedly forward.

She was many miles past any neighbourhood where she was personally known. If she should chance to meet any who knew her, she reflected that the well-known kindness of the family would be of itself a blind to suspicion, as making it an unlikely supposition that she could be a fugitive. As she was also so white as not to be known as of coloured lineage without a critical survey, and her child was white also, it was much easier for her to pass on unsuspected.

On this presumption, she stopped at noon at a neat farm-house, to rest herself, and buy some dinner for her child and self; for as the danger decreased with the distance, the super-natural tension of the nervous system lessened, and she found herself both weary and hungry.

The good woman, kindly and gossiping, seemed rather pleased than otherwise with having somebody come in to talk with; and accepted without examination, Eliza's statement, that she 'was going on a little piece, to spend a week with her friends,' – all which she hoped in her heart might prove strictly true.

An hour before sunset she entered the village of T—, by the Ohio river, weary and foot-sore, but still strong in heart. Her first glance was at the river, which lay like Jordan between her and the Canaan of liberty on the other side.

It was now early spring, and the river was swollen and turbulent; great cakes of floating ice were swinging heavily to and fro in the turbid waters. Owing to the peculiar form of the shore on the Kentucky side, the land bending far out into the water, the ice had been lodged and detained in great quantities, and the narrow channel which swept round the bend was full of ice, piled one cake over another, thus forming a temporary barrier to the descending ice, which lodged, and formed a great undulating raft, filling up the whole river, and extending almost to the Kentucky shore.

Eliza stood for a moment, contemplating this unfavourable

aspect of things, which she saw at once must prevent the usual
ferry-boat from running, and then turned into a small public-
house on the bank, to make a few inquiries.

The hostess, who was busy in various fizzing and stewing
operations, over the fire, preparatory to the evening meal,
stopped with a fork in her hand, as Eliza's sweet and plaintive
voice arrested her.

'What is it?' she said.

'Isn't there any ferry or boat, that takes people over to B—,
now?' she said.

'No, indeed!' said the woman; 'the boats has stopped
running.'

Eliza's look of dismay and disappointment struck the woman,
and she said, inquiringly –

'Maybe you're waiting to get over? – anybody sick? Ye seem
mighty anxious.'

'I've got a child that's very dangerous,' said Eliza. 'I never
heard of it till last night, and I've walked quite a piece to-day, in
hopes to get to the ferry.'

'Well, now, that's onlucky,' said the woman, whose motherly
sympathies were much aroused; 'I'm re'lly consarned for ye.
Solomon!' she cried from the window, towards a small back
building. A man in leather apron and very dirty hands appeared
at the door.

'I say, Sol,' said the woman, 'is that ar man going to tote them
bar'ls over to-night?'

'He said he should try, if 'twas anyway prudent,' said the
man.

'There's a man a piece down here that's going over with some
truck this evening, if he durs' to; he'll be in here to supper to-
night, so you'd better set down and wait. That's a sweet little
fellow,' added the woman, offering him a cake.

But the child, wholly exhausted, cried with weariness.

'Poor fellow! he isn't used to walking, and I've hurried him
on so,' said Eliza.

'Well, take him into this room,' said the woman, opening into
a small bedroom, where stood a comfortable bed. Eliza laid the
weary boy upon it, and held his hands in hers till he was fast
asleep. For her there was no rest. As a fire in her bones, the
thought of the pursuer urged her on; and she gazed with longing

eyes on the sullen, surging waters that lay between her and liberty.

Here we must take our leave of her for the present, to follow the course of her pursuers.

Though Mrs Shelby had promised that the dinner should be hurried on table, yet it was soon seen, as the thing has often been seen before, that it required more than one to make a bargain. So, although the order was fairly given out in Haley's hearing, and carried to Aunt Chloe by at least half-a-dozen juvenile messengers, that dignitary only gave certain very gruff snorts and tosses of her head, and went on with every operation in an unusually leisurely and circumstantial manner.

For some singular reason an impression seemed to reign among the servants generally that missis would not be particularly disobliged by delay; and it was wonderful what a number of counter-accidents occurred constantly to retard the course of things. One luckless wight contrived to upset the gravy, and then gravy had to be got up *de novo*, with due care and formality. Aunt Chloe watching and stirring with dogged precision, answering shortly to all suggestions of haste, that she 'warn't a-going to have raw gravy on the table, to help nobody's catchings.' One tumbled down with the water, and had to go to the spring for more; and another precipitated the butter into the path of events; and there was from time to time, giggling news brought into the kitchen that 'Mas'r Haley was mighty oneasy, and that he couldn't sit in his cheer noways, but was a walkin' and stalkin' to the winders and through the porch.'

'Sarves him right!' said Aunt Chloe, indignantly. 'He'll get wus nor oneasy one of these days, if he don't mend his ways *His* Master'll be sending for him, and then see how he'll look!'

'He'll go to torment, and no mistake,' said little Jake.

'He desarves it,' said Aunt Chloe, grimly; 'he's broke a many, many, many hearts! I tell ye all,' she said, stopping with a fork uplifted in her hands, 'it's like what Mas'r George reads in Ravelations – souls a callin' under the altar! and a callin' on the Lord for vengeance on sich! – and by and by the Lord He'll hear 'em – so He will!'

Aunt Chloe, who was much revered in the kitchen, was listened to with open mouth; and, the dinner being now fairly sent in, the whole kitchen was at leisure to gossip with her, and to listen to her remarks.

'Sich'll be burnt up for ever, and no mistake; won't ther?' said Andy.

'I'd be glad to see it, I'll be boun',' said little Jake.

'Chil'en!' said a voice that made them all start. It was Uncle Tom, who had come in and stood listening to the conversation at the door.

'Chil'en,' he said, 'I'm afeard you don't know what ye're sayin'. Forever is a *dre'ful* word, chil'en; it's awful to think on't. You oughtenter wish that ar to any human critter.'

'We wouldn't to anybody but the soul-drivers,' said Andy; 'nobody can help wishing it to them, they's so awful wicked.'

'Don't natur herself kinder cry out on 'em?' said Aunt Chloe. 'Don't dey tear der sucking baby right off his mother's breast, and sell him? And der little children as is crying and holding on by her clothes, don't they pull 'em off and sells 'em? Don't dey tear wife and husband apart?' said Aunt Chloe, beginning to cry, 'when it's jest takin' the very life on 'em? – and all the while does they feel one bit? don't dey drink, and smoke, and take it oncommon easy? Lor, if the devil don't get them, what's he good for?' And Aunt Chloe covered her face with her checked apron, and began to sob in good earnest.

'Pray for them that 'spitefully use you, the good book says,' says Tom.

'Pray for 'em,' said Aunt Chloe; 'Lor, it's too tough! I can't pray for 'em.'

'It's natur, Chloe, and natur's strong,' said Tom, 'but the Lord's grace is stronger. Besides, you oughter think what an awful state a poor critter's soul's in that'll do them ar things; you oughter thank God that you an't *like* him, Chloe. I'm sure I'd rather be sold ten thousand times over than to have all that ar poor critter's got to answer for.'

'So'd I a heap,' said Jake. 'Lor, *shouldn't* we cotch it, Andy?'

Andy shrugged his shoulders, and gave an acquiescent whistle.

'I'm glad mas'r didn't go off this morning, as he looked to,' said Tom; 'that ar hurt me mor than sellin', it did. Mebbe it might have been natural for him, but 'twould have come desp't hard on me, as has known him from a baby; but I've seen mas'r, and I begin to feel sort o' reconciled to the Lord's will now.

Mas'r couldn't help hisself; he did right, but I'm feared things will be kinder goin' to rack when I'm gone. Mas'r can't be 'spected to be a pryin' round everywhar, as I've done, a keepin' up all the ends. The boys all means well, but they's powerful car'less. That ar troubles me.'

The bell here rung, and Tom was summoned to the parlour.

'Tom,' said his master kindly, 'I want you to notice that I give this gentleman bonds to forfeit a thousand dollars if you are not on the spot when he wants you; he's going to-day to look after his other business, and you can have the day to yourself. Go anywhere you like, boy.'

'Thank you, mas'r,' said Tom.

'And mind yerself,' said the trader, 'and don't come it over your master with any o' yer nigger tricks; for I'll take every cent out of him, if you an't thar. If he'd hear to me, he wouldn't trust any on ye – slippery as eels !'

'Mas'r,' said Tom – and he stood very straight – 'I was jist eight years old when ole missis put you into my arms, and you wasn't a year old. 'Thar,' says she, 'Tom, that's to be *your* young mas'r; take good care on him,' says she. And now I jist ask you, mas'r, have I ever broke word to you, or gone contrary to you, 'specially since I was a Christian ?'

Mr Shelby was fairly overcome, and the tears rose to his eyes.

'My good boy,' said he, 'the Lord knows you say but the truth; and if I was able to help it, all the world shouldn't buy you.'

'And sure as I am a Christian woman,' said Mrs Shelby, 'you shall be redeemed as soon as I can anyway bring together means. Sir,' she said to Haley, 'take good account of who you sell him to, and let me know.'

'Lor, yes, for that matter,' said the trader, 'I may bring him up in a year, not much the wuss for wear, and trade him back.'

'I'll trade with you, then, and make it for your advantage,' said Mrs Shelby.

'Of course,' said the trader, 'all's equal with me; li'ves trade 'em up as down, so I does a good business. All I want is a livin' you know, ma'am; that's all any on us wants, I 'spose.'

Mr and Mr Shelby both felt annoyed and degraded by the familiar impudence of the trader, and yet both saw the absolute necessity of putting a constraint on their feelings. The more hopelessly sordid and insensible he appeared, the greater became Mrs Shelby's dread of his succeeding in re-capturing Eliza and her child, and of course the greater her motive for detaining him by every female artifice. She, therefore, graciously smiled, assented, chatted familiarly, and did all she could to make time pass imperceptibly.

At two o'clock Sam and Andy brought the horses up to the posts, apparently greatly refreshed and invigorated by the scamper of the morning.

Sam was there new oiled from dinner, with an abundance of zealous and ready officiousness. As Haley approached, he was boasting, in flourishing style, to Andy, of the evident and eminent success of the operation, now that he had 'farly come to it.'

'Your master, I s'pose, don't keep no dogs?' said Haley, thoughtfully, as he prepared to mount.

'Heaps on 'em,' said Sam, triumphantly; 'thar's Bruno – he's a roarer! and besides that, 'bout every nigger of us keeps a pup of some natur' or uther.'

'Poh!' said Haley – and he said something else, too, with regard to the said dogs, at which Sam muttered, –

'I don't see no use cussin' on 'em, noway.'

'But your master don't keep no dogs (I pretty much know he don't) for trackin' out niggers?'

Sam knew exactly what he meant, but he kept on a look of earnest and desperate simplicity.

'Our dogs all smells round considerable sharp. I 'spect they's the kind, though they han't never had no practice. They's *far* dogs, though, at most anything, if you'd get 'em started. Here, Bruno,' he called, whistling to the lumbering Newfoundland, who came pitching tumultuously toward them.

'You go hang!' said Haley, getting up. 'Come, tumble up, now.'

Sam tumbled up accordingly, dexterously contriving to tickle Andy as he did so, which occasioned Andy to split out into a laugh, greatly to Haley's indignation, who made a cut at him with his riding-whip.

'I's 'stonished at yer, Andy,' said Sam, with awful gravity. 'This yer's a seris business, Andy. Yer mustn't be a makin' game. This yer an't no way to help mas'r.'

'I shall take the straight road to the river,' said Haley, decidedly, after they had come to the boundaries of the estate. 'I know the way of all of 'em — they makes tracks for the underground.'

'Sartin,' said Sam, 'dat's de idee. Mas'r Haley hits de thing right in de middle. Now, der's two roads to de river — de dirt road and der pike — which mas'r mean to take?'

Andy looked up innocently at Sam, surprised at hearing this new geographical fact, but instantly confirmed what he said by a vehement reiteration.

''Cause,' said Sam, 'I'd rather be 'clined to 'magine that Lizzy'd take de dirt road, bein' it's the least travelled.'

Haley, notwithstanding that he was a very old bird, and naturally inclined to be suspicious of chaff, was rather brought up by this view of the case.

'If yer warn't both on yer such cussed liars now!' he said, contemplatively, as he pondered a moment.

The pensive, reflective tone in which this was spoken appeared to amuse Andy prodigiously, and he drew a little behind and shook so as apparently to run a great risk of falling off his horse, while Sam's face was immovably composed into the most doleful gravity.

'Course,' said Sam, 'mas'r can do as he'd ruther; go de straight road, if mas'r thinks best — it's all one to us. Now, when I study 'pon it, I think de straight road de best *decidedly*.'

'She would naturally go a lonesome way,' said Haley, thinking aloud, and not minding Sam's remark.

'Dar an't no sayin',' said Sam; 'gals is pecular. They never does nothin' ye thinks they will; mose gen'lly the contrary. Gals is nat'lly made contrary; and so, if you thinks they've gone one road, it is sartin you'd better go t'other, and then you'll be sur to find 'em. Now, my private 'pinion is, Lizzy took de dirt road; so I think we'd better take de straight one.'

This profound generic view of the female sex did not seem to dispose Haley particularly to the straight road; and he announced decidedly that he should go the other, and asked Sam when they should come to it.

'A little piece a-head,' said Sam, giving a wink to Andy with the eye which was on Andy's side of the head; and he added gravely, 'but I've studded on de matter, and I'm quite clar we ought not to go dat ar way. I nebber been over it no way. It's despit lonesome, and we might lose our way – what we'd come to, de Lord only knows.'

'Nevertheless,' said Haley, 'I shall go that way.'

'Now I think on't, I think I hearn 'em tell that dat ar road was all fenced up and down by er creek, and thar; an't it, Andy?'

Andy wasn't certain, he'd only 'hearn tell' about that road, but never been over it. In short, he was strictly non-committal.

Haley accustomed to strike the balance of probabilities between lies of greater or lesser magnitude, thought that it lay in favour of the dirt road aforesaid. The mention of the thing he thought he perceived was involuntary on Sam's part at first; and his confused attempts to dissuade him he set down to a desperate lying, on second thoughts, as being unwilling to implicate Eliza.

When, therefore, Sam indicated the road, Haley plunged briskly into it, followed by Sam and Andy.

Now, the road, in fact, was an old one that had formerly been a thoroughfare to the river, but abandoned for many years after the laying of the new pike. It was open for about an hour's ride, and after that it was cut across by various farms and fences. Sam knew this fact perfectly well; indeed, the road had been so long closed up that Andy had never heard of it. He therefore rode along with an air of dutiful submission, only groaning and vociferating occasionally that ''twas desp't rough, and bad for Jerry's foot.'

'Now, I jest give yer warning,' said Haley, 'I know yer; yer won't get me to turn off this yer road, with all yer fussin' – so you shet up!'

'Mas'r will go his own way!' said Sam, with rueful submission, at the same time winking most portentously to Andy, whose delight was now very near the explosive point.

Sam was in wonderful spirits; professed to keep a very brisk look-out – at one time exclaiming that he saw 'a gal's bonnet' on the top of some distant eminence, or calling to Andy 'if that thar wasn't Lizzy down in the hollow' – always making these exclamations in some rough or craggy part of the road, where the sudden quickening of speed was a special inconvenience to all parties concerned, and thus keeping Haley in a state of constant commotion.

After riding about an hour in this way, the whole party made a precipitate and tumultuous descent into a barn-yard belonging to a large farming establishment. Not a soul was in sight, all the hands being employed in the fields; but, as the barn stood conspicuously and plainly square across the road, it was evident that their journey in that direction had reached a decided finale.

'Wan't dar ar what I tell'd mas'r?' said Sam, with an air of injured innocence. 'How does strange gentlemen 'spect to know more about a country dan de natives born and raised?'

'You rascal!' said Haley, 'you knew all about this.'

'Didn't I tell yer I know'd, and yer wouldn't believe me? I tell'd mas'r it was all shet up, and fenced up, and I didn't 'spect we could get through – Andy heard me.'

It was all too true to be disputed, and the unlucky man had to pocket his wrath with the best grace he was able, and all three faced to the right about, and took up their line of march for the highway.

In consequence of all the various delays, it was about three-quarters of an hour after Eliza had laid her child to sleep in the village tavern that the party came riding into the same place. Eliza was standing by the window, looking out in another direction, when Sam's quick eye caught a glimpse of her. Haley and Andy were two yards behind. At this crisis Sam contrived to have his hat blown off, and uttered a loud and characteristic ejaculation, which startled her at once, she drew suddenly back; the whole train swept by the window, round to the front door.

A thousand lives seemed to be concentrated in that one moment to Eliza. Her room opened by a side-door to the river. She caught her child, and sprang down the steps towards it. The trader caught a full glimpse of her, just as she was disappearing down the bank; and throwing himself from his horse, and calling loudly on Sam and Andy, he was after her like a hound after a deer. In that dizzy moment, her feet to her scarce seemed to touch the ground, and a moment brought her to the water's edge. Right on behind they came; and nerved with strength such as God gives only to the desperate, with one wild cry and flying leap, she vaulted sheer over the turbid current by the shore, on to the raft of ice beyond. It was a desperate leap – impossible to anything but madness and despair; and Haley, Sam, and Andy instinctively cried out, and lifted up their hands, as she did it.

The huge green fragment of ice on which she alighted pitched and creaked as her weight came on it, but she stayed there not a moment. With wild cries and desperate energy she leaped to another and still another cake; – stumbling – leaping – slipping – springing upwards again! Her shoes are gone – her stockings cut from her feet – while blood marked every step; but she saw nothing, felt nothing, till dimly, as in a dream, she saw the Ohio side and a man helping her up the bank.

'Yer a brave gal, now, whoever ye ar!' said the man, with an oath.

Eliza recognised the voice and face of a man who owned a farm not far from her old home.

'Oh, Mr Symmes! – save me – do save me – do hide me!' said Eliza.

'Why, what's this?' said the man. 'Why, if 'tant Shelby's gal!'

'My child! – this boy – he'd sold him! There is his mas'r,' said she, pointing to the Kentucky shore. 'O Mr Symmes, you've got a little boy.'

'So I have,' said the man, as he roughly, but kindly, drew her up the steep bank. 'Besides, you are a right brave gal. I like grit wherever I see it.

When they had gained the top of the bank the man paused.

'I'd be glad to do something for ye,' said he, 'but then there's nowhar I could take ye. The best I can do is to tell ye to go *thar*,' said he, pointing to a large white house which stood by itself, off the main street of the village. 'Go thar; they're kind folks. Thar's no kind o' danger but they'll help you – they're up to all that sort o' thing.'

'The Lord bless you!' said Eliza, earnestly.

'No 'casion, no 'casion in the world,' said the man. 'What I've done's of no 'count.'

'And oh, surely, sir, you won't tell any one!'

'Go to thunder, gal! What do you take a feller for? In course not,' said the man. 'Come, now, go along like a likely, sensible gal, as you are. You've arnt your liberty, and you shall have it, for all me.'

The woman folded her child to her bosom, and walked firmly and swiftly away. The man stood and looked after her.

'Shelby, now, mebbe won't think this yer the most neigh-bourly thing in the world; but what's a feller to do? If he catches one of my gals in the same fix, he's welcome to pay back. Somehow I never could see no kind o' critter a strivin' and pantin', and trying to clar theirselves, with the dogs arter 'em, and go agin' 'em. Besides, I don't see no kind of 'casion for me to be hunter and catcher for other folks, neither.'

So spoke this poor, heathenish Kentuckian, who had not been instructed in his constitutional relations, and, consequently, was betrayed into acting in a sort of Christianised manner, which, if he had been better situated and more enlightened, he would not have been left to do.

Haley had stood a perfectly amazed spectator of the scene till Eliza had disappeared up the bank, when he turned a blank, inquiring look, on Sam and Andy.

'That ar was a tolerable fair stroke of business,' said Sam.

'The gal's got seven devils in her, I believe,' said Haley. 'How like a wild cat she jumped!'

'Wal, now,' said Sam, scratching his head, 'I hope mas'r 'll 'scuse us tryin' dat ar road. Don't think I feel spry enough for dat ar, no way!' and Sam gave a hoarse chuckle.

'*You* laugh!' said the trader, with a growl.

'Lord bless you, mas'r, I couldn't help it, now,' said Sam, giving way to the long-pent-up delight of his soul. 'She looked so curi's, a leapin' and springin', ice a crackin', and only to hear her – plump! ker chunk! ker splash! Spring! Lord! how she goes it!' And Sam and Andy laughed till the tears rolled down their cheeks.

'I'll make ye laugh t'other side yer mouths!' said the trader, laying about their heads with his riding-whip.

Both ducked, and ran shouting up the bank, and were on their horses before he was up.

'Good evening, mas'r,' said Sam, with much gravity. 'I berry much 'spect missis be anxious 'bout Jerry. Mas'r Haley won't want us no longer. Missis wouldn't hear of our ridin' the critters over Lizzy's bridge to-night;' and, with a facetious poke into Andy's ribs, he started off, followed by the latter, at full speed, their shouts of laughter coming faintly on the wind.

Chapter 8

ELIZA'S ESCAPE

ELIZA made her desperate retreat across the river just in the dusk of twilight. The grey mist of evening, rising slowly from the river, enveloped her as she disappeared up the bank, and the swollen current and floundering masses of ice presented a hopeless barrier between her and her pursuer. Haley, therefore, slowly and discontentedly returned to the little tavern, to ponder further what was to be done. The woman opened to him the door of a little parlour, covered with a rag carpet, where stood a table with a very shining black oil-cloth, sundry lank, high-backed wood chairs, with some plaster images, in resplendent colours, on the mantelshelf, above a very dimly-smoking grate; a long hard-wood settle extended its uneasy length by the chimney, and here Haley sat him down to meditate on the instability of human hopes and happiness in general.

'What did I want with the little cuss, now,' he said to himself, 'that I should have got myself treed like a 'coon, as I am, this yer way?' and Haley relieved himself by repeating over a not very select litany of imprecations on himself, which, though there was the best possible reason to consider them as true, we shall, as a matter of taste, omit.

He was startled by the loud and dissonant voice of a man who was apparently dismounting at the door. He hurried to the window.

'By the land! if this yer an't the nearest, now, to what I've heard folks call Providence,' said Haley. 'I do b'lieve that ar's Tom Loker.'

Haley hastened out. Standing by the bar, in the corner of the room, was a brawny, muscular man, full six feet in height, and broad in proportion. He was dressed in a coat of buffalo-skin, made with the hair outward, which gave him a shaggy and fierce appearance, perfectly in keeping with the whole air of his physiognomy. In the head and face, every organ and lineament expressive of brutal and unhesitating violence was in a state of the highest possible development. Indeed, could our readers fancy a bull-dog come unto man's estate, and walking about in a hat and coat, they would have no unapt idea of the general style and effect of his physique. He was accompanied by a travelling companion, in many respects an exact contrast to himself. He was short and slender, lithe and cat-like in his motions, and had a peering, mousing expression about his keen black eyes, with which every feature of his face seemed sharpened into sympathy; his thin, long nose ran out as if it was eager to bore into the nature of things in general; his sleek, thin black hair was stuck eagerly forward, and all his motions and evolutions expressed a dry, cautious acuteness. The great big man poured out a big tumbler half full of raw spirits, and gulped it down without a word. The little man stood tip-toe, and putting his head first to one side and then to the other, and snuffing considerately in the directions of the various bottles, ordered at last a mint julep, in a thin and quivering voice, and with an air of great circumspection. When poured out, he took it and looked at it with a sharp, complacent air, like a man who thinks he has done about the right thing, and hit the nail on the head, and proceeded to dispose of it in short and well-advised sips.

'Wal, now, who'd a thought this yer luck 'ad come to me? Why, Loker, how are ye?' said Haley, coming forward and extending his hand to the big man.

'The devil!' was the civil reply. 'What brought you here, Haley?'

The mousing man, who bore the name of Marks, instantly stopped his sipping, and poking his head forward, looked shrewdly on the new acquaintance, as a cat sometimes looks at a moving dry leaf, or some other possible object of pursuit.

'I say, Tom, this yer's the luckiest thing in the world. I'm in a devil of a hobble, and you must help me out.'

'Ugh! aw! like enough!' grunted his complaisant acquaintance. 'A body may be pretty sure of that, when *you're* glad to see 'em: something to be made off of 'em. What's the blow now?'

'You've got a friend here?' said Haley, looking doubtfully at Marks; 'partner, perhaps?'

'Yes, I have. Here Marks! here's that ar feller that I was in with in Natchez.'

'Shall be pleased with his acquaintance,' said Marks, thrusting out a long thin hand, like a raven's claw. 'Mr Haley, I believe?'

'The same, sir,' said Haley. 'And now, gentlemen, seein' as we've met so happily, I think I'll stand up to a small matter of a treat in this here parlour. So, now, old 'coon,' said he to the man at the bar, 'get us hot water, and sugar, and cigars, and plenty of the *real stuff*, and we'll have a blow-out.'

Behold, then, the candles lighted, the fire stimulated to the burning-point in the grate, and our three worthies seated round a table, well spread with all the accessories to good fellowship enumerated before.

Haley began a pathetic recital of his peculiar troubles. Loker shut up his mouth, and listened to him with gruff and surly attention. Marks, who was anxiously and with much fidgeting, compounding a tumbler of punch to his own peculiar taste, occasionally looked up from his employment, and, poking his sharp nose and chin almost into Haley's face, gave the most earnest heed to the whole narrative. The conclusion of it appeared to amuse him extremely, for he shook his shoulders and sides in silence, and perked up his thin lip with an air of great internal enjoyment.

'So, then, ye'r fairly sewed up, an't ye?' he said; 'he! he! he! It's neatly done, too.'

'This yer young-un business makes lots of trouble in the trade,' said Haley, dolefully.

'If we could get a breed of gals that didn't care, now, for their young uns,' said Marks, 'tell ye, I think 'twould be 'bout the greatest mod'rn improvement I knows on;' and Marks patronised his joke by a quiet introductory sniggle.

'Jest so,' said Haley; 'I never couldn't see into it. Young uns is heaps of trouble to 'em – one would think, now, they'd be glad to get clar on em'; but they arn't. And the more trouble a young un is, and the more good for nothing, as a gen'l thing, the tighter they sticks to 'em.'

'Wal, Mr Haley,' said Marks, 'jest pass the hot water. Yes, sir; you say jest what I feel and all'us have. Now, I bought a gal once when I was in the trade, a tight, likely wench she was, too, and quite considerable smart – and she had a young un that was mis'able sickly; it had a crooked back, or something or other, and I jest gin't away to a man that thought he'd take his chance raisin' on't, being it didn't cost nothin' – never thought, yer know, of the gal's takin' on about it – but, Lord, yer oughter seen how she went on! Why, re'lly, she did seem to me to valley the child more 'cause *'twas* sickly and cross, and plagued her; and she warn't making-b'lieve, neither – cried about it, she did, and lopped round, as if she'd lost every friend she had. It re'lly was droll to think on't. Lord, there an't no end to women's notions.'

'Wal, jest so with me,' said Haley. 'Last summer, down on Red River, I got a gal traded off on me, with a likely-lookin' child enough, and his eyes looked as bright as yourn; but come to look, I found him stone-blind. Fact – he was stone-blind. Wal, ye see, I thought there warn't no harm in my jest passing him along, and not sayin' nothin'; and I'd got him nicely swopped off for a keg o'whiskey; but come to get him away from the gal, she was jest like a tiger. So 'twas before we started, and I hadn't got my gang chained up; so what should she do but ups on a cotton-bale, like a cat, ketches a knife from one of the deck hands, and I'll tell ye, she made all fly for a minnit, till she saw 'twan't no use; and she jest turns round and pitches head-first, young un and all, into the river – went down plump, and never ris.'

'Bah!' said Tom Loker, who had listened to these stories with ill-repressed disgust. 'Shif'less, both on ye! *My* gals don't cut up no such shines, I tell ye!'

'Indeed! how do you help it?' said Marks, briskly.

'Help it? why, I buys a gal, and if she's got a young un to be sold, I jest walks up and puts my fist to her face, and says, "Look here, now, if you give me one word out of your head, I'll smash yer face in. I won't hear one word – not the beginning of a word." I says to 'em, "This yer young un's mine and not yourn, and you've no kind o' business with it. I'm going to sell it, first chance; mind you don't cut up none o'yer shines about it, or I'll make ye wish ye'd never been born." I tell ye, they sees it an't no play, when I gets hold. I makes 'em as whist as fishes; and if one on 'em begins and gives a yelp, why'— and Mr Loker brought down his fist with a thump that fully explained the hiatus.

'That ar's what ye may call *emphasis*,' said Marks, poking Haley in the side, and going into another small giggle. 'An't Tom peculiar? he! he! he! I say, Tom, I 'spect you make 'em *understand*, for all niggers' heads is woolly. They don't never have no doubt o' your meaning, Tom. If you an't the devil, Tom, you's his twin-brother; I'll say that for ye.'

Tom received the compliment with becoming modesty, and began to look as affable as was consistent, as John Bunyan says, 'with his doggish nature.'

Haley, who had been imbibing very freely of the staple of the evening, began to feel a sensible elevation and enlargement of his moral faculties – a phenomenon not unusual with gentlemen of a serious and reflective turn, under similar circumstances.

'Wal, now, Tom,' he said, 'ye re'lly is too bad, as I al'ays have told ye. Ye know, Tom, you and I used to talk over these yer matters down in Natchez, and I used to prove to ye that we made full as much, and was as well off for this yer world, by treatin' on 'em well, besides keepin' a better chance for comin' in the kingdom at last, when wust comes to wust, and thar ar'nt nothing else left to get, ye know.'

'Boh!' said Tom, '*don't* I know? – don't make me too sick with any yer stuff – my stomach is a leetle riled, now;' and Tom drank half a glass of raw brandy.

'I say,' said Haley, and leaning back in his chair and gesturing impressively, 'I'll say this, now I al'ays meant to drive my trade so as to make money on't, *fust and foremost*, as much as any man; but then, trade an't everything, and money an't every-thing, 'cause we's all got souls. I don't care, now, who hears me say it – and I think a cussed sight on it, so I may as well come out with it. I b'lieve in religion, and one of these days, when I've got matters tight and snug, I calculate to 'tend to my soul, and them ar matters: and so what's the use of doin' any more wickedness than's re'lly necessary? – it don't seem to me it's 'tall prudent.'

''Tend to yer soul!' repeated Tom contemptuously: 'take a bright look-out to find a soul in you – save yourself any care on that score. If the devil sifts you through a hair sieve, he won't find one.'

'Why, Tom you're cross,' said Haley; 'why can't ye take it pleasant, now, when a feller's talking for your good?'

'Stop that ar jaw o' yourn, there,' said Tom gruffly. 'I can stand most any talk o' yourn but your pious talk – that kills me right up. After all, what's the odds between me and you? 'Tan't that you care one bit more, or have a bit more feelin' – it's clean, sheer, dog meanness, wanting to cheat the devil and save your own skin; don't I see through it? And your "gettin' religion," as you call it, arter all, is too p'isin mean for any crittur; run up a bill with the devil all your life, and then sneak out when pay-time comes! Boh!'

'Come, come, gentlemen, I say, this isn't business,' said Marks. 'There's different ways, you know, of looking at all subjects. Mr Haley is a very nice man, no doubt, and has his own conscience; and, Tom, you have your ways, and very good ones, too, Tom; but quarelling, you know, won't answer no kind of purpose. Let's go to business. Now, Mr Haley, what is it? you want us to undertake to catch this yer gal?'

'The gal's no matter of mine – she's Shelby's; it's only the boy. I was a fool for buying the monkey!'

'You're generally a fool!' said Tom, gruffly.

'Come, now, Loker, none of your huffs,' said Marks, licking his lips; 'you see, Mr Haley's a puttin' us in a way of a good job, I reckon; just hold still – these yer arrangements is my forte. This yer gal, Mr Haley, how is she? what is she?'

'Wal! white and handsome – well brought up. I'd a gin Shelby eight hundred or a thousand, and then made well on her.'

'White and handsome – well brought up!' said Marks, his sharp eyes, nose, and mouth all alive with enterprise. 'Look here, now, Loker, a beautiful opening. We'll do a business here on our own account; we does the catchin'; the boy, of course, goes to Mr Haley – we takes the gal to Orleans to speculate on. An't it beautiful?'

Tom, whose great, heavy mouth had stood ajar during this communication, now suddenly snapped it together, as a big dog closes on a piece of meat, and seemed to be digesting the idea at his leisure.

'Ye see,' said Marks to Haley, stirring his punch as he did so, 'ye see, we has justices convenient at all p'ints along shore that does up any little jobs in our line quite reasonable. Tom, he does

the knockin' down, and that ar; and I come in all dressed up –
shining boots – everything first chop, when the swearin's to be
done. You oughter see, now,' said Marks, in a glow of professional pride, 'how I can tone it off. One day, I'm Mr
Twickem, from New Orleans; 'nother day, I'm just come from
my plantation on Pearl River, where I works seven hundred
niggers; then, again, I come out a distant relation of Henry
Clay, or some old cock in Kentuck. Talents is different you
know. Now, Tom's a roarer when there's any thumping or
fighting to be done; but at lying, he an't good, Tom an't – ye
see it don't come natural to him; but, Lord, if thar's a feller in
the country that can swear to anything and everything, and put
in all the circumstances and flourishes with a longer face, and
carry 't through better 'n I can, why, I'd like to see him, that's
all! I b'lieve, my heart, I could get along, and snake through,
even if justices were more particular than they is. Sometimes I
wish they was more particular; 'twould be a heap more relishin'
if they was – more fun, yer know.'

Tom Loker, who, as we have made it appear, was a man of
slow thoughts and movements, here interrupted Marks by
bringing his heavy fist down on the table, so as to make all ring
again. 'It'll do!' he said.

'Lord bless ye, Tom, ye needn't break all the glasses,' said
Marks; 'save your fist for time o' need.'

'But, gentlemen, an't I to come in for a share of the profits?'
said Haley.

'An't it enough we catch the boy for ye?' said Loker. 'What
do ye want?'

'Wal,' said Haley, 'if I gives you the job, it's worth something
– say ten per cent on the profits, expenses paid.'

'Now,' said Loker, with a tremendous oath, and striking the
table with his heavy fist, 'don't I know you, Dan Haley. Don't
you think to come it over me! Suppose Marks and I have taken
up the catchin' trade, jest to commodate gentlemen like you,
and get nothin' for ourselves? Not by a long chalk! We'll have
the gal out and out, and you keep quiet, or, ye see, we'll have
both – what's to hinder? Han't you show'd us the game? It's as
free to us as you, I hope. If you or Shelby wants to chase us,
look where the partridges was last year: if you find them or us
you're quite welcome.'

'Oh, wal, certainly, jest let it go at that,' said Haley, alarmed; 'you catch the boy for the job; you allers did trade *far* with me, Tom, and was up to yer word.'

'Ye know that,' said Tom; 'I don't pretend none of your snivelling ways, but I won't lie in my 'counts with the devil himself. What I ses I'll do, I will do; you know *that*, Dan Haley.'

'Jes so, jes so, I said so, Tom,' said Haley; 'and if you'd only promise to have the boy for me in a week, at any point you'll name that's all I want.'

'But it an't all I want by a long jump,' said Tom. 'Ye don't think I did business with you, down in Natchez, for nothing, Haley; I've learned to hold an eel when I catch him. You've got to fork over fifty dollars, flat down, or this child don't start a peg. I know yer.'

'Why, when you have a job in hand that may bring a clean profit of somewhere about a thousand or sixteen hundred? Why, Tom, you're onreasonable,' said Haley.

'Yes, and hasn't we business booked for five weeks to come – all we can do? And suppose we leaves all, and goes to bushwhacking round arter yer young un, and finally doesn't catch the gal – and gals allers is the devil *to* catch – what's then; would you pay us a cent – would you? I think I see you a doin' it – ugh! No, no, flap down your fifty. If we get the job, and it pays, I'll hand it back; if we don't, it's for our trouble – that's *far*, an't it, Marks?'

'Certainly, certainly,' said Marks, with a conciliatory tone. 'It's only a retaining fee, you see – he! he! he! – we lawyers, you know. Wal, we must all keep good-natured, keep easy, yer know. Tom 'll have the boy for yer anywhere ye'll name; won't ye, Tom?'

'If we find the young un, I'll bring him on to Cincinnati, and leave him at Granny Belcher's, on the landing,' said Loker.

Marks had got from his pocket a greasy pocket-book, and taking a long paper from thence, he sat down, and fixing his keen black eyes on it, began mumbling over its contents: '"Barnes – Shelby County – boy Jim, three hundred dollars for him, dead or alive. Edwards – Dick and Lucy – man and wife, six hundred dollars; wench Polly and two children – six hundred for her or her head" – I'm jest a running over our business, to see if we can take up this yer handily. Loker,' he said, after a pause, 'we must set Adams and Springer on the track of these yer; they've been booked some time.'

'They'll charge too much,' said Tom.

'I'll manage that ar; they's young in the business, and must 'spect to work cheap,' said Marks, as he continued to read. 'Ther's three on 'em easy cases, 'cause all you've got to do is to shoot 'em, or swear they is shot; they couldn't, of course, charge much for that. Them other cases,' he said, folding the paper, 'will bear puttin' off a spell. So now let's come to the particulars. Now, Mr Haley, you saw this yer gal when she landed?'

'To be sure – plain as I see you.'

'And a man helpin' on her up the bank?' said Loker.

'To be sure, I did.'

'Most likely,' said Marks, 'she's took in somewhere; but where's a question. Tom, what do you say?'

'We must cross the river to-night, no mistake,' said Tom.

'But ther's no boat about,' said Marks. 'The ice is running awfully, Tom; an't it dangerous?'

'Don'no nothing 'bout that, only it's got to be done,' said Tom decidedly.

'Dear me,' said Marks, fidgeting, 'it'll be – I say,' he said, walking to the window, 'it's dark as a wolf's mouth, and Tom'—

'The long and short is, you're scared, Marks; but I can't help that, you've got to go. Suppose you want to lie by a day or two, till the gal's been carried on the underground line up to Sandusky or so, before you start.'

'Oh no; I an't a grain afraid,' said Marks, 'only'—

'Only what?' said Tom.

'Well, about the boat. Yer see there an't any boat.'

'I heard the woman say there was one coming along this evening, and that a man was going to cross over in it. Neck or nothing, we must go with him,' said Tom.

'I s'pose you've got good dogs,' said Haley.

'First-rate,' said Marks. 'But what's the use? you han't got nothing' o' hers to smell on.'

'Yes, I have,' said Haley, triumphantly. 'Here's her shawl she left on the bed in her hurry; she left her bonnet too.'

'That ar's lucky,' said Loker, 'fork over.'

'Though the dogs might damage the gal, if they come on her unawares,' said Haley.

'That ar's a considertion,' said Marks. 'Our dogs tore a feller half to pieces, once, down in Mobile, 'fore we could get 'em off.'

'Well, ye see, for this sort that's to be sold for their looks, that ar won't answer, ye see,' said Haley.

'I do see,' said Marks. 'Besides, if she's got took in, 'tan't no go, neither. Dogs is no 'count in these ver up states where thee critters gets carried; of course, ye can't get on their track. They only does down in plantations, where niggers, when they runs, has to do their own running, and don't get no help.'

'Well,' said Loker, who had stepped out to the bar to make some inquiries, 'they say the man's come with the boat; so, Marks!'

That worthy cast a rueful look at the comfortable quarters he was leaving, but slowly rose to obey. After exchanging a few words of further arrangement, Haley, with visible reluctance, handed over the fifty dollars to Tom, and the worthy trio separated for the night.

If any of our refined and Christian readers object to the society into which this scene introduces them, let us beg them to begin and conquer their prejudices in time. The catching business, we beg to remind them, is rising to the dignity of a lawful and patriotic profession. If all the broad land between the Mississippi and the Pacific becomes one great market for bodies and souls, and human property retains the locomotive tendencies of this nineteenth century, the trader and catcher may yet be among our aristocracy.

While this scene was going on at the tavern, Sam and Andy, in a state of high felicitation pursued their way home.

Sam was in the highest possible feather, and expressed his exultation by all sorts of supernatural howls and ejaculations, by divers odd motions and contortions of his whole system. Sometimes he would sit backward, with his face to the horse's tail and sides, and then, with a whoop and a somerset, come right side up in his place again, and drawing on a grave face, begin to lecture Andy in high-sounding tones for laughing and playing the fool. Anon, slapping his sides with his arms, he would burst forth in peals of laughter, that made the old woods ring as they passed. With all these evolutions, he contrived to keep the horses up to the top of their speed, until, between ten and eleven, their heels resounded on the gravel at the end of the balcony. Mrs Shelby flew to the railings.

'Is that you, Sam? Where are they?'

'Mas'r Haley's a-restin' at the tavern; he's dreful fatigued, missis.'

'And Eliza, Sam?'

'Wal, she's clar 'cross Jordan. As a body may say, in the land o'Canaan.'

'Why, Sam, what *do* you mean?' said Mrs Shelby, breathless and almost faint, as the possible meaning of these words came over her.

'Wal, missis, de Lord He presarves His own. Lizzy's done gone over the river into 'Hio, as 'markably as if the Lord took her over in a charrit of fire and two hosses.'

Sam's vein of piety was always uncommonly fervent in his mistress' presence, and he made great capital of scriptural figures and images.

'Come up here, Sam,' said Mr Shelby, who had followed on to the verandah, 'and tell your mistress what she wants. Come, come, Emily,' said he, passing his arm round her, 'you are cold, and all in a shiver; you allow yourself to feel too much.'

'Feel too much! Am not I a woman – a mother? Are we not both responsible to God for this poor girl? My God, lay not this sin to our charge!'

'What sin, Emily? You see yourself that we have only done what we were obliged to.'

'There's an awful feeling of guilt about it, though,' said Mrs Shelby. 'I can't reason it away.'

'Here, Andy, you nigger, be alive!' called Sam, under the verandah; 'take these yer horses to der barn; don't ye hear mas'r a callin'?' and Sam soon appeared, palm-leaf in hand, at the parlour door.

'Now, Sam, tell us distinctly how the matter was,' said Mr Shelby. 'Where is Eliza, if you know?'

'Wal, mas'r, I saw her with my own eyes a crossin' on the floatin' ice. She crossed most 'markably; it wasn't no less nor a miracle; and I saw a man help her up the 'Hio side, and then she was lost in the dusk.'

'Sam, I think this rather apocryphal – this miracle. Crossing on floating ice isn't so easily done,' said Mr Shelby.

'Easy! couldn't nobody a done it, without de Lord. Why, now,' said Sam, ''twas jist dis yer way. Mas'r Haley, and me, and Andy, we comes up to de little tavern by the river, and I rides a leetle ahead – (I's so zealous to be a cotchin' Lizzy, that I couldn't hold in, no-way) – and when I comes by the tavern winder, sure enough there she was, right in plain sight, and dey diggin' on behind. Wal, I loses off my hat, and sings out nuff to raise the dead. Course Lizzy she hars, and she dodges back, when Mas'r Haley he goes past the door; and then, I tell ye, she clared out de side door; she went down de river bank; Mas'r Haley he seed her, and yelled out, and him, and me, and Andy, we took arter. Down she came to the river, and thar was the current running ten feet wide by the shore, and over t'other side ice a sawin' and a jiggling up and down, kinder as 'twere a great island. We come right behind her, and I thought my soul he'd got her sure enough – when she gin sich a screech as I never hearn, and thar she was, clar over t'other side the current, on the ice, and then on she went, a screeching and a jumpin' – the ice went crack! c'wallop! cracking! chunk! and she a boundin' like a buck! Lord, the spring that ar gal's got in her an't common, I'm o' 'pinion.'

Mrs Shelby sat perfectly silent, pale with excitement, while Sam told his story.

'God be praised, she isn't dead!' said she; 'but where is the poor child now?'

'De Lord will pervide,' said Sam, rolling up his eyes piously. 'As I've been a sayin', dis yer's a providence and no mistake, as missis has allers been a instructin' on us. Thar's allers instruments ris up to do de Lord's will. Now, if't hadn't been for me to-day, she'd a been took a dozen times. Warn't it I started off de hosses dis yer mornin', and kept 'em chasin' till nigh dinner time? And didn't I car Mas'r Haley nigh five miles out of de road, dis evening, or else he'd a come up with Lizzy as easy as a dog arter a 'coon. These yer's all providences.'

'They are a kind of providences that you'll have to be pretty sparing of, Master Sam. I allow no such practices with gentlemen on my place,' said Mr Shelby, with as much sternness as he could command, under the circumstances.

Now, there is no more use in making believe to be angry with a negro than with a child; both instinctively see the true state of the case, through all attempts to affect the contrary; and Sam was in no wise disheartened by this rebuke, though he assumed an air of doleful gravity, and stood with the corners of his mouth lowered in most penitential style.

'Mas'r's quite right – quite; it was ugly on me – there's no disputin' that ar; and of course mas'r and missis wouldn't encourage no such works. I'm sensible of dat ar; but a poor nigger like me's 'mazin' tempted to act ugly sometimes, when fellers will cut up such shines as dat ar Mas'r Haley; he an't no gen'l'man noway: anybody's been raised as I've been can't help a seein' dat ar.'

'Well, Sam,' said Mrs Shelby, 'as you appear to have a proper sense of your errors, you may go now and tell Aunt Chloe she may get you some of that cold ham that was left of dinner to-day. You and Andy must be hungry.'

'Missis is a heap too good for us,' said Sam, making his bow with alacrity, and departing.

It will be perceived, as has been before intimated, that Master Sam had a native talent that might, undoubtedly, have raised him to eminence in political life – a talent of making capital out of everything that turned up, to be invested for his own especial praise and glory; and having done up his piety and humility, as he trusted, to the satisfaction of the parlour, he clapped his palm-leaf on his head, with a sort of rakish, free-and-easy air, and proceeded to the dominions of Aunt Chloe, with the intention of flourishing largely in the kitchen.

'I'll speechify these yer niggers,' said Sam to himself, 'now I've got a chance. Lord, I'll reel it off to make 'em stare!'

It must be observed that one of Sam's especial delights had been to ride in attendance on his master to all kinds of political gatherings, where, roosted on some rail fence, or perched aloft in some tree, he would sit watching the orators, with the greatest apparent gusto, and then, descending among the various brethren of his own colour, assembled on the same errand, he would edify and delight them with the most ludicrous burlesques and imitations, all delivered with the most imperturbable earnestness and solemnity; and though the auditors immediately about him were generally of his own colour, it not unfrequently happened that they were fringed pretty deeply with those of a fairer complexion, who listened, laughing and winking, to Sam's great self-congratulation. In fact, Sam considered oratory as his vocation, and never let slip an opportunity of magnifying his office.

Now, between Sam and Aunt Chloe there had existed, from ancient times, a sort of chronic feud, or rather a decided coolness; but, as Sam was meditating something in the provision department as the necessary and obvious foundation of his operations, he determined, on the present occasion, to be eminently conciliatory; for he well knew that although 'missis' orders' would undoubtedly be followed to the letter, yet he should gain a considerable deal by enlisting the spirit also. He, therefore, appeared before Aunt Chloe with a touchingly sub-dued, resigned expression, like one who has suffered immeasur-able hardships in behalf of a persecuted fellow-creature – enlarged upon the fact that missis had directed him to come to Aunt Chloe for whatever might be wanting to make up the balance in his solids and fluids – and thus unequivocally acknowledged her right and supremacy in the cooking depart-ment, and all thereto pertaining.

The thing took accordingly. No poor, simple, virtuous body was ever cajoled by the attentions of an electioneering politician with more ease than Aunt Chloe was won over by Master Sam's suavities; and if he had been the prodigal son himself, he could not have been overwhelmed with more maternal bountifulness; and he soon found himself seated, happy and glorious, over a large tin pan, containing a sort of *olla podrida* of all that had appeared on the table for two or three days past. Savoury morsels of ham, golden blocks of corn-cake, fragments of pie of every conceivable mathematical figure, chicken wings, gizzards, and drumsticks, all appeared in picturesque confusion; and Sam, as monarch of all he surveyed, sat with his palm-leaf cocked rejoicingly to one side, and patronising Andy at his right hand.

The kitchen was full of all his compeers, who had hurried and crowded in, from the various cabins, to hear the termination of the day's exploits. Now was Sam's hour of glory. The story of the day was rehearsed, with all kinds of ornament and varnish-ing which might be necessary to heighten its effect; for Sam, like some of our fashionable dilettanti, never allowed a story to lose any of its gilding by passing through his hands. Roars of laughter attended the narration, and were taken up and prolonged by all the smaller fry, who were lying, in any quantity, about on the floor, or perched in every corner. In the height of the uproar and laughter, Sam, however, preserved an immovable gravity, only from time to time rolling his eyes up, and giving his auditors divers inexpressibly droll glances, without departing from the sententious elevation of his oratory.

'Yer see, fellow-countrymen,' said Sam, elevating a turkey's leg with energy, 'yer see, now, what dis yer chile's up ter, for 'fendin' yer all – yes, all on yer. For him as tries to get one o' our people, is as good as tryin' to get all; yer see the principle's de same – dat ar's clar. And any one o' these yer drivers that comes smelling round arter any our people, why, he's got *me* in his way; *I'm* the feller he's got to set in with – I'm the feller for ye all to come to, bredren – I'll stand up for yer rights – I'll 'fend 'em to the last breath!'

'Why, but Sam, yer telled me, only this mornin', that you'd help this yer mas'r to cotch Lizzy; seems to me yer talk don't hang together,' said Andy.

'I tell you now, Andy,' said Sam, with awful superiority, 'don't yer be a-talkin' 'bout what yer don't know nothin' on; boys like you, Andy, means well, but they can't be 'spected to collusitate the great principles of action.'

Andy looked rebuked, particularly by the hard word 'collusitate,' which most of the youngerly members of the company seemed to consider as a settler in the case, while Sam proceeded,—

'Dat ar was *conscience*, Andy; when I thought of gwine arter Lizzy, I railly 'spected mas'r was sot dat way. When I found missus was sot the contrar, dat ar was conscience *more yet* – 'cause fellers allers gets more by stickin' to missis' side – so you see I's persistent either way, and sticks up to conscience, and holds on to principles. Yes, *principles*,' said Sam, giving an enthusiastic toss to a chicken's neck – 'what's principles good for, if we isn't persistent, I wanter know? Thar, Andy, you may have dat ar bone, 'tan't picked quite clean.'

Sam's audience hanging on his words with open mouth, he could not but proceed—

'Dis yer matter 'bout persistence, feller niggers,' said Sam, with the air of one entering into an abstruse subject, 'dis yer 'sistency's a thing what an't seed into very clar, by most anybody. Now, yer see, when a feller stands up for a thing one day and night, de contrar de next, folks ses (and nat'rally enough they ses), why he an't persistent – hand me dat ar bit o' corn-cake, Andy. But let's look inter it. I hope the gen'lemen and der fair sex will 'scuse me usin' an or'nary sort o' 'parison. Here ! I'm a tryin' to get top o' der hay. Wal, I puts up my larder dis yer side ; 'tan't no go ; den, 'cause I don' try dere no more, but puts my larder right de contrar side, an't I persistent ? I'm persistent in wanting to get up which ary side my larder is ; don't yer se, all on yer ?'

'It's the only thing ye ever was persistent in, Lord knows !' muttered Aunt Chloe, who was getting rather restive ; the merriment of the evening being to her somewhat after the Scripture comparison – 'like vinegar upon nitre.'

'Yes, indeed !' said Sam, rising, full of supper and glory, for a closing effort. 'Yes, my feller-citizens and ladies of de other sex in general, I has principles – I'm proud to 'oon 'em – they's perquisite to dese yer times, and ter *all* times. I has principles, and I sticks to 'em like forty – jest anything that I thinks is principle, I goes in to't ; I wouldn't mind if dey burn me 'live, I'd walk right up to de stake, I would, and say, Here I comes to shed my last blood fur my principles, fur my country, furder gen'l interests of s'ciety.'

'Well,' said Aunt Chloe, 'one o' yer principles will have to be to get to bed some time to-night, and not be a keepin' everybody up till mornin' ; now, every one of you young uns that don't want to be cracked had better be scase, mighty sudden.'

'Niggers ! all on yer,' said Sam, waving his palm-leaf with benignity, 'I give yer my blessin' : go to bed now, and be good boys.'

And, with this pathetic benediction, the assembly dispersed.

Chapter 9

IN WHICH IT APPEARS THAT A SENATOR IS BUT A MAN

THE light of the cheerful fire shone on the rug and carpet of a cosy parlour, and glittered on the sides of the tea-cups, and well-brightened tea-pot, as Senator Bird was drawing off his boots, preparatory to inserting his feet in a pair of new handsome slippers, which his wife had been working for him while away on his senatorial tour. Mrs Bird, looking the very picture of delight, was superintending the arrangements of the table, ever and anon mingling admonitory remarks to a number of frolicsome juveniles, who were effervescing in all those modes of untold gambol and mischief that had astonished mothers ever since the flood.

'Tom, let the door-knob alone – there's a man ! Mary ! Mary ; don't pull the cat's tail – poor pussy ! Jim, you mustn't climb on that table – no, no ! – You don't know, my dear, what a surprise it is to us all to see you here to-night,' said she, at last, when she found a space to say something to her husband.

'Yes, yes, I thought I'd just make a run down, spend the night, and have a little comfort at home. I'm tired to death, and my head aches !'

Mrs Bird cast a glance at a camphor-bottle, which stood in the half-open closet, and appeared to meditate an approach to it, but her husband interposed.

'No, no, Mary, no doctoring ! a cup of your good hot tea, and some of our good home living, is what I want. It's a tiresome business this legislating !'

And the senator smiled, as if he rather liked the idea of considering himself a sacrifice to his country.

'Well,' said his wife, after the business of the tea-table was getting rather slack, 'and what have they been doing in the Senate ?'

Now, it was a very unusual thing for gentle little Mrs Bird ever to trouble her head with what was going on in the house of the State, very wisely considering that she had enough to do to mind her own. Mr Bird, therefore, opened his eyes in surprise, and said,—

'Not very much of importance.'

'Well; but is it true that they have been passing a law forbidding people to give meat and drink to those poor coloured folks that come along? I heard they were talking of some such law, but I didn't think any Christian legislature would pass it!'

'Why, Mary, you are getting to be a politician all at once.'

'No, nonsense! I wouldn't give a fip for all your politics, generally, but I think this is something downright cruel and unchristian. I hope, my dear, no such law has been passed.'

'There has been a law passed forbidding people to help off the slaves that come over from Kentucky, my dear: so much of that thing has been done by these reckless Abolitionists, that our brethren in Kentucky are very strongly excited, and it seems necessary, and no more than Christian and kind, that something should be done by our State to quiet the excitement.'

'And what is the law? It don't forbid us to shelter these poor creatures a night, does it? and to give 'em something comfortable to eat, and a few old clothes, and send them quietly about their busines?'

'Why, yes, my dear; that would be aiding and abetting, you know.'

Mrs Bird was a timid, blushing little woman, of about four feet in height, and with mild blue eyes, and a peach-blow complexion, and the gentlest, sweetest voice in the world; as for courage, a moderate-sized cock-turkey had been known to put her to rout at the very first gobble, and a stout house-dog of moderate capacity would bring her into subjection merely by a show of his teeth. Her husband and children were her entire world, and in these she ruled more by entreaty and persuasion than by command or argument. There was only one thing that was capable of arousing her, and that provocation came in on the side of her unusually gentle and sympathetic nature; anything in the shape of cruelty would throw her into a passion, which was the more alarming and inexplicable in proportion to the general softness of her nature. Generally the most indulgent and easy to be entreated of all mothers, still her boys had a very reverent remembrance of a most vehement chastisement she once bestowed on them, because she found them leagued with several graceless boys of the neighbourhood stoning a defenceless kitten.

'I'll tell you what,' Master Bill used to say, 'I was scared that time. Mother came at me so that I thought she was crazy, and I was whipped and tumbled off to bed, without any supper, before I could get over wondering what had come about; and, after that, I heard mother crying outside the door, which made me feel worse than all the rest. I'll tell you what,' he'd say, 'we boys never stoned another kitten!'

On the present occasion, Mrs Bird rose quickly, with very red cheeks, which quite improved her general appearance, and walked up to her husband, with quite a resolute air, and said, in a determined tone,—

'Now, John, I want to know if you think such a law as that is right and Christian?'

'You won't shoot me, now, Mary, if I say I do!'

'I never could have thought it of you, John! You didn't vote for it?'

'Even so, my fair politician.'

'You ought to be ashamed, John! Poor, homeless, houseless creatures! It's a shameful, wicked, abominable law, and I'll break it, for one, the first time I get a chance; and I hope I *shall* have a chance, I do! Things have got to a pretty pass, if a woman can't give a warm supper and a bed to poor, starving creatures, just because they are slaves, and have been abused and oppressed all their lives, poor things!'

'But, Mary, just listen to me. Your feelings are all quite right, dear, and interesting, and I love you for them; but then, dear, we mustn't suffer our feelings to run away with our judgment. You must consider it's not a matter of private feeling; there are great public interests involved, there is such a state of public agitation rising, that we must put aside our private feelings.'

'Now, John, I don't know anything about politics, but I can read my Bible; and there I see that I must feed the hungry, clothe the naked, and comfort the desolate; and that Bible I mean to follow.'

'But in cases where your doing so would involve a great public evil'—

'Obeying God never brings on public evils. I know it can't. It's always safest, all round, to – *do as He* bids us.'

'Now, listen to me, Mary, and I can state to you a very clear argument, to show'——

'Oh, nonsense, John! you can talk all night, but you wouldn't do it. I put it to you, John, would *you* now turn away a poor, shivering, hungry creature from your door, because he was a runaway? *Would* you, now?'

Now, if the truth must be told, our senator had the misfortune to be a man who had a particularly humane and accessible nature, and turning away anybody that was in trouble never had been his forte; and what was worse for him in this particular pinch of the argument was, that his wife knew it, and, of course, was making an assault on rather an indefensible point. So he had recourse to the usual means of gaining time for such cases made and provided; he said 'ahem,' and coughed several times, took out his pocket-handkerchief, and began to wipe his glasses. Mrs Bird, seeing the defenceless condition of the enemy's territory, had no more conscience than to push her advantage.

'I should like to see you doing that, John – I really should! Turning a woman out of doors in a snowstorm, for instance, or may be you'd take her up and put her in gaol, wouldn't you? You would make a great hand at that!'

'Of course, it would be a very painful duty,' began Mr Bird, in a moderate tone.

'Duty, John! don't use that word! You know it isn't a duty – it can't be a duty! If folks want to keep their slaves from running away, let 'em treat 'em well – that's my doctrine. If I have slaves (as I hope I never shall have) I'd risk their wanting to run away from me, or you either, John. I tell you folks don't run away when they are happy; and when they do run, poor creatures! they suffer enough with cold, and hunger, and fear, without everybody's turning againt them; and, law or no law, I never will, so help me God!'

'Mary! Mary, my dear, let me reason with you.'

'I hate reasoning, John – especially reasoning on such subjects. There's a way you political folks have of coming round and round a plain right thing; and you don't believe in it yourselves, when it comes to practice. I know *you* well enough, John. You don't believe it's right, any more than I do; and you wouldn't do it any sooner than I.'

At this critical juncture Old Cudjoe, the black man-of-all-work, put his head in at the door, and wished 'Missis would come into the kitchen;' and our senator, tolerably relieved, looked after his little wife with a whimsical mixture of amusement and vexation, and seating himself in the arm-chair, began to read the papers.

After a moment his wife's voice was heard at the door, in a quick earnest tone, 'John! John! I do wish you'd come here a moment.'

He laid down his paper and went into the kitchen, and started, quite amazed at the sight that presented itself. A young and slender woman, with garments torn and frozen, with one shoe gone, and the stocking torn away from the cut and bleeding foot, was laid back in a deadly swoon upon two chairs. There was the impress of the despised race on her face, yet none could help feeling its mournful and pathetic beauty, while its stony sharpness, its cold, fixed, deathly aspect, struck a solemn chill over him. He drew his breath short, and stood in silence. His wife, and their only coloured domestic, old Aunt Dinah, were busily engaged in restorative measures; while old Cudjoe had got the boy on his knee, and was busy pulling off his shoes and stockings, and chafing his little cold feet.

'Sure, now, if she ain't a sight to behold!' said old Dinah, compassionately. ''Pears like 'twas the heat that made her faint. She was tol'able peart when she cum in, and asked if she couldn't warm herself here a spell; and I was just a askin' her where she cum from, and she fainted right down. Never done much hard work, guess, by the looks of her hands.'

'Poor creature!' said Mrs Bird, compassionately, as the woman slowly unclosed her large dark eyes, and looked vacantly at her. Suddenly an expression of agony crossed her face, and she sprang up, saying, 'Oh, my Harry! Have they got him?'

The boy, at this, jumped from Cudjoe's knee, and running to her side, put up his arms. 'Oh, he's here! he's here!' she exclaimed.

'Oh, ma'am!' said she, wildly, to Mrs Bird, 'do protect us! don't let them get him!'

'Nobody shall hurt you here, poor woman,' said Mrs Bird, encouragingly. 'You are safe; don't be afraid.'

'God bless you!' said the woman, covering her face and sobbing; while the little boy, seeing her crying, tried to get into her lap.

With many gentle and womanly offices, which none knew better how to render than Mrs Bird, the poor woman was in time rendered more calm. A temporary bed was provided for her on the settle, near the fire; and, after a short time, she fell into a heavy slumber with the child, who seemed no less weary, soundly sleeping on her arm; for the mother resisted, with nervous anxiety, the kindest attempts to take him from her; and even in sleep her arm encircled him with an unrelaxing clasp, as if she could not even then be beguiled of her vigilant hold.

Mr and Mrs Bird had gone back to the parlour, where, strange as it may appear, no reference was made on either side to the preceding conversation; but Mrs Bird busied herself with her knitting work, and Mr Bird pretended to be reading the paper.

'I wonder who and what she is!' said Mr Bird at last, as he laid it down.

'When she wakes up and feels a little rested, we will see,' said Mr Bird.

'I say, wife!' said Mr Bird, after musing in silence over his newspaper.

'Well, dear?'

'She couldn't wear one of your gowns, could she, by any letting down, or such matter. She seems to be rather larger than you are.'

A quite perceptible smile glimmered on Mrs Bird's face as she answered, 'We'll see.'

Another pause, and Mr Bird again broke out—

'I say, wife!'

'Well! What now?'

'Why, there's that old bombazin cloak that you keep on purpose to put over me when I take my afternoon's nap; you might as well give her that – she needs clothes.'

At this instant Dinah looked in to say that the woman was awake, and wanted to see missis.

Mr and Mrs Bird went into the kitchen, followed by the two eldest boys, the smaller fry having by this time been safely disposed of in bed.

The woman was now sitting up on the settle by the fire. She was looking steadily into the blaze, with a calm, heart-broken expression, very different from her former agitated wildness.

'Did you want me?' said Mrs Bird, in gentle tones. 'I hope you feel better now, poor woman?'

A long-drawn, shivering sigh, was the only answer; but she lifted her dark eyes, and fixed them on her with such a forlorn and imploring expression that the tears came into the little woman's eyes.

'You needn't be afraid of anything; we are friends here, poor woman! Tell me where you came from, and what you want,' said she.

'I came from Kentucky,' said the woman.

'When?' said Mr Bird, taking up the interrogatory.

'To-night.'

'How did you come?'

'I crossed on the ice.'

'Crossed on the ice!' said every one present.

'Yes,' said the woman slowly, 'I did. God helping me, I crossed on the ice; for they were behind me – right behind – and there was no other way!'

'Law, missis,' said Cudjoe, 'the ice is all in broken-up blocks, a swinging and a tettering up and down in the water!'

'I know it was – I know it!' said she, wildly; 'but I did it! I wouldn't have thought I could – I didn't think I should get over, but I didn't care! I could but die, if I didn't. The Lord helped me; nobody knows how much the Lord can help 'em till they try,' said the woman, with a flashing eye.

'Were you a slave?' said Mr Bird.

'Yes, sir; I belonged to a man in Kentucky.'

'Was he unkind to you?'

'No, sir; he was a good master.'

'And was your mistress unkind to you?'

'No, sir – no! my mistress was always good to me.'

'What could induce you to leave a good home, then, and run away, and go through such dangers?'

The woman looked up at Mrs Bird with a keen scrutinising glance, and it did not escape her that she was dressed in deep mourning.

'Ma'am,' she said, suddenly 'have you ever lost a child?'

The question was unexpected, and it was a thrust on a new wound; for it was only a month since a darling child of the family had been laid in the grave.

Mr Bird turned round and walked to the window, and Mrs Bird burst into tears; but recovering her voice, she said—

'Why do you ask that? I have lost a little one.'

'Then you will feel for me. I have lost two, one after another – left 'em buried there when I came away; and I had only this one left. I never slept a night without him; he was all I had. He was my comfort and pride, day and night; and, ma'am, they were going to take him away from me – to *sell* him – sell him down south, ma'am, to go all alone – a baby that had never been away from his mother in his life! I couldn't stand it, ma'am. I knew I never should be good for anything if they did; and when I knew the papers were signed, and he was sold, I took him and came off in the night, and they chased me – the man that bought him, and some of mas'r's folks – and they were coming down right behind me, and I heard 'em. I jumped right on to the ice, and how I got across I don't know; but, first I knew, a man was helping me up the bank.'

The woman did not sob nor weep. She had gone to a place where tears are dry; but every one around her was, in some way characteristic of themselves, showing signs of hearty sympathy.

The two little boys, after a desperate rummaging in their pockets, in search of those pocket-handkerchiefs which mothers know are never to be found there, had thrown themselves disconsolately into the skirts of their mother's gown, where they were sobbing, and wiping their eyes and noses, to their heart's content; Mrs Bird had her face fairly hidden in her pocket-handkerchief; and old Dinah, with tears streaming down her black, honest face, was ejaculating, 'Lord, have mercy on us!' with all the fervour of a camp-meeting; while old Cudjoe, rubbing his eyes very hard with his cuffs, and making a most uncommon variety of wry faces, occasionally responded in the same key, with great fervour. Our senator was a statesman, and of course could not be expected to cry, like other mortals; and so he turned his back to the company, and looked out of the window, and seemed particularly busy in clearing his throat and wiping his spectacle-glasses, occasionally blowing his nose in a manner that was calculated to excite suspicion, had any one been in a state to observe critically.

'How come you to tell me you had a kind master?' he suddenly exclaimed, gulping down very resolutely some kind of rising in his throat, and turning suddenly round upon the woman.

'Because he *was* a kind master – I'll say that of him, anyway; and my mistress was kind; but they couldn't help themselves. They were owing money; and there was some way, I can't tell how, that a man had a hold on them, and they were obliged to give him his will. I listened, and heard him telling mistress that, and she begging and pleading for me, and he told her he couldn't help himself, and that the papers were all drawn; and then it was I took him and left my home, and came away. I knew 'twas no use in my trying to live, if they did it; for 't 'appears like this child is all I have.'

'Have you no husband?'

'Yes, but he belongs to another man. His master is real hard to him, and won't let him come to see me, hardly ever; and he's grown harder and harder upon us, and he threatens to sell him down south. It's like I'll never see *him* again!'

The quiet tone in which the woman pronounced these words might have led a superficial observer to think that she was entirely apathetic; but there was a calm, settled depth of anguish in her large, dark eye, that spoke of something far otherwise.

'And where do you mean to go, my poor woman?' said Mrs Bird.

'To Canada, if I only knew where that was. Is it very far off, is Canada?' said she, looking up, with a simple, confiding air, to Mrs Bird's face.

'Poor thing!' said Mrs Bird involuntarily.

'Is't a very great way off, think?' said the woman, earnestly.

'Much further than you think, poor child!' said Mrs Bird; 'but we will try to think what can be done for you. Here, Dinah, make her up a bed in your own room, close by the kitchen, and I'll think what to do for her in the morning. Meanwhile, never fear, poor woman. Put your trust in God; He will protect you.'

Mrs Bird and her husband re-entered the parlour. She sat down in her little rocking-chair before the fire, swaying thoughtfully to and fro. Mr Bird strode up and down the room, grumbling to himself. 'Pish! pshaw! confounded awkward business!' At length, striding up to his wife, he said—

'I say, wife, she'll have to get away from here this very night. That fellow will be down on the scent bright and early to-morrow morning. If 'twas only the woman, she could lie quiet till it was over; but that little chap can't be kept still by a troop of horse and foot, I'll warrant me; he'll bring it all out, popping his head out of some window or door. A pretty kettle of fish it would be for me, too, to be caught with them both here just now! No; they'll have to be got off to-night.'

'To-night! How is it possible? Where to?'

'Well, I know pretty well where to,' said the senator, beginning to put on his boots, with a reflective air; and, stopping when his leg was half in, he embraced his knee with both hands, and seemed to go off in deep meditation.

'It's a confounded awkward, ugly business,' said he at last, beginning to tug at his boot-straps again, 'and that's a fact!' After one boot was fairly on, the senator sat with the other in his hand, profoundly studying the figure of the carpet. 'It will have to be done, though, for aught I see – hang it all!' And he drew the other boot anxiously on, and looked out of the window.

Now, little Mrs Bird was a discreet woman – a woman who never in her life said, 'I told you so!' and, on the present occasion, though pretty well aware of the shape her husband's meditations were taking, she very prudently forbore to meddle with them, only sat very quietly in her chair, and looked quite ready to hear her liege lord's intentions, when he should think proper to utter them.

'You see,' he said, 'there's my old client, van Trompe, has come over from Kentucky, and set all his slaves free; and he has bought a place seven miles up the creek, there back in the woods, where nobody goes, unless they go on purpose; and it's a place that isn't found in a hurry. There she'd be safe enough; but the plague of the thing is, nobody could drive a carriage there to-night but *me*.'

'Why not? Cudjoe is an excellent driver.'

'Ay, ay, but here it is. The creek has to be crossed twice; and the second crossing is quite dangerous unless one knows it as I do. I have crossed it a hundred times on horseback, and know exactly the turns to take. And so, you see, there's no help for it. Cudjoe must put in the horses, as quietly as may be, about twelve o'clock, and I'll take her over; and then, to give colour to the matter, he must carry me on to the next tavern, to take the stage for Columbus that comes by about three or four, and so it will look as if I had had the carriage only for that. I shall get into business bright and early in the morning. But I'm thinking I shall feel rather cheap there, after all that's been said and done; but, hang it, I can't help it.'

'Your heart is better than your head, in this case, John,' said the wife, laying her little white hand on his. 'Could I ever have loved you, had I not known you better than you know yourself?' And the little woman looked so handsome, with the tears sparkling in her eyes, that the senator thought he must be a decidedly clever fellow to get such a pretty creature into such a passionate admiration of him; and so what could he do but walk off soberly to see about the carriage? At the door, however, he stopped a moment, and then coming back, he said, with some hesitation—

'Mary, I don't know how you'd feel about it, but there's that drawer full of things – of – of – poor little Henry's.' So saying, he turned quickly on his heel, and shut the door after him.

His wife opened the little bedroom door adjoining her room, and, taking the candle, set it down on the top of a bureau there; then from a small recess she took a key, and put it thoughtfully in the lock of a drawer, and made a sudden pause, while two boys, who, boy-like, had followed close on her heels, stood looking, with silent, significant glances, at their mother. And, O mother that reads this, has there never been in your house a drawer, or a closet, the opening of which has been to you like the opening again of a little grave? Ah! happy mother that you are, if it has not been so!

Mrs Bird slowly opened the drawer. There were little coats of many a form and pattern, piles of aprons, and rows of small stockings; and even a pair of little shoes, worn and rubbed at the toes, were peeping from the folds of a paper. There was a toy horse and wagon, a top, a ball – memorials gathered with many a tear and many a heart-break! She sat down by the drawer, and leaning her head on her hands over it, wept till the tears fell through her fingers into the drawer; then, suddenly raising her head, she began, with nervous haste, selecting the plainest and most substantial articles, and gathering them into a bundle.

'Mama,' said one of the boys, gently touching her arm, 'are you going to give away *those* things?'

'My dear boys,' she said, softly and earnestly, 'if our dear, loving little Henry looks down from heaven, he would be glad to have us do this. I could not find it in my heart to give them away to any common person – to anybody that was happy; but I give them to a mother more heart-broken and sorrowful than I am; and I hope God will send His blessing with them!'

There are in this world blessed souls, whose sorrows all spring up into joys for others; whose earthly hopes, laid in the grave with many tears, are the seed from which spring healing flowers and balm for the desolate and the distressed. Among such was the delicate woman who sits there by the lamp, dropping slow tears, while she prepares the memorials of her own lost one for the outcast wanderer.

After a while, Mrs Bird opened a wardrobe, and taking from thence a plain, serviceable dress or two, she sat down busily to her work-table, and, with needle, scissors, and thimble at hand, quietly commenced the 'letting down' process which her husband had recommended, and continued busily at it till the old clock in the corner struck twelve, and she heard the low rattling of wheels at the door.

'Mary,' said her husband, coming in, with his overcoat in his hand, 'you must wake her up now: we must be off.'

Mrs Bird hastily deposited the various articles she had collected in a small plain trunk, and locking it, desired her husband to see it in the carriage, and then proceeded to call the woman. Soon arrayed in a cloak, bonnet, and shawl, that had belonged to her benefactress, she appeared at the door with her child in her arms. Mr Bird hurried her into the carriage, and Mrs Bird pressed on after her to the carriage steps. Eliza leaned out of the carriage, and put out her hand, a hand as soft and beautiful as was given in return. She fixed her large dark eyes, full of earnest meaning, on Mrs Bird's face, and seemed going to speak. Her lips moved, she tried once or twice, but there was no sound, and pointing upward, with a look never to be forgotten, she fell back in the seat and covered her face. The door was shut, and the carriage drove on.

What a situation now, for a patriotic senator, that had been all the week before spurring up the legislature of his native state to pass more stringent resolutions against escaping fugitives, their harbourers and abettors!

Our good senator in his native state had not been exceeded by any of his brethren at Washington, in the sort of eloquence which has won for them immortal renown! How sublimely he had sat with his hands in his pockets, and scouted all sentimental weakness of those who would put the welfare of a few miserable fugitives before great state interests!

He was a bold as a lion about it, and 'mightily convinced' not only himself, but everybody that heard him; but then his idea of a fugitive was only an idea of the letters that spell the word; or, at the most, the image of a little newspaper picture of a man with a stick and bundle, with 'Ran away from the subscriber' under it. The magic of the real presence of distress, the imploring human eye, the frail, trembling human hand, the despairing appeal of helpless agony, these he had never tried. He had never thought that a fugitive might be a hapless mother, a defenceless child, like that one which was now wearing his lost boy's little well-known cap; and so, as our poor senator was not stone or steel, as he was a man, and a downright noble-hearted one, too, he was, as everybody must see, in a sad case for his patriotism. And you need not exult over him, good brother of the Southern States, for we have some inklings that many of you, under similar circumstances, would not do much better. We have reason to know, in Kentucky, as in Mississippi, are noble and generous hearts, to whom never was tale of suffering told in vain. Ah, good brother! is it fair for you to expect of us services which your own brave, honourable heart, would not allow you to render, were you in our place?

Be that as it may, if our good senator was a political sinner, he was in a fair way to expiate it by his night's penance. There had been a long continuous period of rainy weather, and the soft rich earth of Ohio, as every one knows, is admirably suited to the manufacture of mud, and the road was an Ohio railroad of the good old times.

'And pray what sort of a road may that be?' says some eastern traveller, who has been accustomed to connect no ideas with a railroad but those of smoothness or speed.

Know, then, innocent eastern friend, that in benighted regions of the west, where the mud is of unfathomable and sublime depth, roads are made of round rough logs, arranged transversely side by side, and coated over in their pristine freshness with earth, turf, and whatsoever may come to hand, and then the rejoicing native calleth it a road, and straightway essayeth to ride thereupon. In process of time, the rains wash off all the turf and grass aforesaid, move the logs hither and thither, in picturesque positions, up, down, and crosswise, with divers chasms and ruts of black mud intervening.

Over such a road as this our senator went stumbling along, making moral reflections as continuously as under the circumstances could be expected, the carriage proceeding along much as follows: bump! bump! bump! slush! down in the mud! — the senator, woman, and child, reversing their positions so suddenly as to come, without any very accurate adjustment, against the windows of the down-hill side. Carriage sticks fast, while Cudjoe on the outside is heard making a great muster among the horses. After various ineffectual pullings and twitchings, just as the senator is losing all patience, the carriage suddenly rights itself with a bounce, two front wheels go down into another abyss, and senator, woman, and child, all tumble promiscuously on to the front seat; senator's hat is jammed over his eyes and nose quite unceremoniously, and he considers himself fairly extinguished; child cries, and Cudjoe on the outside delivers animated addresses to the horses, who are kicking, and floundering, and straining under repeated cracks of the whip. Carriage springs up with another bounce — down go the hind wheels — senator, woman, and child, fly over on to the back seat, his elbows encountering her bonnet, and both her feet being jammed into his hat, which flies off in the concussion. After a few moments, the 'slough' is passed, and the horses stop, panting; the senator finds his hat, the woman straightens her bonnet and hushes her child, and they brace themselves firmly for what is yet to come.

For a while only the continuous bump! bump! intermingled, just by way of variety, with divers side-plunges and compound shakes; and they begin to flatter themselves that they are not so badly off after all. At last, with a square plunge, which puts all on to their feet and then down into their seats with incredible quickness, the carriage stops, and, after much outside commotion, Cudjoe appears at the door.

'Please, sir, it's powerful bad spot this yer. I don't know how we's to get clar out. I'm a thinkin' we'll have to be a gettin' rails.'

The senator despairingly steps out, picking gingerly for some firm foothold. Down goes one foot an immeasurable depth, he tries to pull it up, loses his balance, and tumbles over into the mud, and is fished out in a very despairing condition by Cudjoe.

But we forbear, out of sympathy to our reader's bones. Western travellers, who have beguiled the midnight hour in the interesting process of pulling down rail fences to pry their carriages out of mud holes, will have a respectful and mournful sympathy with our unfortunate hero. We beg them to drop a silent tear and pass on.

It was full late in the night when the carriage emerged, dripping and bespattered, out of the creek, and stood at the door of a large farmhouse. It took no inconsiderable perseverance to arouse the inmates; but at last the respectable proprietor appeared, and undid the door. He was a great, tall, bristling Orson of a fellow, full six feet and some inches in his stockings, and arrayed in a red flannel hunting-shirt. A very heavy *mat* of sandy hair, in a decidedly tousled condition, and a beard of some days' growth, gave the worthy man an appearance, to say the least, not particularly prepossessing. He stood for a few minutes holding the candle aloft, and blinking on our travellers with a dismal and mystified expression that was truly ludicrous. It cost some effort of our senator to induce him to comprehend the case fully; and while he is doing his best at that, we shall give him a little introduction to our readers.

Honest old John van Trompe was once quite a considerable landholder and slave-owner in the State of Kentucky. Having 'nothing of the bear about him but the skin,' and being gifted by nature with a great, honest, just heart, quite equal to his gigantic frame, he had been for some years witnessing with repressed uneasiness the workings of a system equally bad for oppressor and oppressed. At last, one day John's great heart had swelled altogether too big to wear his bonds any longer; so he just took his pocket-book out of his desk, and went over into Ohio, and bought a quarter of a township of good, rich land, made out free papers for all his people, men, women, and children, packed them up in waggons, and sent them off to settle down; and then honest John turned his face up the creek, and sat quietly down on a snug, retired farm, to enjoy his conscience and his reflections.

'Are you the man that will shelter a poor woman and child from slave-catchers?' said the senator, explicitly.

'I rather think I am,' said honest John, with some considerable emphasis.

'I thought so,' said the senator.

'If there's anybody comes,' said the good man, stretching his tall, muscular form upward, 'why, here I'm ready for him; and I've got seven sons, each six foot high, and they'll be ready for 'em. Give our respects to 'em,' said John; 'tell 'em it's no matter how soon they call, make no kinder difference to us,' said John, running his fingers through the shock of hair that thatched his head, and bursting out into a great laugh.

Weary, jaded, and spiritless, Eliza dragged herself up to the door, with her child lying, in a heavy sleep, on her arm. The rough man held the candle to her face, and, uttering a kind of compassionate grunt, opened the door of a small bedroom adjoining to the large kitchen where they were standing, and motioned her to go in. He took down a candle, and lighting it, set it upon the table, and then addressed himself to Eliza.

'Now, I say, gal, you needn't be a bit afeard, let who will come here. I'm up to all that sort o' thing,' said he, pointing to two or three goodly rifles over the mantelpiece: 'and most people that know me know that 'twouldn't be healthy to try to get anybody out o' my house when I'm agin it. So *now* you jist go to sleep now, as quiet as if yer mother was a rockin' ye,' said he, as he shut the door.

'Why, this is an uncommon handsome un,' he said to the senator. 'Ah, well; handsome uns has the greatest cause to run sometimes, if they has any kind o' feeling, such as decent women should. I know all about that.'

The senator, in a few words, briefly explained Eliza's history.

'O! ou! aw! now, I want to know!' said the good man, pitifully; 'sho! now, sho! That's natur' now, poor crittur! hunted down, now, like a deer — hunted down jest for havin' natural feelin's, and doin' what no kind o' mother could help a doin'! I tell ye what, these yer things make me come the nighest to swearin', now, o' most anything,' said honest John, as he wiped his eyes with the back of a great, freckled, yellow hand.

'I tell ye what, stranger, it was years and years before I'd jine the church, 'cause the ministers round in our parts used to preach that the Bible went in for these ere cuttings up; and I couldn't be up to 'em with their Greek and Hebrew, and so I took up agin 'em Bible and all. I never jined the church till I found a minister that was up to 'em all in Greek and all that, and he said right the contrary; and then I took right hold, and jined the church – I did now, fact,' said John, who had been all this time uncorking some very frisky bottled cider, which at this juncture he presented.

'Ye'd better jest put up here, now, till daylight,' said he, heartily, 'and I'll call up the old woman, and have a bed got ready for you in no time.'

'Thank you, my good friend,' said the senator, 'I must be along, to take the night stage for Columbus.'

'Ah, well, then, if you must, I'll go a piece with you, and show you a cross road that will take you there better than the road you came on. That road's mighty bad.'

John equipped himself, and, with a lantern in hand, was soon seen guiding the senator's carriage towards a road that ran down in a hollow, back of his dwelling. When they parted, the senator put into his hand a ten-dollar bill.

'It's for her,' he said briefly.

Ay, ay,' said John, with equal conciseness. They shook hands and parted.

Chapter 10

THE PROPERTY IS CARRIED OFF

THE February morning looked grey and drizzling through the window of Uncle Tom's cabin. It looked on downcast faces, the images of mournful hearts. The little table stood out before the fire, covered with an ironing-cloth; a coarse but clean shirt or two, fresh from the iron, hung on the back of a chair by the fire, and Aunt Chloe had another spread out before her on the table. Carefully she rubbed and ironed every fold and every hem, with the most scrupulous exactness, every now and then raising her hand to her face to wipe off the tears that were coursing down her cheeks.

Tom sat by, with his Testament open on his knee, and his head leaning upon his hand; but neither spoke. It was yet early, and the children lay all asleep together in their little rude trundle-bed.

Tom, who had to the full the gentle domestic heart, which, woe for them! has been a peculiar characteristic of his unhappy race, got up and walked silently to look at his children.

'It's the last time,' he said.

Aunt Chloe did not answer, only rubbed away over and over on the coarse shirt, already as smooth as hands could make it; and finally setting her iron suddenly down with a despairing plunge, she sat down to the table, and 'lifted up her voice and wept'.

'S'pose we must be resigned; but, O Lord! how ken I? If I know'd anything whar you's goin', or how they'd sarve you! Missis says she'll try and 'deem ye, in a year or two; but, Lor! nobody never comes up that goes down thar! They kills 'em! I've hearn 'em tell how dey works 'em up on dem ar plantations.'

'There'll be the same God there, Chloe, that there is here.'

'Well,' said Aunt Chloe, 's'pose dere will; but de Lord lets dreful things happen, sometimes. I don't seem to get no comfort dat way.'

'I'm in the Lord's hands,' said Tom; 'nothin' can go no furder than He lets it; and thar's *one* thing I can thank Him for. It's *me* that's sold and going down, and not you nur the chil'en. Here you're safe; what comes will come only on me; and the Lord, He'll help me – I know He will.'

Ah, brave, manly heart, smothering thine own sorrow to comfort thy beloved ones! Tom spoke with a thick utterance, and with a bitter choking in his throat – but he spoke brave and strong.

'Let's think on our marcies!' he added tremulously, as if he was quite sure he needed to think on them very hard indeed.

'Marcies!' said Aunt Chloe, 'don't see no marcy in't! tan't right! tan't right it should be so! Mas'r never ought ter left it so that ye *could* be took for his debts. Ye've arn't him all he gets for ye, twice over. He owed ye yer freedom, and ought ter gin't to yer years ago. Mebbe he can't help himself now, but I feel it's wrong. Nothing can't beat that ar out o' me. Sich a faithful crittur as ye've been, and allers sot his business 'fore yer own every way, and reckoned on him more than yer own wife and chil'en! Them as sells heart's love and heart's blood, to get out thar scrapes, de Lord'll be up to 'em!'

'Chloe! now, if ye love me, ye won't talk so, when perhaps jest the last time we'll ever have together! And I'll tell ye, Chloe, it goes agin me to hear one word agin mas'r. Wan't he put in my arms a baby? — it's nature I should think a heap of him. And he couldn't be 'spected to think so much of poor Tom. Mas'rs is used to having all these yer things done for 'em, and nat'lly they don't think so much on't. They can't be 'spected to, no way. Set him 'longside of other mas'rs — who's had the treatment and the livin' I have had? And he never would have let this yer come on me if he could have seed if aforehand. I know he wouldn't.'

'Wal, anyway, thar's wrong about it *somewhar*,' said Aunt Chloe, in whom a stubborn sense of justice was a predominant trait; 'I can't jest make out whar 'tis, but thar's wrong some-whar, I'm *clar* o' that.'

'Yer ought ter look up to the Lord above; He's above all — thar don't a sparrow fall without Him.'

'It don't seem to comfort me, but I 'spect it orter,' said Aunt Cloe. 'But dar's no use talking': I'll jest wet up de corn-cake, and get ye one good breakfast, 'cause nobody knows when you'll get another.'

In order to appreciate the sufferings of the negroes sold south, it must be remembered that all the instinctive affections of that race are peculiarly strong. Their local attachments are very abiding. They are not naturally daring and enterprising, but home-loving and affectionate. Add to this all the terrors with which ignorance invests the unknown, and add to this, again, that selling to the south is set before the negro from childhood as the last severity of punishment. The threat that terrifies more than whipping or torture of any kind is the threat of being sent down river. We have ourselves heard this feeling expressed by them, and seen the unaffected horror with which they will sit in their gossiping hours, and tell frightful stories of that 'down river,' which to them is

> 'That undiscovered country, from whose bourne
> No traveller returns.'

A missionary among the fugitives in Canada told us that many of the fugitives confessed themselves to have escaped from comparatively kind masters, and that they were induced to brave the perils of escape, in almost every case, by the desperate horror with which they regarded being sold south – a doom which was hanging either over themselves or their husbands, their wives, or children. This nerves the African, naturally patient, timid, and unenterprising, with heroic courage, and leads him to suffer hunger, cold, pain, the perils of the wilderness, and the more dread penalties of re-capture.

The simple morning meal now smoked on the table, for Mrs Shelby had excused Aunt Chloe's attendance at the great house that morning. The poor soul had expended all her little energies on this farewell feast – had killed and dressed her choicest chicken, and prepared her corn-cake with scrupulous exactness, just to her husband's taste, and brought out certain mysterious jars on the mantelpiece, some preserves that were never produced except on extreme occasions.

'Lor, Pete,' said Mose, triumphantly, 'ha'n't we got a buster of a breakfast!' at the same time catching at a fragment of the chicken.

Aunt Chloe gave him a sudden box on the ear. 'Thar now! crowing over the last breakfast yer poor daddy's gwine to have to home!'

'O Chloe!' said Tom, gently.

'Wal, I can't help it,' said Aunt Chloe, hiding her face in her apron. 'I's so tossed about, it makes me act ugly.'

The boys stood quite still, looking first at their father and then at their mother, while the baby, climbing up her clothes, began an imperious, commanding cry.

'Thar!' said Aunt Chloe, wiping her eyes and taking up the baby; 'now I's done, I hope – now do eat something. This yer's my nicest chicken. Thar, boys, ye shall have some, poor critturs! Yer mammy's been cross to yer.'

The boys needed no second invitation, and went in with great zeal for the eatables; and it was well they did so, as otherwise there would have been very little performed to any purpose by the party.

'Now,' said Aunt Chloe, bustling about after breakfast, 'I must put up yer clothes. Jest like as not he'll take 'em all away. I know thar ways – mean as dirt, they is! Wal, now, yer flannels for rheumatis is in this corner; so be careful, 'cause there won't nobody make ye no more. Then here's yer old shirts, and these yer is new ones. I toed off these yer stockings last night, and put de ball in 'em to mend with. But Lor! who'll ever mend for ye?' and Aunt Chloe, again over-come, laid her head on the box side, and sobbed. 'To think on't! no crittur to do for ye, sick or well! I don't railly think I ought ter be good now!'

The boys having eaten everything there was on the breakfast-table, began now to take some thought of the case; and seeing their mother crying, and their father looking very sad, began to whimper and put their hands to their eyes. Uncle Tom had the baby on his knee, and was letting her enjoy herself to the utmost extent, scratching his face and pulling his hair, and occasionally breaking out into clamorous explosions of delight, evidently arising out of her own internal reflections.

'Ay, crow away, poor crittur!' said Aunt Chloe; 'ye'll have to come to it, too! Ye'll live to see yer husband sold, or mebbe be sold yerself; and these yer boys, they's to be sold, I s'pose, too, jest like as not, when dey gets good for somethin'; an't no use in niggers havin' nothin'!'

Here one of the boys called out, 'Thar's missis a-comin' in!'

'She can't do no good; what's she coming for?' said Aunt Chloe.

Mrs Shelby entered. Aunt Chloe set a chair for her in a manner decidedly gruff and crusty. She did not seem to notice either the action or the manner. She looked pale and anxious.

'Tom,' she said, 'I come to'—and stopping suddenly, and regarding the silent group, she sat down in the chair, and, covering her face with her handkerchief, began to sob.

'Lor, now, missis, don't – don't!' said Aunt Chloe, bursting out in her turn; and for a few moments they all wept in company. And in those tears they all shed together, the high and the lowly, melted away all the heart-burnings and anger of the oppressed. Oh, ye who visit the distressed, do ye know that everything your money can buy, given with a cold averted face, is not worth one honest tear shed in real sympathy?

'My good fellow,' said Mrs Shelby, 'I can't give you anything to do you any good. If I give you money it will only be taken from you. But I tell you solemnly, and before God, that I will keep trace of you, and bring you back as soon as I can command the money; and, till then, trust in God!'

Here the boys called out that Mas'r Haley was coming, and then an unceremonious kick pushed open the door. Haley stood there in very ill humour, having ridden hard the night before, and being not at all pacified by his ill-success in recapturing his prey.

'Come,' said he, 'ye nigger, ye'r ready? Servant, ma'am,' said he, taking off his hat, as he saw Mrs Shelby.

Aunt Chloe shut and corded the box, and getting up, looked gruffly on the trader, her tears seeming suddenly turned to sparks of fire.

Tom rose up meekly to follow his new master, and raised up his heavy box on his shoulder. His wife took the baby in her arms to go with him to the wagon, and the children, still crying, trailed on behind.

Mrs Shelby, walking up to the trader, detained him for a few moments, talking with him in an earnest manner; and while she was thus talking, the whole family party proceeded to a wagon that stood ready harnessed at the door. A crowd of all the old and young hands on the place stood gathered around it, to bid farewell to their old associate. Tom had been looked up to, both as a head servant and a Christian teacher, by all the place, and there was much honest sympathy and grief about him, particularly among the women.

'Why, Chloe, you bar it better 'n we do!' said one of the women, who had been weeping freely, noticing the gloomy calmness with which Aunt Chloe stood by the wagon.

'I'se done *my* tears!' said she, looking grimly at the trader, who was coming up. 'I does not feel to cry 'fore dat ar old limb, nohow!'

'Get in!' said Haley to Tom, as he strode through the crowd of servants, who looked at him with lowering brows.

Tom got in, and Haley drawing out from under the wagon-seat a heavy pair of shackles, made them fast round each ankle.

A smothered groan of indignation ran through the whole circle, and Mrs Shelby spoke from the verandah, —

'Mr Haley, I assure you that precaution is entirely unnecessary.'

'Don't know, ma'am; I've lost one five hundred dollars from this yer place, and I can't afford to run no more risks.'

'What else could she 'spect on him?' said Aunt Chloe, indignantly; while the two boys, who now seemed to comprehend at once their father's destiny, clung to her gown, sobbing and groaning vehemently.

'I'm sorry,' said Tom, 'that Mas'r George happened to be away.'

George had gone to spend two or three days with a companion on a neighbouring estate, and having departed early in the morning, before Tom's misfortune had been made public, had left without hearing of it.

'Give my love to Mas'r George,' he said earnestly.

Haley whipped up the horse, and with a steady, mournful look, fixed to the last on the old place, Tom was whirled away.

Mr Shelby at this time was not at home. He had sold Tom under the spur of a driving necessity, to get out of the power of a man whom he dreaded, and his first feeling, after the consummation of the bargain, had been that of relief. But his wife's expostulations awoke his half-slumbering regrets; and Tom's manly disinterestedness increased the unpleasantness of his feelings. It was in vain that he said to himself that he had a *right* to do it, that everybody did it, and that some did it without even the excuse of necessity; he could not satisfy his own feelings; and that he might not witness the unpleasant scenes of the consummation, he had gone on a short business tour up the country, hoping that all would be over before he returned.

Tom and Haley rattled on along the dusty road, whirling past every old familiar spot, until the bounds of the estate were fairly passed, and they found themselves out on the open pike. After they had ridden about a mile, Haley suddenly drew up at the door of a blacksmith's shop, when, taking out with him a pair of handcuffs, he stepped into the shop to have a little alteration in them.

'These yer's a little too small for his build,' said Haley, showing the fetters, and pointing out to Tom.

'Lor! now, if thar an't Shelby's Tom. He an't sold him, now?' said the smith.

'Yes he has,' said Haley.

'Now, ye don't! Well, reely,' said the smith, 'who'd a thought it! Why, ye needn't go to fetterin' him up this yer way. He's the faithfullest, best crittur'—

'Yes, yes,' said Haley; 'but your good fellows are just the critturs to want ter run off. Them stupid ones, as doesn't care whar they go, and shiftless, drunken ones, as don't care for nothin', they'll stick by, and like as not be rather pleased to be toted round; but these yer prime fellows they hates it like sin. No way but to fetter 'em; got legs – they'll use 'em, no mistake.'

'Well,' said the smith, feeling among his tools, 'them plantations down thar, stranger, an't jest the place a Kentuck nigger wants to go to; they dies thar tol'able fast, don't they?'

'Wal, yes, tol'able fast, ther dying is; what with the 'climating and one thing and another, they dies so as to keep the market up pretty brisk,' said Haley.

'Wal, now, a feller can't help thinkin' it's a mighty pity to have a nice, quiet, likely fellow, as good un as Tom is, go down to be fairly ground up on one of them ar sugar plantations.'

'Wal, he's got a far chance. I promised to do well by him. I'll get him in house-servant in some good old family, and then if he stands the fever and 'climating, he'll have a berth good as any nigger ought ter ask for.'

'He leaves his wife and chil'en up her, s'pose?'

'Yes! but he'll get another thar. Lord, thar's women enough everywhar,' said Haley.

Tom was sitting very mournfully on the outside of the shop while this conversation was going on. Suddenly he heard the quick, short click of a horse's hoof behind him; and before he could fairly awake from his surprise, young Master George sprang into the wagon, threw his arms tumultuously round his neck, and was sobbing and scolding with energy.

'I declare, it's real mean! I don't care what they say, any of 'em! It's a nasty, mean shame! If I was a man they shouldn't do it – they should not, *so*!' said George, with a kind of subdued howl.

'O Mas'r George! this does me good!' said Tom. 'I couldn't bar to go off without seein' ye! It does me real good, ye can't tell!' Here Tom made some movement of his feet, and George's eye fell on the fetters.

'What a shame!' he exclaimed, lifting his hands. 'I'll knock that old fellow down – I will!'

'No, you won't, Mas'r George; and you must not talk so loud. It won't help me any to anger him.'

'Well, I won't, then, for your sake; but only to think of it – isn't it a shame? They never sent for me, nor sent me any word, and if it hadn't been for Tom Lincoln, I shouldn't have heard it. I tell you, I blew 'em up well, all of 'em, at home!'

'That ar wasn't right, I'm feard, Mas'r George.'

'Can't help it! I say it's a shame! Look here, Uncle Tom,' said he, turning his back to the shop, and speaking in a mysterious tone, '*I've brought you my dollar!*'

'Oh! I couldn't think o' takin' on't, Mas'r George, no ways in the world!' said Tom, quite moved.

'But you *shall* take it!' said George. 'Look here; I told Aunt Chloe I'd do it, and she advised me just to make a hold in it, and put a string through, so you could hang it round your neck, and keep it out of sight; else this mean scamp would take it away. I tell ye, Tom, I want to blow him up! it would do me good!'

'No, don't Mas'r George, for it won't do *me* any good.'

'Well, I won't, for your sake,' said George, busily tying his dollar round Tom's neck; 'but there, now, button your coat tight over it, and keep it, and remember, every time you see it, that I'll come down after you, and bring you back. Aunt Chloe and I have been talking about it. I told her not to fear; I'll see to it, and I'll tease father's life out, if he don't do it.'

'O Mas'r George, ye mustn't talk so 'bout yer father!'

'Lor, Uncle Tom, I don't mean anything bad.'

'And now, Mas'r George,' said Tom, 'ye must be a good boy; 'member how many hearts is sot on ye. Al'ays keep close to yer mother. Don't be getting into any of them foolish ways boys has, of getting too big to mind their mothers. Tell ye what, Mas'r George, the Lord gives good many things twice over; but he don't give ye a mother but once. You'll never see such another woman, Mas'r George, if ye live to be a hundred years old. So now, you hold on to her, and grow up, and be a comfort to her, thar's my own good boy – you will now, won't ye?'

'Yes, I will, Uncle Tom,' said George seriously.

'And be careful of yer speaking, Mas'r George. Young boys, when they comes to your age, is wilful, sometimes – it's natur they should be. But real gentlemen, such as I hopes you'll be, never lets fall no words that isn't 'spectful to thar parents. Ye an't 'fended, Mas'r George?'

'No, indeed, Uncle Tom; you always did give me good advice.'

'I's older, ye know,' said Tom, stroking the boy's fine curly head with his large, strong hand, but speaking in a voice as tender as a woman's, 'and I sees all that's bound up in you. O Mas'r George, you has everything – larnin', privileges, readin', writin' – and you'll grow up to be a great, learned, good man, and all the people on the place and your mother and father 'll be so proud on ye! Be a good mas'r like yer father; and be a Christian, like yer mother. 'Member yer Creator in the days o' yer youth, Mas'r George.'

'I'll be *real* good, Uncle Tom, I tell you,' said George. 'I'm going to be a *first-rater*; and don't you be discouraged. I'll have you back to the place yet. As I told Aunt Chloe this morning, I'll build your house all over, and you shall have a room for a parlour with a carpet on it, when I'm a man. Oh, you'll have good times yet!'

Haley now came to the door, with the handcuffs in his hands.

'Look here now, Mister,' said George, with an air of great superiority, as he got out, 'I shall let father and mother know how you treat Uncle Tom!'

'You're welcome,' said the trader.

'I should think you'd be ashamed to spend all your life buying men and women, and chaining them, like cattle! I should think you'd feel mean!' said George.

'So long as your grand folks wants to buy men and women, I'm as good as they is,' said Haley; ''tan't any meaner sellin' on 'em, than 'tis buyin'!'

'I'll never do either when I'm a man,' said George. 'I'm ashamed this day that I'm a Kentuckian. I always was proud of it before;' and George sat very straight on his horse, and looked round with an air as if he expected the state would be impressed with his opinion.

'Well, good-bye, Uncle Tom; keep a stiff upper lip,' said George.

'Good-bye, Mas'r Geoge,' said Tom, looking fondly and admiringly at him. 'God Almighty bless you! Ah! Kentucky han't got many like you!' he said, in the fulness of his heart, as the frank, boyish face was lost to his view. Away he went, and Tom looked, till the clatter of his horse's heels died away, the last sound or sight of his home. But over his heart there seemed to be a warm spot, where those young hands had placed that precious dollar. Tom put up his hand, and held it close to his heart.

'Now, I tell ye what, Tom,' said Haley, as he came up to the wagon, and threw in the handcuffs, 'I mean to start far with ye, as I gen'ally do with my niggers; and I'll tell ye now, to begin with, you treat me far, and I'll treat you far; I an't never hard on my niggers. Calculates to do the best for 'em I can. Now, ye see, you'd better jest settle down comfortable, and not be tryin' no tricks; because niggers' tricks of all sorts I'm up to, and it's no use. If niggers is quiet, and don't try to get off, they has good times with me; and if they don't, why, it's thar fault, and not mine.'

Tom assured Haley that he had no present intentions of running off. In fact the exhortation seemed rather a superfluous one to a man with a great pair of iron fetters on his feet. But Mr Haley had got in the habit of commencing his relations with his stock with little exhortations, of this nature, calculated, as he deemed, to inspire cheerfulness and confidence, and prevent the necessity of any unpleasant scenes.

And here, for the present, we take our leave of Tom, to pursue the fortunes of other characters in our story.

Chapter 11

IN WHICH PROPERTY GETS INTO AN IMPROPER STATE OF MIND

IT was late in a drizzly afternoon that a traveller alighted at the door of a small country hotel, in the village of N—, in Kentucky. In the bar-room he found assembled quite a miscellaneous company, whom stress of weather had driven to harbour, and the place presented the usual scenery of such reunions. Great, tall, raw-boned Kentuckians, attired in hunting-shirts, and trailing their loose joints over a vast extent of territory, with the easy lounge peculiar to the race – rifles stacked away in the corner, shot-pouches, game-bags, hunting-dogs, and little negroes, all rolled together in the corners – were the characteristic features in the picture. At each end of the fire-place sat a long-legged gentleman, with his chair tipped back, his hat on his head, and the heels of his muddy boots reposing sublimely on the mantelpiece – a position, we will inform our readers, decidedly favourable to the turn of reflection incident to Western taverns, where travellers exhibit a decided preference for this particular mode of elevating their under-standings.

Mine host, who stood behind the bar, like most of his countrymen was great of stature, good-natured, and loose-jointed, with an enormous shock of hair on his head, and a great tall hat on the top of that.

In fact, everybody in the room bore on his head this characteristic emblem of man's sovereignty; whether it were felt hat, palm-leaf, greasy beaver, or fine new chapeau, there it reposed with true republican independence. In truth, it appeared to be the characteristic mark of every individual. Some wore them tipped rakishly on one side – these were your men of humour, jolly free-and-easy dogs; some had them jammed independently down over their noses – these were your hard characters, thorough men, who, when they wore their hats, *wanted* to wear them, and to wear them just as they had a mind to; there were those who had them set far over back – wide-awake men, who wanted a clear prospect; while careless men, who did not know or care how their hats sat, had them shaking about in all directions. The various hats, in fact, were quite a Shakesperian study.

Divers negroes, in very free-and-easy pantaloons, and with no redundancy in the shirt line, were scuttling about, hither and thither, without bringing to pass any very particular results, except expressing a generic willingness to turn over everything in creation generally for the benefit of mas'r and his guests. Add to this picture a jolly, crackling, rollicking fire, going rejoicingly up a great wide chimney – the outer door and every window being set wide open, and the calico window curtain flopping and snapping in a good stiff breeze of damp raw air – and you have an idea of the jollities of a Kentucky tavern.

Your Kentuckian of the present day is a good illustration of the doctrine of transmitted instincts and peculiarities. His fathers were mighty hunters – men who lived in the woods, and slept under the free, open heavens, with the stars to hold their candles; and their descendant to this day always acts as if the house were his camp – wears his hat at all hours, tumbles himself about, and puts his heels on the tops of chairs or mantel-pieces, just as his father rolled on the greensward, and put his upon trees and logs – keeps all the windows and doors open, winter and summer, that he may get air enough for his great lungs – calls everybody 'stranger' with *nonchalant bonhomie*, and is altogether the frankest, easiest, most jovial creature living.

Into such an assembly of the free-and-easy our traveller entered. He was a short, thick-set man, carefully dressed, with a round, good-natured countenance, and something rather fussy and particular in his appearance. He was very careful of his valise and umbrella, bringing them in with his own hands, and resisting, pertinaciously, all offers from the various servants to relieve him of them. He looked round the bar-room with rather an anxious air, and retreating with his valuables to the warmest corner, disposed them under his chair, sat down, and looked rather apprehensively up at the worthy whose heels illustrated the end of the mantelpiece, who was spitting from right to left with a courage and energy rather alarming to gentlemen of weak nerves and particular habits.

'I say, stranger, how are ye?' said the aforesaid gentleman, firing an honorary salute of tobacco-juice in the direction of the new arrival.

'Well, I reckon,' was the reply of the other, as he dodged, with some alarm, the threatening honour.

'Any news?' said the respondent, taking out a strip of tobacco and a large hunting-knife from his pocket.

'Not that I know of,' said the man.

'Chaw?' said the first speaker, handing the old gentleman a bit of his tobacco, with a decidedly brotherly air.

'No, thank ye; it don't agree with me;' said the little man, edging off.

'Don't, eh?' said the other, easily, and stowing away the morsel in his own mouth, in order to keep up the supply of tobacco-juice, for the general benefit of society.

The old gentleman uniformly gave a little start whenever his long-sided brother fired in his direction: and this being observed by his companion, he very good-naturedly turned his artillery to another quarter, and proceeded to storm one of the fire-irons with a degree of military talent fully sufficient to take a city.

'What's that?' said the old gentleman, observing some of the company formed in a group around a large handbill.

'Nigger advertised!' said one of the company, briefly.

Mr Wilson — for that was the old gentleman's name, — rose up, and after carefully adjusting his valise and umbrella, proceeded deliberately to take out his spectacles and fix them on his nose; and, this operation being performed, read as follows:

'Ran away from the subscriber, my mulatto boy, George. Said George six feet in height, a very light mulatto, brown curly hair; is very intelligent, speaks handsomely, can read and write; will probably try to pass for a white man; is deeply scarred on his back and shoulders; has been branded in his right hand with the letter H.

'I will give four hundred dollars for him alive, and the same sum for satisfactory proof that he has been killed.'

The old gentleman read this advertisement from end to end, in a low voice, as if he were studying it.

The long-legged veteran, who had been besieging the fire-irons, as before related, now took down his cumbrous length, and rearing aloft his tall form, walked up to the advertisement, and very deliberately spat a full discharge of tobacco-juice on it.

'There's my mind upon that!' said he, briefly, and sat down again.

'Why, now, stranger, what's that for?' said mine host.

'I'd do it all the same to the writer of that ar paper, if he was here,' said the long man, coolly resuming his old employment of cutting tobacco. 'Any man that owns a boy like that, and can't find any better way o' treating on him *deserves* to lose him. Such papers as these is a shame to Kentucky; that's my mind right out, if anybody wants to know.'

'Well, now, that's a fact,' said mine host, as he made an entry in his book.

'I've got a gang of boys, sir,' said the long man, resuming his attack on the fire-irons, 'and I jest tells 'em – "Boys," says I, – '*run* now! dig! put! jest when ye want too! I never shall come to look after you!' That's the way I keep mine. Let 'em know they are free to run any time, and it jest breaks up their wanting to. More 'n all, I've got free papers for 'em all recorded, in case I gets keeled up any o' these times, and they knows it: I tell ye, stranger, there an't a fellow in our parts gets more out of his niggers than I do. Why, my boys have been to Cincinnati, with five hundred dollars' worth of colts, and brought me back the money, all straight, time and agin. It stands to reason they should. Treat 'em like dogs, and you'll have dogs' works and dogs' actions. Treat 'em like men, and you'll have men's works.' And the honest drover, in his warmth, endorsed this moral sentiment by firing a perfect *feu de joie* at the fire-place.

'I think you're altogether right, friend,' said Mr Wilson; 'and this boy described here *is* a fine fellow – no mistake about that. He worked for me some half-dozen years in my bagging factory, and he was my best hand, sir. He is an ingenious fellow, too; he invented a machine for the cleaning of hemp – a really valuable affair; it's gone into use in several factories. His master holds the patent of it.'

'I'll warrant ye,' said the drover, 'holds it, and makes money out of it, and then turns round and brands the boy in his right hand. If I had a fair chance, I'd mark him, I reckon, so that he'd carry it *one* while.'

'These yer knowin' boys is allers aggravatin' and sarcy,' said a coarse-looking fellow, from the other side of the room; 'that's why they gets cut up and marked so. If they behave themselves, they wouldn't.'

'That is to say, the Lord made 'em men, and it's a hard squeeze getting 'em down into beasts,' said the drover, dryly.

'Bright niggers isn't no kind of 'vantage to their masters,' continued the other, well intrenched in a coarse, unconscious obtuseness, from the contempt of his opponent. 'What's the use o' talents and them things, if you can't get the use on 'em yourself? Why, all the use they make on't is to get round you. I've had one or two of these fellers, and I jest sold 'em down river. I knew I'd got to lose 'em, first or last, if I didn't.'

'Better send orders up to the Lord, to make you a set, and leave out their souls entirely,' said the drover.

Here the conversation was interrupted by the approach of a small one-horse buggy to the inn. It had a genteel appearance and a well-dressed, gentlemanly man sat on the seat, with a coloured servant driving.

The whole party examined the new comer with the interest with which a set of loafers in a rainy day usually examine every new comer. He was very tall, with a dark, Spanish complexion, fine expressive black eyes, and close-curling hair, also of a glossy blackness. His well-formed aquiline nose, straight thin lips, and the admirable contour of his finely-formed limbs, impressed the whole company instantly with the idea of something un-common. He walked easily in among the company, and with a nod indicated to his waiter where to place his trunk, bowed to the company, and with his hat in his hand, walked up leisurely to the bar, and gave in his name as Henry Butler, Oaklands, Shelby County. Turning, with an indifferent air, he sauntered up to the advertisement, and read it over.

'Jim,' he said to his man, 'seems to me we met a boy something like this, up at Bernan's didn't we?'

'Yes, mas'r, said Jim, 'only I an't sure about the hand.'

'Well, I didn't look, of course,' said the stranger, with a careless yawn. Then, walking up to the landlord, he desired him to furnish him with a private apartment, as he had some writing to do immediately.

The landlord was all obsequious, and a relay of about seven

negroes, old and young, male and female, little and big, were soon whizzing about, like a covey of partridges, bustling, hurrying, treading on each other's toes, and tumbling over each other, in their zeal to get mas'r's room ready, while he seated himself easily on a chair in the middle of the room, and entered into conversation with the man who sat next to him.

The manufacturer, Mr Wilson, from the time of the entrance of the stranger, had regarded him with an air of disturbed and uneasy curiosity. He seemed to himself to have met and been acquainted with him somewhere, but he could not recollect. Every few moments, when the man spoke, or moved, or smiled, he would start and fix his eyes on him, and then suddenly withdraw them, as the bright dark eyes met his with such unconcerned coolness. At last, a sudden recollection seemed to flash upon him, for he stared at the stranger with such an air of blank amazement and alarm, that he walked up to him.

'Mr Wilson, I think,' said he, in a tone of recognition, and extending his hand. 'I beg your pardon, I didn't recollect you before. I see you remember me – Mr Butler, of Oaklands, Shelby County.'

'Ye – yes – yes – sir,' said Mr Wilson, like one speaking in a dream.

Just then a negro boy entered, and announced that mas'r's room was ready.

'Jim, see to the trunks,' said the gentleman negligently; then addressing himself to Mr Wilson, he added – ' I should like to have a few moments' conversation with you on business, in my room, if you please.'

Mr Wilson followed him, as one who walks in his sleep; and they proceeded to a large upper chamber, where a new-made fire was crackling, and various servants flying about, putting finishing touches to the arrangements.

When all was done, and the servants departed, the young man deliberately locked the door, and putting the key in his pocket, faced about, and folding his arms on his bosom, looked Mr Wilson full in the face.

'George !' said Mr Wilson.

'Yes, George,' said the young man.

'I couldn't have thought it.'

'I am pretty well disguised, I fancy,' said the young man, with a smile. 'A little walnut bark has made my yellow skin a genteel brown, and I've died my hair black ; so you see I don't answer to the advertisement at all.'

'O George, but this is a dangerous game you are playing. I could not have advised you to it.'

'I can do it on my own responsibility,' said George, with the same proud smile.

We remark, *en passant*, that George was, by his father's side, of white descent. His mother was one of those unfortunates of her race marked out by personal beauty to be the slave of the passions of her possessor, and the mother of children who may never know a father. From one of the proudest families in Kentucky he had inherited a set of fine European features, and a high, indomitable spirit. From his mother he had received only a slight mulatto tinge, amply compensated by its accompanying rich, dark eye. A slight change in the tint of the skin and the colour of his hair had metamorphosed him into the Spanish-looking fellow he then appeared ; and as gracefulness of movement and gentlemanly manners had always been perfectly natural to him, he found no difficulty in playing the bold part he had adopted – that of a gentleman travelling with his domestic.

Mr Wilson, a good-natured but extremely fidgety and cautious old gentleman, ambled up and down the room, appearing, as John Bunyan hath it, 'much tumbled up and down in his mind,' and divided between his wish to help George, and a certain confused notion of maintaining law and order : so as he shambled about, he delivered himself as follows :-

'Well, George, I 'spose you're running away – leaving your lawful master, George – (I don't wonder at it) – at the same time I am sorry, George – yes, decidedly – I think I must say that, George – it's my duty to tell you so.'

'Why are you sorry, sir ?' said George, calmly.

'Why, to see you, as it were, setting yourself in opposition to the laws of your country.'

'*My* country !' said George, with a strong and bitter emphasis ; 'what country have I but the grave ? – and I wish to God that I was laid there !'

'Why, George, no – no – it won't do ; this way of talking is wicked – unscriptural. George, you've got a hard master – in fact, he is – well he conducts himself reprehensibly – I can't pretend to defend him. But you know how the angel commanded Hagar to return to her mistress and submit herself under her hand; and the apostle sent back Onesimus to his master.'

'Don't quote Bible at me that way, Mr Wilson,' said George, with a flashing eye; 'don't! for my wife is a Christian, and I mean to be, if ever I get to where I can; but to quote Bible to a fellow in my circumstances is enough to make him give it up altogether. I appeal to God Almighty; I'm willing to go with the case to Him, and ask Him if I do wrong to seek my freedom.'

'These feelings are quite natural, George,' said the good-natured man, blowing his nose. 'Yes, they're natural, but it is my duty not to encourage 'em in you. Yes, my boy, I'm sorry for you, now; it's a bad case – very bad; but the apostle says, "Let every one abide in the condition in which he is called." We must all submit to the indications of Providence, George – don't you see?'

George stood with his head drawn back, his arms folded tightly over his broad breast, and a bitter smile curling his lips.

'I wonder, Mr Wilson, if the Indians should come and take you a prisoner away from your wife and children, and want to keep you all your life hoeing corn for them, if you'd think it your duty to abide in the condition in which you were called! I rather think that you'd think the first stray horse you could find an indication of Providence – shouldn't you?'

The little old gentleman stared with both eyes at this illustration of the case; but though not much of a reasoner, he had the sense in which some logicians on this particular subject do not excel – that of saying nothing, where nothing could be said. So, as he stood carefully stroking his umbrella, and folding and patting down all the creases in it, he proceeded on with his exhortations in a general way.

'You see, George, you know, now, I always have stood your friend; and whatever I've said, I've said for your good. Now, here, it seems to me, you're running an awful risk. You can't hope to carry it out. If you're taken, it will be worse with you than ever; they'll only abuse you, and half-kill you, and sell you down river.'

'Mr Wilson, I know all this,' said George. 'I *do* run a risk, but—' he threw open his overcoat, and showed two pistols and a bowie-knife. 'There !' he said, 'I'm ready for 'em ! Down south I never *will* go. No ! if it comes to that I can earn myself at least six feet of free soil – the first and last I shall ever own in Kentucky !'

'Why, George, this state of mind is awful ! it's getting really desperate, George ! I'm concerned. Going to break the laws of your country !'

'*My* country again ! Mr Wilson, *you* have a country ; but what country have *I*, or any one like me, born of slave mothers ? What laws are there for us ? We don't make them – we don't consent to them – we have nothing to do with them ; all they do for us is to crush us, and keep us down. Haven't I heard your Fourth-of-July speeches ? Don't you tell us all, once a year, that governments derive their just power from the consent of the governed ? Can't a fellow *think*, that hears such things ? Can't he put this and that together, and see what it comes to ?'

Mr Wilson's mind was one of those that may not unaptly be represented by a bale of cotton – downy, soft, benevolently fuzzy and confused. He really pitied George with all his heart, and had a sort of dim and cloudy perception of the style of feeling that agitated him ; but he deemed it his duty to go on talking *good* to him, with infinite pertinacity.

'George, this is bad. I must tell you, you know, as a friend, you'd better not be meddling with such notions ; they are bad, George, very bad, for boys in your condition – very;' and Mr Wilson sat down to a table, and began nervously chewing the handle of his umbrella.

'See here, now, Mr Wilson,' said George, coming up, and sitting himself determinately down in front of him ; 'Look at me, now. Don't I sit before you, every way, just as much a man as you are ? Look at my face – look at my hands – look at my body,' and the young man drew himself up proudly. 'Why am I *not* a man, as much as anybody ? Well, Mr Wilson, hear what I can tell you. I had a father – one of your Kentucky gentlemen – who didn't think enough of me to keep me from being sold with his dogs and horses, to satisfy the estate, when he died. I saw my mother put up at sheriff's sale, with her seven children. They were sold before her eyes, one by one, all to different masters ; and I was the youngest. She came and kneeled down before old mas'r, and begged him to buy her with me, that she might have at least one child with her; and he kicked her away with his heavy boot. I saw him do it; and the last that I heard was her moans and screams, when I was tied to his horse's neck, to be carried off to his place.'

'Well, then?'

'My master traded with one of the men, and bought my oldest sister. She was a pious, good girl – a member of the Baptist church – and as handsome as my poor mother had been. She was well brought up, and had good manners. At first, I was glad she was bought, for I had one friend near me. I was soon sorry for it. Sir, I have stood at the door and heard her whipped, when it seemed as if every blow cut into my naked heart, and I couldn't do anything to help her; and she was whipped, sir, for wanting to live a decent Christian life, such as your laws give no slave-girl a right to live; and at last I saw her chained with a trader's gang, to be sent to market in Orleans – sent there for nothing else but that – and that's the last I know of her. Well, I grew up – long years and years – no father, no mother, no sister, not a living soul that cared for me more than a dog; nothing but whipping, scolding, starving. Why, sir, I've been so hungry that I have been glad to take the bones they threw to their dogs; and yet, when I was a little fellow, and laid awake whole nights and cried, it wasn't the hunger, it wasn't the whipping, I cried for. No, sir; it was for *my mother* and *my sisters* – it was because I hadn't a friend to love me on earth. I never knew what peace or comfort was. I never had a kind word spoken to me till I came to work in your factory. Mr Wilson, you treated me well; you encouraged me to do well, and to learn to read and write, and to try to make something of myself; and God knows how grateful I am for it. Then, sir, I found my wife; you've seen her, – you know how beautiful she is. When I found she loved me, when I married her, I scarcely could believe I was alive, I was so happy; and sir, she is as good as she is beautiful. But now, what? Why, now comes my master, takes me right away from my work, and my friends, and all I like, and grinds me down into the very dirt! And why? Because, he says, I forgot who I was; he says, to teach me that I am only a nigger! After all and last of all, he comes between me and my wife, and says I shall give her up, and live with another woman. And all this your laws give him power to do, in spite of God or man. Mr

Wilson, look at it! There isn't *one* of all these things, that have broken the hearts of my mother and my sister, and my wife and myself, but your laws allow, and give every man power to do, in Kentucky, and none can say to him nay! Do you call these the laws of *my* country? Sir, I haven't any country, any more than I have any father. But I'm going to have one. I don't want anything of *your* country, except to be let alone – to go peaceably out of it; and when I get to Canada, where the laws will own me and protect me, *that* shall be my country, and its laws I will obey. But if any man tries to stop me, let him take care, for I am desperate. I'll fight for my liberty to the last breath I breathe. You say your fathers did it; if it was right for them, is it right for me?'

This speech, delivered partly while sitting at the table, and partly walking up and down the room – delivered with tears, and flashing eyes, and despairing gestures – was altogether too much for the good-natured old body to whom it was addressed, who had pulled out a great yellow silk pocket-handkerchief, and was mopping up his face with great energy.

'Blast 'em all!' he suddenly broke out. 'Haven't I always said so – the infernal old cusses? I hope I an't swearing now. Well! go a-head, George, go a-head; but, be careful, my boy; don't shoot anybody, George, unless – well – you'd *better* not shoot, I reckon; at least, I wouldn't *hit* anybody, you know. Where is your wife, George?' he added, as he nervously rose, and began walking the room.

'Gone, sir – gone, with her child in her arms, the Lord only knows where. Gone after the north star; and when we ever meet, or whether we meet at all in this world, no creature can tell.'

'Is it possible! astonishing! from such a kind family?'

'Kind families get in debt, and the laws of *our* country allow them to sell the child out of its mother's bosom to pay its master's debts,' said George, bitterly.

'Well, well,' said the honest old man, fumbling in his pocket. 'I s'pose, perhaps, I an't following my judgment – hang it, I *won't* follow my judgment!' he added, suddenly; 'so here, George,' and taking out a roll of bills from his pocket-book, he offered them to George.

'No, my kind, good sir!' said George, 'you've done a great

deal for me, and this might get you into trouble. I have money enough, I hope, to take me as far as I need it.'

'No ; but you must, George. Money is a great help everywhere ; can't have too much, if you get it honestly. Take it – *do* take it, *now* – do, my boy !'

'On condition, sir, that I may repay it at some future time, I will,' said George, taking up the money.

'And now, George, how long are you going to travel in this way ? not long, or far, I hope. It's well carried on, but too bold. And this black fellow, who is he ?'

'A true fellow, who went to Canada more than a year ago. He heard, after he got there, that his master was so angry at him for going off that he whipped his poor old mother ; and he has come all the way back to comfort her, and get a chance to get her away.'

'Has he got her ?'

'Not yet ; he has been hanging about the place, and found no chance yet. Meanwhile, he is going with me as far as Ohio, to put me among friends that helped him, and then he will come back after her.'

'Dangerous, very dangerous !' said the old man.

George drew himself up, and smiled disdainfully.

The old gentleman eyed him from head to foot, with a sort of innocent wonder.

'George, something has brought you out wonderfully. You hold up your head, and speak and move like another man,' said Mr Wilson.

'Because I'm a *free man*' said George, proudly. 'Yes, sir ; I've said "Mas'r" for the last time to any man. *I'm free !*'

'Take care ! You are not sure – you may be taken.'

'All men are free and equal *in the grave*, if it comes to that, Mr Wilson,' said George.

'I'm perfectly dumbfoundered with your boldness !' said Mr Wilson, 'to come right here to the nearest tavern !'

'Mr Wilson, it is *so* bold, and this tavern is *so* near, that they will never think of it ; they will look for me on ahead, and you yourself wouldn't know me. Jim's master don't live in this country ; he isn't known in these parts. Besides, he is given up ; nobody is looking after him, and nobody will take me up from the advertisement, I think.'

'But the mark in your hand?'

George drew off is glove, and showed a newly-healed scar in his hand.

'That is a parting proof of Mr Harris' regard,' he said scornfully. 'A fornight ago, he took it into his head to give it to me, because, he said, he believed I should try to get away one of these days. Looks interesting, doesn't it?' he said, drawing his glove on again.

'I declare, my very blood runs cold when I think of it – your condition and your risks!' said Mr Wilson.

'Mine has run cold a good many years, Mr Wilson; at present, it's about up to the boiling point,' said George.

'Well, my good sir,' continued George, after a few moments' silence, 'I saw you knew me; I thought I'd just have this talk with you, lest your surprised looks should bring me out. I leave early to-morrow morning, before daylight; by to-morrow night I hope to sleep safe in Ohio. I shall travel by daylight, stop at the best hotels, go to the dinner-tables with the lords of the land. So, good-bye, sir; if you hear that I'm taken, you may know that I'm dead!'

George stood up like a rock, and put out his hand with the air of a prince. The friendly little old man shook it heartily, and after a little shower of caution, he took his umbrella, and fumbled his way out of the room.

George stood thoughtfully looking at the door as the old man closed it. A thought seemed to flash across his mind. He hastily stepped to it, and opening it said –

'Mr Wilson, one word more.'

The old gentleman entered again, and George, as before, locked the door, and then stood for a few moments looking on the floor irresolutely. At last, raising his head with a sudden effort –

'Mr Wilson, you have shown yourself a Christian in your treatment of me – I want to ask one last deed of Christian kindness of you.'

'Well, George.'

'Well, sir, what you said was true. I *am* running a dreadful risk. There isn't on earth a living soul to care if I die,' he added, drawing his breath hard, and speaking with a great effort. 'I shall be kicked out and buried like a dog, and nobody'll think of it a day after – *only my poor wife!* Poor soul! she'll mourn and grieve; and if you'd only contrive, Mr Wilson, to send this little pin to her. She gave it to me for a Christmas present, poor child! Give it to her, and tell her I loved her to the last. Will you? *Will* you?' he added earnestly.

'Yes, certainly; poor fellow!' said the old gentleman, taking the pin, with watery eyes, and a melancholy quiver in his voice.

'Tell her one thing,' said George, 'it's my last wish, if she *can* get to Canada, to go there. No matter how kind her mistress is – no matter how much she loves her home; beg her not to go back – for slavery always ends in misery. Tell her to bring up our boy a free man, and then he won't suffer as I have. Tell her this, Mr Wilson, will you?'

'Yes, George, I'll tell her; but I trust you won't die. Take heart, you're a brave fellow. Trust in the Lord, George. I wish in my heart you were safe through though – that's what I do.'

'*Is* there a God to trust in?' said George, in such a tone of bitter despair as arrested the old gentleman's words. 'Oh, I've seen things all my life that have made me feel that there can't be a God. You Christians don't know how these things look to us. There is a God for you, but is there any for us?'

'Oh, now, don't – don't my boy!' said the old man, almost sobbing as he spoke; 'don't feel so. There is – there is; clouds and darkness are round about Him, but righteousness and judgment are the habitation of His throne. There's a *God*, George – believe it; trust in Him, and I'm sure He'll help you. Everything will be set right – if not in this life, in another.'

The real piety and benevolence of the simple old man invested him with a temporary dignity and authority as he spoke. George stopped his distracted walk up and down the room, stood thoughfully a moment, and then said quietly –

'Thank you for saying that, my good friend; I'll *think of that.*'

Chapter 12

SELECT INCIDENT OF LAWFUL TRADE

'In Ramah there was a voice heard, – weeping, and lamentation, and great mourning, Rachel weeping for her children, and would not be comforted.'

Mr Haley and Tom jogged onward in their wagon, each for a time absorbed in his own reflections. Now, the reflections of two men sitting side by side are a curious thing – seated on the same seat, having the same eyes, ears, hands, and organs of all sorts, and having pass before their eyes the same objects: it is wonderful what a variety we shall find in these same reflections!

As, for example, Mr Haley: he thought first of Tom's length, and breadth, and height, and what he would sell for, if he was kept fat and in good case till he got him into market. He thought of how he should make out his gang; he thought of the respective market value of certain supposititious men and women and children who were to compose it, and other kindred topics of the business; then he thought of himself, and how humane he was, that whereas other men chained their 'niggers' hand and foot both, he only put fetters on the feet, and left Tom the use of his hands, as long as he behaved well: and he sighed to think how ungrateful human nature was, so that there was even room to doubt whether Tom appreciated his mercies. He had been taken in so by 'niggers' whom he had favoured; but still he was astonished to consider how good-natured he yet remained!

As to Tom, he was thinking over some words of an unfashionable old book, which kept running through his head, again and again, as follows: 'We have here no continuing city, but we seek one to come; wherefore God himself is not ashamed to be called our God; for He hath prepared for us a city.' These words of an ancient volume, got up principally by 'ignorant and unlearned men,' have, through all time, kept up somehow a strange sort of power over the minds of poor, simple fellows, like Tom. They stir up the soul from its depths, and rouse, as with trumpet call, courage, energy, and enthusiasm, where before was only the blackness of despair.

Mr Haley pulled out of his pocket sundry newpapers, and began looking over their advertisements with absorbed interest. He was not a remarkably fluent reader, and was in the habit of reading in a sort of recitative, half-aloud, by way of calling in his ears to verify the deductions of his eyes. In this tone he slowly recited the following paragraph :-

'EXECUTORS' SALE. – NEGROES ! – Agreeably to order of Court, will be sold, on Tuesday, February 20, before the Court-house door, in the town of Washington, Kentucky, the following negroes : – Hagar, aged 60 ; John aged 30 ; Ben, aged 21 ; Saul, aged 25 ; Albert, aged 14. Sold for the benefit of the creditors and heirs of the estate of Jesse Blutchford, Esq.

'SAMUEL MORRIS ⎫
'THOMAS FLINT   ⎬ *Executors.*'
　　　　　　　⎭

'This yer I must look at, said he to Tom, for want of somebody else to talk to. 'Ye see I am going to get up a prime gang to take down with ye, Tom ; it'll make it sociable and pleasant like – good company will, ye know. We must drive right to Washington first and foremost, and then I'll clap you into jail while I does the business.'

Tom received this agreeable intelligence quite meekly ; simply wondering, in his own heart, how many of these doomed men had wives and children, and whether they would feel as he did about leaving them. It is to be confessed, too, that the *naïve*, off-hand information that he was to be thrown into jail, by no means produced an agreeable impression on a poor fellow who had always prided himself on a strictly honest and upright course of life. Yes, Tom, we must confess it, was rather proud of his honesty, poor fellow – not having very much else to be proud of ; if he had belonged to some of the higher walks of society, he perhaps would never have been reduced to such straits. However, the day wore on, and the evening saw Haley and Tom comfortably accommodated in Washington – the one in a tavern, the other in a jail.

About eleven o'clock the next day a mixed throng was gathered around the court-house steps – smoking, chewing, spitting, swearing, and conversing, according to their respective tastes and turns, waiting for the auction to commence. The men and women to be sold sat in a group apart, talking in a low tone to each other. The woman who had been advertised by the name of Hagar was a regular African in feature and figure. She might have been sixty, but was older than that by hard work and disease, was partially blind, and somewhat crippled with rheumatism. By her side stood her only remaining son, Albert, a bright-looking little fellow of fourteen years. The boy was the only survivor of a large family, who had been successively sold away from her to a southern market. The mother held on to him with both her shaking hands, and eyed with intense trepidation every one who walked up to examine him.

'Don't be fear'd, Aunt Hagar,' said the oldest of the men. 'I spoke to Mas'r Thomas 'bout it, and he thought he might manage to sell you in a lot both together.'

'Dey needn't call me worn out yet,' said she, lifting her shaking hands. 'I can cook yet, and scrub, and scour – I'm wuth a buying, if I do come cheap; tell em dat ar – you *tell* 'em,' she added, earnestly.

Haley here forced his way into the group, walked up to the old man, pulled his mouth open and looked in, felt of his teeth, made him stand and straighten himself, bend his back, and perform various evolutions to show his muscles; and then passed on to the next, and put him through the same trial. Walking up last to the boy, he felt of his arms, straightened his hands, and looked at his fingers, and made him jump, to show his agility.

'He an't gwine to be sold widout me!' said the old woman, with passionate eagerness; 'he and I goes in a lot together; I's rail strong yet, mas'r, and can do heaps o' work – heaps on it, mas'r.'

'On plantation?' said Haley, with a contemptuous glance. 'Likely story!' and, as if satisfied with his examination, he walked out and looked, and stood with his hands in his pockets, his cigar in his mouth, and his hat cocked on one side, ready for action.

'What think of 'em?' said a man who had been following Haley's examination, as if to make up his own mind from it.

'Wal,' said Haley, spitting, 'I shall put in, I think, for the youngerly ones and the boy.'

'They want to sell the boy and the old woman together,' said the man.

'Find it a tight pull; why, she's an old rack o' bones – not worth her salt.'

'You wouldn't then?' said the man.

'Anybody'd be a fool 'twould. She's half blind, crooked with rheumatis, and foolish to boot.'

'Some buys up these yer old critturs, and ses there's a sight more wear in 'em than a body'd think,' said the man reflectively.

'No go, 'tall,' said Haley; 'wouldn't take her for a present – fact: I've *seen*, now.'

'Wal, 'tis kinder pity, now, not to buy her with her son – her heart seems so sot on him; s'pose they fling her in cheap.'

'Them that's got money to spend that ar way, it's all well enough. I shall bid off on that ar boy for a plantation-hand; wouldn't be bothered with her no way – not if they'd give her to me,' said Haley.

'She'll take on desp't,' said the man.

'Nat'lly, she will,' said the trader, coolly.

The conversation was here interrupted by a busy hum in the audience; and the auctioneer, a short, bustling, important fellow, elbowed his way into the crowd. The old woman drew in her breath, and caught instinctively at her son.

'Keep close to your mammy, Albert – close – dey'll put us up togedder,'she said.

'O mammy, I'm fear'd they won't,' said the boy.

'Dey must, child; I can't live, no ways, if they don't,' said the old creature vehemently.

The stentorian tones of the auctioneer, calling out to clear the way, now announced that the sale was about to commence. A place was cleared, and the bidding began. The different men on the list were soon knocked off at prices which showed a pretty brisk demand in the market; two of them fell to Haley.

'Come, now, young un, said the auctioneer, giving the boy a touch with his hammer, 'be up and show your springs, now.'

'Put us two up togedder, togedder – do please, mas'r,' said the old woman, holding fast to her boy.

'Be off,' said the man gruffly, pushing her hands away; 'you come last. Now, darkey, spring;' and, with the word, he pushed the boy toward the block, while a deep heavy groan rose behind him. The boy paused, and looked back; but there was no time to stay, and dashing the tears from his large, bright eyes, he was up in a moment.

His fine figure, alert limbs, and bright face, raised an instant competition, and half-a-dozen bids simultaneously met the ear of the auctioneer. Anxious, half-frightened, he looked from side to side, as he heard the clatter of contending bids – now here, now there – till the hammer fell. Haley had got him. He was pushed from the block towards his new master, but stopped one moment, and looked back, when his poor old mother, trembling in every limb, held out her shaking hands toward him.

'Buy me, too, mas'r; for de dear Lord's sake! – buy me – I shall die if you don't!'

'You'll die if I do, that's the kink of it,' said Haley. 'No!' And he turned on his heel.

The bidding for the poor old creature was summary. The man who had adddressed Haley, and who seemed not destitute of compassion, bought her for a trifle, and the spectators began to disperse.

The poor victims of the sale, who had been brought up in one place together for years, gathered round the despairing old mother, whose agony was pitiful to see.

'Couldn't dey leave me one? Mas'r allers said I should have one – he did,' she repeated over and over, in heartbroken tones.

'Trust in the Lord, Aunt Hagar,' said the oldest of the men, sorrowfully.

'What good will it do?' said she, sobbing passionately.

'Mother! mother! Don't! don't!' said the boy. 'They say you's got a good master.'

'I don't care – I don't care. O Albert! O my boy! you's my last baby. Lord, how ken I?'

'Come, take her off, can't some of ye?' said Haley dryly. 'Don't do no good for her to go on that ar way.'

The old men of the company, partly by persuasion and partly by force, loosed the poor creature's last despairing hold, and as they led her off to her new master's wagon, strove to comfort her.

'Now!' said Haley, pushing his three purchases together, and producing a bundle of handcuffs, which he proceeded to put on their wrists; and fastening each handcuff to a long chain, he drove them before him to the jail.

A few days saw Haley, with his possessions, safely deposited on one of the Ohio boats. It was the commencement of his gang, to be augmented as the boat moved on by various other merchandise of the same kind, which he, or his agent, had stored for him in various points along shore.

The *La Belle Rivière*, as brave and beautiful a boat as ever walked the waters of her namesake river, was floating gaily down the stream, under a brilliant sky, the stripes and stars of free America waving and fluttering overhead; the guards crowded with well-dressed ladies and gentlemen, walking and enjoying the delightful day. All was full of life, buoyant, and rejoicing! all but Haley's gang, who were stored, with other freight, on the lower deck, and who, somehow, did not seem to appreciate their various privileges, as they sat in a knot, talking to each other in low tones.

'Boys,' said Haley, coming up briskly, 'I hope you keep up good heart and are cheerful. Now, no sulks, ye see; keep stiff upper lip, boys; do well by me, and I'll do well by you.'

The boys addressed responded the invariable 'Yes, mas'r,' for ages the watchword of poor Africa; but it's to be owned they did not look particularly cheerful. They had their various little prejudices in favour of wives, mothers, sisters, and children, seen for the last time; and though 'they that wasted them required of them mirth,' it was not instantly forthcoming.

'I've got a wife,' spoke out the article enumerated as 'John, aged thirty,' and he laid his chained hand on Tom's knee, 'and she don't know a word about this, poor girl.'

'Where does she live?' said Tom.

'In a tavern, a piece down here,' said John; 'I wish, now, I *could* see her once more in this world,' he added.

Poor John! It *was* rather natural; and the tears that fell as he spoke came as naturally as if he had been a white man. Tom drew a long breath from a sore heart, and tried, in his poor way, to comfort him.

And overhead, in the cabin, sat fathers and mothers, husbands and wives; and merry, dancing children, moved round among them, like so many little butterflies, and everything was going on quite easy and comfortable.

'O, mamma!' said a boy, who had just come up from below; 'there's a negro trader on board, and he's brought four or five slaves down there.'

'Poor creatures!' said the mother, in a tone between grief and indignation.

'What's that?' said another lady.

'Some poor slaves below,' said the mother.

'And they've got chains on,' said the boy.

'What a shame to our country that such sights are to be seen!' said another lady.

'Oh, there's a great deal to be said on both sides of the subject,' said a genteel woman, who sat at her state-room door, sewing, while her little girl and boy were playing round her. 'I've been south, and I must say I think the negroes are better off than they would be to be free.'

'In some respects, some of them are well off, I grant,' said the lady to whose remark she had answered. 'The most dreadful part of slavery, to my mind, is its outrages on the feelings and affections – the separating of families, for example.'

'That *is* a bad thing, certainly,' said the other lady, holding up a baby's dress she had just completed, and looking intently on its trimmings; 'but then, I fancy, it don't occur often.'

'Oh, it does,' said the first lady, eagerly; 'I've lived many years in Kentucky and Virginia both, and I've seen enough to make one's heart sick. Suppose, ma'am, your two children there, should be taken from you, and sold?'

'We can't reason from our feelings to those of this class of persons,' said the other lady, sorting out some worsteds on her lap.

'Indeed, ma'am, you can know nothing of them if you say so,' answered the first lady, warmly. 'I was born and brought up among them. I know they *do* feel, just as keenly – even more so, perhaps – as we do.'

The lady said 'Indeed!' yawned, and looked out the cabin

window, and finally repeated, for a finale, the remark with which she had begun – 'After all, I think they are better off than they would be to be free.'

'It's undoubtedly the intention of Providence that the African race should be servants – kept in a low condition,' said a grave-looking gentleman in black, a clergyman, seated by the cabin-door. '"Cursed be Canan; a servant of servants shall he be," the Scripture says.'

'I say, stranger, is that ar what that text means?' said a tall man, standing by.

'Undoubtedly. It pleased Providence, for some inscrutable reason, to doom the race to bondage ages ago; and we must not set up our opinion against that.'

'Well, then, we'll all go a-head and buy up niggers,' said the man, 'if that's the way of Providence: won't we, squire?' said he, turning to Haley, who had been standing, with his hands in his pockets, by the stove, and intently listening to the conversation.

'Yes,' continued the tall man; 'we must all be resigned to the decrees of Providence. Niggers must be sold, and trucked round, and kept under; it's what they's made for. 'Pears like this yer view's quite refreshing, an't it, stranger?' said he to Haley.

'I never thought on't,' said Haley. 'I couldn't have said as much, myself; I han't no larning. I took up the trade just to make a living; if 't an't right, I calculated to 'pent on't in time, ye know.'

'And now you'll save yerself the trouble, won't ye?' said the tall man. 'See what 'tis, now, to know Scripture. If ye'd only studied yer Bible, like this yer good man, ye might have know'd it before, and saved ye a heap o' trouble. Ye could jist have said, "Cussed be" – what's his name? – and 'twould all have come right.' And the stranger, who was no other than the honest drover, whom we introduced to our readers in the Kentucky tavern, sat down, and began smoking, with a curious smile on his long, dry face.

A tall, slender young man, with a face expressive of great feeling and intelligence, here broke in, and repeated the words, '"All things whatsoever ye would that men should do unto you, do ye even so unto them." I suppose,' he added, 'that is Scripture, as much as "Cursed be Canan"?'

'Wal, it seems quite *as* plain a text, stranger,' said John, the drover, 'to poor fellows like us, now;' and John smoked on like a volcano.

The young man paused, looked as if he was going to say more, when suddenly the boat stopped, and the company made the usual steamboat rush to see where they were landing.

'Both them ar chaps parsons?' said John to one of the men, as they were going out.

The man nodded.

As the boat stopped, a black woman came running wildly up the plank, darted into the crowd, flew up to where the slave-gang sat, and threw her arms round that unfortunate piece of merchandise before enumerated, 'John, aged thirty,' and with sobs and tears bemoaned him as her husband.

But what needs tell the story, told too oft – every day told – of heartstrings rent and broken – the weak broken and torn for the profit and convenience of the strong! It needs not to be told: every day is telling it – telling it, too, in the ear of One who is not deaf, though He be long silent.

The young man who had spoken for the cause of humanity and God before stood with folded arms, looking on this scene. He turned, and Haley was standing at his side. 'My friend,' he said, speaking with thick utterance, 'how can you, how dare you, carry on a trade like this? Look at those poor creatures! Here I am, rejoicing in my heart that I am going home to my wife and child! and the same bell which is a signal to carry me onward towards them will part this poor man and his wife for ever. Depend upon it, God will bring you into judgment for this.'

The trader turned away in silence.

'I say, now,' said the drover, touching his elbow, 'there's differences in parsons, an't there? "Cussed be Canaan," don't seem to go down with this 'un, does it?'

Haley gave an uneasy growl.

'And that ar an't the worst on't,' said John; 'mabbe it won't go down with the Lord, neither, when ye come to settle with Him, one o' these days, as all on us must, I reckon.'

Haley walked reflectively to the other end of the boat.

'If I make pretty handsomely on one or two next gangs,' he thought, 'I reckon I'll stop off this yer: it's really getting dangerous.' And he took out his pocket-book, and began adding over his accounts – a process which many gentlemen besides Mr Haley have found a specific for an uneasy conscience.

The boat swept proudly away from the shore and all went on merrily, as before. Men talked, and loafed, and read, and smoked. Women sewed, and children played, and the boat passed on her way.

One day, when she lay-to for awhile, at a small town in Kentucky, Haley went up into the place on a little matter of business.

Tom, whose fetters did not prevent his taking a moderate circuit, had drawn near the side of the boat, and stood listlessly gazing over the railings. After a time, he saw the trader returning, with an alert step, in company with a coloured woman, bearing in her arms a young child. She was dressed quite respectably, and a coloured man followed her, bringing along a small trunk. The woman came cheerfully onward, talking, as she came, with the man who bore her trunk, and so passed up the plank into the boat. The bell rung, the steamer whizzed, the engine groaned and coughed, and away swept the boat down the river.

The woman walked forward among the boxes and bales of the lower deck, and sitting down, busied herself with chirrupping to her baby.

Haley made a turn or two about the boat, and then, coming up, seated himself near her, and began saying something to her in an indifferent under-tone.

Tom soon noticed a heavy cloud passing over the woman's brow, and that she answered rapidly, and with great vehemence. 'I don't believe it; I won't believe it!' he heard her say. 'You're jist a foolin' with me.'

'If you won't believe it, look here!' said the man, drawing out a paper; 'this yer's the bill of sale, and there's your master's name to it; and I paid down good solid cash for it, too, I can tell you – so now!'

'I don't believe mas'r would cheat me so; it can't be true!' said the woman with increasing agitation.

'You can ask any of these men here that can read writing. Here!' he said, to a man that was passing by, 'jis read this yer, won't you! This yer gal won't believe me, when I tell her what 'tis.'

'Why, it's a bill of sale, signed by John Fosdick,' said the man, 'making over to you the girl Lucy and her child. It's all straight enough, for aught I see.'

The woman's passionate exclamations collected a crowd around her, and the trader briefly explained to them the cause of the agitation.

'He told me that I was going down to Louisville, to hire out as cook to the same tavern where my husband works; that's what mas'r told me, his own self, and I can't believe he'd lie to me,' said the woman.

'But he has sold you, my poor woman, there's no doubt about it,' said a good-natured looking man, who had been examining the papers; 'he has done it, and no mistake.'

'Then it's no account talking,' said the woman, suddenly growing quite calm; and, clasping her child tighter in her arms, she sat down on her box, turned her back round, and gazed listlessly into the river.

'Going to take it easy, after all!' said the trader. 'Gal's got grit, I see.'

The woman looked calm as the boat went on; and a beautiful, soft, summer breeze passed, like a compassionate spirit, over her head – the gentle breeze that never inquires whether the brow is dusky or fair that it fans. And she saw sunshine sparkling on the water, in golden ripples, and heard gay voices, full of ease and pleasure, talking around her everywhere; but her heart lay as if a great stone had fallen on it. Her baby raised himself up against her, and stroked her cheeks with his little hands; and, springing up and down, crowing and chatting, seemed determined to arouse her. She strained him suddenly and tightly in her arms, and slowly one tear after another fell on his wondering, unconscious face: and gradually she seemed, little by little, to grow calmer, and busied herself with tending and nursing him.

The child, a boy of ten months, was uncommonly large and strong of his age, and very vigorous in his limbs. Never for a moment still, he kept his mother constantly busy in holding him, and guarding his springing activity.

'That's a fine chap!' said a man, suddenly stopping opposite to him, with his hands in his pockets. 'How old is he?'

'Ten months and a half,' said the mother.

The man whistled to the boy, and offered him part of a stick of candy, which he eagerly grabbed at, and very soon had it in a baby's general depository; to wit, his mouth.

'Rum fellow!' said the man. 'Knows what's what!' and he whistled and walked on. When he had got to the other side of the boat, he came across Haley, who was smoking on top of a pile of boxes.

The stranger produced a match and lighted a cigar, saying, as he did so –

'Decentish kind o' wench you've got round there, stranger.'

'Why, I reckon she *is* tol'able fair,' said Haley, blowing the smoke out of his mouth.

'Taking her down south?' said the man.

Haley nodded and smoked on.

'Plantation hand?' said the man.

'Wal,' said Haley, 'I'm filling out an order for a plantation, and I think I shall put her in. They told me she was a good cook, and they can use her for that, or set her at the cotton-picking. She's got the right fingers for that; I looked at 'em. Sell well, either way;' and Haley resumed his cigar.

'They won't want the young 'un on a plantation,' said the man.

'I shall sell him first chance I find,' said Haley, lighting another cigar.

'S'spose you'd be selling him tol'able cheap?' said the stranger, mounting the pile of boxes, and sitting down comfortably.

'Don't know 'bout that,' said Haley; 'he's a pretty smart young 'un – straight, fat, strong: flesh as hard as a brick!'

'Very true; but then there's all the bother and expense of raisin'.'

'Nonsense!' said Haley; 'they is raised as easy as any kind of critter there is going; they an't a bit more trouble than pups. This yer chap will be running all round in a month.'

'I've got a good place for raisin', and I thought of takin' in a little more stock,' said the man. 'One cook lost a young 'un last week – got drowned in the wash-tub, while she was a hangin' out clothes; and I reckon it would be well enough to set her to raisin' this yer.'

Haley and the stranger smoked a while in silence; neither seeming willing to broach the test question of the interview. At last the man resumed: —

'You wouldn't think of wantin' more than ten dollars for that ar chap, seeing you *must* get him off yer hand, anyhow?'

Haley shook his head and spit impressively.

'That won't do, noways,' he said, and began his smoking again.

'Well, stranger, what will you take?'

'Well, now,' said Haley, 'I *could* raise that ar chap myself, or get him raised; he's oncommon likely and healthy, and he'd fetch a hundred dollars six months hence; and, in a year or two, he'd bring two hundred, if I had him in the right spot; so I shan't take a cent less nor fifty for him now.'

'O stranger! that's ridiculous altogether,' said the man.

'Fact!' said Haley, with a decisive nod of his head.

'I'll give thirty for him,' said the stranger, 'but not a cent more.'

'Now, I'll tell ye what I will do,' said Haley, spitting again, with renewed decision. 'I'll split the difference, and say forty-five; and that's the most I will do.'

'Well, agreed!' said the man, after an interval.

'Done!' said Haley. 'Where do you land?'

'At Louisville, said the man.

'Louisville,' said Haley. 'Very fair; we get there about dusk. Chap will be asleep — all fair — get him off quietly, and no screaming — happens beautiful — I like to do everything quietly — I hates all kind of agitation and fluster.' And so, after a transfer of certain bills had passed from the man's pocket-book to the trader's, he resumed his cigar.

It was a bright, tranquil evening when the boat stopped at the wharf at Louisville. The woman had been sitting with her baby in her arms, now wrapped in a heavy sleep. When she heard the name of the place called out, she hastily laid the child down in a little cradle formed by the hollow among the boxes, first carefully spreading under it her cloak, and then she sprung to the side of the boat, in hopes that among the various hotel-waiters that thronged the wharf, she might see her husband. In this hope she pressed forward to the front rails, and stretching far over them, strained her eyes intently on the moving heads on the shore, and the crowd pressed in between her and the child.

'Now's your time,' said Haley, taking the sleeping child up, and handing him to the stranger. 'Don't wake him up and set him to crying, now; it would make a devil of a fuss with the gal.' The man took the bundle carefully, and was soon lost in the crowd that went up the wharf.

When the boat, creaking, and groaning, and puffing, had loosed from the wharf, and was beginning slowly to strain herself along, the woman returned to her old seat. The trader was sitting there – the child was gone!

'Why, why – where?' she began in bewildered surprise.

'Lucy,' said the trader, 'your child's gone; you may as well know it first as last. You see, I know'd you couldn't take him down south; and I got a chance to sell him to a first-rate family, that'll raise him better than you can.'

The trader had arrived at the stage of Christian and political perfection which has been recommended by some preachers and politicians of the north, lately, in which he had completely overcome every humane weakness and prejudice. His heart was exactly where yours, sir, and mine could be brought with proper effort and cultivation. The wild look of anguish and utter despair that the woman cast on him might have disturbed one less practised; but he was used to it. He had seen that same look hundreds of times. You can get used to such things, too, my friend; and it is the great object of recent efforts to make our whole northern community used to them, for the glory of the Union. So the trader only regarded the mortal anguish which he saw working in those dark features, those clenched hands, and suffocating breathings, as necessary incidents of the trade, and merely calculated whether she was going to scream, and get up a commotion on the boat; for, like other supporters of our peculiar institutions, he decidedly disliked agitation.

But the woman did not scream. The shot had passed too straight and direct through the heart for cry or tear.

Dizzily she sat down. Her slack hands fell lifeless by her side. Her eyes looked straight foward, but she saw nothing. All the noise and hum of the boat, the groaning of the machinery, mingled dreamily to her bewildered ear; and the poor, dumb-stricken heart had neither cry nor tear to show for its utter misery. She was quite calm.

The trader, who, considering his advantages, was almost as humane as some of our politicians, seemed to feel called on to administer such consolation as the case admitted ot.

'I know this yer comes kinder hard at first, Lucy,' said he; 'but such a smart, sensible gal as you are, won't give way to it. You see it's *necessary*, and can't be helped.'

'Oh, don't, mas'r, don't !' said the woman, with a voice like one that is smothering.

'You're a smart wench, Lucy,' he persisted. 'I mean to do well by ye, and get ye a nice place down the river; and you'll soon get another husband, such a likely gal as you—'

'Oh, mas'r, if you *only* won't talk to me now,' said the woman, in a voice of such quick and living anguish, that the trader felt that there was something at present in the case beyond his style of operation. He got up, and the woman turned away, and buried her head in her cloak.

The trader walked up and down for a time, and occasionally stopped and looked at her.

'Takes it hard, rather,' he soliloquised; 'but quiet, tho'. Let her sweat a while – she'll come right by and by.'

Tom had watched the whole transaction from first to last, and had a perfect understanding of it results. To him it looked liked something unutterably horrible and cruel, because, poor, ignorant black soul, he had not learned to generalise, and to take enlarged views. If he had only been instructed by certain ministers of Christianity, he might have thought better of it, and seen in it an every-day incident of a lawful trade; a trade which is the vital support of an institution which an American divine[1] tells us, has '*no evils but such as are inseparable from any other relations in social and domestic life*.' But Tom, as we see, being a poor, ignorant fellow, whose reading had been confined entirely to the New Testament, could not comfort and solace himself with views like these. His very soul bled within him for what seemed to him the *wrongs* of the poor suffering thing that lay like a crushed weed on the boxes; the feeling, living, bleeding, yet immortal *thing*, which American state law coolly

[2] Dr Joel Parker, of Philadelphia.

classes with the bundles, and bales, and boxes, among which she is lying.

Tom drew near, and tried to say something; but she only groaned. Honestly, and with tears running down his own cheeks, he spoke of a heart of love in the skies, of a pitying Jesus, and an eternal home; but the ear was deaf with anguish, and the palsied heart could not feel.

Night came on – night, calm, unmoved, and glorious, shining down with her innumerable and solemn angel eyes, twinkling, beautiful, but silent. There was no speech nor language, no pitying voice or helping hand, from that distant sky. One after another the voices of business or pleasure died away; all on the boat were sleeping, and the ripples at the prow were plainly heard. Tom stretched himself out on a box, and there, as he lay, he heard, ever and anon, a smothered sob or cry from the prostrate creature. 'Oh, what shall I do? O Lord! O good Lord, do help me!' and so, ever and anon, until the murmur died away in silence.

At midnight Tom waked with a sudden start. Something black passed quickly by him to the side of the boat, and he heard a splash in the water. No one else saw or heard anything. He raised his head – the woman's place was vacant! He got up, and sought about him in vain. The poor bleeding heart was still at last, and the river rippled and dimpled just as brightly as if it had not closed above it.

Patience! patience! ye whose hearts swell indignant at wrongs like these. Not one throb of anguish, not one tear of the oppressed, is forgotten by the Man of Sorrows, the Lord of Glory. In his patient, generous bosom, he bears the anguish of a world. Bear thou, like him, in patience, and labour in love; for, sure as he is God, 'the year of his redeemed *shall* come.'

The trader waked up bright and early, and came out to see to his live stock. It was now his turn to look about in perplexity.

'Where alive is that gal?' he said to Tom.

Tom, who had learned the wisdom of keeping counsel, did not feel called on to state his observations and suspicions, but said he did not know.

'She surely couldn't have got off in the night at any of the landings, for I was awake and on the look-out whenever the boat stopped. I never trust these yer things to other folks.'

The speech was addressed to Tom quite confidentially, as if it was something that would be specially interesting to him. Tom made no answer.

The trader searched the boat from stem to stern, among boxes, bales, and barrels, around the machinery, by the chimneys, in vain.

'Now, I say, Tom, be fair about this yer,' he said, when, after a fruitless search, he came where Tom was standing. 'You know something about it, now. Don't tell me – I know you do. I saw the gal stretched out here about ten o'clock, and agin at twelve, and agin between one and two; and then at four she was gone, and you was a sleeping right there all the time. Now, you know something – you can't help it.'

'Well, mas'r,' said Tom, 'towards morning something brushed by me, and I kinder half woke; and then I hearn a great splash, and then I clare woke up, and the gal was gone. That's all I know on't.'

The trader was not shocked nor amazed; because, as we said before, he was used to a great many things that you are not used to. Even the awful presence of Death struck no solemn chill upon him. He had seen Death many times – met him in the way of trade, and got acquainted with him – and he only thought of him as a hard customer, that embarrassed his property operations very unfairly; and so he only swore that the gal was a baggage, and that he was devilish unlucky, and that, if things went on in this way, he should not make a cent on the trip. In short, he seemed to consider himself an ill-used man, decidedly; but there was no help for it, as the woman had escaped into a State which *never* will give up a fugitive – not even at the demand of the whole glorious Union. The trader, therefore, sat discontentedly down, with his little account-book, and put down the missing body and soul under the head of *losses*!

'He's a shocking creature, isn't he, this trader? – so unfeeling! It's dreadful, really!'

'Oh, but nobody thinks anything of these traders! They are universally despised – never received into any decent society.'

But who, sir, makes the trader? Who is most to blame? The enlightened, cultivated, intelligent man, who supports the system of which the trader is the inevitable result, or the poor trader himself? You make the public sentiment that calls for his trade, that debauches and depraves him, till he feels no shame in it; and in what are you better than he?

Are you educated and he ignorant, you high and he low, you refined and he coarse, you talented and he simple?

In the day of a future judgment these very considerations may make it more tolerable for him than for you.

In concluding these little incidents of lawful trade, we must beg the world not to think that American legislators are entirely destitute of humanity, as might perhaps be unfairly inferred from the great efforts made in our national body to protect and perpetuate this species of traffic.

Who does not know how our great men are outdoing themselves in declaiming against the *foreign* slave-trade? There are a perfect host of Clarksons and Wilberforces risen up among us on that subject, most edifying to hear and behold. Trading negroes from Africa, dear reader, is so horrid! It is not to be thought of! But trading them from Kentucky — that's quite another thing!

Chapter 13

THE QUAKER SETTLEMENT

A QUIET scene now rises before us. A large, roomy neatly-painted kitchen, its yellow floor glossy and smooth, and without a particle of dust; a neat, well-blacked cooking-stove; rows of shining tin, suggestive of unmentionable good things to the appetite; glossy green wood chairs, old and firm; a small flag-bottomed rocking-chair, with a patch-work cushion in it, neatly contrived out of small pieces of different coloured woollen goods, and a larger sized one, motherly and old, whose wide arms breathed hospitable invitation, seconded by the solicitation of its feather cushions — a real, comfortable, persuasive old chair, and worth, in the way of honest, homely enjoyment, a dozen of your plush or brochetelle drawing-room gentry; and in the chair, gently swaying back and forward, her eyes bent on some fine sewing, sat our old friend Eliza. Yes, there she is, paler and thinner than in her Kentucky home, with a world of quiet sorrow lying under the shadow of her long eyelashes, and marking the outline of her gentle mouth! It was plain to see how old and firm the girlish heart was grown under the discipline of heavy sorrow; and when, anon, her large dark eye was raised to follow the gambols of her little Harry, who was sporting, like some tropical butterfly, hither and thither over the floor, she showed a depth of firmness and steady resolve that was never there in her earlier and happier days.

By her side sat a woman with a bright tin pan in her lap into which she was carefully sorting some dried peaches. She might be fifty-five or sixty; but hers was one of those faces that time seems to touch only to brighten and adorn. The snowy lisse crape cap, made after the strait Quaker pattern, the plain white muslin handkerchief, lying in placid folds across her bosom, the drab shawl and dress, showed at once the community to which she belonged. Her face was round and rosy, with a healthful downy softness, suggestive of a ripe peach. Her hair, partially silvered by age, was parted smoothly back from a high placid forehead, on which time had written no inscription except 'Peace on earth, good will to men;' and beneath shone a large pair of clear, honest, loving, brown eyes; you only needed to look straight into them, to feel that you saw to the bottom of a heart as good and true as ever throbbed in woman's bosom. So much has been said and sung of beautiful young girls, why don't somebody wake up to the beauty of old women? If any want to get up an inspiration under this head, we refer them to our good friend Rachel Halliday, just as she sits there in her little rocking-chair. It had a turn for quacking and squeaking – that chair had – either from having taken cold in early life, or from some asthmatic affection, or perhaps from nervous derangement; but as she gently swung backward and forward, the chair kept up a kind of subdued 'creechy crawchy,' that would have been intolerable in any other chair. But old Simeon Halliday often declared it was as good as any music to him; and the children all avowed that they wouldn't miss of hearing mother's chair for anything in the world. For why? for twenty years or more, nothing but loving words, and gentle moralities, and motherly loving-kindness, had come from that chair – head-aches and heart-aches innumerable had been cured there – difficulties spiritual and temporal solved there – all by one good, loving woman. God bless her!

'And so thee still thinks of going to Canada, Eliza?' she said, as she was quietly looking over her peaches.

'Yes, ma'am,' said Eliza, firmly. 'I must go onward. I dare not stop.'

'And what'll thee do when thee gets there? Thee must think about that, my daughter.'

'My daughter,' came naturally from the lips of Rachel Halliday; for hers was just the face and form that made 'mother' seem the most natural word in the world.

Eliza's hands trembled, and some tears fell on her fine work; but she answered firmly, –

'I shall do – anything I can find. I hope I can find something.'

'Thee knows thee can stay here as long as thee pleases,' said Rachel.

'Oh, thank you,' said Eliza, 'but' – she pointed to Harry – 'I can't sleep nights; I can't rest. Last night I dreamed I saw that man coming into the yard,' she said, shuddering.

'Poor child!' said Rachel, wiping her eyes; 'but thee mustn't feel so. The Lord hath ordered it so that never hath a fugitive been stolen from our village. I trust thine will not be the first.'

The door here opened, and a little, short, round, pincushiony woman stood at the door, with a cheery, blooming face, like a ripe apple. She was dressed, like Rachel, in sober grey, with the muslin folded neatly across her round, plump little chest.

'Ruth Stedman,' said Rachel, coming joyfully forward; 'how is thee, Ruth?' she said, heartily taking both her hands.

'Nicely,' said Ruth, taking off her little drab bonnet, and dusting it with her handkerchief, displaying, as she did so, a round little head, on which the Quaker cap sat with a sort of jaunty air, despite all the stroking and patting of the small fat hands, which were busily applied to arranging it. Certain stray locks of decidedly curly hair, too, had escaped here and there, and had to be coaxed and cajoled into their place again; and then the new comer, who might have been five-and-twenty, turned from the small looking-glass, before which she had been making these arrangements, and looked well pleased – as most people who looked at her might have been: for she was decidedly a wholesome, whole-hearted, chirruping little woman, as ever gladdened man's heart withal.

'Ruth, this friend is Eliza Harris; and this is the little boy I told thee of.'

'I am glad to see thee, Eliza – very,' said Ruth, shaking hands, as if Eliza were an old friend she had long been expecting: 'and this is thy dear boy – I brought a cake for him,' she said, holding out a little heart to the boy, who came up, gazing through his curls, and accepted it shyly.

'Where's thy baby, Ruth?' said Rachel.

'Oh, he's coming; but thy Mary caught him as I came in, and ran off with him to the barn, to show him to the children.'

At this moment the door opened, and Mary, an honest, rosy-looking girl, with large brown eyes, like her mother's, came in with the baby.

'Ah! ha!' said Rachel, coming up, and taking the great, white, fat fellow in her arms; 'how good he looks, and how he does grow!'

'To be sure he does,' said little bustling Ruth, as she took the child, and began taking off a little blue silk hood, and various layers and wrappers of outer garments: and having given a twitch here, and a pull there, and variously adjusted and arranged him, and kissed him heartily, she set him on the floor to collect his thoughts. Baby seemed quite used to this mode of proceeding, for he put his thumb in his mouth (as if it were quite a thing of course), and seemed soon absorbed in his own reflections, while the mother seated herself, and taking out a long stocking of mixed blue and white yarn, began to knit with briskness.

'Mary, thee'd better fill the kettle, hadn't thee?' gently suggested the mother.

Mary took the kettle to the well, and soon re-appearing, placed it over the stove, where it was soon purring and steaming, a sort of censer of hospitality and good cheer. The peaches, moreover, in obedience to a few gentle whispers from Rachel, were soon deposited, by the same hand, in a stew-pan over the fire.

Rachel now took down a snowy moulding-board, and, tying on an apron, proceeded quietly to making up some biscuits, first saying to Mary, 'Mary, hadn't thee better tell John to get a chicken ready?' and Mary disappeared accordingly.

'And how is Abigail Peters?' said Rachel, as she went on with her biscuits.

'Oh, she's better,' said Ruth. 'I was in this morning; made the bed, tidied up the house. Leah Hills went in this afternoon, and baked bread and pies enough to last some days; and I engaged to go back to get her up this evening.'

'I will go in to-morrow, and do any cleaning there may be, and look over the mending,' said Rachel.

'Ah! that is well,' said Ruth. 'I've heard,' she added, 'that Hannah Stanwood is sick. John was up there, last night – I must go there to-morrow.'

'John can come in here to his meals, if thee needs to stay all day,' suggested Rachel.

'Thank thee, Rachel; we'll see to-morrow. But here comes Simeon.'

Simeon Halliday, a tall, straight, muscular man, in drab coat and pantaloons, and broad-brimmed hat, now entered.

'How is thee, Ruth?' he said, warmly, as he spread his broad open hand for her little fat palm; 'and how is John?'

'Oh! John is well, and all the rest of our folks,' said Ruth, cheerily.

'Any news, father?' said Rachel, as she was putting her biscuits into the oven.

'Peter Stebbins told me that they should be along to-night, with *friends*,' said Simeon, significantly, as he was washing his hands at a neat sink, in a little back porch.

'Indeed!' said Rachel, looking thoughtfully, and glancing at Eliza.

'Did thee say thy name was Harris?' said Simeon to Eliza, as he re-entered.

Rachel glanced quickly at her husband, as Eliza tremulously answered – 'Yes;' her fears, ever uppermost, suggesting that possibly there might be advertisements out for her.

'Mother!' said Simeon, standing in the porch, and calling Rachel out.

'What does thee want, father?' said Rachel, rubbing her floury hands, as she went into the porch.

'This child's husband is in the settlement, and will be here to-night,' said Simeon.

'Now, thee doesn't say that, father?' said Rachel, all her face radiant with joy.

'It's really true. Peter was down yesterday, with the wagon, to the other stand, and there he found an old woman and two men, and one said his name was George Harris; and, from what he told of his history, I am certain who he is. He is a bright, likely fellow, too.'

'Shall we tell her now?' said Simeon.

'Let's tell Ruth,' said Rachel. 'Here, Ruth! – come here!'

Ruth, what does thee think?' said Rachel. 'Father says Eliza's husband is in the last company, and will be here to-night.'

A burst of joy from the little Quakeress interrupted the speech. She gave such a bound from the floor, as she clapped her little hands, that two stray curls fell from under her Quaker cap, and lay brightly on her white neckerchief.

'Hush thee, dear!' said Rachel gently; 'hush, Ruth! Tell us; shall we tell her now?'

'Now! to be sure, this very minute. Why, now, suppose 'twas my John, how should I feel? Do tell her right off.'

'Thee uses thyself only to learn how to love thy neighbour, Ruth,' said Simeon, looking with a beaming face on Ruth.

'To be sure. Isn't it what we are made for? If I didn't love John and the baby, I should not know how to feel for her. Come, now, do tell her – do!' and she laid her hands persuasively on Rachel's arm. 'Take her into thy bedroom, there, and let me fry the chicken while thee does it.'

Rachel came out into the kitchen, where Eliza was sewing, and opening the door of a small bedroom, said gently, 'Come in here with me, my daughter; I have news to tell thee.'

The blood flushed in Eliza's pale face; she rose, trembling with nervous anxiety, and looked towards her boy.

'No, no,' said little Ruth, darting up, and seizing her hands. 'Never thee fear; it's good news, Eliza – go in, go in!' And she gently pushed her to the door, which closed after her; and then, turning round, she caught little Harry in her arms, and began kissing him.

'Thee'll see thy father, little one. Does thee know it? Thy

father is coming' she said, over and over again, as the boy looked wonderingly at her.

Meanwhile, within the door, another scene was going on. Rachel Halliday drew Eliza towards her, and said, 'The Lord hath had mercy on thee, daughter; thy husband hath escaped from the house of bondage.'

The blood flushed to Eliza's cheek in a sudden glow, and went back to her heart with as sudden a rush. She sat down pale and faint.

'Have courage, child,' said Rachel, laying her hand on her head. 'He is among friends, who will bring him here to-night.'

'To-night!' Eliza repeated: 'To-night!' The words lost all meaning to her; her head was dreamy and confused; all was mist for a moment.

When she awoke, she found herself snugly tucked up on the bed with a blanket over her, and little Ruth rubbing her hands with camphor. She opened her eyes in a state of dreamy, delicious languor, such as one has who has long been bearing a heavy load, and now feels it gone, and would rest. The tension of the nerves, which had never ceased a moment since the first hour of her flight, had given way, and a strange feeling of security and rest came over her; and, as she lay, with her large dark eyes open, she followed, as in a quiet dream, the motions of those about her. She saw the door open into the other room; saw the supper-table, with its snowy cloth; heard the dreamy murmur of the singing tea-kettle; saw Ruth tripping backward and forward, with plates of cake and saucers of preserves, and ever and anon stopping to put a cake into Harry's hand, or pat his head or twine his long curls round her snowy fingers. She saw the ample motherly form of Rachel, as she ever and anon came to the bedside, and smoothed and arranged something about the bed-clothes, and gave a tuck here and there, by way of expressing her good-will; and was conscious of a kind of sunshine beaming down upon her from her large, clear, brown eyes. She saw Ruth's husband come in – saw her fly up to him, and commence whispering very earnestly, ever and anon, with impressive gesture, pointing her little finger toward the room. She saw her with the baby in her arms, sitting down to tea; she saw them all at table, and little Harry in a high chair, under the shadow of Rachel's ample wing; there were low murmurs of talk, gentle tinkling of tea-spoons and musical clatter of cups and saucers, and all mingled in a delightful dream of rest; and Eliza slept as she had not slept before since the fearful midnight hour when she had taken her child and fled through the frosty starlight.

She dreamed of a beautiful country – a land, it seemed to her, of rest – green shores, pleasant islands, and beautifully glittering water; and there, in a house which kind voices told her was a home, she saw her boy playing, a free and happy child. She heard her husband's footsteps; she felt him coming nearer; his arms were around her, his tears falling on her face, and she awoke! It was no dream. The daylight had long faded; her child lay calmly sleeping by her side; a candle was burning dimly on the stand, and her husband was sobbing by her pillow.

The next morning was a cheerful one at the Quaker house. 'Mother' was up betimes, and surrounded by busy girls and boys, whom we had scarce time to introduce to our readers yesterday, and who all moved obediently to Rachel's gentle 'Thee had better,' or more gentle 'Hadn't thee better?' in the work of getting breakfast; for the breakfast in the luxurious valleys of Indiana is a thing complicated and multiform, and, like picking up the rose-leaves and trimming the bushes in Paradise, asking other hands than those of the original mother. While, therefore, John ran to the spring for fresh water, and Simeon the second sifted meal for corn-cakes, and Mary ground coffee, Rachel moved gently and quietly about, making biscuits, cutting up chicken, and diffusing a sort of sunny radiance over the whole proceeding generally. If there was any danger of friction or collision from the ill-regulated zeal of so many young operators, her gentle 'Come, come!' or 'I wouldn't now,' was quite sufficient to allay the difficulty. Bards have written of the cestus of Venus, that turned the heads of all the world in successive generations. We had rather, for our part, have the cestus of Rachel Halliday, that kept heads from being turned, and made everything go on harmoniously. We think it is more suited to our modern days, decidedly.

While all other preparations were going on, Simeon the elder stood in his shirt-sleeves before a little looking-glass in the corner, engaged in the anti-patriarchal operation of shaving.

Everything went on so sociably, so quietly, so harmoniously, in the great kitchen – it seemed so pleasant to every one to do just what they were doing, there was such an atmosphere of mutual confidence and good fellowship everywhere – even the knives and forks had a social clatter as they went on to the table; and the chicken and ham had a cheerful and joyous fizzle in the pan, as if they rather enjoyed being cooked than otherwise; and when George and Eliza and little Harry came out, they met such a hearty, rejoicing welcome, no wonder it seemed to them like a dream.

At last they were all seated at breakfast, while Mary stood at the stove, baking griddle cakes, which, as they gained the true, exact, golden-brown tint of perfection, were transferred quite handily to the table.

Rachel never looked so truly and benignly happy as at the head of her table. There was so much motherliness and fullheartedness even in the way she passed a plate of cakes or poured a cup of coffee, that it seemed to put a spirit into the food and drink she offered.

It was the first time that ever George had sat down on equal terms at any white man's table; and he sat down, at first, with some constraint and awkwardness; but they all exhaled and went off like fog in the genial morning rays of this simple, overflowing kindess.

This, indeed, was a home – *home* – a word that George had never yet known a meaning for; and a belief in God, and trust in His providence, began to encircle his heart, as, with a golden cloud of protection and confidence, dark, misanthropic, pining, atheistic doubts, and fierce despair, melted away before the light of a living Gospel, breathed in living faces, preached by a thousand unconscious acts of love and good-will, which, like the cup of cold water given in the name of a disciple, shall never lose their reward.

'Father, what if thee should get found out again?' said Simeon second, as he buttered his cake.

'I should pay my fine,' said Simeon, quietly.

'But what if they put thee in prison?'

'Couldn't thee and mother manage the farm?' said Simeon, smiling.

'Mother can do almost everything,' said the boy. 'But isn't it a shame to make such laws?'

'Thee mustn't speak evil of thy rulers, Simeon,' said his father, gravely. 'The Lord only gives us our worldly goods that we may do justice and mercy; if our rulers require a price of us for it, we must deliver it up.'

'Well, I hate those old slaveholders!' said the boy, who felt as unchristian as became any modern reformer.

'I am surprised at thee, son,' said Simeon; 'thy mother never taught thee so. I would do even the same for the slaveholder as for the slave, if the Lord brought him to my door in affliction.'

Simeon second blushed scarlet; but his mother only smiled, and said, 'Simeon is my good boy; he will grow older by and by, and then he will be like his father.'

'I hope, my good sir, that you are not exposed to any difficulty on our account?' said George anxiously.

'Fear nothing, George, for therefore are we sent into the world. If we would not meet trouble for a good cause, we were not worthy of our name.'

'But, for *me*,' said George: 'I could not bear it.'

'Fear not, then, friend George; it is not for thee, but for God and man, we do it,' said Simeon. 'And now thou must lie by quietly this day, and to-night, at ten o'clock, Phineas Fletcher will carry thee onward to the next stand – thee and the rest of thy company. The pursuers are hard after thee; we must not delay.'

'If that is the case, why wait till evening?' said George.

'Thou art safe here by daylight, for every one in the settlement is a Friend, and all are watching. It has been found safer to travel by night.'

Chapter 14

EVANGELINE

'A young star! which shone
O'er life – too sweet an image for such glass!
A lovely being, scarcely formed or moulded:
A rose with all its sweetest leaves yet folded.'

THE Mississippi! How, as by an enchanted wand, have its scenes been changed, since Chateaubriand wrote his prose-poetic description of it, as a river of mighty, unbroken solitudes, rolling amid undreamed wonders of vegetable and animal existence.

But, as in an hour, this river of dreams and wild romance has emerged to a reality scarcely less visionary and splendid. What other river of the world bears on its bosom to the ocean the wealth and enterprise of such another country? – a country whose products embrace all between the tropics and the poles! Those turbid waters, hurrying, foaming, tearing along, an apt resemblance of that headlong tide of business which is poured along its wave by a race more vehement and energetic than any the old world ever saw. Ah! would that they did not also bear along a more fearful freight, the tears of the oppressed, the sighs of the helpless, the bitter prayers of poor, ignorant hearts to an unknown God – unknown, unseen, and silent, but who will yet 'come out of his place to save all the poor of the earth!'

The slanting light of the setting sun quivers on the sea-like expanse of the river; the shivery canes, and the tall, dark cypress, hung with wreaths of dark, funereal moss, glow in the golden ray, as the heavily-laden steamboat marches onward.

Piled with cotton-bales from many a plantation, up over deck and sides, till she seems in the distance a square, massive block of grey, she moves heavily onward to the nearing mart. We must look some time among its crowded decks before we shall find again our humble friend Tom. High on the upper deck, in a little nook among the everywhere predominant cotton bales, at last we may find him.

Partly from confidence inspired by Mr Shelby's representations, and partly from the remarkably inoffensive and quiet character of the man, Tom had insensibly won his way far into the confidence even of such a man as Haley.

At first he had watched him narrowly through the day, and never allowed him to sleep at night unfettered; but the uncomplaining patience and apparent contentment of Tom's manner led him gradually to discontinue these restraints, and for some time Tom had enjoyed a sort of parole of honour, being permitted to come and go freely where he pleased on the boat.

Ever quiet and obliging, and more than ready to lend a hand in every emergency which occurred among the workmen below, he had won the good opinion of all the hands, and spent many hours in helping them with as hearty a good-will as ever he worked on a Kentucky farm.

When there seemed to be nothing for him to do, he would climb to a nook among the cotton-bales of the upper deck, and busy himself in studying over his Bible – and it is there we see him now.

For a hundred or more miles above New Orleans, the river is higher than the surrounding country, and rolls its tremendous volume between massive levees twenty feet in height. The traveller from the deck of the steamer, as from some floating castle top, overlooks the whole country for miles and miles around. Tom, therefore, had spread out full before him, in plantation after plantation, a map of the life to which he was approaching.

He saw the distant slaves at their toil; he saw afar their villages of huts, gleaming out in long rows on many a plantation, distant from the stately mansions and pleasure-grounds of the master; and as the moving picture passed on, his poor foolish heart would be turning backward to the Kentucky farm, with its old shadowy beeches – to the master's house, with its wide, cool halls, and near by, the little cabin, overgrown with the multiflora and bignonia. There he seemed to see familiar faces of comrades, who had grown up with him from infancy; he saw his busy wife, bustling in her preparations for his evening meals; he heard the merry laugh of his boys at their play, and the chirrup of the baby at his knee, and then, with a start, all faded, and he saw again the canebrakes and cypresses and gliding plantations, and heard again the creaking and groaning of the machinery, all telling him too plainly that all that phase of life had gone by for ever.

In such a case you write to your wife, and send messages to your children; but Tom could not write – the mail for him had no existence, and the gulf of separation was unbridged by even a friendly word or signal.

Is it strange, then, that some tears fall on the pages of his Bible, as he lays it on the cotton-bale, and with patient finger, threading his slow way from word to word, traces out its promises? Having learned late in life, Tom was but a slow reader, and passed on laboriously from verse to verse. Fortunate for him was it that the book he was intent on was one which slow reading cannot injure – nay, one whose words, like ingots of gold, seem often to need to be weighed separately, that the mind may take in their priceless value. Let us follow him a moment, as, pointing to each word, and pronouncing each half aloud, he reads –

'Let – not – your – heart – be – troubled. In – my – Father's – house – are – many – mansions. I – go – to – prepare – a – place – for – you.'

Cicero, when he buried his darling and only daughter, had a heart as full of honest grief as poor Tom's – perhaps no fuller, for both were only men; but Cicero could pause over no such sublime words of hope, and look to no such future reunion; and if he *had* seen them, ten to one he would not have believed – he must fill his head first with a thousand questions of authenticity of manuscript, and correctness of translation. But to poor Tom, there it lay, just what he needed, so evidently true and divine that the possibility of a question never entered his simple head. It must be true; for if not true, how could he live?

As for Tom's Bible, though it had no annotations and helps in margin from learned commentators, still it had been embellished with certain way-marks and guide-boards of Tom's own invention, and which helped him more than the most learned expositions could have done. It had been his custom to get the Bible read to him by his master's children, in particular by

young Master George; and as they read he would designate, by
bold strong marks and dashes, with pen and ink, the passages
which more particularly gratified his ear or affected his heart.
His Bible was thus marked through from one end to the other,
with a variety of styles and designations; so he could in a
moment seize upon his favourite passages, without the labour
of spelling out what lay between them; and while it lay there
before him, every passage breathing of some old home scene,
and recalling some past enjoyment, his Bible seemed to him all
of this life that remained, as well as the promise of a future one.

Among the passengers on the boat was a young gentleman of
fortune and family, resident in New Orleans, who bore the
name of St Clare. He had with him a daughter between five and
six years of age, together with a lady, who seemed to claim
relationship to both, and to have the little one especially under
her charge.

Tom had often caught glimpses of this little girl, for she was
one of those busy, tripping creatures that can be no more
contained in one place than a sunbeam or a summer breeze; nor
was she one that, once seen, could be easily forgotten.

Her form was the perfection of childish beauty, without its
usual chubbiness and squareness of outline. There was about it
an undulating and aërial grace, such as one might dream of for
some mythic and allegorical being. Her face was remarkable,
less for its perfect beauty of feature than for a singular and
dreamy earnestness of expression, which made the ideal start
when they looked at her, and by which the dullest and most
literal were impressed, without exactly knowing why. The shape
of her head and the turn of her neck and bust was peculiarly
noble; and the long, golden-brown hair that floated like a cloud
around it, the deep, spiritual gravity of her violet blue eyes,
shaded by heavy fringes of golden brown – all marked her out
from other children, and made every one turn and look after
her, as she glided hither and thither on the boat. Nevertheless,
the little one was not what you would have called either a grave
child or a sad one. On the contrary, an airy and innocent
playfulness seemed to flicker like the shadow of summer leaves
over her childish face and around her buoyant figure. She was
always in motion, always with a half smile on her rosy mouth,
flying hither and thither, with an undulating and cloud-like tread,

singing to herself as she moved, as in a happy dream. Her father
and female guardian were incessantly busy in pursuit of her,
but, when caught, she melted from them again like a summer
cloud: and as no word of chiding or reproof ever fell on her ear
for whatever she chose to do, she pursued her own way all over
the boat. Always dressed in white, she seemed to move like a
shadow through all sorts of places, without contracting spot or
stain; and there was not a corner or nook, above or below,
where those fairy footsteps had not glided, and that visionary
golden head, with its deep blue eyes, fleeted along.

The fireman, as he looked up from his sweaty toil, sometimes
found those eyes looking wonderingly into the raging depths of
the furnace, and fearfully and pityingly at him, as if she thought
him in some dreadful danger. Anon the steersman at the wheel
paused and smiled, as the picture-like head gleamed through the
window of the round-house, and in a moment was gone again.
A thousand times a day rough voices blessed her, and smiles of
unwanted softness stole over hard faces, as she passed; and
when she tripped fearlessly over dangerous places, rough, sooty
hands were stretched involuntarily out to save her, and smooth
her path.

Tom, who had the soft impressible nature of his kindly race,
ever yearning toward the simple and child-like, watched the
little creature with daily increasing interest. To him she seemed
something almost divine; and whenever her golden head and
deep blue eyes peered out upon him from behind some dusky
cotton-bale, or looked down upon him over some ridge of
packages, he half believed that he saw one of the angels stepped
out of his New Testament.

Often and often she walked mournfully round the place where
Haley's gang of men and women sat in their chains. She would
glide in among them, and look at them with an air of perplexed
and sorrowful earnestness; and sometimes she would lift their
chains with her slender hands, and then sigh woefully, as she
glided away. Several times she appeared suddenly among them,
with her hands full of candy, nuts, and oranges, which she
would distribute joyfully to them, and then be gone again.

Tom watched the little lady a great deal, before he ventured
on any overtures towards acquaintanceship. He knew an abundance of simple acts to propitiate and invite the approaches of

the little people, and he resolved to play his part right skilfully. He could cut cunning little baskets out of cherry-stones, could make grotesque faces on hickory nuts, or odd-jumping figures out of elder-pith, and he was a very Pan in the manufacture of whistles of all sizes and sorts. His pockets were full of miscellaneous articles of attraction, which he had hoarded in days of old for his master's children, and which he now produced, with commendable prudence and economy, one by one, as overtures for acquaintance and friendship.

The little one was shy, for all her busy interest in everything going on, and it was not easy to tame her. For a while, she would perch like a canary-bird on some box or package near Tom, while busy in the little arts aforenamed, and take from him, with a kind of grave bashfulness, the little articles he offered. But at last they got on quite confidential terms.

'What's little missy's name?' said Tom at last, when he thought matters were ripe to push such an inquiry.

'Evangeline St Clare,' said the little one, 'though papa and everybody else call me Eva. Now, what's your name?'

'My name's Tom; the little chil'en used to call me Uncle Tom, way back thar in Kentuck.'

'Then I mean to call you Uncle Tom, because, you see, I like you,' said Eva. 'So, Uncle Tom, where are you going?'

'I don't know, Miss Eva.'

'Don't know?' said Eva.

'No. I am going to be sold to somebody. I don't know who.'

'My papa can buy you,' said Eva, quickly; 'and if he buys you, you will have good times. I mean to ask him to, this very day.'

'Thank you, my little lady,' said Tom.

The boat here stopped at a small landing to take in wood, and Eva, hearing her father's voice, bounded nimbly away. Tom rose up, and went forward to offer his service in wooding, and soon was busy among the hands.

Eva and her father were standing together by the railings to see the boat start from the landing-place, the wheel had made two or three revolutions in the water, when, by some sudden movement, the little one suddenly lost her balance, and fell sheer over the side of the boat into the water. Her father, scarce knowing what he did, was plunging in after her, but was held back by some behind him, who saw that more efficient aid had followed his child.

Tom was standing just under her, on the lower deck, as she fell. He saw her strike the water and sink, and was after her in a moment. A broad-chested, strong-armed fellow, it was nothing for him to keep afloat in the water, till, in a moment or two, the child rose to the surface, and he caught her in his arms, and, swimming with her to the boat-side, handed her up, all dripping, to the grasp of hundreds of hands, which, as if they had all belonged to one man, were stretched eagerly out to receive her. A few moments more, and her father bore her, dripping and senseless, to the ladies' cabin, where, as is usual in cases of the kind, there ensued a very well-meaning and kind-hearted strife among the female occupants generally, as to who should do the most things to make a disturbance, and to hinder her recovery in every way possible.

It was a sultry close day, the next day, as the steamer drew near to New Orleans. A general bustle of expectation and preparation was spread through the boat; in the cabin, one and another were gathering their things together and arranging them preparatory to going ashore. The steward and chamber-maid, and all, were busily engaged in cleaning, furbishing, and arranging the splendid boat, preparatory to a grand *entrée*.

On the lower deck sat our friend Tom, with his arms folded, and anxiously, from time to time, turning his eyes towards a group on the other side of the boat.

There stood the fair Evangeline, a little paler than the day before, but otherwise exhibiting no traces of the accident which had befallen her. A graceful, elegantly-formed young man, stood by her, carelessly leaning one elbow on a bale of cotton, while a large pocket-book lay open before him. It was quite evident, at a glance, that the gentleman was Eva's father. There was the same noble cast of head, the same large blue eyes, the same golden-brown hair; yet the expression was wholly different. In the large, clear blue eyes, though in form and colour exactly similar, there was wanting that misty, dreamy depth of expression; all was clear, bold, and bright, but with a light wholly of this world: the beautifully-cut mouth had a proud and somewhat sarcastic expression, while an air of free-and-easy superiority sat not ungracefully in every turn and movement of his fine form. He was listening with a good-humoured, negligent air, half comic, half contemptuous, to Haley, who was very volubly expatiating on the quality of the article for which they were bargaining.

'All the moral and Christian virtues bound in black morocco, complete !' he said, when Haley had finished. 'Well, now, my good fellow, what's the damage ? as they say in Kentucky ; in short what's to be paid out for this business ? How much are you going to cheat me, now ? Out with it !'

'Wal,' said Haley, 'if I should say thirteen hundred dollars far that ar fellow, I shouldn't but just save myself — I shouldn't, now, re'ly.'

'Poor fellow !' said the young man, fixing his keen, mocking blue eye on him ; 'but I suppose you would let me have him for that, out of a particular regard for me !'

'Well, the young lady here seems to be sot on him, and nat'lly enough.'

'Oh, certainly, there's a call on your benevolence, my friend. Now, as a matter of Christian charity, how cheap could you afford to let him go, to oblige a young lady that's particular sot on him ?'

'Wal, now, just think on't,' said the trader ; 'just look at them limbs — broad-chested, strong as a horse. Look at his head ; them high forrads al'ays shows calculatin' niggers, that'll do any kind o' thing. I've marked that ar. Now, a nigger of that ar heft and build is worth considerable, just, as you may say, for his body, supposin' he's stupid ; but come to put in his calculatin' faculties, and them which I can show he has oncommon, why, of course, it makes him come higher. Why, that ar fellow managed his master's whole farm. He has a strornary talent for business.'

'Bad, bad, very bad ; knows altogether too much !' said the young man, with the same mocking smile playing about his mouth. 'Never will do in the world. Your smart fellows are always running off, stealing horses, and raising the devil generally. I think you'll have to take off a couple of hundred for his smartness.'

'Wal, there might be something in that ar, if it warn't for his character ; but I can show recommends from his master and others, to prove he is one of your real pious — the most humble, prayin', pious critter ye ever did see. Why, he's been called a preacher in them parts he came from.'

'And I might use him for a family chaplain, possibly,' added the young man, dryly. 'That's quite an idea. Religion is a remarkably scarce article at our house.'

'You're joking, now.'

'How do you know I am? Didn't you just warrant him for a preacher? Has he been examined by any synod or council? Come, hand over your papers.'

If the trader had not been sure, by a certain good-humoured twinkle in the large blue eye, that all this banter was sure, in the long run, to turn out a cash concern, he might have been somewhat out of patience; as it was, he laid down a greasy pocket-book on the cotton bales, and began anxiously studying over certain papers in it, the young man standing by the while, looking down on him with an air of careless, easy drollery.

'Papa, do buy him! it's no matter what you pay,' whispered Eva softly, getting up on a package, and putting her arm around her father's neck. 'You have money enough, I know. I want him.'

'What for, pussy? Are you going to use him for a rattle-box, or a rocking-horse, or what?'

'I want to make him happy.'

'An original reason, certainly.'

Here the trader handed up a certificate, signed by Mr Shelby, which the young man took with the tips of his long fingers, and glanced over carelessly.

'A gentlemanly hand,' he said, 'and well spelt, too. Well, now, but I'm not sure, after all, about this religion,' said he, the old wicked expression returning to his eye; 'the country is almost ruined with pious white people; such pious politicians as we have just before elections – such pious goings on in all departments of church and state, that a fellow does not know who'll cheat him next. I don't know, either, about religion's being up in the market, just now. I have not looked in the papers lately, to see how it sells. How many hundred dollars, now, do you put on for this religion?'

'You like to be a jokin', now,' said the trader; 'but then there's *sense* under all that ar. I know there's differences in religion. Some kinds is mis'rable: there's your meetin' pious;

there's your singin', roarin' pious; them ar an't no account, in black or white: but these rayly is; and I've seen it in niggers as often as any, your rail softly, quiet, stiddy, honest pious, that the hull world couldn't tempt 'em to do nothing that they thinks is wrong; and ye see in this letter what Tom's old master says about him.'

'Now,' said the young man, stooping gravely over his book of bills, 'if you can assure me that I really can buy *this* kind of pious, and that it will be set down to my account in the book up above, as something belonging to me, I wouldn't care if I did go a little extra for it. How d'ye say?'

'Wal, railly, I can't do that,' said the trader. 'I'm a thinking that every man'll have to hand on his own hook, in them ar quarters.'

'Rather hard on a fellow that pays extra on religion, and can't trade with it in the State where he wants it most, an't it, now?' said the young man, who had been making out a roll of bills while he was speaking. 'There, count your money, old boy!' he added, as he handed the roll to the trader.

'All right,' said Haley, his face beaming with delight; and pulling out an old inkhorn, he proceeded to fill out a bill of sale, which, in a few moments, he handed to the young man.

'I wonder, now, if I was divided up and inventoried,' said the latter, as he ran over the paper, 'how much I might bring. Say so much for the shape of my head, so much for a high forehead, so much for arms, and hands, and legs, and then so much for education, learning, talent, honesty, religion! Bless me! there would be small charge on that last, I'm thinking. But come, Eva,' he said; and taking the hand of his daughter, he stepped across the boat, and carelessly putting the tip of his finger under Tom's chin, said, good-humouredly, 'Look up, Tom, and see how you like your new master.'

Tom looked up. It was not in nature to look into that gay, young, handsome face, without a feeling of pleasure; and Tom felt the tears start in his eyes as he said, heartily, 'God bless you, mas'r!'

'Well, I hope he will. What's your name? Tom? Quite as likely to do it for your asking as mine, from all accounts. Can you drive horses, Tom?'

'I've been al'ays used to horses,' said Tom. 'Mas'r Shelby raised heaps on 'em.'

'Well, I think I shall put you in coachy, on condition that you won't be drunk more than once a week, unless in cases of emergency, Tom.'

Tom looked surprised and rather hurt, and said, 'I never drink, mas'r.'

'I've heard that story before, Tom; but then we'll see. It will be a special accommodation to all concerned if you don't. Never mind, my boy,' he added, good-humouredly, seeing Tom still look grave; 'I don't doubt you mean to do well.'

'I sartin do, mas'r,' said Tom.

'And you shall have good times,' said Eva. 'Papa is very good to everybody, only he always will laugh at them.'

'Papa is much obliged to you for his recommendation,' said St Clare, laughing, as he turned on his heel, and walked away.

Chapter 15

OF TOM'S NEW MASTER, AND VARIOUS OTHER MATTERS

SINCE the thread of our humble hero's life has now become interwoven with that of higher ones, it is necessary to give some brief introduction to them.

Augustine St Clare was the son of a wealthy planter of Louisiana. The family had its origin in Canada. Of two brothers, very similar in temperament and character, one had settled on a flourishing farm in Vermont, and the other became an opulent planter in Louisiana. The mother of Augustine was a Huguenot French lady, whose family had emigrated to Louisiana during the days of its early settlement. Augustine and another brother were the only children of their parents. Having inherited from his mother an exceeding delicacy of constitution, he was, at the instance of physicians, during many years of his boyhood, sent to the care of his uncle in Vermont, in order that his constitution might be strengthened by the cold of a more bracing climate.

In childhood he was remarkable for an extreme and marked sensitiveness of character, more akin to the softness of woman than the ordinary hardness of his own sex. Time, however, overgrew this softness with the rough bark of manhood, and but few knew how living and fresh it still lay at the core. His talents were of the very first order, although his mind showed a preference always for the ideal and the aesthetic; and there was about him that repugnance to the actual business of life which is the common result of this balance of the faculties. Soon after the completion of his college course, his whole nature was kindled into one intense and passionate effervescence of romantic passion. His hour came – the hour that comes only once; his star rose in the horizon – that star that rises so often in vain, to be remembered only as a thing of dreams; and it rose for him in vain. To drop the figure, he saw and won the love of a high-minded and beautiful woman, in one of the northern states, and they were affianced. He returned south to make arrangements for their marriage, when, most unexpectedly, his letters were returned to him by mail, with a short note from her guardian, stating to him that ere this reached him the lady would be the wife of another. Stung to madness, he vainly hoped, as many another has done, to fling the whole thing from his heart by one desperate effort. Too proud to supplicate or seek explanation, he threw himself at once into a whirl of fashionable society, and in a fortnight from the time of the fatal letter was the accepted lover of the reigning belle of the season; and as soon as arrangements could be made, he became the husband of a fine figure, a pair of bright, dark eyes, and a hundred thousand dollars; and, of course, everbody thought him a happy fellow.

The married couple were enjoying their honeymoon, and entertaining a brilliant circle of friends in their splendid villa near Lake Pontchartrain, when one day a letter was brought to him in *that* well-remembered writing. It was handed to him while he was in full tide of gay and successful conversation, in a whole room-full of company. He turned deadly pale when he saw the writing, but still preserved his composure, and finished the playful warfare of badinage which he was at the moment carrying on with a lady opposite; and, a short time after, was missed from the circle. In his room, alone, he opened and read the letter, now worse than idle and useless to be read. It was from her, giving a long account of a persecution to which she had been exposed by her guardian's family, to lead her to unite herself with their son; and she related how, for a long time, his letters had ceased to arrive; how she had written time and again, till she became weary and doubtful; how her health had failed under her anxieties, and how, at last, she had discovered the whole fraud which had been practised on them both. The letter ended with expressions of hope and thankfulness, and professions of undying affection, which were more bitter than death to the unhappy young man. He wrote to her immediately :

'I have received yours – but too late. I believed all I heard. I was desperate. *I am married*, and all is over. Only forget – it is all that remains for either of us.'

And thus ended the whole romance and ideal of life for Augustine St Clare; but the *real* remained – the *real*, like the flat, bare, oozy tide-mud, when the blue sparkling wave, with all its company of gliding boats and white-winged ships, its music of oars and chiming water, has gone down, and there it lies, flat, slimy, bare – exceedingly real.

Of course, in a novel, people's hearts break, and they die, and that is the end of it; and in a story this is very convenient. But in real life we do not die when all that makes life bright dies to us. There is a most busy and important round of eating, drinking, dressing, walking, visiting, buying, selling, talking, reading, and all that makes up what is commonly called *living*, yet to be gone through; and this yet remained to Augustine. Had his wife been a whole woman, she might yet have done something – as woman can – to mend the broken threads of life, and weave again into a tissue of brightness. But Marie St Clare could not even see that they had been broken. As before stated, she consisted of a fine figure, a pair of splendid eyes, and a hundred thousand dollars; and none of these items were precisely the ones to minister to a mind diseased.

When Augustine, pale as death, was found lying on the sofa, and pleaded sudden sick-headache as the cause of his distress, she recommended to him to smell of hartshorn; and when the paleness and headache came on week after week, she only said that she never thought Mr St Clare was sickly; but it seemed he was very liable to sick-headaches, and that it was a very unfortunate thing for her, because he didn't enjoy going into company with her, and it seemed odd to go so much alone, when they were just married. Augustine was glad in his heart that he had married so undiscerning a woman; but as the gloss and civilities of the honeymoon wore away he discovered that a beautiful young woman, who has lived all her life to be caressed and waited on, might prove quite a hard mistress in domestic life. Marie never had possessd much capability of affection, or much sensibility; and the little that she had had been merged into a most intense and unconscious selfishness; a selfishness the more hopeless from its quiet obtuseness, its utter ignorance of any claims but her own. From her infancy she had been surrounded with servants, who lived only to study her caprices; the idea that they had either feelings or rights had never dawned upon her, even in distant perspective. Her father, whose only child she had been, had never denied her anything that lay within the compass of human possibility; and when she entered life, beautiful, accomplishd, and an heiress, she had, of course, all the eligibles and non-eligibles of the other sex sighing at her feet, and she had no doubt that Augustine was a most fortunate man in having obtained her. It is a great mistake to suppose that a woman with no heart will be an easy creditor in the exchange of affection. There is not on earth a more merciless exactor of love from others than a thoroughly selfish woman; and the more unlovely she grows, the more jealously and scrupulously she exacts love, to the uttermost farthing. When, therefore, St Clare began to drop off those gallantries and small attentions which flowed at first through the habitude of courtship, he found his sultana no way ready to resign her slave; there were abundance of tears, poutings, and small tempests; there were discontents, pinings, upbraidings. St Clare was good-natured and self-indulgent, and sought to buy off with presents and flatteries; and when Marie became mother to a beautiful daughter, he really felt awakened for a time to something like tenderness.

St Clare's mother had been a woman of uncommon elevation and purity of character, and he gave to this child his mother's name, fondly fancying that she would prove a reproduction of her image. The thing had been remarked with petulant jealousy by his wife, and she regarded her husband's absorbing devotion to the child with suspicion and dislike; all that was given to her seemed so much taken from herself. From the time of the birth of this child her health gradually sunk. A life of constant inaction, bodily and mental – the friction of ceaseless *ennui* and discontent, united to the ordinary weakness which attended the period of maternity – in course of a few years changed the blooming young belle into a yellow, faded, sickly woman, whose time was divided among a variety of fanciful diseases, and who considered herself, in every sense, the most ill-used and suffering person in existence.

There was no end of her various complaints; but her principal forte appeared to lie in sick-headache, which sometimes would confine her to her room three days out of six. As, of course, all family arrangements fell into the hands of servants, St Clare found his *ménage* anything but comfortable. His only daughter was exceedingly delicate, and he feared that, with no one to look after her and attend to her, her health and life might yet fall a sacrifice to her mother's inefficiency. He had taken her with him on a tour to Vermont, and had persuaded his cousin, Miss Ophelia St Clare, to return with him to his southern residence; and they are now returning on this boat, where we have introduced them to our readers.

And now, while the distant domes and spires of New Orleans rise to our view, there is yet time for an introduction to Miss Ophelia.

Whoever has travelled in the New England States will remember, in some cool village, the large farm-house, with its clean-swept grassy yard, shaded by the dense and massive foliage of the sugar-maple; and remember the air of order and stillness, of perpetuity and unchanging repose, that seemed to breathe over the whole place. Nothing lost, or out of order, not a picket loose in the fence, not a particle of litter in the turfy yard, with its clumps of lilac-bushes growing up under the windows. Within, he will remember wide, clean rooms, where nothing ever seems to be doing or going to be done, where everything is once and for ever rigidly in place, and where all household arrangements move with the punctual exactness of the old clock in the corner. In the family 'keeping-room,' as it is termed, he will remember the staid, respectable old book-case, with its glass doors, where Rollin's *History*, Milton's *Paradise Lost*, Bunyan's *Pilgrim's*

Progress, and Scott's *Family Bible*, stand side by side in decorous order, with multitudes of other books, equally solemn and respectable. There are no servants in the house, but the lady in the snowy cap, with the spectacles, who sits sewing every afternoon among her daughters, as if nothing ever had been done, or were to be done – she and her girls, in some long-forgotten forepart of the day, '*did up the work*,' and for the rest of the time, probably at all hours when you would see them, it is '*done up*.' The old kitchen-floor never seems stained or spotted; the tables, the chairs, and the various cooking utensils, never seem deranged or disordered: though three and sometimes four meals a day are got there, though the family washing and ironing is there performed, and though pounds of butter and cheese are in some silent and mysterious manner there brought into existence.

On such a farm, in such a house and family, Miss Ophelia had spent a quiet existence of some forty-five years, when her cousin invited her to visit his southern mansion. The eldest of a large family, she was still considered by her father and mother as one of 'the children,' and the proposal that she should go to *Orleans* was a most momentous one to the family circle. The old grey-headed father took down Morse's *Atlas* out of the bookcase, and looked out the exact latitude and longitude; and read Flint's *Travels in the South and West*, to make up his own mind as to the nature of the country.

The good mother inquired, anxiously, 'if Orleans wasn't an awful wicked place;' saying, 'that it seemed to her most equal to going to the Sandwich Islands, or any where among the heathen.'

It was known at the minister's, and at the doctor's, and at Miss Peabody's milliner's shop, that Ophelia St Clare was 'talking about going away down to Orleans with her cousin; and, of course, the whole village could do no less than help this very important process of *talking about* the matter. The minister, who inclined strongly to Abolitionist views, was quite doubtful whether such a step might not tend somewhat to encourage the southerners in holding on to their slaves; while the doctor, who was a stanch Colonisationist, inclined to the opinion that Miss Ophelia ought to go, to show the Orleans people that we don't think hardly of them, after all. He was of opinion, in fact, that southern people needed encouraging.

When, however, the fact that she had resolved to go was fully before the public mind, she was solemnly invited out to tea by all her friends and neighbours for the space of a fortnight, and her prospects and plans duly canvassed and inquired into. Miss Mosely, who came into the house to help to do the dressmaking, acquired daily accessions of importance from the developments with regard to Miss Ophelia's wardrobe which she had been enabled to make. It was credibly ascertained that Squire Sinclare, as his name was commonly contracted in the neighbourhood, had counted out fifty dollars, and given them to Miss Ophelia, and told her to buy any clothes she thought best; and that two new silk dresses, and a bonnet, had been sent for from Boston. As to the propriety of this extraordinary outlay, the public mind was divided; some affirming that it was well enough, all things considered, for once in one's life, and others stoutly affirming that the money had better have been sent to the missionaries; but all parties agreed that there had been no such parasol seen in those parts as had been sent on from New York, and that she had one silk dress that might fairly be trusted to stand alone, whatever might be said of its mistress. There were credible rumours, also, of a hemstitched pocket-handkerchief; and report even went so far as to state that Miss Ophelia had one pocket-handkerchief with lace all around it – it was even added that it was worked in the corners; but this latter point was never satisfactorily ascertained, and remains, in fact, unsettled to this day.

Miss Ophelia, as you now behold her, stands before you, in a very shining brown linen travelling-dress, tall, square-formed, and angular. Her face was thin, and rather sharp in its outlines; the lips compressed, like those of a person who is in the habit of making up her mind definitely on all subjects; while the keen, dark eyes had a peculiarly searching, advised movement, and travelled over everything, as if they were looking for something to take care of.

All her movements were sharp, decided, and energetic; and, though she was never much of a talker, her words were remarkably direct and to the purpose when she did speak.

In her habits, she was a living impersonation of order, method, and exactness. In punctuality, she was as inevitable as a clock, and as inexorable as a railroad engine; and she held in most decided contempt and abomination anything of a contrary character.

The great sin of sins, in her eyes – the sum of all evils – was expressed by one very common and important word in her vocabulary – 'shiftlessness.' Her finale and ultimatum of contempt consisted in a very emphatic pronunciation of the word 'shiftless;' and by this she characterised all modes of procedure which had not a direct and inevitable relation to accomplishment of some purpose then definitely had in mind. People who did nothing, or who did not know exactly what they were going to do, or who did not take the most direct way to accomplish what they set their hands to, were objects of her entire contempt; a contempt shown less frequently by anything she said than by a kind of stony grimness, as if she scorned to say anything about the matter.

As to mental cultivation, she had a clear, strong, active mind, was well and thoroughly read in history and the older English classics, and thought with great strength within certain narrow limits. Her theological tenets were all made up, labelled in the most positive and distinct forms and put by, like the bundles in her patch trunk; there were just so many of them, and there were never to be any more. So, also, were her ideas with regard to most matters of practical life – such as housekeeping in all its branches, and the various political relations of her native village. And, underlaying all, deeper than anything else, higher and broader, lay the strongest principle of her being – conscientiousness. Nowhere is conscience so dominant and all-absorbing as with New England women. It is the granite formation, which lies deepest, and rises out, even to the tops of the highest mountains.

Miss Ophelia was the absolute bond-slave of the 'ought.' Once make her certain that the 'path of duty,' as she commonly phrased it, lay in any given direction, and fire and water could not keep her from it. She would walk straight down into a well, or up to a loaded cannon's mouth, if she were only quite sure that there the path lay. Her standard of right was so high, so all-embracing, so minute, and making so few concessions to human frailty, that though she strove with heroic ardour to reach it, she never actually did so, and of course was burdened with a constant and often harassing sense of deficiency. This gave a severe and somewhat gloomy cast to her religious character.

But how in the world can Miss Ophelia get along with Augustine St Clare – gay, easy, unpunctual, unpractical, sceptical, – in short, walking with impudent and nonchalant freedom over every one of her most cherished habits and opinions?

To tell the truth, then, Miss Ophelia loved him. When a boy, it had been hers to teach him his catechism, mend his clothes, comb his hair, and bring him up generally in the way he should go; and her heart having a warm side to it, Augustine had, as he usually did with most people, monopolised a large share of it for himself, and therefore it was that he succeeded very easily in persuading her that the 'path of duty' lay in the direction of New Orleans, and that she must go with him to take care of Eva, and keep everything from going to wreck and ruin during the frequent illnesses of his wife. The idea of a house without anybody to take care of it went to her heart; then she loved the lovely little girl, as few could help doing; and though she regarded Augustine as very much of a heathen, yet she loved him, laughed at his jokes, and forbore with his failings, to an extent which those who knew him thought perfectly incredible. But what more or other is to be known of Miss Ophelia, our reader must discover by a personal acquaintance.

There she is, sitting now in her state room, surrounded by a mixed multitude of little and big carpet-bags, boxes, baskets, each containing some separate responsibility which she is tying, binding up, packing or fastening, with a face of great earnestness.

'Now, Eva, have you kept count of your things? Of course you haven't – children never do: there's the spotted carpet-bag and the little blue band-box with your best bonnet – that's two; then the India-rubber satchel is three; and my tape and needle-box is four; and my band-box, five; and my collar-box, six; and that little hair trunk, seven. What have you done with your sunshade? Give it to me, and let me put a paper round it, and tie it to my umbrella with my shade: there now.'

'Why, aunty, we are only going up home – what is the use?'

'To keep it nice, child; people must take care of their things if they ever mean to have anything. And now, Eva, is your thimble put up?'

'Really, aunty, I don't know.'

'Well, never mind; I'll look your box over. – Thimble, wax, two spoons, scissors, knife, tape-needle; all right – put it in here. What did you ever do, child, when you were coming on with only your papa? I should have thought you'd lost everything you had.'

'Well, aunty, I did lose a great many; and then, when we stopped anywhere, papa would buy some more of whatever it was.'

'Mercy on us, child, what a way!'

'It was a very easy way, aunty,' said Eva.

'It's a dreadful shiftless one,' said aunty.

'Why, aunty, what'll you do now?' said Eva. 'That trunk is too full to be shut down.'

'It *must* shut down,' said aunty, with the air of a general, as she squeezed the things in, and sprung upon the lid; still a little gap remained about the mouth of the trunk.

'Get up here, Eva!' said Miss Ophelia, courageously; 'what has been done can be done again. This trunk has *got to be* shut and locked, – there are no two ways about it.'

And the trunk, intimidated, doubtless, by this resolute statement, gave in. The hasp snapped sharply in its hole, and Miss Ophelia turned the key, and pocketed it in triumph.

'Now we're ready. Where's your papa? I think it time this baggage was set out. Do look out, Eva, and see if you see your papa.'

'Oh, yes, he's down the other end of the gentlemen's cabin, eating an orange.'

'He can't know how near we are coming,' said aunty; 'hadn't you better run and speak to him?'

'Papa never is in a hurry about anything,' said Eva, 'and we haven't come to the landing. Do step on the guards, aunty. Look! there's our house, up that street!'

The boat now began, with heavy groans, like some vast, tired monster, to prepare to push up among the multiplied steamers at the levee. Eva joyously pointed out the various spires, domes, and way-marks, by which she recognised her native city.

'Yes, yes, dear; very fine,' said Miss Ophelia. 'But mercy on us! the boat has stopped! where is your father?'

And now ensued the usual turmoil of landing – waiters

running twenty ways at once – men tugging trunks, carpet-bags, boxes – women anxiously calling to their children, and every-body crowding in a dense mass to the plank towards the landing.

Miss Ophelia seated herself resolutely on the lately van-quished trunk, and marshalling all her goods and chattels in fine military order, seemed resolved to defend them to the last.

'Shall I take your trunk, ma'am?' 'Shall I take your baggage?' 'Let me 'tend to your baggage, missis.' 'Shan't I carry out these yer, missis?' rained down upon her unheeded. She sat with grim determination, upright as a darning-needle stuck in a board, holding on to her bundle of umbrella and parasols, and replying with a determination that was enough to strike dismay even into a hackman, wondering to Eva, in each interval, 'what upon earth her papa could be thinking of; he couldn't have fallen over, now – but something must have happened;' and just as she had begun to work herself into a real distress, he came up with his usually careless motion, and giving Eva a quarter of the orange he was eating, said –

'Well, Cousin Vermont, I suppose you are all ready?'

'I've been ready, waiting, nearly an hour,' said Miss Ophelia; 'I began to be really concerned about you.'

'That's a clever fellow, now,' said he. 'Well, the carriage is waiting, and the crowd are now off, so that one can walk out in a decent and Christian manner, and not be pushed and shoved. Here,' he added to a driver who stood behind him, 'take these things.'

'I'll go and see to his putting them in,' said Miss Ophelia.

'Oh, pshaw! cousin; what's the use?' said St Clare.

'Well, at any rate, I'll carry this, and this, and this,' said Miss Ophelia, singling out three boxes and a small carpet-bag.

'My dear Miss Vermont, positively you mustn't come the Green Mountains over us that way. You must adopt at least a piece of southern principle, and not walk out under all that load. They'll take you for a waiting-maid; give them to this fellow; he'll put them down as if they were eggs, now.'

Miss Ophelia looked despairingly as her cousin took all her treasures from her, and rejoiced to find herself once more in a carriage with them in a state of preservation.

'Where's Tom?' said Eva.

'Oh, he's on the outside, pussy. I'm going to take Tom up to mother for a peace-offering, to make up for that drunken fellow that upset the carriage.'

'Oh, Tom will make a splendid driver, I know,' said Eva; 'he'll never get drunk.'

The carriage stopped in front of an ancient mansion, built in the odd mixture of Spanish and French style, of which there are specimens in some parts of New Orleans. It was built in the Moorish fashion – a square building enclosing a court-yard, into which the carriage drove through an arched gateway. The court, in the inside, had evidently been arranged to gratify a picturesque and voluptuous ideality. Wide galleries ran all around the four sides, whose Moorish arches, slender pillars, and arabesque ornaments, carried the mind back, as in a dream, to the reign of Oriental romance in Spain. In the middle of the court, a fountain threw high its silvery water, falling in a never-ceasing spray into a marble basin, fringed with a deep border of fragrant violets. The water in the fountain, pellucid as crystal, was alive with myriads of gold and silver fishes, twinkling and darting through it like so many living jewels. Around the fountain ran a walk, paved with a mosaic of pebbles, laid in various fanciful patterns; and this again was surrounded by turf, smooth as green velvet, while a carriage-drive enclosed the whole. Two large orange-trees, now fragrant with blossoms, threw a delicious shade; and, ranged in a circle round upon the turf, were marble vases of arabesque sculpture, containing the choicest flowering plants of the tropics. Huge pomegranate trees, with their glossy leaves and flame-coloured flowers, dark-leaved Arabian jessamines, with their silvery stars, geraniums, luxuriant roses bending beneath their heavy abundance of flowers, golden jessamines, lemon-scented verbena, all united their bloom and fragrance, while here and there a mystic old aloe, with its strange, massive leaves, sat looking like some hoary old enchanter, sitting in weird grandeur among the more perishable bloom and fragrance around it.

The galleries that surrounded the court were festooned with a curtain of some kind of Moorish stuff, and could be drawn down at pleasure to exclude the beams of the sun. On the whole, the appearance of the place was luxurious and romantic.

As the carriage drove in, Eva seemed like a bird ready to burst from a cage, with the wild eagerness of her delight.

'Oh, isn't it beautiful, lovely! My own, dear, darling home!'
she said to Miss Ophelia. 'Isn't it beautiful?'

''Tis a pretty place,' said Miss Ophelia, as she alighted;
'though it looks rather old and heathenish to me.'

Tom got down from the carriage, and looked about with an
air of calm, still enjoyment. The negro, it must be remembered,
is an exotic of the most gorgeous and superb countries of the
world, and he has deep in his heart a passion for all that is
splendid, rich, and fanciful; a passion which, rudely indulged
by an untrained taste, draws on them the ridicule of the colder
and more correct white race.

St Clare, who was in his heart a poetical voluptuary, smiled
as Miss Ophelia made her remark on his premises, and, turning
to Tom, who was standing looking round, his beaming black
face perfectly radiant with admiration, he said –

'Tom, my boy, this seems to suit you.'

'Yes, mas'r, it looks about the right thing,' said Tom.

All this passed in a moment, while trunks were being hustled
off, hackman paid, and while a crowd of all ages and sizes –
men, women, and children, came running through the galleries,
both above and below, to see mas'r come in. Foremost among
them was a highly-dressed young mulatto man, evidently a very
distingué personage, attired in the ultra extreme of the mode,
and gracefully waving a scented cambric handkerchief in his
hand.

This personage had been exerting himself, with great alacrity,
in driving all the flock of domestics to the other end of the
verandah.

'Back! all of you. I am ashamed of you,' he said in a tone of
authority. 'Would you intrude on master's domestic relations,
in the first hour of his return?'

All looked abashed at this elegant speech, delivered with quite
an air, and stood huddled together at a respectful distance,
except two stout porters, who came up and began conveying
away the baggage.

Owing to Mr Adolph's systematic arrangements, when St
Clare turned round from paying the hackman, there was nobody
in view but Mr Adolph himself, conspicuous in satin vest, gold
guard-chain, and white pants, and bowing with inexpressible
grace and suavity.

'Ah, Adolph, is it you?' said his master, offering his hand to him; 'how are you, boy?' while Adolph poured forth, with great fluency, an extemporary speech, which he had been preparing, with great care, for a fortnight before.

'Well, well,' said St Clare, passing on, with his usual air of negligent drollery, 'that's very well got up, Adolph. See that the baggage is well bestowed. I'll come to the people in a minute;' and so saying, he led Miss Ophelia to a large parlour that opened on to the verandah.

While this had been passing, Eva had flown like a bird through the porch and parlour, to a little boudoir opening likewise on the verandah.

A tall, dark-eyed, sallow woman, half rose from a couch on which she was reclining.

'Mamma!' said Eva, in a sort of rapture, throwing herself on her neck, and embracing her over and over again.

'That'll do – take care, child – don't you make my head ache!' said the mother, after she had languidly kissed her.

St Clare came in, embraced his wife, in true, orthodox, husbandly fashion, and then presented to her his cousin. Marie lifted her large eyes on her cousin with an air of some curiosity, and received her with languid politeness. A crowd of servants now pressed to the entry door, and among them a middle-aged mulatto woman, of very respectable appearance, stood fore-most, in a tremor of expectation and joy, at the door.

'Oh, there's Mammy!' said Eva, as she flew across the room and, throwing herself into her arms, she kissed her repeatedly.

This woman did not tell her that she made her head ache, but, on the contrary, she hugged her, and laughed, and cried, till her sanity was a thing to be doubted of; and when released from her, Eva flew from one to another, shaking hands and kissing, in a way that Miss Ophelia afterwards declared fairly turned her stomach.

'Well!' said Miss Ophelia, 'you southern children can do something that *I* couldn't.'

'What, now, pray?' said St Clare.

'Well, I want to be kind to everybody, and I wouldn't have anything hurt; but, as to kissing—'

'Niggers,' said St Clare, 'that you're not up to; eh?'

'Yes, that's it. How can she?'

St Clare laughed as he went into the passage. 'Halloa! here, what's to pay out here? Here, you all – Mammy, Jimmy, Polly, Sukey – glad to see mas'r?' he said, as he went shaking hands from one to another. 'Look out for the babies!' he added, as he stumbled over a sooty little urchin, who was crawling upon all-fours. 'If I step upon anybody, let 'em mention it.'

There was an abundance of laughing and blessing mas'r, as St Clare distributed small pieces of change among them.

'Come, now, take yourselves off, like good boys and girls,' he said; and the whole assemblage, dark and light, disappeared through a door into a large verandah, followed by Eva, who carried a large satchel, which she had been filling with apples, nuts, candy, ribbons, laces, and toys of every description, during her whole homeward journey.

As St Clare turned to go back, his eye fell upon Tom, who was standing uneasily, shifting from one foot to the other, while Adolph stood negligently leaning against the banisters, examining Tom through an opera-glass, with an air that would have done credit to any dandy living.

'Puh! you puppy,' said his master, striking down the opera-glass; 'is that the way you treat your company? Seems to me, Dolph,' he added, laying his finger on the elegant figured satin vest that Adolph was sporting, 'seems to me that's *my* vest.'

'Oh! master, this vest all stained with wine! – of course a gentleman in master's standing never wears a vest like this. I understood I was to take it. It does for a poor nigger-feller, like me.'

And Adolph tossed his head, and passed his fingers through his scented hair, with a grace.

'So, that's it, is it?' said St Clare, carelessly. 'Well, here, I'm gong to show this Tom to his mistress, and then you take him to the kitchen; and mind you don't put on any of your airs to him. He's worth two such puppies as you.'

'Master always will have his joke,' said Adolph, laughing. 'I'm delighted to see master in such spirits.'

'Here, Tom,' said St Clare, beckoning.

Tom entered the room. He looked wistfully on the velvet carpets, and the before unimagined splendours of mirrors, pictures, statues, and curtains, and, like the Queen of Sheba before Solomon, there was no more spirit in him. He looked afraid even to set his feet down.

'See here, Marie,' said St Clare to his wife, 'I've bought you a coachman, at last, to order. I tell you he's a regular hearse for blackness and sobriety, and will drive you like a funeral, if you want. Open your eyes, now, and look at him. Now, don't say I never think about you when I'm gone.'

Marie opened her eyes, and fixed them on Tom, without rising.

'I know he'll get drunk,' she said.

'No, he's warranted a pious and sober article.'

'Well, I hope he may turn out well,' said the lady; 'it's more than I expect, though.'

'Dolph,' said St Clare, 'show Tom downstairs; and mind yourself,' he added; 'remember what I told you.'

Adolph tripped gracefully forward, and Tom, with lumbering tread, went after.

'He's a perfect behemoth!' said Marie.

'Come, now, Marie,' said St Clare, seating himself on a stool beside her sofa, 'be gracious, and say something pretty to a fellow.'

'You've been gone a fortnight beyond the time,' said the lady, pouting.

'Well, you know I wrote you the reason.'

'Such a short, cold letter!' said the lady.

'Dear me! the mail was just going, and it had to be that or nothing.'

'That's just the way always,' said the lady; 'always something to make your journeys long, and letters short.'

'See here, now,' he added, drawing an elegant velvet case out of his pocket, and opening it, 'here's a present I got for you in New York.' It was a daguerreotype, clear and soft as an engraving, representing Eva and her father sitting hand in hand.

Marie looked at it with a dissatisfied air.

'What made you sit in such an awkward position?' she said.

'Well, the position may be a matter of opinion; but what do you think of the likeness?'

'If you don't think anything of my opinion in one case, I suppose you wouldn't in another,' said the lady, shutting the daguerreotype.

'Hang the woman!' said St Clare, mentally; but aloud he added, 'Come, now, Marie, what do you think of the likeness? Don't be nonsensical, now.'

'It's very inconsiderate of you, St Clare,' said the lady, 'to insist on my talking and looking at things. You know I've been lying all day with the sick-headache; and there's been such a tumult made ever since you came, I'm half dead.'

'You're subject to the sick-headache, ma'am?' said Miss Ophelia, suddenly rising from the depths of the large armchair, where she had sat quietly, taking an inventory of the furniture, and calculating its expense.

'Yes, I'm a perfect martyr to it,' said the lady.

'Juniper-berry tea is good for sick-headache,' said Miss Ophelia; 'at least, Augustine, Deacon Abraham Perry's wife used to say so; and she was a great nurse.'

'I'll have the first juniper-berries that get ripe in our garden by the lake brought in for that especial purpose,' said St Clare, gravely pulling the bell as he did so; 'meanwhile, cousin, you must be wanting to retire to your apartment, and refresh yourself a little after your journey. Dolph,' he added, 'tell Mammy to come here.' The decent mulatto woman whom Eva had caressed to rapturously soon entered; she was dressed neatly, with a high red and yellow turban on her head, the recent gift of Eva, and which the child had been arrranging on her head. 'Mammy,' said St Clare, 'I put this lady under your care; she is tired, and wants rest. Take her to her chamber, and be sure she is made comfortable;' and Miss Ophelia disappeared in the rear of Mammy.

Chapter 16

TOM'S MISTRESS AND HER OPINIONS

'AND now, Marie,' said St Clare, 'your golden days are dawning. Here is our practical, business-like New England cousin, who will take the whole budget of cares off your shoulders, and give you time to refresh yourself, and grow young and handsome. The ceremony of delivering the keys had better come off forthwith.'

This remark was made at the breakfast-table, a few mornings after Miss Ophelia had arrived.

'I'm sure she's welcome,' said Marie, leaning her head languidly on her hand. 'I think she'll find one thing, if she does, and that is, that it's we mistresses that are the slaves, down here.'

'Oh, certainly, she will discover that, and a world of wholesome truths besides, no doubt,' said St Clare.

'Talk about our keeping slaves, as if we did it for our *convenience*,' said Marie. 'I'm sure, if we consulted *that*, we might let them all go at once.'

Evangeline fixed her large, serious eyes on her mother's face, with an earnest and perplexed expression, and said simply, 'What do you keep them for, mamma?'

'I don't know, I'm sure, except for a plague; they are the plague of my life. I believe that more of my ill-health is caused by them than by any one thing; and ours, I know, are the very worst that ever anybody was plagued with.'

'Oh, come, Marie, you've got the blues this morning,' said St Clare. 'You know 'tisn't so. There's Mammy, the best creature living – what could you do without her?'

'Mammy is the best I ever knew,' said Marie; 'and yet Mammy, now, is selfish – dreadfully selfish; it's the fault of the whole race.'

'Selfishness *is* a dreadful fault,' said St Clare, gravely.

'Well, now, there's Mammy,' said Marie; 'I think it's selfish of her to sleep so sound nights; she knows I need little attentions almost every hour, when my worst turns are on, and yet she's so hard to wake. I absolutely am worse, this very morning, for the efforts I had to make to wake her last night.'

'Hasn't she sat up with you a good many nights lately, mamma?' said Eva.

'How should you know that?' said Marie, sharply; 'she's been complaining, I suppose.'

'She didn't complain; she only told me what bad nights you'd had – so many in succession!'

'Why don't you let Jane or Rosa take her place a night or two,' said St Clare, 'and let her rest?'

'How can you propose it?' said Marie. 'St Clare, you really are inconsiderate! So nervous as I am, the least breath disturbs me; and a strange hand about me would drive me absolutely frantic. If Mammy felt the interest in me she ought to, she'd wake easier – of course she would. I've heard of people who had such devoted servants, but it never was *my* luck;' and Marie sighed.

Miss Ophelia had listened to this conversation with an air of shrewd, observant gravity; and she still kept her lips tightly compressed, as if determined fully to ascertain her longitude and position, before she committed herself.

'Now, Mammy has a *sort* of goodness,' said Marie; 'she's smooth and respectable, but she's selfish at heart. Now, she never will be done fidgeting and worrying about that husband of hers. You see, when I was married and came to live here, of course I had to bring her with me, and her husband, my father couldn't spare. He was a blacksmith, and, of course, very necessary; and I thought and said, at the time, that Mammy and he had better give each other up, as it wasn't likely to be convenient for them ever to live together again. I wish now I'd insisted on it, and married Mammy to somebody else; but I was foolish and indulgent, and didn't want to insist. I told Mammy at the time that she mustn't ever expect to see him more than once or twice in her life again, for the air of father's place doesn't agree with my health, and I can't go there; and I advised her to take up with somebody else; but no – she wouldn't.

Mammy has a kind of obstinacy about her, in spots, that everybody don't see as I do.'

'Has she children ?' said Miss Ophelia.

'Yes ; she has two.'

'I suppose she feels the separation from them ?'

'Well, of course, I couldn't bring them. They were little dirty things – I couldn't have them about ; and, besides, they took up too much of her time ; but I believe that Mammy has always kept up a sort of sulkiness about this. She won't marry anybody else ; and I do believe now, though she knows how necessary she is to me, and how feeble my health is, she would go back to her husband to-morrow, if she only could. I *do*, indeed,' said Marie ; 'they are just so selfish, now, the best of them.'

'It's distressing to reflect upon,' said St Clare, dryly.

Miss Ophelia looked keenly at him, and saw the flush of mortification and repressed vexation, and the sarcastic curl of the lip, as he spoke.

'Now, Mammy has always been a pet with me,' said Marie. 'I wish some of your northern servants could look at her closets of dresses, – silks and muslins, and one real linen cambric, she has hanging there. I've worked sometimes whole afternoons, trimming her caps, and getting her ready to go to a party. As to abuse, she don't know what it is. She never was whipped more than once or twice in her whole life. She has her strong coffee or her tea every day, with white sugar in it. It's abominable, to be sure ; but St Clare will have high life below stairs, and they, every one of them, live just as they please. The fact is, our servants are over-indulged. I suppose it is partly our fault that they are selfish, and act like spoiled children ; but I've talked to St Clare till I am tired.'

'And I, too,' said St Clare, taking up the morning paper.

Eva, the beautiful Eva, had stood listening to her mother, with that expression of deep and mystic earnestness which was peculiar to her. She walked softly round to her mother's chair, and put her arms round her neck.

'Well, Eva, what now ?' said Marie

'Mamma, couldn't I take care of you one night – just one ? I know I shouldn't make you nervous, and I shouldn't sleep. I often lie awake nights thinking—'

'Oh, nonsense, child – nonsense!' said Marie; 'you are such a strange child!'

'But may I, mamma? I think,' she said timidly, 'that Mammy isn't well. She told me her head ached all the time lately.'

'Oh, that's just one of Mammy's fidgets! Mammy is just like all the rest of them – makes such a fuss about every little headache or finger-ache; it'll never do to encourage it – never! I'm principled about this matter,' said she, turning to Miss Ophelia, 'you'll find the necessity of it. If you encourage servants in giving way to every little disagreeable feeling, and complaining of every little ailment, you'll have your hands full. I never complain myself – nobody knows what I endure. I feel it a duty to bear it quietly, and I do.'

Miss Ophelia's round eyes expressed an undisguised amazement at this peroration, which struck St Clare as so supremely ludicrous that he burst into a loud laugh.

'St Clare always laughs when I make the least allusion to my ill-health,' said Marie, with the voice of a suffering martyr. 'I only hope the day won't come when he'll remember it!' and Marie put her handkerchief to her eyes.

Of course there was rather a foolish silence. Finally, St Clare got up, looked at his watch, and said he had an engagement down street. Eva tripped away after him, and Miss Ophelia and Marie remained at the table alone.

'Now, that's just like St Clare!' said the latter, withdrawing her handkerchief with somewhat of a spirited flourish, when the criminal to be affected by it was no longer in sight. 'He never realises, never can, never will, what I suffer, and have for years. If I was one of the complaining sort, or ever made any fuss about my ailments, there would be some reason for it. Men do get tired, naturally, of a complaining wife. But I've kept things to myself, and borne, and borne, till St Clare has got in the way of thinking I can bear anything.'

Miss Ophelia did not exactly know what she was expected to answer to this.

While she was thinking what to say, Marie gradually wiped away her tears, and smoothed her plumage in a general sort of way, as a dove might be supposed to make toilet after a shower, and began a housewifely chat with Miss Ophelia, concerning cupboards, closets, linen-presses, store-rooms, and other matters, of which the latter was, by common understanding, to assume the direction – giving her so many cautions, directions, and charges, that a head less systematic and business-like than Miss Ophelia's would have been utterly dizzied and confounded.

'And now,' said Marie, 'I believe I've told you everything; so that, when my next sick turn comes on, you'll be able to go forward entirely, without consulting me; only about Eva – she requires watching.'

'She seems to be a good child, very,' said Miss Ophelia; 'I never saw a better child.'

'Eva's peculiar,' said her mother, 'very. There are things about her so singular: she isn't like me, now, a particle:' and Marie sighed, as if this was a truly melancholy consideration.

Miss Ophelia in her own heart said, 'I hope she isn't,' but had prudence enough to keep it down.

'Eva always was disposed to be with servants; and I think that well enough with some children. Now, I always played with father's little negroes – it never did me any harm. But Eva somehow always seems to put herself on an equality with every creature that comes near her. It's a strange thing about the child. I never have been able to break her off it. St Clare, I believe, encourages her in it. The fact is, St Clare indulges every creature under this roof but his own wife.'

Again Miss Ophelia sat in blank silence.

'Now, there's no way with servants,' said Marie, 'but to *put them down*, and keep them down. It was always natural to me, from a child. Eva is enough to spoil a whole house-full. What she will do when she comes to keep house herself, I'm sure I don't know. I hold to being *kind* to servants – I always am; but you must make 'em *know their place*. Eva never does; there's no getting into the child's head the first beginning of an idea what a servant's place is! You heard her offering to take care of me nights, to let Mammy sleep! That's just a specimen of the way the child would be doing all the time, if she was left to herself.'

'Why,' said Miss Ophelia bluntly, 'I suppose you think your servants are human creatures, and ought to have some rest when they are tired?'

'Certainly, of course. I'm very particular in letting them have everything that comes convenient – anything that doesn't put one at all out of the way, you know. Mammy can make up her sleep, some time or other; there's no difficulty about that. She's the sleepiest concern that ever I saw; sewing, standing, or sitting, that creature will go to sleep, and sleep anywhere and everywhere. No danger but Mammy gets sleep enough. But this treating servants as if they were exotic flowers or china vases is really ridiculous,' said Marie, as she plunged languidly into the depths of a voluminous and pillowy lounge, and drew towards her an elegant cut-glass vinaigrette. 'You see,' she continued, in a faint and lady-like voice, like the last dying breath of an Arabian jessamine, or something equally ethereal, 'you see, Cousin Ophelia, I don't often speak of myself. It isn't my *habit*; 'tisn't agreeable to me. In fact, I haven't strength to it. But there are points where St Clare and I differ. St Clare never understood me, never appreciated me. I think it lies at the root of all my ill-health. St Clare means well, I am bound to believe; but men are constitutionally selfish and inconsiderate to woman. That, at least, is my impression.'

Miss Ophelia, who had not a small share of the genuine New England caution, and a very particular horror of being drawn into family difficulties, now began to foresee something of this kind impending: so, composing her face into a grim neutrality, and drawing out of her pocket about a yard and a quarter of stocking, which she kept as a specific against what Dr Watts asserts to be a personal habit of Satan when people have idle hands, she proceeded to knit most energetically, shutting her lips together in a way that said, as plain as words could, 'You needn't try to make me speak. I don't want anything to do with your affairs' – in fact, she looked about as sympathising as a stone lion. But Marie didn't care for that. She had got somebody to talk to, and she felt it her duty to talk, and that was enough; and reinforcing herself by smelling again at her vinaigrette, she went on.

'You see, I brought my own property and servants into the connection when I married St Clare, and I am legally entitled to manage them my own way. St Clare had his fortune and his servants, and I'm well enough content he should manage them his way; but St Clare will be interfering. He has wild extravagant notions about things, particularly about the treatment of servants. He really does act as if he set his servants before me, and before himself, too; for he lets them make him all sorts of trouble, and never lifts a finger. Now, about some things, St Clare is really frightful – he frightens me – good-natured as he looks, in general. Now, he has set down his foot that, come what will, there shall not be a blow struck in this house, except what he or I strike; and he does it in a way that I really dare not cross him. Well, you may see what that leads to; for St Clare wouldn't raise his hand, if every one of them walked over him, and I – you see how cruel it would be to require me to make the exertion. Now, you know these servants are nothing but grown-up children.'

'I don't know anything about it, and I thank the Lord that I don't!' said Miss Ophelia, shortly.

'Well, but you will have to know something, and know it to your cost, if you stay here. You don't know what a provoking, stupid, careless, unreasonable, childish, ungrateful set of wretches they are.'

Marie seemed wonderfully supported, always, when she got upon this topic; and she now opened her eyes, and seemed quite to forget her languor.

'You don't know, and you can't, the daily, hourly trials that beset a housekeeper from them, everywhere and every way. But it's no use to complain to St Clare. He talks the strangest stuff. He says we have made them what they are, and ought to bear with them. He says their faults are all owing to us, and that it would be cruel to make the fault and punish it too. He says we shouldn't do any better, in their place; just as if one could reason from them to us, you know.'

'Don't you believe that the Lord made them of one blood with us?' said Miss Ophelia, shortly.

'No, indeed, not I! A pretty story, truly! They are a degraded race.'

'Don't you think they've got immortal souls?' said Miss Ophelia, with increasing indignation.

'Oh, well,' said Marie, yawning, 'that, of course – nobody doubts that. But as to putting them on any sort of equality with us, you know, as if we could be compared, why, it's impossible! Now, St Clare really has talked to me as if keeping Mammy from her husband was like keeping me from mine. There's no comparing in this way. Mammy couldn't have the feelings that I should. It's a different thing altogether – of course, it is; and yet St Clare pretends not to see it. And just as if Mammy could love her little dirty babies as I love Eva! Yet St Clare once really and soberly tried to persuade me that it was my duty, with my weak health, and all I suffer, to let Mammy go back, and take somebody else in her place. That was a little too much even for *me* to bear. I don't often show my feelings. I make it a principle to endure everything in silence; it's a wife's hard lot, and I bear it. But I did break out, that time; so that he has never alluded to the subject since. But I know by his looks, and little things that he says, that he thinks so as much as ever; and it's so trying, so provoking!'

Miss Ophelia looked very much as if she was afraid she should say something; but she rattled away with her needles in a way that had volumes of meaning in it, if Marie could only have understood it.

'So, you just see,' she continued, 'what you've got to manage. A household without any rule; where servants have it all their own way, do what they please, and have what they please, except so far as I, with my feeble health, have kept up government. I keep my cowhide about, and sometimes I do lay it on; but the exertion is always too much for me. If St Clare would only have this thing done as others do—'

'And how's that?'

'Why, send them to the calaboose, or some of the other places, to be flogged. That's the only way. If I wasn't such a poor, feeble piece, I believe I should manage with twice the energy that St Clare does.'

'And how does St Clare contrive to manage?' said Miss Ophelia. 'You say he never strikes a blow.'

'Well, men have a more commanding way, you know; it is easier for them; besides, if you ever looked full in his eye, it's peculiar – that eye – and if he speaks decidedly, there's a kind of flash. I'm afraid of it, myself; and the servants know they must mind. I couldn't do as much by a regular storm and scolding as St Clare can be one turn of his eye, if once he is in earnest. Oh, there's no trouble about St Clare; that's the reason he has no more feeling for me. But you'll find, when you come to manage, that there's no getting along without severity – they are so bad, so deceitful, so lazy.'

'The old tune,' said St Clare, sauntering in. 'What an awful account these wicked creatures will have to settle, at last, especially for being lazy! You see, cousin,' said he, as he stretched himself at full length on a lounge opposite to Marie, 'it's wholly inexcusable in them, in the light of the example that Marie and I set them, this laziness.'

'Come, now, St Clare, you are too bad!' said Marie.

'Am I, now? Why, I thought I was talking good, quite remarkably for me. I try to enforce your remarks, Marie, always.'

'You know you meant no such thing, St Clare,' said Marie.

'Oh, I must have been mistaken, then. Thank you, my dear, for setting me right.'

'You do really try to be provoking,' said Marie.

'Oh, come, Marie, the day is growing warm, and I have just had a long quarrel with Dolph, which has fatigued me excessively; so, pray be agreeable now, and let a fellow repose in the light of your smile.'

'What's the matter about Dolph?' asked Marie. 'That fellow's impudence had been growing to a point that is perfectly intolerable to me. I only wish I had the undisputed management of him a while. I'd bring him down.'

'What you say, my dear, is marked with your usual acuteness and good sense,' said St Clare. 'As to Dolph, the case is this: that he has so long been engaged in imitating my graces and perfections, that he has at last really mistaken himself for his master; and I have been obliged to give him a little insight into his mistake.'

'How?' said Marie.

'Why, I was obliged to let him understand explicitly that I preferred to keep *some* of my clothes for my own personal wearing; also, I put his magnificence upon an allowance of Cologne water, and actually was so cruel as to restrict him to one dozen of my cambric handkerchiefs. Dolph was particularly huffy about it, and I had to talk to him like a father to bring him round.'

'Oh! St Clare, when will you learn how to treat your servants? It's abominable, the way you indulge them!' said Marie.

'Why, after all, what's the harm of the poor dog's wanting to be like his master? and if I haven't brought him up any better than to find his chief good in Cologne and cambric handkerchiefs, why shouldn't I give them to him?'

'And why haven't you brought him up better?' said Miss Ophelia, with blunt determination.

'Too much trouble; laziness, cousin, laziness – which ruins more souls than you can shake a stick at. If it weren't for laziness, I should have been a perfect angel, myself. I'm inclined to think that laziness is what your old Dr Botherem, up in Vermont, used to call the "essence of moral evil." It's an awful consideration, certainly.'

'I think you slaveholders have an awful responsibility upon you,' said Miss Ophelia. 'I wouldn't have it for a thousand worlds. You ought to educate your slaves, and treat them like reasonable creatures, like immortal creatures, that you've got to stand before the bar of God with. That's my mind,' said the good lady, breaking suddenly out with a tide of zeal that had been gaining strength in her mind all the morning.

'Oh! come, come,' said St Clare, getting up quickly; 'what do you know about us?' And he sat down to the piano, and rattled off a lively piece of music. St Clare had a decided genius for music. His touch was brilliant and firm, and his fingers flew over the keys with a rapid and bird-like motion, airy, and yet decided. He played piece after piece, like a man who is trying to play himself into a good humour. After pushing the music aside, he rose up, and said gaily, 'Well, now, cousin, you've given us a good talk, and done your duty; on the whole, I think the better of you for it. I make no manner of doubt that you threw a very diamond of truth at me, though you see it hit me so directly in the face, that it wasn't exactly appreciated at first.'

'For my part, I don't see any use in such sort of talk,' said Marie. 'I'm sure, if anybody does more for servants than we do, I'd like to know who: and it don't do 'em a bit good – not a particle; they get worse and worse. As to talking to them, or anything like that, I'm sure I have talked till I was tired and hoarse, telling them their duty, and all that; and I'm sure they can go to church when they like, though they don't understand a word of the sermon, more than so many pigs, so it isn't of any great use for them to go, as I see; but they do go, and so they have every chance: but, as I said before, they are a degraded race, and always will be, and there isn't any help for them; you can't make anything of them, if you try. You see, cousin Ophelia, I've tried, and you haven't; I was born and bred among them, and I know.'

Miss Ophelia thought she had said enough, and therefore sat silent. St Clare whistled a tune.

'St Clare, I wish you wouldn't whistle,' said Marie; 'it makes my head worse.'

'I won't,' said St Clare. 'Is there anything else you wouldn't wish me to do?'

'I wish you *would* have some kind of sympathy for my trials; you never have any feeling for me.'

'My dear accusing angel!' said St Clare.

'It's provoking to be talked to in that way.'

'Then, how will you be talked to? I'll talk to order – anyway you'll mention, only to give satisfaction.'

A gay laugh from the court rang through the silken curtains of the verandah. St Clare stepped out, and lifting up the curtain, laughed too.

'What is it?' said Miss Ophelia, coming to the railing.

There sat Tom, on a little mossy seat in the court, every one of his button-holes stuck full of cape jessamines, and Eva, gaily laughing, was hanging a wreath of roses round his neck; and then she sat down on his knee, like a chip sparrow, still laughing.

'O Tom, you look so funny.'

Tom had a sober, benevolent smile, and seemed, in his quiet way, to be enjoying the fun quite as much as his little mistress. He lifted his eyes, when he saw his master, with a half-deprecating, apologetic air.

'How can you let her?' said Miss Ophelia.

'Why not?' said St Clare.

'Why, I don't know, it seems so dreadful!'

'You would think no harm in a child's caressing a large dog, even if he was black; but a creature that can think, and reason, and feel, and is immortal, you shudder at: confess it, cousin. I know the feeling among some of you northerners well enough. Not that there is a particle of virtue in our not having it; but custom with us does what Christianity ought to do – obliterates the feeling of personal prejudice. I have often noticed, in my travels north, how much stronger this was with you than with us. You loathe them as you would a snake or a toad, yet you are indignant at their wrongs. You would not have them abused, but you don't want to have anything to do with them yourselves. You would send them to Africa, out of your sight and smell, and then send a missionary or two to do up all the self-denial of elevating them compendiously. Isn't that it?'

'Well, cousin,' said Miss Ophelia, thoughtfully, 'there may be some truth in this.'

'What would the poor and lowly do without children?' said St Clare, leaning on the railing, and watching Eva as she tripped off, leading Tom with her. 'Your little child is your only true democrat. Tom, now, is a hero to Eva; his stories are wonders in her eyes, his songs and Methodist hymns are better than an opera, and the traps and little bits of trash in his pocket a mine of jewels, and he the most wonderful Tom that ever wore a black skin. This is one of the roses of Eden that the Lord has dropped down expressly for the poor and lowly, who get few enough of any other kind.'

'It's strange, cousin,' said Miss Ophelia; 'one might almost think you were a *professor*, to hear you talk.'

'A professor?' said St Clare.

'Yes; a professor of religion.'

'Not at all; not a professor, as your town folks have it; and, what is worse, I'm afraid, not a *practiser*, either.'

'What makes you talk so, then?'

'Nothing is easier than talking,' said St Clare. 'I believe Shakespeare makes somebody say, "I could sooner show twenty what were good to be done, than be one of the twenty to follow my own showing." Nothing like division of labour. My forte lies in talking, and yours, cousin, lies in doing.'

In Tom's external situation, at this time, there was, as the world says, nothing to complain of. Little Eva's fancy for him – the instinctive gratitude and loveliness of a noble nature – had led her to petition her father that he might be her especial attendant, whenever she needed the escort of a servant, in her walks or rides; and Tom had general orders to let everything else go, and attend to Miss Eva whenever she wanted him – orders which our readers may fancy were far from disagreeable to him. He was kept well dressed, for St Clare was fastidiously particular on this point. His stable services were merely a sinecure, and consisted in a daily care and inspection, and directing an under-servant in his duties; for Marie St Clare declared that she could not have any smell of the horses about him when he came near her, and that he must positively not be put to any service that would make him unpleasant to her, as her nervous system was entirely inadequate to any trial of that nature: one snuff of anything disagreeable, being, according to her account, quite sufficient to close the scene, and put an end to all her earthly trials at once. Tom, therefore, in his well-brushed broadcloth suit, smooth beaver, glossy boots, faultless wristbands and collar, with his grave, good-natured black face, looked respect-able enough to be a bishop of Carthage, as men of his colour were in other ages.

Then, too, he was in a beautiful place, a consideration to which his sensitive race are never indifferent; and he did enjoy with a quiet joy the birds, the flowers, the fountains, the perfume, and light and beauty of the court, the silken hangings, and pictures, and lustres, and statuettes, and gilding, that made the parlours within a kind of Aladdin's palace to him.

If ever Africa shall show an elevated and cultivated race – and come it must, some time, her turn to figure in the great drama of human improvement – life will awake there with a gorgeous-ness and splendour of which our cold western tribes faintly have conceived. In that far-off mystic land of gold, and gems, and spices, and waving palms, and wondrous flowers, and miracu-lous fertility, will awake new forms of art, new styles of splendour; and the negro race, no longer despised and trodden down, will, perhaps, show forth some of the latest and most magnificent revelations of human life. Certainly they will, in their gentleness, their lowly docility of heart, their aptitude to repose on a superior mind and rest on a higher power, their childlike simplicity of affection, and facility of forgiveness. In all these they will exhibit the highest form of the peculiarly *Chris-tian life*, and, perhaps, as God chasteneth whom he loveth, he hath chosen poor Africa in the furnace of affliction, to make her the highest and noblest in that kingdom which he will set up when every other kingdom has been tried and failed; for the first shall be last, and the last first.

Was this what Marie St Clare was thinking of, as she stood,

gorgeously dressed, on the verandah, on Sunday morning, clasping a diamond bracelet on her slender wrist? Most likely it was. Or, if it wasn't that, it was something else; for Marie patronised good things, and she was going now, in full force – diamonds, silk, and lace, and jewels and all – to a fashionable church, to be very religious. Marie always made a point to be very pious on Sundays. There she stood, so slender, so elegant, so airy and undulating in all her motions, her lace scarf enveloping her like a mist. She looked a graceful creature, and she felt very good and very elegant indeed. Miss Ophelia stood at her side, a perfect contrast. It was not that she had not as handsome a silk dress and shawl, and as fine a pocket-handkerchief; but stiffness and squareness, and bolt-uprightness, enveloped her with as indefinite yet appreciable a presence as did grace her elegant neighbour; not the grace of God, however – that is quite another thing.

'Where's Eva?' said Marie.

'The child stopped on the stairs, to say something to Mammy.'

And what was Eva saying to Mammy on the stairs? Listen, reader, and you will hear, though Marie does not.

'Dear Mammy, I know your head is aching dreadfully.'

'Lord bless you, Miss Eva, my head allers aches lately! You don't need to worry.'

'Well, I'm glad you're going out; and here – 'and the little girl threw her arms around her – 'Mammy, you shall take my vinaigrette.'

'What! your beautiful gold thing, thar, with them diamonds! Lor, miss, 'twouldn't be proper, noways.'

'Why not? You need it, and I don't. Mamma always uses it for headache, and it'll make you feel better. No, you shall take it, to please me, now.'

'Do hear the darling talk!' said Mammy, as Eva thrust it into her bosom, and, kissing her, ran downstairs to her mother.

'What were you stopping for?'

'I was just stopping to give Mammy my vinaigrette, to take to church with her.'

'Eva!' said Marie, stamping impatiently, 'your gold vinaigrette to *Mammy*! When will you learn what's *proper*? Go right and take it back this moment!'

Eva looked downcast and aggrieved, and turned slowly.

'I say, Marie, let the child alone; she shall do as she pleases,' said St Clare.

'St Clare, how will she ever get along in the world?' said Marie.

'The Lord knows,' said St Clare; 'but she'll get along in heaven better than you or I.'

'O papa, don't,' said Eva, softly touching his elbow; 'it troubles mother.'

'Well, cousin, are you ready to go to meeting?' said Miss Ophelia, turning square about on St Clare.

'I'm not going, thank you.'

'I do wish St Clare ever would go to church,' said Marie; 'but he hasn't a particle of religion about him. It really isn't respectable.'

'I know it,' said St Clare. 'You ladies go to church to learn how to get along in the world, I suppose, and your piety sheds respectability on us. If I did go at all, I would go where Mammy goes: there's something to keep a fellow awake there, at least.'

'What! those shouting Methodists? Horrible!' said Marie.

'Anything but the dead sea of your respectable churches, Marie. Positively, it's too much to ask of a man. Eva, do you like to go? Come, stay at home and play with me.'

'Thank you, papa, but I'd rather go to church.'

'Isn't it dreadful tiresome?' said St Clare.

'I think it is tiresome, some,' said Eva, 'and I am sleepy, too; but I try to keep awake.'

'What do you go for, then?'

'Why, you know, papa,' she said in a whisper, 'cousin told me that God wants to have us; and he gives us everything, you know; and it isn't much to do it, if he wants us to. It isn't so very tiresome, after all.'

'You sweet little obliging soul!' said St Clare, kissing her; 'go along, that's a good girl, and pray for me.'

'Certainly, I always do,' said the child, as she sprang after her mother into the carriage.

St Clare stood on the steps and kissed his hand to her as the carriage drove away; large tears were in his eyes.

'O Evangeline! rightly named,' he said; 'hath not God made thee an evangel to me?'

So he felt a moment; and then he smoked a cigar, and read

the *Picayune*, and forgot his little gospel. Was he much unlike other folks?

'You see, Evangeline,' said her mother, 'it's always right and proper to be kind to servants, but it isn't proper to treat them *just* as we would our relations, or people in our own class of life. Now, if Mammy was sick, you wouldn't want to put her in your own bed?'

'I should feel just like it, mamma,' said Eva, 'because then it would be handier to take care of her, and because, you know, my bed is better than hers.'

Marie was in utter despair at the entire want of moral perception evinced in this reply.

'What can I do to make this child understand me?' she said.

'Nothing,' said Miss Ophelia, significantly.

Eva looked sorry and disconcerted for a moment, but children, luckily, do not keep to one impression long; and in a few moments she was merrily laughing at various things which she saw from the carriage windows as it rattled along.

'Well, ladies,' said St Clare, as they were comfortably seated at the dinner-table, 'and what was the bill of fare at church to-day?'

'Oh, Dr G— preached a splendid sermon!' said Marie. 'It was just such a sermon as you ought to hear; it expressed all my views exactly.'

'It must have been very improving,' said St Clare. 'The subject must have been an extensive one.'

'Well, I mean all my views about society and such things,' said Marie. 'The text was, "He hath made everything beautiful in its season;" and he showed how all the orders and distinctions in society came from God; and that it was so appropriate, you know, and beautiful, that some should be high and some low, and that some were born to rule and some to serve, and all that, you know; and he applied it so well to all this ridiculous fuss that is made about slavery, and he proved distinctly that the Bible was on our side, and supported all our institutions so convincingly. I only wish you'd heard him.'

'Oh, I didn't need it,' said St Clare. 'I can learn what does me as much good as that from the *Picayune* any time, and smoke a cigar besides; which I can't do, you know, in a church.'

'Why,' said Miss Ophelia, 'don't you believe in these views?'

'Who – I? You know I'm such a graceless dog that these religious aspects of such subjects don't edify me much. If I was to say anything on this slavery matter, I would say out, fair and square, "We're in for it; we've got 'em and mean to keep 'em" – it's for our convenience and our interest; for that's the long and short of it; that's just the whole of what all this sanctified stuff amounts to, after all; and, I think that will be intelligible to everybody, everywhere.'

'I do think, Augustine, you are so irreverent!' said Marie. 'I think it's shocking to hear you talk.'

'Shocking! it's the truth. This religious talk on such matters, why don't they carry it a little further, and show the beauty, in its season, of a fellow's taking a glass too much, and sitting a little too late over his cards and various providential arrangements of that sort, which are pretty frequent among us young men; we'd like to hear that those are right and godly, too.'

'Well,' said Miss Ophelia, 'do you think slavery right or wrong?'

'I'm not going to have any of your horrid New England directness, cousin,' said St Clare, gaily. 'If I answer that question, I know you'll be at me with half-a-dozen others, each one harder than the last; and I'm not a going to define my position. I am one of the sort that lives by throwing stones at other people's glass-house; but I never mean to put up one for them to stone.'

'That's just the way he's always talking,' said Marie; 'you can't get any satisfaction out of him. I believe it's just because he don't like religion that he's always running out in this way he's been doing.'

'Religion!' said St Clare, in a tone that made both ladies look at him. 'Religion! Is what you hear at church religion? Is that which can bend and turn, and descend and ascend, to fit every crooked phase of selfish, worldly society, religion? Is that religion which is less scrupulous, less generous, less just, less considerate for man than even my own ungodly, worldly, blinded nature? No! When I look for a religion, I must look for something above me, and not something beneath.'

'Then you don't believe that the Bible justifies slavery?' said Miss Ophelia.

'The Bible was my *mother*'s book,' said St Clare. 'By it she lived and died, and I would be very sorry to think it did. I'd as soon desire to have it proved that my mother could drink brandy, chew tobacco, and swear, by way of satisfying me that I did right in doing the same. It wouldn't make me at all more satisfied with these things in myself, and it would take from me the comfort of respecting her; and it really is a comfort, in this world, to have anything one can respect. In short, you see,' said he, suddenly resuming his gay tone, 'all I want is that different things be kept in different boxes. The whole frame-work of society, both in Europe and America, is made up of various things which will not stand the scrutiny of any very ideal standard of morality. It's pretty generally understood that men don't aspire after the absolute right, but only to do about as well as the rest of the world. Now, when any one speaks up, like a man, and says slavery is necessary to us, we can't get along without it, we should be beggared if we give it up, and, of course, we mean to hold on to it – this is strong, clear, well-defined language; it has the respectability of truth to it; and if we may judge by their practice, the majority of the world will bear us out in it. But when he begins to put on a long face, and snuffle, and quote Scripture, I incline to think he isn't much better than he should be.'

'You are very uncharitable,' said Marie.

'Well,' said St Clare, 'suppose that something should bring down the price of cotton once and for ever, and make the whole slave property a drug in the market; don't you think we should soon have another version of the Scripture doctrine. What a flood of light would pour into the church, all at once, and how immediately it would be discovered that everything in the Bible and reason went the other way!'

'Well, at any rate,' said Marie, as she reclined herself on a lounge, 'I'm thankful I'm born where slavery exists; and I believe it's right – indeed I feel it must be; and, at any rate, I'm sure I couldn't get along without it.'

'I say, what do you think, pussy?' said her father to Eva, who came in at this moment, with a flower in her hand.

'What about, papa?'

'Why, which do you like the best; to live as they do at your uncle's, up in Vermont, or to have a house full of servants, as we do?'

'Oh, of course, our way is the pleasantest,' said Eva.

'Why so ?' said St Clare, stoking her head.

'Why, it makes so many more round you to love, you know,' said Eva, looking up earnestly.

'Now, that's just like Eva,' said Marie; 'just one of her odd speeches.'

'Is it an odd speech, papa ?' said Eva, whisperingly, as she got upon his knee.

'Rather, as this world goes, pussy,' said St Clare. 'But where has my little Eva been, all dinner-time ?'

'Oh, I've been up in Tom's room, hearing him sing, and Aunt Dinah gave me my dinner.'

'Hearing Tom sing, eh ?'

'Oh, yes! He sings such beautiful things about the New Jerusalem, and bright angels, and the land of Canaan.'

'I dare say : it's better than the opera, isn't it ?'

'Yes ; and he's going to teach them to me.'

'Singing-lessons, eh ? – you *are* coming on.'

'Yes, he sings for me, and I read to him in my Bible ; and he explains what it means, you know.'

'On my word,' said Marie, laughing, 'that is the latest joke of the season.'

'Tom isn't a bad hand, now, at explaining Scripture, I'll dare swear,' said St Clare. 'Tom has a natural genius for religion. I wanted the horses out early this morning, and I stole up to Tom's cubiculum there, over the stables, and there I heard him holding a meeting by himself; and, in fact, I haven't heard anything quite so savoury as Tom's prayer this some time. He put in for me with a zeal that was quite apostolic.'

'Perhaps he guessed you were listening. I've heard of that trick before.'

'If he did, he wasn't very politic; for he gave the Lord his opinion of me pretty freely. Tom seemed to think there was decidedly room for improvement in me, and seemed very earnest that I should be converted.

'I hope you'll lay it to heart,' said Miss Ophelia.

'I suppose you are much of the same opinion,' said St Clare. 'Well, we shall see – shan't we, Eva ?'

Chapter 17

THE FREE MAN'S DEFENCE

THERE was a gentle bustle at the Quaker house, as the afternoon drew to a close. Rachel Halliday moved quietly to and fro, collecting from her household stores such needments as could be arranged in the smallest compass, for the wanderers who were to go forth that night. The afternoon shadows stretched eastward, and the round red sun stood thoughtfully on the horizon, and his beams shone yellow and calm into the little bedroom where George and his wife were sitting. He was sitting with his child on his knee, and his wife's hand in his. Both looked thoughtful and serious, and traces of tears were on their cheeks.

'Yes, Eliza,' said George, 'I know all you say is true. You are a good child – a great deal better than I am; and I will try to do as you say. I'll try to act worthy of a free man. I'll try to feel like a Christian. God almighty knows that I've meant to do well – tried hard to do well – when everything has been against me; and now I'll forget all the past, and put away every hard and bitter feeling, and read my Bible, and learn to be a good man.'

'And when we get to Canada,' said Eliza, 'I can help you. I can do dressmaking very well; and I understand fine washing and ironing; and between us we can find something to live on.'

'Yes, Eliza, so long as we have each other and our boy. O Eliza, if these people only knew what a blessing it is for a man to feel that his wife and child belong to *him*! I've often wondered to see men that could call their wives and children *their own*, fretting and worrying about anything else. Why, I feel rich and strong, though we have nothing but our bare hands. I feel as if I could scarcely ask God for any more. Yes, though I've worked hard every day till I am twenty-five years old, and have not a cent of money, nor a roof to cover me, nor a spot of land to call my own, yet if they will only let me alone now, I will be satisfied

– thankful; I will work, and send back the money for you and my boy. As to my old master, he has been paid five times over for all he ever spent for me. I don't owe him anything.'

'But yet we are not quite out of danger,' said Eliza; 'we are not yet in Canada.'

'True,' said George: 'but it seems as if I smelt the free air, and it makes me strong.'

At this moment voices were heard in the outer apartment, in earnest conversation, and very soon a rap was heard on the door. Eliza started and opened it.

Simeon Halliday was there, and with him a Quaker brother, whom he introduced as Phineas Fletcher. Phineas was tall and lathy, red-haired, with an expression of great acuteness and shrewdness in his face. He had not the placid, quiet, unworldly air of Simeon Halliday; on the contrary, a particularly wide-awake and *au-fait* appearance, like a man who rather prides himself on knowing what he is about, and keeping a bright look-out ahead; peculiarities which sorted rather oddly with his broad brim and formal phraseology.

'Our friend Phineas hath discovered something of importance to the interest of thee and thy party, George,' said Simeon: 'it were well for thee to hear it.'

'That I have,' said Phineas, 'and it shows the use of a man's always sleeping with one ear open in certain places, as I've always said. Last night I stopped at a little lone tavern, back on the road. Thee remembers the place, Simeon, where we sold some apples, last year, to that fat woman with the great ear-rings. Well, I was tired with hard driving; and, after my supper, I stretched myself down on a pile of bags in the corner, and pulled a buffalo over me, to wait till my bed was ready; and what does I do, but get fast asleep.'

'With one ear open, Phineas?' said Simeon, quietly.

'No! I slept, ears and all, for an hour or two, for I was pretty well tired; but when I came to myself a little, I found that there were some men in the room, sitting round a table, drinking and talking; and I thought, before I made much muster, I'd just see what they were up to, especially as I heard them say something about the Quakers. "So," says one, "they are up in the Quaker settlement, no doubt," says he. Then I listened with both ears, and I found that they were talking about this very party. So I lay and heard them lay off all their plans. This young man, they said, was to be sent back to Kentucky, to his master, who was going to make an example of him, to keep all niggers from running away; and his wife two of them were going to run down to New Orleans to sell, on their own account, and they calculated to get sixteen or eighteen hundred dollars for her; and the child, they said, was going to a trader, who had bought him; and then there was the boy Jim, and his mother, they were to go back to their masters in Kentucky. They said that there were two constables, in a town a little piece ahead, who would go in with 'em to get 'em taken up, and the young woman was to be taken before a judge: and one of the fellows, who is small and smooth-spoken, was to swear to her for his property, and get her delivered over to him to take south. They've got a right notion of the track we are going to-night; and they'll be down after us, six or eight strong. So, now, what's to be done?'

The group that stood in various attitudes, after this communication, were worthy of a painter. Rachel Halliday, who had taken her hands out of a batch of biscuit to hear the news, stood with them upraised and floury, and with a face of the deepest concern. Simeon looked profoundly thoughtful; Eliza had thrown her arms around her husband, and was looking up to him. George stood with clenched hands and glowing eyes, and looking as any other man might look whose wife was to be sold at auction, and son sent to a trader, all under the shelter of a Christian nation's laws.

'What *shall* we do, George?' said Eliza, faintly.

'I know what *I* shall do,' said George, as he stepped into the little room, and began examining his pistols.

'Ay, ay,' said Phineas, nodding his head to Simeon; 'thou seest, Simeon, how it will work.'

'I see,' said Simeon, sighing; 'I pray it come not to that.'

'I don't want to involve any one with or for me,' said George. 'If you will lend me your vehicle and direct me, I will drive alone to the next stand. Jim is a giant in strength, and brave as death and despair, and so am I.'

'Ah, well, friend,' said Phineas, 'but thee'll need a driver, for all that. Thee's quite welcome to do all the fighting, thee knows; but I know a thing or two about the road that thee doesn't.'

'But I don't want to involve you,' said George.

'Involve?' said Phineas, with a curious and keen expression of face. 'When thee does involve me, please to let me know.'

'Phineas is a wise and skilful man,' said Simeon. 'Thee does well, George, to abide by his judgment; and,' he added, laying his hand kindly on George's shoulder, and pointing to the pistols, ' be not over-hasty with these – young blood is hot.'

'I will attack no man,' said George. 'All I ask of this country is to be let alone, and I will go out peaceably; but' – he paused, and his brow darkened and his face worked – 'I've had a sister sold in that New Orleans market. I know what they are sold for; and am I going to stand by and see them take my wife and sell her, when God has given me a pair of strong arms to defend her? No; God help me! I'll fight to the last breath, before they shall take my wife and son. Can you blame me?'

'Mortal man cannot blame thee, George. Flesh and blood could not do otherwise,' said Simeon. 'Woe unto the world because of offences, but woe unto them through whom the offence cometh.'

'Would not even you, sir, do the same, in my place?'

'I pray that I be not tried,' said Simeon; 'the flesh is weak.'

'I think my flesh would be pretty tolerable strong in such a case,' said Phineas, stretching out a pair of arms like the sails of a windmill. 'I an't sure, friend George, that I shouldn't hold a fellow for thee if thee had any accounts to settle with him.'

'If man should *ever* resist evil,' said Simeon, 'then George should feel free to do it now: but the leaders of our people taught a more excellent way; for the wrath of man worketh not the righteousness of God: but it goes sorely against the corrupt will of man, and none can receive it save they to whom it is given. Let us pray the Lord that we be not tempted.'

'And so *I* do,' said Phineas; 'but if we are tempted too much—why, let them look out, that's all.'

'It's quite plain thee wasn't born a Friend,' said Simeon, smiling. 'The old nature hath its way in thee pretty strong as yet.'

To tell the truth, Phineas had been a hearty two-fisted back-woodsman, a vigorous hunter, and a dead shot at a buck; but having wooed a pretty Quakeress, had been moved by the power of her charms to join the society in his neighbourhood; and though he was an honest, sober, and efficient member, and nothing particular could be alleged against him, yet the more spiritual among them could not but discern an exceeding lack of savour in his developments.

'Friend Phineas will ever have ways of his own,' said Rachel Halliday, smiling; 'but we all think that his heart is in the right place, after all.'

'Well,' said George, 'isn't best that we hasten our flight?'

'I got up at four o'clock, and came on with all speed, full two or three hours ahead of them, if they start at the time they planned. It isn't safe to start till dark, at any rate; for there are some evil persons in the villages ahead, that might be disposed to meddle with us, if they saw our wagon, and that would delay us more than the waiting; but in two hours I think we may venture. I will go over to Michael Cross, and engage him to come behind on his swift nag, and keep a bright look-out on the road, and warn us if any company of men come on. Michael keeps a horse that can soon get ahead of most other horses; and he could shoot ahead and let us know, if there were any danger. I am going out now to warn Jim and the old woman to be in readiness, and to see about the horse. We have a pretty fair start, and stand a good chance to get to the stand before they can come up with us. So, have good courage, friend George; this isn't the first ugly scrape that I've been in with thy people,' said Phineas, as he closed the door.

'Phineas is pretty shrewd,' said Simeon. 'He will do the best that can be done for thee, George.'

'All I am sorry for,' said George, 'is the risk to you.'

'Thee'll much oblige us, friend George, to say no more about that. What we do we are conscience-bound to do, we can do no other way. And now, mother,' said he, turning to Rachel, 'hurry thy preparations for these friends, for we must not send them away fasting.'

And while Rachel and her children were busy making corn-cake, and cooking ham and chicken, and hurrying on the *et ceteras* of the evening meal, George and his wife sat in their little room with their arms folded about each other, in such talk as husband and wife have when they know that a few hours may part them for ever.

'Eliza,' said George, 'people that have friends and houses, and lands, and money, and all those things, *can't* love as we do, who have nothing but each other. Till I knew you, Eliza, no creature ever had loved me, but my poor heartbroken mother and sister. I saw poor Emily that morning the trader carried her off. She came to the corner where I was lying asleep, and said, "Poor George, your last friend is going. What will become of you, poor boy?" And I got up and threw my arms round her, and cried and sobbed, and she cried too; and those were the last kind words I got for ten long years; and my heart all withered up, and felt as dry as ashes, till I met you. And your loving me – why it was almost like raising one from the dead! I've been a new man ever since! And now, Eliza, I'll give my last drop of blood, but they *shall not* take you from me. Whoever gets you must walk over my dead body.'

'O Lord, have mercy!' said Eliza, sobbing. 'If he will only let us get out of this country together, that is all we ask.'

'Is God on their side?' said George, speaking less to his wife than pouring out his own bitter thoughts. 'Does he see all they do? Why does he let such things happen? and they tell us that the Bible is on their side; certainly all the power is. They are rich, and healthy, and happy; they are members of churches, expecting to go to heaven; and they get along so easy in the world, and have it all their own way; and poor, honest, faithful Christians – Christians as good or better than they – are lying in the very dust under their feet. They buy 'em and sell 'em, and make trade of their hearts' blood, and groans and tears – and God *lets* them.'

'Friend George,' said Simeon, from the kitchen, 'listen to this Psalm; it may do thee good.'

George drew his seat near the door, and Eliza, wiping her tears, came forward also to listen, while Simeon read as follows:

' "But as for me, my feet were almost gone; my steps had well-nigh slipped. For I was envious of the foolish, when I saw the prosperity of the wicked. They are not in trouble like other men, neither are they plagued like other men. Therefore pride compasseth them as a chain; violence covereth them as a garment. Their eyes stand out with fatness; they have more than heart could wish. They are corrupt, and speak wickedly concerning oppression; they speak loftily. Therefore his people return, and the waters of a full cup are wrung out to them, and they say, How doth God know? and, Is there knowledge in the Most High?" Is not that the way thee feels, George?'

'It is so, indeed,' said George, 'as well as I could have written it myself.'

'Then, hear,' said Simeon: '"When I thought to know this it was too painful for me, until I went unto the sanctuary of God. Then understood I their end. Surely thou didst set them in slippery places, thou castedst them down to destruction. As a dream when one awaketh, so, O Lord, when thou awakest thou shalt despise their image. Nevertheless, I am continually with thee; thou hast holden me by my right hand. Thou shalt guide me by thy counsel, and afterwards receive me to glory. It is good for me to draw near unto God. I have put my trust in the Lord God."'

The words of holy trust, breathed by the friendly old man, stole like sacred music over the harassed and chafed spirit of George; and after he ceased he sat with a gentle and subdued expression on his fine features.

'If this world were all, George,' said Simeon, 'thee might, indeed, ask, Where is the Lord? But it is often those who have least of all in this life whom He chooseth for the kingdom. Put thy trust in Him, and, no matter what befalls thee here, He will make all right hereafter.'

If these words had been spoken by some easy, self-indulgent exhorter, from whose mouth they might have come merely as pious and rhetorical flourish, proper to be used to people in distress, perhaps they might not have had much effect; but coming from one who daily and calmly risked fine and imprisonment for the cause of God and man, they had a weight that could not be felt, and both the poor, desolate fugitives, found calmness and strength breathing into them from it.

And now Rachel took Eliza's hand kindly, and led the way to the supper-table. As they were sitting down, a light tap sounded at the door, and Ruth entered.

'I just ran in,' she said, 'with these little stockings for the boy – three pair, nice, warm, woollen ones. It will be so cold, thee knows, in Canada. Does thee keep up good courage, Eliza?' she added, tripping round to Eliza's side of the table, and shaking her warmly by the hand, and slipping a seed-cake into Harry's hand. 'I brought a little parcel of these for him,' she said, tugging at her pocket to get out the package. 'Children, thee knows, will always be eating.'

'Oh, thank you; you are too kind,' said Eliza.

'Come, Ruth, sit down to supper,' said Rachel.

'I couldn't any way. I left John with the baby, and some biscuits in the oven; and I can't stay a moment, else John will burn up all the biscuits, and give the baby all the sugar in the bowl. That's the way he does,' said the little Quakeress, laughing. 'So, good bye, Eliza; good bye, George; the Lord grant thee a safe journey;' and with a few tripping steps Ruth was out of the apartment.

A little while after supper a large covered wagon drew up before the door; the night was clear starlight, and Phineas jumped briskly down from his seat to arrange his passengers. George walked out of the door, with his child on one arm and his wife on the other. His step was firm, his face settled and resolute. Rachel and Simeon came out after them.

'You get out a moment,' said Phineas, to those inside, 'and let me fix the back of the wagon, there, for the womenfolk and the boy.'

'Here are the two buffaloes,' said Rachel. 'Make the seats as comfortable as may be; it's hard riding all night.'

Jim came out first, and carefully assisted out his old mother, who clung to his arm and looked anxiously about, as if she expected the pursuer every moment.

'Jim, are your pistols all in order?' said George, in a low, firm voice.

'Yes, indeed,' said Jim.

'And you've no doubt what you shall do if they come?'

'I rather think I haven't,' said Jim, throwing open his broad chest, and taking a deep breath. 'Do you think I'll let them get mother again?'

During this brief colloquy Eliza had been taking her leave of her kind friend Rachel, and was handed into the carriage by Simeon, and, creeping into the back part with her boy, sat down among the buffalo-skins. The old woman was next handed in and seated, and George and Jim placed on a rough board seat front of them, and Phineas mounted in front.

'Farewell, my friends!' said Simeon, from without.

'God bless you!' answered all from within.

And the wagon drove off, rattling and jolting over the frozen road.

There was no opportunity for conversation, on account of the roughness of the way, and the noise of the wheels. The vehicle therefore rumbled on, through long, dark stretches of woodland, over wide dreary plains, up hills and down valleys, and on, on, on they jogged, hour after hour. The child soon fell asleep, and lay heavily in his mother's lap. The poor, frightened old woman at last forgot her fears; and even Eliza, as the night waned, found all her anxieties insufficient to keep her eyes from closing. Phineas seemed, on the whole, the briskest of the company, and beguiled his long drive with whistling certain very un-Quaker-like songs as he went on.

But about three o'clock George's ear caught the hasty and decided click of a horse's hoof coming behind them at some distance, and jogged Phineas by the elbow. Phineas pulled up his horses and listened.

'That must be Michael,' he said; 'I think I know the sound of his gallop;' and he rose up and stretched his head anxiously back over the road.

A man riding in hot haste was now dimly descried at the top of a distant hill.

'There he is, I do believe!' said Phineas. George and Jim both sprang out of the wagon, before they knew what they were doing. All stood intensely silent, with their faces turned towards the expected messenger. On he came. Now he went down into a valley, where they could not see him; but they heard the sharp, hasty tramp, rising nearer and nearer; at last they saw him emerge on the top of an eminence, within hail.

'Yes, that's Michael!' said Phineas; and, raising his voice, 'Halloa, there, Michael!'

'Phineas! is that thee?'

'Yes; what news? – they coming?'

'Right on behind, eight or ten of them, hot with brandy, swearing and foaming like so many wolves!'

And just as he spoke a breeze brought the faint sound of galloping horsemen towards them.

'In with you – quick, boys, in!' said Phineas. 'If you must fight, wait till I get you a piece a-head.' And, with the word, both jumped in, and Phineas lashed the horses to a run, the horseman keeping close beside them. The wagon rattled, jumped, almost flew, over the frozen ground; but plainer, and still plainer, came the noise of pursuing horsemen behind. The women heard it, and, looking anxiously out, saw, far in the rear, on the brow of a distant hill, a party of men looming up against the red-streaked sky of early dawn. Another hill, and their pursuers had evidently caught sight of their wagon, whose white, cloth-covered top, made it conspicuous at some distance, and a loud yell of brutal triumph came forward on the wind. Eliza sickened, and strained her child closer to her bosom; the old woman prayed and groaned, and George and Jim clenched their pistols with the grasp of despair. The pursuers gained on them fast; the carriage made a sudden turn, and brought them near a ledge of a steep overhanging rock, that rose in an isolated ridge or clump in a large lot, which was, all around it, quite clear and smooth. This isolated pile, or range of rocks, rose up black and heavy against the brightening sky, and seemed to promise shelter and concealment. It was a place well known to Phineas, who had been familiar with the spot in his hunting days; and it was to gain this point he had been racing his horses.

'Now for it!' said he, suddenly checking his horses, and springing from his seat to the ground. 'Out with you, in a twinkling, every one, and up into these rocks with me. Michael, thee tie thy horse to the wagon, and drive ahead to Amariah's, and get him and his boys to come back and talk to these fellows.'

In a twinkling they were all out of the carriage.

'There,' said Phineas, catching up Harry, 'you, each of you, see to the women; and run, *now*, if you ever *did* run.'

There needed no exhortation. Quicker than we can say it, the whole party were over the fence, making with all speed for the rocks, while Michael, throwing himself from his horse, and fastening the bridle to the wagon, began driving it rapidly away.

'Come ahead!' said Phineas, as they reached the rocks, and saw, in the mingled starlight and dawn, the traces of a rude but plainly marked footpath leading up among them; 'this is one of our old hunting dens. Come up!'

Phineas went before, springing up the rocks like a goat, with the boy in his arms. Jim came second, bearing his trembling old mother over his shoulder, and George and Eliza brought up the rear. The party of horsemen came up to the fence, and, with mingled shouts and oaths, were dismounting, to prepare to follow them. A few moments' scrambling brought them to the top of the ledge; the path then passed between a narrow defile, where only one could walk at a time, till suddenly they came to a rift or chasm more than a yard in breadth, and beyond which lay a pile of rocks, separate from the rest of the ledge, standing full thirty feet high, with its sides steep and perpendicular as those of a castle. Phineas easily leaped the chasm, and sat down the boy on a smooth, flat platform of crisp white moss, that covered the top of the rock.

'Over with you!' he called: 'spring, now, once, for your lives!' said he, as one after another sprang across. Several fragments of loose stone formed a kind of breastwork, which sheltered their position from the observation of those below.

'Well, here we all are,' said Phineas, peeping over the stone breastwork to watch the assailants, who were coming tumultuously up under the rocks. 'Let 'em get us, if they can. Whoever comes here has to walk single file between those two rocks, in fair range of your pistols, boys, d'ye see?'

'I do see,' said George; 'and now, as this matter is ours, let us take all the risk, and do all the fighting.'

'Thee's quite welcome to do the fighting, George,' said Phineas, chewing some checkerberry-leaves as he spoke; 'but I may have the fun of looking on, I suppose. But see, these fellows are kinder debating down there, and looking up, like hens when they are going to fly up on to the roost. Hadn't thee better give 'em a word of advice, before they come up, just to tell 'em handsomely they'll be shot if they do?'

The party beneath, now more apparent in the light of the dawn, consisted of our old acquaintances, Tom Loker and Marks, with two constables, and a posse consisting of such rowdies at the last tavern as could be engaged by a little brandy to go and help the fun of trapping a set of niggers.

'Well, Tom, yer coons are farly treed,' said one.

'Yes, I see 'em go up right here,' said Tom; 'and here's a path. I'm for going right up. They can't jump down in a hurry, and it won't take long to ferret 'em out.'

'But, Tom, they might fire at us from behind the rocks,' said Marks. 'That would be ugly, you know.'

'Ugh!' said Tom, with a sneer. 'Always for saving your skin, Marks! No danger! Niggers are too plaguy scared!'

'I don't know why I *shouldn't* save my skin,' said Marks. 'It's the best I've got; and niggers *do* fight like the devil, sometimes.'

At this moment George appeared on the top of a rock above them, and, speaking in a calm, clear voice, said —

'Gentlemen, who are you, down there, and what do you want?'

'We want a party of runaway niggers,' said Tom Loker. 'One George Harris, and Eliza Harris, and their son, and Jim Selden, and an old woman. We've got the officers here, and a warrant to take 'em; and we're going to have 'em too. D'ye hear? An't you George Harris, that belongs to Mr Harris, of Shelby county, Kentucky?'

'I am George Harris. A Mr Harris, of Kentucky, did call me his property. But now I'm a free man, standing on God's free soil; and my wife and my child I claim as mine. Jim and his mother are here. We have arms to defend ourselves, and we mean to do it. You can come up, if you like; but the first one of you that comes within the range of our bullets is a dead man, and the next, and the next; and so on till the last.'

'Oh, come! come!' said a short, puffy man, stepping forward, and blowing his nose as he did so. 'Young man, this an't no kind of talk at all for you. You see, we're officers of justice. We've got the law on our side, and the power, and so forth; so you'd better give up peaceably, you see; for you'll certainly have to give up at last.'

'I know very well that you've got the law on your side, and the power,' said George, bitterly. 'You mean to take my wife to sell in New Orleans, and put my boy like a calf in a trader's pen, and send Jim's old mother to the brute that whipped and abused her before, because he couldn't abuse her son. You want to send Jim and me back to be whipped and tortured, and ground down under the heels of them that you call masters; and your laws *will* bear you out in it — more shame for you and them! But you haven't got us. We don't own your laws; we don't own your country; we stand here as free, under God's sky, as you are; and, by the great God that made us, we'll fight for our liberty till we die.'

George stood out in fair sight on the top of the rocks, as he made his declaration of independence; the glow of dawn gave a flush to his swarthy cheek, and bitter indignation and despair gave fire to his dark eye; and, as if appealing from man to the justice of God, he raised his hand to heaven as he spoke.

If it had been only a Hungarian youth, now, bravely defending in some mountain fastness the retreat of fugitives escaping from Austria into America, this would have been sublime heroism; but as it was a youth of African descent, defending the retreat of fugitives through America into Canada, of course we are too well instructed and patriotic to see any heroism in it; and if any of our readers do, they must do it on their own private responsibility. When despairing Hungarian fugitives make their way, against all the search-warrants and authorities of their lawful government, to America, press and political cabinet ring with applause and welcome. When despairing African fugitives do the same thing, it is—what *is* it?

Be it as it may, it is certain that the attitude, eye, voice, manner of the speaker, for a moment struck the party below to silence. There is something in boldness and determination that for a time hushes even the rudest nature. Marks was the only one who remained wholly untouched. He was deliberately cocking his pistol, and in the momentary silence that followed George's speech, he fired at him.

'Ye see, ye get jist as much for him dead as alive in Kentucky,' he said, coolly, as he wiped his pistol on his coat-sleeve.

George sprang backwards – Eliza uttered a shriek – the ball had passed close to his hair, had nearly grazed the cheek of his wife, and stuck in the tree above.

'It's nothing, Eliza,' said George, quickly.

'Thee'd better keep out of sight, with thy speechifying,' said Phineas; 'they're mean scamps.'

'Now, Jim,' said George, 'look that your pistols are all right and watch that pass with me. The first man that shows himself I fire at; you take the second, and so on. It won't do, you know, to waste two shots on one.'

'But what if you don't hit?'

'I *shall* hit,' said George, coolly.

'Good! Now, there's stuff in that fellow,' muttered Phineas, between his teeth.

The party below, after Marks had fired, stood, for a moment, rather undecided.

'I think you must have hit some on 'em,' said one of the men. 'I heard a squeal!'

'I'm going right up for one,' said Tom. 'I never was afraid of niggers, and I ain't going to be now. Who goes after?' he said, springing up the rocks.

George heard the words distinctly. He drew up his pistol, examined it, pointed it towards that point in the defile where the first man would appear.

One of the most courageous of the party followed Tom, and, the way being thus made, the whole party began pushing up the rock – the hindermost pushing the front ones faster than they would have gone of themselves. On they came, and in a moment the burly form of Tom appeared in sight, almost at the verge of the chasm.

George fired – the shot entered his side; but though wounded he would not retreat, but, with a yell like that of a mad bull, he was leaping right across the chasm into the party.

'Friend,' said Phineas, suddenly stepping to the front, and meeting him with a push from his long arms, 'thee isn't wanted here.'

Down he fell into the chasm, crackling down among trees, bushes, logs, loose stones, till he lay, bruised and groaning, thirty feet below. The fall might have killed him, had it not been broken and moderated by his clothes catching in the branches of a large tree; but he came down with some force, however – more than was at all agreeable or convenient.

'Lord, help us! they are perfect devils!' said Marks, heading the retreat down the rocks with much more of a will than he had joined the ascent, while all the party came tumbling precipitately after him – the fat constable, in particular, blowing and puffing in a very energetic manner.

'I say, fellers,' said Marks, 'you jist go round and pick up Tom, there, while I run and get on to my horse, to go back for help – that's you;' and without minding the hooting and jeers of his company, Marks was as good as his word, and was soon seen galloping away.

'Was ever such a sneaking varmint?' said one of the men. 'To come on his business, and he clear out and leave us this yer way!'

'Well, we must pick up that feller,' said another. 'Cuss me if I much care whether he is dead or alive.'

The men, led by the groans of Tom, scrambled and crackled through stumps, logs, and bushes, to where that hero lay groaning and swearing with alternate vehemence.

'Ye keep it a-going pretty loud, Tom,' said one. 'Ye much hurt?'

'Don't know. Get me up can't ye? Blast that infernal Quaker! If it had not been for him, I'd a pitched some on 'em down here, to see how they liked it.'

With much labour and groaning, the fallen hero was assisted to rise; and, with one holding him up under each shoulder, they got him as far as the horses.

'If you could only get me a mile back to that ar tavern. Give me a handkerchief or something, to stuff into this place, and stop this infernal bleeding.'

George looked over the rocks, and saw them trying to lift the burly form of Tom into the saddle. After two or three ineffectual attempts, he reeled, and fell heavily to the ground.

'Oh, I hope he isn't killed!' said Eliza, who, with all the party, stood watching the proceeding.

'Why not?' said Phineas. 'Serves him right.'

'Because after death comes the judgment,' said Eliza.

'Yes,' said the old woman, who had been groaning and praying, in her Methodist fashion, during all the encounter, 'it is an awful case for the poor crittur's soul.'

'On my word, they're leaving him, I do believe,' said Phineas.

It was true; for, after some appearance of irresolution and consultation, the whole party got on their horses and rode away. When they were quite out of sight, Phineas began to bestir himself.

'Well, we must go down and walk a piece,' he said. 'I told Michael to go forward and bring help, and be along back here with the wagon; but we shall have to walk a piece along the road, I reckon, to meet them. The Lord grant he be along soon! It's early in the day: there won't be much travel afoot yet awhile; we an't much more than two miles from our stopping-place. If the road hadn't been so rough last night, we could have outrun 'em entirely.'

As the party neared the fence, they discovered in the distance, along the road, their own wagon coming back, accompanied by some men on horseback.

'Well, now, there's Michael, and Stephen, and Amariah,' exclaimed Phineas, joyfully. 'Now we *are* made – as safe as if we'd got there.'

'Well, do stop, then,' said Eliza, 'and do something for that poor man; he's groaning dreadfully.'

'It would be no more than Christian,' said George; 'let's take him up and carry him on.'

'And doctor him up among the Quakers!' said Phineas; 'pretty well, that! Well, I don't care if we do. Here, let's have a look at him!' and Phineas, who, in the course of his hunting and backwoods life, had acquired some rude experience of surgery, kneeled down by the wounded man, and began a careful examination of his condition.

'Marks,' said Tom, feebly; 'is that you, Marks?'

'No, I reckon 't an't, friend,' said Phineas. 'Much Marks cares for thee, if his own skin's safe. He's off, long ago.'

'I believe I'm done for,' said Tom. 'The cussed sneaking dog, to leave me to die alone! My poor old mother always told me 't would be so.'

'La, sakes! jist hear the poor crittur. He's got a mammy, now,' said the old negress. 'I can't help kinder pityin' on him.'

'Softly, softly; don't thee snap and snarl, friend,' said Phineas, as Tom winced and pushed his hand away. 'Thee has no chance, unless I stop the bleeding.' And Phineas busied himself with making some off-hand surgical arrangements with his own pocket-handkerchief, and such as could be mustered in the company.

'You pushed me down there,' said Tom, faintly.

'Well, if I hadn't, thee would have pushed us down, thee sees,' said Phineas, as he stooped to apply his bandage. 'There, there – let me fix this bandage. We mean well to thee; we bear no malice. Thee shall be taken to a house where they'll nurse thee first-rate – as well as thy own mother could.'

Tom groaned, and shut his eyes. In men of his class, vigour and resolution are entirely a physical matter, and ooze out with the flowing of the blood; and the gigantic fellow really looked piteous in his helplessness.

The other party now came up. The seats were taken out of the wagon. The buffalo-skins, doubled in fours, were spread all along one side, and four men, with great difficulty, lifted the heavy form of Tom into it. Before he was gotten in, he fainted entirely. The old negress, in the abundance of her compassion, sat down on the bottom, and took his head in her lap. Eliza, George and Jim, bestowed themselves, as well as they could, in the remaining space, and the whole party set forward.

'What do you think of him?' said George, who sat by Phineas, in front.

'Well, it's only a pretty deep flesh-wound; but then tumbling and scratching down that place didn't help him much. It has bled pretty freely – pretty much dreaned him out, courage and all; but he'll get over it, and may be learn a thing or two by it.'

'I'm glad to hear you say so,' said George. 'It would always be a heavy thought to me if I'd caused his death, even in a just cause.'

'Yes,' said Phineas, 'killing is an ugly operation, any way they'll fix it, man or beast. I've been a great hunter in my day, and I tell thee I've seen a buck that was shot down, and a dying, look that way on a feller with his eye that it reely most made a feller feel wicked for killing on him; and human creatures is a more serious consideration yet, bein', as thy wife says, that the judgment comes to 'em after death. So I don't know as our people's notions on these matters is too strict; and, considerin' how I was raised, I fell in with them pretty considerably.'

'What shall you do with this poor fellow?' said George.

'Oh, carry him along to Amariah's. There's old Grandmam Stephens there – Dorcas, they call her – she's most an amazin' nurse. She takes to nursing real natural, and an't never better suited than when she gets a sick body to tend. We may reckon on turning him over to her for a fortnight or so.'

A ride of about an hour more brought the party to a neat farm-house, where the weary travellers were received to an abundant breakfast. Tom Loker was soon carefully deposited in a much cleaner and softer bed than he had ever been in the habit of occupying. His wound was carefully dressed and bandaged, and he lay languidly opening and shutting his eyes on the white window-curtains and gently-gliding figures of his sick room, like a weary child. And here, for the present, we shall take leave of one party.

Chapter 18

MISS OPHELIA'S EXPERIENCES AND OPINIONS

OUR friend Tom, in his own simple musings, often compared his more fortunate lot, in the bondage into which he was cast, with that of Joseph in Egypt; and, in fact, as time went on, and he developed more and more under the eye of his master, the strength of the parallel increased.

St Clare was indolent and careless of money. Hitherto the providing and marketing had been principally done by Adolph, who was, to the full, as careless and extravagant as his master; and, between them both, they had carried on the dispersing process with great alacrity. Accustomed, for many years, to regard his master's property as his own care, Tom saw, with an uneasiness he could scarcely repress, the wasteful expenditure of the establishment: and, in the quiet indirect way which his class often acquire, would sometimes make his own suggestions.

St Clare at first employed his occasionally; but, struck with his soundness of mind and good business capacity, he confided in him more and more, till gradually all the marketing and providing for the family were entrusted to him.

'No, no, Adolph,' he said, one day, as Adolph was deprecating the passing of power out of his hands; 'let Tom alone. You only understand what you want — Tom understands cost and come too; and there may be some end to money, by and by, if we don't let somebody do that.'

Trusted to an unlimited extent by a careless master, who handed him a bill without looking at it, and pocketed the change without counting it, Tom had every facility and temptation to dishonesty; and nothing but an impregnable simplicity of nature, strengthened by Christian faith, could have kept him from it. But, to that nature, the very unbounded trust reposed in him was bond and seal for the most scrupulous accuracy.

With Adolph the case had been different. Thoughtless and self-indulgent, and unrestrained by a master who found it easier to indulge than to regulate, he had fallen into an absolute confusion as to *meum* and *tuum* with regard to himself and his master, which sometimes troubled even St Clare. His own good sense taught him that such a training of his servants was unjust and dangerous. A sort of chronic remorse went with him everywhere, although not strong enough to make any decided change in his course; and this very remorse reacted again into indulgence. He passed lightly over the most serious faults, because he told himself that, if he had done his part, his dependants had not fallen into them.

Tom regarded his gay, airy, handsome young master, with an odd mixture of fealty, reverence, and fatherly solicitude. That he never read the Bible; never went to church; that he jested and made free with any and everything that came in the way of his wit; that he spent his Sunday evenings at the opera or theatre; that he went to wine-parties, and clubs, and suppers, oftener than was at all expedient – were all things that Tom could see as plainly as anybody, and on which he based a conviction that 'mas'r wasn't a Christian;' a conviction, however, which he would have been very slow to express to any one else, but on which he founded many prayers, in his own simple fashion, when he was by himself in his little dormitory. Not that Tom had not his own way of speaking his mind occasionally, with something of that tact often observable in his class; as, for example, the very day after the Sabbath we have described, St Clare was invited out to a convivial party of choice spirits, and was helped home, between one and two o'clock at night, in a condition when the physical had decidedly attained the upper hand of the intellectual. Tom and Adolph assisted to get him composed for the night, the latter in high spirits, evidently regarding the matter as a good joke, and laughing heartily at the rusticity of Tom's horror, who really was simple enough to lie awake most of the rest of the night, praying for his young master.

'Well, Tom, what are you waiting for?' said St Clare, the next day, as he sat in his library, in dressing-gown and slippers. St Clare had just been intrusting Tom with some money, and various commissions. 'Isn't all right there, Tom?' he added, as Tom still stood waiting.

'I'm 'fraid not, mas'r,' said Tom, with a grave face.

St Clare laid down his paper, and set down his coffee-cup, and looked at Tom.

'Why, Tom, what's the case? You look as solemn as a coffin.'

'I feel very bad, mas'r. I al'ays have thought that mas'r would be good to everybody.'

'Well, Tom, haven't I been? Come, now, what do you want? There's something you haven't got, I suppose, and this is the preface.'

'Mas'r al'ays been good to me. I haven't nothing to complain of, on that head. But there is one that mas'r isn't good to.'

'Why, Tom, what's got into you? Speak out; what do you mean?'

'Last night, between one and two, I thought so. I studied upon the matter then. Mas'r isn't good to *himself*.'

Tom said this with his back to his master, and his hand on the door-knob. St Clare felt his face flush crimson, but he laughed.

'Oh, that's all, is it?' he said gaily.

'All!' said Tom, turning suddenly round and falling on his knees. 'O, my dear young mas'r! I'm 'fraid it will be *loss of all – all* – body and soul. The good Book says, "it biteth like a serpent and stingeth like an adder," my dear mas'r!'

Tom's voice choked, and the tears ran down his cheeks.

'You poor silly fool!' said St Clare, with tears in his own eyes. 'Get up, Tom: I'm not worth crying over.'

But Tom wouldn't rise, and looked imploring.

'Well, I won't go to any more of their cursed nonsense, Tom,' said St Clare; 'on my honour, I won't. I don't know why I haven't stopped long ago. I've always despised *it*, and myself for it; so now, Tom, wipe your eyes, and go about your errands. Come, come,' he added, 'no blessings. I'm not so wonderfully good now,' he said, as he gently pushed Tom to the door. 'There, I'll pledge my honour to you, Tom, you don't see me so again,' he said; and Tom went off, wiping his eyes, with great satisfaction.

'I'll keep my faith with him, too,' said St Clare, as he closed the door.

And St Clare did so; for gross sensualism, in any form, was not the peculiar temptation of his nature.

But, all this time, who shall detail the tribulations manifold of our friend Miss Ophelia, who had begun the labours of a Southern housekeeper?

There is all the difference in the world in the servants of Southern establishments, according to the character and capacity of the mistresses who have brought them up.

South as well as north, there are women who have an extraordinary talent for command and tact in educating. Such are enabled, with apparent ease, and without severity, to subject to their will, and bring into harmonious and systematic order, the various members of their small estate, to regulate their peculiarities, and so balance and compensate the deficiencies of one by the excess of another as to produce a harmonious and orderly system.

Such a housekeeper was Mrs Shelby, whom we have already described; and such our readers may remember to have met with. If they are not common at the South, it is because they are not common in the world. They are to be found there as often as anywhere; and, when existing, find in that peculiar state of society a brilliant opportunity to exhibit their domestic talent.

Such a housekeeper Marie St Clare was not, nor her mother before her. Indolent and childish, unsystematic and improvident, it was not to be expected that servants trained under her care should not be so likewise; and she had very justly described to Miss Ophelia the state of confusion she would find in the family, though she had not ascribed it to the proper cause.

The first morning of her regency, Miss Ophelia was up at four o'clock; and having attended to all the adjustments of her own chamber, as she had done ever since she came there, to the great amazement of the chambermaid, she prepared for a vigorous onslaught on the cupboards and closets of the establishment, of which she had the keys.

The store-room, the linen presses, the china closet, the kitchen and cellar, that day, all went under an awful review. Hidden things of darkness were brought to light to an extent that alarmed all the principalities and powers of kitchen and chamber, and caused many wonderings and murmurings about 'dese yer northern ladies' from the domestic cabinet.

Old Dinah, the head cook, and principal of all rule and authority in the kitchen department, was filled with wrath at what she considered an invasion of privilege. No feudal baron in Magna Charta times could have more thoroughly resented some incursion of the Crown.

Dinah was a character in her own way, and it would be injustice to her memory not to give the reader a little idea of her. She was a native and essential cook, as much as Aunt Chloe – cooking being an indigenous talent of the African race; but Chloe was a trained and methodical one, who moved in an orderly domestic harness, while Dinah was a self-taught genius, and, like geniuses in general, was positive, opinionated, and erratic, to the last degree.

Like a certain class of modern philosophers, Dinah perfectly scorned logic and reason in every shape, and always took refuge in intuitive certainty; and here she was perfectly impregnable. No possible amount of talent or authority, or explanation, could ever make her believe that any other way was better than her own, or that the course she had pursued in the smallest matter could be in the least modified. This had been a conceded point with her old mistress, Marie's mother, and 'Miss Marie,' as Dinah always called her young mistress, even after her marriage, found it easier to submit than contend; and so Dinah had ruled supreme. This was the easier, in that she was perfect mistress of that diplomatic art which unites the utmost subservience of manner with the utmost inflexibility as to measure.

Dinah was mistress of the whole art and mystery of excuse-making in all its branches. Indeed, it was an axiom with her that the cook can do no wrong; and a cook in a Southern kitchen finds abundance of heads and shoulders on which to lay off every sin and frailty, so as to maintain her own immaculateness entire. If any part of the dinner was a failure, there were fifty indisputably good reasons for it; and it was the fault undeniably of fifty other people whom Dinah berated with unsparing zeal.

But it was very seldom that there was any failure in Dinah's last results. Though her mode of doing everything was peculiarly meandering and circuitous, and without any sort of calculation as to time and place, – though her kitchen generally looked as if it had been arranged by a hurricane blowing through it, and she had about as many places for each cooking utensil as there were days in the year, – yet, if one would have patience to wait her own good time, up would come her dinner in perfect order, and in a style of preparation with which an epicure could find no fault.

It was now the season of incipient preparation for dinner. Dinah, who required large intervals of reflection and repose, and was studious of ease in all her arrangements, was seated on the kitchen floor, smoking a short stumpy pipe, to which she was much addicted, and which she always kindled up, as a sort of censer, whenever she felt the need of an inspiration in her arrangements. It was Dinah's mode of invoking the domestic Muses.

Seated around her were various members of that rising race with which a Southern household abounds, engaged in shelling peas, peeling potatoes, picking pin-feathers out of fowls, and other preparatory arrangements, Dinah every once in a while interrupting her meditations to give a poke or a rap on the head to some of the young operators, with the pudding-stick that lay by her side. In fact, Dinah ruled over the woolly heads of the younger members with a rod of iron, and seemed to consider them born for no earthly purpose but to 'save her steps,' as she phrased it. It was the spirit of the system under which she had grown up, and she carried it out to its full extent.

Miss Ophelia, after passing on her reformatory tour through all the other parts of the establishment, now entered the kitchen. Dinah had heard, from various sources, what was going on, and resolved to stand on defensive and conservative ground, mentally determined to oppose and ignore every new measure, without any actual and observable contest.

The kitchen was a large brick-floored apartment, with a great old-fashioned fireplace stretching along one side of it, an arrangement which St Clare had vainly tried to persuade Dinah to exchange for the convenience of a modern cook-stove. Not she. No Puseyite, or Conservative of any school, was ever more inflexibly attached to time-honoured inconveniences than Dinah.

When St Clare had first returned from the north, impressed with the system and order of his uncle's kitchen arrangements, he had largely provided his own with an array of cupboards, drawers, and various apparatus, to induce systematic regulation, under the sanguine illusion that it would be of any possible assistance to Dinah in her arrangements. He might as well have provided them for a squirrel or a magpie. The more drawers and closets there were, the more hiding-holes could Dinah make for the accommodation of old rags, hair-combs, old shoes, ribbons, cast-off artificial flowers, and other articles of *virtù*, wherein her soul delighted.

When Miss Ophelia entered the kitchen, Dinah did not rise, but smoked on in sublime tranquillity, regarding her movements obliquely out of the corner of her eye, but apparently intent only on the operations around her.

Miss Ophelia commenced opening a set of drawers.

'What is this drawer for, Dinah ?' she said.

'It's handy for most anything, missis,' said Dinah. So it appeared to be. From the variety it contained, Miss Ophelia pulled out first a fine damask table-cloth stained with blood, having evidently been used to envelop some raw meat.

'What's this, Dinah ? You don't wrap up meat in your mistress's best table-cloths ?'

'O Lor, missis, no ; the towels was all a missin' – so I jest did it. I laid out to wash that ar – that's why I put in thar.'

'Shiftless !' said Miss Ophelia to herself, proceeding to tumble over the drawer, where she found a nutmeg-grater and two or three nutmegs, a Methodist hymn-book, a couple of soiled Madras handkerchiefs, some yarn and knitting work, a paper of tobacco and a pipe, a few crackers, one or two gilded china saucers with some pomade in them, one or two thin old shoes, a piece of flannel carefully pinned up enclosing some small white onions, several damask table napkins, some coarse crash towels, some twine and darning-needles, and several broken papers, from which sundry sweet herbs were sifting into the drawer.

'Where do you keep your nutmegs, Dinah ?' said Miss Ophelia, with the air of one who prayed for patience.

'Most anywhere, missis ; there's some in that cracked teacup, up there, and there's some over in that ar cupboard.'

'Here are some in the grater,' said Miss Ophelia, holding them up.

'Laws, yes, I put 'em there this morning. I likes to keep my things handy,' said Dinah. 'You, Jake! what are you stopping for! You'll cotch it! Be still, thar!' she added, with a dive of her stick at the criminal.

'What's this?' said Miss Ophelia, holding up the saucer of pomade.

'Laws, it's my har *grease*; I put it thar to have it handy.'

'Do you use your mistress's best saucers for that?'

'Law! it was cause I was driv, and in sich a hurry; I was gwine to change it this very day.'

'Here are two damask table-napkins.'

'Them table-napkins I put thar to get 'em washed out, some day.'

'Don't you have some place here on purpose for things to be washed?'

'Well, Mas'r St Clare got dat ar chest, he said, for dat; but I likes to mix up biscuit and hev my things on it some days, and then it an't handy a liftin' up the lid.'

'Why don't you mix your biscuits on the pastry-table, there?'

'Law, missis, it gets sot so full of dishes, and one thing and another, der an't no room, noways'—

'But you should *wash* your dishes, and clear them away.'

'Wash my dishes!' said Dinah; in a high key, as her wrath began to rise over her habitual respect of manner. 'What does ladies know 'bout work, I want to know? When 'd mas'r ever get his dinner if I was to spend all my time a washin' and a puttin' up dishes? Miss Marie never told me so, nohow.'

'Well, here are these onions.'

'Laws, yes!' said Dinah; 'that *is* whar I put 'em now. I couldn't 'member. Them's particular onions I was a savin' for dis yer very stew. I'd forgot they was in dat ar old flannel.'

Miss Ophelia lifted out the sifting paper of sweet herbs.

'I wish missis wouldn't touch dem ar. I likes to keep my things where I knows whar to go to 'em,' said Dinah, rather decidedly.

'But you don't want these holes in the papers.'

'Them's handy for siftin' on't out,' said Dinah.

'But you see it spills all over the drawer.'

'Laws, yes! if missis will go a tumblin' things all up so, it will.

Missis has spilt lots dat ar way,' said Dinah, coming uneasily to the drawers. 'If missis only will go up stars till my clarin'-up time comes, I'll have everything right; but I can't do nothin' when ladies is round, a henderin'. You, Sam, don't you gib the baby dat ar sugar-bowl. I'll crack ye over, if you don't mind!'

'I'm going through the kitchen, and going to put everything in order, *once*, Dinah; and then I'll expect you to *keep* it so.'

'Lor, now! Miss Phelia, dat ar an't no way for ladies to do. I never did see ladies doin' no sich; my old missis nor Miss Marie never did, and I don't see no kinder need on't;' and Dinah stalked indignantly about, while Miss Ophelia piled and sorted dishes, emptied dozens of scattering bowls of sugar into one receptacle, sorted napkins, table-cloths, and towels for washing; washing, wiping, and arranging with her own hands, and with a speed and alacrity which perfectly amazed Dinah.

'Lor, now! if dat ar de way dem northern ladies do, dey an't ladies, nohow,' she said to some of her satellites, when at a safe hearing distance. 'I has things as straight as anybody, when my clarin'-up time comes; but I don't want ladies round a henderin' and getting my things all where I can't find 'em.'

To do Dinah justice, she had, at regular periods, paroxysms of reformation and arrangement, which she called, 'clarin'-up times,' when she would begin with great zeal, and turn every drawer and closet wrong side outward, on to the floor or tables, and make the ordinary confusion sevenfold more confounded. Then she would light her pipe, and leisurely go over her arrangements, looking things over, and discoursing upon them; making all the young fry scour most vigorously on the tin things, and keeping up for several hours a most energetic state of confusion, which she would explain to the satisfaction of all inquirers by the remark that she was a 'clarin' up.' 'She couldn't hev things a gwine on so as they had been, and she was gwine to make these yer young ones keep better order;' for Dinah herself somehow indulged the illusion that she, herself, was the soul of order, and it was only the *young uns*, and the everybody else in the house, that were the cause of anything that fell short of perfection in this respect. When all the tins were scoured, and the tables scrubbed snowy white, and everything that could offend tucked out of sight in holes and corners, Dinah would dress herself up in a smart dress, clean apron, and high, brilliant

Madras turban, and tell all marauding 'young uns,' to keep out of the kitchen, for she was gwine to have things kept nice. Indeed, these periodic seasons were often an inconvenience to the whole household; for Dinah would contract such an immoderate attachment to her scoured tin, as to insist upon it that it shouldn't be used again for any possible purpose, at least till the ardour of the 'clarin'-up' period abated.

Miss Ophelia, in a few days, thoroughly reformed every department of the house to a systematic pattern; but her labours in all departments that depended on the co-operation of servants were like those of Sisyphus or the Danaides. In despair, she one day appealed to St Clare.

'There is no such thing as getting anything like system in this family!'

'To be sure there isn't,' said St Clare.

'Such shiftless management, such waste, such confusion, I never saw!'

'I dare say you didn't.'

'You would not take it so coolly if you were housekeeper.'

'My dear cousin, you may as well understand, once for all, that we masters are divided into two classes, oppressors and oppressed. We who are good-natured and hate severity, make up our minds to a good deal of inconvenience. If we *will keep* a shambling, loose, untaught set in the community, for our convenience, why, we must take the consequence. Some rare cases I have seen of persons who, by a peculiar tact, can produce order and system without severity; but I'm not one of them, and so I made up my mind, long ago, to let things go just as they do. I will not have the poor devils thrashed and cut to pieces, and they know it; and, of course, they know the staff is in their own hands.'

'But to have no time, no place, no order – all going on in this shiftless way!'

'My dear Vermont, you natives up by the North Pole set an extravagant value on time! What on earth is the use of time to a fellow who has twice as much of it as he knows what to do with? As to order and system, where there is nothing to be done but to lounge on the sofa and read, an hour sooner or later in breakfast or dinner isn't of much account. Now, there's Dinah gets you a capital dinner – soup, ragout, roast fowl, dessert, ice creams and all – and she creates it all out of Chaos and old Night down there in that kitchen. I think it really sublime, the way she manages. But, heaven bless us! if we are to go down there, and view all the smoking and squatting about, the hurryscurryation of the preparatory process, we should never eat more! My good cousin, absolve yourself from that! It's more than a Catholic penance, and does no more good. You'll only lose your own temper, and utterly confound Dinah. Let her go her own way.'

'But, Augustine, you don't know how I found things.'

'Don't I? Don't I know that the rolling-pin is under her bed, and the nutmeg-grater in her pocket with her tobacco – that there are sixty-five different sugar-bowls, one in every hole in the house – that she washes dishes with a dinner napkin one day and with the fragment of an old petticoat the next! But the upshot is, she gets up glorious dinners, makes superb coffee; and you must judge her as warriors and statesmen are judged, by *her success*.'

'But the waste – the expense!'

'Oh, well! Lock everything you can, and keep the key. Give out by driblets, and never inquire for odds and ends – it isn't best.'

'That troubles me, Augustine. I can't help feeling as if these servants were not *strictly honest*. Are you sure they can be relied on?'

Augustine laughed immoderately at the grave and anxious face with which Miss Ophelia propounded the question.

'Oh, cousin, that's too good. *Honest*! – as if that's a thing to be expected! Honest! – why, of course, they aren't. Why should they be? What upon earth is to make them so?'

'Why don't you instruct?'

'Instruct! Oh, fiddlestick! What instructing do you think I should do! I look like it! As to Marie, she has spirit enough, to be sure, to kill off a whole plantation; if I'd let her manage; but she wouldn't get the cheatery out of them.'

'Are there no honest ones?'

'Well, now and then one, whom Nature makes so impracticably simple, truthful, and faithful, that the worst possible influence can't destroy it. But, you see, from the mother's breast the coloured child feels and sees that there are none but

underhand ways open to it. It can get along no other way with
its parents, its mistress, its young master and missie play-fellows.
Cunning and deception become necessary, inevitable habits. It
isn't fair to expect anything else of him. He ought not to be
punished for it. As to honesty, the slave is kept in that dependent, semi-childish state, that there is no making him realise the
rights of property, or feel that his master's goods are not his
own, if he can get them. For my part I don't see how they *can*
be honest. Such a fellow as Tom here is, is a moral miracle!'

'And what becomes of their souls?' said Miss Ophelia.

'That isn't my affair, as I know of,' said St Clare; 'I am only
dealing in facts of the present life. The fact is, that the whole
race are pretty generally understood to be turned over to the
devil, for our benefit, in this world, however it may turn out in
another!'

'This is perfectly horrible!' said Miss Ophelia; 'you ought to
be ashamed of yourselves!'

'I don't know as I am. We are in pretty good company, for all
that,' said St Clare, 'as people in the broad road generally are.
Look at the high and the low, all the world over, and it's the
same story; the lower class used up, body, soul, and spirit, for
the good for the upper. It is so in England; it is so everywhere;
and yet all Christendom stands aghast, with virtuous indignation, because we do the thing in a little different shape from
what they do it.'

'It isn't so in Vermont.'

'Ah, well, in New England, and in the free States, you have
the better of us, I grant. But there's the bell; so, cousin, let us
for a while lay aside our sectional prejudices, and come out to
dinner.'

As Miss Ophelia was in the kitchen in the latter part of the
afternoon, some of the sable children called out, 'La sakes!
thar's Prue a coming, grunting along like she allers does.'

A tall, bony, coloured woman now entered the kitchen,
bearing on her head a basket of rusks and hot rolls.

'Ho, Prue! you've come,' said Dinah.

Prue had a peculiar scowling expression of countenance, and
a sullen grumbling voice. She set down her basket, squatted
herself down, and resting her elbows on her knees said, –

'O Lord! I wish I's dead!'

'Why do you wish you were dead?' said Miss Ophelia.

'I'd be out of my misery,' said the woman gruffly, without taking her eyes from the floor.

'What need you getting drunk, then, and cutting up, Prue?' said a spruce quadroon chambermaid, dangling, as she spoke, a pair of coral ear-drops.

The woman looked at her with a sour, surly glance.

'May be you'll come to it, one of these yer days. I'd be glad to see you, I would; then you'll be glad of a drop, like me, to forget your misery.'

'Come, Prue,' said Dinah, 'let's look at your rusks. Here's missis will pay for them.'

Miss Ophelia took out a couple of dozen.

'Thar's some tickets in that ar old cracked jug on the top shelf,' said Dinah. 'You, Jake, climb up and get it down.'

'Tickets – what are they for?' said Miss Ophelia.

'We buy tickets of her mas'r, and she gives us bread for 'em.'

'And they counts my money and tickets, when I gets home, to see if I's got the change; and if I han't they half kills me.'

'And serves you right,' said Jane, the pert chambermaid, 'if you will take their money to get drunk on. That's what she does, missis.'

'And that's what I *will* do; I can't live no other ways – drink and forget my misery.'

'You are very wicked and very foolish,' said Miss Ophelia, 'to steal your master's money to make yourself a brute with.'

'It's mighty likely, missis; but I will do it – yes, I will. O Lord! I wish I's dead, I do; I wish I's dead, and out of my misery!' and slowly and stiffly the old creature rose, and got her basket on her head again; but before she went out she looked at the quadroon girl, who still stood playing with her ear-drops.

'Ye think ye're mighty fine with them ar, a frolickin', and a tossin' your head, and a lookin' down on everybody. Well, never mind – you may live to be a poor, old cut-up crittur, like me. Hope to the Lord ye will, I do; then see if ye won't drink – drink – drink – yerself into torment; and sarve ye right, too – ugh!' and, with a malignant howl the woman left the room.

'Disgusting old beast!' said Adolph, who was getting his master's shaving-water. 'If I was her master, I'd cut her up worse then she is.'

'Ye couldn't do that ar, no ways,' said Dinah. 'Her back's a far sight now – she can't never get a dress together over it.'

'I think such low creatures ought not to be allowed to go round to genteel families,' said Miss Jane. 'What do you think, Mr St Clare?' she said, coquettishly tossing her head at Adolph.

It must be observed that, among other appropriations from his master's stock, Adolph was in the habit of adopting his name and address; and that the style under which he moved, among the coloured circles of New Orleans, was that of *Mr St Clare*.

'I'm certainly of your opinion, Miss Benoir,' said Adolph.

Benoir was the name of Marie St Clare's family, and Jane was one of her servants.

'Pray, Miss Benoir, may I be allowed to ask if those drops are for the ball to-morrow night? They are certainly bewitching!'

'I wonder, now, Mr St Clare, what the impudence of you men will come to!' said Jane, tossing her pretty head till the ear-drops twinkled again. 'I shan't dance with you for a whole evening, if you go to asking me any more questions.'

'Oh, you couldn't be so cruel, now! I was just dying to know whether you would appear in your pink tarletane,' said Adolph.

'What is it?' said Rosa, a bright, piquant little quadroon, who came skipping downstairs at this moment.

'Why, Mr St Clare's so impudent!'

'On my honour,' said Adolph, 'I'll leave it to Miss Rosa, now.'

'I know he's always a saucy creature,' said Rosa, poising herself on one of her little feet, and looking maliciously at Adolph. 'He's always geting me so angry with him.'

'O ladies, ladies, you will certainly break my heart, between you,' said Adolph. 'I shall be found dead in my bed some morning, and you'll have it to answer for.'

'Do hear the horrid creature talk!' said both ladies, laughing immoderately.

'Come, clar out, you! I can't have you cluttering up the kitchen,' said Dinah, 'in my way, foolin' round here.'

'Aunt Dinah's glum, because she can't go to the ball,' said Rosa.

'Don't want none o' your light-coloured balls,' said Dinah; 'cuttin' round, makin' b'lieve you's white folks. Arter all, you's niggers, much as I am.'

'Aunt Dinah greases her wool stiff, every day, to make it lie straight,' said Jane.

'And it will be wool, after all,' said Rosa, maliciously shaking down her long, silky curls.

'Well, in the Lord's sight, an't wool as good as har, any time?' said Dinah. 'I'd like to have missus say which is worth the most – a couple such as you, or one like me. Get out wid ye, ye trumpery – I won't have ye round!'

Here the conversation was interrupted in a two-fold manner. St Clare's voice was heard at the head of the stairs, asking Adolph if he meant to stay all night with his shaving-water; and Miss Ophelia, coming out of the dining-room, said –

'Jane and Rosa, what are you wasting your time for here? Go in and attend to your muslins.'

Our friend Tom, who had been in the kitchen during the conversation with the old rusk-woman, had followed her out into the street. He saw her go on, giving every once in a while a suppressed groan. At last she set her basket down on a doorstep, and began arranging the old faded shawl which covered her shoulders.

'I'll carry your basket a piece,' said Tom, compassionately.

'Why should ye?' said the woman. 'I don't want no help.'

'You seem to be sick, or in trouble, or somethin',' said Tom.

'I an't sick,' said the woman, shortly.

'I wish,' said Tom, looking at her earnestly, 'I wish I could persuade you to leave off drinking. Don't you know it will be the ruin of ye, body and soul?'

'I knows I'm gwine to torment,' said the woman, sullenly. 'Ye don't need to tell me that ar. I's ugly – I's wicked – I's gwine straight to torment. O Lord! I wish I's thar!'

Tom shuddered at these frightful words, spoken with a sullen, impassioned earnestness.

'O Lord have mercy on ye! poor crittur. Han't ye never heard of Jesus Chrsit?'

'Jesus Christ! – who's He?'

'Why, He's *the Lord*,' said Tom.

'I think I've hearn tell o' the Lord, and the judgment and torment. I've hearn o' that.'

'But didn't anybody ever tell you of the Lord Jesus, that loved us poor sinners, and died for us?'

'Don't know nothin' 'bout that,' said the woman; 'nobody han't never loved me, since my old man died.'

'Where was you raised?' said Tom.

'Up in Kentuck. A man kept me to breed chil'en for market, and sold 'em as fast as they got big enough; last of all, he sold me to a speculator, and my master got me o' him.'

'What set you into this bad way of drinkin'?'

'To get shet o' my misery. I had one child after I come here; and I thought then I'd have one to raise, cause mas'r wasn't a speculator. It was the peartest little thing! and missis she seemed to think a heap on't, at first; it never cried — it was likely and fat. But missis tuck sick, and I tended her; and I tuck the fever, and my milk all left me, and the child it pined to skin and bone, and missis wouldn't buy milk for it. She wouldn't hear to me, when I telled her I hadn't milk. She said she knowed I could feed it on what other folks eat; and the child kinder pined and cried, and cried, and cried, day and night, and got all gone to skin and bones, and missis got sot agin it, and she said 'twarn't nothin' but crossness. She wished it was dead, she said; and she wouldn't let me have it o' nights, cause, she said, it kept me awake, and made me good for nothing. She made me sleep in her room; and I had to put it a way off in a little kind o' garret, and thar it cried itself to death, one night. It did; and I tuck to drinkin', to keep its crying out of my ears! I did — and I will drink! I will, if I do go to torment for it! Mas'r says I shall go to torment, and I tell him I've got thar now!'

'O ye por crittur!' said Tom, 'han't nobody never telled ye how the Lord Jesus loved ye, and died for ye? Han't they telled ye, that He'll help ye, and ye can go to heaven, and have rest, at last?'

'I looks like gwine to heaven,' said the woman; 'an't thar where white folks is gwine? S'pose they'd have me thar? I'd rather go to torment, and get away from mas'r and missis. I had so,' she said, as, with her usual groan, she got her basket on her head, and walked sullenly away.

Tom turned, and walked sorrowfully back to the house. In the court he met little Eva — a crown of tuberoses on her head, and her eyes radiant with delight.

'O Tom! here you are. I'm glad I've found you. Papa says you may get out the ponies and take me in my little new carriage,' she said, catching his hand. 'But what's the matter, Tom? – you look sober.'

'I feel bad, Miss Eva,' said Tom, sorrowfully. 'But I'll get the horses for you.'

'But do tell me, Tom, what is the matter. I saw you talking to cross old Prue.'

Tom, in simple, earnest phrase, told Eva the woman's history. She did not exclaim, or wonder, or weep, as other children do. Her cheeks grew pale, and a deep, earnest shadow passed over her eyes. She laid both hands on the bosom, and sighed heavily.

Chapter 19

MISS OPHELIA'S EXPERIENCES
AND OPINIONS, CONTINUED

'TOM, you needn't get me the horses. I don't want to go,' she said.

'Why not, Miss Eva?'

'These things sink into my heart, Tom,' said Eva; 'they sink into my heart,' she repeated earnestly. 'I don't want to go;' and she turned from Tom, and went into the house.

A few days after another woman came, in old Prue's place, to bring the rusks; Miss Ophelia was in the kitchen.

'Lor!' said Dinah, 'what's got Prue?'

'Prue isn't comin' any more,' said the woman, mysteriously.

'Why not?' said Dinah, 'she an't dead, is she?'

'We doesn't exactly know. She's down cellar,' said the woman, glancing at Miss Ophelia.

After Miss Ophelia had taken the rusks, Dinah followed the woman to the door.

'What *has* got Prue, anyhow?' she said.

The woman seemed desirous yet reluctant to speak, and answered in a low, mysterious tone, –

'Well, you mustn't tell nobody. Prue, she got drunk agin – and they had her down cellar – and thar they left her all day; and I hearn 'em saying that the *flies had got to her* – and *she's dead*!'

Dinah held up her hands, and, turning, saw close by her side the spirit-like form of Evangeline, her large, mystic eyes dilated with horror, and every drop of blood driven from her lips and cheeks.

'Lor bless us! Miss Eva's gwine to faint away! What got us all, to let her har such talk? Her pa'll be rail mad.'

'I sha'n't faint, Dinah,' said the child, firmly; 'and why shouldn't I hear it? It an't so much for me to hear it as for poor Prue to suffer it.'

'*Lor sakes*! it isn't for sweet delicate young ladies like you – these yer stories isn't; it's enough to kill 'em!'

Eva sighed again, and walked upstairs with a slow and melancholy step.

Miss Ophelia anxiously inquired the woman's story. Dinah gave a very garrulous version of it, to which Tom added the particulars which he had drawn from her on that morning.

'An abominable business – perfectly horrible!' she exclaimed, as she entered the room where St Clare lay, reading his paper.

'Pray, what iniquity has turned up now?' said he.

'What now? why those folks have whipped Prue to death!' said Miss Ophelia, going on, with great strength of detail into the story, and enlarging on its most shocking particulars.

'I thought it would come to that some time,' said St Clare, going on with his paper.

'Thought so! – an't you going to *do* anything about it?' said Miss Ophelia, 'Haven't got any *selectmen*, or anybody to interfere and look after such matters?'

'It's commonly supposed that the *property* interest is a sufficient guard in these cases. If people choose to ruin their own possessions, I don't know what's to be done. It seems the poor creature was a thief and a drunkard; and so there won't be much hope to get up sympathy for her.'

'It is perfectly outrageous – it is horrid, Augustine! It will certainly bring down vengeance upon you.'

'My dear cousin, I didn't do it, and I can't help it; I would, if I could. If low-minded, brutal people, will act like themselves, what am I to do? They have absolute control; they are irresponsible despots. There would be no use in interfering;

there is no law that amounts to anything practically for such a case. The best we can do is to shut our eyes and ears, and let it alone. It's the only resource left us.'

'How can you shut your eyes and ears? How can you let such things alone?'

'My dear child, what do you expect? Here is a whole class – debased, uneducated, indolent, provoking – put, without any sort of terms or conditions, entirely into the hands of such people as the majority in our world are; people who have neither consideration nor self-control, who haven't even an enlightened regard to their own interest – for that's the case with the largest half of mankind. Of course, in a community so organised, what can a man of honourable and humane feelings do, but shut this eyes all he can, and harden his heart? I can't buy every poor wretch I see. I can't turn knight-errant, and undertake to redress every individual case of wrong in such a city as this. The most I can do is to try and keep out of the way of it.'

St Clare's fine countenance was for a moment overcast; he looked annoyed: but, suddenly calling up a gay smile, he said –

'Come, cousin, don't stand there looking like one of the Fates; you've only seen a peep through the curtain – a specimen of what is going on the world over, in some shape or other. If we are to be prying and spying into all the dismals of life, we should have no heart to anything. 'Tis like looking too close into the details of Dinah's kitchen;' and St Clare lay back on the sofa and busied himself with his paper.

Miss Ophelia sat down and pulled out her knitting-work, and sat there, grim with indignation. She knit and knit; but while she mused the fire burned. At last she broke out –

'I tell you, Augustine, I can't get over things so, if you can. It's a perfect abomination for you to defend such a system – that's *my* mind!'

'What now?' said St Clare, looking up. 'At it again, eh?'

'I say it's perfectly abominable for you to defend such a system!' said Miss Ophelia, with increasing warmth.

'*I* defend it, my dear lady? Who ever said I did defend it?' said St Clare.

'Of course you defend it – you all do – all you Southerners. What do you have slaves for, if you don't?'

'Are you such a sweet innocent as to suppose nobody in this world ever does what they don't think is right? Don't you, or didn't you ever, do anything that you did not think quite right?'

'If I do I repent of it, I hope,' said Miss Ophelia, rattling her needles with energy.

'So do I,' said St Clare, peeling his orange; 'I'm repenting of it all the time.'

'What do you keep on doing it for?'

'Didn't you ever keep on doing wrong after you'd repented, my good cousin?'

'Well, only when I've been very much tempted,' said Miss Ophelia.

'Well, I'm very much tempted,' said St Clare; 'that's just my difficulty.'

'But I always resolve I won't, and try to break it off.'

'Well, I have been resolving I won't, off and on, these ten years,' said St Clare; 'but I haven't, somehow, got clear. Have you got clear of all your sins, cousin?'

'Cousin Augustine,' said Miss Ophelia, seriously, and laying down her knitting-work, 'I suppose I deserve that you should reprove my short-comings. I know all you say is true enough; nobody else feels them more than I do: but it does seem to me, after all, there is some difference between me and you. It seems to me that I would cut off my right hand sooner than keep on, from day to day, doing what I thought was wrong. But then my conduct is so inconsistent with my profession, I don't wonder you reprove me.'

'Oh, now, cousin,' said Augustine, sitting down on the floor, and laying his head back in her lap, 'don't take on so awfully serious! You know what a good-for-nothing, saucy boy I always was. I love to poke you up – that's all – just to see you get earnest. I do think you are desperately, distressingly good; it tires me to death to think of it.'

'But this is a serious subject, my boy, Auguste,' said Miss Ophelia, laying her hand on his forehead.

'Dismally so,' said he; 'and I – well, I never want to talk seriously in hot weather. What with mosquitoes and all, a fellow can't get himself up to any very sublime moral flights; and I believe,' said St Clare, suddenly rousing himself up, 'there's a theory now! I understand now why northern nations are always more virtuous than southern ones – I see into that whole subject.'

'O Auguste, you are a sad rattlebrain!'

'Am I? Well, so I am, I suppose, but for once I will be serious, now; but you must hand that basket of oranges – you see you'll have to "stay me with flagons and comfort me with apples" if I'm going to make this effort. Now,' said Augustine, drawing the basket up, 'I'll begin: When, in the course of human events, it becomes necessary for a fellow to hold two or three dozen of his fellow worms in captivity, a decent regard to the opinions of society requires—'

'I don't see that you are growing more serious,' said Miss Ophelia.

'Wait – I'm coming on – you'll hear. The short of the matter is, cousin,' said he, his handsome face suddenly settling into an earnest and serious expression, 'on this abstract question of slavery there can, as I think, be but one opinion. Planters, who have money to make by it – clergymen, who have planters to please – politicians, who want to rule by it – may warp and bend language and ethics to a degree that shall astonish the world at their ingenuity! They can press Nature and the Bible, and nobody knows what else, into the service; but, after all, neither they nor the world believe in it one particle the more. It comes from the devil, that's the short of it; and, to my mind, it's a pretty respectable specimen of what he can do in his own line.'

Miss Ophelia stopped her knitting, and looked surprised; and St Clare, apparently enjoying her astonishment, went on.

'You seem to wonder; but if you will get me fairly at it, I'll make a clean breast of it. This cursed business, accursed of God and man, what is it? Strip it of all its ornament, run it down to the root and nucleus of the whole, and what is it? Why, because my brother Quashy is ignorant and weak, and I am intelligent and strong – because I know how, and *can* do it – therefore, I may steal all he has, keep it, and give him only such and so much as suits my fancy. Whatever is too hard, too dirty, too disagreeable for me, I may set Quashy to doing. Because I don't like work, Quashy shall work. Because the sun burns me, Quashy shall stay in the sun. Quashy shall earn the money, and I will spend it. Quashy shall lie down in every puddle, that I may walk over dryshod. Quashy shall do my will, and not his, all the days of his mortal life, and have such a chance of getting to heaven at last as I find convenient. This I take to be about what slavery *is*. I defy anybody on earth to read our slave-code, as it stands in our law-books, and make anything else of it. Talk of the *abuses* of slavery! Humbug! The *thing itself* is the essence of all abuse! And the only reason why the land don't sink under it, like Sodom and Gomorrah, is because it is *used* in a way infinitely better than it is. For pity's sake, for shame's sake, because we are men born of women, and not savage beasts, many of us do not, and dare not – we would *scorn* to use the full power which our savage laws put into our hands. And he who goes the furthest, and does the worst, only uses within limits the power that the law gives him.'

St Clare has started up, and, as his manner was when excited, was walking, with hurried steps, up and down the floor. His fine face, classic as that of a Greek statue, seemed actually to burn with the fervour of his feelings. His large blue eyes flashed, and he gestured with an unconscious eagerness. Miss Ophelia had never seen him in this mood before, and she sat perfectly silent.

'I declare to you,' said he, suddenly stopping before his cousin – 'it's no sort of use to talk or to feel on this subject – but I declare to you, there have been times when I have thought, if the whole country would sink, and hide all this injustice and misery from the light, I would willingly sink with it. When I have been travelling up and down on our boats, or about on my collecting tours, and reflected that every brutal, disgusting, mean, low-lived fellow I met, was allowed by our laws to become absolute despot of as many men, women, and children, as he could cheat, steal, or gamble money enough to buy – when I have seen such men in actual ownership of helpless children, of young girls and women – I have been ready to curse my country, to curse the human race!'

'Augustine! Augustine!' said Miss Ophelia, 'I'm sure you've said enough. I never, in my life, heard anything like this; even at the North.'

'At the North!' said St Clare, with a sudden change of expression, and resuming something of his habitual careless tone. 'Pooh! you northern folks are cold-blooded; you are cool in everything! You can't begin to curse up hill and down, as we can when we get fairly at it.'

'Well, but the question is'—said Miss Ophelia.

'Oh, yes, to be sure, the *question is* – and a deuce of a question it is! – How came *you* in this state of sin and misery? Well, I shall answer in the good old words you used to teach me, Sundays. I came so by ordinary generation. My servants were my father's, and, what is more, my mother's; and now they are mine, they and their increase, which bids fair to be a pretty considerable item. My father, you know, came first from New England; and he was just such another man as your father – a regular old Roman; upright, energetic, noble-minded, with an iron will. Your father settled down in New England, to rule over rocks and stones, and to force an existence out of Nature; and mine settled in Louisiana, to rule over men and women, and force an existence out of them. My mother,' said St Clare, getting up and walking to a picture at the end of the room, and gazing upward with a face fervent with veneration, '*she was divine*! Don't look at me so! – you know what I mean! She probably was of mortal birth; but as far as ever I could observe, there was no trace of any human weakness or error about her; and everybody that lives to remember her, whether bond or free, servant, acquaintance, relation, all say the same. Why, cousin, that mother has been all that has stood between me and utter unbelief for years. She was a direct embodiment and personification of the New Testament – a living fact, to be accounted for, and to be accounted for in no other way than by its truth. O mother! mother!' said St Clare, clasping his hands in a sort of transport; and then suddenly checking himself, he came back, and seating himself on an ottoman, he went on: –

'My brother and I were twins; and they say, you know, that twins ought to resemble each other; but we were in all points a contrast. He had black, fiery eyes, coal-black hair, a strong, fine Roman profile, and a rich brown complexion. I had blue eyes, golden hair, a Greek outline, and fair complexion. He was active and observing, I dreamy and inactive. He was generous to his friends and equals, but proud, dominant, overbearing to inferiors, and utterly unmerciful to whatever set itself up against him. Truthful we both were; he from pride and courage, I from a sort of abstract ideality. We loved each other about as boys generally do, off and on, and in general; he was my father's pet, and I my mother's.

'There was a morbid sensitiveness and acuteness of feeling in me on all possible subjects, of which he and my father had no kind of understanding, and with which they could have no possible sympathy. But mother did; and so, when I had quarrelled with Alfred, and father looked sternly on me, I used to go off to mother's room, and sit by her. I remember just how she used to look, with her pale cheeks, her deep, soft, serious eyes, her white dress – she always wore white – and I used to think of her whenever I read in Revelation about the saints that were arrayed in fine linen, clean and white. She had a great deal of genius of one sort or another, particularly in music, and she used to sit at her organ, playing fine old majestic music of the Catholic church, and singing with a voice more like an angel than a mortal woman; and I would lay my head down on her lap, and cry, and dream, and feel – oh, immeasurably! – things that I had no language to say!

'In those days, this matter of slavery had never been canvassed as it has now; nobody dreamed of any harm in it.

'My father was a born aristocrat. I think, in some pre-existent state, he must have been in the higher circles of spirits, and brought all his old court pride along with him; for it was ingrain, bred in the bone, though he was originally of poor and not in any way of noble family. My brother was begotten in his image.

'Now, an aristocrat, you know, the world over, has no human sympathies, beyond a certain line in society. In England the line is in one place, in Burmah in another, and in America in another; but the aristocrat of all these countries never goes over it. What would be hardship and distress and injustice in his own class, is a cool matter of course in another one. My father's dividing line was that of colour. *Among his equals*, never was a man more just and generous; but he considered the negro, through all possible gradations of colour, as an intermediate link between man and animals, and graded all his ideas of justice or generosity on this hypothesis. I suppose, to be sure, if anybody had asked him, plump and fair, whether they had human immortal souls, he might have hemmed and hawed, and said "Yes." But my father was not a man much troubled with spiritualism; religious sentiment he had none, beyond a veneration for God, as decidedly the head of the upper classes.

'Well, my father worked some five hundred negroes; he was an inflexible, driving, punctilious business man; everything was to move by system – to be sustained with unfailing accuracy and precision. Now, if you take into account that all this was to be worked out by a set of lazy, twaddling, shiftless labourers, who had grown up all their lives in the absence of every possible motive to learn how to do anything but "shirk," as you Vermonters say, you'll see that there might naturally be on his plantation a great many things that looked horrible and distressing to a sensitive child like me.

'Besides all, he had an overseer – a great, tall slab-sided, two-fisted, renegade son of Vermont (begging your pardon), who had gone through a regular apprenticeship in hardness and brutality, and taken his degree to be admitted to practice. My mother never could endure him, nor I; but he obtained an entire ascendency over my father; and this man was the absolute despot of the estate.

'I was a little fellow then, but I had the same love that I have now for all kinds of human things – a kind of passion for the study of humanity, come in what shape it would. I was found in the cabins and among the field-hands a great deal, and, of course, was a great favourite; and all sorts of complaints and grievances were breathed in my ear, and I told them to mother, and we, between us, formed a sort of committee for a redress of grievances. We hindered and repressed a great deal of cruelty, and congratulated ourselves on doing a vast deal of good, till, as often happens, my zeal overacted. Stubbs complained to my father that he couldn't manage the hands, and must resign his position. Father was a fond, indulgent husband, but a man that never flinched from anything that he thought necessary; and so he put down his foot, like a rock, between us and the field-hands. He told my mother, in language perfectly respectful and deferential, but quite explicit, that over the house-servants she should be entire mistress, but that with the field-hands he could allow no interference. He revered and respected her above all living things; but he would have said it all the same to the Virgin Mary herself, if she had come in the way of his system.

'I used sometimes to hear my mother reasoning cases with

him – endeavouring to excite his sympathies. He would listen to the most pathetic appeals with the most discouraging politeness and equanimity. "It all resolves itself into this," he would say; "must I part with Stubbs, or keep him? Stubbs is the soul of punctuality, honesty, and efficiency, a thorough business hand, and as humane as the general run. We can't have perfection; and if I keep him, I must sustain his administration as a *whole*, even if there are, now and then, things that are exceptional. All government includes some necessary hardness. General rules will bear hard on particular cases." This last maxim my father seemed to consider a settler in most alleged cases of cruelty. After he had said *that*, he commonly drew up his feet on the sofa, like a man that has disposed of a business, and betook himself to a nap or the newspaper, as the case might be.

'The fact is, my father showed the exact sort of talent for a statesman. He could have divided Poland as easily as an orange, or trod on Ireland as quietly and systematically as any man living. At last my mother gave up, in despair. It never will be known, till the last account, what noble and sensitive natures like hers have felt, cast, utterly helpless, into what seems to them an abyss of injustice and cruelty, and which seems so to nobody about them. It has been an age of long sorrow of such natures, in such a hell-begotten sort of world as ours. What remained for her but to train her children in her own views and sentiments? Well, after all you say about training, children will grow up substantially what they *are* by nature and only that. From the cradle, Alfred was an aristocrat; and as he grew up, instinctively, all his sympathies and all his reasonings were in that line, and all mother's exhortations went to the winds. As to me, they sunk deep into me. She never contradicted, in form, anything that my father said, or seemed directly to differ from him; but she impressed, burnt into my very soul, with all the force of her deep, earnest nature, an idea of the dignity and worth of the meanest human soul. I have looked in her face with solemn awe, when she would point up to the stars in the evening, and say to me, "See there, Auguste! the poorest, meanest soul on our place will be living, when all these stars are gone for ever – will live as long as God lives!"

'She had some fine old paintings; one, in particular, of Jesus healing a blind man. They were very fine, and used to impress me strongly. "See, there, Auguste," she would say; "the blind man was a beggar, poor and loathsome; therefore he would not heal him *afar off*! he called him to him, and put *his hands on him*! Remember this, my boy." If I had lived to grow up under her care, she might have stimulated me to I know not what of enthusiasm. I might have been a saint, reformer, martyr – but, alas! I went from her when I was only thirteen, and I never saw her again.'

St Clare rested his head on his hands, and did not speak for some minutes. After a while he looked up, and went on: –

'What poor, mean trash this whole business of human virtue is! A mere matter, for the most part, of latitude and longitude, and geographical position, acting with natural temperament. The greater part is nothing but an accident. Your father, for example, settles in Vermont, in a town where all are, in fact, free and equal; becomes a regular church member and deacon, and in due time joins an Abolitionist society, and thinks us all little better than heathens. Yet he us, for all the world, in constitution and habit, a duplicate of my father. I can see it leaking out in fifty different ways – just that same strong, overbearing, dominant spirit. You know very well how impossible it is to persuade some of the folks in your village that Squire Sinclair does not feel above them. The fact is, though he has fallen on democratic times, and embraced a democratic theory, he is to the heart an aristocrat, as much as my father, who ruled over five or six hundred slaves.'

Miss Ophelia felt rather disposed to cavil at this picture, and was laying down her knitting to begin, but St Clare stopped her.

'Now I know every word you are going to say. I do not say they *were* alike, in fact. One fell into a condition where everything acted against the natural tendency, and the other where everything acted for it; and so one turned out a pretty wilful, stout, overbearing old democrat, and the other a wilful, stout old despot. If both had owned plantations in Louisiana, they would have been as like as two old bullets cast in the same mould!'

'What an undutiful boy you are!' said Miss Ophelia.

'I don't mean them any disrespect,' said St Clare. 'You know irreverence is not my forte. But to go back to my history: –

'When father died, he left the whole property to us twin boys, to be divided as we should agree. There does not breathe on God's earth a nobler-souled, more generous fellow, than Alfred, in all that concerns his equals; and we got on admirably with this property question, without a single unbrotherly word or feeling. We undertook to work the plantation together; and Alfred, whose outward life and capabilities had double the strength of mine, became an enthusiastic planter, and a wonderfully successful one.

'But two years' trial satisfied me that I could not be a partner in that matter. To have a great gang of seven hundred, whom I could not know personally, or feel any individual interest in, bought and driven, housed, fed, worked like so many horned cattle, trained up to military precision – the question of how little of life's commonest enjoyments would keep them in working order, being a constantly recurring problem, the *necessity* of drivers and overseers, the ever-necessary whip, first, last, and only argument – the whole thing was insufferably disgusting and loathsome to me; and when I thought of my mother's estimate of one poor human soul, it became even frightful.

'It's all nonsense to talk to me about slaves *enjoying* all this ! To this day I have no patience with the unutterable trash that some of your patronising Northerners have made up, as in their zeal to apologise for our sins. We all know better. Tell me that any man living wants to work all his days, from day-dawn till dark, under the constant eye of a master, without the power of putting forth one irresponsible volition, on the same dreary, monotonous, unchanging toil, and all for two pairs of pantaloons and a pair of shoes a-year, with enough food and shelter to keep him in working order ! Any man who thinks that human beings can, as a general thing, be made about as comfortable that way as any other, I wish he might try it. I'd buy the dog and work him, with a clear conscience !'

'I always have supposed,' said Miss Ophelia, 'that you, all of you, approved of these things, and thought them *right* – according to Scripture.'

'Humbug ! we are not quite reduced to that yet. Alfred, who is as determined a despot as ever walked, does not pretend to this kind of defence; no, he stands, high and haughty, on that good, old, respectable ground, *the right of the strongest*; and he says, and I think quite sensibly, that the American planter is "only doing, in another form, what the English aristocracy and capitalists are doing by the lower classes," that is, I take it, *appropriating* them, body and bone, soul and spirit, to their use and convenience. He defends both – and I think, at least, *consistently*. He says that there can be no high civilisation without enslavement of the masses, either nominal or real. There must, he says, be a lower class given up to physical toil and confined to an animal nature ; and a higher one thereby acquires leisure and wealth for a more expanded intelligence and improvement, and becomes the directing soul of the lower. So he reasons, because, as I said, he is born an aristocrat ; so I don't believe, because I was born a democrat.'

'How in the world can the two things be compared ?' said Miss Ophelia. 'The English labourer is not sold, traded, parted from his family, whipped.'

'He is as much at the will of his employer as if he were sold to him. The slave-owner can whip his refractory slave to death – the capitalist can starve him to death. As to family security, it is hard to say which is the worst – to have one's children sold, or see them starve to death at home.'

'But it's no kind of apology for slavery, to prove that it isn't worse than some other bad thing.'

'I didn't give it for one – nay, I'll say, besides, that ours is the more bold and palpable infringement of human rights. Actually buying a man up, like a horse – looking at his teeth, cracking his joints, and trying his paces, and then paying down for him – having speculators, breeders, traders, and brokers in human bodies and souls – sets the thing before the eyes of the civilised world in a more tangible form, though the thing done be, after all, in its nature, the same : that is, appropriating one set of human beings to the use and improvement of another, without any regard to their own.'

'I never thought of the matter in this light,' said Miss Ophelia.

'Well, I've travelled in England some, and I've looked over a good many documents as to the state of their lower classes ; and I really think there is no denying Alfred, when he says that his slaves are better off than a large class of the population of England. You see, you must not infer, from what I have told you, that Alfred is what is called a hard master ; for he isn't. He is despotic, and unmerciful to insubordination ; he would shoot a fellow down with as little remorse as he would shoot a buck, if he opposed him. But, in general, he takes a sort of pride in having his slaves comfortably fed and accommodated.

'When I was with him, I insisted that he should do something for their instruction; and to please me, he did get a chaplain, and used to have them catechised Sundays, though I believe, in his heart, that he thought it would do about as much good to set a chaplain over his dogs and horses. And the fact is, that a mind stupefied and animalised by every bad influence from the hour of birth, spending the whole of every week-day in unreflecting toil, cannot be done much with by a few hours on Sunday. The teachers of Sunday-schools among the manufacturing population of England, and among plantation-hands in our country, could perhaps testify to the same result, *there and here*. Yet some striking exceptions there are among us, from the fact that the negro is naturally more impressible to religious sentiment than the white.'

'Well,' said Miss Ophelia, 'how came you to give up your plantation life?'

'Well, we jogged on together some time, till Alfred saw plainly that I was no planter. He thought it absurd, after he had reformed, and altered, and improved everywhere, to suit my notions, that I still remained unsatisfied. The fact was, it was, after all, the THING that I hated – the using these men and women, the perpetuation of all this ignorance, brutality, and vice – just to make money for me!

'Besides, I was always interfering in the details. Being myself one of the laziest of mortals, I had altogether too much fellow-feeling for the lazy; and when poor, shiftless dogs put stones at the bottom of their cotton baskets to make them weigh heavier, or filled their sacks with dirt, with cotton at the top, it seemed so exactly like what I should do if I were they, I couldn't and wouldn't have them flogged for it. Well, of course, there was an end of plantation discipline; and Alf and I came to about the same point that I and my respected father did, years before. So he told me that I was a womanish sentimentalist, and would never do for business life; and advised me to take the bank-stock and the New Orleans family mansion, and go to writing poetry, and let him manage the plantation. So we parted, and I came here.'

'But why didn't you free your slaves?'

'Well, I wasn't up to that. To hold them as tools for money-making, I could not; have them to help spend money, you know, didn't look quite so ugly to me. Some of them were old house-servants, to whom I was much attached; and the younger ones were children to the old. All were well satisfied to be as they were.' He paused, and walked reflectively up and down the room.

'There was,' said St Clare, 'a time in my life when I had plans and hopes of doing something in this world, more than to float and drift. I had vague, indistinct yearnings to be a sort of emancipator – to free my native land from this spot and stain. All young men have had such fever-fits, I suppose, some time – but then'—

'Why didn't you?' said Miss Ophelia; 'you ought not to put your hand to the plough, and look back.'

'Oh, well, things didn't go with me as I expected, and I got the despair of living that Solomon did. I suppose it was a necessary incident to wisdom in us both; but, somehow or other, instead of being actor and regenerator in society, I became a piece of drift-wood, and have been floating and eddying about, ever since. Alfred scolds me every time we meet, and he has the better of me, I grant; for he really does something. His life is a logical result of his opinions, and mine is a contemptible *non sequitur*.'

'My dear cousin, can you be satisfied with such a way of spending your probation?'

'Satisfied! Was I not just telling you I despised it? But then, to come back to this point – we were on this liberation business. I don't think my feelings about slavery are peculiar. I find many men who, in their hearts, think of it just as I do. The land groans under it; and bad as it is for the slave, it is worse, if anything, for the master. It takes no spectacles to see that a great class of vicious, improvident, degraded people, among us, are an evil to us, as well as to themselves. The capitalist and aristocrat of England cannot feel that as we do, because they do not mingle with the class they degrade as we do. They are in our houses; they are the associates of our children, and they form their minds faster than we can; for they are a race that children always will cling to and assimilate with. If Eva, now, was not

more angel than ordinary, she would be ruined. We might as
well allow the small-pox to run among them, and think our
children would not take it, as to let them be uninstructed and
vicious, and think our children will not be affected by that. Yet
our laws positively and utterly forbid any efficient general
educational system, and they do it wisely, too; for just begin
and thoroughly educate one generation, and the whole thing
would be blown sky high. If we did not give them liberty, they
would take it.'

'And what do you think will be the end of this?' said Miss
Ophelia.

'I don't know. One thing is certain – that there is a mustering
among the masses, the world over; and there is a *dies iræ*
coming on, sooner or later. The same thing is working, in
Europe, in England, and in this country. My mother used to tell
me of a millennium that was coming, when Christ should reign,
and all men should be free and happy. And she taught me, when
I was a boy, to pray, "Thy kingdom come." Sometimes I think
all this sighing, and groaning, and stirring among the dry bones
foretells what she used to tell me was coming. But who may
abide the day of his appearing?'

'Augustine, sometimes I think you are not far from the
kingdom,' said Miss Ophelia, laying down her knitting, and
looking anxiously at her cousin.

'Thank you for your good opinion; but it's up and down with
me – up to heaven's gate in theory, down to earth's dust in
practice. But there's the tea-bell – do let's go – and don't say,
now, I haven't had one downright serious talk for once in my
life.'

At table, Marie alluded to the incident of Prue. 'I suppose
you'll think, cousin,' she said, 'that we are all barbarians.'

'I think that's a barbarous thing,' said Miss Ophelia; 'but I
don't think you are all barbarians.'

'Well, now,' said Marie, 'I know it's impossible to get along
with some of these creatures. They are so bad they ought not to
live. I don't feel a particle of sympathy for such cases. If they'd
only behave themselves, it would not happen.'

'But, mamma,' said Eva, 'the poor creature was unhappy;
that's what made her drink.'

'Oh, fiddlestick! as if that were any excuse! I'm unhappy,

very often. I presume,' she said, pensively, 'that I've had greater trials than ever she had. It's just because they are so bad. There's some of them that you cannot break in by any kind of severity. I remember father had a man that was so lazy he would run away just to get rid of work, and lie round in the swamps, stealing and doing all sorts of horrid things. That man was caught and whipped, time and again, and it never did him any good; and the last time he crawled off, though he couldn't but just go, he died in the swamp. There was no sort of reason for it, for father's hands were always treated kindly.'

'I broke a fellow in, once,' said St Clare, 'that all the overseers and masters had tried their hands on in vain.'

'You!' said Marie; 'well, I'd be glad to know when *you* ever did anything of the sort.'

'Well, he was a powerful, gigantic fellow — a native-born African; and he appeared to have the rude instinct of freedom in him to an uncommon degree. He was a regular African lion. They called him Scipio. Nobody could do anything with him; and he was sold round from overseer to overseer, till at last Alfred bought him, because he thought he could manage him. Well, one day he knocked down the overseer, and was fairly off into the swamps. I was on a visit to Alf's plantation, for it was after we had dissolved partnership. Alfred was greatly exasperated, but I told him that it was his own fault, and laid him any wager that I could break the man; and finally it was agreed that, if I caught him, I should have him to experiment on. So they mustered out a party of some six or seven, with guns and dogs, for the hunt. People, you know, can get up just as much enthusiasm in hunting a man as a deer, if it is only customary; in fact, I got a little excited myself, though I had only put in as a sort of mediator, in case he was caught.

'Well, the dogs bayed and howled, and we rode and scampered, and finally we started him. He ran and bounded like a buck, and kept us well in the rear for some time; but at last he got caught in an impenetrable thicket of cane: then he turned to bay, and I tell you he fought the dogs right gallantly. He dashed them to right and left, and actually killed three of them with only his naked fists, when a shot from a gun brought him down, and he fell, wounded and bleeding, almost at my feet. The poor fellow looked up at me with manhood and despair both in his eye. I kept back the dogs and the party, as they came pressing up, and claimed him as my prisoner. It was all I could do to keep them from shooting him, in the flush of success; but I persisted in my bargain, and Alfred sold him to me. Well, I took him in hand, and in one fortnight I had him tamed down as submissive and tractable as heart could desire.'

'What in the world did you do to him?' said Marie.

'Well, it was quite a simple process. I took him to my own room, had a good bed made for him, dressed his wounds, and tended him myself, until he got fairly on his feet again. And in process of time, I had free papers made out for him, and told him he might go where he liked.'

'And did he go?' said Miss Ophelia.

'No. The foolish fellow tore the paper in two, and absolutely refused to leave me. I never had a braver, better fellow – trusty and true as steel. He embraced Christianity afterwards, and became as gentle as a child. He used to oversee my place on the lake, and did it capitally, too. I lost him the first cholera season. In fact, he laid down his life for me. For I was sick, almost to death; and when, through the panic, everybody else fled, Scipio worked for me like a giant, and actually brought me back into life again. But, poor fellow! he was taken, right after, and there was no saving him. I never felt anybody's loss more.'

Eva had come gradually nearer and nearer to her father, as he told the story – her small lips apart, her eyes wide and earnest with absorbing interest.

As he finished, she suddenly threw her arms around his neck, burst into tears, and sobbed convulsively.

'Eva, dear child! what is the matter?' said St Clare, as the child's small frame trembled and shook with the violence of her feelings. 'This child,' he added, 'ought not to hear any of this kind of thing – she's nervous.'

'No, papa, I'm not nervous,' said Eva, controlling herself suddenly, with a strength of resolution singular in such a child. 'I'm not nervous, but these things *sink into my heart*.'

'What do you mean, Eva?'

'I can't tell you, papa. I think a great many thoughts. Perhaps some day I shall tell you.'

'Well, think away, dear – only don't cry and worry your

papa,' said St Clare. 'Look here – see what a beautiful peach I have got for you!'

Eva took it, and smiled, though there was still a nervous twitching about the corners of her mouth.

'Come, look at the gold-fish,' said St Clare, taking her hand and stepping on to the verandah. A few moments, and merry laughs were heard through the silken curtains, as Eva and St Clare were pelting each other with roses, and chasing each other among the alleys of the court.

There is danger that our humble friend Tom be neglected amid the adventures of the higher born; but if our readers will accompany us up to a little loft over the stable, they may, perhaps, learn a little of his affairs. It was a decent room, containing a bed, a chair, and a small, rough stand, where lay Tom's Bible and hymn-book; and where he sits, at present, with his slate before him, intent on something that seems to cost him a great deal of anxious thought.

The fact was, that Tom's home yearnings had become so strong, that he had begged a sheet of writing-paper of Eva; and, mustering up all his small stock of literary attainment acquired by Mas'r George's instructions, he conceived the bold idea of writing a letter; and he was busy now, on his slate, getting out his first draught. Tom was in a good deal of trouble, for the forms of some of the letters he had forgotten entirely, and of what he did remember he did not know exactly which to use. And while he was working, and breathing very hard in his earnestness, Eva alighted like a bird on the round of his chair behind him and peeped over his shoulder.

'O Uncle Tom! what funny things you *are* making, there!'

'I'm trying to write to my poor old woman, Miss Eva, and my little chil'en,' said Tom, drawing the back of his hand over his eyes; 'but, somehow, I'm feared I shan't make it out.'

'I wish I could help you, Tom! I've learnt to write some. Last year I could make all the letters, but I'm afraid I've forgotten.'

So Eva put her little golden head close to his, and the two commenced a grave and anxious discussion, each one equally earnest, and about equally ignorant; and, with a deal of consulting and advising over every word, the composition began, as they both felt very sanguine, to look quite like writing.

'Yes, Uncle Tom, it really begins to look beautiful,' said Eva, gazing delighted on it. 'How pleased your wife'll be, and the poor little children! Oh, it's a shame you ever had to go away from them! I mean to ask papa to let you go back, some time.'

'Missis said that she would send down money for me, as soon as they could get it together,' said Tom. 'I'm 'spectin' she will. Young Mas'r George, he said he'd come for me; and he gave me this yer dollar as a sign;' and Tom drew from under his clothes the precious dollar.

'Oh, he'll certainly come, then!' said Eva. 'I'm so glad!'

'And I wanted to send a letter, you know, to let 'em know whar I was, and tell poor Chloe that I was well off, 'cause she felt so dreadful, poor soul!'

'I say, Tom!' said St Clare's voice, coming in at the door at this moment.

Tom and Eva both started.

'What's here?' said St Clare, coming up and looking at the slate.

'Oh, it's Tom's letter. I'm helping him to write it,' said Eva; 'isn't it nice?'

'I wouldn't discourage either of you,' said St Clare, 'but I rather think, Tom, you'd better get me to write your letter for you. I'll do it, when I come home from my ride.'

'It's very important he should write,' said Eva, 'because his mistress is going to send down money to redeem him you know, papa; he told me they told him so.'

St Clare thought in his heart that this was probably only one of those things which good-natured owners say to their servants, to alleviate their horror of being sold, without any intention of fulfilling the expectation thus excited. But he did not make any audible comment upon it — only ordered Tom to get the horses out for a ride.

Tom's letter was written in due form for him that evening, and safely lodged in the post-office.

Miss Ophelia still persevered in her labours in the house-keeping line. It was universally agreed among all the household, from Dinah down to the youngest urchin, that Miss Ophelia was decidedly 'curis' — a term by which a southern servant implies that his or her betters don't exactly suit them.

The higher circle in the family — to wit, Adolph, Jane, and

Rosa – agreed that she was no lady; ladies never kept working about as she did; that she had no *air* at all; and they were surprised that she should be any relation of the St Clares. Even Marie declared that it was absolutely fatiguing to see Cousin Ophelia always so busy. And, in fact, Miss Ophelia's industry was so incessant as to lay some foundation for the complaint. She sewed and stitched away from daylight to dark, with the energy of one who is pressed on by some immediate urgency; and then, when the light faded, and the work was folded away, with one turn out came the ever-ready knitting-work, and there she was again, going on as briskly as ever. It really was a labour to see her.

Chapter 20

TOPSY

ONE morning, while Miss Ophelia was busy in some of her domestic cares, St Clare's voice was heard calling her at the foot of the stairs.

'Come down here, cousin; I've something to show you.'

'What is it?' said Miss Ophelia, coming down, with her sewing in her hand.

'I've made a purchase for your department – see here,' said St Clare; and, with the word, he pulled along a little negro girl, about eight or nine years of age.

She was one of the blackest of her race; and her round shining eyes, glittering as glass beads, moved with quick and restless glances over everything in the room. Her mouth, half open with astonishment at the wonders of the new mas'r's parlour, displayed a white and brilliant set of teeth. Her woolly hair was braided in sundry little tails, which stuck out in every direction. The expression of the face was an odd mixture of shrewdness and cunning, over which was oddly drawn, like a kind of veil, an expression of the most doleful gravity and solemnity. She was dressed in a single filthy, ragged garment, made of bagging; and stood with her hands demurely folded before her. Altogether, there was something odd and goblin-like about her appearance – something, as Miss Ophelia afterwards said, 'so heathenish,' as to inspire that good lady with utter dismay; and, turning to St Clare, she said, –

'Augustine, what in the world have you brought that thing here for?'

'For you to educate, to be sure, and train in the way she should go. I thought she was rather a funny specimen in the Jim Crow line. Here, Topsy,' he added, giving a whistle, as a man would to call the attention of a dog, 'give us a song, now, and show us some of your dancing.'

The black, glassy eyes glittered with a kind of wicked drollery, and the thing struck up, in a clear shrill voice, an odd negro melody, to which she kept time with her hands and feet, spinning round, clapping her hands, knocking her knees together, in a wild, fantastic sort of time, and producing in her throat all those odd guttural sounds which distinguish the native music of her race; and finally, turning a summerset or two, and giving a prolonged closing note, as odd and unearthly as that of a steam-whistle, she came suddenly down on the carpet, and stood with her hands folded, and a most sanctimonious expression of meekness and solemnity over her face, only broken by the cunning glances which she shot askance from the corners of her eyes.

Miss Ophelia stood silent, perfectly paralysed with amazement.

St Clare, like a mischievous fellow as he was, appeared to enjoy her astonishment; and, addressing the child again, said, –

'Topsy, this is your new mistress. I'm going to give you up to her; see, now, that you behave yourself.'

'Yes, mas'r,' said Topsy, with a sanctimonious gravity, her wicked eyes twinkling as she spoke.

'You're going to be good, Topsy, you understand,' said St Clare.

'Oh, yes, mas'r,' said Topsy, with another twinkle, her hands still devoutly folded.

'Now, Augustine, what upon earth is this for?' said Miss Ophelia. 'Your house is so full of these little plagues, now, that

a body can't set their foot down without treading on 'em. I get
up in the morning, and find one asleep behind the door, and see
one black head poking out from under the table, one lying on
the door-mat; and they are mopping, and mowing, and grinning
between all the railings, and tumbling over the kitchen floor!
What on earth did you want to bring this one for?'

'For you to educate — didn't I tell you? You're always
preaching about educating. I thought I would make you a
present of a fresh-caught specimen, and let you try your hand
on her, and bring her up in the way she should go.'

'*I* don't want her, I am sure; I have more to do with 'em now
than I want to.'

'That's you Christians, all over. You'll get up a society, and
get some poor missionary to spend all his days among just such
heathen. But let me see one of you that would take one into
your house with you, and take the labour of their conversion on
yourselves! No; when it comes to that, they are dirty and
disagreeable, and it's too much care, and so on.'

'Augustine, you know I didn't think of it in that light,' said
Miss Ophelia, evidently softening. 'Well, it might be a real
missionary work,' said she, looking rather more favourably on
the child.

St Clare had touched the right string. Miss Ophelia's conscientiousness was ever on the alert. 'But,' she added, 'I really didn't
see the need of buying this one — there are enough now in your
house to take all my time and skill.'

'Well, then, cousin,' said St Clare, drawing her aside, 'I ought
to beg your pardon for my good-for-nothing speeches. You are
so good, after all, that there's no sense in them. Why, the fact is,
this concern belonged to a couple of drunken creatures that
keep a low restaurant, that I have to pass by every day, and I
was tired of hearing her screaming, and them beating and
swearing at her. She looked bright and funny, too, as if
something might be made of her; so I bought her, and I'll give
her to you. Try, now, and give her a good orthodox New
England bringing-up, and see what it'll make of her. You know
I haven't any gift that way, but I'd like you to try.'

'Well, I'll do what I can,' said Miss Ophelia; and she
approched her new subject very much as a person might be

supposed to approach a black spider, supposing him to have benevolent designs toward it.

'She's dreadfully dirty, and half-naked,' she said.

'Well, take her downstairs, and make some of them clean and clothe her up.'

Miss Ophelia carried her to the kitchen regions.

'Don't see what Mas'r St Clare wants of 'nother nigger!' said Dinah, surveying the new arrival with no friendly air. 'Won't have her round under *my* feet, *I* know!'

'Pah!' said Rosa and Jane, with supreme disgust; 'let her keep out of our way! What in the world mas'r wanted another of these low niggers for, I can't see!'

'You go long! No more nigger dan you be, Miss Rosa,' said Dinah, who felt this last remark a reflection on herself. 'You seem to tink yourself white folks. You an't nerry one, black *nor* white. I'd like to be one or turrer.'

Miss Ophelia saw that there was nobody in the camp that would undertake to oversee the cleansing and dressing of the new arrival; and so she was forced to do it herself, with some very ungracious and reluctant assistance from Jane.

It is not for ears polite to hear the particulars of the first toilet of a neglected, abused child. In fact, in this world, multitudes must live and die in a state that it would be too great a shock to the nerves of their fellow-mortals even to hear described. Miss Ophelia had a good, strong, practical deal of resolution; and she went through all the disgusting details with heroic thorough-ness, though it must be confessed, with no very gracious air – for endurance was the utmost to which her principles could bring her. When she saw, on the back and shoulders of the child, great welts and calloused spots, ineffaceable marks of the system under which she had grown up thus far, her heart became pitiful within her.

'See there!' said Jane, pointing to the marks, 'don't that show she's a limb? We'll have fine works with her I reckon. I hate these nigger young uns! so disgustin'! I wonder that mas'r would buy her.'

The 'young un' alluded to heard all these comments with the subdued and doleful air which seemed habitual to her, only scanning, with a keen and furtive glance of her flickering eyes, the ornaments which Jane wore in her ears. When arrayed at last in a suit of decent and whole clothing, her hair cropped short to her head, Miss Ophelia, with some satisfaction, said she looked more Christian-like than she did, and in her own mind began to mature some plans for her instruction.

Sitting down before her, she began to question her.

'How old are you, Topsy?'

'Dun no, missis,' said the image, with a grin that showed all her teeth.

'Don't know how old you are? Didn't anybody ever tell you? Who was your mother?'

'Never had none,' said the child, with another grin.

'Never had any mother! What do you mean? Where were you born?'

'Never was born!' persisted Topsy, with another grin, that looked so goblin-like, that, if Miss Ophelia had been at all nervous, she might have fancied that she had got hold of some sooty gnome from the land of Diablerie; but Miss Ophelia was not nervous, but plain and business-like, and she said, with some sternness —

'You mustn't answer me in that way, child; I'm not playing with you. Tell me where you were born, and who your father and mother were.'

'Never was born,' reiterated the creature, more emphatically; 'never had no father nor mother, nor nothin'. I was raised by a speculator, with lots of others. Old Aunt Sue used to take car on us.'

The child was evidently sincere; and Jane, breaking into a short laugh, said —

'Laws, missis, there's heaps of 'em. Speculators buys 'em up cheap, when they's little, and gets 'em raised for market.'

'How long have you lived with your master and mistress?'

'Dun no, missis.'

'Is it a year, or more, or less?'

'Dun no, missis.'

'Laws, missis, those low negroes, they can't tell; they don't know anything about time,' said Jane: 'they don't know what a year is; they don't know their own ages.'

'Have you ever heard anything about God, Topsy?'

The child looked bewildered, but grinned as usual.

'Do you know who made you?'

'Nobody, as I knows on,' said the child, with a short laugh.

The idea appeared to amuse her considerably; for her eyes twinkled, and she added –

'I 'spect I grow'd. Don't think nobody never made me.'

'Do you know how to sew?' said Miss Ophelia, who thought she would turn her inquiries to something more tangible.

'No, missis.'

'What can you do? – what did you do for your master and mistress?'

'Fetch water, and wash dishes, and rub knives, and wait on folks.'

'Were they good to you?'

"Spect they was,' said the child, scanning Miss Ophelia cunningly.

Miss Ophelia rose from this encouraging colloquy; St Clare was leaning over the back of her chair.

'You find virgin soil there, cousin; put in your own ideas – you won't find many to pull up.'

Miss Ophelia's ideas of education, like all her other ideas, were very set and definite, and of the kind that prevailed in New England a century ago, and which are still preserved in some very retired and unsophisticated parts, where there are no railroads. As nearly as could be expressed, they could be comprised in very few words; to teach them to mind when they were spoken to; to teach them the catechism, sewing, and reading; and to whip them if they told lies. And though, of course, in the flood of light that is now poured on education, these are left far away in the rear, yet it is an undisputed fact that our grandmothers raised some tolerably fair men and women under this *régime*, as many of us can remember and testify. At all events, Miss Ophelia knew of nothing else to do, and therefore applied her mind to her heathen with the best diligence she could command.

The child was announced and considered in the family as Miss Ophelia's girl; and, as she was looked upon with no gracious eye in the kitchen, Miss Ophelia resolved to confine her sphere of operation and instruction chiefly to her own chamber. With a self-sacrifice which some of our readers will appreciate, she resolved, instead of comfortably making her own bed, sweeping and dusting her own chamber – which she had hitherto done, in utter scorn of all offers of help from the chambermaid of the establishment – to condemn herself to the martyrdom of instructing Topsy to perform these operations. Ah, woe the day ! Did any of our readers ever do the same, they will appreciate the amount of her self-sacrifice.

Miss Ophelia began with Topsy by taking her into her chamber the first morning, and solemnly commencing a course of instruction in the art and mystery of bed-making.

Behold, then, Topsy, washed and shorn of all the little braided tails wherein her heart had delighted, arrayed in a clean gown, with well-starched apron, standing reverently before Miss Ophelia, with an expression of solemnity well befitting a funeral.

'Now, Topsy, I'm going to show you just how my bed is to be made. I am very particular about my bed. You must learn exactly how to do it.'

'Yes, ma'am,' says Topsy, with a deep sigh, and a face of woeful earnestness.

'Now, Topsy, look here : this is the hem of the sheet – this is the right side of the sheet, and this is the wrong : will you remember ?'

'Yes, ma'am,' says Topsy, with another sigh.

'Well, now, the under sheet you must bring over the bolster – so – and tuck it clear down under the mattress nice and smooth – so ; do you see ?'

'Yes, ma'am,' said Topsy, with profound attention.

'But the upper sheet,' said Miss Ophelia, 'must be brought down in this way, and tucked under firm and smooth at the foot – so – the narrow hem at the foot.'

'Yes, ma'am,' said Topsy, as before ; but we will add, what Miss Ophelia did not see, that, during the time when the good lady's back was turned, in the zeal of her manipulations, the young disciple had contrived to snatch a pair of gloves and a ribbon, which she had adroitly slipped into her sleeves, and stood with her hands dutifully folded, as before.

'Now, Topsy, let's see *you* do this,' said Miss Ophelia, pulling off the clothes, and seating herself.

Topsy, with great gravity and adroitness, went through the exercise completely to Miss Ophelia's satisfaction ; smoothing the sheets, patting out every wrinkle, and exhibiting, through the whole process, a gravity and seriousness with which her instructress was greatly edified. By an unlucky slip, however, a fluttering fragment of the ribbon hung out of one of her sleeves, just as she was finishing, and caught Miss Ophelia's attention. Instantly, she pounced upon it. 'What's this? You naughty, wicked child – you've been stealing this!'

The ribbon was pulled out of Topsy's own sleeve, yet was she not in the least disconcerted; she only looked at it with an air of the most surprised and unconscious innocence.

'Laws! why that ar's Miss Feely's ribbon, ain't it? How could it a got in my sleeve?'

'Topsy, you naughty girl, don't you tell me a lie; you stole that ribbon!'

'Missis, I declar for't, I didn't; never seed it till dis yer blessed minnit.'

'Topsy,' said Miss Ophelia, 'don't you know it's wicked to tell lies.'

'I never tell no lies, Miss Feely,' said Topsy, with virtuous gravity; 'it's jist the truth I've been a tell'in now, and an't nothin' else.'

'Topsy, I shall have to whip you, if you tell lies so.'

'Law, missis, if you's to whip all day, couldn't say no other way,' said Topsy, beginning to blubber. 'I never seed dat ar, it must a got caught in my sleeve. Miss Feely must have left it on the bed, and it got caught in the clothes, and so got in my sleeve.'

Miss Ophelia was so indignant at the barefaced lie, that she caught the child and shook her.

'Don't you tell me that again.'

The shake brought the gloves on to the floor, from the other sleeve.

'There you!' said Miss Ophelia, 'will you tell me now you didn't steal the ribbon?'

Topsy now confessed to the gloves, but still persisted in denying the ribbon.

'Now, Topsy,' said Miss Ophelia, 'if you'll confess all about it, I won't whip you this time.' Thus adjured, Topsy confessed to the ribbon and gloves, with woeful protestations of penitence.

'Well, now, tell me. I know you must have taken other things since you have been in the house, for I let you run about all day yesterday. Now, tell me if you took anything, and I shan't whip you.'

'Law, missis! I took Miss Eva's red thing she wars on her neck.'

'You did, you naughty child! Well, what else?'

'I took Rosa's yer-rings – them red ones.'

'Go bring them to me this minute, both of 'em.'

'Laws, missis, I can't – they's burnt up!'

'Burnt up? – what a story! Go get 'em, or I'll whip you.'

Topsy, with loud protestations, and tears, and groans, declared that she *could* not. 'They's burnt up – they was.'

'What did you burn 'em up for?' said Miss Ophelia.

''Cause I's wicked – I is. I's mighty wicked, anyhow. I can't help it.'

Just at this moment Eva came innocently into the room, with the identical coral necklace on her neck.

'Why, Eva, where did you get your necklace?' said Miss Ophelia.

'Get it? Why, I've had it on all day,' said Eva.

'Did you have it on yesterday?'

'Yes; and what is funny, aunty, I had it on all night. I forget to take it off when I went to bed.'

Miss Ophelia looked perfectly bewildered; the more so as Rosa at that instant came into the room, with a basket of newly-ironed linen poised on her head, and the coral ear-drops shaking in her ears.

'I'm sure I can't tell anything what to do with such a child!' she said, in despair. 'What in the world did you tell me you took those things for, Topsy?'

'Why, missis said I must 'fess; and I couldn't think of nothin' else to 'fess,' said Topsy, rubbing her eyes.

'But, of course, I didn't want you to confess things you didn't do,' said Miss Ophelia; 'that's telling a lie, just as much as the other.'

'Laws, now, is it?' said Topsy, with an air of innocent wonder.

'La, there an't any such thing as truth in that limb,' said Rosa, looking indignantly at Topsy. 'If I was Mas'r St Clare, I'd whip her till the blood run, I would! I'd let her catch it!'

'No, no, Rosa,' said Eva, with an air of command, which the

child could assume at times, 'you mustn't talk so, Rosa. I can't bear to hear it.'

'La, sakes! Miss Eva, you's so good, you don't know nothing how to get along with niggers. There's no way but cut 'em well up, I tell ye.'

'Rosa,' said Eva, 'hush! Don't you say another word of that sort,' and the eye of the child flashed, and her cheek deepened in colour.

Rosa was cowed in a moment.

'Miss Eva has got the St Clare blood in her, that's plain. She can speak for all the world just like her papa,' she said, as she passed out of the room.

Eva stood looking at Topsy.

There stood the two children, representatives of the two extremes of society. The fair, high-bred child, with her golden hair, her deep eyes, her spiritual, noble brow, and prince-like movements; and her black, keen, subtle, cringing, yet acute neighbour. They stood the representatives of their races. The Saxon, born of ages of cultivation, command, education, physical and moral eminence; the Afric, born of ages of oppression, ignorance, toil, and vice!

Something, perhaps, of such thoughts struggled through Eva's mind. But a child's thoughts are rather dim, undefined instincts; and in Eva's noble nature many such were yearning and working, for which she had no power of utterance. When Miss Ophelia expatiated on Topsy's naughty, wicked conduct, the child looked perplexed and sorrowful, but said, sweetly –

'Poor Topsy, why need you steal? You're going to be taken good care of now. I'm sure I'd rather give you anything of mine than have you steal it.'

It was the first word of kindness the child had ever heard in her life; and the sweet tone and manner struck strangely on the wild, rude heart, and a sparkle of something like a tear shone in the keen, round, glittering eye; but it was followed by a short laugh and habitual grin. No! the ear that has never heard anything but abuse is strangely incredulous of anything so heavenly as kindness; and Topsy only thought Eva's speech something funny and inexplicable – she did not believe it.

But what was to be done with Topsy? Miss Ophelia found the case a puzzler; her rules for bringing up didn't seem to apply. She thought she would take time to think of it; and, by the way of gaining time, and in hope of some indefinite moral virtues supposed to be inherent in dark closets, Miss Ophelia shut Topsy up in one till she had arranged her ideas further on the subject.'

'I don't see,' said Miss Ophelia to St Clare, 'how I'm going to manage that child, without whipping her.'

'Well, whip her, then, to your heart's content; I'll give you full power to do what you like.'

'Children always have to be whipped,' said Miss Ophelia; 'I never heard of bringing them up without.'

'Oh, well, certainly,' said St Clare; 'do as you think best. Only I'll make one suggestion: I've seen this child whipped with a poker, knocked down with a shovel or tongs, whichever came handiest; and, seeing that she is used to that style of operation, I think your whippings will have to be pretty energetic to make much impression.'

'What is to be done with her, then?' said Ophelia.

'You have started a serious question,' said St Clare; 'I wish you'd answer it. What is to be done with a human being that can be governed only by the lash? – *that* fails – it's a very common state of things down here.'

'I'm sure I don't know; I never saw such a child as this.'

'Such children are very common among us, and such men and women too. How are they to be governed?' said St Clare.

'I'm sure it's more than I can say,' said Miss Ophelia.

'Or I either,' said St Clare. 'The horrid cruelties and outrages that once and a while find their way into the papers – such cases as Prue's, for example – what do they come from? In many cases, it is a gradual hardening process on both sides – the owner growing more and more cruel, as the servants more and more callous. Whipping and abuse are like laudanum; you have to double the dose as the sensibilities decline. I saw this very early when I became an owner; and I resolved never to begin, because I did not know when I should stop; and I resolved, at least, to protect my own moral nature. The consequence is, that my servants act like spoiled children; but I think that better than for us both to be brutalised together. You have talked a great deal about our responsibilities in educating, cousin. I really wanted you to *try* with one child, who is a specimen of thousands among us.'

'It is your system makes such children,' said Miss Ophelia.

'I know it; but they are *made* – they exist – and what *is* to be done with them?'

'Well, I can't say I thank you for the experiment. But, then, as it appears to be a duty, I shall persevere and try, and do the best I can,' said Miss Ophelia; and Miss Ophelia, after this, did labour, with a commendable degree of zeal and energy, on her new subject. She instituted regular hours and employments for her, and undertook to teach her to read and to sew.

In the former art the child was quick enough. She learned her letters as if by magic; and was very soon able to read plain reading; but the sewing was a more difficult matter. The creature was as lithe as a cat, and as active as a monkey, and the confinement of sewing was her abomination; so she broke her needles, threw them slily out of windows, or down in chinks of the walls; she tangled, broke, and dirtied her thread, or, with a sly movement, would throw a spool away altogether. Her motions were almost as quick as those of a practised conjuror, and her command of her face quite as great; and though Miss Ophelia could not help feeling that so many accidents could not possibly happen in succession, yet she could not, without a watchfulness which would leave her no time for anything else, detect her.

Topsy was soon a noted character in the establishment. Her talent for every species of drollery, grimace, and mimicry – for dancing, tumbling, climbing, singing, whistling, imitating every sound that hit her fancy – seemed inexhaustible. In her play-hours she invariably had every child in the establishment at her heels, open-mouthed with admiration and wonder – not excepting Miss Eva, who appeared to be fascinated by her wild diablerie, as a dove is sometimes charmed by a glittering serpent. Miss Ophelia was uneasy that Eva should fancy Topsy's society so much, and implored St Clare to forbid it.

'Poh! let the child alone,' said St Clare. 'Topsy will do her good.'

'But so depraved a child – are you not afraid she will teach her some mischief?'

'She can't teach her mischief; she might teach it to some

children, but evil rolls off Eva's mind like dew off a cabbage-leaf – not a drop sinks in.'

'Don't be too sure,' said Miss Ophelia. 'I know I'd never let a child of mine play with Topsy.'

'Well, your children needn't,' said St Clare, 'but mine may; if Eva could have been spoiled, it would have been done years ago.'

Topsy was at first despised and contemned by the upper servants: they soon found reason to alter their opinion. It was very soon discovered that whoever cast an indignity on Topsy was sure to meet with some inconvenient accident shortly after – either a pair of ear-rings or some cherished trinket would be missing, or an article of dress would be suddenly found utterly ruined, or the person would stumble accidentally into a pail of hot water, or a libation of dirty slop would unaccountably deluge them from above when in full gala dress; and on all these occasions, when investigation was made, there was nobody found to stand sponsor for the indignity. Topsy was cited, and had up before all the domestic judicatories, time and again; but always sustained her examinations with most edifying innocence and gravity of appearance. Nobody in the world ever doubted who did the things; but not a scrap of direct evidence could be found to establish the suppositions, and Miss Ophelia was too just to feel at liberty to proceed to any lengths without it.

The mischiefs done were always so nicely timed, also, as further to shelter the aggressor. Thus, the times for revenge on Rosa and Jane, the two chambermaids, were always chosen in those seasons when (as not unfrequently happened) they were in disgrace with their mistress, when any complaint from them would of course meet with no sympathy. In short, Topsy soon made the household understand the propriety of letting her alone; and she was let alone accordingly.

Topsy was smart and energetic in all manual operations, learning everything that was taught her with surprising quickness. With a few lessons she had learned to do the proprieties of Miss Ophelia's chamber in a way with which even that particular lady could find no fault. Mortal hands could not lay spread smoother, adjust pillows more accurately, sweep and dust and arrange more perfectly, than Topsy, when she chose – but she didn't very often choose. If Miss Ophelia, after three or four days of careful and patient supervision, was so sanguine as to suppose that Topsy had at last fallen into her way, could do without overlooking, and so go off and busy herself about something else, Topsy would hold a perfect carnival of confusion for some one or two hours. Instead of making the bed, she would amuse herself with pulling off the pillow-cases, butting her woolly head among the pillows, till it would sometimes be grotesquely ornamented with feathers sticking out in various directions; she would climb the posts, and hang head downward from the tops; flourish the sheets and spreads all over the apartment; dress the bolster up in Miss Ophelia's night-clothes, and enact various scenic performances with that – singing and whistling, and making grimaces at herself in the looking-glass; in short, as Miss Ophelia phrased it, 'raising Cain' generally.

On one occasion, Miss Ophelia found Topsy with her very best scarlet India Canton crape shawl wound round her head for a turban, going on with her rehearsals before the glass in great style – Miss Ophelia having, with carelessness most unheard of in her, left the key for once in her drawer.

'Topsy!' she would say, when at the end of all patience, 'what does make you act so?'

'Dun no, missis – I 'spects 'cause I's so wicked!'

'I don't know anything what I shall do with you, Topsy.'

'Law, missis, you must whip me; my old missis allers whipped me. I an't used to workin' unless I gets whipped.'

'Why, Topsy, I don't want to whip you. You can do well, if you've a mind to; what is the reason you won't?'

'Laws, missis, I's used to whippin'; I 'spects it's good for me.'

Miss Ophelia tried the recipe, and Topsy invariably made a terrible commotion, screaming, groaning, and imploring; though half an hour afterwards, when roosted on some projection of the balcony, and surrounded by a flock of admiring 'young uns,' she would express the utmost contempt of the whole affair.

'Law, Miss Feely whip! – wouldn't kill a skeeter, her whippins. Oughter see how old mas'r made the flesh fly; old mas'r know'd how!'

Topsy always made great capital of her own sins and enormities, evidently considering them as something peculiarly distinguishing.

'Law, you niggers,' she would say to some of her auditors, 'does you know you's all sinners? Well, you is, everybody is. White folks is sinners, too – Miss Feely says so; but I 'spects niggers is the biggest ones; but lor! ye an't any on ye up to me. I's so awful wicked there can't nobody do nothin' with me. I used to keep old missis a swarin' at me half de time. I 'spects I's the wickedest crittur in the world;' and Topsy would cut a summerset, and come up brisk and shining on to a higher perch, and evidently plume herself on the distinction.

Miss Ophelia busied herself very earnestly on Sundays, teaching Topsy the catechism. Topsy had an uncommon verbal memory, and committed with a fluency that greatly encouraged her instructress.

'What good do you expect it is going to do her?' said St Clare.

'Why, it always has done children good. It's what children always have to learn, you know,' said Miss Ophelia.

'Understand it or not?' said St Clare.

'Oh, children never understand it at the time; but after they are grown up, it'll come to them.'

'Mine hasn't come to me yet,' said St Clare, 'though I'll bear testimony that you put it into me pretty thoroughly when I was a boy.'

'Ah, you were always good at learning, Augustine. I used to have great hopes of you,' said Miss Ophelia.

'Well, haven't you now?' said St Clare.

'I wish you were as good as you were when you were a boy, Augustine.'

'So do I, that's a fact, cousin,' said St Clare. 'Well, go ahead and catechise Topsy; maybe you'll make out something yet.'

Topsy, who had stood like a black statue during this discussion, with hands decently folded, now, at a signal from Miss Ophelia, went on: –

'Our first parents, being left to the freedom of their own will, fell from the state wherein they were created.'

Topsy's eyes twinkled, and she looked inquiringly.

'What is it, Topsy?' said Miss Ophelia.

'Please, missis, was dat ar state Kentuck?'

'What state, Topsy?'

'Dat state dey fell out of. I used to hear mas'r tell how we came down from Kentuck.'

St Clare laughed.

'You'll have to give her a meaning, or she'll make one,' said he. 'There seems to be a theory of emigration suggested there.'

'O Augustine, be still!' said Miss Ophelia: 'how can I do anything if you'll be laughing?'

'Well, I won't disturb the exercises again, on my honour;' and St Clare took his paper into the parlour, and sat down till Topsy had finished her recitations. They were all very well, only that now and then she would oddly transpose some important words, and persist in the mistake, in spite of every effort to the contrary; and St Clare, after all his promises of goodness, took a wicked pleasure in these mistakes, calling Topsy to him whenever he had a mind to amuse himself, and getting her to repeat the offending passages, in spite of Miss Ophelia's remonstrances.

'How do you think I can do anything with the child, if you will go on so, Augustine?' she would say.

'Well, it is too bad; I won't again; but I do like to hear the droll little image stumble over those big words!'

'But you confirm her in the wrong way.'

'What's the odds? One word is as good as another to her.'

'You wanted me to bring her up right; and you ought to remember she is a reasonable creature and be careful of your influence over her.'

'Oh, dismal! so I ought; but, as Topsy herself says, I's so wicked!'

In very much this way Topsy's training proceeded, for a year or two — Miss Ophelia worrying herself from day to day with her as a kind of chronic plague, to whose inflictions she became, in time, as accustomed as persons sometimes do to the neuralgia or sick-headache.

St Clare took the same kind of amusement in the child that a man might in the tricks of a parrot or a pointer. Topsy, whenever her sins brought her into disgrace in other quarters, always took refuge behind his chair; and St Clare, in one way or other, would make peace for her. From him she got many a stray picayune, which she laid out in nuts and candies, and distributed, with careless generosity, to all the children in the family; for Topsy, to do her justice, was good-natured and liberal, and only spiteful in self-defence. She is fairly introduced into our *corps de ballet*, and will figure from time to time, in her turn, with other performers.

Chapter 21

KENTUCK

OUR readers may not be unwilling to glance back, for a brief interval, at Uncle Tom's Cabin, on the Kentucky farm, and see what has been transpiring among those whom he had left behind.

It was late in the summer afternoon, and the doors and windows of the large parlour all stood open, to invite any stray breeze that might feel in a good humour to enter. Mr Shelby sat in a large hall opening into the room, and running through the whole length of the house to a balcony on either end. Leisurely tipped back in one chair, with his heels in another, he was enjoying his after-dinner cigar. Mrs Shelby sat in the door, busy about some fine sewing; she seemed like one who had something on her mind, which she was seeking an opportunity to introduce.

'Do you know,' she said, 'that Chloe has had a letter from Tom?'

'Ah! has she? Tom's got some friend there, it seems. How is the old boy?'

'He has been bought by a very fine family, I should think,' said Mrs Shelby; 'is kindly treated, and has not much to do.'

'Ah! well, I'm glad of it – very glad,' said Mr Shelby, heartily. 'Tom, I suppose, will get reconciled to a southern residence – hardly want to come up here again.'

'On the contrary, he inquires very anxiously,' said Mrs Shelby, 'when the money for his redemption is to be raised.'

'I'm sure *I* don't know,' said Mr Shelby. 'Once get business running wrong, there does seem to be no end to it. It's like jumping from one bog to another, all through a swamp; borrow of one to pay another, and then borrow of another to pay one – and these confounded notes falling due before a man has time to smoke a cigar and turn round – dunning letters and dunning messages – all scamper and hurry-scurry.'

'It does seem to me, my dear, that something might be done to straighten matters. Suppose we sell off all the horses, and sell one of your farms, and pay up square?'

'Oh! ridiculous, Emily! You are the finest woman in Kentucky, but still you haven't sense to know that you don't understand business; women never do, and never can.'

'But, at least,' said Mrs Shelby, 'could you not give me some little insight into yours? – a list of all your debts, at least, and of all that is owed to you, and let me try and see if I can't help you to economise.'

'Oh, bother! don't plague me, Emily! – I can't tell exactly. I know somewhere about what things are likely to be; but there's no trimming and squaring my affairs, as Chloe trims crusts off her pies. You don't know anything about business, I tell you.'

And Mr Shelby, not knowing any other way of enforcing his ideas, raised his voice; a mode of arguing very convenient and convincing, when a gentleman is discussing matters of business with his wife.

Mrs Shelby ceased talking, with something of a sigh. The fact was, that though, as her husband had stated, she was a woman, she had a clear, energetic, practical mind, and a force of character every way superior to that of her husband; so that it would not have been so very absurd a supposition to have allowed her capable of managing, as Mr Shelby supposed. Her heart was set on performing her promise to Tom and Aunt Chloe, and she sighed as discouragements thickened around her.

'Don't you think we might, in some way, contrive to raise that money? Poor Aunt Chloe! her heart is so set on it!'

'I'm sorry if it is. I think I was premature in promising. I'm not sure, now, but it's the best way to tell Chloe, and let her make up her mind to it. Tom'll have another wife in a year or two, and she had better take up with somebody else.'

'Mr Shelby, I have taught my people that their marriages are as sacred as ours. I never could think of giving Chloe such advice.'

'It's a pity, wife, that you have burdened them with a morality above their condition and prospects. I always thought so.'

'It's only the morality of the Bible, Mr Shelby.'

'Well, well, Emily, I don't pretend to interfere with your religious notions, only they seem extremely unfitted for people in that condition.'

'They are, indeed,' said Mrs Shelby; 'and that is why, from my soul, I hate the whole thing. I tell you, my dear, *I* cannot absolve myself from the promises I make to these helpless creatures. If I can get the money no other way, I will take music scholars; I could get enough, I know, and earn the money myself.'

'You wouldn't degrade yourself that way, Emily? I never could consent to it.'

'Degrade! would it degrade me as much as to break my faith with the helpless? No, indeed!'

'Well, you are always heroic and transcendental,' said Mr Shelby, 'but I think you had better think before you undertake such a piece of Quixotism.'

Here the conversation was interrupted by the appearance of Aunt Chloe, at the end of the verandah.

'If you please, missis' – she said.

'Well, Chloe, what is it?' said her mistress, rising, and going to the end of the balcony.

'If missis would come and look at dis yer lot o' poetry.'

Chloe had a particular fancy for calling poultry poetry, an application of language in which she always persisted, notwithstanding frequent corrections and advisings from the young members of the family.

'La sakes!' she would say, 'I can't see; one jis good as turrer, poetry suthin' good, any how;' and so poetry Chloe continued to call it.

Mrs Shelby smiled as she saw a prostrate lot of chickens and ducks, over which Chloe stood, with a very grave face of consideration.

'I'm a thinkin' whether missis would be a havin' a chicken pie o' dese yer.'

'Really, Aunt Chloe I don't much care; serve them any way you like.'

Chloe stood handling them over abstractedly, it was quite

evident that the chickens were not what she was thinking of. At last, with the short laugh with which her tribe often introduce a doubtful proposal, she said –

'Laws me, missis, what should mas'r and missis be a troublin' theirselves 'bout de money, and not a usin' what right in der hands?' and Chloe laughed again.

'I don't understand you, Chloe,' said Mrs Shelby, nothing doubting, from her knowledge of Chloe's manner, that she had heard every word of the conversation that had passed between her and her husband.

'Why, laws me, missis!' said Chloe, laughing again, 'other folks hire out der niggers, and makes money on 'em! Don't keep sich a tribe eatin' 'em out of house and home.'

'Well, Chloe, who do you propose that we should hire out?'

'Laws! I ain't a proposin' nothin'; only Sam he said der was one of dese yer *perfectioners*, dey calls 'em, in Louisville, said he wanted a good hand at cake and pastry, and said he'd give four dollars a-week to one, he did.'

'Well, Chloe?'

'Well, laws, I's a thinkin', missis, it's time Sally was put along to be doin' something. Sally's been under my care, now, dis some time, and she does most as well as me, considerin'; and if missis would only let me go, I would help fetch up de money. I an't afraid to put my cake, nor pies nother, 'long side no *perfectioner's*.'

'Confectioner's, Chloe.'

'Law sakes, missis! 't an't no odds; words is so curis, can't never get 'em right!'

'But, Chloe, do you want to leave your children?'

'Laws, missis! de boys is big enough to do day's works; dey does well enough; and Sally, she'll take de baby – she's such a peart young un, she won't take no looking arter.'

'Louisville is a good way off.'

'Law sakes! who's afeard? it's down river, somer near my old man, perhaps?' said Chloe, speaking the last in the tone of a question, and looking at Mrs Shelby.

'No, Chloe; it's many a hundred miles off,' said Mrs Shelby.

Chloe's countenance fell.

'Never mind; your going there shall bring you nearer, Chloe.

Yes, you may go; and your wages shall every cent of them be laid aside for your husband's redemption.'

As when a bright sunbeam turns a dark cloud to silver, so Chloe's dark face brightened immediately; it really shone.

'Laws! if missis isn't too good! I was thinking of dat ar very thing; cause I shouldn't need no clothes, nor shoes, nor nothin'. I could save every cent. How many weeks is der in a yer, missis?'

'Fifty-two,' said Mrs Shelby.

'Laws! now, dere is? and four dollars for each on 'em. Why, how much dat ar be?'

'Two hundred and eight dollars,' said Mrs Shelby.

'Why-e,' said Chloe, with an accent of surprise and delight; 'and how long would it take me to work it out, missis?'

'Some four or five years, Chloe; but then you needn't do it all, I shall add something to it.'

'I wouldn't hear to missis' givin' lessons nor nothin'. Mas'r's quite right in dat ar; 'twouldn't do no ways. I hope none our family ever be brought to dat ar, while I's got hands.'

'Don't fear, Chloe; I'll take care of the honour of the family,' said Mrs Shelby, smiling. 'But when do you expect to go?'

'Well, I warn't spectin' nothin'; only Sam, he's a gwine to de river with some colts, and he said I could go 'long with him; so I jest put my things together. If missis was willin' I'd go with Sam to-morrow mornin', if missis would write my pass, and write me a commendation.'

'Well, Chloe, I'll attend to it, if Mr Shelby has no objections. I must speak to him.'

Mrs Shelby went upstairs, and Aunt Chloe, delighted, went out to her cabin, to make her preparation.

'Law sakes, Mas'r George! ye didn't know I's a gwine to Louisville to-morrow!' she said to George, as entering her cabin, he found her busy in sorting over her baby's clothes. 'I thought I'd jist look over Sis's things, and get 'em straightened up. But I'm gwine, Mas'r George – gwine to have four dollars a-week; and missis is gwine to lay it all up, to buy back my old man again!'

'Whew!' said George 'here's a stroke of business, to be sure! How are you going?'

'To-morrow, wid Sam. And now Mas'r George, I knows

you'll jist sit down and write to my old man, and tell him all about it – won't ye ?'

'To be sure,' said George ; 'Uncle Tom'll be right glad to hear from us. I'll go right in the house for paper and ink ; and then, you know, Aunt Chloe, I can tell about the new colts and all.'

'Sartin, sartin, Mas'r George ; you go 'long, and I'll get ye up a bit o' chicken, or some sich : ye won't have many more suppers wid your poor old aunty.'

Chapter 22

'THE GRASS WITHERETH – THE FLOWER FADETH'

LIFE passes with us all, a day at a time ; so it passed with our friend Tom, till two years were gone. Though parted from all his soul held dear, and though often yearning for what lay beyond, still was he never positively and consciously miserable ; for, so well is the harp of human feeling strung, that nothing but a crash that breaks every string can wholly mar its harmony ; and, on looking back to seasons which in review appear to us as those of deprivation and trial, we can remember that each hour, as it glided, brought its diversions and alleviations, so that, though not happy wholly, we were not, either, wholly miserable.

Tom read, in his only literary cabinet, of one who had 'learned, in whatsoever state he was, therewith to be content.' It seemed to him good and reasonable doctrine, and accorded well with the settled and thoughtful habit which he had acquired from the reading of that same book.

His letter homeward, as we related in the last chapter, was in due time answered by Master George, in a good, round, school-boy hand, that Tom said might be read 'most acrost the room.' It contained various refreshing items of home intelligence, with which our reader is fully acquainted ; stated how Aunt Chloe had been hired out to a confectioner in Louisville, where her skill in the pastry line was gaining wonderful sums of money, all of which, Tom was informed, was to be laid up to go to make up the sum of his redemption money; Mose and Pete were thriving, and the baby was trotting all about the house, under the care of Sally and the family generally.

Tom's cabin was shut up for the present; but George expatiated brilliantly on ornaments and additions to be made to it when Tom came back.

The rest of this letter gave a list of George's school studies, each one headed by a flourishing capital; and also told the names of four new colts that had appeared on the premises since Tom left; and stated, in the same connection, that father and mother were well. The style of the letter was decidedly concise and terse; but Tom thought it the most wonderful specimen of composition that had appeared in modern times. He was never tired of looking at it, and even held a council with Eva on the expediency of getting it framed, to hang up in his room. Nothing but the difficulty of arranging it so that both sides of the page would show at once, stood in the way of this undertaking.

The friendship between Tom and Eva had grown with the child's growth. It would be hard to say what place she held in the soft, impressible heart of her faithful attendant. He loved her as something frail and earthly, yet almost worshipped her as something heavenly and divine. He gazed on her as the Italian sailor gazes on his image of the child Jesus – with a mixture of reverence and tenderness; and to humour her graceful fancies, and meet those thousand simple wants which invest childhood like a many-coloured rainbow was Tom's chief delight. In the market, at morning, his eyes were always on the flower-stalls for rare bouquets for her, and the choicest peach or orange was slipped into his pocket to give to her when he came back; and the sight that pleased him most was her sunny head looking out at the gate for his distant approach, and her childish question, 'Well, Uncle Tom, what have you got for me to-day?'

Nor was Eva less zealous in kind offices, in return. Though a child, she was a beautiful reader: a fine, musical ear, a quick, poetic fancy, and an instinctive sympathy with what is grand and noble, made her such a reader of the Bible as Tom had never before heard. At first she read to please her humble friend; but soon her own earnest nature threw out its tendrils, and wound itself around the majestic book; and Eva loved it, because it woke in her strange yearnings, and strong, dim emotions, such as impassioned, imaginative children love to feel.

The parts that pleased her most were the Revelation and the Prophecies – parts whose dim and wondrous imagery and fervent language impressed her the more, that she questioned vainly of their meaning; and she and her simple friend, the old child and the young one, felt just alike about it. All that they knew was, that they spoke of a glory to be revealed – a wondrous something yet to come, wherein their soul rejoiced, yet knew not why; and though it be not so in the physical, yet in moral science that which cannot be understood is not always profitless. For the soul awakes a trembling stranger, between two dim eternities – the eternal past, the eternal future. The light shines only on a small space around her; therefore she needs must yearn towards the unknown and the voices and shadowy movings which come to her from out the cloudy pillar of inspiration have each one echoes and answers in her own expecting nature. Its mystic imageries are so many talismans and gems inscribed with unknown hieroglyphics; she folds them in her bosom, and expects to read them when she passes beyond the veil.

At this time in our story, the whole St Clare establishment is, for the time being, removed to their villa on Lake Pontchartrain. The heats of summer had driven all who were able to leave this sultry and unhealthy city to seek the shores of the lake, and its cool sea-breezes.

St Clare's villa was an East Indian cottage, surrounded by light verandahs of bamboo-work, and opening on all sides into gardens and pleasure-grounds. The common sitting-room opened on to a large garden, fragrant with every picturesque plant and flower of the tropics, where winding paths ran down to the very shores of the lake, whose silvery sheet of water lay there rising and falling in the sunbeams – a picture never for an hour the same, yet every hour more beautiful.

It is now one of those intensely golden sunsets which kindles the whole horizon into one blaze of glory, and makes the water another sky. The lake lay in rosy or golden streaks, save where white-winged vessels glided hither and thither, like so many spirits, and little golden stars twinkled through the glow, and looked down at themselves as they trembled in the water.

Tom and Eva were seated on a little mossy seat, in an arbour at the foot of the garden. It was Sunday evening, and Eva's Bible lay open on her knee. She read, 'And I saw a sea of glass, mingled with fire.'

'Tom,' said Eva, suddenly stopping, and pointing to the lake, 'there 'tis.'

'What, Miss Eva ?'

'Don't you see – there ?' said the child, pointing to the glassy water, which, as it rose and fell, reflected the golden glow of the sky. 'There's a "sea of glass, mingled with fire."'

'True enough, Miss Eva,' said Tom ; and Tom sang –

> 'Oh, had I the wings of the morning,
>   I'd fly away to Canaan's shore :
> Bright angels should convey me home,
>   To the New Jerusalem.'

'Where do you suppose New Jerusalem is, Uncle Tom ?' said Eva.

'Oh, up in the clouds, Miss Eva.'

'Then I think I see it,' said Eva. 'Look in those clouds ! they look like great gates of pearl ; and you can see beyond them – far, far off – it's all gold. Tom, sing about "spirits bright."'

Tom sang the words of a well-known Methodist hymn –

> 'I see a band of spirits bright,
>   That taste the glories there :
> They all are robed in spotless white,
>   And conquering palms they bear.'

'Uncle Tom, I've seen *them*,' said Eva.

Tom had no doubt of it at all ; it did not surprise him in the least. If Eva had told him she had been to heaven, he would have thought it entirely probable.

'They come to me sometimes in my sleep, those spirits ;' and Eva's eyes grew dreamy, and she hummed, in a low voice –

> 'They all are robed in spotless white,
>   And conquering palms they bear.'

'Uncle Tom,' said Eva, 'I am going there.'

'Where, Miss Eva ?'

The child rose, and pointed her little hand to the sky; the glow of evening lit her golden hair and flushed cheek with a kind of unearthly radiance, and her eyes were bent earnestly on the skies.

'I'm going *there* !' she said, 'to the spirits bright, Tom; *I'm going, before long.*'

The faithful old heart felt a sudden thrust; and Tom thought how often he had noticed, within six months, that Eva's little hands had grown thinner, and her skin more transparent, and her breath shorter; and how, when she ran or played in the garden, as she once could for hours, she became soon so tired and languid. He had heard Miss Ophelia speak often of a cough, that all her medicaments could not cure; and even now that fervent cheek and little hand were burning with hectic fever; and yet the thought of Eva's words suggested had never come to him till now.

Has there ever been a child like Eva ? Yes, there have been; but their names are always on grave-stones, and their sweet smiles, their heavenly eyes, their singular words and ways, are among the buried treasures of yearning hearts. In how many families do you hear the legend that all the goodness and graces of the living are nothing to the peculiar charms of one who *is not* ! It is as if Heaven had an especial band of angels, whose office it was to sojourn for a season here, and endear to them the wayward human heart, that they might bear it upward with them in their homeward flight. When you see that deep, spiritual light in the eye – when the little soul reveals itself in words sweeter and wiser than the ordinary words of children – hope not to retain that child; for the seal of Heaven is on it, and the light of immortality looks out from its eyes.

Even so, beloved Eva ! fair star of thy dwelling ! Thou art passing away; but they that love thee dearest know it not.

The colloquy between Tom and Eva was interrupted by a hasty call from Miss Ophelia.

'Eva – Eva ! – why, child, the dew is falling you mustn't be out there !'

Eva and Tom hastened in.

Miss Ophelia was old, and skilled in the tactics of nursing.

She was from New England, and knew well the first guileful footsteps of that soft, insidious disease, which sweeps away so many of the fairest and loveliest, and, before one fibre of life seems broken, seals them irrevocably for death.

She had noted the slight, dry cough, the daily brightening cheek; nor could the lustre of the eye and the airy buoyancy born of fever deceive her.

She tried to communicate her fears to St Clare; but he threw back her suggestions with a restless petulance, unlike his usual careless good-humour.

'Don't be croaking, cousin – I hate it!' he would say; 'don't you see that the child is only growing? Children always lose strength when they grow fast.'

'But she has that cough!'

'Oh, nonsense of that cough – it is not anything! She has taken a little cold, perhaps.'

'Well, that was just the way Eliza Jane was taken, and Ellen and Maria Sanders.

'Oh, stop these hobgoblin nurse-legends! You old hands get so wise, that a child cannot cough or sneeze, but you see desperation and ruin at hand. Only take care of the child, keep her from the night air, and don't let her play too hard, and she'll do well enough.'

So St Clare said; but he grew nervous and restless. He watched Eva feverishly day by day, as might be told by the frequency with which he repeated over that 'the child was quite well' – that there wasn't anything in that cough – it was only some little stomach affection, such as children often had. But he kept by her more than before, took her oftener to ride with him, brought home, every few days, some receipt or strengthening mixture – 'not,' he said, 'that the child *needed* it, but then it would not do her any harm.'

If it must be told, the thing that struck a deeper pang to his heart than anything else was the daily increasing maturity of the child's mind and feelings. While still retaining a child's fanciful graces, yet she often dropped, unconsciously, words of such a reach of thought, and strange unworldly wisdom, that they seemed to be an inspiration. At such times, St Clare would feel a sudden thrill, and clasp her in his arms as if that fond clasp could save her; and his heart rose up with wild determination to keep her, never to let her go.

The child's whole heart and soul seemed absorbed in works of love and kindness. Impulsively generous she had always been, but there was a touching and womanly thoughtfulness about her now that every one noticed. She still loved to play with Topsy and the various coloured children; but she now seemed rather a spectator than an actor of their plays, and she would sit for half an hour at a time laughing at the odd tricks of Topsy — and then a shadow would seem to pass across her face, her eyes grew misty, and her thoughts were afar.

'Mamma,' she said suddenly, to her mother, one day, 'why don't we teach our servants to read?'

'What a question, child! People never do.'

'Why don't they?' said Eva.

'Because it is no use for them to read. It don't help them to work any better, and they are not made for anything else.'

'But they ought to read the Bible, mamma, to learn God's will.'

'Oh, they can get that read to them all *they* need.'

'It seems to me, mamma, the Bible is for every one to read themselves. They need it a great many times when there is nobody to read it.'

'Eva, you are an odd child,' said her mother.

'Miss Ophelia has taught Topsy to read,' continued Eva.

'Yes, and you see how much good it does. Topsy is the worst creature I ever saw!'

'Here's poor Mammy!' said Eva. 'She loves the Bible so much, and wishes so she could read! And what will she do when I can't read to her?'

Marie was busy, turning over the contents of a drawer, as she answered, —

'Well, of course, by and by, Eva, you will have other things to think of, besides reading the Bible round to servants. Not but that is very proper; I've done it myself, when I had health. But when you come to be dressing and going into company, you won't have time. See here!' she added, 'these jewels I'm going to give you when you come out. I wore them to my first ball. I can tell you, Eva, I made a sensation.'

Eva took the jewel-case, and lifted from it a diamond necklace. Her large, thoughtful eyes rested on them, but it was plain her thoughts were elsewhere.

'How sober you look, child!' said Marie.

'Are these worth a great deal of money, mamma?'

'To be sure they are. Father sent to France for them. They are worth a small fortune.'

'I wish I had them,' said Eva, 'to do what I pleased with!'

'What would you do with them?'

'I'd sell them, and buy a place in the free States, and take all our people there, and hire teachers, to teach them to read and write.'

Eva was cut short by her mother's laughing.

'Set up a boarding-school! Wouldn't you teach them to play on the piano, and paint on velvet?'

'I'd teach them to read their own Bible, and write their own letters, and read letters that are written to them,' said Eva, steadily. 'I know, mamma, it does come very hard on them that they can't do these things. Tom feels it – Mammy does – a great many of them do. I think it's wrong.'

'Come, come, Eva; you are only a child! You know nothing about these things,' said Marie; 'besides, your talking makes my head ache.'

Marie always had a headache on hand for any conversation that did not exactly suit her. Eva stole away; but after that, she assiduously gave Mammy reading lessons.

Chapter 23

HENRIQUE

ABOUT this time, St Clare's brother Alfred, with his eldest son, a boy of twelve, spent a day or two with the family at the lake.

No sight could be more singular and beautiful than that of these twin brothers. Nature, instead of instituting resemblances between them, had made them opposites on every point; yet a mysterious tie seemed to unite them in a closer friendship than ordinary.

They used to saunter, arm in arm, up and down the alleys and walks of the garden – Augustine, with his blue eyes and golden hair, his ethereally flexible form and vivacious features; and Alfred, dark-eyed, with haughty Roman profile, firmly-knit limbs, and decided bearing. They were always abusing each other's opinions and practices, and yet never a whit the less absorbed in each other's society; in fact, the very contrariety seemed to unite them, like the attraction between opposite poles of the magnet.

Henrique, the eldest son of Alfred, was a noble, dark-eyed, princely boy, full of vivacity and spirit; and, from the first moment of introduction, seemed to be perfectly fascinated by the spirituelle graces of his cousin Evangeline.

Eva had a little pet pony, of a snowy whiteness. It was easy as a cradle, and as gentle as its little mistress; and this pony was now brought up to the back verandah by Tom, while a little mulatto boy of about thirteen led along a small black Arabian, which had just been imported, at a great expense, for Henrique.

Henrique had a boy's pride in his new possession; and as he advanced and took the reins out of the hands of his little groom, he looked carefully over him, and his brow darkened.

'What's this, Dodo, you little lazy dog! you haven't rubbed my horse down this morning.'

'Yes, mas'r,' said Dodo, submissively; 'he got that dust on his own self.'

'You rascal, shut your mouth!' said Henrique, violently raising his riding-whip. 'How dare you speak!'

The boy was a handsome, bright-eyed mulatto, of just Henrique's size, and his curling hair hung round a high, bold forehead. He had white blood in his veins, as could be seen by the quick flush in his cheek, and the sparkle of his eye, as he eagerly tried to speak.

'Mas'r Henrique— !' he began.

Henrique struck him across the face with his riding-whip, and, seizing one of his arms, forced him on to his knees, and beat him till he was out of breath.

'There, you impudent dog! Now will you learn not to answer

back when I speak to you? Take the horse back, and clean him properly. I'll teach you your place!'

'Young mas'r,' said Tom, 'I 'specs what he was gwine to say was, that the horse would roll when he was bringing him up from the stable; he's so full of spirits – that's the way he got that dirt on him: I looked to his cleaning.'

'You hold your tongue till you're asked to speak!' said Henrique, turning on his heel, and walking up the steps to speak to Eva, who stood in her riding-dress.

'Dear cousin, I'm sorry this stupid fellow has kept you waiting,' he said. 'Let's sit down here, on this seat, till they come. What's the matter, cousin? – you look sober.'

'How could you be so cruel and wicked to poor Dodo?' said Eva.

'Cruel – wicked!' said the boy, with unaffected surprise. 'What do you mean, dear Eva?'

'I don't want you to call me dear Eva, when you do so,' said Eva.

'Dear cousin, you don't know Dodo; it's the only way to manage him, he's so full of lies and excuses. The only way is to put him down at once – not let him open his mouth; that's the way papa manages.'

'But Uncle Tom said it was an accident, and he never tells what isn't true.'

'He's an uncommon old nigger, then!' said Henrique. 'Dodo will lie as fast as he can speak.'

'You frighten him into deceiving, if you treat him so.'

'Why, Eva, you've really taken such a fancy to Dodo, that I shall be jealous.'

'But you beat him, and he didn't deserve it.'

'Oh, well, it may go for some time when he does, and don't get it. A few cuts never come amiss with Dodo – he's a regular spirit, I can tell you; but I won't beat him again before you, if it troubles you.'

Eva was not satisfied, but found it in vain to try to make her handsome cousin understand her feelings.

Dodo soon appeared with the horses.

'Well, Dodo, you've done pretty well this time,' said his young master, with a more gracious air. 'Come, now, and hold Miss Eva's horse, while I put her on to the saddle.'

Dodo came and stood by Eva's pony. His face was troubled; his eyes looked as if he had been crying.

Henrique, who valued himself on his gentlemanly adroitness in all matters of gallantry, soon had his fair cousin in the saddle, and, gathering the reins, placed them in her hands.

But Eva bent to the other side of the horse, where Dodo was standing, and said, as he relinquished the reins, 'That's a good boy, Dodo – thank you !'

Dodo looked up in amazement into the sweet young face : the blood rushed to his cheeks and the tears to his eyes.

'Here, Dodo,' said his master, imperiously.

Dodo sprang and held the horse while his master mounted.

'There's a picayune for you to buy candy with, Dodo,' said Henrique; 'go get some.'

And Henrique cantered down the walk after Eva. Dodo stood looking after the two children. One had given him money; and one had given him what he wanted far more – a kind word kindly spoken. Dodo had been only a few months away from his mother. His master had bought him at a slave warehouse, for his handsome face, to be a match to the handsome pony; and he was now getting his breaking in, at the hands of his young master.

The scene of the beating had been witnessed by the two brothers St Clare, from another part of the garden.

Augustine's cheek flushed; but he only observed, with his usual sarcastic carelessness, 'I suppose that's what we may call republican education, Alfred ?'

'Henrique is a devil of a fellow, when his blood's up,' said Alfred, carelessly.

'I suppose you consider this an instructive practice for him,' said Augustine, dryly.

'I couldn't help it if I didn't. Henrique is a regular little tempest – his mother and I have given him up long ago. But, then, that Dodo is a perfect sprite – no amount of whipping can hurt him.'

'And this by way of teaching Henrique the first verse of a republican's catechism, "All men are born free and equal ?" '

'Poh !' said Alfred, 'one of Tom Jefferson's pieces of French sentiment and humbug. It's perfectly ridiculous to have that going the rounds among us to this day.'

'I think it is,' said St Clare, significantly.

'Because,' said Alfred, 'we can see plainly enough that all men are *not* born free, nor born equal; they are born anything else. For my part, I think half this republican talk is sheer humbug. It is the educated, the intelligent, the wealthy, the refined, who ought to have equal rights, and not the *canaille*.'

'If you can keep the *canaille* of that opinion,' said Augustine. 'They took *their* turn once, in France.'

'Of course, they must be *kept down*, consistently, steadily, as I *should*,' said Alfred, setting his foot hard down, as if he were standing on somebody.

'It makes a terrible slip when they get up,' said Augustine: 'in St Domingo, for instance.'

'Poh!' said Alfred, 'we'll take care of that in this country. We must set our face against all this educating, elevating talk, that is getting about now; the lower class must not be educated.'

'That is past praying for,' said Augustine; 'educated they will be, and we have only to say how. Our system is educating them in barbarism and brutality. We are breaking all humanising ties, and making them brute beasts; and, if they get the upper hand, such we shall find them.'

'They never shall get the upper hand!' said Alfred.

'That's right,' said St Clare; 'put on the steam, fasten down the escape-valve, and sit on it, and see where you'll land.'

'Well,' said Alfred, 'we *will* see. I'm not afraid to sit on the escape-valve, as long as the boilers are strong, and the machinery works well.'

'The nobles in Louis XVI's time thought just so; and Austria and Pius IX think so now: and, some pleasant morning, you may all be caught up to meet each other in the air, *when the boilers burst*.'

'*Dies declarabit*,' said Alfred, laughing.

'I tell you,' said Augustine, 'if there is anything that is revealed with the strength of a divine law in our times, it is that the masses are to rise, and the under class become the upper one.'

'That's one of your red republican humbugs, Augustine! Why didn't you ever take to the stump? You'd make a famous stump orator! Well, I hope I shall be dead before this millennium of your greasy masses comes on.'

'Greasy or not greasy, they will govern *you*, when their time comes,' said Augustine; 'and they will be just such rulers as you make them. The French noblesse chose to have the people "*sans culottes*," and they had "*sans culotte* governors to their hearts' content. The people of Hayti' –

'Oh, come, Augustine! as if we hadn't enough of that abominable, contemptible Hayti! The Haytians were not Anglo-Saxons; if they had been, there would have been another story. The Anglo-Saxon is the dominant race of the world, and *is to be so.*'

'Well, there is a pretty fair infusion of Anglo-Saxon blood among our slaves now,' said Augustine. 'There are plenty among them who have only enough of the African to give a sort of tropical warmth and fervour to our calculating firmness and foresight. If ever the San Domingo hour comes, Anglo-Saxon blood will lead on the day. Sons of white feathers, with all our haughty feelings burning in their veins, will not always be bought and sold and traded. They will rise, and raise with them their mothers' race.'

'Stuff! – nonsense!'

'Well,' said Augustine, 'there goes an old saying to this effect: "As it was in the days of Noah, so shall it be; they ate, they drank, they planted, they builded, and knew not till the flood came and took them."'

'On the whole, Augustine, I think your talents might do for a circuit rider,' said Alfred, laughing. 'Never you fear for us! possession is our nine points. We've got the power. This subject race!' said he, stamping firmly, 'is down, and shall *stay* down! We have energy enough to manage our own powder.'

'Sons trained like your Henrique will be grand guardians of your powder-magazines,' said Augustine; 'so cool and self-possessed! The proverb says, "They that cannot govern themselves cannot govern others."'

'There is a trouble there,' said Alfred thoughtfully; 'there's no doubt that our system is a difficult one to train children under. It gives too free scope to the passions, altogether, which, in our climate, are hot enough. I find trouble with Henrique. The boy is generous and warm-hearted, but a perfect fire-cracker when excited. I believe I shall send him north for his education, where obedience is more fashionable, and where he will associate more with equals and less with dependants.'

'Since training children is the staple work of the human race,' said Augustine, 'I should think it something of a consideration that our system does not work well there.'

'It does not for some things,' said Alfred; 'for others, again, it does. It makes boys manly and courageous; and the very vices of an abject race tend to strengthen in them the opposite virtues. I think Henrique, now, has a keener sense of the beauty of truth, from seeing lying and deception the universal badge of slavery.'

'A Christian-like view of the subject, certainly!' said Augustine.

'It's true, Christian-like or not; and is about as Christian-like as most other things in the world,' said Alfred.

'That may be,' said St Clare.

'Well, there's no use in talking, Augustine. I believe we've been round and round this old track five hundred times, more or less. What do you say to a game of backgammon?'

The two brothers ran up the verandah steps, and were soon seated at a light bamboo stand, with a backgammon-board between them. As they were setting their men, Alfred said, –

'I tell you, Augustine, if I thought as you do, I should do something.'

'I dare say you would – you are one of the doing sort; but what?'

'Why, elevate your own servants, for a specimen,' said Alfred, with a half-scornful smile.

'You might as well set Mount Ætna on them flat, and tell them to stand up under it, as tell me to elevate my servants under all the superincumbent mass of society upon them. One man can do nothing, against the whole action of a community. Education, to do anything, must be a state education; or there must be enough agreed in it to make it current.'

'You take the first throw,' said Alfred; and the brothers were soon lost in the game, and heard no more till the scraping of horses' feet was heard under the verandah.

'There come the children,' said Augustine, rising. 'Look here, Alf! Did you ever see anything so beautiful?' And, in truth, it *was* a beautiful sight. Henrique, with his bold brow, and dark, glossy curls, and glowing cheek, was laughing gaily, as he bent towards his fair cousin, as they came on. She was dressed in a blue riding-dress, with a cap of the same colour. Exercise had given a brilliant hue to her cheeks, and heightened the effect of her singularly transparent skin and golden hair.

'Good heavens! what perfectly dazzling beauty!' said Alfred. 'I tell you, Augustine, won't she make some hearts ache, one of these days!'

'She will, too truly – God knows, I'm afraid so!' said St Clare, in a tone of sudden bitterness, as he hurried down to take her off her horse.

'Eve, darling! you're not much tired?' he said, as he clasped her in his arms.

'No, papa,' said the child; but her short, hard breathing alarmed her father.

'How could you ride so fast, dear? You know it's bad for you.'

'I felt so well, papa, and liked it so much, I forgot.'

St Clare carried her in his arms into the parlour, and laid her on the sofa.

'Henrique, you must be careful of Eva,' said he; 'you mustn't ride fast with her.

'I'll take her under my care,' said Henrique, seating himself by the sofa, and taking Eva's hand.

Eva soon found herself much better. Her father and uncle resumed their game, and the children were left together.

'Do you know, Eva, I'm so sorry papa is only going to stay two days here, and then I shan't see you again for ever so long! If I stay with you, I'll try to be good, and not be cross to Dodo, and so on. I don't mean to treat Dodo ill; but you know I've got such a quick temper. I'm not really bad to him, though. I give him a picayune, now and then; and you see he dresses well. I think, on the whole, Dodo's pretty well off.'

'Would you think you were well off, if there were not one creature in the world near you to love you?'

'I? Well, of course not.'

'And you have taken Dodo away from all the friends he ever had, and now he has not a creature to love him: nobody can be good that way.'

'Well, I can't help it, as I know of. I can't get his mother, and I can't love him myself, nor anybody else, as I know of.'

'Why can't you?' said Eva.

'*Love* Dodo! Why, Eva, you wouldn't have me! I may *like* him well enough; but you don't *love* your servants.'

'I do, indeed.'

'How odd!'

'Don't the Bible say we must love everybody?'

'Oh, the Bible! To be sure, it says a great many such things; but then nobody ever thinks of doing them – you know, Eva, nobody does.'

Eva did not speak; her eyes were fixed and thoughtful for a few moments.

'At any rate,' she said, 'dear cousin, do love poor Dodo, and be kind to him, for my sake!'

'I could love anything for your sake, dear cousin; for I really think you are the loveliest creature that I ever saw!' And Henrique spoke with an earnestness that flushed his handsome face. Eva received it with perfect simplicity, without even a change of feature; merely saying, 'I'm glad you feel so, dear Henrique! I hope you will remember.'

The dinner-bell put an end to the interview.

Chapter 24

FORESHADOWINGS

Two days after this, Alfred St Clare and Augustine parted; and Eva, who had been stimulated by the society of her young cousin to exertions beyond her strength, began to fail rapidly. St Clare was at last willing to call in medical advice, a thing from which he had always shrunk, because it was the admission of an unwelcome truth. But for a day or two Eva was so unwell as to be confined to the house, and the doctor was called.

Marie St Clare had taken no notice of the child's gradually decaying health and strength, because she was completely absorbed in studying out two or three new forms of disease to which she believed she herself was a victim. It was the first principle of Marie's belief that nobody ever was or could be so great a sufferer as *herself*; and therefore she always repelled quite indignantly any suggestion that any one around her could be sick. She was always sure in such a case that it was nothing but laziness or want of energy, and that if they had had the suffering *she* had they would soon know the difference.

Miss Ophelia had several times tried to awaken her maternal fears about Eva, but to no avail.

'I don't see as anything ails the child,' she would say; 'she runs about and plays.'

'But she has a cough.'

'Cough! you don't need to tell me about a cough. I've always been subject to a cough all my days. When I was of Eva's age, they thought I was in a consumption. Night after night Mammy used to sit up with me. Oh, Eva's cough is not anything!'

'But she gets weak, and is short-breathed.'

'Law! I've had that years and years; it's only a nervous affection.'

'But she sweats so, nights!'

'Well, I have these ten years. Very often, night after night, my clothes will be wringing wet. There won't be a dry thread in my night-clothes, and the sheets will be so that Mammy has to hang them up to dry! Eva doesn't sweat anything like that!'

Miss Ophelia shut her mouth for a season. But now that Eva was fairly and visibly prostrated, and a doctor called, Marie all on a sudden took a new turn.

She knew it she said, she always felt it, that she was destined to be the most miserable of mothers. Here she was, with her wretched health, and her only darling child going down to the grave before her eyes? And Marie routed up Mammy nights, and rumpussed and scolded with more energy than ever all day, on the strength of this new misery.

'My dear Marie, don't talk so!' said St Clare. 'You ought not to give up the case so, at once.'

'You have not a mother's feelings, St Clare! You never could understand me! — you don't now.'

'But don't talk so, as if it were a gone case!'

'I can't take it as indifferently as you can, St Clare. If *you* don't feel when your only child is in this alarming state, *I* do. It's a blow too much for me, with all I was bearing before.'

'It's true,' said St Clare, 'that Eva is very delicate – *that* I always knew; and that she has grown so rapidly as to exhaust her strength; and that her situation is critical. But just now she is only prostrated by the heat of the weather, and by the excitement of her cousin's visit, and the exertions she made. The physician says there is room for hope.'

'Well, of course, if you can look on the bright side, pray do; it's a mercy if people haven't sensitive feelings in this world. I am sure I wish I didn't feel as I do – it only makes me completely wretched! I wish I *could* be as easy as the rest of you!'

And the 'rest of them' had good reason to breathe the same prayer, for Marie paraded her new misery as the reason and apology for all sorts of inflictions on every one about her. Every word that was spoken by anybody, everything that was done or was not done everywhere, was only a new proof that she was surrounded by hard-hearted, insensible beings who were unmindful of her peculiar sorrows. Poor Eva heard some of these speeches; and nearly cried her little eyes out in pity for her mamma, and in sorrow that she should make her so much distress.

In a week or two there was a great improvement of symptoms – one of those deceitful lulls by which her inexorable disease so often beguiles the anxious heart, even on the verge of the grave. Eva's step was again in the garden – in the balconies; she played and laughed again, and her father, in a transport, declared that they should soon have her as hearty as anybody. Miss Ophelia and the physician alone felt no encouragement from this illusive truce. There was one other heart, too, that felt the same certainty, and that was the little heart of Eva. What is it that sometimes speaks in the soul so calmly, so clearly, that its earthly time is short? Is it the secret instinct of decaying nature, or the soul's impulsive throb, as immortality draws on? Be it what it may, it rested in the heart of Eva, a calm, sweet, prophetic certainty that Heaven was near; calm as the light of sunset, sweet as the bright stillness of autumn: there her little heart reposed, only troubled by sorrow for those who loved her so dearly.

For the child, though nursed so tenderly, and though life was unfolding before her with every brightness that love and wealth could give, had no regret for herself in dying.

In that Book which she and her simple old friend had read so much together, she had seen and taken to her young heart the image of One who loved the little child; and as she gazed and mused, he had ceased to be an image and a picture of the distant past, and come to be a living, all-surrounding reality. His love enfolded her childish heart with more than mortal tenderness; and it was to Him, she said, she was going, and to His home.

But her heart yearned with sad tenderness for all that she was to leave behind – her father most; for Eva, though she never distinctly thought so, had an instinctive perception that she was more in his heart than any other. She loved her mother because she was so loving a creature, and all the selfishness that she had seen in her only saddened and perplexed her; for she had a child's implicit trust that her mother could not do wrong. There was something about her that Eva never could make out; and she always smoothed it over with thinking that, after all, it was mamma, and she loved her very dearly indeed.

She felt, too, for those fond, faithful servants, to whom she was as daylight and sunshine. Children do not usually generalise; but Eva was an uncommonly mature child, and the things that she had witnessed of the evils of the system under which they were living had fallen, one by one, into the depths of her thoughtful, pondering heart. She had vague longings to do something for them – to bless and save not only them, but all in their condition – longings that contrasted sadly with the feebleness of her little frame.

'Uncle Tom,' she said, one day, when she was reading to her friend, 'I can understand why Jesus *wanted* to die for us.'

'Why, Miss Eva?'

'Because I've felt so, too.'

'What is it, Miss Eva? – I don't understand.'

'I can't tell you; but when I saw those poor creatures on the boat, you know, when you came up and I, some had lost their mothers, and some their husbands, and some mothers cried for their little children; and when I heard about poor Prue – oh, wasn't that dreadful? – and a great many other times I've felt that I would be glad to die, if my dying could stop all this misery. I *would die* for them, Tom, if I could,' said the child, earnestly, laying her little thin hand on his.

Tom looked at the child with awe: and when she, hearing her

father's voice, glided away, he wiped his eyes many times as he looked after her.

'It's jest no use tryin' to keep Miss Eva here,' he said to Mammy, whom he met a moment after. 'She's got the Lord's mark in her forehead.'

'Ah, yes, yes!' said Mammy, raising her hands; 'I've allers said so. She wasn't never like a child that's to live – there was allers something deep in her eyes. I've told missis so many the time; it's a comin' true – we all sees it – dear, little, blessed lamb!'

Eva came tripping up the verandah steps to her father. It was late in the afternoon, and the rays of the sun formed a kind of glory behind her, as she came forward in her white dress, with her golden hair and glowing cheeks, her eyes unnaturally bright with the slow fever that burned in her veins.

St Clare had called her to show a statuette that he had been buying for her; but her appearance, as she came on, impressed him suddenly and painfully. There is a kind of beauty so intense, yet so fragile, that we cannot bear to look at it. Her father folded her suddenly in his arms, and almost forgot what he was going to tell her.

'Eva, dear, you are better nowadays, are you not?'

'Papa,' said Eva, with sudden firmness, 'I've had things I wanted to say to you a great while. I want to say them now, before I get weaker.'

St Clare trembled as Eva seated herself on his lap. She laid her head on his bosom and said –

'It's all no use, papa, to keep it to myself any longer. The time is coming that I'm going to leave you. I am going, and never to come back!' and Eva sobbed.

'Oh, now, my dear little Eva!' said St Clare, trembling as he spoke, but speaking cheerfully, 'you've got nervous and low-spirited: you mustn't indulge such gloomy thoughts. See here, I've bought a statuette for you!'

'No, papa,' said Eva, putting it gently away, 'don't deceive yourself! I am *not* any better – I know it perfectly well; and I am going before long. I am not nervous – I am not low-spirited. If it were not for you, papa, and my friends, I should be perfectly happy. I want to go – I long to go!'

'Why, dear child, what has made your poor little heart so

sad ? You have had everything to make you happy that could be given you ?'

'I had rather be in heaven, though – only, for my friends' sake I would be willing to live. There are a great many things here that make me sad, that seem dreadful to me. I had rather be there; but I don't want to leave you – it almost breaks my heart !'

'What makes you sad, and seems dreadful, Eva ?'

'Oh, things that are done and done all the time. I feel sad for our poor people; they love me dearly, and they are all good and kind to me. I wish, papa, they were all *free*.'

'Why, Eva, child, don't you think they are well enough off now ?'

'Oh, but, papa, if anything should happen to you, what would become of them ? There are very few men like you, papa. Uncle Alfred isn't like you, and mamma isn't; and then think of poor old Prue's owners ! What horrid things people do, and can do !' And Eva shuddered.

'My dear child, you are too sensitive. I'm sorry I ever let you hear such stories.'

'Oh, that's what troubles me, papa. You want me to live so happy, and never to have any pain, never suffer anything, not even hear a sad story, when other poor creatures have nothing but pain and sorrow all their lives; it seems selfish. I ought to know such things – I ought to feel about them. Such things always sunk into my heart, they went down deep; I've thought and thought about them. Papa, isn't there any way to have all slaves made free ?'

'That's a difficult question, dearest. There's no doubt that this way is a very bad one, a great many people think so; I do myself. I heartily wish that there were not a slave in the land, but then I don't know what is to be done about it.'

'Papa, you are such a good man, and so noble, and kind, and you always have a way of saying things that is so pleasant; couldn't you go all round and try to persuade people to do right about this ? When I am dead, papa, then you will think of me, and do it for my sake. I would do it if I could.'

'When you are dead, Eva !' said St Clare, passionately. 'Oh, child, don't talk to me so ! You are all I have on earth.'

'Poor old Prue's child was all that she had; and yet she had to hear it crying, and she couldn't help it! Papa, these poor creatures love their children as much as you do me. Oh, do something for them! There's poor Mammy loves her children; I've seen her crying when she talked about them. And Tom loves his children; and it's dreadful, papa, that such things are happening all the time!'

'There, there, darling,' said St Clare, soothingly; 'only don't distress yourself, and don't talk of dying, and I will do anything you wish.'

'And promise me, dear father, that Tom shall have his freedom as soon as —' She stopped, and said in a hesitating tone – 'I am gone!'

'Yes, dear, I will do anything in the world – anything you could ask me to.'

'Dear papa,' said the child, laying her burning cheek against his, 'how I wish we could go together.'

'Where, dearest?' said St Clare.

'To our Saviour's home; it's so sweet and peaceful there – it is all so loving there!' The child spoke unconsciously, as of a place where she had often been. 'Don't you want to go, papa?' she said.

St Clare drew her closer to him, but was silent.

'You will come to me,' said the child, speaking in a voice of calm certainty, which she often used unconsciously.

'I shall come after you. I shall not forget you.'

The shadows of the solemn evening closed round them deeper and deeper, as St Clare sat silently holding the little frail form to his bosom. He saw no more the deep eyes, but the voice came over him as a spirit voice; and, as in a sort of judgment vision, his whole past life rose in a moment before his eyes – his mother's prayers and hymns – his own early yearnings and aspirings for good; and, between them and this hour, years of worldliness and scepticism, and what man calls respectable living. We can think *much*, very much, in a moment. St Clare saw and felt many things, but spoke nothing; and, as it grew darker, he took his child to her bedroom, and when she was prepared for rest he sent away the attendants, and rocked her in his arms, and sung to her till she was asleep.

Chapter 25

THE LITTLE EVANGELIST

It was Sunday afternoon. St Clare was stretched on a bamboo lounge in the verandah, solacing himself with a cigar. Marie lay reclined on a sofa, opposite the window opening on the verandah, closely secluded, under an awning of transparent gauze, from the outrages of the mosquitos, and languidly holding in her hand an elegantly bound prayer-book. She was holding it because it was Sunday, and she imagined she had been reading it – though, in fact, she had been only taking a succession of short naps, with it open in her hands.

Miss Ophelia, who, after some rummaging, had hunted up a small Methodist meeting within riding distance, had gone out, with Tom as driver, to attend it, and Eva had accompanied them.

'I say, Augustine,' said Marie, after dozing a while, 'I must send to the city after my old Doctor Posey; I'm sure I've got the complaint of the heart.'

'Well; why need you send for him? This doctor that attends Eva seems skilful.'

'I would not trust him in a critical case,' said Marie, 'and I think I may say mine is becoming so! I've been thinking of it these two or three nights past; I have such distressing pains, and such strange feelings.'

'O Marie, you are blue; I don't believe it's heart-complaint.'

'I dare say *you* don't,' said Marie; 'I was prepared to expect *that*. You can be alarmed enough if Eva coughs or has the least thing the matter with her, but you never think of me.'

'If it's particularly agreeable to you to have heart-disease, why, I'll try and maintain you have it,' said St Clare; 'I didn't know it was.'

'Well, I only hope you won't be sorry for this when it's too late!' said Marie; 'but, believe it or not, my distress about Eva, and the exertions I have made with that dear child, have developed what I have long suspected.'

What the *exertions* were which Marie referred to it would have been difficult to state. St Clare quietly made this commentary to himself, and went on smoking, like a hard-hearted wretch of a man as he was, till a carriage drove up before the verandah, and Eva and Miss Ophelia alighted.

Miss Ophelia marched straight to her own chamber, to put away her bonnet and shawl, as was always her manner, before she spoke a word on any subject; while Eva came at St Clare's call, and was sitting on his knee, giving him an account of the services they had heard.

They soon heard loud exclamations from Miss Ophelia's room (which, like the one in which they were sitting, opened on to the verandah), and violent reproof addressed to somebody.

'What new witchcraft has Topsy been brewing?' asked St Clare. 'That commotion is of her raising, I'll be bound!'

And, in a moment after, Miss Ophelia, in high indignation, came dragging the culprit along.

'Come out here, now!' she said. 'I *will* tell your master.'

'What's the case now?' said Augustine.

'The case is that I cannot be plagued with this child any longer! It's past all bearing; flesh and blood cannot endure it! Here, I locked her up, and gave her a hymn to study; and what does she do, but spy out where I put my key, and has gone to my bureau, and got a bonnet-trimming, and cut it all to pieces to make dolls' jackets! I never saw anything like it in my life.'

'I told you, cousin,' said Marie, 'that you'd find out that these creatures can't be brought up without severity. If I had *my* way, now,' she said, looking reproachfully at St Clare, 'I'd send that child out, and have her thoroughly whipped; I'd have her whipped till she couldn't stand!'

'I don't doubt it,' said St Clare. 'Tell me of the lovely rule of women! I never saw above a dozen women that wouldn't half kill a horse, or a servant, either, if they had their own way with them, let alone a man.'

'There is no use in this shilly-shally way of yours, St Clare!' said Marie. 'Cousin is a woman of sense, and she sees it now as plain as I do.'

Miss Ophelia had just the capability of indignation that

belongs to the thorough-paced housekeeper, and this had been pretty actively roused by the artifice and wastefulness of the child; in fact, many of my lady readers must own that they should have felt just so in her circumstances; but Marie's words went beyond her, and she felt less heat.

'I wouldn't have the child treated so for the world,' she said; 'but I am sure, Augustine, I don't know what to do. I've taught and taught, I've talked till I'm tired, I've whipped her, I've punished her in every way I can think of; and still she's just what she was at first.'

'Come here, Topsy, you monkey!' said St Clare, calling the child up to him.

Topsy came up; her round, hard eyes glittering and blinking with a mixture of apprehensiveness and their usual odd drollery.

'What makes you behave so?' said St Clare, who could not help being amused with the child's expression.

''Spects it's my wicked heart,' said Topsy, demurely; 'Miss Feely says so.'

'Don't you see how much Miss Ophelia has done for you? She says she has done everything she can think of.'

'Lor, yes, mas'r! old missis used to say so, too. She whipped me a heap harder, and used to pull my hair, and knock my head agin the door; but it didn't do me no good! I 'spects, if they's to pull every spear o' har out o' my head, it wouldn't do no good neither – I's so wicked! Laws! I's nothin' but a nigger, noways!'

'Well, I shall have to give her up,' said Miss Ophelia; 'I can't have that trouble any longer.'

'Well, I'd just like to ask one question,' said St Clare.

'What is it?'

'Why, if your Gospel is not strong enough to save one heathen child, that you can have at home here, all to yourself, what's the use of sending one or two poor missionaries off with it among thousands of just such? I suppose this child is about a fair sample of what thousands of your heathen are.'

Miss Ophelia did not make an immediate answer; and Eva, who had stood a silent spectator of the scene thus far, made a silent sign to Topsy to follow her. There was a little glass-room at the corner of the verandah, which St Clare used as a sort of reading-room; and Eva and Topsy disappeared into this place.

'What's Eva going about now?' said St Clare; 'I mean to see.'

And, advancing on tiptoe, he lifted up a curtain that covered the glass-door, and looked in. In a moment, laying his finger on his lips, he made a silent gesture to Miss Ophelia to come and look. There sat the two children on the floor, with their side faces towards them – Topsy with her usual air of careless drollery and unconcern; but, opposite to her, Eva, her whole face fervent with feeling, and tears in her large eyes.

'What does make you so bad, Topsy? Why won't you try and be good? Don't you love *anybody*, Topsy?'

'Dunno nothing 'bout love; I loves candy and sich, that's all,' said Topsy.

'But you love your father and mother?'

'Never had none, ye know. I telled ye that, Miss Eva.'

'Oh, I know,' said Eva sadly; 'but hadn't you any brother or sister, or aunt, or'—

'No, none on 'em – never had nothing nor nobody.'

'But, Topsy, if you'd only try to be good, you might—'

'Couldn't never be nothin' but a nigger, if I was ever so good,' said Topsy. 'If I could be skinned, and come white, I'd try then.'

'But people can love you, if you are black, Topsy. Miss Ophelia would love you if you were good.'

Topsy gave the short, blunt laugh, that was her common mode of expressing incredulity.

'Don't you think so?' said Eva.

'No; she can't bar me, 'cause I'm a nigger! – she'd's soon have a toad touch her. There can't nobody love niggers, and niggers can't do nothin'. *I* don't care,' said Topsy, beginning to whistle.

'O Topsy, poor child, *I* love you!' said Eva, with a sudden burst of feeling, and laying her little, thin, white hand on Topsy's shoulder; 'I love you, because you haven't had any father, or mother, or friends – because you've been a poor, abused child! I love you, and I want you to be good. I am very unwell, Topsy, and I think I shan't live a great while, and it really grieves me to have you be so naughty. I wish you would try to be good, for my sake; it's only a little while I shall be with you.'

The round, keen eyes of the black child were overcast with tears; large, bright drops rolled heavily down, one by one, and fell on the little white hand. Yes, in that moment a ray of real belief, a ray of heavenly love, had penetrated the darkness of her heathen soul! She laid her head down between her knees, and wept and sobbed; while the beautiful child, bending over her, looked like the picture of some bright angel stooping to reclaim a sinner.

'Poor Topsy!' said Eva, 'don't you know that Jesus loves all alike? He is just as willing to love you as me. He loves you just as I do, only more, because he is better. He will help you to be good, and you can go to heaven at last, and be an angel for ever, just as much as if you were white. Only think of it, Topsy, *you* can be one of those spirits bright Uncle Tom sings about.'

'O dear Miss Eva! dear Miss Eva!' said the child, 'I will try! I will try! I never did care nothin' about it before.'

St Clare at this instant dropped the curtain. 'It puts me in mind of mother,' he said to Miss Ophelia. 'It is true what she told me: if we want to give sight to the blind, we must be willing to do as Christ did – call them to us, and *put our hands on them.*'

'I've always had a prejudice against negroes,' said Miss Ophelia; 'and it's a fact, I never could bear to have that child touch me; but I didn't think she knew it.'

'Trust any child to find that out,' said St Clare; 'there's no keeping it from them. But I believe that all the trying in the world to benefit a child, and all the substantial favours you can do them, will never excite one emotion of gratitude while that feeling of repugnance remains in the heart; it's a queer kind of fact, but so it is.'

'I don't know how I can help it,' said Miss Ophelia; 'they *are* disagreeable to me – this child in particular. How can I help feeling so.'

'Eva does, it seems.'

'Well, she's so loving! After all, though, she's no more than Christ-like,' said Miss Ophelia; 'I wish I were like her. She might teach me a lesson.'

'It wouldn't be the first time a little child had been used to instruct an old disciple, if it *were* so,' said St Clare.

Chapter 26

DEATH

'Weep not for those whom the veil of the tomb,
In life's early morning, hath hid from our eyes.'

EVA's bedroom was a spacious apartment, which, like the other rooms in the house, opened on to the broad verandah. The room communicated, on one side, with her father and mother's apartments; on the other, with that appropriated to Miss Ophelia. St Clare had gratified his own eye and taste, in furnishing this room in a style that had a peculiar keeping with the character of her for whom it was intended. The windows were hung with curtains of rose-coloured and white muslin; the floor was spread with a matting which had been ordered in Paris, to a pattern of his own device, having round it a border of rose-buds and leaves, and a centre-piece with full-blown roses. The bedstead, chairs, and lounges were of bamboo, wrought in peculiarly graceful and fanciful patterns. Over the head of the bed was an alabaster bracket, on which a beautiful sculptured angel stood, with drooping wings, holding out a crown of myrtle-leaves. From this depended, over the bed, light curtains of rose-coloured gauze, striped with silver, supplying that protection from mosquitos which is an indispensable addition to all sleeping accommodation in that climate. The graceful bamboo lounges were amply supplied with cushions of rose-coloured damask, while over them, depending from the hands of sculptured figures, were gauze curtains similar to those of the bed. A light, fanciful bamboo table stood in the middle of the room, where a Parian vase, wrought in the shape of a white lily, with its buds, stood, ever filled with flowers. On this table lay Eva's books and little trinkets, with an elegantly-wrought alabaster writing-stand, which her father had supplied to her when he saw her trying to improve herself in writing. There was a fireplace in the room, and on the marble mantel above stood a beautifully-wrought statuette of Jesus receiving little children, and on either side marble vases, for which it was Tom's pride and delight to offer bouquets every morning. Two or three exquisite paintings of children, in various attitudes, embellished the wall. In short, the eye could turn nowhere without meeting images of childhood, of beauty, and of peace. Those little eyes never opened, in the morning light, without falling on something which suggested to the heart soothing and beautiful thoughts.

The deceitful strength which had buoyed Eva up for a little while was fast passing away; seldom and more seldom her light footstep was heard in the verandah, and oftener and oftener she was found reclined on a little lounge by the open window, her large, deep eyes fixed on the rising and falling waters of the lake.

It was towards the middle of the afternoon, as she was so reclining – her Bible half-open, her little transparent fingers lying listlessly between the leaves – suddenly she heard her mother's voice, in sharp tones, in the verandah.

'What now, you baggage? what new piece of mischief? You've been picking the flowers, eh?' and Eva heard the sound of a smart slap.

'Law, missis! they's for Miss Eva,' she heard a voice say, which she knew belonged to Topsy.

'Miss Eva! A pretty excuse! you suppose she wants *your* flowers, you good-for-nothing nigger! Get along off with you!'

In a moment, Eva was off from her lounge, and in the verandah.

'Oh, don't, mother! I should like the flowers; do give them to me; I want them!'

'Why, Eva, your room is full now.'

'I can't have too many,' said Eva. 'Topsy, do bring them here.'

Topsy, who had stood sullenly, holding down her head, now came up and offered her flowers. She did it with a look of hesitation and bashfulness, quite unlike the eldritch boldness and brightness which was usual with her.

'It's a beautiful bouquet!' said Eva, looking at it.

It was rather a singular one – a brilliant scarlet-geranium, and one single white japonica, with its glossy leaves. It was tied up with an evident eye to the contrast of colour, and the arrangement of every leaf had carefully been studied.

Topsy looked pleased, as Eva said, 'Topsy, you arrange flowers very prettily. Here,' she said, 'is this vase, I haven't any flowers for. I wish you'd arrange something every day for it.'

'Well, that's odd!' said Marie. 'What in the world do you want that for?'

'Never mind, mamma; you'd as lief as not Topsy should do it – had you not?'

'Of course, anything you please, dear! Topsy, you hear your young mistress; see that you mind.'

Topsy made a short curtsey, and looked down; and, as she turned away, Eva saw a tear roll down her dark cheek.

'You see, mamma, I knew poor Topsy wanted to do something for me,' said Eva to her mother.

'Oh, nonsense! it's only because she likes to do mischief. She knows she mustn't pick flowers – so she does it; that's all there is to it. But, if you fancy to have her pluck them, so be it.'

'Mamma, I think Topsy is different from what she used to be; she's trying to be a good girl.'

'She'll have to try a good while before *she* gets to be good,' said Marie, with a careless laugh.

'Well, you know, mamma, poor Topsy! everything has always been against her.'

'Not since she's been here, I'm sure. If she hasn't been talked to, and preached to, and every earthly thing done that anybody could do; and she's just so ugly, and always will be: you can't make anything of the creature!'

'But, mamma, it's so different to be brought up as I've been, with so many friends, so many things to make me good and happy; and to be brought up as she's been, all the time till she came here!'

'Most likely,' said Marie, yawning. 'Dear me, how hot it is!'

'Mamma, you believe, don't you, that Topsy could become an angel, as well as any of us, if she were a Christian?'

'Topsy! what a ridiculous idea! Nobody but you would ever think of it. I suppose she could, though.'

'But, mamma, isn't God her Father, as much as ours? Isn't Jesus her Saviour?'

'Well, that may be. I suppose God made everybody,' said Marie. 'Where is my smelling-bottle?'

'It's such a pity – oh ! *such* a pity !' said Eva, looking out on the distant lake, and speaking half to herself.

'What's a pity ?' said Marie.

'Why, that any one, who could be a bright angel, and live with angels, should go all down, down, down, and nobody help them ! Oh, dear !'

'Well, we can't help it; it's no use worrying, Eva ! I don't know what's to be done; we ought to be thankful for our own advantages.'

'I hardly can be,' said Eva; 'I'm so sorry to think of poor folks that haven't any.'

'That's odd enough,' said Marie. 'I'm sure my religion makes me thankful for my advantages.'

'Mamma,' said Eva, 'I want to have some of my hair cut off – a good deal of it.'

'What for ?' said Marie.

'Mamma, I want to give some away to my friends, while I am able to give it to them myself. Won't you ask aunty to come and cut it for me ?'

Marie raised her voice, and called Miss Ophelia from the other room.

The child half rose from her pillow as she came in, and shaking down her long golden brown curls, said, rather playfully, 'Come, aunty, shear the sheep.'

'What's that ?' said St Clare, who had just then entered with some fruit he had been out to get for her.

'Papa, I just want aunty to cut off some of my hair; there's too much of it, and it makes my head hot. Besides, I want to give some of it away.'

Miss Ophelia came with her scissors.

'Take care, don't spoil the looks of it !' said her father; 'cut underneath, where it won't show. Eva's curls are my pride.'

'O papa !' said Eva, sadly.

'Yes, and I want them kept handsome against the time I take you up to your uncle's plantation, to see Cousin Henrique,' said St Clare, in a gay tone.

'I shall never go there, papa; I am going to a better country. Oh, do believe me ! Don't you see, papa, that I get weaker every day ?'

'Why do you insist that I shall believe such a cruel thing, Eva?' said her father.

'Only because it is *true*, papa; and if you will believe it now, perhaps you will get to feel about it as I do.'

St Clare closed his lips, and stood gloomily eyeing the long beautiful curls, which, as they were separated from the child's head, were laid, one by one, in her lap. She raised them up, looked earnestly at them, twined them around her thin fingers, and looked from time to time anxiously at her father.

'It's just what I've been foreboding,' said Marie; 'it's just what has been preying on my health from day to day, bringing me downward to the grave, though nobody regards it. I have seen this long. St Clare, you will see, after a while, that I was right.'

'Which will afford you great consolation, no doubt!' said St Clare, in a dry, bitter tone.

Marie lay back on a lounge, and covered her face with her cambric handkerchief.

Eva's clear blue eye looked earnestly from one to the other. It was the calm, comprehending gaze of a soul half loosed from its earthly bonds; it was evident she saw, felt, and appreciated the difference between the two.

She beckoned with her hand to her father. He came, and sat down by her.

'Papa, my strength fades away every day, and I know I must go. There are some things I want to say and do, that I ought to do; and you are so unwilling to have me speak a word on this subject. But it must come; there's no putting it off. Do be willing I should speak now!'

'My child, I *am* willing,' said St Clare, covering his eyes with one hand, and holding up Eva's hand with the other.

'Then I want to see all our people together. I have some things I *must* say to them,' said Eva.

'*Well!*' said St Clare, in a tone of dry endurance.

Miss Ophelia despatched a messenger, and soon the whole of the servants were convened in the room.

Eva lay back on her pillows, her hair hanging loosely about her face, her crimson cheeks contrasting painfully with the intense whiteness of her complexion and the thin contour of her limbs and features, and her large, soul-like eyes, fixed earnestly on every one.

The servants were struck with a sudden emotion. The spiritual face, the long locks of hair cut off and lying by her, her father's averted face, and Marie's sobs, struck at once upon the feelings of a sensitive and impressible race; and as they came in they looked one on another, sighed, and shook their heads. There was a deep silence, like that of a funeral.

Eva raised herself, and looked long and earnestly round at every one. All looked sad and apprehensive. Many of the women hid their faces in their aprons.

'I sent for you all, my dear friends,' said Eva, 'because I love you. I love you all; and I have something to say to you, which I want you always to remember. . . . I am going to leave you. In a few more weeks, you will see me no more—'

Here the child was interrupted by bursts of groans, sobs, and lamentations, which broke from all present, and in which her slender voice was lost entirely. She waited a moment, and then, speaking in a tone that checked the sobs of all, she said –

'If you love me, you must not interrupt me so. Listen to what I say. I want to speak to you about your souls. . . . Many of you, I am afraid, are very careless. You are thinking only about this world. I want you to remember that there is a beautiful world, where Jesus is. I am going there, and you can go there; it is for you, as much as me. But if you want to go there, you must not live idle, careless, thoughtless lives; you must be Christians. You must remember that each one of you can become angels, and be angels for ever. . . . If you want to be Christians, Jesus will help you. You must pray to him; you must read—'

The child checked herself, looked piteously at them, and said sorrowfully –

'Oh, dear! you *can't* read. Poor souls!' and she hid her face in the pillow and sobbed, while many a smothered sob from those she was addressing, who were kneeling on the floor, aroused her.

'Never mind,' she said, raising her face and smiling brightly through her tears, 'I have prayed for you; and I know Jesus will help you, even if you can't read. Try all to do the best you can; pray every day; ask Him to help you, and get the Bible read to you whenever you can; and I think I shall see you all in heaven.'

'Amen,' was the murmured response from the lips of Tom and Mammy, and some of the elder ones, who belonged to the Methodist church. The younger and more thoughtless ones, for the time completely overcome, were sobbing, with their heads bowed upon their knees.

'I know,' said Eva, 'you all love me.'

'Yes; oh, yes! indeed we do. Lord bless her!' was the involuntary answer of all.

'Yes, I know you do. There isn't one of you that hasn't always been very kind to me; and I want to give you something that, when you look at, you shall always remember me. I'm going to give all of you a curl of my hair; and, when you look at it, think that I loved you and am gone to heaven, and that I want to see you all there.'

It is impossible to describe the scene, as, with tears and sobs, they gathered round the little creature, and took from her hands what seemed to them a last mark of her love. They fell on their knees; they sobbed, and prayed, and kissed the hem of her garment; and the elder ones poured forth words of endearment, mingled in prayers and blessings, after the manner of their susceptible race.

As each one took their gift, Miss Ophelia, who was apprehensive for the effect of all this excitement on her little patient, signed to each one to pass out of the apartment.

At last, all were gone but Tom and Mammy.

'Here, Uncle Tom,' said Eva, 'is a beautiful one for you. Oh, I am so happy, Uncle Tom, to think I shall see you in heaven, for I'm sure I shall; and Mammy, dear, good, kind Mammy!' she said, fondly throwing her arms round her old nurse, 'I know you'll be there, too.'

'O Miss Eva, don't see how I can live without ye, no how!' said the faithful creature. ''Pears like it's just taking everything off the place to oncet!' and Mammy gave way to a passion of grief.

Miss Ophelia pushed her and Tom gently from the apartment, and thought they were all gone; but as she turned, Topsy was standing there.

'Where did you start up from?' she said, suddenly.

'I was here,' said Topsy, wiping the tears from her eyes.

'O Miss Eva, I've been a bad girl; but won't you give *me* one, too?'

'Yes, poor Topsy! to be sure I will. There – every time you look at that, think that I loved you, and wanted you to be a good girl!'

'O Miss Eva, I *is* trying!' said Topsy, earnestly; 'but Lor, it's so hard to be good! 'Pears like I ain't used to it, noways!'

'Jesus knows it, Topsy; he is sorry for you; he will help you.'

Topsy, with her eyes hid in her apron, was silently passed from the apartment by Miss Ophelia; but, as she went, she hid the precious curl in her bosom.

All being gone, Miss Ophelia shut the door. That worthy lady had wiped away many tears of her own during the scene, but concern for the consequence of such an excitement to her young charge was uppermost in her mind.

St Clare had been sitting, during the whole time, with his hand shading his eyes, in the same attitude. When they were all gone, he sat so still.

'Papa!' said Eva, gently laying her hand on his.

He gave a sudden start and shiver, but made no answer.

'Dear papa!' said Eva.

'I *cannot*,' said St Clare, rising, 'I *cannot* have it so! The Almighty hath dealt *very bitterly* with me!' and St Clare pronounced these words with a bitter emphasis indeed.

'Augustine! has not God a right to do what He will with his own?' said Miss Ophelia.

'Perhaps so; but that doesn't make it any easier to bear,' said he, with a dry, hard, tearless manner, as he turned away.

'Papa, you break my heart!' said Eva, rising and throwing herself into his arms; 'you must not feel so!' and the child sobbed and wept with a violence which alarmed them all, and turned her father's thoughts at once to another channel.

'There, Eva – there, dearest! Hush! hush! I was wrong; I was wicked. I will feel any way, do any way – only don't distress yourself; don't sob so. I will be resigned; I was wicked to speak as I did.'

Eva soon lay like a wearied dove in her father's arms; and he, bending over her, soothed her by every tender word he could think of.

Marie rose and threw herself out of the apartment into her own, when she fell into violent hysterics.

'You didn't give me a curl, Eva,' said her father, smiling sadly.

'They are all yours, papa,' said she, smiling – 'yours and mamma's; and you must give dear aunty as many as she wants. I only gave them to our poor people myself, because you know, papa, they might be forgotten when I am gone, and because I hoped it might help them remember ... You are a Christian, are you not, papa?' said Eva, doubtfully.

'Why do you ask me?'

'I don't know. You are so good, I don't see how you can help it.'

'What is being a Christian, Eva?'

'Loving Christ most of all,' said Eva.

'Do you, Eva?'

'Certainly I do.'

'You never saw him,' said St Clare.

'That makes no difference,' said Eva. 'I believe him, and in a few days I shall *see* him;' and the young face grew fervent, radiant with joy.

St Clare said no more. It was a feeling which he had seen before in his mother; but no chord within vibrated to it.

Eva after this declined rapidly; there was no more any doubt of the event; the fondest hope could not be blinded. Her beautiful room was avowedly a sick room; and Miss Ophelia day and night performed the duties of a nurse – and never did her friends appreciate her value more than in that capacity. With so well-trained a hand and eye, such perfect adroitness and practice in every art which could promote neatness and comfort, and keep out of sight every disagreeable incident of sickness – with such a perfect sense of time, such a clear, untroubled head, such exact accuracy in remembering every prescription and direction of the doctor's – she was everything to him. They who had shrugged their shoulders at her little peculiarities and setnesses, so unlike the careless freedom of southern manners, acknowledged that now she was the exact person that was wanted.

Uncle Tom was much in Eva's room. The child suffered much from nervous restlessness, and it was a relief to her to be carried; and it was Tom's greatest delight to carry her little frail form in his arms, resting on a pillow, now up and down her room, now out into the verandah; and when the fresh sea-breezes blew from the lake, and the child felt freshest in the morning, he would sometimes walk with her under the orange trees in the garden, or, sitting down in some of their old seats, sing to her their favourite old hymns.

Her father often did the same thing; but his frame was slighter; and when he was weary, Eva would say to him, –

'O papa, let Tom take me. Poor fellow! it pleases him; and you know it's all he can do now, and he wants to do something!'

'So do I, Eva,' said her father.

'Well, papa, you can do everything, and are everything to me. You read to me – you sit up nights – and Tom has only this one thing, and his singing; and I know, too, he does it easier than you can. He carries me so strong!'

The desire to do something was not confined to Tom. Every servant in the establishment showed the same feeling, and in their way did what they could.

Poor Mammy's heart yearned towards her darling; but she found no opportunity, night or day, as Marie declared that the state of her mind was such, it was impossible for her to rest; and, of course, it was against her principles to let any one else rest. Twenty times in a night Mammy would be roused to rub her feet, to bathe her head, to find her pocket-handkerchief, to see what the noise was in Eva's room, to let down a curtain because it was too light, or to put it up because it was too dark; and, in the day-time, when she longed to have some share in the nursing of her pet, Marie seemed unusually ingenious in keeping her busy anywhere and everywhere all over the house, or about her own person; so that stolen interviews and momentary glimpses were all she could obtain.

'I feel it my duty to be particularly careful of myself, now,' she would say, 'feeble as I am, and with the whole care and nursing of that dear child upon me.'

'Indeed, my dear,' said St Clare, 'I thought our cousin relieved you of that.'

'You talk like a man, St Clare – just as if a mother *could* be relieved of the care of a child in that state; but, then, it's all alike – no one ever knows what I feel! I can't throw things off, as you do.'

St Clare smiled. You must excuse him, he couldn't help it – for St Clare could smile yet. For so bright and placid was the farewell voyage of the little spirit – by such sweet and fragrant breezes was the small bark borne towards the heavenly shores – that it was impossible to realise that it was death that was approaching. The child felt no pain – only a tranquil, soft weakness, daily and almost insensibly increasing; and she was so beautiful, so loving, so trustful, so happy, that one could not resist the soothing influence of that air of innocence and peace which seemed to breathe around her. St Clare found a strange calm coming over him. It was not hope – that was impossible; it was not resignation; it was only a calm resting in the present, which seemed so beautiful that he wished to think of no future. It was like that hush of spirit which we feel amid the bright, mild woods of autumn, when the bright hectic flush is on the trees, and the last lingering flowers by the brook; and we joy in it all the more, because we know that soon it will all pass away.

The friend who knew most of Eva's own imaginings and fore-shadowings was her faithful bearer, Tom. To him she said what she would not disturb her father by saying. To him she imparted those mysterious intimations which the soul feels, as the cords begin to unbind ere it leaves its clay for ever.

Tom, at last, would not sleep in his room, but lay all night in the outer verandah, ready to rouse at every call.

'Uncle Tom, what alive have you taken to sleeping anywhere and everywhere, like a dog, for?' said Miss Ophelia. 'I thought you was one of the orderly sort, that liked to lie in bed in a Christian way.'

'I do, Miss Feely,' said Tom, mysteriously. 'I do, but now—'

'Well, what now?'

'We mustn't speak loud; Mas'r St Clare won't hear on't; but, Miss Feely, you know there must be somebody watchin' for the bridegroom.'

'What do you mean, Tom?'

'You know it says in Scripture, "At midnight there was a great cry made, Behold the bridegroom cometh." That's what I'm 'spectin' now every night, Miss Feely – and I couldn't sleep out o' hearin no ways.'

'Why, Uncle Tom, what makes you think so?'

'Miss Eva, she talks to me. The Lord, he sends his messenger in the soul. I must be thar, Miss Feely; for when that ar blessed child goes into the kingdom, they'll open the door so wide, we'll all get a look in at the glory, Miss Feely.'

'Uncle Tom, did Miss Eva say she felt more unwell than usual to-night?'

'No; but she told me this morning she was coming nearer – thar's them that tells it to the child, Miss Feely. It's the angels. "It's the trumpet sound afore the break o' day,"' said Tom, quoting from a favourite hymn.

This dialogue passed between Miss Ophelia and Tom, between ten and eleven one evening, after her arrangements had all been made for the night, when, on going to bolt her outer door, she found Tom stretched along by it, in the outer verandah.

She was not nervous or impressible; but the solemn, heartfelt manner struck her. Eva had been unusually bright and cheerful that afternoon, and had sat raised in her bed, and looked over all her little trinkets and precious things, and designated the friends to whom she would have them given; and her manner was more animated, and her voice more natural, than they had known it for weeks. Her father had been in in the evening, and had said that Eva appeared more like her former self than ever she had done since her sickness; and when he kissed her for the night, he said to Miss Ophelia; 'Cousin, we may keep her with us, after all; she is certainly better,' and he had retired with a lighter heart in his bosom than he had had there for weeks.

But at midnight – strange, mystic hour, when the veil between the frail present and the eternal future grows thin – then came the messenger!

There was a sound in that chamber, first of one who stepped quickly. It was Miss Ophelia, who had resolved to sit up all night with her little charge, and who, at the turn of the night, had discerned what experienced nurses significantly call a 'change.' The outer door was quickly opened, and Tom, who was watching outside, was on the alert in a moment.

'Go for the doctor, Tom! lose not a moment,' said Miss Ophelia; and, stepping across the room, she rapped at St Clare's door.

'Cousin,' she said, 'I wish you would come.'

Those words fell on his heart like clods upon a coffin. Why

did they? He was up and in the room in an instant, and bending over Eva, who still slept.

What was it he saw that made his heart stand still? Why was no word spoken between the two? Thou canst say, who hast seen that same expression on the face dearest to thee; that look, indescribable, hopeless, unmistakable, that says to thee that thy beloved is no longer thine.

On the face of the child, however, there was no ghastly imprint – only a high and almost sublime expression – the over-shadowing presence of spiritual natures, the dawning of immortal life in that childish soul.

They stood there so still, gazing upon her, that even the ticking of the watch seemed too loud. In a few moments Tom returned with the doctor. He entered, gave one look, and stood silent as the rest.

'When did this change take place?' said he, in a low whisper, to Miss Ophelia.

'About the turn of the night,' was the reply.

Marie, roused by the entrance of the doctor, appeared hurriedly from the next room.

'Augustine! Cousin! – Oh! – what?' – she hurriedly began.

'Hush!' said St Clare hoarsely; '*she is dying*!'

Mammy heard the words, and flew to awaken the servants. The house was soon roused – lights were seen, footsteps heard, anxious faces thronged the verandah, and looked tearfully through the glass doors; but St Clare heard and said nothing; he saw only *that look* on the face of the little sleeper.

'Oh, if she would only wake, and speak once more!' he said; and, stooping over her, he spoke in her ear – 'Eva, darling!'

The large blue eyes unclosed – a smile passed over her face; she tried to raise her head, and to speak.

'Do you know me, Eva?'

'Dear papa,' said the child with a last effort, throwing her arms about his neck. In a moment they dropped again; and, as St Clare raised his head, he saw a spasm of mortal agony pass over the face – she struggled for breath, and threw up her little hands.

'O God, this is dreadful!' he said, turning away in agony and wringing Tom's hand, scarce conscious what he was doing. 'O Tom, my boy, it is killing me!'

Tom had his master's hands between his own; and, with tears streaming down his dark cheeks, looked up for help where he had always been used to look.

'Pray that this may be cut short!' said St Clare; 'this wrings my heart!'

'Oh, bless the Lord! it's over – it's over, dear mas'r!' said Tom; 'look at her.'

The child lay panting on her pillows, as one exhausted – the large clear eyes rolled up and fixed. Ah, what said those eyes, that spoke so much of heaven? Earth was passed, and earthly pain; but so solemn, so mysterious, was the triumphant brightness of that face, that it checked even the sobs of sorrow. They pressed around her breathless stillness.

'Eva!' said St Clare, gently.

She did not hear.

'O Eva, tell us what you see! What is it?' said her father.

A bright, a glorious smile passed over her face, and she said, brokenly – 'Oh! love – joy – peace!' gave one sigh, and passed from death unto life!

'Farewell, beloved child! the bright, eternal doors have closed after thee; we shall see thy sweet face no more. Oh, woe for them who watched thy entrance into heaven, when they shall wake and find only the cold grey sky of daily life, and thou gone for ever!'

Chapter 27

'THIS IS THE LAST OF EARTH'

THE statuettes and pictures in Eva's room were shrouded in white napkins, and only hushed breathings and muffled footfalls were heard there, and the light stole in solemnly through windows partially darkened by closed blinds.

The bed was draped in white; and there, beneath the drooping angel-figure, lay a little sleeping form – sleeping never to waken!

There she lay, robed in one of the simple white dresses she had been wont to wear when living; the rose-coloured light through the curtains cast over the icy coldness of death a warm glow. The heavy eyelashes drooped softly on the pure cheek; the head was turned a little to one side, as if in natural sleep, but there was diffused over every lineament of the face that high celestial expression, that mingling of rapture and repose, which showed it was no earthly or temporary sleep, but the long, sacred rest which 'He giveth to his beloved.'

There is no death to such as thou, dear Eva! neither darkness nor shadow of death; only such a bright fading as when the morning star fades in the golden dawn. Thine is the victory without the battle – the crown without the conflict.

So did St Clare think, as, with folded arms, he stood there gazing. Ah! who shall say what he did think? for, from the hour that voices had said, in the dying chamber, 'She is gone,' it had been all a dreary mist, a heavy 'dimness of anguish.' He had heard voices around him; he had had questions asked, and answered them; they had asked him when he would have the funeral, and where they should lay her; and he had answered impatiently, that he cared not.

Adolph and Rosa had arranged the chamber; volatile, fickle, and childish as they generally were, they were soft-hearted and full of feeling; and while Miss Ophelia presided over the general details of order and neatness, it was their hands that added those soft, poetic touches to the arrangements, that took from the death-room the grim and ghastly air which too often marks a New England funeral.

There were still flowers on the shelves – all white, delicate, and fragrant, with graceful, drooping leaves. Eva's little table, covered with white, bore on it her favourite vase, with a single white moss rose-bud in it. The folds of the drapery, the fall of the curtains had been arranged, and re-arranged, by Adolph and Rosa, with that nicety of eye which characterises their race. Even now, while St Clare stood there thinking, little Rosa tripped softly into the chamber with a basket of white flowers. She stepped back when she saw St Clare, and stopped respectfully; but, seeing that he did not observe her, she came forward to place them around the dead. St Clare saw her as in a dream, while she placed in the small hands a fair cape of jessamine, and, with admirable taste, disposed other flowers around the couch.

The door opened again, and Topsy, her eyes swelled with crying, appeared, holding something under her apron. Rosa made a quick, forbidding gesture; but she took a step into the room.

'You must go out,' said Rosa, in a sharp positive whisper; '*you* haven't any business here!'

'Oh, do let me! I brought a flower – such a pretty one!' said Topsy, holding up a half-blown tea rose-bud. 'Do let me put just one there.'

'Get along!' said Rosa, more decidedly.

'Let her stay!' said St Clare, suddenly stamping his foot. 'She shall come.'

Rosa suddenly retreated, and Topsy came forward and laid her offering at the feet of the corpse; then suddenly, with a wild and bitter cry, she threw herself on the floor alongside the bed, and wept and moaned aloud.

Miss Ophelia hastened into the room, and tried to raise and silence her; but in vain.

'O Miss Eva! O Miss Eva! I wish I's dead, too – I do!'

There was a piercing wildness in the cry; the blood flushed into St Clare's white, marble-like face, and the first tears he had shed since Eva died stood in his eyes.

'Get up, child,' said Miss Ophelia, in a softened voice; 'don't cry so. Miss Eva is gone to heaven; she is an angel.'

'But I can't see her!' said Topsy. 'I never shall see her!' and she sobbed again.

They all stood a moment in silence.

'*She* said she *loved* me,' said Topsy – 'she did! Oh, dear! oh, dear! there ain't *nobody* left now – there ain't!'

'That's true enough,' said St Clare; 'but do,' he said to Miss Ophelia, 'see if you can't comfort the poor creature.'

'I jist wish I hadn't never been born,' said Topsy. 'I didn't want to be born, no ways; and I don't see no use on't.'

Miss Ophelia raised her gently but firmly, and took her from the room; but, as she did so, some tears fell from her eyes.

'Topsy, you poor child,' she said, as she led her into her room, 'don't give up! *I* can love you, though I am not like that dear little child. I hope I've learnt something of the love of Christ from her. I can love you; I do, and I'll try to help you to grow up a good Christian girl.'

Miss Ophelia's voice was more than her words, and more than that were the honest tears that fell down her face. From that hour she acquired an influence over the mind of the destitute child that she never lost.

'O, my Eva, whose little hour on earth did so much of good,' thought St Clare, 'what account have I to give for my long years?'

There were, for a while, soft whisperings and foot-falls in the chamber, as one after another stole in, to look at the dead; and then came the little coffin; and then there was a funeral, and carriages drove to the door, and strangers came and were seated; and there were white scarfs and ribbons, and crape bands, and mourners dressed in black crape; and there were words read from the Bible, and prayers offered; and St Clare lived, and walked, and moved, as one who has shed every tear. To the last he saw only one thing, that golden head in the coffin; but then he saw the cloth spread over it, the lid of the coffin closed; and he walked, when he was put beside the others, down to a little place at the bottom of the garden, and there, by the mossy seat where she and Tom had talked, and sung, and read so often, was the little grave. St Clare stood beside it – looked vacantly down; he saw them lower the little coffin; he heard dimly, the solemn words, 'I am the Resurrection and the Life; he that believeth in me, though he were dead, yet shall he live,' and as the earth was cast in and filled up the little grave, he could not realise that it was his Eva that they were hiding from his sight.

Nor was it – not Eva, but only the frail seed of that bright, immortal form with which she shall yet come forth, in the day of the Lord Jesus!

And then all were gone, and the mourners went back to the place which should know her no more; and Marie's room was darkened, and she lay on the bed, sobbing and moaning in uncontrollable grief, and calling every moment for the attentions of all her servants. Of course, they had no time to cry – why should they? The grief was *her* grief, and she was fully convinced that nobody on earth did, could, or would feel it as she did.

'St Clare did not shed a tear,' she said, 'he didn't sympathise with her; it was perfectly wonderful to think how hard-hearted and unfeeling he was, when he must know how she suffered.'

So much are people the slave of their eye and ear, that many of the servants really thought that missis was the principal sufferer in the case, especially as Marie began to have hysterical spasms, and sent for the doctor, and at last declared herself dying; and in the running and scampering, and bringing up hot bottles, and heating of flannels, and chafing, and fussing, that ensued, there was quite a diversion.

Tom, however, had a feeling at his own heart, that drew him to his master. He followed him wherever he walked, wistfully and sadly, and when he saw him sitting, so pale and quiet, in Eva's room, holding before his eyes her little open Bible, though seeing no letter or word of what was in it, there was more sorrow to Tom in that still, fixed, tearless eye, than in all Marie's moans and lamentations.

In a few days the St Clare family were back again in the city; Augustine, with the restlessness of grief, longing for another scene, to change the current of his thoughts. So they left the house and garden, with its little grave, and came back to New Orleans; and St Clare walked the streets busily, and strove to fill up the chasm in his heart with hurry and bustle, and change of place; and people who saw him in the street, or met him at the café, knew of his loss only by the weed on his hat; for there he was, smiling and talking, and reading the newspaper, and speculating on politics, and attending to business matters; and who could see that all this smiling outside was but a hollow shell over a heart that was a dark and silent sepulchre?

'Mr St Clare is a singular man,' said Marie to Miss Ophelia, in a complaining tone. 'I used to think, if there was anything in the world he did love, it was our dear little Eva; but he seems to be forgetting her very easily. I cannot ever get him to talk about her. I really did think he would show more feeling.'

'Still waters run deepest, they used to tell me,' said Miss Ophelia, oracularly.

'Oh, I don't believe in such things; it's all talk. If people have feeling, they will show it – they can't help it; but, then, it's a great misfortune to have feeling. I'd rather have been made like St Clare. My feelings prey upon me so!'

'Sure, missis, Mas'r St Clare is getting thin as a shader. They say he don't never eat nothin',' said Mammy. 'I know he don't forget Miss Eva; I know there couldn't nobody – dear, little, blessed cretur!' she added, wiping her eyes.

'Well, at all events, he has no consideration for me,' said Marie; 'he hasn't spoken one word of sympathy, and he must know how much more a mother feels than any man can.'

'The heart knoweth its own bitterness,' said Miss Ophelia, gravely.

'That's just what I think. I know just what I feel – nobody else seems to. Eva used to, but she's gone!' and Marie lay back on her lounge, and began to sob disconsolately.

Marie was one of those unfortunately constituted mortals, in whose eyes whatever is lost and gone assumes a value which it never had in possession. Whatever she had, she seemed to survey only to pick flaws in it; but, once fairly away, there was no end to her valuation of it.

While this conversation was taking place in the parlour, another was going on in St Clare's library.

Tom, who was always uneasily following his master about, had seen him go to the library, some hours before, and, after vainly waiting for him to come out, determined, at last, to make an errand in. He entered softly. St Clare lay on his lounge at the further end of the room. He was lying on his face, with Eva's Bible open before him, at a little distance. Tom walked up, and stood by the sofa. He hesitated; and, while he was hesitating, St Clare suddenly raised himself up. The honest face, so full of grief, and with such an imploring expression of affection and sympathy, struck his master. He laid his hand on Tom's, and bowed down his forehead on it.

'O Tom, my boy, the whole world is as empty as an egg shell.'

'I know it, mas'r – I know it,' said Tom. 'But, oh, if mas'r could only look up – up where our dear Miss Eva is – up to the dear Lord Jesus!'

'Ah, Tom! I do look up; but the trouble is, I don't see anything when I do. I wish I could.'

Tom sighed heavily.

'It seems to be given to children, and poor honest fellows like you, to see what we can't,' said St Clare. 'How comes it?'

'Thou hast "hid from the wise and prudent, and revealed unto babes," ' murmured Tom, ' "even so, Father, for so it seemed good in thy sight." '

'Tom, I don't believe – I can't believe; I've got the habit of doubting,' said St Clare. 'I want to believe this Bible, and I can't.'

'Dear mas'r, pray to the good Lord – "Lord, I believe; help thou my unbelief." '

'Who knows anything about anything?' said St Clare, his eyes wandering dreamily, and speaking to himself. 'Was all that beautiful love and faith only one of the ever-shifting phases of human feeling, having nothing real to rest on, passing away with the little breath? And is there no more Eva – no heaven – no Christ – nothing?'

'O dear mas'r, there is! I know it; I'm sure of it,' said Tom, falling on his knees. 'Do, do, dear mas'r, believe it!'

'How do you know there's any Christ, Tom? You never saw the Lord.'

'Felt him in my soul, mas'r – feel him now! O mas'r, when I was sold away from my old woman and the children, I was jest a'most broke up. I felt as if there warn't nothing left; and then the good Lord he stood by me, and he says, "Fear not, Tom;" and he brings light and joy into a poor feller's soul – makes all peace; and I's so happy, and loves everybody, and feels willin' jest to be the Lord's, and have the Lord's will done, and be put jest where the Lord wants to put me. I know it couldn't come from me, cause I's a poor, complainin' cretur; it comes from the Lord; and I know he's willing to do for mas'r.'

Tom spoke with fast-running tears and choking voice. St Clare leaned his head on his shoulder, and wrung the hard, faithful, black hand.

'Tom, you love me,' he said.

'I's willin' to lay down my life, this blessed day, to see mas'r a Christian.'

'Poor, foolish boy,' said St Clare, half raising himself. 'I'm not worth the love of one good, honest heart like yours.'

'O mas'r, dere's more than me loves you – the blessed Lord Jesus loves you.'

'How do you know that Tom?' said St Clare.

'Feels it in my soul. O mas'r! "the love of Christ, that passeth knowledge." '

'Singular!' said St Clare, turning away, 'that the story of a man that lived and died eighteen hundred years ago can affect people so yet. But he was no man,' he added suddenly. 'No man ever had such long and living power! Oh, that I could believe what my mother taught me, and pray as I did when *I* was a boy!'

'If mas'r pleases,' said Tom, 'Miss Eva used to read this so beautifully. I wish mas'r be so good as read it. Don't get no readin', hardly, now Miss Eva's gone.'

The chapter was the eleventh of John – the touching account of the raising of Lazarus. St Clare read it aloud, often pausing to wrestle down feelings which were aroused by the pathos of the story. Tom knelt before him, with clasped hands, and with an absorbed expression of love, trust, adoration, on his quiet face.

'Tom,' said his master, 'this is all *real* to you!'

'I can jest fairly *see* it, mas'r,' said Tom.

'I wish I had your eyes, Tom.'

'I wish to the dear Lord mas'r had!'

'But, Tom, you know that I have a great deal more knowledge than you. What if I should tell you that I don't believe this Bible?'

'O mas'r!' said Tom, holding up his hands, with a deprecating gesture.

'Wouldn't it shake your faith some, Tom?'

'Not a grain,' said Tom.

'Why, Tom, you must know I know the most.'

'O mas'r, haven't you jest read how He hides from the wise and prudent, and reveals unto babes? But mas'r wasn't in earnest, for sartin, now?' said Tom anxiously.

'No, Tom, I was not. I don't disbelieve, and I think there is reason to believe; and still I don't. It's a troublesome bad habit I've got, Tom.'

'If mas'r would only pray!'

'How do you know I don't, Tom?'

'Does mas'r?'

'I would, Tom, if there was anybody there when I pray; but it's all speaking unto nothing, when I do. But come, Tom, you pray, now, and show me how.'

Tom's heart was full; he poured it out in prayer, like waters that have been long suppressed. One thing was plain enough; Tom thought there was somebody to hear, whether there were or not. In fact, St Clare felt himself borne, on the tide of his faith and feeling, almost to the gates of that heaven he seemed so vividly to conceive. It seemed to bring him nearer to Eva.

'Thank you, my boy,' said St Clare, when Tom rose. 'I like to hear you, Tom; but go, now, and leave me alone: some other time I'll talk more.'

Tom silently left the room.

Chapter 28

REUNION

Week after week glided away in the St Clare mansion, and the waves of life settled back to their usual flow where that little bark had gone down. For how imperiously, how coolly, in disregard of all one's feeling, does the hard, cold, uninteresting course of daily realities move on! Still must we eat, and drink, and sleep and wake again – still bargain, buy, sell, ask and answer questions – pursue, in short, a thousand shadows, though all interest in them be over; the cold, mechanical habit of living remaining, after all vital interest in it has fled.

All the interests and hopes of St Clare's life had unconsciously wound themselves around this child. It was for Eva that he had managed his property; it was for Eva that he had planned the disposal of his time; and, to do this and that for Eva – to buy, improve, alter and arrange, or dispose something for her – had been so long his habit, that, now she was gone, there seemed nothing to be thought of, and nothing to be done.

True, there was another life – a life which, once believed in, stands as a solemn, significant figure before the otherwise unmeaning ciphers of time, changing them to orders of mysterious, untold value. St Clare knew this well, and often, in many a weary hour, he heard that slender, childish voice calling him to the skies, and saw that little hand pointing to him the way of life; but a heavy lethargy of sorrow lay on him – he could not arise. He had one of those natures which could better and more clearly conceive of religious things from its own perceptions and instincts, than many a matter-of-fact and practical Christian. The gift to appreciate and the sense to feel the finer shades and relations of moral things, often seems an attribute of those whose whole life shows a careless disregard of them. Hence Moore, Byron, Goethe, often speak words more wisely descriptive of the true religious sentiment, than another man whose whole life is governed by it. In such minds, disregard of religion is a more fearful treason – a more deadly sin.

St Clare had never pretended to govern himself by any religious obligation; and a certain fineness of nature gave him such an instinctive view of the extent of the requirements of Christianity, that he shrank, by anticipation, from what he felt would be the exactions of his own conscience, if he once did resolve to assume them. For, so inconsistent is human nature, especially in the ideal, that not to undertake a thing at all seems better than to undertake and come short.

Still St Clare was in many respects another man. He read his little Eva's Bible seriously and honestly; he thought more soberly and practically of his relations to his servants – enough to make him extremely dissatisfied with both his past and present course; and one thing he did, soon after his return to New Orleans, and that was to commence the legal steps necessary to Tom's emancipation, which was to be perfected as soon as he could get through the necessary formalities. Meantime, he attached himself to Tom more and more, every day. In all the wide world, there was nothing that seemed to remind him so much of Eva; and he would insist on keeping him constantly about him, and, fastidious and unapproachable as he was with regard to his deeper feelings, he almost thought aloud to Tom. Nor would any one have wondered at it, who had seen the expression of affection and devotion with which Tom continually followed his young master.

'Well, Tom,' said St Clare, the day after he had commenced the legal formalities for his enfranchisement, 'I'm going to make a free man of you; so, have your trunk packed, and get ready to set out for Kentuck.'

The sudden light of joy that shone in Tom's face as he raised his hands to heaven, his emphatic 'Bless the Lord!' rather discomposed St Clare; he did not like it that Tom should be so ready to leave him.

'You haven't had such very bad times here, that you need be in such a rapture, Tom,' he said dryly.

'No, no, mas'r! tan't that – it's bein' a *free man*! That's what I'm joyin' for.'

'Why, Tom, don't you think, for your own part, you've been better off than to be free?'

'*No, indeed*, Mas'r St Clare,' said Tom, with a flash of energy. 'No, indeed!'

'Why, Tom, you couldn't possibly have earned, by your work, such clothes and such living as I have given you.'

'Knows all that, Mas'r St Clare; mas'r's been too good: but, mas'r, I'd rather have poor clothes, poor house, poor everything, and have 'em *mine*, than have the best, and have 'em any man's else! I had so, mas'r; I think it's natur, mas'r!'

'I suppose so, Tom; and you'll be going off and leaving me, in a month or so,' he added, rather discontentedly. 'Though why you shouldn't, no mortal knows,' he said, in a gayer tone; and, getting up, he began to walk the floor.

'Not while mas'r is in trouble,' said Tom. 'I'll stay with mas'r as long as he wants me – so as I can be any use.'

'Not while I'm in trouble, Tom?' said St Clare, looking sadly out of the window. . . . 'And when will *my* trouble be over?'

'When Mas'r St Clare's a Christian,' said Tom.

'And you really mean to stay by till that day comes?' said St Clare, half-smiling as he turned from the window, and laid his hand on Tom's shoulder. 'Ah, Tom, you soft, silly boy! I won't keep you till that day. Go home to your wife and children, and give my love to all.'

'I's faith to believe that day will come,' said Tom, earnestly, and with tears in his eyes; 'the Lord has a work for mas'r.'

'A work, eh?' said St Clare; 'well, now, Tom, give me your views on what sort of a work it is; let's hear.'

'Why, even a poor fellow like me has a work from the Lord; and Mas'r St Clare, that has larnin', and riches, and friends, such he might do for the Lord!'

'Tom, you seem to think the Lord needs a great deal done for him,' said St Clare, smiling.

'We does for the Lord when we does for his critturs,' said Tom.

'Good theology, Tom; better than Dr B. preaches, I dare swear,' said St Clare.

The conversation was here interrupted by the announcement of some visitors.

Marie St Clare felt the loss of Eva as deeply as she could feel anything; and as she was a woman that had a great faculty of making everybody unhappy when she was, her immediate attendants had still stronger reason to regret the loss of their young mistress, whose winning ways and gentle intercessions had so often been a shield to them from the tyrannical and selfish exactions of her mother. Poor old Mammy, in particular, whose heart, severed from all natural domestic ties, had consoled itself with this one beautiful being, was almost heartbroken. She cried day and night, and was, from excess of sorrow, less skilful and alert in her ministrations on her mistress than usual, which drew down a constant storm of invectives on her defenceless head.

Miss Ophelia felt the loss; but, in her good and honest heart, it bore fruit unto everlasting life. She was more softened, more gentle; and though equally assiduous in every duty, it was with a chastened and quiet air, as one who communed with her own heart not in vain. She was more diligent in teaching Topsy – taught her mainly from the Bible – did not any longer shrink from her touch, or manifest an ill-repressed disgust, because she felt none. She viewed her now through the softened medium that Eva's hand had first held before her eyes, and saw in her only an immortal creature, whom God had sent to be led by her to glory and virtue. Topsy did not become at once a saint; but the life and death of Eva did work a marked change in her. The callous indifference was gone; there was now sensibility, hope, desire, and the striving for good – a strife irregular, interrupted, suspended oft, but yet renewed again.

One day, when Topsy had been sent for by Miss Ophelia, she came, hastily thrusting something into her bosom.

'What are you doing there, you limb? You've been stealing something, I'll be bound,' said the imperious little Rosa, who had been sent to call her, seizing her, at the same time, roughly by the arm.

'You go 'long, Miss Rosa!' said Topsy, pulling from her; ''tan't none o' your business!'

'None o' your sa'ce!' said Rosa. 'I saw you hiding something – I know yer tricks;' and Rosa seized her arm, and tried to force her hand into her bosom, while Topsy, enraged, kicked and fought valiantly for what she considered her rights. The clamour and confusion of the battle drew Miss Ophelia and St Clare both to the spot.

'She's been stealing!' said Rosa.

'I han't neither!' vociferated Topsy, sobbing with passion.

'Give me that, whatever it is!' said Miss Ophelia, firmly.

Topsy hesitated; but, on a second order, pulled out of her bosom a little parcel done up in the foot of one of her own old stockings.

Miss Ophelia turned it out. There was a small book which had been given to Topsy by Eva, containing a single verse of Scripture, arranged for every day in the year, and in a paper the curl of hair that she had given her on that memorable day when she had taken her last farewell.

St Clare was a good deal affected at the sight of it; the little book had been rolled in a long strip of black crape, torn from the funeral weeds.

'What did you wrap *this* round the book for?' said St Clare, holding up the crape.

'Cause – cause – cause 'twas Miss Eva. Oh, don't take 'em away, please!' she said: and sitting flat down on the floor, and putting her apron over her head, she began to sob vehemently.

It was a curious mixture of the pathetic and the ludicrous – the little old stocking – black crape – text-book – fair, soft curl – and Topsy's utter distress.

St Clare smiled; but there were tears in his eyes, as he said, –

'Come, come – don't cry; you shall have them!' and putting them together, he threw them into her lap, and drew Miss Ophelia with him into the parlour.

'I really think you can make something of that concern,' he said, pointing with his thumb backward over his shoulder. 'Any mind that is capable of a *real sorrow* is capable of good. You must try and do something with her.'

'The child has improved greatly,' said Miss Ophelia. 'I have great hopes of her; but, Augustine,' she said, laying her hand on his arm, 'one thing I want to ask; whose is this child to be? – yours or mine?'

'Why, I gave her to *you*,' said Augustine.

'But not legally; I want her to be mine legally,' said Miss Ophelia.

'Whew! cousin,' said Augustine. 'What will the Abolition Society think? They'll have a day of fasting appointed for this backsliding, if you become a slave-holder!'

'Oh, nonsense! I want her mine, that I may have a right to take her to the free States, and give her her liberty, that all I am trying to do be not undone.'

'Oh, cousin, what an awful "doing evil that good may come!" I can't encourage it.'

'I don't want you to joke, but to reason,' said Miss Ophelia. 'There is no use in my trying to make this child a Christian child unless I save her from all the chances and reverses of slavery; and, if you really are willing I should have her, I want you to give me a deed of gift, or some legal paper.'

'Well, well,' said St Clare, 'I will!' and he sat down, and unfolded a newspaper to read.

'But I want it done now,' said Miss Ophelia.

'What's your hurry?'

'Because now is the only time there ever is to do a thing in,' said Miss Ophelia. 'Come, now, here's a paper, pen, and ink; just write a paper.'

St Clare, like most men of his class of mind, cordially hated the present tense of action, generally; and therefore he was considerably annoyed by Miss Ophelia's downrightness.

'Why, what's the matter?' said he. 'Can't you take my word? One would think you had taken lessons of the Jews, coming at a fellow so!'

'I want to make sure of it,' said Miss Ophelia. 'You may die, or fail, and then Topsy be hustled off to auction, spite of all I can do.'

'Really, you are quite provident. Well, seeing I'm in the hands of a Yankee, there is nothing for it but to concede;' and St Clare rapidly wrote off a deed of gift, which, as he was well versed in the forms of law, he could easily do, and signed his name to it in sprawling capitals, concluding by a tremendous flourish.

'There, isn't that black and white, now, Miss Vermont?' he said, as he handed it to her.

'Good boy,' said Miss Ophelia, smiling. 'But must it not be witnessed?'

'Oh, bother! – yes. Here,' he said, opening the door into Marie's apartment, 'Marie, cousin wants your autograph; just put your name down here.'

'What's this?' said Marie, as she ran over the paper. 'Ridiculous! I thought cousin was too pious for such horrid things,' she added, as she carelessly wrote her name; 'but if she has a fancy for that article, I'm sure she's welcome.'

'There, now, she's yours, body and soul,' said St Clare, handing the paper.

'No more mine now than she was before,' said Miss Ophelia. 'Nobody but God has a right to give her to me; but I can protect her now.'

'Well, she's yours by a fiction of law, then,' said St Clare, as he turned back into the parlour, and sat down to his paper.

Miss Ophelia, who seldom sat much in Marie's company, followed him into the parlour, having first carefully laid away the paper.

'Augustine,' she said, suddenly, as she sat knitting, 'have you ever made any provision for your servants, in case of your death?'

'No,' said St Clare, as he read on.

'Then all your indulgence to them may prove a great cruelty, by and by.'

St Clare had often thought the same thing himself; but he answered negligently –

'Well, I mean to make a provision, by and by.'

'When?' said Miss Ophelia.

'Oh, one of these days.'

'What if you should die first?'

'Cousin, what's the matter?' said St Clare, laying down his paper, and looking at her. 'Do you think I show symptoms of yellow fever or cholera, that you are making post-mortem arrangements with such zeal?'

'"In the midst of life we are in death,"' said Miss Ophelia.

St Clare rose up, and laying the paper down, carelessly walked to the door that stood open on the verandah, to put an end to a conversation that was not agreeable to him. Mechanically he repeated the last word again – '*Death*!' – and, as he leaned against the railings and watched the sparkling water as it rose and fell in the fountain, and, as in a dim and dizzy haze, saw the flowers and trees and vases of the courts, he repeated again the mystic word, so common in every mouth, yet of such fearful power – 'DEATH!' 'Strange that there should be such a word,' he said, 'and such a thing, and we ever forget it; that one should be living, warm and beautiful, full of hopes, desires, and wants one day, and the next be gone, utterly gone, and for ever!'

It was a warm, golden evening; and as he walked to the other end of the verandah, he saw Tom busily intent on his Bible, pointing, as he did so, with his finger to each successive word, and whispering them to himself with an earnest air.

'Want me to read to you, Tom?' said St Clare, seating himself carelessly by him.

'If Mas'r pleases,' said Tom, gratefully; 'mas'r makes it so much plainer.'

St Clare took the book and glanced at the place, and began reading one of the passages which Tom had designated by the heavy marks around it. It ran as follows: –

'When the Son of Man shall come in his glory, and all his holy angels with him, then shall he sit upon the throne of his glory; and before him shall be gathered all nations: and he shall separate them one from another, as a shepherd divideth his sheep from the goats.' St Clare read on in an animated voice, till he came to the last of the verses.

'Then shall the King say unto them on his left hand, Depart from me, ye cursed, into everlasting fire: for I was an hungered, and ye gave me no meat: I was thirsty, and ye gave me no drink: I was a stranger, and ye took me not in: naked, and ye clothed me not: I was sick, and in prison, and ye visited me not. Then shall they answer unto him, Lord, when saw we thee an hungered, or athirst, or a stranger, or naked, or sick, or in prison, and did not minister unto thee? Then shall he say unto them, Inasmuch as ye did it not to one of the least of these my brethren, ye did it not to me.'

St Clare seemed struck with this last passage, for he read it twice – the second time slowly, and as if he were revolving the words in his mind.

'Tom,' he said, 'these folks that get such hard measure seem to have been doing just what I have – living good, easy, respectable lives; and not troubling themselves to inquire how many of their brethren were hungry or athirst, or sick, or in prison.'

Tom did not answer.

St Clare rose up and walked thoughtfully up and down the verandah, seeming to forget everything in his own thoughts; so absorbed was he, that Tom had to remind him twice that the tea-bell had rung, before he could get his attention.

St Clare was absent and thoughtful all tea-time. After tea, he and Marie and Miss Ophelia took possession of the parlour, almost in silence.

Marie disposed herself on a lounge, under a silken mosquito curtain, and was soon sound asleep. Miss Ophelia silently busied herself with her knitting. St Clare sat down to the piano, and began playing a soft and melancholy movement with the Æolian accompaniment. He seemed in a deep reverie, and to be soliloquising to himself by music. After a little, he opened one of the drawers, took out an old music-book, whose leaves were yellow with age, and began turning it over.

'There,' he said to Miss Ophelia, 'this was one of my mother's books, and here is her handwriting – come and look at it. She copied and arranged this from Mozart's Requiem.' Miss Ophelia came accordingly.

'It was something she used to sing often,' said St Clare. 'I think I can hear her now.'

He struck a few majestic chords, and began singing that grand old Latin piece, the 'Dies Iræ.'

Tom, who was listening in the outer verandah, was drawn by the sound to the very door, where he stood earnestly. He did not understand the words, of course; but the music and manner of singing appeared to affect him strongly, especially when St Clare sang the more pathetic parts. Tom would have sympathised more heartily, if he had known the meaning of the beautiful words: –

> 'Recordare, Jesu pie,
> Quod sum causa tuæ viæ,

Ne me perdas illa die :
Quærens me, sedisti lassus,
Redemisti crucem passus,
Tantus labor non sit cassus.'[1]

St Clare threw a deep and pathetic expression into the words ; for the shadowy veil of years seemed drawn away, and he seemed to hear his mother's voice leading his. Voice and instrument seemed both living, and threw out with vivid sympathy those strains which the ethereal Mozart first conceived as his own dying requiem.

When St Clare had done singing, he sat leaning his head upon his hand a few moments, and then began walking up and down the floor.

'What a sublime conception is that of a last judgment !' said he. 'A righting of all the wrongs of ages ! – a solving of all moral problems, by an unanswerable wisdom ! It is, indeed, a wonderful image.'

'It is a fearful one to us,' said Miss Ophelia.

'It ought to be to me, I suppose,' said St Clare, stopping thoughtfully. 'I was reading to Tom this afternoon that chapter in Matthew that gives an account of it, and I have been quite struck with it. One should have expected some terrible enormities charged to those who are excluded from Heaven, as the reason ; but no – they are condemned for *not* doing positive good, as if that included every possible harm.'

'Perhaps,' said Miss Ophelia, 'it is impossible for a person who does no good not to do harm.'

'And what,' said St Clare, speaking abstractedly, but with deep feeling, 'what shall be said of one whose own heart, whose education, and the wants of society, have called in vain to some noble purpose ; who has floated on a dreamy, neutral spectator of the struggles, agonies, and wrongs of man, when he should have been a worker ?'

---

[1] These lines have been thus inadequately translated : –

> 'Think, O Jesus, for what reason
> Thou endured'st earth's spite and treason,
> Nor me lose, in that dread season.
> Seeking me, thy worn feet hasted,
> On the cross thy soul death tasted ;
> Let not all these toils be wasted.'

'I should say,' said Miss Ophelia, 'that he ought to repent, and begin now.'

'Always practical and to the point!' said St Clare, his face breaking out into a smile. 'You never leave me any time for general reflections, cousin; you always bring me short up against the actual present; you have a kind of eternal *now*, always in your mind.'

'*Now* is all the time I have anything to do with,' said Miss Ophelia.

'Dear little Eva – poor child!' said St Clare, 'she had set her simple little soul on a good work for me.'

It was the first time since Eva's death that he had ever said as many words as these of her, and he spoke now evidently repressing very strong feeling.

'My view of Christianity is such,' he added, 'that I think no man can consistently profess it without throwing the whole weight of his being against this monstrous system of injustice that lies at the foundation of all our society; and, if need be, sacrificing himself in the battle. That is, I mean that *I* could not be a Christian otherwise, though I have certainly had intercourse with a great many enlightened and Christian people who did no such thing; and I confess that the apathy of religious people on this subject, their want of perception of wrongs that filled me with horror, have engendered in me more scepticism than any other thing.'

'If you knew all this,' said Miss Ophelia, 'why didn't you do it?'

'Oh, because I have had only that kind of benevolence which consists in lying on a sofa, and cursing the church and clergy for not being martyrs and confessors. One can see, you know, very easily, how others ought to be martyrs.'

'Well, are you going to do differently now?' said Miss Ophelia.

'God only knows the future,' said St Clare. 'I am braver than I was, because I have lost all; and he who has nothing to lose can afford all risks.'

'And what are you going to do?'

'My duty, I hope, to the poor and lowly, as fast as I find it out,' said St Clare, 'beginning with my own servants for whom I have yet done nothing; and perhaps, at some future day, it may appear that I can do something for a whole class, something to save my country from the disgrace of that false position in which she now stands before all civilised nations.'

'Do you suppose it possible that a nation ever will voluntarily emancipate?' said Miss Ophelia.

'I don't know,' said St Clare. 'This is a day of great deeds. Heroism and disinterestedness are rising up, here and there, in the earth. The Hungarian nobles set free millions of serfs, at an immense pecuniary loss; and, perhaps, among us may be found generous spirits, who do not estimate honour and justice by dollars and cents.'

'I hardly think so,' said Miss Ophelia.

'But suppose we should rise up to-morrow and emancipate, who would educate these millions, and teach them how to use their freedom? They never would rise to do much among us. The fact is, we are too lazy and unpractical ourselves ever to give them much of an idea of that industry and energy which is necessary to form them into men. They will have to go north, where labour is the fashion – the universal custom; and tell me, now, is there enough Christian philanthropy among your northern states to bear with the process of their education and elevation? You send thousands of dollars to foreign missions; but could you endure to have the heathen sent into your towns and villages, and give your time and thoughts, and money, to raise them to the Christian standard? That's what I want to know. If we emancipate, are you willing to educate? How many families in your town would take in a negro man and woman, teach them, bear with them, and seek to make them Christians? How many merchants would take Adolph, if I wanted to make him a clerk; or mechanics, if I wanted him taught a trade? If I wanted to put Jane and Rosa to a school, how many schools are there in the northern states that would take them in? how many families that would board them? and yet they are as white as many a woman, north or south. You see, cousin, I want justice done us. We are in a bad position. We are the more *obvious* oppressors of the negro; but the unchristian prejudice of the north is an oppressor almost equally severe.'

'Well, cousin, I know it is so,' said Miss Ophelia. 'I know it was so with me, till I saw it was my duty to overcome it; but I trust I have overcome it, and I know there are many good people at the north who in this matter need only to be *taught* what their duty is to do it. It would certainly be a greater self-denial to receive heathen among us than to send missionaries to them ; but I think we would do it.'

'*You* would, I know,' said St Clare. 'I'd like to see anything you wouldn't do, if you thought it your duty !'

'Well, I'm not uncommonly good,' said Miss Ophelia. 'Others would, if they saw things as I do. I intend to take Topsy home, when I go. I suppose our folks will wonder, at first ; but I think they will be brought to see as I do. Besides, I know there are many people at the north who do exactly what you said.'

'Yes, but they are a minority ; and if we should begin to emancipate to any extent, we should soon hear from you.'

Miss Ophelia did not reply. There was a pause of some moments ; and St Clare's countenance was overcast by a sad, dreamy expression.

'I don't know what makes me think of my mother so much to-night,' he said. 'I have a strange kind of feeling, as if she were near me. I keep thinking of things she used to say. Strange what brings these past things so vividly back to us, sometimes !'

St Clare walked up and down the room for some minutes more, and then said –

'I believe I'll go down street, a few moments, and hear the news to-night.'

He took his hat, and passed out.

Tom followed him to the passage, out of the court, and asked if he should attend him.

'No, my boy,' said St Clare. 'I shall be back in an hour.'

Tom sat down in the verandah. It was a beautiful moonlight evening, and he sat watching the rising and falling spray of the fountain, and listening to its murmur. Tom thought of his home, and that he should soon be a free man, and able to return to it at will. He thought how he should work to buy his wife and boys. He felt the muscles of his brawny arms with a sort of joy, as he thought they would soon belong to himself, and how much they could do to work out the freedom of his family. Then he thought of his noble young master, and, ever second to that, came the habitual prayer that he had always offered for him ; and then his thoughts passed on to the beautiful Eva, whom he now thought of among the angels; and he thought till he almost fancied that the bright face and golden hair were looking upon him, out of the spray of the fountain. And, so musing, he fell asleep, and dreamed he saw her coming bounding towards him, just as she used to come, with a wreath of jessamine in her hair, her cheeks bright, and her eyes radiant with delight; but, as he looked, she seemed to rise from the ground; her cheeks wore a paler hue – her eyes had a deep, divine radiance, a golden halo seemed around her head – and she vanished from his sight; and Tom was awakened by a loud knocking, and the sound of many voices at the gate.

He hastened to undo it; and, with smothered voices, and heavy tread, came several men, bringing a body, wrapped in a cloak, and lying on a shutter. The light of the lamp fell full on the face; and Tom gave a wild cry of amazement and despair, that rang through all the galleries, as the men advanced with their burden to the open parlour door, where Miss Ophelia still sat knitting.

St Clare had turned into a café, to look over an evening paper. As he was reading, an affray arose between two gentlemen in the room, who were both partially intoxicated. St Clare and one or two others made an effort to separate them, and St Clare received a fatal stab in the side with a bowie-knife, which he was attempting to wrest from one of them.

The house was full of cries and lamentations, shrieks and screams; servants frantically tearing their hair, throwing themselves on the ground, or running distractedly about lamenting. Tom and Miss Ophelia alone seemed to have any presence of mind; for Marie was in strong hysteric convulsions. At Miss Ophelia's direction, one of the lounges in the parlour was hastily prepared, and the bleeding form laid upon it. St Clare had fainted, through pain and loss of blood; but as Miss Ophelia applied restoratives, he revived, opened his eyes, looked fixedly on them, looked earnestly around the room, his eyes travelling wistfully over every object, and finally they rested on his mother's picture.

The physician now arrived, and made his examination. It was evident, from the expression of his face, that there was no hope; but he applied himself to dressing the wound, and he and Miss Ophelia and Tom proceeded composedly with this work, amid the lamentations and sobs and cries of the affrighted servants, who had clustered about the doors and windows of the verandah.

'Now,' said the physician, 'we must turn all these creatures out; all depends on his being kept quiet.'

St Clare opened his eyes, and looked fixedly on the distressed beings whom Miss Ophelia and the doctor were trying to urge from the apartment. 'Poor creatures !' he said, and an expression of bitter self-reproach passed over his face. Adolph absolutely refused to go. Terror had deprived him of all presence of mind; he threw himself along on the floor, and nothing could persuade him to rise. The rest yielded to Miss Ophelia's urgent representations, that their master's safety depended on their stillness and obedience.

St Clare could say but little; he lay with his eyes shut, but it was evident that he wrestled with bitter thoughts. After a while, he laid his hand on Tom's, who was kneeling beside him, and said, 'Tom ! poor fellow !'

'What, mas'r ?' said Tom, earnestly.

'I am dying !' said St Clare, pressing his hand; 'pray !'

'If you would like a clergyman—' said the physician.

St Clare hastily shook his head, and said again to Tom, more earnestly, 'Pray !'

And Tom did pray, with all his mind and strength, for the soul that was passing – the soul that seemed looking so steadily and mournfully from those large, melancholy blue eyes. It was literally prayer offered with strong crying and tears.

When Tom ceased to speak, St Clare reached out and took his hand, looking earnestly at him, but saying nothing. He closed his eyes, but still retained his hold; for, in the gates of eternity, the black hand and the white hold each other with an equal clasp. He murmured softly to himself, at broken intervals,

> 'Recordare, Jesu pie –
>
> Ne me perdas – illa die
> Quærens me – sedisti lassus.'

It was evident that the words he had been singing that evening were passing through his mind – words of entreaty addressed to

Infinite Pity. His lips moved at intervals, as parts of the hymn fell brokenly from them.

'His mind is wandering,' said the doctor.

'No! it is coming HOME at last!' said St Clare, energetically; 'at last! at last!'

The effort of speaking exhausted him. The sinking paleness of death fell on him; but with it there fell, as if shed from the wings of some pitying spirit, a beautiful expression of peace, like that of a wearied child who sleeps.

So he lay for a few moments. They saw that the mighty hand was on him. Just before the spirit parted, he opened his eyes, with a sudden light, as of joy and recognition, and said, '*Mother*!' and then he was gone!

Chapter 29

THE UNPROTECTED

WE hear often of the distress of the negro servants on the loss of a kind master, and with good reason; for no creature on God's earth is left more utterly unprotected and desolate than the slave in these circumstances.

The child who has lost a father has still the protection of friends and of the law; he is something, and can do something – has acknowledged rights and position; the slave has none. The law regards him, in every respect, as devoid of rights, as a bale of merchandise. The only possible acknowledgment of any of the longings and wants of a human and immortal creature which are given to him, comes to him through the sovereign and irresponsible will of his master; and when that master is stricken down, nothing remains.

The number of those men who know how to use wholly irresponsible power humanely and generously is small. Everybody knows this and the slave knows it best of all; so that he feels that there are ten chances of his finding an abusive and tyrannical master, to one of his finding a considerate and kind one. Therefore is it that the wail over a kind master is loud and long, as well it may be.

When St Clare breathed his last, terror and consternation took hold of his household. He had been stricken down so in a moment, in the flower and strength of his youth! Every room and gallery of the house resounded with sobs and shrieks of despair.

Marie, whose nervous system had been enervated by a constant course of self-indulgence, had nothing to support the terror of the shock, and, at the time her husband breathed his last, was passing from one fainting-fit to another; and he to whom she had been joined in the mysterious tie of marriage passed from her for ever, without the possibility of even a parting word.

Miss Ophelia, with characteristic strength and self-control, had remained with her kinsman to the last — all eye, all ear, all attention, doing everything of the little that could be done, and joining with her whole soul in the tender and impassioned prayers which the poor slave had poured forth for the soul of his dying master.

When they were arranging him for his last rest, they found upon his bosom a small, plain miniature case, opening with a spring. It was the miniature of a noble and beautiful female face; and on the reverse, under a crystal, a lock of dark hair. They laid them back on the lifeless breast — dust to dust — poor mournful relics of early dreams, which once made that cold heart beat so warmly!

Tom's whole soul was filled with thoughts of eternity; and while he ministered around the lifeless clay, he did not once think that the sudden stroke had left him in hopeless slavery. He felt at peace about his master; for in that hour when he had poured forth his prayer into the bosom of his Father, he had found an answer of quietness and assurance springing up within himself. In the depths of his own affectionate nature he felt able to perceive something of the fulness of Divine love; for an oracle hath thus written: 'He that dwelleth in love dwelleth in God, and God in him.' Tom hoped and trusted, and was at peace.

But the funeral passed, with all its pageant of black crape, and prayers, and solemn faces; and back rolled the cool, muddy waves of everyday life; and up came the everlasting hard inquiry of 'What is to be done next?'

It rose to the mind of Marie, as, dressed in loose mourning robes, and surrounded by anxious servants, she sat up in a great easy-chair, and inspected samples of crape and bombazine. It rose to Miss Ophelia, who began to turn her thoughts towards her northern home. It rose, in silent terrors to the minds of the servants, who well knew the unfeeling, tyrannical character of the mistress in whose hands they were left. All knew very well that the indulgences which had been accorded to them were not from their mistress, but from their master; and that, now he was gone, there would be no screen between them and every tyrannous infliction which a temper soured by affliction might devise.

It was about a fortnight after the funeral, that Miss Ophelia, busied one day in her apartment, heard a gentle tap at the door. She opened it, and there stood Rosa, the pretty young quadroon whom we have before often noticed, her hair in disorder, and her eyes swelled with crying.

'O Miss Feely,' she said, falling on her knees, and catching the skirt of her dress, '*do, do* go to Miss Marie for me! do plead for me! She's goin' to send me out to be whipped – look there!' And she handed to Miss Ophelia a paper.

It was an order, written in Marie's delicate Italian hand, to the master of a whipping establishment, to give the bearer fifteen lashes.

'What have you been doing?' said Miss Ophelia.

'You know, Miss Feely, I've got such a bad temper; it's very bad of me. I was trying on Miss Marie's dress, and she slapped my face; and I spoke out before I thought, and was saucy; and she said that she'd bring me down, and have me know, once for all, that I wasn't going to be so topping as I had been; and she wrote this, and says I shall carry it. I'd rather she'd kill me, right out.'

Miss Ophelia stood considering, with the paper in her hand.

'You see, Miss Feely,' said Rosa, 'I don't mind the whipping so much, if Miss Marie or you was to do it; but, to be sent to a *man* – and such a horrid man! the shame of it, Miss Feely!'

Miss Ophelia well knew that it was the universal custom to send women and young girls to whipping-houses, to the hands of the lowest of men – men vile enough to make this their profession – there to be subjected to brutal exposure and shameful correction. She had *known* it before; but hitherto she had never realised it, till she saw the slender form of Rosa almost convulsed with distress. All the honest blood of woman-hood, the strong New England blood of liberty, flushed to her cheeks, and throbbed bitterly in her indignant heart; but, with habitual prudence and self-control, she mastered herself, and crushing the paper firmly in her hand, she merely said to Rosa –

'Sit down, child, while I go to your mistress.'

'Shameful! monstrous! outrageous!' she said to herself, as she was crossing the parlour.

She found Marie sitting up in her easy-chair, with Mammy standing by her combing her hair; Jane sat on the ground before her, busy in chafing her feet.

'How do you find yourself to-day?' said Miss Ophelia.

A deep sigh and a closing of the eyes was the only reply for a moment; and then Marie answered, 'Oh, I don't know, cousin; I suppose I'm as well as I ever shall be!' And Marie wiped her eyes with a cambric handkerchief, bordered with an inch deep of black.

'I came,' said Miss Ophelia, with a short dry cough, such as commonly introduces a difficult subject, – 'I came to speak with you about poor Rosa.'

Marie's eyes were open wide enough now, and a flush rose to her sallow cheeks, as she answered sharply, –

'Well! what about her?'

'She is very sorry for her fault.'

'She is, is she? She'll be sorrier before I've done with her! I've endured that child's impudence long enough; and now I'll bring her down – I'll make her lie in the dust.'

'But could not you punish her some other way, some way that would be less shameful?'

'I mean to shame her; that's just what I want. She has all her life presumed on her delicacy, and her good looks, and her lady-like airs, till she forgets who she is; and I'll give her one lesson that will bring her down, I fancy!'

'But, cousin, consider that, if you destroy delicacy and a sense of shame in a young girl, you deprave her very fast.'

'Delicacy!' said Marie, with a scornful laugh; 'a fine word for such as she! I'll teach her, with all her airs, that she's no better than the raggedest black wench that walks the streets! She'll take no more airs with me!'

'You will answer to God for such cruelty,' said Miss Ophelia with energy.

'Cruelty! I'd like to know what the cruelty is? I wrote orders for only fifteen lashes, and told him to put them on lightly. I'm sure there's no cruelty there!'

'No cruelty!' said Miss Ophelia. 'I'm sure any girl might rather be killed outright!'

'It might seem so to anybody with your feelings, but all these creatures get used to it; it's the only way they can be kept in order. Once let them feel that they are to take any airs about delicacy, and all that, and they'll run all over you, just as my servants always have. I've begun now to bring them under; and I'll have them all to know that I'll send one out to be whipped as soon as another, if they don't mind themselves!' said Marie, looking around her decidedly.

Jane hung her head and cowered at this, for she felt as if it was particularly directed to her. Miss Ophelia sat for a moment, as if she had swallowed some explosive mixture, and were ready to burst. Then, recollecting the utter uselessness of contention with such a nature, she shut her lips resolutely, gathered herself up, and walked out of the room.

It was hard to go back and tell Rosa that she could do nothing for her; and, shortly after, one of the man-servants came to say that her mistress had ordered him to take Rosa with him to the whipping-house, whither she was hurried, in spite of her tears and entreaties.

A few days after, Tom was standing musing by the balconies, when he was joined by Adolph, who, since the death of his master, had been entirely crestfallen and disconsolate. Adolph knew that he had always been an object of dislike to Marie, but while his master lived he had paid but little attention to it. Now that he was gone, he had moved about in daily dread and trembling, not knowing what might befall him next. Marie had held several consultations with her lawyer. After communicating with St Clare's brother, it was determined to sell the place and all the servants, except her own personal property, and these she intended to take with her, and go back to her father's plantation.

'Do ye know, Tom, that we've all got to be sold?' said Adolph.

'How did you hear that?' said Tom.

'I hid myself behind the curtains when missis was talking with the lawyer. In a few days we shall all be sent off to auction, Tom.'

'The Lord's will be done!' said Tom, folding his arms and sighing heavily.

'We'll never get another such a master,' said Adolph, apprehensively; 'but I'd rather be sold than take my chance under missis.'

Tom turned away; his heart was full. The hope of liberty, the thought of distant wife and children, rose up before his patient soul, as to the mariner shipwrecked almost in port rises the vision of the church-spire and loving roofs of his native village, seen over the top of some black wave only for one last farewell. He drew his arms tightly over his bosom, and choked back the bitter tears, and tried to pray. The poor old soul had such a singular, unaccountable prejudice in favour of liberty, that it was a hard wrench for him; and the more he said 'Thy will be done,' the worse he felt.

He sought Miss Ophelia who, ever since Eva's death, had treated him with marked and respectful kindness.

'Miss Feely,' he said, 'Mas'r St Clare promised me my freedom. He told me that he had begun to take it out for me; and now, perhaps, if Miss Feely would be good enough to speak about it to missis, she would feel like goin' on with it, as it was Mas'r St Clare's wish.'

'I'll speak for you, Tom, and do my best,' said Miss Ophelia; 'but if it depends on Mrs St Clare, I can't hope much for you: nevertheless, I will try.'

This incident occurred a few days after that of Rosa, while Miss Ophelia was busied in preparations to return north.

Seriously reflecting within herself, she considered that perhaps she had shown too hasty a warmth of language in her former interview with Marie; and she resolved that she would now endeavour to moderate her zeal, and to be as conciliatory as possible. So the good soul gathered herself up, and, taking her knitting, resolved to go into Marie's room, be as agreeable as possible, and negotiate Tom's case with all the diplomatic skill of which she was mistress.

She found Marie reclining at length upon a lounge, supporting herself on one elbow by pillows, while Jane, who had been out shopping, was displaying before her certain samples of thin black stuffs.

'That will do,' said Marie, selecting one; 'only I'm not sure about its being properly mourning.'

'Laws, missis,' said Jane volubly, 'Mrs General Derbennon wore just this very thing after the General died, last summer; it makes up lovely!'

'What do you think?' said Marie to Miss Ophelia.

'It's a matter of custom, I suppose,' said Miss Ophelia. 'You can judge about it better than I.'

'The fact is,' said Marie, 'that I haven't a dress in the world that I can wear; and, as I am going to break up the establishment and go off next week, I must decide upon something.'

'Are you going so soon?'

'Yes. St Clare's brother has written, and he and the lawyer think that the servants and furniture had better be put up at auction, and the place left with our lawyer.'

'There's one thing I wanted to speak with you about,' said Miss Ophelia. 'Augustine promised Tom his liberty, and began the legal forms necessary to it. I hope you will use your influence to have it perfected.'

'Indeed, I shall do no such thing!' said Marie, sharply. 'Tom is one of the most valuable servants on the place; it couldn't be afforded any way. Besides, what does he want of liberty? He's a great deal better off as he is.'

'But he does desire it very earnestly, and his master promised it,' said Miss Ophelia.

'I dare say he does want it,' said Marie; 'they all want it, just because they are a discontented set, always wanting what they haven't got. Now I'm principled against emancipating in any case. Keep a negro under the care of a master, and he does well enough and is respectable; but set them free, and they get lazy and won't work, and take to drinking, and go all down to be mean, worthless fellows. I've seen it tried hundreds of times. It's no favour to set them free.'

'But Tom is so steady, industrious, and pious.'

'Oh, you needn't tell me! I've seen a hundred like him. He'll do very well as long as he's taken care of, that's all.'

'But then, consider,' said Miss Ophelia, 'when you set him up for sale, the chances of his getting a bad master.'

'Oh, that's all humbug!' said Marie. 'It isn't one time in a hundred that a good fellow gets a bad master; most masters are good, for all the talk that is made. I've lived and grown up here in the South, and I never yet was acquainted with a master that didn't treat his servants well, quite as well as is worth while. I don't feel any fears on that head.'

'Well,' said Miss Ophelia, energetically. 'I know it was one of the last wishes of your husband, that Tom should have his liberty; it was one of the promises that he made to dear little Eva on her death-bed, and I should not think you would feel at liberty to disregard it.'

Marie had her face covered with her handkerchief at this appeal, and began sobbing and using her smelling-bottle with great vehemence.

'Everybody goes against me,' she said. 'Everybody is so inconsiderate! I shouldn't have expected that *you* would bring up all these remembrances of my troubles to me; it's so inconsiderate! But nobody ever does consider – my trials are so peculiar! It is so hard that, when I had only one daughter, she should have been taken! – and I'm so hard to be suited! – he should be taken! And you seem to have so little feeling for me, and keep bringing it up to me so carelessly – when you know how it overcomes me! I suppose you mean well; but it is very inconsiderate, very!' And Marie sobbed, and gasped for breath, and called Mammy to open the window, and to bring her the camphor-bottle, and to bathe her head and unhook her dress; and, in the general confusion that ensued, Miss Ophelia made her escape to her apartment.

She saw at once that it would do no good to say anything more, for Marie had an indefinite capacity for hysteric fits; and after this, whenever her husband's or Eva's wishes with regard to the servants were alluded to, she always found it convenient to set one in operation. Miss Ophelia therefore did the next best thing she could for Tom; she wrote a letter to Mrs Shelby for him, stating his troubles, and urging them to send to his relief.

The next day, Tom and Adolph, and some half-dozen other servants, were marched down to a slave-warehouse to await the convenience of the trader, who was going to make up a lot for auction.

Chapter 30

THE SLAVE WAREHOUSE

A SLAVE warehouse! Perhaps some of my readers conjure up horrible visions of such a place. They fancy some foul, obscure den, some horrible *Tartarus 'informis, ingens, cui lumen ademptum.'* But no, innocent friend! in these days men have learned the art of sinning expertly and genteelly, so as not to shock the eyes and senses of respectable society. Human property is high in the market; and is therefore well fed, well cleaned, tended and looked after, that it may come to sale sleek, and strong, and shining. A slave warehouse in New Orleans is a house externally not much unlike many others, kept with neatness; and where every day you may see arranged, under a sort of shed along the outside, rows of men and women, who stand there as a sign of the property sold within.

Then you shall be courteously entreated to call and examine, and shall find an abundance of husbands and wives, brothers, sisters, fathers, mothers, and young children, to be 'sold separately or in lots, to suit the convenience of the purchaser;' and that soul immortal, once bought with blood and anguish by the Son of God, when the earth shook, and the rocks rent, and the graves were opened, can be sold, leased, mortgaged, exchanged for groceries or dry goods, to suit the phases of trade or the fancy of the purchaser.

It was a day or two after the conversation between Marie and Miss Ophelia, that Tom, Adolph, and about half a dozen others of the St Clare estate, were turned over to the loving-kindness of Mr Skeggs, the keeper of a dépôt on — street, to await the auction, next day.

Tom had with him quite a sizable trunk full of clothing, as had most others of them. They were ushered for the night into a long room, where many other men of all ages, sizes, and shades of complexion, were assembled, and from which roars of laughter and unthinking merriment were proceeding.

'Ah, ah! that's right. Go it, boys! – go it!' said Mr Skeggs, the keeper. 'My people are always so merry; Sambo, I see!' he said, speaking approvingly to a burly negro who was performing tricks of low buffoonery, which occasioned the shouts which Tom had heard.

As might be imagined, Tom was in no humour to join these proceedings; and, therefore, setting his trunk as far as possible from the noisy group, he sat down on it and leaned his face against the wall.

The dealers in the human article make scrupulous and systematic efforts to promote noisy mirth among them, as a means of drowning reflection and rendering them insensible to their condition. The whole object of the training to which the negro is put, from the time he is sold in the northern market till he arrives south, is systematically directed toward making him callous, unthinking, and brutal. The slave-dealer collects his gang in Virginia or Kentucky, and drives them to some convenient, healthy place – often a watering-place – to be fattened. Here they are fed full daily; and, because some are inclined to pine, a fiddle is kept commonly going among them, and they are made to dance daily; and he who refuses to be merry – in whose soul thoughts of wife, or child, or home, are too strong for him to be gay – is marked as sullen and dangerous, and subjected to all the evils which the ill-will of an utterly irresponsible and hardened man can inflict upon him. Briskness, alertness, and cheerfulness of appearance, especially before observers, are constantly enforced upon them, both by the hope of thereby getting a good master, and the fear of all that the driver may bring upon them if they prove unsaleable.

'What dat ar nigger doin' here?' said Sambo, coming up to Tom, after Mr Skeggs had left the room. Sambo was a full black, of great size, very lively, voluble, and full of trick and grimace.

'What you doin' here?' said Sambo, coming up to Tom, and poking him facetiously in the side. 'Meditatin', eh?'

'I am to be sold at the auction to-morrow!' said Tom, quietly.

'Sold at auction — haw! haw! boys, an't this yer fun? I wish't I was gwine that ar way! — tell ye, wouldn't I make 'em laugh? But how is it — dis yer whole lot gwine to-morrow?' said Sambo, laying his hand freely on Adolph's shoulder.

'Please to let me alone!' said Adolph, fiercely, straightening himself up with extreme disgust.

'Law, now, boys! dis yer's one o' yer white niggers — kind o' cream colour, ye know, scented!' said he, coming up to Adolph and snuffing. 'O Lor! he'd do for a tobaccer-shop; they could keep him to scent snuff! Lor, he'd keep a whole shop a gwine — he would!'

'I say, keep off, can't you!' said Adolph, enraged.

'Lor, now, how touchy we is — we white niggers! Look at us, now!' and Sambo gave a ludicrous imitation of Adolph's manner; 'here's de airs and graces. We's been in a good family, I 'spects.'

'Yes,' said Adolph; 'I had a master that could have bought you all for old truck!'

'Laws, now, only think,' said Sambo, 'the gentlemens that we is!'

'I belonged to the St Clare family,' said Adolph proudly.

'Lor, you did! Be hanged if they ar'n't lucky to get shet of ye. 'Spects they's gwine to trade ye off with a lot o' cracked tea-pots and sich like!' said Sambo, with a provoking grin.

Adolph, enraged at this taunt, flew furiously at his adversary, swearing and striking on every side of him. The rest laughed and shouted, and the uproar brought the keeper to the door.

'What now, boys? Order, order!' he said, coming in and flourishing a large whip.

All fled in different directions, except Sambo, who, presuming on the favour which the keeper had to him as a licensed wag, stood his ground, ducking his head with a facetious grin whenever the master made a dive at him.

'Lor, mas'r, 'tan't us — we's reg'lar stiddy — it's these yer new hands; they's real aggravatin' — kinder pickin' at us, all time!'

The keeper at this turned upon Tom and Adolph, and distributed a few kicks and cuffs without much inquiry, and, leaving general orders for all to be good boys and go to sleep, left the apartment.

While this scene was going on in the men's sleeping-room, the reader may be curious to take a peep at the corresponding apartment alotted to the women. Stretched out in various attitudes over the floor, he may see numberless sleeping forms of every shade of complexion, from the purest ebony to white, and of all years, from childhood to old age, lying now asleep. Here is a fine bright girl, of ten years, whose mother was sold out yesterday, and who to-night cried herself to sleep when nobody was looking at her. Here, a worn old negress, whose thin arms and callous fingers tell of hard toil, waiting to be sold to-morrow, as a cast-off article, for what can be got for her; and some forty or fifty others, with heads variously enveloped in blankets or articles of clothing, lie stretched around them. But, in a corner, sitting apart from the rest, are two females of a more interesting appearance than common. One of these is a respectably-dressed mulatto woman between forty and fifty, with soft eyes and a gentle and pleasing physiognomy. She has on her head a high-raised turban, made of a gay red Madras handkerchief, of the first quality, and her dress is neatly fitted, and of good material, showing that she has been provided for with a careful hand. By her side, and nestling closely to her, is a young girl of fifteen – her daughter. She is a quadroon, as may be seen from her fairer complexion, though her likeness to her mother is quite discernible. She has the same soft dark eye, with longer lashes, and her curling hair is of a luxuriant brown. She also is dressed with great neatness, and her white, delicate hands betray very little acquaintance with servile toil. These two are to be sold to-morrow, in the same lot with the St Clare servants; and the gentleman to whom they belong, and to whom the money for their sale is to be transmitted, is a member of a Christian church in New York, who will receive the money, and go thereafter to the sacrament of his Lord and theirs, and think no more of it.

These two, whom we shall call Susan and Emmeline, had been the personal attendants of an amiable and pious lady of New Orleans, by whom they had been carefully and piously instructed and trained. They had been taught to read and write, diligently instructed in the truths of religion, and their lot had been as happy a one as in their condition it was possible to be. But the only son of their protectress had the management of her property; and, by carelessness and extravagance, involved it to a large amount, and at last failed. One of the largest creditors was the respectable firm of B. and Co., in New York. B. and Co. wrote to their lawyer in New Orleans, who attached the real estate (these two articles and a lot of plantation hands formed the most valuable part of it), and wrote word to that effect to New York. Brother B. being, as we have said, a Christian man, and a resident in a free State, felt some uneasiness on the subject. He didn't like trading in slaves and souls of men – of course he didn't; but then there were thirty thousand dollars in the case, and that was rather too much money to be lost for a principle; and so, after much considering, and asking advice from those that he knew would advise to suit him, Brother B. wrote to his lawyer to dispose of the business in the way that seemed to him the most suitable, and remit the proceeds.

The day after the letter arrived in New Orleans, Susan and Emmeline were attached, and sent to the dépôt to await a general auction on the following morning; and as they glimmer faintly upon us in the moonlight which steals through the grated window, we may listen to their conversation. Both are weeping, but each quietly, that the other may not hear.

'Mother, just lay your head on my lap, and see if you can't sleep a little,' says the girl, trying to appear calm.

'I haven't any heart to sleep, Em! I can't. It's the last night we may be together!'

'Oh, mother, don't say so! Perhaps we shall get sold together – who knows?'

'If 'twas anybody's else case, I should say so too, Em,' said the woman; 'but I'm so feared of losin' you that I don't see anything but the danger.'

'Why, mother? The man said we were both likely, and would sell well.'

Susan remembered the man's looks and words. With a deadly sickness at her heart, she remembered how he had looked at Emmeline's hands, and lifted up her curly hair, and pronounced her a first-rate article. Susan had been trained as a Christian, brought up in the daily reading of the Bible, and had the same horror of her child's being sold to a life of shame that any other

Christian mother might have; but she had no hope – no protection.

'Mother, I think we might do first-rate, if you could get a place as cook, and I as chambermaid, or seamstress, in some family. I dare say we shall. Let's both look as bright and lively as we can, and tell all we can do, and perhaps we shall,' said Emmeline.

'I want you to brush your hair all back straight to-morrow,' said Susan.

'What for, mother? I don't look near so well that way.'

'Yes; but you'll sell better so.'

'I don't see why,' said the child.

'Respectable families would be more apt to buy you if they saw you looked plain and decent, as if you wasn't trying to look handsome. I know their ways better'n you do,' said Susan.

'Well, mother, then I will.'

'And, Emmeline, if we shouldn't ever see each other again after to-morrow – if I'm sold way up on a plantation somewhere, and you somewhere else – always remember how you've been brought up, and all missis has told you. Take your Bible with you, and your hymn-book; and if you're faithful to the Lord, he'll be faithful to you.'

So speaks the poor soul in sore discouragement; for she knows that to-morrow any man, however vile and brutal, however godless and merciless, if he only has money to pay for her, may become owner of her daughter, body and soul; and then how is the child to be faithful? She thinks of all this as she holds her daughter in her arms, and wishes that she were not so handsome and attractive. It seems almost an aggravation to her to remember how purely and piously, how much above the ordinary lot she has been brought up. But she has no resort but to *pray*; and many such prayers to God have gone up from those same trim, neatly-arranged, respectable slave-prisons – prayers which God has not forgotten, as coming days shall show; for it is written, 'Whoso causeth one of these little ones to offend, it were better for him that a mill-stone were hanged about his neck, and that he were drowned in the depths of the sea.'

The soft, earnest, quiet moonbeam looks in fixedly, marking the bars of the grated windows on the prostrate, sleeping forms. The mother and daughter are singing together a wild and melancholy dirge, common as a funeral hymn among the slaves, –

'Oh, where is weeping Mary?
Oh, where is weeping Mary?
  'Rived in the goodly land.
She is dead, and gone to heaven;
She is dead, and gone to heaven;
  'Rived in the goodly land.

These words, sung by voices of a peculiar and melancholy sweetness, in an air which seemed like the sighing of earthly despair after heavenly hope, floated through the dark prison-rooms with a pathetic cadence, as verse after verse was breathed out, –

'Oh, where are Paul and Silas?
'Oh, where are Paul and Silas?
  Gone to the goodly land.
They are dead and gone to heaven;
They are dead and gone to heaven;
  'Rived in the goodly land.'

Sing on, poor souls! The night is short, and the morning will part you for ever!

But now it is morning, and everything is astir, and the worthy Mr Skeggs is busy and bright, for a lot of goods is to be fitted out for auction. There is a brisk look-out on the toilet; injunctions passed around to every one to put on their best faces and be spry; and now all are arranged in a circle for a last review, before they are marched up to the Bourse.

Mr Skeggs, with his palmetto on, and his cigar in his mouth, walks around to put farewell touches on his wares.

'How's this?' he said, stepping in front of Susan and Emmeline. 'Where's your curls, gal?'

The girl looked timidly at her mother, who, with the smooth adroitness common among her class, answers, –

'I was telling her last night to put up her hair smooth and neat, and not havin' it flying about in curls – looks more respectable so!'

'Bother!' said the man, peremptorily, turning to the girl. 'You go right along, and curl yourself real smart !' he added, giving a crack to a rattan he held in his hand; 'and be back in quick time, too ! You go and help her,' he added to the mother. 'Them curls may make a hundred dollars' difference in the sale of her.'

Beneath a splendid dome were men of all nations, moving to and fro over the marble *pavé*. On every side of the circular were little tribunes, or stations, for the use of speakers and auctioneers. Two of these, on opposite sides of the area, were now occupied by brilliant and talented gentlemen, enthusiastically forcing up, in English and French commingled, the bids of connoisseurs in their various wares. A third one, on the other side, still unoccupied, was surrounded by a group waiting the moment of sale to begin. And here we may recognise the St Clare servants, Tom, Adolph, and others; and there, too, Susan and Emmeline, awaiting their turn, with anxious and dejected faces. Various spectators, intending to purchase, or not to purchase, as the case might be, gathered around the group, handling, examining, and commenting on their various points and faces, with the same freedom that a set of jockeys discuss the merits of a horse.

'Holloa, Alf ! what brings you here ?' said a young exquisite, slapping the shoulder of a sprucely dressed young man, who was examining Adolph through an eyeglass.

'Well, I was wanting a valet, and I heard that St Clare's lot was going. I thought I'd just look at his'—

'Catch me ever buying any of St Clare's people ! Spoilt niggers, every one ! Impudent as the devil !' said the other.

'Never fear that !' said the first. 'If I get 'em, I'll soon have their airs out of them; they'll soon find that they've another kind of master to deal with than Monsieur St Clare. 'Pon my word, I'll buy that fellow. I like the shape of him.'

'You'll find it'll take all you've got to keep him. He's deucedly extravagant !'

'Yes, but my lord will find that he *can't* be extravagant with *me*. Just let him be sent to the calaboose a few times, and thoroughly dressed down ! I'll tell you if it don't bring him to a sense of his ways ! Oh, I'll reform him, up hill and down – you'll see ! I buy him, that's flat !'

Tom had been standing wistfully examining the multitude of

faces thronging around him for one whom he would wish to call master; and if you should ever be under the necessity, sir, of selecting out of two hundred men one who was to become your absolute owner and disposer, you would perhaps realise, just as Tom did, how few there were that you would feel at all comfortable in being made over to. Tom saw abundance of men, great, burly, gruff men; little, chirping, dried men; long-favoured, lank, hard men; and every variety of stubbed-looking, commonplace men, who pick up their fellow-men as one picks up chips, putting them into the fire or a basket with equal unconcern, according to their convenience; but he saw no St Clare.

A little before the sale commenced, a short, broad, muscular man, in a checked shirt considerably open at the bosom, and pantaloons much the worse for dirt and wear, elbowed his way through the crowd, like one who is going actively into a business; and, coming up to the group, began to examine them systematically. From the moment that Tom saw him approaching, he felt an immediate and revolting horror at him, that increased as he came near. He was evidently, though short, of gigantic strength. His round, bullet head, large, light-grey eyes, with their shaggy, sandy eyebrows, and stiff, wiry, sunburnt air, were rather unprepossessing items, it is to be confessed; his large, coarse mouth was distended with tobacco, the juice of which from time to time, he ejected from him with great decision and explosive force; his hands were immensely large, hairy, sunburnt, freckled, and very dirty, and garnished with long nails, in a very foul condition. This man proceeded to a very free personal examination of the lot. He seized Tom by the jaw, and pulled open his mouth to inspect his teeth; made him strip up his sleeve, to show his muscle; turned him round, make him jump and spring, to show his paces.

'Where was you raised?' he added briefly to these investigations.

'In Kintuck, mas'r,' said Tom, looking about as if for deliverance.

'What have you done?'

'Had care of mas'r's farm,' said Tom.

'Likely story!' said the other shortly, as he passed on. He paused a moment before Dolph; then spitting a discharge of

tobacco-juice on his well-blacked boots, and giving a contemptuous umph, he walked on. Again he stopped before Susan and
Emmeline. He put out his heavy, dirty hand, and drew the girl
towards him; passed it over her neck and bust, felt her arms,
looked at her teeth, and then pushed her back against her
mother, whose patient face showed the suffering she had been
going through at every motion of the hideous stranger.

The girl was frightened, and began to cry.

'Stop that, you minx!' said the salesman; 'no whimpering
here, the sale is going to begin.' And accordingly the sale begun.

Adolph was knocked off at a good sum, to the young
gentleman who had previously stated his intention of buying
him; and the other servants of the St Clare lot went to various
bidders.

'Now, up with you, boy! d'ye hear?' said the auctioneer to
Tom.

Tom stepped upon the block, gave a few anxious looks
round; all seemed mingled in a common, indistinct noise – the
clatter of the salesman crying off his qualifications in French
and English, the quick fire of French and English bids; and
almost in a moment came the final thump of the hammer, and
the clear ring on the last syllable of the word '*dollars*,' as the
auctioneer announced his price, and Tom was made over. He
had a master!

He was pushed from the block; the short, bullet-headed man,
seizing him roughly by the shoulder, pushed him to one side,
saying, in harsh voice, 'Stand there, *you*!'

Tom hardly realised anything; but still the bidding went on –
rattling, clattering, now French, now English. Down goes the
hammer again, – Susan is sold. She goes down from the block,
stops, looks wistfully back; her daughter stretches her hands
towards her. She looks with agony in the face of the man who
has bought her – a respectable middle-aged man, of benevolent
countenance.

'O mas'r, please do buy my daughter!'

'I'd like to, but I'm afraid I can't afford it,' said the gentleman,
looking with painful interest as the young girl mounted the
block, and looked around her with a frightened and timid
glance.

The blood flushes painfully in her otherwise colourless cheek, her eyes have a feverish fire, and her mother groans to see that she looks more beautiful than she ever saw her before. The auctioneer sees his advantage, and expatiates volubly in mingled French and English, and bids rise in rapid succession.

'I'll do anything in reason,' said the benevolent-looking gentleman, pressing in, and joining with the bids. In a few moments they have run beyond his purse. He is silent; the auctioneer grows warmer; but bids gradually drop off. It lies now between an aristocratic old citizen and our bullet-headed acquaintance. The citizen bids for a few turns, contemptuously measuring his opponent; but the bullet-head has the advantage over him, both in obstinacy and concealed length of purse, and the controversy lasts but a moment; the hammer falls – he has got the girl, body and soul, unless God help her!

Her master is Mr Legree who owns a cotton plantation on the Red River. She is pushed along in the same lot with Tom and two other men, and goes off, weeping as she goes.

The benevolent gentleman is sorry; but then the thing happens every day! One sees girls and mothers crying at these sales *always*! it can't be helped, etc.; and he walks off with his acquisition in another direction.

Two days after the lawyer of the Christian firm of B. and Co., New York, sent on their money to them. On the reverse of that draft, so obtained, let them write these words of the great Paymaster, to whom they shall make up their account in a future day: – '*When he maketh inquisition for blood, he forgetteth not the cry of the humble!*'

Chapter 31

THE MIDDLE PASSAGE

'Thou art of purer eyes than to behold evil, and canst not look upon iniquity: wherefore lookest thou upon them that deal treacherously, and holdest thy tongue when the wicked devoureth the man that is more righteous than he?' – *Hab*. i. 13.

ON the lower part of a small mean boat, on the Red River, Tom sat – chains on his wrists, chains on his feet, and a weight heavier than chains lay on his heart. All had faded from his sky – moon and star; all had passed by him, as the trees and banks were now passing, to return no more. Kentucky home, with wife and children, and indulgent owners; St Clare home, with all its refinements and splendours; the golden head of Eva, with its saint-like eyes; the proud, gay, handsome, seeming careless, yet ever-kind St Clare; hours of ease and indulgent leisure – all gone! and in place thereof, *what* remains?

It is one of the bitterest apportionments of a lot of slavery, that the negro, sympathetic and assimilative, after acquiring, in a refined family, the tastes and feelings which form the atmosphere of such a place, is not the less liable to become the bond-slave of the coarsest and most brutal – just as a chair or table, which once decorated the superb saloon, comes, at last, battered and defaced, to the bar-room of some filthy tavern, or some low haunt of vulgar debauchery. The great difference is, that the table and chair cannot feel, and the *man* can; for even a legal enactment that he shall be 'taken, reputed, adjudged in law, to be a chattel personal,' cannot blot out his soul, with its own private little world of memories, hopes, loves, fears, and desires.

Mr Simon Legree, Tom's master, had purchased slaves at one place and another, in New Orleans, to the number of eight, and driven them, handcuffed, in couples of two and two, down to the good steamer *Pirate*, which lay at the levee, ready for a trip up the Red River.

Having got them fairly on board, and the boat being off, he came round, with that air of efficiency which ever characterised him, to take a review of them. Stopping opposite to Tom, who had been attired for sale in his best broadcloth suit, with well-starched linen and shining boots, he briefly expressed himself as follows : –

'Stand up.'

Tom stood up.

'Take off that stock !' and as Tom, encumbered by his fetters, proceeded to do it, he assisted him, by pulling it, with no gentle hand, from his neck, and putting it in his pocket.

Legree now turned to Tom's trunk, which, previous to this, he had been ransacking, and, taking from it a pair of old pantaloons and a dilapidated coat, which Tom had been wont to put on about his stable-work, he said, liberating Tom's hands from the handcuffs, and pointing to a recess in among the boxes –

'You go there, and put these on.'

Tom obeyed, and in a few moments returned.

'Take off your boots,' said Mr Legree.

Tom did so.

'There,' said the former, throwing him a pair of coarse, stout shoes, such as were common among the slaves, 'put these on.'

In Tom's hurried exchange he had not forgotten to transfer his cherished Bible to his pocket. It was well he did so ; for Mr Legree, having refitted Tom's handcuffs, proceeded deliberately to investigate the contents of his pockets. He drew out a silk handkerchief, and put it into his own pocket. Several little trifles, which Tom had treasured, chiefly because they had amused Eva, he looked upon with a contemptuous grunt, and tossed them over his shoulder into the river.

Tom's Methodist hymn-book, which, in his hurry, he had forgotten, he now held up and turned over.

'Humph ! pious, to be sure. So, what's yer name ? – you belong to the Church, eh ?'

'Yes, mas'r,' said Tom, firmly.

'Well, I'll soon have *that* out of you. I have none o' yer bawling, praying, singing niggers on my place ; so remember.

Now, mind yourself,' he said, with a stamp and a fierce glance of his grey eye, directed at Tom, '*I'm* your Church now! You understand – you've got to be as *I* say.'

Something within the silent black man answered *No*! and, as if repeated by an invisible voice, came the words of an old prophetic scroll, as Eva had often read them to him – 'Fear not; for I have redeemed thee. I have called thee by my name. Thou art MINE!'

But Simon Legree heard no voice. That voice is one he never shall hear. He only glared for a moment on the downcast face of Tom, and walked off. He took Tom's trunk, which contained a very neat and abundant wardrobe, to the forecastle, where it was soon surrounded by various hands of the boat. With much laughing, at the expense of niggers who tried to be gentlemen, the articles very readily were sold to one another, and the empty trunk finally put up at auction. It was a good joke, they all thought, especially to see how Tom looked after his things, as they were going this way and that; and then the auction of the trunk, that was funnier than all, and occasioned abundant witticisms.

This little affair being over, Simon sauntered up again to his property.

'Now, Tom, I've relieved you of any extra baggage, you see. Take mighty good care of them clothes. It'll be long enough before you get more. I go in for making niggers careful; one suit has to do for one year, on my place.'

Simon next walked up to the place where Emmeline was sitting, chained to another woman.

'Well, my dear,' he said, chucking her under the chin, 'keep up your spirits.'

The involuntary look of horror, fright, and aversion with which the girl regarded him, did not escape his eye. He frowned fiercely.

'None o' your shines, gal! You's got to keep a pleasant face when I speak to ye – d'ye hear? And you, you old yellow poco moonshine!' he said, giving a shove to the mulatto woman to whom Emmeline was chained, 'don't you carry that sort of face! You's got to look chipper, I tell yer!'

'I say, all on ye,' he said, retreating a pace or two back, 'look at me – look at me – look me right in the eye – *straight*, now !' said he, stamping his foot at every pause.

As, by a fascination, every eye was now directed to the glaring, greenish-grey eye of Simon.

'Now,' said he, doubling his great, heavy fist into something resembling a blacksmith's hammer, 'd'ye see this fist ? Heft it !' he said, bringing it down on Tom's hand. 'Look at these yer bones ! Well, I tell ye this yer fist has got as hard as iron *knocking down niggers*. I never seen the nigger yet I couldn't bring down with one crack,' said he, bringing his fist down so near to the face of Tom that he winked and drew back. 'I don't keep none o' yer cussed overseers; I does my own overseering; and I tell you things *is* seen to. You's every one on ye got to toe the mark, I tell ye; quick – straight – the moment I speak. That's the way to keep in with me. You won't find no soft spot in me, nowhere. So, now, mind yourselves; for I don't show no mercy !'

The women involuntarily drew in their breath, and the whole gang sat with downcast, dejected faces. Meanwhile, Simon turned on his heel, and marched up to the bar of the boat for a dram.

That's the way I begin with my niggers,' he said to a gentlemanly man who had stood by him during his speech. 'It's my system to begin strong – just let'm know what to expect.'

'Indeed !' said the stranger, looking upon him with the curiosity of a naturalist studying some out-of-the-way specimen.

'Yes, indeed. I'm none o' yer gentlemen planters, with lily fingers, to slop round and be cheated by some old cuss of an overseer ! Just feel of my knuckles, now; look at my fist. Tell ye, sir, the flesh on't has come jest like a stone, practising on niggers – feel on it.'

The stranger applied his fingers to the implement in question, and simply said –

''Tis hard enough; and I suppose,' he added, 'practice has made your heart just like it.'

'Why, yes, I may say so,' said Simon, with a hearty laugh. 'I reckon ther's as little soft in me as in any one going. Tell you, nobody comes it over me ! Niggers never gets round me, neither with squalling nor soft soap – that's a fact !'

'You have a fine lot there.'

'Real,' said Simon. 'There's that Tom, they tell'd me he was suthin' uncommon. I paid a little high for him, tending him for a driver and a managing chap; only get the notions out that he's larn't by bein' treated as niggers never ought to be, he'll do prime! The yellow woman I got took in in. I rayther think she sickly, but I shall put her through for what's she's worth. She may last a year or two. I don't go for savin' niggers. Use up and buy more's my way; makes you less trouble, and I'm quite sure it comes cheaper in the end;' and Simon sipped his glass.

'And how long do they generally last?' said the stranger.

'Well, donno; 'cordin' as their constitution is. Stout fellers last six or seven years; trashy ones gets worked up in two or three. I used to, when I fust begun, have considerable trouble fussin' with 'em and trying to make 'em hold out – doctorin' on 'em up when they's sick, and givin' on 'em clothes and blankets, and what not, tryin' to keep 'em all sort o' decent and comfortable. Law, 'twasn't no sort o' use; I just put 'em straight through, sick or well. When one nigger's dead, I buy another; and I find it comes cheaper and easier, every way.'

The stranger turned away, and seated himself beside a gentleman who had been listening to the conversation with repressed uneasiness.

'You must not take that fellow to be any specimen of Southern planters,' said he.

'I should hope not,' said the young gentleman, with emphasis.

'He is a mean, low, brutal fellow,' said the other.

'And yet your laws allow him to hold any number of human beings subject to his absolute will, without even a shadow of protection; and, low as he is, you cannot say there are not many such.'

'Well,' said the other, 'there are also many considerate and humane men among planters.'

'Granted,' said the young man; 'but, in my opinion it is you considerate, humane men, that are responsible for all the brutality and outrage wrought by these wretches; because if it were not for your sanction and influence, the whole system could not keep foot-hold for an hour. If there were no planters except such as that one,' said he, pointing with his finger to Legree, who stood with his back to them, 'the whole thing would go down like a millstone. It is your respectability and humanity that licenses and protects his brutality.'

'You certainly have a high opinion of my good nature,' said the planter, smiling; 'but I advise you not to talk quite so loud, as there are people on board the boat who might not be quite so tolerant to opinion as I am. You had better wait till I get up to my plantation, and there you may abuse us all, quite at your leisure.'

The young gentleman coloured and smiled, and the two were soon busy in a game of backgammon. Meanwhile, another conversation was going on in the lower part of the boat, between Emmeline and the mulatto women with whom she was confined. As was natural, they were exchanging with each other some particulars of their history.

'Who did you belong to?' said Emmeline.

'Well, my mas'r was Mr Ellis — lived on Levee Street. P'raps you've seen the house?'

'Was he good to you?' said Emmeline.

'Mostly, till he tuk sick. He's lain sick, off and on, more than six months, and been orful oneasy. 'Pears like he warnt willin' to have nobody rest, day or night; and got so curous, there couldn't nobody suit him. 'Pears like he just grew crosser every day; kept me up nights till I got fairly beat out, and couldn't keep awake no longer; and cause I got to sleep one night, Lors, he talk so orful to me, and he tell me he'd sell me to just the hardest master he could find; and he'd promised me my freedom, too, when he died.'

'Had you any friends?' said Emmeline.

'Yes, my husband; he's a blacksmith. Mas'r gen'ly hired him out. They took me off so quick, I didn't even have time to see him; and I's got four children. Oh, dear me!' said the woman, covering her face with her hands.

It is a natural impulse in every one when they hear a tale of distress, to think of something to say by way of consolation. Emmeline wanted to say something, but she could not think of anything to say. What was there to be said? As by a common consent, they both avoided, with fear and dread, all mention of the horrible man who was now their master.

True, there is religious trust for even the darkest hour. The mulatto woman was a member of the Methodist church, and had an unenlightened but very sincere spirit of piety. Emmeline had been educated much more intelligently – taught to read and write, and diligently instructed in the Bible, by the care of a faithful and pious mistress; yet, would it not try the faith of the firmest Christian, to find themselves abandoned apparently of God, in the grasp of ruthless violence? How much more must it shake the faith of Christ's poor little ones, weak in knowledge and tender in years!

The boat moved on – freighted with its weight of sorrow – up the red, muddy, turbid current, through the abrupt, tortuous windings of the Red River; and sad eyes gazed wearily on the steep red-clay banks, as they glided by in dreary sameness. At last the boat stopped at a small town, and Legree with his party disembarked.

Chapter 32

DARK PLACES

'The dark places of the earth are full of the habitations of cruelty.'

TRAILING wearily behind a rude wagon, and over a ruder road, Tom and his associates faced onward.

In the wagon was seated Simon Legree; and the two women, still fettered together, were stowed away with some baggage in the back part of it, and the whole company were seeking Legree's plantation, which lay a good distance off.

It was a wild, forsaken road, now winding through dreary pine barrens, where the wind whispered mournfully, and now over long causeways, through long cypress swamps, the doleful trees rising out of the slimy, spongy ground, hung with long wreaths of funereal black moss, while ever and anon the loathsome form of the moccasin snake might be seen sliding among broken stumps and shattered branches that lay here and there, rotting in the water.

It is disconsolate enough, this riding, to the stranger, who, with well-filled pocket and well-appointed horse, threads the lonely way on some errand of business; but wilder, drearier, to the man enthralled, whom every weary step bears further from all that man loves and prays for.

So one should have thought that witnessed the sunken and dejected expression on those dark faces; the wistful, patient weariness, with which those sad eyes rested on object after object that passed them in their sad journey.

Simon rode on, however, apparently well pleased, occasionally pulling away at a flask of spirit, which he kept in his pocket.

'I say *you*!' he said, as he turned back and caught a glance at the dispirited faces behind him; 'strike up a song, boys – come!'

The men looked at each other, and the '*come*' was repeated, with a smart crack of the whip which the driver carried in his hands. Tom began a Methodist hymn –

> 'Jerusalem, my happy home,
>   Name ever dear to me!
> When shall my sorrows have an end?
>   Thy joys, when shall—'

'Shut up, you black cuss!' roared Legree; 'did ye think I wanted any o' yer infernal old Methodism? I say, tune up, now, something real rowdy – quick!'

One of the other men struck up one of those unmeaning songs common among the slaves –

> 'Mas'r seed me cotch a coon,
>   High, boys, high!
> He laugh'd to split – d'ye see the moon?
>   Ho! ho! ho! boys, ho!
>   Ho! yo! hi – e! oh!'

The singer appeared to make up the songs to his own pleasure, generally hitting on rhyme, without much attempt at reason; and all the party took up the chorus at intervals –

> 'Ho! ho! ho! boys, ho!
> High – e – oh! high – e – oh!'

It was sung very boisterously, and with a forced attempt at merriment; but no wail of despair, no words of impassioned prayer, could have had such a depth of woe in them as the weld notes of the chorus. As if the poor, dumb heart, threatened – prisoned – took refuge in that inarticulate sanctuary of music, and found there a language in which to breathe its prayer to God! There was a prayer in it which Simon could not hear. He only heard the boys singing noisily, and was well pleased; he was making them 'keep up their spirits.'

'Well, my little dear,' said he, turning to Emmeline, and laying his hand on her shoulder, 'we're almost home!'

When Legree scolded and stormed, Emmeline was terrified; but when he laid his hand on her, and spoke as he now did, she felt as if she had rather he would strike her. The expression of his eyes made her soul sick, and her flesh creep. Involuntarily she clung closer to the mulatto woman by her side, as if she were her mother.

'You didn't ever wear ear-rings,' he said, taking hold of her small ear with his coarse fingers.

'No, mas'r!' said Emmeline, trembling and looking down.

'Well, I'll give you a pair when we get home, if you're a good girl. You needn't be so frightened; I don't mean to make you work very hard. You'll have fine times with me, and live like a lady – only be a good girl.'

Legree had been drinking to that degree that he was inclining to be very gracious; and it was about this time that the enclosures of the plantation rose to view. The estate had formerly belonged to a gentleman of opulence and taste, who had bestowed some considerable attention to the adornment of his grounds. Having died insolvent, it had been purchased, at a bargain, by Legree, who used it, as he did everything else, merely as an implement for money-making. The place had that ragged, forlorn appearance, which is always produced by the evidence that the care of the former owner has been left to go to utter decay.

What was once a smooth-shaven lawn before the house, dotted here and there with ornamental shrubs, was now covered with frowsy tangled grass, with horse-posts set up here and there in it where the turf was stamped away, and the ground littered with broken pails, cobs of corn, and other slovenly remains. Here and there a mildewed jessamine or honeysuckle hung raggedly from some ornamental support, which had been pushed to one side by being used as a horse-post. What once was a large garden was now all grown over with weeds, through which, here and there, some solitary exotic reared its forsaken head. What had been a conservatory had now no window-sashes, and on the mouldering shelves stood some dry, forsaken flower-pots, with sticks in them, whose dried leaves showed they had once been plants.

The wagon rolled up a weedy gravel-walk, under a noble avenue of China trees, whose graceful forms and ever-springing foliage seemed to be the only things there that neglect could not daunt or alter – like noble spirits, so deeply rooted in goodness as to flourish and grow stronger amid discouragement and decay.

The house had been large and handsome. It was built in a manner common at the South; a wide verandah of two stories running round every part of the house, into which every outer door opened, the lower tier being supported by brick pillars.

But the place looked desolate and uncomfortable; some windows stopped up with boards, some with shattered panes, and shutters hanging by a single hinge – all telling of coarse neglect and discomfort.

Bits of board, straw, old decayed barrels and boxes, garnished the ground in all directions; and three or four ferocious-looking dogs, roused by the sound of the wagon-wheels, came tearing out, and were with difficulty restrained from laying hold of Tom and his companions, by the efforts of the ragged servants who came after them.

'Ye see what ye'd get!' said Legree, caressing the dogs with grim satisfaction, and turning to Tom and his companions; 'Ye see what ye'd get if ye try to run off. These yer dogs has been raised to track niggers; and they'd jest as soon chaw one on ye up as eat their supper. So, mind yerself! How now, Sambo!' he said to a ragged fellow, without any brim to his hat, who was officious in his attentions. 'How have things been going?'

'Fust rate, mas'r.'

'Quimbo,' said Legree to another, who was making zealous demonstrations to attract his attention, 'ye minded what I telled ye?'

'Guess I did, didn't I?'

These two coloured men were the two principal hands on the

plantation. Legree had trained them in savageness and brutality as systematically as he had his bull-dogs; and, by long practice in hardness and cruelty, brought their whole nature to about the same range of capacities. It is a common remark, and one that is thought to militate strongly against the character of the race, that the negro overseer is always more tyrannical and cruel than the white one. This is simply saying that the negro mind has been more crushed and debased than the white. It is no more true of this race than of every oppressed race, the world over. The slave is always a tyrant, if he can get a chance to be one.

Legree, like some potentates we read of in history, governed his plantation by a sort of resolution of forces. Sambo and Quimbo cordially hated each other; the plantation hands, one and all, cordially hated them; and by playing off one against another he was pretty sure, through one or the other of the three parties, to get informed of whatever was on foot in the place.

Nobody can live entirely without social intercourse; and Legree encouraged his two black satellites to a kind of coarse familiarity with him – a familiarity, however, at any moment liable to get one or the other of them into trouble; for, on the slightest provocation, one of them always stood ready at a nod to be a minister of his vengeance on the other.

As they stood there now by Legree, they seemed an apt illustration of the fact that brutal men are lower even than animals. Their coarse, dark, heavy features; their great eyes, rolling enviously on each other; their barbarous, guttural, half-brute intonation; their dilapidated garments fluttering in the wind – were all in admirable keeping with the vile and unwholesome character of everything about the place.

'Here, you Sambo,' said Legree, 'take these yer boys down to the quarters; and here's a gal I've got for *you*,' said he, as he separated the mulatto woman from Emmeline and pushed her towards him. 'I promised to bring you one, you know.'

The woman gave a sudden start, and, drawing back, said suddenly –

'O mas'r! I left my old man in New Orleans.'

'What of that you—! won't you want one here? None o' your words – go 'long!' said Legree, raising his whip.

'Come, mistress,' he said to Emmeline, 'you go in here with me.'

A dark, wild face was seen, for a moment, to glance at the

window of the house; and, as Legree opened the door, a female voice said something in a quick imperative tone. Tom, who was looking with anxious interest after Emmeline, as she went in, noticed this, and heard Legree answer angrily, 'You may hold your tongue! I'll do as I please, for all you!'

Tom heard no more; for he was soon following Sambo to the quarters. The quarters was a little sort of street of rude shanties, in a row, in a part of the plantation far off from the house. They had a forlorn, brutal, forsaken air. Tom's heart sank when he saw them. He had been comforting himself with the thought of a cottage, rude, indeed, but one which he might make neat and quiet, and where he might have a shelf for his Bible, and a place to be alone out of his labouring hours. He looked into several; they were mere rude shells, destitute of any species of furniture, except a heap of straw foul with dirt, spread confusedly over the floor, which was merely the bare ground, trodden hard by the tramping of innumerable feet.

'Which of these will be mine?' said he to Sambo, submissively.

'Dunno; ken turn in here, I s'pose,' said Sambo; '"spect thar's room for another thar; thar's a pretty smart heap o' niggers to each on 'em now; sure I dunno what I's to do with more.'

It was late in the evening when the weary occupants of the shanties came flocking home – men and women, in soiled and tattered garments, surly and uncomfortable, and in no mood to look pleasantly on newcomers. The small village was alive with no inviting sounds; hoarse, guttural voices contending at the hand-mills where their morsel of hard corn was yet to be ground into meal, to fit it for the cake that was to constitute their only supper. From the earliest dawn of the day they had been in the fields, pressed to work under the driving lash of the overseers; for it was now in the very heat and hurry of the season, and no means were left untried to press every one up to the top of their capabilities. 'True,' says the negligent lounger, 'picking cotton isn't hard work.' Isn't it? And it isn't much inconvenience, either, to have one drop of water fall on your head; yet the worst torture of the Inquisition is produced by drop after drop, drop after drop, falling moment after moment, with monotonous succession, on the same spot; and work in itself not hard becomes so by being pressed, hour after hour, with unvarying, unrelenting sameness, with not even the consciousness of free-will to take from its tediousness. Tom looked in vain among the gang, as they poured along, for companionable faces. He saw only sullen, scowling, embruted men, and feeble, discouraged women, or women that were not women – the strong pushing away the weak – the gross, unrestricted animal selfishness of human beings, of whom nothing good was expected and desired; and who, treated in every way like brutes, had sunk as nearly to their level as it was possible for human beings to do. To a late hour in the night the sound of the grinding was protracted; for the mills were few in number compared with the grinders, and the weary and feeble ones were driven back by the strong, and came on last in their turn.

'Ho, yo!' said Sambo, coming to the mulatto woman, and throwing down a bag of corn before her, 'what a cuss yo name?'

'Lucy,' said the woman.

'Wal, Lucy, yo my woman now. Yo grind dis yer corn, and get *my* supper baked, ye har?'

'I an't your woman, and I won't be!' said the woman, with the sharp sudden courage of despair; 'you go 'long!'

'I'll kick yo, then!' said Sambo, raising his foot threateningly.

'Ye may kill me, if ye choose – the sooner the better. Wish't I was dead!' said she.

'I say, Sambo, you go to spilin' the hands, I'll tell mas'r o' you,' said Quimbo, who was busy at the mill, from which he had viciously driven two or three tired women, who were waiting to grind their corn.

'And I'll tell him ye won't let the women come to the mills, yo old nigger!' said Sambo. 'Yo jes keep to yo own row.'

Tom was hungry with his day's journey, and almost faint for want of food.

'Thar, yo!' said Quimbo, throwing down a coarse bag, which contained a peck of corn; 'thar, nigger, grab – take car on't, yo won't get no more *dis* yer week.'

Tom waited till a late hour to get a place at the mills; and then, moved by the utter weariness of two women, whom he saw trying to grind their corn there, he ground for them, put together the decaying brands of the fire, where many had baked cakes before them, and then went about getting his own supper. It was a new kind of work there – a deed of charity, small as it was; but it woke an answering touch in their hearts – and expression of womanly kindness came over their hard faces. They mixed his cake for him, and tended its baking; and Tom sat down by the light of the fire, and drew out his Bible – for he had need of comfort.

'What's that?' said one of the women.

'A Bible,' said Tom.

'Good Lord! han't seen un since I was in Kentuck.'

'Was you raised in Kentuck?' said Tom, with interest.

'Yes, and well raised, too; never 'spected to come to dis yer!' said the woman sighing.

'What's dat ar book, any way?' said the other woman.

'Why, the Bible.'

'Laws a me, what's dat?' said the woman.

'Do tell! you never hearn on't?' said the other woman. 'I used to har missis a readin' on't, sometimes, in Kentuck; but, laws o' me! we don't har nothin' here but crackin' and swarin'.'

'Read a piece, anyways!' said the first woman, curiously, seeing Tom attentively poring over it.

Tom read, 'Come unto Me, all ye that labour and are heavy laden, and I will give you rest.'

'Them's good words enough,' said the woman; 'who says 'em?'

'The Lord,' said Tom.

'I jest wish I know'd whar to find Him,' said the woman; 'I would go. 'Pears like I never should get rested agin. My flesh is fairly sore, and I tremble all over, every day, and Sambo's allers a jawin' at me, 'cause I doesn't pick faster; and nights it's most midnight 'fore I can get my supper; and then 'pears like I don't turn over and shut my eyes 'fore I hear de horn blow to get up, and at it agin in de mornin'. If I knew whar de Lord was, I'd tell him.'

'He's here, he's everywhere,' said Tom.

'Lor! you an't gwine to make me believe dat ar! I know de Lord an't here,' said the woman; ''tan't no use talking, though. I's jest gwine to camp down, and sleep while I ken.'

The women went off to their cabins, and Tom sat alone by the smouldering fire, that flickered up redly in his face.

The silver, fair-browed moon rose in the purple sky, and looked down, calm and silent, as God looks on the scene of misery and oppression – looked calmly on the lone black man, as he sat with his arms folded, and his Bible on his knee.

'Is God here?' Ah! how is it possible for the untaught heart to keep its faith, unswerving, in the face of dire misrule, and palpable, unrebuked injustice? In that simple heart waged a fierce conflict: the crushing sense of wrong, the foreshadowing of a whole life of future misery, the wreck of all past hopes, mournfully tossing in the soul's sight, like dead corpses of wife, and child, and friend, rising from the dark wave, and surging in the face of the half-drowned mariner! Ah, was it easy *here* to believe and hold fast the great pass-word of Christian faith, that 'God Is, and is the REWARDER of them that diligently seek Him?'

Tom rose, disconsolate, and stumbled into the cabin that had been allotted to him. The floor was already strewn with weary sleepers, and the foul air of the place almost repelled him; but the heavy night dews were chill and his limbs weary, and wrapping about him a tattered blanket, which formed his only bedclothing, he stretched himself in the straw, and fell asleep.

In dreams, a gentle voice came over his ear; he was sitting on the mossy seat in the garden by Lake Pontchartrain, and Eva, with her serious eyes bent downward, was reading to him from the Bible; and he heard her read: —

'When thou passest through the waters, I will be with thee; and the rivers, they shall not overflow thee; when thou walkest through the fire thou shalt not be burned, neither shall the flame kindle upon thee: for I am the Lord thy God, the Holy One of Israel, thy Saviour.'

Gradually the words seemed to melt and fade, as in a divine music; the child raised her deep eyes, and fixed them lovingly on him, and rays of warmth and comfort seemed to go from them to his heart; and, as if wafted on the music, she seemed to rise on shining wings, from which flakes and spangles of gold fell off like stars, and she was gone.

Tom woke. Was it a dream? Let it pass for one. But who shall say that the sweet young spirit, which in life so yearned to comfort and console the distressed, was forbidden of God to assume this ministry after death?

> 'It is a beautiful belief,
>   That ever round our head
> Are hovering, on angel wings,
>   The spirits of the dead.'

Chapter 33

CASSY

'And behold the tears of such as were oppressed, and they had no comforter; and on the side of their oppressors there was *power*, but they had no comforter.' – *Eccl.* iv. 1.

IT took but a short time to familiarise Tom with all that was to be hoped or feared in his new way of life. He was an expert and efficient workman in whatever he undertook; and was, both from habit and principle, prompt and faithful. Quiet and peaceable in his disposition, he hoped, by unremitting diligence, to avert from himself at least a portion of the evils of his condition. He saw enough of abuse and misery to make him sick and weary; but he determined to toil on with religious patience, committing himself to Him that judgeth righteously, not without hope that some way of escape might yet be opened to him.

Legree took silent note of Tom's availability. He rated him as a first-class hand; and yet he felt a secret dislike to him – the native antipathy of bad to good. He saw plainly that when, as was often the case, his violence and brutality fell on the helpless, Tom took notice of it; for, so subtle is the atmosphere of opinion, that it will make itself felt without words, and the opinion even of a slave may annoy a master. Tom in various ways manifested a tenderness of feeling, a commiseration for his fellow-sufferers, strange and new to them, which was watched with a jealous eye by Legree. He had purchased Tom with a view of eventually making him a sort of overseer, with whom he might at times entrust his affairs in short absences; and, in his view, the first, second, and third requisite for that place was *hardness*. Legree made up his mind that, as Tom was not hard to his hand, he would harden him forthwith; and some few weeks after Tom had been on the place he determined to commence the process.

One morning, when the hands were mustered for the field, Tom noticed with surprise a new-comer among them, whose appearance excited his attention. It was a woman, tall and slenderly formed, with remarkably delicate hands and feet, and dressed in neat and respectable garments. By the appearance of her face, she might have been between thirty-five and forty; and it was a face that, once seen, could never be forgotten – one of those that at a glance seem to convey to us an idea of a wild, painful, and romantic history. Her forehead was high, and her eyebrows marked with beautiful clearness. Her straight, well-formed nose, her finely-cut mouth, and the graceful contour of her head and neck, showed that she must once have been beautiful; but her face was deeply wrinkled with lines of pain, and of proud and bitter endurance. Her complexion was sallow and unhealthy, her cheeks thin, her features sharp, and her whole form emaciated. But her eye was the most remarkable feature – so large, so heavily black, overshadowed by long lashes of equal darkness, and so wildly, mournfully despairing. There was a fierce pride and defiance in every line of her face, in every curve of the flexible lip, in every motion of her body; but in her eye was a deep, settled night of anguish – an expression so hopeless and unchanging as to contrast fearfully with the scorn and pride expressed by her whole demeanour.

Where she came from, or who she was, Tom did not know. The first thing he did know, she was walking by his side, erect and proud, in the dim grey of the dawn. To the gang, however, she was known: for there was much looking and turning of heads, and a smothered yet apparent exultation among the miserable, ragged, half-starved creatures by whom she was surrounded.

'Got to come to it at last – glad of it!' said one.

'He! he! he!' said another; 'you will know how good it is misse!'

'We'll see her work!'

'Wonder if she'll get a cutting up, at night, like the rest of us!'

'I'd be glad to see her down for a flogging, I'll bound!' said another.

The woman took no notice of these taunts, but walked on with the same expression of angry scorn, as if she heard nothing. Tom had always lived among refined and cultivated people, and he felt intuitively, from her air and bearing, that she belonged to that class; but how or why she could be fallen to those degrading circumstances he could not tell. The woman neither looked at him nor spoke to him, though, all the way to the field, she kept close at his side.

Tom was soon busy at his work; but, as the woman was at no great distance from him, he often glanced an eye to her, at her work. He saw at a glance that her native adroitness and handiness made the task to her an easier one that it proved to many. She picked very fast and very clean, and with an air of scorn, as if she despised both the work and the disgrace and humiliation of the circumstances in which she was placed.

In the course of the day, Tom was working near the mulatto woman who had been bought in the same lot with himself. She was evidently in a condition of great suffering, and Tom often heard her praying, as she wavered and trembled, and seemed about to fall down. Tom silently, as he came near to her, transferred several handfuls of cotton from his own sack to hers.

'Oh, don't, don't!' said the woman, looking surprised; 'it'll get you into trouble.'

Just then Sambo came up. He seemed to have a special spite against this woman; and, flourishing his whip, said, in brutal, guttural tones, 'What dis yer, Luce – foolin' a'? and, with the word, kicking the woman with his heavy cow-hide shoe, he struck Tom across the face with his whip.

Tom silently resumed his task; but the woman, before at the last point of exhaustion, fainted.

'I'll bring her to!' said the driver, with a brutal grin. 'I'll give her something better than camphire!' and, taking a pin from his coat-sleeve, he buried it to the head in her flesh. The woman groaned, and half rose. 'Get up, you beast, and work, will yer, or I'll show you a trick more!'

The woman seemed stimulated, for a few moments, to an unnatural strength, and worked with desperate eagerness.

'See that you keep to dat ar,' said the man, 'or yer'll wish yer's dead to-night, I reckin'!'

'That I do now!' Tom heard her say; and again he heard her say, 'Oh Lord, how long? O Lord, why don't you help us?'

At the risk of all that he might suffer, Tom came forward again, and put all the cotton in his sack into the woman's.

'Oh, you mustn't! you donno what they'll do to ye!' said the woman.

'I can bar it,' said Tom, 'better'n you;' and he was at his place again. It passed in a moment.

Suddenly the stranger woman whom we have described, and who had, in the course of her work, come near enough to hear Tom's last words, raised her heavy black eyes, and fixed them for a second on him; then, taking a quantity of cotton from her basket, she placed it in his.

'You know nothing about this place,' she said, 'or you wouldn't have done that. When you've been here a month, you'll be done helping anybody; you'll find it hard enough to take care of your own skin.'

'The Lord forbid, missis!' said Tom, using instinctively to his field companion the respectful form proper to the high-bred with whom he had lived.

'The Lord never visits these parts,' said the woman, bitterly, as she went nimbly forward with her work; and again the scornful smile curled her lips.

But the action of the woman had been seen by the driver across the field; and flourishing his whip, he came up to her.

'What! what!' he said to the woman with an air of triumph, 'YOU a foolin'? Go along! yer under me now – mind yourself, or yer'll cotch it!'

A glance like sheet-lightning suddenly flashed from those black eyes; and, facing about, with quivering lip and dilated nostrils, she drew herself up, and fixed a glance, blazing with rage and scorn, on the driver.

'Dog!' she said, 'touch *me*, if you dare! I've power enough yet to have you torn by the dogs, burnt alive, cut to inches! I've only to say the word!'

'What de devil you here for, den?' said the man, evidently cowed, and sullenly retreating a step or two. 'Didn't mean no harm, Misse Cassy!'

'Keep your distance, then!' said the woman. And, in truth, the man seemed greatly inclined to attend to something at the other end of the field, and started off in quick time.

The woman suddenly turned to her work, and laboured with a despatch that was perfectly astonishing to Tom. She seemed to work by magic. Before the day was through, her basket was filled, crowded down, and piled, and she had several times put largely into Tom's. Long after dusk, the whole weary train, with their baskets on their heads, defiled up to the building appropriated to the storing and weighing the cotton. Legree was there, busily conversing with the two drivers.

'Dat ar Tom's gwine to make a powerful deal o' trouble; kept aputtin' into Lucy's basket. One o' these yer dat will get all der niggers to feelin' 'bused, if mas'r don't watch him!' said Sambo.

'Hey-dey! The black cuss!' said Legree. 'He'll have to get a breakin' in – won't he, boys?'

Both negroes grinned a horrid grin at this intimation.

'Ay, ay! let Mas'r Legree alone for breakin' in! De debil heself couldn't beat mas'r at dat!' said Quimbo.

'Wal, boys, the best way is to give him the flogging to do till he gets over his notions. Break him in!'

'Lord, mas'r 'll have hard work to get dat out o'him!'

'It'll have to come out of him though!' said Legree, as he rolled his tobacco in his mouth.

'Now, dars Lucy – de aggravatinest, ugliest wench on de place!' pursued Sambo.

'Take care, Sam; I shall begin to think what's the reason for your spite agin Lucy.'

'Well, mas'r knows she sot herself up agin mas'r, and wouldn't have me when he tell'd her to.'

'I'd a flogged her into't,' said Legree, spitting; 'only there's such a press o' work, it don't seem wuth a while to upset her jist now. She's slender; but these yer slender gals will bear half killin' to get their own way!'

'Wal, Lucy was real aggravatin' and lazy, sulkin' round; wouldn't do nothin' – and Tom he tuck up for her.'

'He did, eh? Wal, then, Tom shall have the pleasure of flogging her. It'll be a good practice for him, and he won't put it on to the gal like you devils, neither.'

'Ho, ho! haw! haw! haw!' laughed both the sooty wretches; and the diabolical sounds seemed, in truth, a not unapt expression of the fiendish character which Legree gave them.

'Wal, but, mas'r, Tom and Misse Cassy, and dey among 'em, filled Lucy's basket. I ruther guess der weight's in it, mas'r.'

'*I do the weighing!*' said Legree, emphatically.

Both the drivers again laughed their diabolical laugh.

'So !' he added, 'Misse Cassy did her day's work.'

'She picks like de debil and all his angels !'

'She's got 'em all in her, I believe !' said Legree ; and growling a brutal oath, he proceeded to the weighing-room.

Slowly the weary, dispirited creatures wound their way into the room, and, with crouching reluctance, presented their baskets to be weighed.

Legree noted on a slate, on the side of which was pasted a list of names, the amount.

Tom's basket was weighed and approved ; and he looked with an anxious glance for the success of the woman he had befriended.

Tottering with weakness, she came forward, and delivered her basket. It was of full weight, as Legree well perceived ; but, affecting anger, he said : –

'What, you lazy beast ! short again ! Stand aside, you'll catch it, pretty soon !'

The woman gave a groan of utter despair, and sat down on a board.

The person who had been called Misse Cassy now came forward, and, with a haughty, negligent air, delivered her basket. As she delivered it, Legree looked in her eyes with a sneering yet inquiring glance.

She fixed her black eyes steadily on him, her lips moved slightly, and she said something in French. What it was, no one knew ; but Legree's face became perfectly demoniacal in its expression as she spoke ; he half raised his hand, as if to strike – a gesture which she regarded with fierce disdain, as she turned and walked away.

'And now,' said Legree, 'come here, you Tom. You see, I told ye I didn't buy ye jest for the common work. I mean to promote ye, and make a driver of ye : and to-night ye may jest as well begin to get yer hand in. Now, ye jest take this yer gal and flog her ; ye've seen enough on't to know how.'

'I beg mas'r's pardon,' said Tom ; 'hope's mas'r won't set me at that. It's what I an't used to – never did – and can't do, no way possible.'

'Ye'll larn a pretty smart chance of things ye never did know, before I've done with ye !' said Legree, taking up a cow-hide, and striking Tom a heavy blow across the cheek, and following up the infliction by a shower of blows.

'There;' he said, as he stopped to rest; 'now will ye tell me ye can't do it?'

'Yes, mas'r,' said Tom, putting up his hand to wipe the blood that trickled down his face. 'I'm willin' to work, night and day, and work while there's life and breath in me; but this yer thing I can't feel it right to do; and, mas'r, I *never* shall do it – *never*!'

Tom had a remarkably smooth, soft voice, and an habitually respectful manner, that had given Legree an idea that he would be cowardly, and easily subdued. When he spoke these last words, a thrill of amazement went through every one; the poor woman clasped her hands, and said, 'O Lord!' and every one involuntarily looked at each other and drew in their breath, as if to prepare for the storm that was about to burst.

Legree looked stupefied and confounded; but at last burst forth, –

'What! ye blasted black beast! tell *me* ye don't think it *right* to do what I tell ye! What have any of you cussed cattle to do with thinking what's right? I'll put a stop to it! Why, what do ye think ye are? Maybe ye think ye'r a gentleman, master Tom, to be telling your master what's right, and what an't. So you pretend it's wrong to flog the gal?'

'I think so, mas'r,' said Tom. 'The poor crittur's sick and feeble; 'twould be downright cruel, and it's what I never will do, or begin to. Mas'r, if you mean to kill me, kill me; but, as to my raising my hand agin any one here, I never shall – I'll die first!'

Tom spoke in a mild voice, but with a decision that could not be mistaken. Legree shook with anger; his greenish eyes glared fiercely, and his very whiskers seemed to curl with passion; but like some ferocious beast, that plays with its victim before he devours it, he kept back his strong impulse to proceed to immediate violence, and broke out into bitter raillery.

'Well, here's a pious dog, at last let down among us sinners! – a saint, a gentleman, and no less, to talk to us sinners about our sins. Powerful holy critter he must be! Here, you rascal, you make believe to be so pious – didn't you never hear, out of yer Bible, "Servants, obey your masters?" An't I your master? Didn't I pay down twelve hundred dollars, cash, for all there is inside yer old cussed black shell? An't yer mine, now, body and soul?' he said, giving Tom a violent kick with his heavy boot! 'tell me!'

In the very depth of physical suffering, bowed by brutal oppression, this question shot a gleam of joy and triumph through Tom's soul. He suddenly stretched himself up, and looking earnestly to heaven, while the tears and blood that flowed down his face mingled, he exclaimed, –

'No, no, no! my soul an't yours, mas'r! You haven't bought it – ye can't buy it! It has been bought and paid for by One that's able to keep it. No matter, no matter, you can't harm me!'

'I can't!' said Legree, with a sneer; 'we'll see – we'll see! Here, Sambo! Quimbo! give this dog such a breakin' in as he won't get over this month!'

The two gigantic negroes that now laid hold of Tom, with fiendish exultation in their faces, might have formed no unapt personification of powers of darkness. The poor woman screamed with apprehension, and all rose, as by a general impulse, while they dragged him unresisting from the place.

Chapter 34

THE QUADROON'S STORY

'And behold the tears of such as were oppressed; and on the side of their oppressors there was power. Wherefore I praised the dead that are already dead more than the living which are yet alive.' – *Eccl.* iv. 1, 2.

IT was late at night, and Tom lay groaning and bleeding alone, in an old forsaken room of the gin-house, among pieces of broken machinery, piles of damaged cotton, and other rubbish which had there accumulated.

The night was damp and close, and the thick air swarmed

with myriads of mosquitos, which increased the restless torture of his wounds; whilst a burning thirst – a torture beyond all others – filled up the uttermost measure of physical anguish.

'Oh good Lord! *Do* look down – give me the victory! – give me the victory over all!' prayed poor Tom, in his anguish.

A footstep entered the room behind him, and the light of a lantern flashed on his eyes.

'Who's there? Oh, for the Lord's massy, please give me some water!'

The woman Cassy – for it was she – set down her lantern, and, pouring water from a bottle, raised his head, and gave him drink. Another and another cup were drained, with feverish eagerness.

'Drink all ye want,' she said; 'I knew how it would be. It isn't the first time I've been out in the night, carrying water to such as you.'

'Thank you, missis,' said Tom, when he had done drinking.

'Don't call me missis! I'm a miserable slave like yourself – a lower one than you can ever be!' said she bitterly. 'But now,' said she, going to the door, and dragging in a small palliasse, over which she had spread linen cloths wet with cold water, 'try, my poor fellow, to roll yourself on to this.'

Stiff with wounds and bruises, Tom was a long time in accomplishing this movement; but when done, he felt a sensible relief from the cooling application to his wounds.

The woman, whom long practice with the victims of brutality had made familiar with many healing arts, went on to make many applications to Tom's wounds, by means of which he was soon somewhat relieved.

'Now,' said the woman, when she had raised his head on a roll of damaged cotton, which served for a pillow, 'there's the best I can do for you.'

Tom thanked her; and the woman, sitting down on the floor, drew up her knees, and embracing them with her arms, looked fixedly before her, with a bitter and painful expression of countenance. Her bonnet fell back, and long wavy streams of black hair fell around her singular and melancholy face.

'It's no use, my poor fellow,' she broke out, at last, 'it's of no use, this you've been trying to do. You were a brave fellow – you had the right on your side; but it's all in vain, and out of

the question, for you to struggle. You are in the devil's hands;
he is the strongest, and you must give up.'

Give up! and had not human weakness and physical agony
whispered that before? Tom started; for the bitter woman, with
her wild eyes and melancholy voice, seemed to him an embodiment of the temptation with which he had been wrestling.

'Oh Lord! O Lord!' he groaned, 'how can I give up?'

'There's no use calling on the Lord — he never hears,' said the
woman, steadily. 'There isn't any God, I believe; or, if there is,
he's taken sides against us. All goes against us, heaven and earth.
Everything is pushing us into hell. Why shouldn't we go?'

Tom closed his eyes, and shuddered at the dark, atheistic
words.

'You see,' said the woman, '*you* don't know anything about
it — I do. I've been on this place five years, body and soul, under
this man's foot, and I hate him as I do the devil! Here you are,
on a lone plantation, ten miles from any other, in the swamps;
not a white person here who could testify if you were burned
alive — if you were scalded, cut into inch-pieces, set up for the
dogs to tear, or hung up and whipped to death. There's no law
here, of God or man, that can do you or any one of us the least
good; and this man! there's no earthly thing that he's too good
to do. I could make any one's hair rise, and their teeth chatter,
if I should only tell what I've seen and been knowing to here, —
and it's no use resisting! Did I *want* to live with him? Wasn't I
a woman delicately bred? and he — God in heaven! what was
he, and is he? And yet I've lived with him these five years, and
cursed every moment of my life — night and day! And now he's
got a new one — a young thing, only fifteen; and she brought
up, she says, piously. Her good mistress taught her to read the
Bible, and she's brought her Bible here — to hell with her!' And
the woman laughed a wild and doleful laugh, that rang with a
strange supernatural sound through the old ruined shed.

Tom folded his hands; all was darkness and horror.

'O Jesus! Lord Jesus! have you quite forgot us poor critturs?'
burst forth, at last. 'Help, Lord, I perish!'

The woman sternly continued: —

'And what are these miserable low dogs you work with, that
you should suffer on their account? Every one of them would
turn against you the first time they got a chance. They are all of

'em as low and cruel to each other as they can be; and there's no use in your suffering to keep from hurting them.'

'Poor critturs!' said Tom, 'what made 'em cruel? And if I give out, I shall get used to't, and grow, little by little, just like 'em! No, no, missis! I've lost everything – wife, and children, and home, and a kind mas'r – and he would have set me free, if he'd only lived a week longer. I've lost everything in *this* world, and it's clean gone for ever – and now I *can't* lose heaven, too; no, I can't get to be wicked, besides all!'

'But it can't be that the Lord will lay sin to our account,' said the woman; 'He won't charge it to us, when we're forced to it; He'll charge it to them that drove us to it.'

'Yes,' said Tom; 'but that won't keep us from growing wicked.' If I get to be as hard-hearted as that ar Sambo, and as wicked, 't won't make much odds to me how I come so; it's the *bein' so* – that ar's what I'm a dreadin'.'

The woman fixed a wild and startled look on Tom, as if a new thought had struck her; and then, heavily groaning, said –

'O God a' mercy! you speak the truth! Oh – oh – oh!' And, with groans, she fell on the floor, like one crushed and writhing under the extremity of mental anguish.

There was a silence awhile, in which the breathing of both parties could be heard, when Tom faintly said, 'Oh, please, missis!'—

The woman suddenly rose up, with her face composed to its usual stern, melancholy expression.

'Please, missis, I saw 'em throw my coat in that ar' corner, and in my coat-pocket is my Bible – if missis would please get it for me.'

Cassy went and got it. Tom opened at once to a heavily-marked passage, much worn, of the last scenes in the life of Him by whose stripes we are healed.

'If missis would only be so good as read that ar' – it's better than water.'

Cassy took the book, with a dry, proud air, and looked over the passage. She then read aloud, in a soft voice, and with a beauty of intonation that was peculiar, that touching account of anguish and of glory. Often, as she read, her voice faltered, and sometimes failed her altogether, when she would stop, with an air of frigid composure, till she had mastered herself. When she came to the touching words, 'Father, forgive them, for they know not what they do,' she threw down the book, and burying her face in the heavy masses of her hair, she sobbed aloud, with a convulsive violence.

Tom was weeping also, and occasionally uttering a smothered ejaculation.

'If we only could keep up to that ar'?' said Tom – 'it seemed to come so natural to him, and we have to fight so hard for't! O Lord, help us! O blessed Lord Jesus, do help us!'

'Missis,' said Tom, after a while, 'I can see that somehow you're quite 'bove me in everything; but there's one thing missis might learn even from poor Tom. Ye said the Lord took sides against us, because he lets us be 'bused and knocked round; but ye see what come on his own Son – the blessed Lord of Glory. Wa'nt he al'ays poor? and have we, any on us, yet come so low as he come? The Lord han't forgot us – I'm sartin, o' that ar'. If we suffer with Him, we shall also reign, Scripture says; but if we deny Him, He also will deny us. Didn't they all suffer – the Lord and all His? It tells how they were stoned and sawn asunder, and wandered about in sheepskins and goatskins, and was destitute, afflicted, tormented. Sufferin' an't no reason to make us think the Lord's turned agin us; but jest the contrary, if we only hold on to him, and doesn't give up to sin.'

'But why does He put us where we can't help but sin?' said the woman.

'I think we *can* help it,' said Tom.

'You'll see,' said Cassy. 'What'll you do? To-morrow they'll be at you again. I know 'em, I have seen all their doings; I can't bear to think of all they'll bring you to – and they'll make you out at last!'

'Lord Jesus!' said Tom, 'you *will* take care of my soul! O Lord, do! – don't let me give out!'

'Oh, dear,' said Cassy, 'I've heard all this crying and praying before; and yet they've been broken down and brought under. There's Emmeline, she's trying to hold on, and you're trying – but what use? You must give up, or be killed by inches.'

'Well, then, I *will* die!' said Tom. 'Spin it out as long as they can, they can't help my dying some time! – and after that, they can't do no more. I'm clar! I'm set! I *know* the Lord'll help me, and bring me through.'

The woman did not answer; she sat with her black eyes intently fixed on the floor.

'Maybe it's the way,' she murmured to herself; 'but those that *have* given up, there's no hope for them – none! We live in filth and grow loathsome, till we loathe ourselves! And we long to die, and we don't dare to kill ourselves. No hope! no hope! no hope! – this girl now – just as old as I was. You see me now,' she said, speaking to Tom very rapidly, 'see that I am! Well, I was brought up in luxury. The first I remember is playing about, when I was a child, in splendid parlours – when I was kept dressed up like a doll, and company and visitors used to praise me. There was a garden opening from the saloon windows; and there I used to play hide-and-go-seek, under the orange-trees, with my brothers and sisters. I went to a convent, and there I learned music, French, and embroidery, and what not; and when I was fourteen, I came out to my father's funeral. He died very suddenly, and when the property came to be settled, they found that there was scarcely enough to cover the debts; and when the creditors took an inventory of the property, I was set down in it. My mother was a slave woman, and my father had always meant to set me free, but he had not done it, and so I was set down in the list. I'd always known who I was, but never thought much about it. Nobody ever expects that a strong healthy man is agoing to die. My father was a well man only four hours before he died – it was one of the first cholera cases in New Orleans. The day after the funeral my father's wife took her children, and went up to her father's plantation. I thought they treated me strangely, but didn't know. There was a young lawyer whom they left to settle the business; and he came every day, and was about the house, and spoke very politely to me. He brought with him one day a young man, whom I thought the handsomest I had ever seen. I shall never forget that evening; I walked with him in the garden. I was lonesome and full of sorrow, and he was so kind and gentle to me; and he told me, that he had seen me before I went to the convent, and that he had loved me a great while, and that he would be my friend and protector. In short, though he didn't tell me, he had paid two thousand dollars for me, and I was

his property. I became his willingly, for I loved him. Loved!'
said the woman, stopping, 'Oh, how I *did* love that man! How
I love him now, and always shall while I breathe! He was so
beautiful, so high, so noble! He put me into a beautiful house,
with servants, horses, and carriages, and furniture, and dresses.
Everything that money could buy he gave me; but I didn't set
any value on all that, I only cared for him. I loved him better
than my God and my own soul; and, if I tried, I couldn't do any
other way from what he wanted me to.

   'I wanted only one thing – I did want him to *marry* me. I
thought, if he loved me as he said he did, and if I was what he
seemed to think I was, he would be willing to marry me and set
me free. But he convinced me that it would be impossible; and
he told me that if we were only faithful to each other, it was
marriage before God. If that is true, wasn't I that man's wife?
Wasn't I faithful? For seven years didn't I study every look and
motion, and only live and breathe to please him. He had the
yellow fever, and for twenty days and nights I watched with him
– I alone, and gave him all his medicine, and did everything for
him; and then he called me his good angel, and said I'd saved
his life. We had two beautiful children. The first was a boy, and
we called him Henry; he was the image of his father – he had
such beautiful eyes, such a forehead, and his hair hung all in
curls around it – and he had all his father's spirit, and his talent
too. Little Elsie, he said, looked like me. He used to tell me that
I was the most beautiful woman in Louisiana, he was so proud
of me and the children. He used to love to have me dress them
up, and take them and me about in an open carriage, and hear
the remarks that people would make on us; and he used to fill
my ears constantly with the fine things that were said in praise
of me and the children. Oh, those were happy days! I thought I
was as happy as any one could be; but then there came evil
times. He had a cousin come to New Orleans who was his
particular friend – he thought all the world of him; but, from
the first time I saw him, I couldn't tell why, I dreaded him, for I
felt sure he was going to bring misery on us. He got Henry to
going out with him, and often he would not come home nights
till two or three o'clock. I did not dare say a word; for Henry
was so high-spirited, I was afraid to. He got him to the gaming-
houses; and he was one of the sort that when he once got agoing

there, there was no holding back. And then he introduced him to another lady, and I saw soon that his heart was gone from me. He never told me, but I saw it — I knew it day after day. I felt my heart breaking, but I could not say a word. At this the wretch offered to buy me and the children of Henry, to clear off his gambling debts, which stood in the way of his marrying as he wished — and *he sold us*. He told me one day that he had business in the country; and should be gone two or three weeks. He spoke kinder than usual, and said he should come back; but it didn't deceive me; I knew that the time had come; I was just like one turned into stone; I couldn't speak nor shed a tear. He kissed me and kissed the children a good many times, and went out. I saw him get on his horse, and I watched him till he was quite out of sight; and then I fell down and fainted.

'Then *he* came, the cursed wretch! he came to take possession. He told me that he had bought me and my children, and showed me the papers. I cursed him before God, and told him I'd die sooner than live with him.

'"Just as you please," said he; "but if you don't behave reasonably I'll sell both the children, where you shall never see them again." He told me that he always had meant to have me, from the first time he saw me; and that he had drawn Henry on, and got him in debt, on purpose to make him willing to sell me. That he got him in love with another woman; and that I might know, after all that, that he should not give up for a few airs and tears, and things of that sort.

'I gave up, for my hands were tied. He had my children; whenever I resisted his will anywhere, he would talk about selling them, and he made me as submissive as he desired. Oh, what a life it was! to live with my heart breaking, every day — to keep on, on, on, loving, when it was only misery; and to be bound, body and soul, to one I hated. I used to love to read to Henry, to play to him, to waltz with him, and sing to him; but everything I did for this one was a perfect drag — yet I was afraid to refuse anything. He was very imperious and harsh to the children. Elsie was a timid little thing; but Henry was bold and high-spirited, like his father, and he had never been brought under in the least by any one. He was always finding fault, and quarrelling with him; and I used to live in daily fear and dread. I tried to make the child respectful — I tried to keep them apart, for I held on to those children like death; but it did no good. *He sold both those children.* He took me to ride one day, and when I came home they were nowhere to be found! He told me he had sold them; he showed me the money, the price of their blood. Then it seemed as if all good forsook me. I raved and cursed – cursed God and man; and, for a while, I believe, he really was afraid of me. But he didn't give up so. He told me that my children were sold, but whether I ever saw their faces again depended on him; and that if I wasn't quiet, they should smart for it. Well, you can do anything with a woman when you've got her children. He made me submit; he made me be peaceable; he flattered me with hopes that perhaps he would buy them back; and so things went on a week or two. One day I was out walking, and passed by the calaboose; I saw a crowd about the gate, and heard a child's voice – and suddenly my Henry broke away from two or three men who were holding him, and ran, screaming, and caught my dress. They came up to him, swearing dreadfully; and one man, whose face I shall never forget, told him that he wouldn't get away so; that he was going with him into the calaboose, and he'd get a lesson there he'd never forget. I tried to beg and plead – they only laughed; the poor boy screamed and looked into my face, and held on to me, until, in tearing him off, they tore the skirt of my dress half away; and they carried him in screaming "Mother! mother! mother!" There was one man stood there seemed to pity me. I offered him all the money I had if he'd only interfere. He shook his head, and said that the man said the boy had been impudent and disobedient, ever since he bought him; that he was going to break him in once for all. I turned and ran; and every step of the way I thought that I heard him scream. I got into the house, ran all out of breath to the parlour, where I found Butler. I told him, and begged him to go and interfere. He only laughed and told me the boy had got his desserts. He'd got to be broken in – the sooner the better; "what did I expect?" he asked.

'It seemed to me something in my head snapped at that moment. I felt dizzy and furious. I remember seeing a great sharp bowie-knife on the table; I remember something about catching it, and flying upon him! and then all grew dark, and I didn't know any more – not for days and days.

'When I came to myself, I was in a nice room; but not mine.

An old woman tended me; and a doctor came to see me, and there was a great deal of care taken of me. After a while I found that he had gone away, and left me at this house to be sold; and that's why they took such pains with me.

'I didn't mean to get well, and hoped I shouldn't; but, in spite of me, the fever went off, and I grew healthy, and finally got up. They made me dress up every day; and gentlemen used to come in and stand and smoke their cigars, and look at me, and ask questions, and debate my price. I was so gloomy and silent that none of them wanted me. They threatened to whip me if I wasn't gayer, and didn't take some pains to make myself agreeable. At length, one day, came a gentleman named Stuart. He seemed to have some feeling for me; he saw that something dreadful was on my heart, and he came to see me alone a great many times, and finally persuaded me to tell him. He bought me at last, and promised to do all he could to find and buy back my children. He went to the hotel where my Henry was; they told him he had been sold to a planter up on Pearl River; that was the last that I ever heard. Then he found where my daughter was; an old woman was keeping her. He offered an immense sum for her, but they would not sell her. Butler found out that it was for me he wanted her; and he sent me word that I should never have her. Captain Stuart was very kind to me; he had a splendid plantation, and took me to it. In the course of a year I had a son born. Oh! that child! – how I loved it! How just like my poor Henry the little thing looked! But I had made up my mind – yes, I had, I would never again let a child live to grow up! I took the little fellow in my arms, when he was two weeks old, and kissed him and cried over him; and then I gave him laudanum, and held him close to my bosom while he slept to death. How I mourned and cried over it! and who ever dreamed that it was anything but a mistake that had made me give it the laudanum? but it's one of the few things that I'm glad of now. I am not sorry to this day; he, at least, is out of pain. What better than death could I give him, poor child? After a while the cholera came, and Captain Stuart died; everybody died that wanted to live: and I – I, though I went down to death's door – I *lived*! Then I was sold, and passed from hand to hand, till I grew faded and wrinkled, and I had a fever; and then this wretch bought me, and brought me here – and here I am!'

The woman stopped. She had hurried on through her story with a wild, passionate utterance; sometimes seeming to address it to Tom, and sometimes speaking as in a soliloquy. So vehement and overpowering was the force with which she spoke, that, for a season, Tom was beguiled even from the pain of his wounds; and, raising himself on one elbow, watched her, as she paced restlessly up and down, her long black hair swaying heavily about her as she moved.

'You tell me,' she said, after a pause, 'that there is a God – a God that looks down and sees all these things. Maybe it's so. The sisters in the convent used to tell me of a day of judgment, when everything is coming to light; won't there be vengeance then!

'They think it's nothing what we suffer – nothing what our children suffer! It's all a small matter; yet I've walked the streets when it seemed as if I had misery enough in my one heart to sink the city. I've wished the houses would fall on me, or the stones sink under me. Yes! and in the judgment day I will stand up before God, a witness against those that have ruined me and my children, body and soul!

'When I was a girl I thought I was religious; I used to love God and prayer. Now I'm a lost soul, pursued by devils that torment me day and night; they keep pushing me on and on – and I'll do it, too, some of these days!' she said, clenching her hand, while an insane light glanced in her heavy black eyes. 'I'll send him where he belongs – a short way, too – one of these nights, if they burn me alive for it.' A wild, long laugh rang through the deserted room, and ended in a hysteric sob; she threw herself on the floor in convulsive sobbings and struggles.

In a few moments the frenzy fit seemed to pass off; she rose slowly, and seemed to collect herself.

'Can't I do anything more for you, my poor fellow?' she said, approaching where Tom lay; 'shall I give you some more water?'

There was a graceful and compassionate sweetness in her voice and manner, as she said this, that formed a strange contrast with the former wildness.

Tom drank the water, and looked earnestly and pitifully into her face.

'O missis, I wish you'd go to Him that can give you living waters !'

'Go to him ! Where is he ? Who is he ?' said Cassy.

'Him that you read of to me – the Lord.'

'I used to see the picture of him over the altar, when I was a girl,' said Cassy, her dark eyes fixing themselves in an expression of mournful reverie ; 'but *he isn't here.* There's nothing here but sin, and long, long, long despair ! Oh !' She laid her hand on her breast, and drew in her breath, as if to lift a heavy weight.

Tom looked as if he would speak again, but she cut him short with a decided gesture.

'Don't talk, my poor fellow. Try to sleep if you can.' And, placing water in his reach, and making whatever little arrangements for his comfort she could, Cassy left the shed.

Chapter 35

THE TOKENS

'And slight withal may be the things that bring
Back on the heart the weight which it would fling
Aside for ever ; it may be a sound,
A flower, the wind, the ocean, which shall wound –
Striking the electric chain wherewith we're darkly bound.'
Childe Harold's Pilgrimage, Canto iv.

THE sitting-room of Legree's establishment was a large, long room, with a wide, ample fireplace. It had once been hung with a showy and expensive paper, which now hung mouldering, torn, and discoloured, from the damp walls. The place had that peculiar sickening, unwholesome smell, compounded of mingled damp, dirt, and decay, which one often notices in close old houses. The wall-paper was defaced, in spots, by slops of beer and wine ; or garnished with chalk memorandums ; and long sums footed up, as if somebody had been practising arithmetic there. In the fireplace stood a brazier full of burning charcoal; for, though the weather was not cold, the evenings always seemed damp and chilly in that great room; and Legree, moreover, wanted a place to light his cigars, and heat his water for punch. The ruddy glare of the charcoal displayed the confused and unpromising aspect of the room – saddles, bridles, several sorts of harness, riding-whips, overcoats, and various articles of clothing, scattered up and down the room in confused variety; and the dogs, of which we have before spoken, had encamped themselves among them, to suit their own taste and convenience.

Legree was just mixing himself a tumbler of punch, pouring his hot water from a cracked and broken-nosed pitcher, grumbling, as he did so –

'Plague on that Sambo, to kick up this yer row between me and the new hands! The fellow won't be fit to work for a week now – right in the press of the season!'

'Yes, just like you,' said a voice behind his chair. It was the woman Cassy, who had stolen upon his soliloquy.

'Ha! You she-devil! you've come back, have you?'

'Yes, I have,' she said coolly; 'come to have my own way, too!'

'You lie, you jade! I'll be up to my word. Either behave yourself, or stay down to the quarters, and fare and work with the rest.'

'I'd rather ten thousand times,' said the women, 'live in the dirtiest hole at the quarters than be under your hoof!'

'But you *are* under my hoof, for all that,' said he, turning upon her with a savage grin; 'that's one comfort. So, sit down here on my knee, my dear, and hear to reason,' said he, laying hold on her wrist.

'Simon Legree, take care!' said the woman, with a sharp flash of her eye – a glance so wild and insane in its light as to be almost appalling. 'You're afraid of me, Simon,' she said deliberately, 'and you've reason to be! But be careful, for I've got the devil in me!'

The last words she whispered in a hissing tone, close to his ear.

'Get out! I believe, to my soul, you have!' said Legree, pushing her from him, and looking uncomfortably at her. 'After all, Cassy,' he said, 'why can't you be friends with me as you used to ?'

'Used to !' said she bitterly. She stopped short – a world of choking feelings, rising in her heart, kept her silent.

Cassy had always kept over Legree the kind of influence that a strong, impassioned woman can ever keep over the most brutal man; but of late she had grown more and more irritable and restless under the hideous yoke of her servitude, and her irritability at times broke out into raving insanity; and this liability made her a sort of object of dread to Legree, who had that superstitious horror of insane persons which is common to coarse and uninstructed minds. When Legree brought Emmeline to the house, all the smouldering embers of womanly feeling flashed up in the worn heart of Cassy, and she took part with the girl; and a fierce quarrel ensued between her and Legree. Legree, in a fury, swore she should be put to field-service if she would not be peaceable. Cassy, with proud scorn, declared she *would* go to the field. And she worked there one day, as we have described, to show how perfectly she scorned the threat.

Legree was secretly uneasy all day, for Cassy had an influence over him from which he could not free himself. When she presented her basket at the scales, he had hoped for some concession, and addressed her in a short of half conciliatory, half scornful tone; and she had answered with the bitterest contempt.

The outrageous treatment of poor Tom had roused her still more; and she had followed Legree to the house with no particular intention but to upbraid him for his brutality.

'I wish, Cassy,' said Legree, 'you'd behave yourself decently.'

'*You* talk about behaving decently ! And what have you been doing? You, who haven't even sense enough to keep from spoiling one of your best hands, right in the most pressing season, just for your devilish temper !'

'I was a fool, it's a fact, to let any such brangle come up,' said Legree; 'but when the boy set up his will, he had to be broke in.'

'I reckon you won't break *him* in !'

'Won't I ?' said Legree, rising passionately. 'I like to know if I won't ! He'll be the first nigger that ever came it round me ! I'll break every bone in his body but he *shall* give up !'

Just then the door opened and Sambo entered. He came forward bowing, and holding out something in a paper.

'What's that, you dog?' said Legree.

'It's a witch thing, mas'r!'

'A what?'

'Something that niggers gets from witches. Keeps 'em from feelin' when they's flogged. He had tied it round his neck with a black string.'

Legree, like most godless and cruel men, was superstitious. He took the paper, and opened it uneasily.

There dropped out of it a silver dollar, and a long, shining curl of fair hair – hair which, like a living thing, twined itself round Legree's fingers.

'Damnation!' he screamed in sudden passion, stamping on the floor, and pulling furiously at the hair, as if it burned him. 'Where did this come from? Take it off! – burn it up! – burn it up!' he screamed, tearing it off and throwing it into the charcoal. 'What did you bring it to me for?'

Sambo stood with his heavy mouth wide open, and aghast with wonder; and Cassy, who was preparing to leave the apartment, stopped, and looked at him in perfect amazement.

'Don't you bring me any more of your devilish things!' said he, shaking his fist at Sambo, who retreated hastily towards the door; and, picking up the silver dollar, he sent it smashing through the window-pane out into the darkness.

Sambo was glad to make his escape. When he was gone, Legree seemed a little ashamed of his fit of alarm. He sat doggedly down in his chair, and began sullenly sipping his tumbler of punch.

Cassy prepared herself for going out, unobserved by him; and slipped away to minister to poor Tom, as we have already related.

And what was the matter with Legree? and what was there in a simple curl of fair hair to appal that brutal man, familiar with any form of cruelty? To answer this, we must carry the reader backward in his history. Hard and reprobate as the godless man seemed now, there had been a time when he had been rocked on the bosom of a mother – cradled with prayers and pious hymns – his now seared brow bedewed with the waters of holy baptism. In early childhood a fair-haired woman had led him, at the sound of Sabbath bell, to worship and to pray. For in New England that mother had trained her only son with long, unwearied love, and patient prayers. Born of a hard-tempered sire, on whom that gentle woman had wasted a world of unvalued love, Legree had followed in the steps of his father. Boisterous, unruly, and tyrannical, he despised all her counsel, and would none of her reproof; and, at an early age, broke from her to seek his fortunes at sea. He never came home but once after; and then his mother, with the yearning of a heart that must love something, and has nothing else to love, clung to him, and sought, with passionate prayers and entreaties, to win him from a life of sin to his soul's eternal good.

That was Legree's day of grace. Then good angels called him; then he was almost persuaded, and Mercy held him by the hand. His heart inly relented – there was a conflict – but sin got the victory, and he set all the force of his rough nature against the conviction of his conscience. He drank and swore, was wilder and more brutal than ever. And one night, when his mother, in the last agony of her despair, knelt at his feet, he spurned her from him, threw her senseless on the floor, and, with brutal curses, fled to his ship. The next Legree heard of his mother was when one night, as he was carousing among drunken companions, a letter was put into his hand. He opened it, and a lock of long, curling hair fell from it, and twined about his fingers. The letter told him his mother was dead, and that, dying, she blessed and forgave him.

There is a dread, unhallowed necromancy of evil, that turns things sweetest and holiest to phantoms of horror and affright. That pale, loving mother – her dying prayers, her forgiving love – wrought in that demoniac heart of sin only as a damning sentence, bringing with it a fearful looking for of judgment and fiery indignation. Legree burned the hair, and burned the letter; and when he saw them hissing and crackling in the flame, inly shuddered as he thought of everlasting fires. He tried to drink, and revel, and swear away the memory; but often, in the deep night, whose solemn stillness arraigns the bad soul in forced communion with herself, he had seen that pale mother rising by his bedside, and felt the soft twining of that hair around his fingers till the cold sweat would roll down his face, and he would spring from his bed in horror. Ye who have wondered to hear, in the same evangel, that 'God is love,' and that 'God is a consuming fire,' see ye not how, to the soul resolved in evil, perfect love is the most fearful torture, the seal and sentence of the direst despair?

'Blast it!' said Legree to himself, as he sipped his liquor, 'where did he get that? If it didn't look just like – whoo! I thought I'd forgot that. Curse me if I think there's any such thing as forgetting anything, any how – hang it! I'm lonesome! I mean to call Em. She hates me – the monkey! I don't care – I'll *make* her come!'

Legree stepped out into a large entry, which went upstairs, by what had formerly been a superb winding-staircase; but the passage-way was dirty and dreary, encumbered with boxes and unsightly litter. The stairs, uncarpeted, seemed winding up, in the gloom, to nobody knew where. The pale moonlight streamed through a shattered fanlight over the door, the air was unwholesome and chilly, like that of a vault.

Legree stopped at the foot of the stairs, and heard a voice singing. It seemed strange and ghost-like in that dreary old house, perhaps because of the already tremulous state of his nerves. Hark! what is it?

A wild, pathetic voice, chants a hymn common among the slaves:

'Oh there'll be mourning, mourning, mourning,
Oh there'll be mourning, at the judgment-seat of Christ!'

'Blast the girl!' said Legree. 'I'll choke her – Em! Em!' he called harshly: but only a mocking echo from the walls answered him. The sweet voice still sung on: –

'Parents and children there shall part
Parents and children there shall part
Shall part to meet no more!'

And clear and loud swelled through the empty halls the refrain –

'Oh there'll be mourning, mourning, mourning,
Oh there'll be mourning, at the judgment-seat of Christ!'

Legree stopped. He would have been ashamed to tell of it, but large drops of sweat stood on his forehead, his heart beat heavy and thick with fear; he even thought he saw something white rising and glimmering in the gloom before him, and shuddered to think what if the form of his dead mother should suddenly appear to him.

'I know one thing,' he said to himself, as he stumbled back in the sitting-room, and sat down; 'I'll let that fellow alone after this! What did I want of his cussed paper? I b'lieve I am bewitched, sure enough! I've been shivering and sweating ever since! Where did he get that hair? It couldn't have been *that*! I burnt *that* up, I know I did! It would be a joke if hair could rise from the dead!'

Ah, Legree! that golden tress *was* charmed; each hair had in it a spell of terror and remorse for thee, and was used by a mightier power to bind thy cruel hands from inflicting uttermost evil on the helpless!

'I say,' said Legree, stamping and whistling to the dogs, 'wake up, some of you, and keep me company!' but the dogs only opened one eye at him sleepily, and closed it again.

'I'll have Sambo and Quimbo up here to sing, and dance one of their hell dances, and keep off these horrid notions,' said Legree; and, putting on his hat, he went on to the verandah and blew a horn, with which he commonly summoned his two sable drivers.

Legree was often wont, when in a gracious humour, to get these two worthies into his sitting-room, and, after warming them up with whisky, amuse himself by setting them to singing, dancing, or fighting, as the humour took him.

It was between one and two o'clock at night, as Cassy was returning from her ministrations to poor Tom, that she heard the sound of wild shrieking, whooping, hallooing, and singing from the sitting-room, mingled with the barking of dogs, and other symptoms of general uproar.

She came up on the verandah steps, and looked in. Legree and both the drivers, in a state of furious intoxication, were singing, whooping, upsetting chairs, and making all manner of ludicrous and horrid grimaces at each other.

She rested her small, slender hand on the window-blind, and looked fixedly at them. There was a world of anguish, scorn, and fierce bitterness in her black eyes as she did so. 'Would it be a sin to rid the world of such a wretch?' she said to herself.

She turned hurriedly away, and, passing round to a back door, glided upstairs, and tapped at Emmeline's door.

Chapter 36

EMMELINE AND CASSY

CASSY entered the room, and found Emmeline sitting, pale with fear, in the furthest corner of it. As she came in, the girl started up nervously; but, on seeing who it was, rushed forward, and, catching her arm, said, 'O, Cassy, is it you? I'm so glad you've come! I was afraid it was—. Oh, you don't know what a horrid noise there has been downstairs all this evening!'

'I ought to know,' said Cassy, dryly. 'I've heard it often enough!'

'O Cassy, do tell me; couldn't we get away from this place? I don't care where – into the swamp among the snakes – anywhere! *Couldn't* we get *somewhere* away from here?'

'Nowhere but into our graves,' said Cassy.

'Did you ever try?'

'I've seen enough of trying, and what comes of it?' said Cassy.

'I'd be willing to live in the swamps, and gnaw the bark from trees. I an't afraid of snakes! I'd rather have one near me than him,' said Emmeline, eagerly.

'There have been a good many here of your opinion,' said Cassy. 'But you could not stay in the swamps – you'd be tracked by the dogs, and brought back, and then – then – '

'What would he do?' said the girl, looking with breathless interest into her face.

'What *wouldn't* he do, you'd better ask,' said Cassy. 'He's learned his trade well among the pirates in the West Indies. You wouldn't sleep much if I should tell you things I've seen – things that he tells of, sometimes, for good jokes. I've heard screams here that I haven't been able to get out of my head for weeks and weeks. There's a place way out down by the quarters, where you can see a black, blasted tree, and the ground all covered with black ashes. Ask any one what was done there, and see if they will dare to tell you.'

'Oh, what do you mean ?'

'I won't tell you. I hate to think of it. And I tell you, the Lord only knows what we may see to-morrow, if that poor fellow holds out as he's begun.'

'Horrid !' said Emmeline, every drop of blood receding from her cheeks. 'O Cassy, do tell me what I shall do !'

'What I've done. Do the best you can ; do what you must, and make it up in hating and cursing.'

'He wanted to make me drink some of his hateful brandy,' said Emmeline ; 'and I hate it so—'

'You'd better drink,' said Cassy. 'I hated it, too ; and now I can't live without it. One must have something ; things don't look so dreadful when you take that.'

'Mother used to tell me never to touch any such thing,' said Emmeline.

'*Mother* told you !' said Cassy, with a thrilling and bitter emphasis on the word mother. 'What use is it for mothers to say anything ? You are all to be bought and paid for, and your souls belong to whoever gets you. That's the way it goes. I say, *drink* brandy : drink all you can, and it'll make things come easier.'

'O Cassy ! do pity me !'

'Pity you ! don't I ? Haven't I a daughter ? – Lord knows where she is, and whose she is now ! Going the way her mother went before her, I suppose, and that her children must go after her ! There's no end to the curse for ever !'

'I wish I'd never been born !' said Emmeline, wringing her hands.

'That's an old wish with me,' said Cassy. 'I've got used to wishing that. I'd die, if I dared to,' she said, looking out into the darkness with that still, fixed despair, which was the habitual expression of her face when at rest.

'It would be wicked to kill one's self,' said Emmeline.

'I don't know why ; no wickeder than things we live and do day after day. But the sisters told me things when I was in the convent that make me afraid to die. If it would only be the end of us, why then—'

Emmeline turned away and hid her face in her hands.

While this conversation was passing in the chamber, Legree, overcome with his carouse, had sank to sleep in the room below. Legree was not an habitual drunkard. His coarse, strong nature, craved and could endure a continual stimulation, that would have utterly wrecked and crazed a finer one. But a deep underlying spirit of cautiousness prevented his often yielding to appetite in such measure as to lose control of himself.

This night, however, in his feverish efforts to banish from his mind those fearful elements of woe and remorse which woke within him, he had indulged more than common; so that, when he had discharged his sable attendants, he fell heavily on a settle in the room, and was sound asleep.

Oh, how dares the bad soul to enter the shadowy world of sleep? – that land whose dim outlines lie so fearfully near to the mystic scene of retribution! Legree dreamed. In his heavy and feverish sleep a veiled form stood beside him, and laid a cold, soft hand upon him. He thought he knew who it was; and shuddered, with creeping horror, though the face was veiled. Then he thought he felt *that hair* twining round his fingers; and then, that it slid smoothly round his neck, and tightened, and tightened, and he could not draw his breath; and then he thought voices *whispered* to him – whispers that chilled him with horror. Then it seemed to him he was on the edge of a frightful abyss, holding on and struggling in mortal fear, while dark hands stretched up, and were pulling him over; and Cassy came behind him, laughing, and pushed him. And then rose up that solemn veiled figure, and drew aside the veil. It was his mother; and she turned away from him, and he fell down, down, down, amid a confused noise of shrieks, and groans, and shouts of demon laughter: – and Legree awoke.

Calmly the rosy hue of dawn was stealing into the room. The morning star stood, with its solemn, holy eye of light, looking down on the man of sin, from out the brightening sky. Oh, with what freshness, what solemnity and beauty, is each new day born; as if to say to insensate men, 'Behold! thou hast one more chance! *Strive* for immortal glory!' There is no speech nor language where this voice is not heard; but the bold, bad man, heard it not. He woke with an oath and a curse. What to him was the gold and purple, the daily miracle of morning! What to him the sanctity of that star which the Son of God has hallowed as his own emblem? Brute-like, he saw without perceiving; and, stumbling forward, poured out a tumbler of brandy, and drank half of it.

'I've had a h—l of a night!' he said to Cassy, who just then entered from an opposite door.

'You'll get plenty of the same sort by and by,' said she, dryly.

'What do you mean, you minx?'

'You'll find out, one of these days,' returned Cassy in the same tone. 'Now, Simon, I've one piece of advice to give you.'

'The devil you have!'

'My advice is,' said Cassy steadily, as she began adjusting some things about the room, 'that you let Tom alone.'

'What business is't of yours?'

'What? To be sure, I don't know what it should be. If you want to pay twelve hundred for a fellow, and use him right up in the press of the season, just to serve your own spite, it's no business of mine. I've done what I could for him.'

'You have? What business have you meddling in my matters?'

'None, to be sure. I've saved you some thousands of dollars, at different times, by taking care of your hands – that's all the thanks I get. If your crop comes shorter into market than any of theirs, you won't lose your bet, I suppose? Tomkins won't lord it over you, I suppose; and you'll pay down your money like a lady, won't you? I think I see you doing it!'

Legree, like many other planters, had but one form of ambition – to have in the heaviest crop of the season; and he had several bets on this very present season pending in the next town. Cassy, therefore, with woman's tact, touched the only string that could be made to vibrate.

'Well, I'll let him off at what he's got,' said Legree; 'but he shall beg my pardon, and promise better fashions.'

'That he won't do,' said Cassy.

'Won't, eh?'

'No, he won't,' said Cassy.

'I'd like to know *why*, mistress,' said Legree, in the extreme of scorn.

'Because he's done right, and he knows it, and won't say he's done wrong.'

'Who a cuss cares what he knows? The nigger shall say what I please, or—'

'Or you'll lose your bet on the cotton crop, by keeping him out of the field just at this very press.'

'But he *will* give up, course he will ; don't I know what niggers is ? He'll beg like a dog this morning.'

'He won't, Simon ; you don't know this kind. You may kill him by inches, you won't get the first word of confession out of him.'

'We'll see. Where is he ?' said Legree, going out.

'In the waste-room of the gin-house,' said Cassy.

Legree, though he talked so stoutly to Cassy, still sailed forth from the house with a degree of misgiving which was not common with him. His dreams of the past night, mingled with Cassy's prudential suggestions, considerably affected his mind. He resolved that nobody should be witness of his encounter with Tom, and determined, if he could not subdue him by bullying, to defer his vengeance to be wreaked in a more convenient season.

The solemn light of dawn, the angelic glory of the morning-star, had looked in through the rude window of the shed where Tom was lying, and, as if descending on that star-beam, came the solemn words, 'I am the root and offspring of David, and the bright and morning-star.' The mysterious warnings and intimations of Cassy, so far from discouraging his soul, in the end had roused it as with a heavenly call. He did not know but that the day of his death was dawning in the sky ; and his heart throbbed with solemn throes of joy and desire, as he thought that the wondrous *all* on which he had often pondered, the great white throne, with its ever radiant rainbow ; the white-robed multitude, with voices as many waters ; the crowns, the palms, the harps – might all break upon his vision before that sun should set again ; and therefore, without shuddering or trembling, he heard the voice of his persecutor as he drew near.

'Well, my boy,' said Legree, with a contemptuous kick, 'how do you find yourself ? Didn't I tell yer I could larn yer a thing or two ? How do you like it, eh ? How did yer whaling agree with yer, Tom ? An't quite so crank as ye was last night ? Ye couldn't treat a poor sinner now to a bit of a sermon, could yer, eh ?'

Tom answered nothing.

'Get up, you beast !' said Legree, kicking him again.

This was a difficult matter for one so bruised and faint, and, as Tom made efforts to do so, Legree laughed brutally.

'What makes ye so spry this morning, Tom? Cotched cold, maybe, last night.'

Tom by this time had gained his feet, and was confronting his master with a steady, unmoved front.

'The devil you can!' said Legree, looking him over. 'I believe you haven't got enough yet. Now, Tom, get right down on yer knees and beg my pardon for yer shines last night.'

Tom did not move.

'Down, you dog!' said Legree, striking him with his riding-whip.

'Mas'r Legree,' said Tom, 'I can't do it. I did only what I thought was right. I shall do just so again, if ever the time comes. I never will do a cruel thing, come what may.'

'Yes; but ye don't know what may come, Master Tom. Ye think what you've got is something. I tell you 'tant anything – nothing a 'tall. How would ye like to be tied to a tree, and have a slow fire lit up around ye? Wouldn't that be pleasant – eh, Tom?'

'Mas'r,' said Tom, 'I know ye can do dreadful things; but' – he stretched himself upward and clasped his hands – 'but after ye've killed the body, there an't no more ye can do. And oh, there's all ETERNITY to come after that!'

ETERNITY! The word thrilled through the black man's soul with light and power as he spoke – it thrilled through the sinner's soul, too, like the bite of a scorpion. Legree gnashed on him with his teeth, but rage kept him silent; and Tom, like a man disenthralled, spoke in a clear and cheerful voice.

'Mas'r Legree, as ye bought me, I'll be a true and faithful servant to ye. I'll give ye all the work of my hands, all my time, all my strength; but my soul I won't give up to mortal man. I will hold on to the Lord, and put his commands before all, die or live, you may be sure on't. Mas'r Legree, I an't a grain afeared to die. I'd as soon die as not. Ye may whip me, starve me, burn me – it'll only send me sooner where I want to go.'

'I'll make ye give out, though, 'fore I've done!' said Legree, in a rage.

'I shall have *help*,' said Tom. 'You'll never do it.'

'Who the devil's going to help you?' said Legree, scornfully.

'The Lord Almighty !' said Tom.

'D—n you !' said Legree, as with one blow of his fist he felled Tom to the earth.

A cold soft hand fell on Legree's at this moment. He turned – it was Cassy's ; but the cold soft touch recalled his dream of the night before, and, flashing through the chambers of his brain, came all the fearful images of the night-watches, with a portion of the horror that accompanied them.

'Will you be a fool ? said Cassy in French. 'Let him go ! Let me alone to get him fit to be in the field again. Isn't it just as I told you ?'

They say the alligator and the rhinoceros, though enclosed in bullet-proof mail, have each a spot where they are vulnerable ; and fierce, reckless, unbelieving reprobates, have commonly this point in superstitious dread.

Legree turned away, determined to let the point go for the time.

'Well, have it your own way,' he said doggedly to Cassy. 'Hark ye !' he said to Tom, 'I won't deal with ye now, because the business is pressing, and I want all my hands ; but I *never* forget. I'll score it against ye, and some time I'll have my pay out o' yer old black hide – mind ye !'

Legree turned, and went out.

'There you go,' said Cassy, looking darkly after him ; 'your reckoning's to come yet ! My poor fellow, how are you ?'

'The Lord God hath sent his angel, and shut the lion's mouth for this time,' said Tom.

'For this time to be sure,' said Cassy ; 'but now you've got his ill-will upon you, to follow you, day in, day out, hanging like a dog on your throat ! sucking your blood, bleeding away your life, drop by drop ! I know the man !'

Chapter 37

LIBERTY

'No matter with what solemnities he may have been devoted upon the altar of slavery, the moment he touches the sacred soil of Britain, the altar and the god sink together in the dust, and he stands redeemed, regenerated and disenthralled, by the irresistible genius of universal emancipation.' – CURRAN.

A WHILE we must leave Tom in the hands of his persecutors, while we turn to pursue the fortunes of George and his wife, whom we left in friendly hands in a farm-house on the road-side.

Tom Loker we left groaning and touzling in a most immaculately clean Quaker bed, under the motherly supervision of Aunt Dorcas, who found him to the full as tractable a patient as a sick bison.

Imagine a tall, dignified, spiritual woman, whose clear muslin cap shades waves of silvery hair, parted on a broad, clear forehead, which overarches thoughtful grey eyes; a snowy handkerchief of lisse crape is folded neatly across her bosom; her glossy brown silk dress rustles peacefully as she glides up and down the chamber.

'The devil !' says Tom Loker, giving a great throw to the bed-clothes.

'I must request thee, Thomas, not to use such language,' says Aunt Dorcas, as she quietly re-arranged the bed.

'Well, I won't, granny, if I can help it,' says Tom; 'but it is enough to make a fellow swear, so cursedly hot !'

Dorcas removed a comforter from the bed, straightened the clothes again, and tucked them in till Tom looked something like a chrysalis, remarking, as she did so –

'I wish, friend, thee would leave off cursing and swearing, and think upon thy ways.'

'What the devil,' said Tom, 'should I think of *them* for ? Last thing ever *I* want to think of – hang it all !' And Tom flounced over, untucking and disarranging everything in a manner frightful to behold.

'That fellow and gal are here, I s'pose ?' said he sullenly, after a pause.

'They are so,' said Dorcas.

'They'd better be off up to the lake,' said Tom; 'the quicker the better.'

'Probably they will do so,' said Aunt Dorcas, knitting peacefully.

'And hark ye,' said Tom; 'we've got correspondents in Sandusky that watch the boats for us. I don't care if I tell now. I hope they *will* get away, just to spite Marks – the cursed puppy ! – d—n him !'

'Thomas !' said Dorcas.

'I tell you, granny, if you bottle a fellow up too tight, I shall split,' said Tom, 'But about the gal – tell 'em to dress her up some way so's to alter her. Her description's out in Sandusky.'

'We will attend to that matter,' said Dorcas, with characteristic composure.

As we at this place take leave of Tom Loker, we may as well say that, having lain three weeks at the Quaker dwelling, sick with a rheumatic fever, which set in in company with his other afflictions, Tom arose from his bed a somewhat sadder and wiser man; and, in place of slave-catching, betook himself to life in one of the new settlements, where his talents developed themselves more happily in trapping bears, wolves, and other inhabitants of the forest, in which he made himself quite a name in the land. Tom always spoke reverently of the Quakers. 'Nice people,' he would say; 'wanted to convert me, but couldn't come it exactly. But tell ye what, stranger, they do fix up a sick fellow first-rate, no mistake ! Make jist the tallest kind o' broth and knicknacks.'

As Tom had informed them that their party would be looked for in Sandusky, it was thought prudent to divide them. Jim, with his old mother, was forwarded separately; and, a night or two after, George and Eliza, with their child, were driven privately into Sandusky, and lodged beneath a hospitable roof, preparatory to taking their last passage on the lake.

Their night was now far spent, and the morning star of liberty rose fair before them. Liberty; electric word! What is it? Is there anything more in it than a name, a rhetorical flourish? Why, men and women of America, does your hearts' blood thrill at that word, for which your fathers bled and your braver mothers were willing that their noblest and best should die?

Is there anything in it glorious and dear for a nation, that is not also glorious and dear for a man? What is freedom to a nation, but freedom to the individuals in it? What is freedom to that young man who sits there with his arms folded over his broad chest, the tint of African blood in his cheek, its dark fires in his eye – what is freedom to George Harris? To your fathers, freedom was the right of a nation to be a nation. To him, it is the right of a man to be a man and not a brute; the right to call the wife of his bosom his wife, and to protect her from lawless violence; the right to protect and educate his child; the right to have a home of his own, a religion of his own, a character of his own, unsubject to the will of another. All these thoughts were rolling and seething in George's breast, as he was pensively leaning his head on his hand, watching his wife, as she was adapting to her slender and pretty form the articles of man's attire, in which it was deemed safest she should make her escape.

'Now for it,' said she, as she stood before the glass, and shook down her silky abundance of black curly hair. 'I say, George, it's almost a pity, isn't it?' she said, as she held up some of it playfully. 'Pity it's all got to come off?'

George smiled sadly, and made no answer.

Eliza turned to the glass, and the scissors glittered as one long lock after another was detached from her head.

'There now, that'll do,' she said, taking up a hair-brush; 'now for a few fancy touches.'

'There, an't I a pretty young fellow?' she said, turning round to her husband, laughing and blushing at the same time.

'You always will be pretty, do what you will,' said George.

'What does make you so sober?' said Eliza, kneeling on one knee and laying her hand on his. 'We are only within twenty-four hours of Canada, they say. Only a day and a night on the lake, and then – oh, then!'

'Oh, Eliza!' said George, drawing her towards him; 'that is it! Now my fate is all narrowing down to a point. To come so near, to be almost in sight, and then lose all ! I should never live under it, Eliza.'

'Don't fear,' said his wife hopefully. 'The good Lord would not have brought us so far if he didn't mean to carry us through. I seem to feel him with us, George.'

'You are a blessed woman, Eliza !' said George, clasping her with a convulsive grasp. 'But – oh, tell me ! can this great mercy be for us ? Will these years and years of misery come to an end ? – shall we be free ?'

'I am sure of it, George,' said Eliza, looking upward, while tears of hope and enthusiasm shone on her long, dark lashes. 'I feel it in me, that God is going to bring us out of bondage this very day.'

'I will believe you, Eliza,' said George, rising suddenly up. 'I will believe; come, let's be off. Well, indeed,' said he, holding her off at arm's length, and looking admiringly at her, 'you *are* a pretty little fellow. That crop of little, short curls is quite becoming. Put on your cap. So – a little to one side. I never saw you look quite so pretty. But it's almost time for the carriage; I wonder if Mrs Smyth has got Harry rigged ?'

The door opened, and a respectable middle-aged woman entered, leading little Harry, dressed in girl's clothes.

'What a pretty girl he makes,' said Eliza, turning him round. 'We call him Harriet, you see; don't the name come nicely ?'

The child stood gravely regarding his mother in her new and strange attire, observing a profound silence, and occasionally drawing deep sighs, and peeping at her from under his dark curls.

'Does Harry know mamma ?' said Eliza, stretching her hands towards him.

The child clung shyly to the woman.

'Come, Eliza, why do you try to coax him, when you know that he has got to be kept away from you ?'

'I know it's foolish,' said Eliza, 'yet I can't bear to have him turn away from me. But come – where's my cloak ? Here – how is it men put on cloaks, George ?'

'You must wear it so,' said her husband, throwing it over his shoulders.

'So then,' said Eliza, imitating the motion; 'and I must stamp, and take long steps, and try to look saucy.'

'Don't exert yourself,' said George. 'There is, now and then, a modest young man; and I think it would be easier for you to act that character.'

'And these gloves! mercy upon us!' said Eliza, 'why, my hands are lost in them.'

'I advise you to keep them on pretty strictly,' said George. 'Your little slender paw might bring us all out. Now, Mrs Smyth, you are to go under our charge, and be our aunty – you mind.'

'I've heard,' said Mrs Smyth, 'that there have been men down, warning all the packet-captains against a man and woman, with a little boy.'

'They have!' said George. 'Well, if we see any such people we can tell them.'

A hack now drove to the door, and the friendly family who had received the fugitives crowded around them with farewell greetings.

The disguises the party had assumed were in accordance with the hints of Tom Loker. Mrs Smyth, a respectable woman from the settlement in Canada, whither they were fleeing, being fortunately about crossing the lake to return thither, had consented to appear as the aunt of little Harry; and, in order to attach him to her, he had been allowed to remain, the two last days, under her sole charge; and an extra amount of petting, joined to an indefinite amount of seed-cakes and candy, had cemented a very close attachment on the part of the young gentleman.

The hack drove to the wharf. The two young men, as they appeared, walked up the plank into the boat, Eliza gallantly giving her arm to Mrs Smyth, and George attending to their baggage.

George was standing at the captain's office, settling for his party, when he overheard two men talking by his side.

'I've watched every one that came on board,' said one; 'and I know they're not on this boat.'

The voice was that of the clerk of the boat. The speaker whom he addressed was our sometime friend Marks, who, with that valuable perseverance which characterised him, had come on to Sandusky, seeking whom he might devour.

'You would scarcely know the woman from a white one,' said

Marks. 'The man is a very light mulatto. He has a brand in one of his hands.'

The hand with which George was taking the tickets and change trembled a little; but he turned coolly round, fixed an unconcerned glance on the face of the speaker, and walked leisurely toward another part of the boat, where Eliza stood waiting for him.

Mrs Smyth, with little Harry, sought the seclusion of the ladies' cabin, where the dark beauty of the supposed little girl drew many flattering comments from the passengers.

George had the satisfaction, as the bell rang out its farewell peal, to see Marks walk down the plank to the shore; and drew a long sigh of relief when the boat had put a returnless distance between them.

It was a superb day. The blue waves of Lake Erie danced rippling and sparkling in the sunlight. A fresh breeze blew from the shore, and the lordly boat ploughed her way right gallantly onward.

Oh, what an untold world there is in one human heart! Who thought, as George walked calmly up and down the deck of the steamer, with his shy companion at his side, of all that was burning in his bosom? The mighty good that seemed approaching seemed too good, too fair, even to be a reality; and he felt a jealous dread every moment of the day that something would rise to snatch it from him.

But the boat swept on – hours fleeted, and, at last, clear and full rose the blessed English shore – shores charmed by a mighty spell – with one touch to dissolve every incantation of slavery, no matter in what language pronounced, or by what national power confirmed.

George and his wife stood arm in arm as the boat neared the small town of Amherstberg, in Canada. His breath grew thick and short; a mist gathered before his eyes; he silently pressed the little hand that lay trembling on his arm. The bell rang – the boat stopped. Scarcely seeing what he did, he looked out his baggage, and gathered his little party. The little company were landed on the shore. They stood still till the boat had cleared; and then, with tears and embracings, the husband and wife, with their wondering child in their arms, knelt down and lifted up their hearts to God!

"'T was something like the burst from death to life ;
From the grave's cerements to the robes of heaven ;
From sin's dominion, and from passion's strife,
To the pure freedom of a soul forgiven ;
Where all the bonds of death and hell are riven,
And mortal puts on immortality,
When Mercy's hand hath turned the golden key,
And Mercy's voice hath said, "Rejoice, thy soul is free !" '

The little party were soon guided by Mrs Smyth to the hospitable abode of a good missionary, whom Christian charity has placed here as a shepherd to the outcast and wandering, who are constantly finding an asylum on this shore.

Who can speak the blessedness of that first day of freedom ? Is not the *sense* of liberty a higher and a finer one than any of the five ? To move, speak, and breathe, go out and come in, unwatched and free from danger ! Who can speak the blessings of that rest which comes down on the free man's pillow, under laws which ensure to him the rights that God has given to man ? How fair and precious to that mother was that sleeping child's face, endeared by the memory of a thousand dangers ! How impossible was it to sleep in the exuberant possession of such blessedness ! And yet these two had not one acre of ground, not a roof that they could call their own ; they had spent their all, to the last dollar. They had nothing more than the birds of the air, or the flowers of the field – yet they could not sleep for joy. 'O ye who take freedom from man, with what words shall ye answer it to God ?'

Chapter 38

THE VICTORY

'Thanks be unto God, who giveth us the victory.'

HAVE not many of us, in the weary way of life, felt, in some hours, how far easier it were to die than to live?

The martyr, when faced even by a death of bodily anguish and horror, finds in the very terror of his doom a strong stimulant and tonic. There is a vivid excitement, a thrill and fervour, which may carry through any crisis of suffering that is the birth-hour of eternal glory and rest.

But to live, to wear on day after day of mean, bitter, low, harassing servitude, every nerve damped and depressed, every power of feeling gradually smothered – this long and wasting heart-martyrdom, this slow, daily bleeding away of the inward life, drop by drop, hour after hour – this is the true searching test of what there may be in man or woman.

When Tom stood face to face with his persecutor, and heard his threats, and thought in his very soul that his hour was come, his heart swelled bravely in him, and he thought he could bear torture and fire, bear anything, with the vision of Jesus and heaven but just a step beyond; but when he was gone, and the present excitement passed off, came back the pain of his bruised and weary limbs, came back the sense of his utterly degraded, hopeless, forlorn estate: and the day passed wearily enough.

Long before his wounds were healed, Legree insisted that he should be put to the regular field-work; and then came day after day of pain and weariness, aggravated by every kind of injustice and indignity that the ill-will of a mean and malicious mind could devise. Whoever, in *our* circumstances, has made trial of pain, even with all the alleviations which for us usually attend it, must know the irritation that comes with it. Tom no longer wondered at the habitual surliness of his associates; nay, he found the placid, sunny temper which had been the habitude of his life broken in on and sorely strained by the inroads of the same thing. He had flattered himself on leisure to read his Bible, but there was no such thing as leisure there. In the height of the season, Legree did not hesitate to press all his hands through Sundays and week-days alike. Why shouldn't he? He made more cotton by it, and gained his wager; and if it wore out a few more hands, he could buy better ones. At first Tom used to read a verse or two of his Bible, by the flicker of the fire, after he had returned from his daily toil; but, after the cruel treatment he received, he used to come home so exhausted that his head swam and his eyes failed when he tried to read, and he was fain to stretch himself down with the others in utter exhaustion.

Is it strange that the religious peace and trust which had upborne him hitherto should give way to tossings of soul and despondent darkness. The gloomiest problem of this mysterious life was constantly before his eyes: souls crushed and ruined, evil triumphant, and God silent. It was weeks and months that Tom wrestled, in his own soul, in darkness and sorrow. He thought of Miss Ophelia's letter to his Kentucky friends and would pray earnestly that God would send him deliverance; and then he would watch, day after day, in the vague hope of seeing somebody sent to redeem him; and, when nobody came, he would crush back to his soul bitter thoughts – that it was vain to serve God, that God had forgotten him. He sometimes saw Cassy; and sometimes, when summoned to the house, caught a glimpse of the dejected form of Emmeline, but held very little communion with either; in fact, there was no time for him to commune with anybody.

One evening he was sitting in utter dejection and prostration by a few decayed brands, where his coarse supper was baking. He put a few bits of brushwood on the fire, and strove to raise the light, and then drew his worn Bible from his pocket. There were all the marked passages which had thrilled his soul so often – words of patriarchs and seers, poets and sages, who from early time had spoken courage to man – voices from the great cloud of witnesses who ever surround us in the race of life. Had the word lost its power, or could the failing eye and weary sense no longer answer to the touch of that mighty inspiration? Heavily sighing, he put it in his pocket. A coarse laugh roused him; he looked up – Legree was standing opposite to him.

'Well, old boy,' he said, 'you find your religion don't work, it seems! I thought I should get that through your wool at last.'

The cruel taunt was more than hunger, and cold, and nakedness. Tom was silent.

'You were a fool, said Legree; 'for I meant to do well by you when I bought you. You might have been better off than Sambo, or Quimbo either, and had easy times; and, instead of getting cut up and thrashed every day or two, ye might have had liberty to lord it round, and cut up the other niggers; and ye might have had, now and then, a good warming of whiskey-punch. Come, Tom, don't you think you'd better be reasonable? Heave that ar old pack of trash in the fire and join my church!'

'The Lord forbid!' said Tom, fervently.

'You see the Lord an't going to help you; if he had been, he wouldn't have let *me* get you! This yer religion is all a mess of lying trumpery, Tom. I know all about it. Ye'd better hold to me; I'm somebody, and can do something!'

'No, mas'r,' said Tom, 'I'll hold on. The Lord may help me, or not help; but I'll hold to Him, and believe Him to the last!'

'The more fool you!' said Legree, spitting scornfully at him, and spurning him with his foot. 'Never mind, I'll chase you down yet, and bring you under, you'll see!' and Legree turned away.

When a heavy weight presses the soul to the lowest level at which endurance is possible, there is an instant and desperate effort of every physical and moral nerve to throw off the weight; and hence the heaviest anguish often precedes a return tide of joy and courage. So was it now with Tom. The atheistic taunts of his cruel master sunk his before dejected soul to the lowest ebb; and though the hand of faith still held to the eternal Rock, it was with a numb, despairing grasp. Tom sat like one stunned at the fire. Suddenly everything around him seemed to fade, and a vision rose before him of One crowned with thorns, buffeted and bleeding. Tom gazed in awe and wonder at the majestic patience of the face; the deep pathetic eyes thrilled him to his inmost heart; his soul woke, as, with floods of emotion, he stretched out his hands and fell upon his knees; when gradually the vision changed, the sharp thorns became rays of glory, and in splendour inconceivable he saw that same face bending compassionately towards him, and a voice said, 'He that overcometh shall sit down with me on my throne, even as I also overcame, and am set down with my Father on his throne.'

How long Tom lay there he knew not. When he came to himself, the fire was gone out, his clothes were wet with the chill and drenching dews; but the dread soul-crisis was past, and, in the joy that filled him, he no longer felt hunger, cold, degradation, disappointment, wretchedness. From his deepest soul, he that hour loosed and parted from every hope in the life that now is, and offered his own will an unquestioning sacrifice to the Infinite. Tom looked up to the silent, ever-living stars, types of the angelic hosts who ever look down on man; and the solitude of the night rung with the triumphant words of a hymn, which he had sung often in happier days, but never with such feeling as now: --

> 'The earth shall be dissolved like snow,
>   The sun shall cease to shine;
> But God, who called me here below,
>   Shall be for ever mine.
>
> 'And when this mortal life shall fail,
>   And flesh and sense shall cease,
> I shall possess within the veil
>   A life of joy and peace.
>
> 'When we've been there ten thousand years
>   Bright shining like the sun,
> We've no less days to sing God's praise
>   Than when we first begun.'

Those who have been familiar with the religious histories of the slave-population, know that relations like what we have narrated are very common among them. We have heard some from their own lips of a very touching and affecting character. The psychologist tells us of a state in which the affections and images of the mind become so dominant and overpowering, that they press into their service the outward senses, and make them give tangible shape to the inward imagining. Who shall measure what an all-pervading Spirit may do with these capabilities of our mortality, or the ways in which He may encourage the desponding souls of the desolate? If the poor forgotten slave believes that Jesus hath appeared and spoken to him, who shall contradict him? Did He not say that His mission in all ages was to bind up the broken-hearted, and set at liberty them that are bruised?

When the dim grey of dawn woke the slumberers to go forth to the field, there was among those tattered and shivering wretches one who walked with an exultant tread; for firmer than the ground he trod on was his strong faith in almighty, eternal Love. Ah, Legree! try all your forces now! Utmost agony, woe, degradation, want, and loss of all things, shall only hasten on the process by which he shall be made a king and a priest unto God!

From this time, an inviolable sphere of peace encompassed the lowly heart of the oppressed one – an ever-present Saviour hallowed it as a temple. Past now the bleeding of earthly regrets – past its fluctuations of hope, and fear, and desire – the human will, bent and bleeding, and struggling long, was now entirely merged in the divine. So short now seemed the remaining voyage of life – so near, so vivid, seemed eternal blessedness – that life's uttermost woes fell from him unharming.

All noticed the change in his appearance. Cheerfulness and alertness seemed to return to him, and a quietness which no insult or injury could ruffle seemed to possess him.

'What the devil's got into Tom?' Legree said to Sambo. 'A while ago he was all down in the mouth, and now he's peart as a cricket.'

'Dunno, mas'r; gwine to run off, mebbe.'

'Like to see him try that,' said Legree, with a savage grin; 'wouldn't we, Sambo?'

'Guess we would! haw! haw! ho!' said the sooty gnome, laughing obsequiously. 'Lord, de fun! To see him stickin' in the mud, chasin' and tearin' through de bushes, dogs a-holdin' on to him! Lord, I laughed fit to split, dat ar' time we cotched Molly. I thought they'd had her all stripped up afore I could get 'em off. She car's de marks o' dat ar' spree yet.'

'I reckon she will to her grave,' said Legree. 'But now, Sambo, you look sharp! If the nigger's got anything of this sort going, trip him up.'

'Mas'r, let me 'lone for dat!' said Sambo. 'I'll tree de coon! Ho! ho! ho!'

This was spoken as Legree was getting on to his horse to go to the neighbouring town. That night, as he was returning, he thought he would turn his horse and ride round the quarters, and see if all was safe.

It was a superb moonlight night, and the shadows of the graceful china-trees lay minutely pencilled on the turf below, and there was that transparent stillness in the air which it seems almost unholy to disturb. Legree was at a little distance from the quarters when he heard the voice of some one singing. It was not a usual sound there, and he paused to listen. A musical tenor voice sung —

> 'When I can read my title clear
>   To mansions in the skies,
> I bid farewell to every fear,
>   And wipe my weeping eyes.
>
> 'Should earth against my soul engage,
>   And hellish darts be hurled,
> Then I can smile at Satan's rage,
>   And face a frowning world.
>
> 'Let cares like a wild deluge come,
>   And storms of sorrow fall,
> May I but safely reach my home,
>   My God, my heaven, my all!'

'So ho!' said Legree to himself, 'he thinks so, does he? How I hate these cursed Methodist hymns! Here, you nigger!' said he, coming suddenly out upon Tom, and raising his riding-whip, 'how dare you be gettin' up this yer row, when you ought to be in bed? Shut yer old black gash, and get along in with you.'

'Yes, mas'r,' said Tom, with ready cheerfulness, as he rose to go in.

Legree was provoked beyond measure by Tom's evident happiness! and, riding up to him, belaboured him over his head and shoulders.

'There, you dog,' he said, 'see if you feel so comfortable after that!'

But the blows fell now only on the outer man, and not, as

before, on the heart. Tom stood perfectly submissive; and yet Legree could not hide from himself that his power over his bond-thrall was somehow gone. And as Tom disappeared in his cabin, and he wheeled his horse suddenly round, there passed through his mind one of those vivid flashes that often send the lightning of conscience across the dark and wicked soul. He understood full well that it was God who was standing between him and his victim, and he blasphemed Him. That submissive and silent man, whom taunts, nor threats, nor stripes, nor cruelties could disturb, roused a voice within him, such as of old his Master roused in the demoniac soul, saying, 'What have we to do with thee, thou Jesus of Nazareth? Art thou come to torment us before the time?'

Tom's whole soul overflowed with compassion and sympathy for the poor wretches by whom he was surrounded. To him it seemed as if his life-sorrows were now over, and as if, out of that strange treasury of peace and joy with which he had been endowed from above, he longed to pour out something for the relief of their woes. It is true, opportunities were scanty; but on the way to the fields and back again, and during the hours of labour, chances fell in his way of extending a helping hand to the weary, the disheartened and discouraged. The poor, worn-down, brutalised creatures, at first could scarcely comprehend this; but when it was continued week after week, and month after month, it began to awaken long-silent chords in their benumbed hearts. Gradually and imperceptibly the strange, silent, patient man, who was ready to bear every one's burden, and sought help from none – who stood aside for all, and came last, and took least, yet was foremost to share his little all with any who needed – the man who, in cold nights, would give up his tattered blanket to add to the comfort of some woman who shivered with sickness, and who filled the baskets of the weaker ones in the field, at the terrible risk of coming short in his own measure – and who, though pursued with unrelenting cruelty by their common tyrant, never joined in uttering a word of reviling or cursing – this man as last began to have a strange power over them; and when the more pressing season was past, and they were allowed again their Sundays for their own use, many would gather together to hear from him of Jesus. They would gladly have met to hear, and pray, and sing, in some place together; but Legree would not permit it, and more than once broke up such attempts with oaths and brutal execrations, so that the blessed news had to circulate from individual to individual. Yet who can speak the simple joy with which some of those poor outcasts, to whom life was a joyless journey to a dark unknown, heard of a compassionate Redeemer and a heavenly home? It is the statement of missionaries that, of all races of the earth, none have received the Gospel with such eager docility as the African. The principle of reliance and unquestioning faith which is its foundation is more a native element in this race than any other; and it has so often been found among them, that a stray seed of truth, borne on some breeze of accident into hearts the most ignorant, has sprung up into fruit, whose abundance has shamed that of higher and more skilful culture.

The poor mulatto woman, whose simple faith had been well nigh crushed and overwhelmed by the avalanche of cruelty and wrong which had fallen upon her, felt her soul raised up by the hymns and passages of Holy Writ which this lowly missionary breathed into her ear in intervals, as they were going to and returning from work; and even the half-crazed and wandering mind of Cassy was soothed and calmed by his simple and unobtrusive influences.

Stung to madness and despair by the crushing agonies of a life, Cassy had often resolved in her soul an hour of retribution, when her hand should avenge on her oppressor all the injustice and cruelty to which she had been witness, or which *she* had in her own person suffered.

One night, after all in Tom's cabin were sunk in sleep, he was suddenly aroused by seeing her face at the hole between the logs that served for a window. She made a silent gesture for him to come out.

Tom came out the door. It was between one and two o'clock at night – broad, calm, still moonlight. Tom remarked, as the light of the moon fell upon Cassy's large, black eyes, that there was a wild and peculiar glare in them, unlike their wonted fixed despair.

'Come here, Father Tom,' she said, laying her small hand on his wrist, and drawing him forward with a force as if the hand were of steel; 'come here – I've news for you.'

'What, Misse Cassy?' said Tom, anxiously.

'Tom, wouldn't you like your liberty?'

'I shall have it, misse, in God's time,' said Tom.

'Ay, but you may have it to-night,' said Cassy, with a flash of sudden energy. 'Come on.'

Tom hesitated.

'Come!' said she in a whisper, fixing her black eyes on him. 'Come along! He's asleep – sound. I put enough into his brandy to keep him so. I wish I'd had more, I shouldn't have wanted you. But come, the back door is unlocked; there is an axe there. I put it there – his room door is open; I'll show you the way. I'd a done it myself, only my arms are so weak. Come along!'

'Not for ten thousand worlds, misse!' said Tom firmly, stopping and holding her back, as she was pressing forward.

'But think of all these poor creatures,' said Cassy. 'We might set them all free, and go somewhere in the swamps and find an island and live by ourselves; I've heard of its being done. Any life is better than this.'

'No!' said Tom firmly. 'No! good never comes of wickedness. I'd sooner chop my right hand off!'

'Then *I* shall do it,' said Cassy, turning.

'O Misse Cassy!' said Tom, throwing himself before her, 'for the dear Lord's sake that died for ye, don't sell your precious soul to the devil that way! Nothing but evil will come of it. The Lord hasn't called us to wrath. We must suffer, and wait His time.'

'Wait!' said Cassy. 'Haven't I waited? – waited till my head is dizzy and my heart sick? What has he made me suffer? What has he made hundreds of poor creatures suffer? Isn't he wringing the life-blood out of you! I'm called on! they call me! His time's come, and I'll have his heart's blood!'

'No, no, no!' said Tom, holding her small hands, which were clenched with spasmodic violence. 'No, ye poor, lost soul, that ye mustn't do! The dear, blessed Lord, never shed no blood but his own, and that he poured out for us when we was enemies. Lord, help us to follow his steps and love our enemies!'

'Love!' said Cassy, with a fierce glare, 'love *such* enemies! It isn't in flesh and blood.'

'No, misse, it isn't,' said Tom, looking up; 'but *He* gives it to us, and that's the *victory*. When we can love and pray over all and through all, the battle's past and the victory's come – glory be to God!' And, with streaming eyes and choking voice, the black man looked up to heaven.

And this, O Africa! – latest called of nations, called to the crown of thorns, the scourge, the bloody sweat, the cross of agony – this is to be *thy* victory; by this shalt thou reign with Christ when his kingdom shall come on earth.

The deep fervour of Tom's feelings, the softness of his voice, his tears, fell like dew on the wild, unsettled spirit of the poor woman. A softness gathered over the lurid fires of her eye; she looked down, and Tom could feel the relaxing muscles of her hands as she said –

'Didn't I tell you that evil spirits followed me? O Father Tom, I can't pray! I wish I could. I never have prayed since my children were sold! What you say must be right – I know it must; but when I try to pray, I can only hate and curse. I can't pray!'

'Poor soul,' said Tom, compassionately. 'Satan desires to have ye, and sift ye as wheat. I pray the Lord for ye. O Misse Cassy, turn to the dear Lord Jesus. He came to bind up the broken-hearted, and comfort all that mourn!'

Cassy stood silent, while large, heavy tears dropped from her downcast eyes.

'Misse Cassy,' said Tom, in a hesitating tone, after surveying her a moment in silence, 'if ye only could get away from here – if the thing was possible – I'd 'vise ye and Emmeline to do it; that is, if ye could go without blood-guiltiness – not otherwise.'

'Would you try it with us, Father Tom?'

'No,' said Tom; 'time was when I would; but the Lord's given me a work among these yer poor souls, and I'll stay with 'em and bear my cross with 'em till the end. It's different with you; it's a snare to you – it's more'n you can stand; and you'd better go, if you can.'

'I know no way but through the grave,' said Cassy. 'There's no beast or bird but can find a home somewhere, even the snakes and the alligators have their places to lie down and be quiet; but there's no place for us. Down in the darkest swamps the dogs will hunt us out, and find us. Everybody and everything is against us, even the very beasts side against us; and where shall we go?'

Tom stood silent; at length he said –

'Him that saved Daniel in the den of lions – that saved the children in the fiery furnace – Him that walked on the sea and bade the winds be still – He's alive yet; and I've faith to believe He can deliver you. Try it, and I'll pray with all my might for you.'

By what strange law of mind is it that an idea long overlooked, and trodden under foot as a useless stone, suddenly sparkles out in new light, as a discovered diamond?

Cassy had often revolved, for hours, all possible or probable schemes of escape, and dismissed them all as hopeless and impracticable; but at this moment there flashed through her mind a plan, so simple and feasible in all its details, as to awaken an instant hope.

'Father Tom, I'll try it!' she said suddenly.

'Amen!' said Tom. 'The Lord help ye!'

Chapter 39

THE STRATAGEM

'The way of the wicked is as darkness; they know not at what they stumble.'

THE garret of the house that Legree occupied, like most other garrets, was a great desolate space, dusty, hung with cobwebs, and littered with cast-off lumber. The opulent family that had inhabited the house in the days of its splendour had imported a great deal of splendid furniture, some of which they had taken away with them, while some remained standing desolate in mouldering, unoccupied rooms, or stored away in this place. One or two immense packing-boxes, in which this furniture was brought, stood against the sides of the garret. There was a small window there, which let in through its dingy, dusty panes, a scanty, uncertain light on the tall, high-backed chairs and dusty tables, that had once seen better days. Altogether, it was a weird and ghostly place; but, ghostly as it was, it wanted not in legends among the superstitious negroes to increase its terrors. Some few years before, a negro woman who had incurred Legree's displeasure was confined there for several weeks. What passed there we do not say; the negroes used to whisper darkly to each other; but it was known that the body of the unfortunate creature was one day taken down from there, and buried; and after that it was said that oaths and cursings, and the sound of violent blows, used to ring through that old garret, and mingled with wailings and groans of despair. Once, when Legree chanced to overhear something of this kind, he flew into a violent passion, and swore that the next one that told stories about that garret should have an opportunity of knowing what was there, for he would chain him up there for a week. This hint was enough to repress talking, though, of course, it did not disturb the credit of the story in the least.

Gradually the staircase that led to the garret, and even the passage-way to the staircase, were avoided by every one in the house, from every one fearing to speak of it, and the legend was gradually falling into desuetude. It had suddenly occurred to Cassy to make use of the superstitious excitability which was so great in Legree for the purpose of her liberation, and that of her fellow sufferer.

The sleeping-room of Cassy was directly under the garret. One day, without consulting Legree, she suddenly took it upon her, with some considerable ostentation, to change all the furniture and appurtenances of the room to one at some considerable distance. The under-servants, who were called on to effect this movement, were running and bustling about with great zeal and confusion, when Legree returned from a ride.

'Halloa! you Cass!' said Legree; 'what's in the wind now?'

'Nothing; only I choose to have another room,' said Cassy, doggedly.

'And what for, pray?' said Legree.

'I choose to,' said Cassy.

'The devil you do! And what for?'

'I'd like to get some sleep, now and then.'

'Sleep! well, what hinders your sleeping?'

'I could tell, I suppose, if you want to hear,' said Cassy, drily.

'Speak out, you minx !' said Legree.

'Oh ! nothing. I suppose it wouldn't disturb *you* ! Only groans, and people scuffling, and rolling round on the garret-floor half the night, from twelve to morning.'

'People up garret !' said Legree, uneasily, but forcing a laugh ; 'who are they, Cassy ?'

Cassy raised her sharp black eyes, and looked in the face of Legree with an expression that went through his bones as she said, 'To be sure, Simon, who are they ? I'd like to have *you* tell me. You don't know, I suppose !'

With an oath, Legree struck at her with his riding-whip ; but she glided to one side, and passed through the door, and looking back, said, 'If you'll sleep in that room, you'll know all about it. Perhaps you'd better try it !' and then immediately she shut and locked the door.

Legree blustered and swore, and threatened to break down the door; but apparently thought better of it, and walked uneasily into the sitting-room. Cassy perceived that her shaft had struck home; and from that hour, with the most exquisite address, she never ceased to continue the train of influences she had begun.

In a knot-hole in the garret she had inserted the neck of an old bottle, in such a manner that when there was the least wind, most doleful and lugubrious wailing sounds proceeded from it, which, in a high wind, increased to a perfect shriek, such as to credulous and superstitious ears might easily seem to be that of horror and despair.

These sounds were from time to time heard by the servants, and revived in full force the memory of the old ghost legend. A superstitious creeping horror seemed to fill the house; and though no one dared to breathe it to Legree, he found himself encompassed by it as by an atmosphere.

No one is so thoroughly superstitious as the godless man. The Christian is composed by the belief of a wise, all-ruling Father, whose presence fills the void unknown with light and order ; but to the man who has dethroned God the spirit-land is, indeed, in the words of the Hebrew poet, 'a land of darkness and the shadow of death,' without any order, where the light is as darkness. Life and death to him are haunted grounds, filled with goblin forms of vague and shadowy dread.

Legree had had the slumbering moral element in him roused by his encounters with Tom – roused, only to be resisted by the determinate force of evil; but still there was a thrill and commotion of the dark, inner world, produced by every word, or prayer, or hymn, that reacted in superstitious dread.

The influence of Cassy over him was of a strange and singular kind. He was her owner, her tyrant, and tormentor. She was, as he knew, wholly, and without any possibility of help or redress, in his hands; and yet so it is, that the most brutal man cannot live in constant association with a strong female influence, and not be greatly controlled by it. When he first bought her, she was, as she had said, a woman delicately bred; and then he crushed her, without scruple, beneath the foot of his brutality. But as time, and debasing influences and despair, hardened womanhood within her and waked the fires of fiercer passions, she had become, in a measure, his mistress, and he alternately tyrannised over and dreaded her.

This influence had become more harassing and decided, since partial insanity had given a strange, weird, unsettled cast to all her words and language.

A night or two after this, Legree was sitting in the old sitting-room, by the side of a flickering wood fire, that threw uncertain glances round the room. It was a stormy, windy night, such as raises whole squadrons of nondescript noises in rickety old houses. Windows were rattling, shutters flapping, the wind carousing, rumbling, and tumbling down the chimney, and every once in a while puffing out smoke and ashes, as if a legion of spirits were coming after them. Legree laid down his paper, and seeing an old book lying on the table, which he had noticed Cassy reading the first part of the evening, took it up and began to turn it over. It was one of those collections of stories of bloody murders, ghostly legends, and supernatural visitations, which, coarsely got up and illustrated, have a strange fascination for one who once begins to read them.

Legree poohed and pished, but read, turning page after page, till, finally, after reading some way, he threw down the book with an oath.

'You don't believe in ghosts, do you, Cass?' said he, taking the tongs and settling the fire. 'I thought you'd more sense than to let noises scare *you*.'

'No matter what I believe,' said Cassy, sullenly.

'Fellows used to try to frighten me with their yarns at sea,' said Legree. 'Never come it round me that way. I'm too tough for any such trash, tell ye.'

Cassy sat looking intently at him in the shadow of the corner. There was that strange light in her eyes that always impressed Legree with uneasiness.

'Them noises was nothing but rats and the wind,' said Legree. 'Rats will make a devil of a noise. I used to hear 'em sometimes down in the hold of a ship; and wind – Lord's sake! ye can make anything out o' wind.'

Cassy knew Legree was uneasy under her eyes, and therefore she made no answer, but sat fixing them on him with that strange, unearthly expression as before.

'Come, speak out, woman – don't you think so?' said Legree.

'Can rats walk down stairs, and come walking through the entry, and open a door when you've locked it and set a chair against it?' said Cassy; 'and come walk, walk, walking right up to your bed, and put out their hand, so?'

Cassy kept her glittering eyes fixed on Legree as she spoke, and he stared at her like a man in the nightmare, till, when she finished by laying her hand, icy cold, on his, he sprang back with an oath.

'Woman! What do you mean? Nobody did!'

'Oh, no – of course not – did I say they did?' said Cassy, with a smile of chilling derision.

'But – did – have you really seen? Come, Cass, what is it now – speak out!'

'You may sleep there yourself,' said Cassy, 'if you want to know.'

'Did it come from the garret, Cassy?'

'*It* – what?' said Cassy.

'Why, what you told of.'

'I didn't tell you anything,' said Cassy, with dogged sullenness.

Legree walked up and down the room uneasily.

'I'll have this yer thing examined. I'll look into it this very night. I'll take my pistols'—

'Do,' said Cassy; 'sleep in that room. I'd like to see you doing it. Fire your pistols – do!'

Legree stamped his foot, and swore violently.

'Don't swear,' said Cassy; 'nobody knows who may be hearing you. Hark! What was that?'

'What?' said Legree, starting.

A heavy old Dutch clock, that stood in the corner of the room, began, and slowly struck twelve.

For some reason or other Legree neither spoke nor moved; a vague horror fell on him; while Cassy, with a keen, sneering glitter in her eyes, stood looking at him, counting the strokes.

'Twelve o'clock; well, *now* we'll see,' said she, turning and opening the door into the passage-way, and standing as if listening.

'Hark! What's that?' said she, raising her finger.

'It's only the wind,' said Legree. 'Don't you hear how cursedly it blows?'

'Simon, come here!' said Cassy in a whisper, laying her hand on his, and leading him to the foot of the stairs; 'do you know what *that* is? Hark!'

A wild shriek came pealing down the stairway. It came from the garret. Legree's knees knocked together; his face grew white with fear.

'Hadn't you better get your pistols?' said Cassy, with a sneer that froze Legree's blood. 'It's time this thing was looked into, you know. I'd like to have you go up now; *they're at it.*'

'I won't go!' said Legree, with an oath.

'Why not? There an't any such things as ghosts, you know! Come!' and Cassy flitted up the winding stairway, laughing, and looking back after him. 'Come on.'

'I believe you *are* the devil!' said Legree. 'Come back, you hag! – come back, Cass! You shan't go!'

But Cassy laughed wildly, and fled on. He heard her open the entry doors that led to the garret. A wild gust of wind swept down extinguishing the candle he held in his hand, and with it the fearful, unearthly screams; they seemed to be shrieked in his very ear.

Legree fled frantically into the parlour, whither, in a few moments, he was followed by Cassy, pale, calm, cold as an avenging spirit, and with that same fearful light in her eye.

'I hope you are satisfied,' said she.

'Blast you, Cass!' said Legree.

'What for?' said Cassy. 'I only went up and shut the doors.

What's the matter with that garret, Simon, do you suppose?'
said she.

'None of your business!' said Legree.

'Oh, it an't? Well,' said Cassy, 'at any rate, I'm glad *I* don't
sleep under it.'

Anticipating the rising of the wind that very evening, Cassy
had been up and opened the garret-window. Of course, the
moment the doors were opened, the wind had drafted down,
and extinguished the light.

This may serve as a specimen of the game that Cassy played
with Legree, until he would sooner have put his head into a
lion's mouth than to have explored that garret. Meanwhile, in
the night, when everybody else was asleep, Cassy slowly and
carefully accumulated there a stock of provisions sufficient to
afford subsistence for some time; she transferred, article by
article, a greater part of her own and Emmeline's wardrobe. All
things being arranged, they only waited a fitting opportunity to
put their plan in execution.

By cajoling Legree, and taking advantage of a good-natured
interval, Cassy had got him to take her with him to the
neighbouring town, which was situated directly on the Red
River. With a memory sharpened to almost preternatural clearness, she remarked every turn in the road, and formed a mental
estimate of the time to be occupied in traversing it.

At the time when all was matured for action, our readers may,
perhaps, like to look behind the scenes, and see the final *coup
d'état*.

It was now near evening. Legree had been absent, on a ride to
a neighbouring farm. For many days Cassy had been unusually
gracious and accommodating in her humours; and Legree and
she had been, apparently, on the best of terms. At present, we
may behold her and Emmeline, in the room of the latter, busy
in sorting and arranging two small bundles.

'There, these will be large enough,' said Cassy. 'Now, put on
your bonnet, and let's start: it's just about the right time.'

'Why, they can see us yet,' said Emmeline.

'I mean they shall,' said Cassy, coolly. 'Don't you know that
they must have their chase after us, at any rate. The way of the
thing is to be just this. We will steal out of the back door, and
run down by the quarters. Sambo or Quimbo will be sure to see

us. They will give chase, and we will get into the swamp; then, they can't follow us any further till they go up and give the alarm, and turn out the dogs, and so on; and while they are blundering round, and tumbling over each other, as they always do, you and I will just slip along to the creek that runs back of the house, and wade along in it till we get opposite the back door. That will put the dogs all at fault; for scent won't lie in the water. Every one will run out of the house to look after us, and then we'll whip in at the back door, and up into the garret, where I have got a nice bed made up in one of the great boxes. We must stay in that garret a good while; for, I tell you, he will raise heaven and earth after us. He'll muster some of those old overseers on the other plantations, and have a great hunt; and they'll go over every inch of ground in that swamp. He makes it his boast that nobody ever got away from him. So let him hunt at his leisure.'

'Cassy, how well you have planned it!' said Emmeline. 'Who ever would have thought of it but you?'

There was neither pleasure nor exultation in Cassy's eyes — only a despairing firmness.

'Come,' she said, reaching her hand to Emmeline.

The two fugitives glided noiselessly from the house, and flitted, through the gathering shadows of evening, along by the quarters. The crescent moon, set like a silver signet in the western sky, delayed a little the approach of night. As Cassy expected, when quite near the verge of the swamps that encircled the plantation, they heard a voice calling to them to stop. It was not Sambo, however, but Legree, who was pursuing them with violent execrations. At the sound, the feebler spirit of Emmeline gave way; and, laying hold of Cassy's arm, she said, 'O, Cassy, I'm going to faint!'

'If you do, I'll kill you!' said Cassy, drawing a small, glittering stiletto, and flashing it before the eyes of the girl.

The diversion accomplished the purpose. Emmeline did not faint, and succeeded in plunging with Cassy into a part of the labyrinth of swamp, so deep and dark that it was perfectly hopeless for Legree to think of following them without assistance.

'Well,' said he, chuckling brutally, 'at any rate, they've got themselves into a trap now – the baggages! They're safe enough. They shall sweat for it!'

'Hulloa, there! Sambo! Quimbo! All hands!' called Legree, coming to the quarters when the men and women were just returning from work. 'There's two runaways in the swamps. I'll give five dollars to any nigger as catches 'em. Turn out the dogs! Turn out Tiger, and Fury, and the rest!'

The sensation produced by this news was immediate. Many of the men sprang forward officiously to offer their services, either from the hope of the reward, or from that cringing subserviency which is one of the most baleful effects of slavery. Some ran one way, and some another. Some were uncoupling the dogs, whose hoarse, savage bay, added not a little to the animation of the scene.

'Mas'r, shall we shoot 'em if we can't cotch 'em?' said Sambo, to whom his master brought a rifle.

'You may fire on Cass, if you like; it's time she was gone to the devil, where she belongs; but the gal, not,' said Legree. 'And now, boys, be spry and smart. Five dollars for him that gets 'em; and a glass of spirits to every one of you, anyhow.'

The whole band, with the glare of blazing torches, and whoop, and shout, and savage yell, of man and beast, proceeded down to the swamp, followed at some distance by every servant in the house. The establishment was, of a consequence, wholly deserted when Cassy and Emmeline glided into it the back way. The whooping and shouts of their pursuers were still filling the air; and, looking from the sitting-room windows, Cassy and Emmeline could see the troop, with the flambeaux, just dispersing themselves along the edge of the swamp.

'See there!' said Emmeline, pointing to Cassy; 'the hunt is begun! Look how those lights dance about! Hark! the dogs! Don't you hear? If we were only *there*, our chance wouldn't be worth a picayune. Oh, for pity's sake, do let's hide ourselves. Quick!'

There's no occasion for hurry,' said Cassy, coolly; 'they are all out after the hunt – that's the amusement of the evening! We'll go upstairs by and by. Meanwhile,' said she, deliberately taking a key from the pocket of a coat that Legree had thrown down in his hurry, 'meanwhile I shall take something to pay our passage.'

She unlocked the desk, took from it a roll of bills, which she counted over rapidly.

'Oh, don't let us do that!' said Emmeline.

'Don't!' said Cassy, 'why not? Would you have us starve in the swamps, or have that that will pay our way to the free States? Money will do anything, girl.' And as she spoke she put the money in her bosom.

'It would be stealing,' said Emmeline, in a distressed whisper.

'Stealing!' said Cassy, with a scornful laugh. 'They who steal body and soul needn't talk to us. Every one of these bills is stolen – stolen from poor, starving, sweating creatures, who must go to the devil at last for his profit. Let *him* talk about stealing! But come, we may as well go up garret; I've got a stock of candles there, and some books to pass away the time. You may be pretty sure they wont come *there* to inquire after us. If they do, I'll play ghost for them.'

When Emmeline reached the garret, she found an immense box, in which some heavy pieces of furniture had once been brought, turned on its side, so that the opening faced the wall, or rather the eaves. Cassy lit a small lamp, and, creeping round under the eaves, they established themselves in it. It was spread with a couple of small mattresses and some pillows; a box near by was plentifully stored with candles, provisions, and all the clothing necessary to their journey, which Cassy had arranged into bundles of an astonishingly small compass.

'There,' said Cassy, as she fixed the lamp into a small hook, which she had driven into the side of the box for that purpose; 'This is to be our home for the present. How do you like it?'

'Are you sure they won't come and search the garret?'

'I'd like to see Simon Legree doing that,' said Cassy. 'No, indeed, he will be too glad to keep away. As to the servants, they would any of them stand and be shot sooner than show their faces here.'

Somewhat reassured, Emmeline settled herself back on her pillow.

'What did you mean, Cassy, by saying you would kill me?' she said simply.

'I meant to stop you fainting,' said Cassy, 'and I did do it. And now I tell you, Emmeline, you must make up your mind *not* to faint, let what will come; there's no sort of need of it. If I had not stopped you, that wretch might have had his hands on you now.'

Emmeline shuddered.

The two remained some time in silence. Cassy busied herself with a French book; Emmeline, overcome with the exhaustion, fell into a doze, and slept some time. She was awakened by loud shouts and outcries, the tramp of horses' feet, and the baying of dogs. She started up with a faint shriek.

'Only the hunt coming back,' said Cassy, coolly; 'never fear. Look out of this knot-hole. Don't you see 'em all down there? Simon has to give it up for this night. Look, how muddy his horse is, flouncing about in the swamp; the dogs, too, look rather crest-fallen. Ah, my good sir! you'll have to try the race again and again – the game isn't there'

'Oh, don't speak a word!' said Emmeline; 'what if they should hear you?'

'If they do hear anything, it will make them very particular to keep away,' said Cassy. 'No danger; we may make any noise we please, and it will only add to the effect.'

At length the stillness of midnight settled down over the house. Legree, cursing his ill luck, and vowing dire vengeance on the morrow, went to bed.

Chapter 40

THE MARTYR

'Deem not the just by Heaven forgot!
     Though life its common gifts deny –
Though, with a crush'd and bleeding heart,
     And spurn'd of man, he goes to die!
For God hath mark'd each sorrowing day,
     And number'd every bitter tear;
And heaven's long years of bliss shall pay
     For all his children suffer here.' – BRYANT.

THE longest way must have its close – the gloomiest night will wear on to a morning. An eternal, inexorable lapse of moments is ever hurrying the day of the evil to an eternal night, and the night of the just to an eternal day. We have walked with our humble friend thus far in the valley of slavery; first, through flowery fields of ease and indulgence, then through heart-breaking separations from all that man holds dear. Again, we have waited with him in a sunny island, where generous hands concealed his chains with flowers; and, lastly, we have followed him when the last ray of earthly hope went out in night, and seen how, in the blackness of earthly darkness, the firmament of the unseen has blazed with stars of new and significant lustre.

The morning-star now stands over the tops of the mountains, and gales and breezes, not of earth, show that the gates of day are unclosing.

The escape of Cassy and Emmeline irritated the before surly temper of Legree to the last degree; and his fury, as was to be expected, fell upon the defenceless head of Tom. When he hurriedly announced the tidings among his hands, there was a sudden light in Tom's eye, a sudden upraising of his hands, that did not escape him. He saw that he did not join the muster of the pursuers. He thought of forcing him to do it; but having had, of old, experience of his inflexibility when commanded to take part in any deed of inhumanity, he would not, in his hurry, stop to enter into any conflict with him.

Tom, therefore, remained behind, with a few who had learned of him to pray, and offered up prayers for the escape of the fugitives.

When Legree returned, baffled and disappointed, all the long-working hatred of his soul towards his slave began to gather in a deadly and desperate form. Had not this man braved him – steadily, powerfully, resistlessly – ever since he bought him? Was there not a spirit in him which, silent as it was, burned on him like the fires of perdition?

'I *hate* him!' said Legree, that night, as he sat up in his bed; 'I *hate* him! And isn't he MINE? Can't I do what I like with him? Who's to hinder, I wonder?' And Legree clenched his fist and shook it as if he had something in his hands that he could rend in pieces.

But then Tom was a faithful, valuable servant; and although

Legree hated him the more for that, yet the consideration was still somewhat of a restraint to him.

The next morning he determined to say nothing, as yet; to assemble a party from some neighbouring plantations, with dogs; and guns; to surround the swamp, and go about the hunt systematically. If it succeeded, well and good; if not, he would summon Tom before him, and – his teeth clenched and his blood boiled – *then* he would break that fellow down, or – there was a dire inward whisper, to which his soul assented.

Ye say that the *interest* of the master is a sufficient safeguard for the slave. In the fury of man's mad will, he will wittingly, and with open eye, sell his own soul to the devil to gain his ends; and will he be more careful of his neighbour's body?

'Well,' said Cassy, the next day, from the garret, as she reconnoitred through the knot-hole, 'the hunt's going to begin again to-day!'

Three or four mounted horsemen were curvetting about, on the space front of the house; and one or two leashes of strange dogs were struggling with the negroes who held them, baying and barking at each other.

The men are, two of them, overseers of plantations in the vicinity; and others were some of Legree's associates at the tavern-bar of a neighbouring city, who had come for the interest of the sport. A more hard-favoured set, perhaps, could not be imagined. Legree was serving brandy profusely round among them, as also among the negroes who had been detailed from the various plantations for this service; for it was an object to make every service of this kind among the negroes as much of a holiday as possible.

Cassy placed her ear at the knot-hole; and, as the morning air blew directly towards the house, she could overhear a good deal of the conversation. A grave sneer overcast the dark, severe gravity of her face, as she listened, and heard them divide out the ground, discuss the rival merits of the dogs, give orders about firing, and the treatment of each in case of capture.

Cassy drew back; and, clasping her hands, looked upward, and said, 'O great Almighty God! we are *all* sinners; but what have *we* done, more than all the rest of the world, that we should be treated so?'

There was a terrible earnestness in her face and voice as she spoke.

'If it wasn't for *you*, child,' she said, looking at Emmeline, 'I'd *go* out to them; and I'd thank any one of them that *would* shoot me down; for what use will freedom be to me? Can it give me back my children, or make me what I used to be?'

Emmeline, in her child-like simplicity, was half afraid of the dark moods of Cassy. She looked perplexed, but made no answer. She only took her hand, with a gentle, caressing movement.

'Don't!' said Cassy, trying to draw it away; 'you'll get me to loving you; and I never mean to love anything again!'

'Poor Cassy!' said Emmeline, 'don't feel so! If the Lord gives us liberty, perhaps He'll give you back your daughter. At any rate, I'll be like a daughter to you. I know I'll never see my poor old mother again! I shall love you, Cassy, whether you love me or not!'

The gentle, child-like spirit conquered. Cassy sat down by her, put her arm round her neck, stroked her soft brown hair; and Emmeline then wondered at the beauty of her magnificent eyes, now soft with tears.

'O Em!' said Cassy, 'I've hungered for my children, and thirsted for them, and my eyes fail with longing for them. Here! here!' she said, striking her breast, 'it's all desolate, all empty! If God would give me back my children, then I could pray.'

'You must trust Him, Cassy,' said Emmeline; 'He is our Father!'

'His wrath is upon us,' said Cassy; 'He has turned away in anger.'

'No, Cassy! He will be good to us. Let us hope in Him,' said Emmeline. 'I always have had hope.'

The hunt was long, animated, and thorough, but unsuccessful; and, with grave, ironic exultation, Cassy looked down on Legree as, weary and dispirited, he alighted from his horse.

'Now, Quimbo,' said Legree, as he stretched himself down in the sitting-room, 'you just go and walk that Tom up here, right away! The old cuss is at the bottom of this yer whole matter; and I'll have it out of his old black hide, or I'll know the reason why!'

Sambo and Quimbo both, though hating each other, were joined in one mind by a no less cordial hatred of Tom. Legree had told them at first that he had bought him for a general overseer in his absence; and this had begun an ill-will on their part, which had increased in their debased and servile natures, as they saw him becoming obnoxious to their master's displeasure. Quimbo, therefore, departed with a will to execute his orders.

Tom heard the message with a forewarning heart; for he knew all the plan of the fugitives' escape, and the place of their present concealment. He knew the deadly character of the man he had to deal with, and his despotic power. But he felt strong in God to meet death, rather than betray the helpless.

He set his basket down by the row, and, looking up, said, 'Into Thy hands I commend my spirit! Thou hast redeemed me, O Lord God of truth!' and then quietly yielded himself to the rough, brutal grasp with which Quimbo seized him.

'Ay, ay!' said the giant, as he dragged him along, 'ye'll cotch it, now! I'll boun' mas'r's back's up high! No sneaking out, now! Tell ye ye'll get it, and no mistake! See how ye'll look now, helpin' mas'r's niggers to run away! See what ye'll get!'

The savage words, none of them reached that ear – a higher voice there was saying, 'Fear not them that kill the body, and after that have no more that they can do.' Nerve and bone of that poor man's body vibrated to those words, as if touched by the finger of God; and he felt the strength of a thousand souls in one. As he passed along, the trees and bushes, the huts of his servitude, the whole scene of his degradation, seemed to whirl by him, as the landscape by the rushing car. His soul throbbed – his home was in sight – and the hour of release seemed at hand.

'Well, Tom,' said Legree, walking up and seizing him grimly by the collar of his coat, and speaking through his teeth, in a paroxysm of determined rage, 'do you know I've made up my mind to KILL you?'

'It's very likely, mas'r,' said Tom, calmly.

'I have, said Legree, with grim, terrible calmness, 'done – just – that – thing, Tom, unless you tell me what you know about these yer gals!'

Tom stood silent.

'D'ye hear?' said Legree, stamping, with a roar like that of an incensed lion. 'Speak!'

'*I ha'nt got nothing to tell, mas'r,*' said Tom, with a slow, firm, deliberate utterance.

'Do you dare to tell me, ye old black Christian, ye don't *know*?' said Legree.

Tom was silent.

'Speak!' thundered Legree, striking him furiously. 'Do you know anything?'

'I know, mas'r; but I can't tell anything. *I can die!*'

Legree drew in a long breath; and, suppressing his rage, took Tom by the arm, and, approaching his face almost to his, said, in a terrible voice, 'Hark'e, Tom — ye think 'cause I've let you off before, I don't mean what I say; but this time I've *made up my mind*, and counted the cost. You've always stood it out agin' me — now I'll *conquer ye or kill ye!* — one or t'other. I'll count every drop of blood there is in you, and take 'em, one by one, till ye give up!'

Tom looked up to his master, and answered, 'Mas'r, if you was sick, or in trouble, or dying, and I could save ye, I'd *give* ye my heart's blood; and if taking every drop of blood in this poor old body would save your precious soul, I'd give 'em freely, as the Lord gave His for me. O mas'r, don't bring this great sin on your soul! It will hurt you more than 'twill me! Do the worst you can, my troubles 'll be over soon; but if ye don't repent, yours won't *never* end!'

Like a strange snatch of heavenly music, heard in the lull of a tempest, this burst of feeling made a moment's blank pause. Legree stood aghast, and looked at Tom; and there was such a silence that the tick of the old clock could be heard, measuring, with silent touch, the last moments of mercy and probation to that hardened heart.

It was but a moment. There was one hesitating pause, one irresolute, relenting thrill, and the spirit of evil came back, with sevenfold vehemence; and Legree, foaming with rage, smote his victim to the ground.

Scenes of blood and cruelty are shocking to our ear and heart. What man has nerve to do, man has not nerve to hear. What brother-man and brother-Christian must suffer cannot be told us, even in our secret chamber, it so harrows up the soul. And yet, O my country! these things are done under the shadow of thy laws! O Christ! thy Church sees them, almost in silence!

But of old there was One whose suffering changed an instrument of torture, degradation, and shame, into a symbol of glory, honour, and immortal life; and where His Spirit is, neither degrading stripes, nor blood, nor insults, can make the Christian's last struggle less than glorious.

Was he alone that long night, whose brave, loving spirit was bearing up, in that old shed, against buffeting and brutal stripes?

Nay! There stood by him ONE, seen by him alone, 'like unto the Son of God.'

The tempter stood by him, too, blinded by furious, despotic will, every moment pressing him to shun that agony by the betrayal of the innocent. But the brave, true heart was firm on the Eternal Rock. Like his Master, he knew that, if he saved others, himself he could not save; nor could utmost extremity wring from him words, save of prayer and holy trust.

'He's most gone, mas'r,' said Sambo, touched, in spite of himself, by the patience of his victim.

'Pay away till he gives up! Give it to him! give it to him!' shouted Legree. 'I'll take every drop of blood he has, unless he confesses.'

Tom opened his eyes, and looked upon his master. 'Ye poor, miserable critter!' he said, 'there an't no more ye can do! I forgive ye, with all my soul!' and he fainted entirely away.

'I b'lieve my soul he's done for, finally,' said Legree, stepping forward to look at him. 'Yes, he is! Well, his mouth's shut up at last, that's one comfort!'

Yes, Legree; but who shall shut up that voice in thy soul — that soul, past repentance, past prayer, past hope, in whom the fire that never shall be quenched is already burning?

Yet Tom was not quite gone. His wondrous words and pious prayers had struck upon the hearts of the imbruted blacks who had been the instruments of cruelty upon him; and the instant Legree withdrew they took him down, and in their ignorance, sought to call him back to life — as if *that* were any favour to him.

'Sartin, we's been doin' a dreful wicked thing!' said Sambo; 'hopes mas'r 'll have to 'count for it, and not we.'

They washed his wounds – they provided a rude bed of some refuse cotton for him to lie down on; and one of them, stealing up to the house, begged a drink of brandy of Legree, pretending that he was tired, and wanted it for himself. He brought it back, and poured it down Tom's throat.

'O Tom!' said Quimbo, 'we's been awful wicked to ye!'

'I forgive ye, with all my heart!' said Tom, faintly.

'O Tom! do tell us who is *Jesus*, anyhow!' said Sambo, 'Jesus, that's been a standin' by you so, all this night. – Who is he?'

The word roused the failing, fainting spirit. He poured forth a few energetic sentences of that wondrous One – His life, His death, His everlasting presence, and power to save.

They wept – both the savage men.

'Why didn't I never hear this before?' said Sambo; 'but I do believe! – I can't help it! Lord Jesus, have mercy on us!'

'Poor critters!' said Tom, 'I'd be willing to bar' all I have, if it'll only bring ye to Christ! O Lord! give me these two more souls, I pray.'

That prayer was answered!

Chapter 41

THE YOUNG MASTER

Two days after, a young man drove a light wagon up through the avenue of China trees, and throwing the reins hastily on the horses' necks, sprang out and inquired for the owner of the place.

It was George Shelby; and to show how he came to be there, we must go back in our story.

The letter of Miss Ophelia to Mrs Shelby had, by some unfortunate accident, been detained for a month or two at some remote post-office, before it reached its destination; and, of course, before it was received, Tom was already lost to view among the distant swamps of the Red River.

Mrs Shelby read the intelligence with the deepest concern; but any immediate action upon it was an impossibility. She was then in attendance on the sick-bed of her husband, who lay delirious in the crisis of a fever. Master George Shelby, who, in the interval, had changed from a boy to a tall young man, was her constant and faithful assistant, and her only reliance in superintending his father's affairs. Miss Ophelia had taken the precaution to send them the name of the lawyer who did business for the St Clares; and the most that in the emergency could be done was, to address a letter of inquiry to him. The sudden death of Mr Shelby a few days after, brought, of course, an absorbing pressure of other interests for a season.

Mr Shelby showed his confidence in his wife's ability, by appointing her sole executrix upon his estates; and thus immediately a large and complicated amount of business was brought upon her hands.

Mrs Shelby, with characteristic energy, applied herself to the work of straightening the entangled web of affairs, and she and George were for some time occupied with collecting and examining accounts, selling property and settling debts; for Mrs Shelby was determined that everything should be brought into tangible and recognisable shape, let the consequences to her prove what they might. In the meantime, they received a letter from the lawyer, to whom Miss Ophelia had referred them, saying that he knew nothing of the matter; that the man was sold at a public auction, and that, beyond receiving the money, he knew nothing of the affair.

Neither George nor Mrs Shelby could be easy at this result; and, accordingly, some six months after, the former, having business for his mother down the river, resolved to visit New Orleans in person, and push his inquiries, in hopes of discovering Tom's whereabouts and restoring him.

After some months of unsuccessful search, by the merest accident, George fell in with a man in New Orleans who happened to be possessed of the desired information; and with his money in his pocket, our hero took steamboat for Red River, resolving to find out and repurchase his old friend.

He was soon introduced into the house, where he found Legree in the sitting-room.

Legree received the stranger with a kind of surly hospitality.

'I understand,' said the young man, 'that you bought, in New Orleans, a boy named Tom. He used to be on my father's place, and I came to see if I couldn't buy him back.'

Legree's brow grew dark, and he broke out passionately: 'Yes, I did buy such a fellow, and a h—l of a bargain I had of it, too! The most rebellious, saucy, impudent dog! Set up my niggers to run away, got off two gals worth eight hundred or a thousand dollars a-piece. He owned to that, and when I bid him tell me where they was, he up and said he knew, but he wouldn't tell; and stood to it, though I gave him the cussedest flogging I ever gave nigger yet. I b'lieve he is trying to die; but I don't know as he'll make it out.'

'Where is he?' said George, impetuously. 'Let me see him.' The cheeks of the young man were crimson, and his eyes flashed fire; but he prudently said nothing as yet.

'He's in dat ar shed,' said a little fellow, who stood holding George's horse.

Legree kicked the boy, and swore at him; but George, without saying another word, turned and strode to the spot.

Tom had been lying two days since the fatal night; not suffering, for every nerve of suffering was blunted and destroyed. He lay, for the most part, in a quiet stupor; for the laws of a powerful and well-knit frame would not at once release the imprisoned spirit. By stealth, there had been there, in the darkness of the night, poor desolate creatures, who stole from their scanty hours' rest, that they might repay to him some of those ministrations of love in which he had always been so abundant. Truly, those poor disciples had little to give – only the cup of cold water; but it was given with full hearts.

Tears had fallen on that honest, insensible face – tears of late repentance in the poor, ignorant heathen, who his dying love and patience had awakened to repentance, and bitter prayers breathed over him to a late-found Saviour, of whom they scarce knew more than the name, but whom the yearning ignorant heart of man never implores in vain.

Cassy, who had glided out of her place of concealment, and, by over-hearing, learned the sacrifice that had been made for her and Emmeline, had been there the night before, defying the danger of detection; and, moved by the few last words which the affectionate soul had yet strength to breathe, the long winter of despair, the ice of years, had given way, and the dark, despairing woman, had wept and prayed.

When George entered the shed, he felt his head giddy and his heart sick.

'Is it possible ? — is it possible ?' said he, kneeling down by him. 'Uncle Tom ! my poor — poor old friend !'

Something in the voice penetrated to the ear of the dying. He moved his head gently, smiled, and said, —

> 'Jesus can make a dying bed
>   Feel soft as downy pillows are.'

Tears which did honour to his manly heart fell from the young man's eyes as he bent over his poor friend.

'O dear Uncle Tom ! do wake — do speak once more ! Look up ! Here's Mas'r George — your own little Mas'r George. Don't you know me ?'

'Mas'r George !' said Tom, opening his eyes, and speaking in a feeble voice, 'Mas'r George !' He looked bewildered.

Slowly the idea seemed to fill his soul; and the vacant eye became fixed and brightened, the whole face lighted up, the hard hands clasped, and tears ran down the cheeks.

'Bless the Lord ! it is — it is — it's all I wanted ! They haven't forgot me. It warms my soul; it does my old heart good ! Now I shall die content ! Bless the Lord, O my soul !'

'You shan't die ! you *mustn't* die, nor think of it ! I've come to buy you, and take you home,' said George, with impetuous vehemence.

'O Mas'r George, you're too late. The Lord's bought me, and is going to take me home — and I long to go. Heaven is better than Kintuck.'

'Oh, don't die ! It'll kill me ! — it'll break my heart to think what you've suffered — and lying in this old shed, here ! Poor, poor fellow !'

'Don't call me poor fellow !' said Tom, solemnly. 'I *have* been poor fellow, but that's all past and gone now. I'm right in the door, going into glory; O Mas'r George ! *Heaven has come* ! I've got the victory ! — the Lord Jesus has given it to me ! Glory be to His name !'

George was awe-struck at the force, the vehemence, the power with which these broken sentences were uttered. He sat gazing in silence.

Tom grasped his hand, and continued – 'Ye mustn't, now, tell Chloe, poor soul! how ye found me; 'twould be so dreffful to her. Only tell her ye found me going into glory; and that I couldn't stay for no one. And tell her the Lord stood by me everywhere and al'ays, and made everything light and easy. And oh, the poor chil'en, and the baby – my old heart's been most broke for 'em, time and agin. Tell 'em all to follow me – follow me! Give my love to mas'r, and dear good missis – and everybody in the place! Ye don't know. 'Pears like I loves 'em all. I loves every creatur', every whar! – it's nothing *but* love! O Mas'r George! what a thing 'tis to be a Christian!'

At this moment Legree sauntered up to the door of the shed, looked in with a dogged air of affected carelessness, and turned away.

'The old Satan!' said George, in his indignation. 'It's a comfort to think the devil will pay *him* for this some of these days!'

'Oh, don't! – oh, ye mustn't!' said Tom, grasping his hand; 'he's a poor mis'able critter. It's awful to think on't! Oh if he only could repent, the Lord would forgive him now; but I'm feared he never will.'

'I hope he won't!' said George. 'I never want to see him in heaven.'

'Hush, Mas'r George! it worries me. Don't feel so. He an't done me no real harm – only opened the gate of the kingdom for me; that's all!'

At this moment the sudden flush of strength which the joy of meeting his young master had infused into the dying man gave way. A sudden sinking fell upon him; he closed his eyes; and that mysterious and sublime change passed over his face that told the approach of other worlds.

He began to draw his breath with long, deep inspirations; and his broad chest rose and fell heavily. The expression of his face was that of a conqueror.

'Who – who – who shall separate us from the love of Christ?' he said, in a voice that contended with mortal weakness; and with a smile he fell asleep.

George sat fixed with solemn awe. It seemed to him that the

place was holy; and as he closed the lifeless eyes, and rose up from the dead, only one thought possessed him – that expressed by his simple old friend, 'What a thing it is to be a Christian!'

He turned. Legree was standing sullenly behind him.

Something in that dying scene had checked the natural fierceness of youthful passion. The presence of the man was simply loathsome to George; and he felt only an impulse to get away from him, with as few words as possible.

Fixing his keen, dark eyes on Legree, he simply said, pointing to the dead, 'You have got all you ever can of him. What shall I pay you for the body? I will take it away, and bury it decently.'

'I don't sell dead niggers,' said Legree, doggedly. 'You are welcome to bury him where and when you like.'

'Boys,' said George, in an authoritative tone to two or three negroes who were looking at the body, 'help me lift him up, and carry him to my wagon; and get me a spade.'

One of them ran for a spade; the other two assisted George to carry the body to the wagon.

George neither spoke to nor looked at Legree, who did not countermand his orders, but stood whistling with an air of forced unconcern. He sulkily followed them to where the wagon stood at the door.

George spread his cloak in the wagon, and had the body carefully disposed of in it, moving the seat so as to give it room. Then he turned, fixed his eyes on Legree, and said, with forced composure –

'I have not as yet said to you what I think of this most atrocious affair; this is not the time and place. But, sir, this innocent blood shall have justice. I will proclaim this murder. I will go to the very first magistrate, and expose you.'

'Do!' said Legree, snapping his fingers scornfully. 'I'd like to see you doing it. Where you going to get witnesses? – how you going to prove it? Come, now!'

George saw at once the force of this defiance. There was not a white person on the place; and, in all Southern courts, the testimony of coloured blood is nothing. He felt at that moment as if he could have rent the heavens with his heart's indignant cry for justice; but in vain.

'After all, what a fuss for a dead nigger!' said Legree.

The word was as a spark to a powder-magazine. Prudence

was never a cardinal virtue of the Kentucky boy. George turned, and, with one indignant blow, knocked Legree flat upon his face; and as he stood over him, blazing with wrath and defiance, he would have formed no bad personification of his great namesake triumphing over the dragon.

Some men, however, are decidedly bettered by being knocked down. If a man lays them fairly flat in the dust, they seem immediately to conceive a respect for him; and Legree was one of this sort. As he rose, therefore, and brushed the dust from his clothes, he eyed the slowly-retreating wagon with some evident consideration; nor did he open his mouth till it was out of sight.

Beyond the boundaries of the plantation George had noticed a dry, sandy knoll, shaded by a few trees; there they made the grave.

'Shall we take off the cloak, mas'r?' said the negroes, when the grave was ready.

'No, no; bury it with him. It's all I can give you now, poor Tom, and you shall have it.'

They laid him in; and the men shovelled away silently. They banked it up, and laid green turf over it.

'You may go, boys,' said George, slipping a quarter into the hand of each. They lingered about, however.

'If young mas'r would please buy us—', said one.

'We'd serve him so faithful', said the other.

'Hard times here, mas'r!' said the first. 'Do, mas'r, buy us, please!'

'I can't – I can't,' said George, with difficulty, motioning them off; 'it's impossible!'

The poor fellows looked dejected, and walked off in silence.

'Witness, eternal God,' said George, kneeling on the grave of his poor friend, 'oh, witness that, from this hour, I will do *what one man can* to drive out this curse of slavery from my land!'

There is no monument to mark the last resting-place of our friend. He needs none. His Lord knows where he lies, and will raise him up immortal, to appear with him when he shall appear in his glory.

Pity him not! Such a life and death is not for pity. Not in the riches of omnipotence is the chief glory of God, but in self-denying, suffering love. And blessed are the men whom he calls to fellowship with him, bearing their cross after him with patience. Of such it is written, 'Blessed are they that mourn, for they shall be comforted.'

Chapter 42

AN AUTHENTIC GHOST STORY

FOR some remarkable reason, ghostly legends were uncommonly rife, about this time, among the servants on Legree's place.

It was whisperingly asserted that footsteps, in the dead of night, had been heard descending the garret-stairs, and patrolling the house. In vain the doors of the upper entry had been locked; the ghost either carried a duplicate key in its pocket, or availed itself of a ghost's immemorial privilege of coming through the keyhole, and promenaded as before, with a freedom that was alarming.

Authorities were somewhat divided as to the outward form of the spirit, owing to a custom quite prevalent among negroes – and, for aught we know, among whites too – of invariably shutting the eyes, and covering up heads under blankets, petticoats, or whatever else might come in use for a shelter, on these occasions. Of course, as everybody knows, when the bodily eyes are thus out of the lists, the spiritual eyes are uncommonly vivacious and perspicacious; and therefore there were abundance of full-length portraits of the ghost, abundantly sworn and testified to, which as is often the case with portraits, agreed with each other in no particular, except the common family peculiarity of the ghost tribe – the wearing of a *white sheet*. The poor souls were not versed in ancient history, and did not know that Shakespeare had authenticated this costume, by telling how

'the *sheeted* dead
Did squeak and gibber in the streets of Rome;'

and therefore their all hitting upon this is a striking fact in pneumatology, which we recommend to the attention of spiritual media generally.

Be it as it may, we have private reasons for knowing that a tall figure in a white sheet did walk, at the most approved ghostly hours, around the Legree premises – pass out the doors, glide about the house – disappear at intervals, and, reappearing, pass up the silent stair-way, into that fatal garret; and that, in the morning, the entry doors were all found shut and locked as firm as ever.

Legree could not help overhearing this whispering; and it was all the more exciting to him from the pains that were taken to conceal it from him. He drank more brandy than usual; held up his head briskly, and swore louder than ever in the day-time; but he had bad dreams, and the visions of his head on his bed were anything but agreeable. The night after Tom's body had been carried away he rode to the next town for a carouse, and had a high one. Got home late and tired; locked his door, took out the key, and went to bed.

After all, let a man take what pains he may to hush it down, a human soul is an awful, ghostly, unquiet possession for a bad man to have. Who knows the metes and bounds of it? Who knows all its awful perhapses – those shudderings and tremblings, which it can no more live down than it can outlive its own eternity! What a fool is he who locks his door to keep out spirits, who has in his own bosom a spirit he dares not meet alone – whose voice, smothered far down, and piled over with mountains of earthliness, is yet like the forewarning trumpet of doom!

But Legree locked his door and set a chair against it; he set a night-lamp at the head of his bed; and he put his pistols there. He examined the catches and fastenings of the windows, and then swore 'he didn't care for the devil and his angels,' and went to sleep.

Well, he slept, for he was tired – slept soundly. But, finally, there came over his sleep a shadow – a horror – an apprehension of something dreadful hanging over him. It was his mother's shroud, he thought; but Cassy had it, holding it up, and showing it to him. He heard a confused noise of screams and groanings; and with it all, he knew he was asleep, and he struggled to wake himself. He was half awake. He was sure something was coming into his room. He knew the door was opening, but he could not stir hand or foot. At last he turned, with a start; the door *was* open, and he saw a hand putting out his light.

It was a cloudy, misty moonlight, and there he saw it! — something white, gliding in! He heard the still rustle of its ghostly garments. It stood still by his bed: a cold hand touched his; a voice said three times, in a low, fearful whisper, 'Come! come! come!' And while he lay sweating with terror, he knew not when or how, the thing was gone. He sprang out of bed, and pulled at the door. It was shut and locked, and the man fell down in a swoon.

After this, Legree became a harder drinker than ever before. He no longer drank cautiously, prudently, but imprudently and recklessly.

There were reports around the country, soon after, that he was sick and dying. Excess had brought on that frightful disease that seems to throw the lurid shadows of a coming retribution back into the present life. None could bear the horrors of that sick room, when he raved and screamed, and spoke of sights which almost stopped the blood of those who heard him; and, at his dying bed, stood a stern, white inexorable figure, saying 'Come! come! come!'

By a singular coincidence, on the very night that this vision appeared to Legree, the house-door was found open in the morning, and some of the negroes had seen two white figures gliding down the avenue towards the highroad.

It was near sunrise when Cassy and Emmeline paused, for a moment, in a little knot of trees near the town.

Cassy was dressed after the manner of the Creole Spanish ladies — wholly in black. A small black bonnet on her head, covered by a veil thick with embroidery, concealed her face. It had been agreed that, in their escape, she was to personate the character of a Creole lady, and Emmeline that of her servant.

Brought up, from early life, in connection with the highest society, the language, movements, and air of Cassy, were all in agreement with this idea; and she had still enough remaining with her of a once splendid wardrobe, and sets of jewels, to enable her to personate the thing to advantage.

She stopped in the outskirts of the town, where she had

noticed trunks for sale, and purchased a handsome one. This she requested the man to send along with her. And, accordingly, thus escorted by a boy wheeling her trunk, and Emmeline behind her, carrying her carpet-bag and sundry bundles, she made her appearance at the small tavern, like a lady of consideration.

The first person that struck her, after her arrival, was George Shelby, who was staying there, awaiting the next boat.

Cassy had remarked the young man from her loophole in the garret, and seen him bear away the body of Tom, and observed, with secret exultation, his rencontre with Legree. Subsequently, she had gathered, from the conversations she had overheard among the negroes, as she glided about in her ghostly disguise after nightfall, who he was, and in what relation he stood to Tom. She, therefore, felt an immediate accession of confidence when she found that he was, like herself, awaiting the next boat.

Cassy's air and manner, address, and evident command of money, prevented any rising disposition to suspicion in the hotel. People never inquire too closely into those who are fair on the main point of paying well – a thing which Cassy had foreseen when she provided herself with money.

In the edge of the evening, a boat was heard coming along, and George Shelby handed Cassy aboard, with the politeness which comes naturally to every Kentuckian, and exerted himself to provide her with a good stateroom.

Cassy kept her room and bed, on pretext of illness, during the whole time they were on Red River; and was waited on with obsequious devotion by her attendant.

When they arrived at the Mississippi River, George, having learned that the course of the strange lady was upward, like his own, proposed to take a stateroom for her on the same boat with himself – good-naturedly compassionating her feeble health, and desirous to do what he could to assist her.

Behold, therefore, the whole party safely transferred to the good steamer *Cincinnati*, and sweeping up the river under a powerful head of steam.

Cassy's health was much better. She sat upon the guards, came to the table, and was remarked upon in the boat as a lady that must have been very handsome.

From the moment that George got the first glimpse of her

face, he was troubled with one of those fleeting and indefinite likenesses which almost everybody can remember, and has been, at times, perplexed with. He could not keep himself from looking at her, and watching her perpetually. At table, or sitting at her stateroom door, still she would encounter the young man's eye fixed on her, and politely withdrawn, when she showed, by her countenance, that she was sensible of the observation.

Cassy became uneasy. She began to think that he suspected something; and finally resolved to throw herself entirely on his generosity, and entrusted him with her whole history.

George was heartily disposed to sympathise with any one who had escaped from Legree's plantation – a place that he could not remember or speak of with patience; and, with the courageous disregard of consequences which is characteristic of his age and state, he assured her that he would do all in his power to protect and bring them through.

The next stateroom to Cassy's was occupied by a French lady, named de Thoux, who was accompanied by a fine little daughter, a child of some twelve summers.

This lady, having gathered from George's conversation that he was from Kentucky, seemed evidently disposed to cultivate his acquaintance; in which design she was seconded by the graces of her little girl, who was about as pretty a plaything as ever diverted the weariness of a fortnight's trip on a steamboat.

George's chair was often placed at her stateroom door; and Cassy, as she sat upon the guards, could hear their conversation.

Madame de Thoux was very minute in her inquiries as to Kentucky, where she said she had resided in a former period of her life. George discovered, to his surprise, that her former residence must have been in his own vicinity; and her inquiries showed knowledge of people and things in his region that was perfectly surprising to him.

'Do you know,' said Madame de Thoux to him one day, 'of any man in your neighbourhood of the name of Harris?'

'There is an old fellow of that name lives not far from my father's place,' said George. 'We never have had much intercourse with him, though.'

'He is a large slave-owner, I believe?' said Madame de Thoux, with a manner which seemed to betray more interest than she was exactly willing to show.

'He is,' said George, looking rather surprised at her manner.

'Did you ever know of his having – perhaps you may have heard of his having a mulatto boy, named George ?'

'Oh, certainly – George Harris – I know him well ; he married a servant of my mother's, but has escaped now to Canada.'

'He has ?' said Madame de Thoux, quickly. 'Thank God !'

George looked a surprised inquiry, but said nothing.

Madame de Thoux leaned her head on her hand, and burst into tears. 'He is my brother !' she said.

'Madame !' said George, with a strong accent of surprise.

'Yes,' said Madame de Thoux, lifting her head proudly, and wiping her tears ; 'Mr Shelby, George Harris is my brother !'

'I am perfectly astonished,' said George, pushing back his chair a pace or two, and looking at Madame de Thoux.

'I was sold to the South when he was a boy,' said she. 'I was bought by a good and generous man. He took me with him to the West Indies, set me free, and married me. It is but lately that he died, and I was coming up to Kentucky to see if I could find and redeem my brother.'

'I have heard him speak of a sister Emily, that was sold South,' said George.

'Yes, indeed ! I am the one,' said Madame de Thoux. 'Tell me what sort of a—'

'A very fine young man,' said George, 'notwithstanding the curse of slavery that lay on him. He sustained a first-rate character, both for intelligence and principle. I know, you see,' he said, 'because he married in our family.'

'What sort of a girl ?' said Madame de Thoux, eagerly.

'A treasure !' said George. 'A beautiful, intelligent, amiable girl. Very pious. My mother had brought her up, and trained her as carefully, almost, as a daughter. She could read and write, embroider and sew beautifully, and was a beautiful singer.'

'Was she born in your house ?' said Madame de Thoux.

'No. Father bought her once, in one of his trips to New Orleans, and brought her up as a present to mother. She was about eight or nine years old, then. Father would never tell mother what he gave for her ; but, the other day, on looking over his old papers, we came across the bill of sale. He paid an extravagant sum for her, to be sure – I suppose, on account of her extraordinary beauty.'

George sat with his back to Cassy, and did not see the absorbed expression of her countenance as he was giving these details.

At this point of the story she touched his arm, and, with a face perfectly white with interest, said, 'Do you know the names of the people he bought her of?'

'A man of the name of Simmons, I think, was the principal in the transaction – at least, I think that was the name on the bill of sale.'

'O my God!' said Cassy, and fell insensible on the floor of the cabin.

George was wide-awake now, and so was Madame de Thoux. Though neither of them could conjecture what was the cause of Cassy's fainting – still they made all the tumult which is proper in such cases – George upsetting a wash-pitcher, and breaking two tumblers, in the warmth of his humanity; and various ladies in the cabin, hearing that somebody had fainted, crowded the stateroom door, and kept out all the air they possibly could; so that, on the whole, everything was done that could be expected!

Poor Cassy, when she recovered, turned her face to the wall, and wept and sobbed like a child – perhaps, mother, you can tell what she was thinking of! Perhaps you cannot; but she felt as sure, in that hour, that God had had mercy on her, and that she should see her daughter – as she did months afterwards – when – but we anticipate.

Chapter 43

RESULTS

THE rest of our story is soon told. George Shelby, interested, as any other young man might be, by the romance of the incident, no less than by feelings of humanity, was at pains to send to Cassy, the bill of sale of Eliza, whose date and name all corresponded with her own knowledge of facts, and left no doubt upon her mind as to the identity of her child. It remained now only for her to trace out the path of the fugitives.

Madame de Thoux and she, thus drawn together by the singular coincidence of their fortunes, proceeded immediately to Canada, and began a tour of inquiry among the stations where the numerous fugitives from slavery are located. At Amherstberg they found the missionary with whom George and Eliza had taken shelter on their first arrival in Canada, and through him were enabled to trace the family to Montreal.

George and Eliza had now been five years free. George had found constant occupation in the shop of a worthy machinist, where he had been earning a competent support for his family, which, in the meantime, had been increased by the addition of another daughter.

Little Harry, a fine bright boy, had been put to a good school, and was making rapid proficiency in knowledge.

The worthy pastor of the station in Amherstberg, where George had first landed, was so much interested in the statements of Madame de Thoux and Cassy, that he yielded to the solicitations of the former to accompany them to Montreal in their search – she bearing all the expense of the expedition.

The scene now changes to a small, neat tenement, in the outskirts of Montreal; the time, evening. A cheerful fire blazes on the hearth; a tea-table, covered with a snowy cloth, stands prepared for the evening meal. In one corner of the room was a table covered with a green cloth, where was an open writing-desk, pens, paper, and over it a shelf of well-selected books.

This was George's study. The same zeal for self-improvement which had led him to steal the much-coveted arts of reading and writing, amid all the toils and discouragements of his early life, still led him to devote all his leisure time to self-cultivation.

At this present time he is seated at the table, making notes from a volume of the family library he has been reading.

'Come, George,' says Eliza, 'you've been gone all day. Do put down that book, and let's talk, while I'm getting tea – do.'

And little Eliza seconds the effort by toddling up to her father, and trying to pull the book out of his hand, and install herself on his knee as a substitute.

'Oh, you little witch!' says George, yielding as, in such circumstances, man always must.

'That's right,' says Eliza, as she begins to cut a loaf of bread. A little older she looks; her form a little fuller; her hair more matronly than of yore; but evidently contented and happy as woman need be.

'Harry, my boy, how did you come on in that sum to-day?' says George, as he lays his hand on his son's head.

Harry has lost his long curls; but he can never lose those eyes and eyelashes, and that fine, bold brow, that flushes with triumph, as he answers, 'I did it, every bit of it, *myself*, father, and *nobody* helped me.'

'That's right,' says his father; 'depend on yourself, my son. You have a better chance than ever your poor father had.'

At this moment there is a rap at the door, and Eliza goes and opens it. The delighted, 'Why – this you?' calls up her husband, and the good pastor of Amherstberg is welcomed. There are two women with him, and Eliza asks them to sit down.

Now, if the truth must be told, the honest pastor had arranged a little programme, according to which this affair was to develop itself; and, on the way up, all had very cautiously and prudently exhorted each other not to let things out, except according to previous arrangement.

What was the good man's consternation, therefore, just as he had motioned to the ladies to be seated, and was taking out his pocket-handkerchief to wipe his mouth, so as to proceed to his introductory speech in good order, when Madame de Thoux upset the whole plan by throwing her arms around George's neck, and letting all out at once, by saying, 'O George! don't you know me? I am your sister Emily!'

Cassy had seated herself more composedly, and would have carried on her part very well, had not Eliza suddenly appeared before her in exact shape and form, every outline and curl, just as her daughter was when she saw her last. The little thing peered up in her face, and Cassy caught her up in her arms, pressed her to her bosom, saying, what at the moment she really believed, 'Darling, I'm your mother!'

In fact, it was a troublesome matter to do up exactly in proper order; but the good pastor at last succeeded in getting everybody quiet, and delivering the speech with which he had intended to open the exercises, and in which, at last, he succeeded so well, that his whole audience were sobbing about him in a manner that ought to satisfy any orator, ancient or modern.

They knelt together, and the good man prayed – for there are some feelings so agitated and tumultuous, that they can find rest only by being poured into the bosom of almightly Love – and then, rising up, the new-found family embraced each other, with a holy trust in Him who, from such peril and dangers, and by such unknown ways, had brought them together.

The notebook of a missionary among the Canadian fugitives contains truth stranger than fiction. How can it be otherwise, when a system prevails which whirls families and scatters their members, as the wind whirls and scatters the leaves of autumn? These shores of refuge, like the eternal shore, often unite again, in glad communion, hearts that for long years have mourned each other as lost. And affecting beyond expression is the earnestness with which every new arrival among them is met, if perchance it may bring tidings of mother, sister, child, or wife, still lost to view in the shadows of slavery.

Deeds of heroism are wrought here more than those of romance, when, defying torture and braving death itself, the fugitive voluntarily threads his way back to the terrors and perils of that dark land, that he may bring out his sister, or mother, or wife.

One young man, of whom a missionary has told us, twice recaptured, and suffering shameful stripes for his heroism, had escaped again; and in a letter which we heard read, tells his friends that he is going back a third time, that he may, at last, bring away his sister. My good sir, is this man a hero or a criminal ? Would not you do as much for your sister ? And can you blame him ?

But to return to our friends, whom we left wiping their eyes and recovering themselves from too great and sudden a joy. They are now seated around the social board, and are getting decidedly companionable ; only that Cassy who keeps little Eliza on her lap, occasionally squeezes the little thing in a manner that rather astonishes her, and obstinately refuses to have her mouth stuffed with cake to the extent the little one desires, alleging, what the child rather wonders at, that she has got something better than cake, and doesn't want it.

And, indeed, in two or three days such a change has passed over Cassy that our readers would scarcely know her. The despairing, haggard expression of her face had given way to one of gentle trust. She seemed to sink at once into the bosom of the family, and take the little ones into her heart, as something for which it long had waited. Indeed, her love seemed to flow more naturally to the little Eliza than to her own daughter, for she was the exact image and body of the child whom she had lost. The little one was a flowery bond between mother and daughter, through whom grew up acquaintanceship and affection. Eliza's steady, consistent piety, regulated by the constant reading of the sacred word, made her a proper guide for the shattered and wearied mind of her mother. Cassy yielded at once, and with her whole soul, to every good influence, and became a devout and tender Christian.

After a day or two, Madame de Thoux told her brother more particularly of her affairs. The death of her husband had left her an ample fortune, which she generously offered to share with the family. When she asked George what way she could best apply it for him, he answered, 'Give me an education, Emily ; that has always been my heart's desire. Then I can do all the rest.'

On mature deliberation, it was decided that the whole family should go, for some years, to France, whither they sailed, carrying Emmeline with them.

The good looks of the latter won the affection of the first

mate of the vessel, and shortly after entering the port, she became his wife.

George remained four years at a French university, and applying himself with an unintermitted zeal, obtained a very thorough education.

Political troubles in France at last led the family again to seek an asylum in this country.

George's feelings and views, as an educated man, may be best expressed in a letter to one of his friends : –

'I feel somewhat at a loss as to my future course. True, as you have said to me, I might mingle in the circles of the whites in this country, my shade of colour is so slight, and that of my wife and family scarce perceptible. Well, perhaps on sufferance, I might. But, to tell you the truth, I have no wish to.

'My sympathies are not for my father's race, but for my mother's. To him I was no more than a fine dog or horse; to my poor heart-broken mother I was a *child;* and, though I never saw her after the cruel sale that separated us till she died, yet I *know* she always loved me dearly. I know it by my own heart. When I think of all she suffered, of my own early sufferings, of the distress and struggles of my heroic wife, of my sister, sold in the New Orleans slave-market – though I hope to have no unchristian sentiments, yet I may be excused for saying, I have no wish to pass for an American, or to identify myself with them.

'It is with the oppressed, enslaved African race that I cast in my lot; and if I wished anything, I would wish myself two shades darker, rather than one lighter.

'The desire and yearning of my soul is for an African *nationality.* I want a people that shall have a tangible, separate existence of its own; and where am I to look for it? Not in Hayti; for in Hayti they had nothing to start with. A stream cannot rise above its fountain. The race that formed the character of the Haytians was a worn-out, effeminate one, and, of course, the subject race will be centuries in rising to anything.

'Where, then, shall I look? On the shores of Africa I see a republic – a republic formed of picked men, who, by energy and self-educating force, have, in many cases, individually, raised themselves above a condition of slavery. Having gone through a preparatory stage of feebleness, this republic has at last become an acknowledged nation on the face of the earth – acknowledged by both France and England. There it is my wish to go, and find myself a people.

'I am aware, now, that I shall have you all against me; but, before you strike, hear me. During my stay in France, I have followed up, with intense interest, the history of my people in America. I have noted the struggle between Abolitionist and Colonisationist, and have received some impressions, as a distant spectator, which could never have occurred to me as a participator.

'I grant that this Liberia may have subserved all sorts of purposes, by being played off in the hands of our oppressors, against us. Doubtless the scheme may have been used, in unjustifiable ways, as a means of retarding our emancipation. But the question to me is, Is there not a God above all man's schemes? May He not have overruled all their designs, and founded for us a nation by them?

'In these days a nation is born in a day. A nation starts now with all the great problems of republican life and civilisation wrought out to its hand; it has not to discover, but only to apply. Let us, then, all take hold together with all our might, and see what we can do with this new enterprise, and the whole splendid continent of Africa opens before us and our children. *Our nation* shall roll the tide of civilisation and Christianity along its shores, and plant there mighty republics, that, growing with the rapidity of tropical vegetation, shall be for all coming ages.

'Do you say that I am deserting my enslaved brethren? I think not. If I forget them one hour, one moment of my life, so may God forget me? But what can I do for them here? Can I break their chains? No, not as an individual; but let me go and form part of a nation, which shall have a voice in the councils of nations, and then we can speak. A nation has a right to argue, remonstrate, implore, and present the cause of its race, which an individual has not.

'If Europe ever becomes a grand council of free nations – as I trust in God it will – if there serfdom, and all unjust and oppressive social inequalities, are done away; and if they, as France and England have done, acknowledge our position –

then, in the great congress of nations, we will make our appeal, and present the cause of our enslaved and suffering race; and it cannot be that free, enlightened America, will not then desire to wipe from her escutcheon that bar sinister which disgraces her among nations, and is as truly a curse to her as to the enslaved.

'But, you will tell me, our race have equal rights to mingle in the American republic as the Irishman, the German, the Swede. Granted, they have. We *ought* to be free to meet and mingle – to rise by our individual worth, without any consideration of caste or colour; and they who deny us this right are false to their own professed principles of human equality. We ought, in particular, to be allowed *here*. We have *more* than the rights of common men – we have the claim of an injured race for reparation. But, then, *I do not want it;* I want a country, a nation, of my own. I think that the African race has peculiarities yet to be unfolded in the light of civilisation and Christianity, which, if not the same with those of the Anglo-Saxon, may prove to be, morally, of even a higher type.

'To the Anglo-Saxon race have been entrusted the destinies of the world, during its pioneer period of struggle and conflict. To that mission its stern, inflexible, energetic elements were well adapted; but, as a Christian, I look for another era to arise. On its borders I trust we stand; and the throes that now convulse the nations are, to my hope, but the birth-pangs of an hour of universal peace and brotherhood.

'I trust that the development of Africa is to be essentially a Christian one. If not a dominant and commanding race, they are, at least, an affectionate, magnanimous, and forgiving one. Having been called in the furnace of injustice and oppression, they have need to bind closer to their hearts that sublime doctrine of love and forgiveness, through which alone they are to conquer, which it is to be their mission to spread over the continent of Africa.

'In myself, I confess I am feeble for this – full half the blood in my veins is the hot and hasty Saxon; but I have an eloquent preacher of the Gospel ever by my side, in the person of my beautiful wife. When I wander, her gentler spirit ever restores me, and keeps before my eyes the Christian calling and mission of our race. As a Christian patriot, as a teacher of Christianity, I go to *my country* – my chosen, my glorious Africa! – and to her, in my heart, I sometimes apply those splendid words of prophecy, "Whereas thou hast been forsaken and hated, so that no man went through thee; *I* will make thee an eternal excellence, a joy of many generations!"

'You will call me an enthusiast: you will tell me that I have not well considered what I am undertaking. But I have considered, and counted the cost. I go to *Liberia*, not as to an Elysium of romance, but as to *a field of work*. I expect to work with both hands – to work *hard;* to work against all sorts of difficulties and discouragements; and to work till I die. This is what I go for; and in this I am quite sure I shall not be disappointed.

'Whatever you may think of my determination, do not divorce me from your confidence; and think that, in whatever I do, I act with a heart wholly given to my people.

'GEORGE HARRIS.'

George, with his wife, children, sister, and mother, embarked for Africa some few weeks after. If we are not mistaken, the world will yet hear from him there.

Of our other characters we have nothing very particular to write, except a word relating to Miss Ophelia and Topsy, and a farewell chapter, which we shall dedicate to George Shelby.

Miss Ophelia took Topsy home to Vermont with her, much to the surprise of that grave deliberate body whom a New Englander recognises under the term 'Our folks.' 'Our folks,' at first, thought it an odd and unnecessary addtion to their well-trained domestic establishment; but, so thoroughly efficient was Miss Ophelia in her conscientious endeavour to do her duty by her *élève*, that the child rapidly grew in grace and in favour with the family and neighbourhood. At the age of womanhood she was, by her own request, baptised, and became a member of the Christian Church in the place; and showed so much intelligence, activity, and zeal, and desire to do good in the world, that she was at last recommended and approved as a missionary to one of the stations in Africa; and we have heard that the same activity and ingenuity which, when a child, made her so multi-form and restless in her developments, is now employed, in a safer and wholesomer manner, in teaching the children of her own country.

P.S. – It will be a satisfaction to some mother also to state, that some inquiries which were set on foot by Madame de Thoux have resulted recently in the discovery of Cassy's son. Being a young man of energy, he had escaped some years before his mother, and been received and educated by friends of the oppressed in the north. He will soon follow his family to Africa.

Chapter 44

THE LIBERATOR

GEORGE SHELBY had written to his mother merely a line, stating the day that she might expect him home. Of the death-scene of his old friend he had not the heart to write. He had tried several times, and only succeeded in half-choking himself; and invariably finished by tearing up the paper, wiping his eyes, and rushing somewhere to get quiet.

There was a pleased bustle all through the Shelby mansion that day in expectation of the arrival of young Mas'r George.

Mrs Shelby was seated in her comfortable parlour, where a cheerful hickory fire was dispelling the chill of the late autumn evening. A supper-table, glittering with plate and cut glass, was set out, on whose arrangements our former friend, old Chloe, was presiding.

Arrayed in a new calico dress, with clean, white apron, and high, well-starched turban, her black polished face glowing with satisfaction, she lingered, with needless punctiliousness, around the arrangements of the table, merely as an excuse for talking a little to her mistress.

'Laws, now! won't it look natural to him?' she said. 'Thar – I set his plate just whar he likes it – round by the fire. Mas'r George allers wants de warm seat. Oh, go way. Why didn't Sally get out de *best* teapot – de little new one Mas'r George got for missis, Christmas? I'll have it out! And missis has heard from Mas'r George?' she said, inquiringly.

'Yes, Chloe; but only a line, just to say he would be home to-night, if he could – that's all.'

'Didn't say nothin' 'bout my old man, s'pose?' said Chloe, still fidgeting with the teacups.

'No, he didn't. He did not speak of anything, Chloe. He said he would tell all when he got home.'

'Jes like Mas'r George, he's allers so ferce for tellin' everything hisself. I allers minded dat ar in Mas'r George. Don't see, for my part, how white people gen'lly can bar to hev to write things much as they do – writin' 's such slow, oneasy kind o' work.'

Mrs Shelby smiled.

'I'm a thinkin' my old man won't know de boys and de baby. Lor'! she's the biggest gal, now; good she is, too, and peart, Polly is. She's out to the house, now, watchin' de hoecake. I's got jist de very pattern my old man liked so much a-bakin'. Jist sich as I gin him the morning he was took off. Lord bless us! how I felt dat ar morning!'

Mrs Shelby sighed, and felt a heavy weight on her heart, at this allusion. She had felt uneasy ever since she received her son's letter, lest something should prove to be hidden behind the veil of silence which he had drawn.

'Missis had got dem bills?' said Chloe, anxiously.

'Yes, Chloe.'

'Cause I wants to show my old man dem very bills de perfectioner gave me. "And," says he, "Chloe, I wish you'd stay longer." "Thank you, mas'r," says I, "I would, only my old man's coming home, and missis, she can't do without me no longer." There's jist what I told him. Berry nice man, dat Mas'r Jones was.'

Chloe had pertinaciously insisted that the very bills in which her wages had been paid should be preserved to show to her husband, in memorial of her capability; and Mrs Shelby had readily consented to humour her in the request.

'He won't know Polly – my old man won't. Laws, it's five year since they tuk him! She was a baby den – couldn't but jist stand. Remember how tickled he used to be, 'cause she would keep a fallin' over, when she sot out to walk. Laws a me!'

The rattling of wheels now was heard.

'Mas'r George!' said Aunt Chloe, starting to the window. Mrs Shelby ran to the entry door, and was folded in the arms of her son. Aunt Chloe stood anxiously straining her eyes out into the darkness.

'O *poor* Aunt Chloe !' said George, stopping compassionately, and taking her hard black hand between both his. 'I'd have given all my fortune to have brought him with me, but he's gone to a better country.'

There was a passionate exclamation from Mrs Shelby, but Aunt Chloe said nothing.

The party entered the supper-room. The money of which Chloe was so proud was still lying on the table.

'Thar,' said she, gathering it up, and holding it with a trembling hand to her mistress, 'don't never want to see nor hear on't again. Jist as I knew 'twould be – sold and murdered on dem ar' old plantations !'

Chloe turned, and was walking proudly out of the room. Mrs Shelby followed her softly, and took one of her hands, drew her down into a chair, and sat down by her.

'My poor, good Chloe !' said she.

Chloe leaned her head on her mistress's shoulder, and sobbed out, 'O missis ! 'scuse me, my heart's broke – dat's all !'

'I know it is,' said Mrs Shelby, as her tears fell fast; 'and *I* cannot heal it, but Jesus can. He healeth the broken-hearted, and bindeth up their wounds.'

There was a silence for some time, and all wept together. At last, George, sitting down beside the mourner, took her hand, and, with simple pathos, repeated the triumphant scene of her husband's death, and his last messages of love.

About a month after this, one morning, all the servants of the Shelby estate were convened together in the great hall that ran through the house, to hear a few words from their young master.

To the surprise of all, he appeared among them with a bundle of papers in his hand, containing a certificate of freedom to every one on the place, which he read successively, and presented, amid the sobs and tears and shouts of all present.

Many, however, pressed around him, earnestly begging him not to send them away ; and, with anxious faces, tendering back their free papers.

'We don't wan't to be no freer than we are. We's allers had all we wanted. We don't want to leave the ole place, and mas'r and missis, and de rest !'

'My good friends,' said George, as soon as he could get a silence, 'there'll be no need for you to leave me. The place wants as many hands to work it as it did before. We need the same about the house that we did before. But you are now free men and free women. I shall pay you wages for your work such as we shall agree on. The advantage is, that in case of my getting in debt or dying – things that might happen – you cannot now be taken up and sold. I expect to carry on the estate, and to teach you what, perhaps, it will take you some time to learn – how to use the rights I give you as free men and women. I expect you to be good, and willing to learn; and I trust in God that I shall be faithful, and willing to teach. And now, my friends, look up, and thank God for the blessing of freedom.'

An aged, patriarchal negro, who had grown grey and blind on the estate, now rose, and lifting his trembling hand, said 'Let us give thanks unto the Lord!' As all kneeled by one consent, a more touching and hearty Te Deum never ascended to heaven, though borne on the peal of organ, bell, and cannon, than came from that honest old heart.

On rising, another struck up a Methodist hymn, of which the burden was:

> 'The year of Jubilee is come –
> Return, ye ransomed sinners, home.'

'One thing more,' said George, as he stopped the congratulations of the throng. 'You all remember our good old Uncle Tom?'

George here gave a short narration of the scene of his death, and of his loving farewell to all on the place, and added, –

'It was on his grave, my friends, that I resolved, before God, that I would never own another slave while it was possible to free him: that nobody, through me, should ever run the risk of being parted from home and friends, and dying on a lonely plantation, as he died. So, when you rejoice in your freedom, think that you owe it to that good old soul, and pay it back in kindness to his wife and children. Think of your freedom, every time you see UNCLE TOM'S CABIN; and let it be a memorial to put you all in mind to follow in his steps, and be as honest, and faithful, and Christian as he was.'

Chapter 45

CONCLUDING REMARKS

THE writer has often been inquired of, by correspondents from different parts of the country, whether this narrative is a true one; and to these inquiries she will give one general answer.

The separate incidents that compose the narrative are to a very great extent authentic, occurring, many of them, either under her own observation, or that of her personal friends. She or her friends have observed characters the counterpart of almost all that are here introduced; and many of the sayings are word for word as heard herself or reported to her.

The personal appearance of Eliza, the character ascribed to her, are sketches drawn from life. The incorruptible fidelity, piety, and honesty of Uncle Tom, had more than one development to her personal knowledge. Some of the most deeply tragic and romantic, some of the most terrible incidents, have also their parallel in reality. The incident of the mother's crossing the Ohio River on the ice is a well-known fact. The story of 'Old Prue' (Chapter 19.) was an incident that fell under the personal observation of a brother of the writer, then collecting-clerk to a large mercantile house in New Orleans. From the same source was derived the character of the planter, Legree. Of him her brother thus wrote, speaking of visiting his plantation on a collecting tour: 'He actually made me feel of his fist, which was like a blacksmith's hammer or a nodule of iron, telling me that it was "calloused with knocking down niggers." When I left the plantation I drew a long breath, and felt as if I had escaped from an ogre's den.'

That the tragical fate of Tom, also, has too many times had its parallel, there are living witnesses all over our land to testify. Let it be remembered that in all Southern states it is a principle of jurisprudence that no person of coloured lineage can testify in a suit against a white, and it will be easy to see that such a case may occur wherever there is a man whose passions out-weigh his interests, and a slave who has manhood or principle enough to resist his will. There is actually nothing to protect the slave's life but the *character* of the master. Facts too shocking to be contemplated occasionally force their way to the public ear, and the comment that one often hears made on them is more shocking than the thing itself. It is said, 'Very likely such cases may now and then occur, but they are no sample of general practice.' If the laws of New England were so arranged that a master could *now and then* torture an apprentice to death without a possibility of being brought to justice, would it be received with equal composure? Would it be said, 'These cases are rare, and no samples of general practice'? This injustice is an *inherent* one in the slave system, it cannot exist without it.

The public and shameless sale of beautiful mulatto and quadroon girls has acquired a notoriety from the incidents following the capture of the *Pearl*. We extract the following from the speech of the Hon. Horace Mann, one of the legal counsel for the defendants in that case. He says: 'In that company of seventy-six persons, who attempted, in 1848, to escape from the District of Columbia in the schooner *Pearl*, and whose officers I assisted in defending, there were several young and healthy girls, who had those peculiar attractions of form and feature which connoisseurs prize so highly. Elizabeth Russell was one of them. She immediately fell into the slave-trader's fangs, and was doomed for the New Orleans market. The hearts of those that saw her were touched with pity for her fate. They offered eighteen hundred dollars to redeem her; and some there were who offered to give that would not have much left after the gift; but the fiend of a slave-trader was inexorable. She was despatched to New Orleans: but, when about half way there, God had mercy on her, and smote her with death. There were two girls named Edmundson in the same company. When about to be sent to the same market, an older sister went to the shambles to plead with the wretch who owned them, for the love of God to spare his victims. He bantered her, telling what fine dresses and fine furniture they would have. "Yes," she said, "that may do very well in this life, but what will become of them in the next?" They, too, were sent to New Orleans; but were afterwards redeemed at an enormous ransom and brought back.' Is it not plain from this, that the histories of Emmeline and Cassy may have many counterparts?

Justice, too, obliges the author to state that the fairness of mind and generosity attributed to St Clare are not without a parallel, as the following anecdote will show. A few years since, a young Southern gentleman was in Cincinnati, with a favourite servant, who had been his personal attendant from a boy. The young man took advantage of this opportunity to secure his own freedom, and fled to the protection of a Quaker, who was quite noted in affairs of this kind. The owner was exceedingly indignant. He had always treated the slave with such indulgence, and his confidence in his affection was such, that he believed he must have been practised upon to induce him to revolt from him. He visited the Quaker, in high anger; but being possessed of uncommon candour and fairness, was soon quieted by his arguments and representations. It was a side of the subject which he never had heard – never had thought on; and he immediately told the Quaker that, if his slave would to his own face, say, that it was his desire to be free, he would liberate him. An interview was forthwith procured, and Nathan was asked by his young master whether he had ever had any reason to complain of his treatment, in any respect.

'No, mas'r,' said Nathan; 'you've always been good to me.'

'Well, then, why do you want to leave me?'

'Mas'r may die, and then who get me? – I'd rather be a free man.'

After some deliberation, the young master replied, 'Nathan, in your place I think I should feel very much so myself. You are free.'

He immediately made him out free papers; deposited a sum of money in the hands of the Quaker, to be judiciously used in assisting him to start in life, and left a very sensible and kind letter of advice to the young man. That letter was for some time in the writer's hands.

The author hopes she has done justice to that nobility, generosity, and humanity, which in many cases characterise individuals at the South. Such instances save us from utter despair of our kind. But she asks any person, who knows the world, are such characters *common* anywhere?

For many years of her life, the author avoided all reading

upon or allusion to the subject of slavery, considering it as too painful to be inquired into, and one which advancing light and civilisation would certainly live down. But, since the legislative Act of 1850, when she heard, with perfect surprise and consternation, Christian and humane people actually recommending the remanding escaped fugitives into slavery, as a duty binding on good citizens – when she heard on all hands, from kind, compassionate, and estimable people, in the free states of the North, deliberations and discussions as to what Christian duty could be on this head – she could only think, these men and Christians cannot know what slavery is; if they did, such a question could never be open for discussion. And from this arose a desire to exhibit it in a *living dramatic reality*. She has endeavoured to show it fairly, in its best and its worst phases. In its *best* aspect, she has, perhaps, been successful; but, oh, who shall say what yet remains untold in that valley and shadow of death that lies the other side?

To you, generous, noble-minded men and women of the South – you, whose virtue and magnanimity, and purity of character, are the greater for the severer trial it has encountered – to you is her appeal. Have you not, in your own secret souls, in your own private conversings, felt that there are woes and evils in this accursed system far beyond what are here shadowed, or can be shadowed? Can it be otherwise? Is *man* ever a creature to be trusted with wholly irresponsible power? And does not the slave system, by denying the slave all legal right of testimony, make every individual owner an irresponsible despot? Can anybody fail to make the inference what the practical result will be? If there is, as we admit, a public sentiment among you, men of honour, justice, and humanity, is there not also another kind of public sentiment among the ruffian, the brutal, and debased? And cannot the ruffian, the brutal, the debased, by slave law, own just as many slaves as the best and purest? Are the honourable, the just, the high-minded, and compassionate, the majority anywhere in this world?

The slave-trade is now, by American law, considered as piracy. But a slave-trade as systematic as ever was carried on on the coast of Africa is an inevitable attendant and result of American slavery. And its heart-break and its horrors, *can* they be told?

The writer has given only a faint shadow, a dim picture, of the anguish and despair that are at this very moment riving thousands of hearts, shattering thousands of families, and driving a helpless and sensitive race to frenzy and despair. There are those living who know the mothers whom this accursed traffic has driven to the murder of their children, and themselves seeking in death a shelter from woes more dreaded than death. Nothing of tragedy can be written, can be spoken, can be conceived, that equals the frightful reality of scenes daily and hourly acting on our shores, beneath the shadow of American law, and the shadow of the cross of Christ.

And now, men and women of America, is this a thing to be trifled with, apologised for, and passed over in silence? Farmers of Massachusetts, of New Hampshire, of Vermont, of Connecticut, who read this book by the blaze of your winter-evening fire – strong-hearted, generous sailors and ship-owners of Maine – is this a thing for you to countenance and encourage? Brave and generous men of New York, farmers of rich and joyous Ohio, and ye of the wide prairie States, answer, is this a thing for you to protect and countenance? And you, mothers of America – you, who have learned, by the cradles of your own children, to love and feel for all mankind, by the sacred love you bear your child; by your joy in his beautiful, spotless infancy; by the motherly pity and tenderness with which you guide his growing years; by the anxieties of his education; by the prayers you breathe for his soul's eternal good – I beseech you, pity the mother who has all your affections, and not one legal right to protect, guide, or educate the child of her bosom! By the sick hour of your child; by those dying eyes, which you can never forget; by those last cries that wrung your heart when you could neither help nor save; by the desolation of that empty cradle, that silent nursery, I beseech you, pity those mothers that are constantly made childless by the American slave-trade! And say, mothers of America, is this a thing to be defended, sympathised with, passed over in silence?

Do you say that the people of the free states have nothing to do with it, and can do nothing? Would to God this were true! But it is not true. The people of the free states have defended, encouraged, and participated; and are more guilty for it, before

God, than the South, in that they have *not* the apology of education or custom.

If the mothers of the free states had all felt as they should in times past, the sons of the free states would have not have been the holders, and proverbially the hardest masters, of slaves; the ,ons of the free states would not have connived at the extension of slavery in our national body; the sons of the free states would not, as they do, trade the souls and bodies of men as an equivalent to money in their mercantile dealings. There are multitudes of slaves temporarily owned and sold again, by merchants in Northern cities; and shall the whole guilt or obloquy of slavery fall only on the South?

Northern men, Northern mothers, Northern Christians, have something more to do than denounce their brethren at the South; they have to look to the evil among themselves.

But what can any individual do? Of that every individual can judge. There is one thing that every individual can do, they can see to it that *they feel right*. An atmosphere of sympathetic influence encircles every human being; and the man or woman who *feels* strongly, healthily, and justly, on the great interests of humanity, is a constant benefactor to the human race. See, then, to your symphathies in this matter! Are they in harmony with the symphathies of Christ? or are they swayed and perverted by the sophistries of worldly policy?

Christian men and women of the North; still further, you have another power: you can *pray!* Do you believe in prayer? or has it become an indistinct apostolic tradition? You pray for the heathen abroad, pray also for the the heathen at home. And pray for those distressed Christians whose whole chance of religious improvement is an accident of trade and sale – from whom any adherence to the morals of Christianity is, in many cases, an impossibility, unless they have given them from above the courage and grace of martyrdom.

But still more. On the shores of our free states are emerging the poor, shattered, broken remnants of families, men and women escaped, by miraculous providences, from the surges of slavery, feeble in knowledge, and, in many cases, infirm in moral constitution, from a system which confounds and confuses every principle of Christianity and morality. They come to seek a refuge among you; and they come to seek education, knowledge, Christianity.

What do you owe to these poor unfortunates, O Christians? Does not every American Christian owe to the African race some effort at reparation for the wrongs that the American nation has brought upon them? Shall the doors of churches and school-houses be shut upon them? Shall States arise and shake them out? Shall the Church of Christ hear in silence the taunt that is thrown at them, and shrink away from the helpless hand that they stretch out, and by her silence, encourage the cruelty that would chase them from our borders? If it must be so, it will be a mournful spectacle. If it must be so, the country will have reason to tremble, when it remembers that the fate of nations is in the hands of One who is very pitiful, and of tender compassion.

Do you say, 'We don't want them here; let them go to Africa?'

That the providence of God has provided a refuge in Africa is, indeed, a great and noticeable fact; but that is no reason why the Church of Christ should throw off that responsibility to this outcast race which her profession demands of her.

To fill up Liberia with an ignorant, inexperienced, half-barbarised race, just escaped from the chains of slavery, would be only to prolong for ages the period of struggle and conflict which attends the inception of new enterprises. Let the Church of the North receive these poor sufferers in the spirit of Christ; receive them to the educating advantages of Christian republican society and schools, until they have attained to somewhat of a moral and intellectual maturity, and then assist them in their passage to those shores where they may put in practice the lessons they have learned in America.

There is a body of men in the North, comparatively small, who have been doing this; and, as the result, this country has already seen examples of men, formerly slaves, who have rapidly acquired property, reputation, and education. Talent has been developed, which, considering the circumstances, is certainly remarkable; and, for moral traits of honesty, kindness, tenderness of feeling, for heroic efforts and self-denials, endured for the ransom of brethren and friends yet in slavery, they have been remarkable to a degree that, considering the influence under which they were born, is surprising.

The writer has lived, for many years, on the frontier-line of slave states, and has had great opportunities of observation among those who formerly were slaves. They have been in her family as servants; and, in default of any other school to receive them, she has, in many cases, had them instructed in a family school, with her own children. She has also the testimony of missionaries among the fugitives in Canada in coincidence with her own experience; and her deductions, with regard to the capabilities of the race, are encouraging in the highest degree.

The first desire of the emancipated slave, generally, is for *education*. There is nothing that they are not willing to give or do to have their children instructed; and, so far as the writer has observed herself, or taken the testimony of teachers among them, they are remarkably intelligent and quick to learn. The results of schools founded for them by benevolent individuals in Cincinnati fully establish this.

The author gives the following statement of facts, on the authority of Professor C.E. Stowe, then of Lane Seminary, Ohio, with regard to emancipated slaves, now resident in Cincinnati; given to show the capability of the race, even without any very particular assistance or encouragement.

The initial letters alone are given. They are all residents of Cincinnati.

'B—. Furniture-maker; twenty years in this city; worth ten thousand dollars, all his own earnings; a Baptist.

'C—. Full black; stolen from Africa; sold in New Orleans; been free fifteen years; paid for himself six hundred dollars; a farmer; owns several farms in Indiana; Presbyterian; probably worth fifteen or twenty thousand dollars, all earned by himself.

'K—. Full black; dealer in real estate; worth thirty thousand dollars; about forty years old; free six years; paid eighteen hundred dollars for his family; member of the Baptist Church; received a legacy from his master, which he has taken good care of and increased.

'G—. Full black; coal-dealer; about thirty years old; worth eighteen thousand dollars; paid for himself twice, being once defrauded to the amount of sixteen hundred dollars; made all his money by his own efforts — much of it while a slave, hiring his time of his master, and doing business for himself; a fine, gentlemanly fellow.

'W—. Three-fourths black; barber and waiter; from Kentucky; nineteen years free; paid for self and family over three thousand dollars; worth twenty thousand dollars, all his own earnings; deacon in the Baptist Church.

'G. D—. Three-fourths black; white-washer; from Kentucky; nine years free; paid fifteen hundred dollars for self and family; recently died, aged sixty; worth six thousand dollars.'

Professor Stowe says, 'With all these, except G—, I have been, for some years, personally acquainted, and make my statements from my own knowledge.'

The writer well remembers an aged coloured women, who was employed as a washerwoman in her father's family. The daughter of this women married a slave. She was a remarkably active and capable young women, and by her industry and thrift, and the most persevering self-denial, raised nine hundred dollars for her husband's freedom, which she paid, as she raised it, into the hands of his master. She yet wanted a hundred dollars of the price when he died. She never recovered any of the money.

These are but few facts among multitudes which might be adduced to show the self-denial, energy, patience, and honesty which the slave has exhibited in a state of freedom.

And let it be remembered that these individuals have thus bravely succeeded in conquering for themselves comparative wealth and social position in the face of every disadvantage and discouragement. The coloured man, by the law of Ohio, cannot be a voter, and, till within a few years, was even denied the right of testimony in legal suits with the white. Nor are these instances confined to the State of Ohio. In all states of the Union we see men, but yesterday burst from the shackles of slavery who, by a self-educating force, which cannot be too much admired, have risen to highly respectable stations in society. Pennington among clergymen, Douglas and Ward among editors, are well-known instances.

If this persecuted race, with every discouragement and disadvantage, have done thus much, how much more they might do, if the Christian Church would act towards them in the spirit of her Lord!

This is an age of the world when nations are trembling and

convulsed. A mighty influence is abroad, surging and heaving the world, as with an earthquake. And is America safe? Every nation that carries in its bosom great and unredressed injustice has in it the elements of this last convulsion.

For what is this mighty influence thus rousing in all nations and languages those groanings that cannot be uttered for man's freedom and equality?

O Church of Christ, read the signs of the times! Is not this power the Spirit of HIM whose kingdom is yet to come, and whose will to be done on earth as it is in heaven?

But who may abide the day of his appearing? 'For that day shall burn as an oven: and he shall appear as a swift witness against those that oppress the hireling in his wages, the widow and the fatherless, and that *turn aside the stranger in his right*: and he shall break in pieces the oppressor.'

Are not these dread words for a nation bearing in her bosom so mighty an injustice? Christians! every time that you pray that the kingdom of Christ may come, can you forget that prophecy associates, in dread fellowship, the *day of vengeance* with the year of his redeemed?

A day of grace is yet held out to us. Both North and South have been guilty before God; and the *Christian Church* has a heavy account to answer. Not by combining together to protect injustice and cruelty, and making a common capital of sin, is this Union to be saved – but by repentance, justice, and mercy; for not surer is the eternal law by which the millstone sinks in the ocean, than that stronger law by which injustice and cruelty shall bring on nations the wrath of Almighty God!

NARRATIVE OF THE
LIFE OF
FREDERICK DOUGLASS,
AN AMERICAN SLAVE

Preface

IN THE month of August, 1841, I attended an anti-slavery convention in Nantucket, at which it was my happiness to become acquainted with Frederick Douglass, the writer of the following Narrative. He was a stranger to nearly every member of that body; but, having recently made his escape from the southern prison-house of bondage, and feeling his curiosity excited to ascertain the principles and measures of the abolitionists, – of whom he had heard a somewhat vague description while he was a slave, – he was induced to give his attendance, on the occasion alluded to, though at that time a resident in New Bedford.

Fortunate, most fortunate occurrence! – fortunate for the millions of his manacled brethren, yet panting for deliverance from their awful thraldom! – fortunate for the cause of negro emancipation, and of universal liberty! – fortunate for the land of his birth, which he has already done so much to save and bless! – fortunate for a large circle of friends and acquaintances, whose sympathy and affection he has strongly secured by the many sufferings he has endured, by his virtuous traits of character, by his ever abiding remembrance of those who are in bonds, as being bound with them! – fortunate for the multitudes, in various parts of our republic, whose minds he has enlightened on the subject of slavery, and who have been melted to tears by his pathos, or roused to virtuous indignation by his stirring eloquence against the enslavers of men! – fortunate for himself, as it at once brought him into the field of public usefulness, 'gave the world assurance of a man,' quickened the slumbering energies of his soul, and consecrated him to the great work of breaking the rod of the oppressor, and letting the oppressed go free!

I shall never forget his first speech at the convention – the extraordinary emotion it excited in my own mind – the powerful impression it created upon a crowded auditory, completely taken by surprise – the applause which followed from the beginning to the end of his felicitous remarks. I think I never hated slavery so intensely as at that moment; certainly, my perception of the enormous outrage which is inflicted by it, on the godlike nature of its victims, was rendered far more clear than ever. There stood one, in physical proportion and stature commanding and exact – in intellect richly endowed – in natural eloquence a prodigy – in soul manifestly 'created but a little lower than the angels' – yet a slave, ay, a fugitive slave – trembling for his safety, hardly daring to believe that on the American soil, a single white person could be found who would befriend him at all hazards, for the love of God and humanity ! Capable of high attainments as an intellectual and moral being – needing nothing but a comparatively small amount of cultivation to make him an ornament to society and a blessing to his race – by the law of the land, by the voice of the people, by the terms of the slave code, he was only a piece of property, a beast of burden, a chattel personal, nevertheless !

A beloved friend from New Bedford prevailed on Mr Douglass to address the convention. He came forward to the platform with a hesitancy and embarrassment, necessarily the attendants of a sensitive mind in such a novel position. After apologizing for his ignorance, and reminding the audience that slavery was a poor school for the human intellect and heart, he proceeded to narrate some of the facts in his own history as a slave, and in the course of his speech gave utterance to many noble thoughts and thrilling reflections. As soon as he had taken his seat, filled with hope and admiration, I rose, and declared that Patrick Henry, of revolutionary fame, never made a speech more eloquent in the cause of liberty, than the one we had just listened to from the lips of that hunted fugitive. So I believed at that time – such is my belief now. I reminded the audience of the peril which surrounded this self-emancipated young man at the North – even in Massachusetts, on the soil of the Pilgrim Fathers, among the descendants of revolutionary sires ; and I appealed to them, whether they would ever allow him to be carried back into slavery – law or no law, constitution or no constitution. The response was unanimous and in thunder-tones – 'NO !' 'Will you succor and protect him as a brother-man – a resident of the old Bay State?' 'YES!' shouted the whole mass, with an energy so startling, that the ruthless tyrants south of Mason and Dixon's line might almost have heard the mighty burst of feeling, and recognized it as the pledge of an invincible determination, on the part of those who gave it, never to betray him that wanders, but to hide the outcast, and firmly to abide the consequences.

It was at once deeply impressed upon my mind, that, if Mr Douglass could be persuaded to consecrate his time and talents to the promotion of the anti-slavery enterprise, a powerful impetus would be given to it, and a stunning blow at the same time inflicted on northern prejudice against a colored complexion. I therefore endeavored to instill hope and courage into his mind, in order that he might dare to engage in a vocation so anomalous and responsible for a person in his situation; and I was seconded in this effort by warm-hearted friends, especially by the late General Agent of the Massachusetts Anti-Slavery Society, Mr John A. Collins, whose judgment in this instance entirely coincided with my own. At first, he could give no encouragement; with unfeigned diffidence, he expressed his conviction that he was not adequate to the performance of so great a task; the path marked out was wholly an untrodden one; he was sincerely apprehensive that he should do more harm than good. After much deliberation, however, he consented to make a trial; and ever since that period, he has acted as a lecturing agent, under the auspices either of the American or the Massachusetts Anti-Slavery Society. In labors he has been most abundant; and his success in combating prejudice, in gaining proselytes, in agitating the public mind, has far surpassed the most sanguine expectations that were raised at the commencement of his brilliant career. He has borne himself with gentleness and meekness, yet with true manliness of character. As a public speaker, he excels in pathos, wit, comparison, imitation, strength of reasoning, and fluency of language. There is in him that union of head and heart, which is indispensable to an englightenment of the heads and a winning of the hearts of others. May his strength continue to be equal to his day! May he continue to 'grow in grace, and in the knowledge of God,' that he may be increasingly serviceable in the cause of bleeding humanity, whether at home or abroad!

It is certainly a very remarkable fact, that one of the most efficient advocates of the slave population, now before the public, is a fugitive slave, in the person of Frederick Douglass; and that the free colored population of the United States are as ably represented by one of their own number, in the person of Charles Lenox Remond, whose eloquent appeals have extorted the highest applause of multitudes on both sides of the Atlantic. Let the calumniators of the colored race despise themselves for their baseness and illiberality of spirit, and henceforth cease to talk of the natural inferiority of those who require nothing but time and opportunity to attain to the highest point of human excellence.

It may, perhaps, be fairly questioned, whether any other portion of the population of the earth could have endured the privations, sufferings and horrors of slavery, without having become more degraded in the scale of humanity than the slaves of African descent. Nothing has been left undone to cripple their intellects, darken their minds, debase their moral nature, obliterate all traces of their relationship to mankind; and yet how wonderfully they have sustained the mighty load of a most frightful bondage, under which they have been groaning for centuries! To illustrate the effect of slavery on the white man, – to show that he has no powers of endurance, in such a condition, superior to those of his black brother – Daniel O'Connell, the distinguished advocate of universal emancipation, and the mightiest champion of prostrate but not conquered Ireland, relates the following anecdote in a speech delivered by him in the Conciliation Hall, Dublin, before the Loyal National Repeal Association, March 31, 1845. 'No matter,' said Mr O'Connell, 'under what specious term it may disguise itself, slavery is still hideous. *It has a natural, an inevitable tendency to brutalize every noble faculty of man.* An American sailor, who was cast away on the shore of Africa, where he was kept in slavery for three years, was, at the expiration of that period, found to be imbruted and stultified – he had lost all reasoning power; and having forgotten his native language, could only utter some savage gibberish between Arabic and English, which nobody could understand, and which even he himself found difficulty in pronouncing. So much for the humanizing influence of the domestic instutitution!' Admitting this to have been an extraordinary case of mental deterioration, it proves at least that the white slave can sink as low in the scale of humanity as the black one.

Mr Douglass has very properly chosen to write his own Narrative, in his own style, and according to the best of his ability, rather than to employ some one else. It is, therefore, entirely his own production; and, considering how long and dark was the career he had to run as a slave – how few have been his opportunities to improve his mind since he broke his iron fetters – it is, in my judgment, highly creditable to his head and heart. He who can peruse it without a tearful eye, a heaving breast, an afflicted spirit – without being filled with an unutterable abhorrence of slavery and all its abettors, and animated with a determination to seek the immediate overthrow of that execrable system – without trembling for the fate of this country in the hands of a righteous God, who is ever on the side of the oppressed, and whose arm is not shortened that it cannot save – must have a flinty heart, and be qualified to act the part of a trafficker 'in slaves and the souls of men.' I am confident that it is essentially true in all its statements; that nothing has been set down in malice, nothing exaggerated, nothing drawn from the imagination; that it comes short of the reality, rather than overstates a single fact in regard to slavery as it is. The experience of Frederick Douglass, as a slave, was not a peculiar one; his lot was not especially a hard one; his case may be regarded as a very fair specimen of the treatment of slaves in Maryland, in which State it is conceded that they are better fed and less cruelly treated than in Georgia, Alabama, or Louisiana. Many have suffered incomparably more, while very few on the plantations have suffered less, than himself. Yet how deplorable was his situation! what terrible chastisements were inflicted upon his person! what still more shocking outrages were perpetrated upon his mind! with all his noble powers and sublime aspirations, how like a brute was he treated, even by those professing to have the same mind in them that was in Christ Jesus! to what dreadful liabilities was he continually subjected! how destitute of friendly counsel and aid, even in his greatest extremities! how heavy was the midnight of woe which shrouded in blackness the last ray of hope, and filled the future with terror and gloom! what longings after freedom took possession of his breast, and how his misery augmented, in proportion as he grew reflective and intelligent – thus demonstrating that a happy slave is an extinct man! how he thought, reasoned, felt, under the lash of the driver, with the chains upon his limbs! what perils he encountered in his endeavors to escape from his horrible doom! and how signal have been his deliverance and preservation in the midst of a nation of pitiless enemies!

This Narrative contains many affecting incidents, many passages of great eloquence and power; but I think the most thrilling one of them all is the description Douglass gives of his feelings, as he stood soliloquizing respecting his fate, and the chances of his one day being a freeman, on the banks of the Chesapeake Bay – viewing the receding vessels as they flew with their white wings before the breeze, and apostrophizing them as animated by the living spirit of freedom. Who can read that passage, and be insensible to its pathos and sublimity? Compressed into it is a whole Alexandrian library of thought, feeling, and sentiment – all that can, all that need be urged, in the form of expostulation, entreaty, rebuke, against that crime of crimes, – making man the property of his fellow-man! O, how accursed is that system, which entombs the godlike mind of man, defaces the divine image, reduces those who by creation were crowned with glory and honor to a level with four-footed beasts, and exalts the dealer in human flesh above all that is called God! Why should its existence be prolonged one hour? Is it not evil, only evil, and that continually? What does its presence imply but the absence of all fear of God, all regard for man, on the part of the people of the United States? Heaven speed its eternal overthrow!

So profoundly ignorant of the nature of slavery are many persons, that they are stubbornly incredulous whenever they read or listen to any recital of the cruelties which are daily inflicted on its victims. They do not deny that the slaves are held as property; but that terrible fact seems to convey to their minds no idea of injustice, exposure to outrage, or savage barbarity. Tell them of cruel scourgings, of mutilations and brandings, of scenes of pollution and blood, of the banishment of all light and knowledge, and they affect to be greatly indignant at such enormous exaggerations, such wholesale misstatements, such abominable libels on the character of the southern planters! As if all these direful outrages were not the natural results of slavery! As if it were less cruel to reduce a human being to the condition of a thing, than to give him a severe flagellation, or to deprive him of necessary food and clothing! As if whips, chains, thumb-screws, paddles, bloodhounds, overseers, drivers, patrols, were not all indispensable to keep the slaves down, and to give protection to their ruthless oppressors! As if, when the marriage institution is abolished, concubinage, adultery, and incest, must not necessarily abound; when all the rights of humanity are annihilated, any barrier remains to protect the victim from the fury of the spoiler; when absolute power is assumed over life and liberty, it will not be wielded with destructive sway! Skeptics of this character abound in society. In some few instances, their incredulity arises from a want of reflection; but, generally, it indicates a hatred of the light, a desire to shield slavery from the assaults of its foes, a contempt of the colored race, whether bond or free. Such will try to discredit the shocking tales of slaveholding cruelty which are recorded in this truthful Narrative; but they will labor in vain. Mr Douglass has frankly disclosed the place of his birth, the names of those who claimed ownership in his body and soul, and the names also of those who committed the crimes which he has alleged against them. His statements, therefore, may easily be disproved, if they are untrue.

In the course of his Narrative, he relates two instances of murderous cruelty — in one of which a planter deliberately shot a slave belonging to a neighboring plantation, who had unintentionally gotten within his lordly domain in quest of fish; and in the other, an overseer blew out the brains of a slave who had fled to a stream of water to escape a bloody scourging. Mr Douglass states that in neither of these instances was any thing done by way of legal arrest or judicial investigation. The Baltimore American, of March 17, 1845, relates a similar case of atrocity, perpetrated with similar impunity — as follows: — 'Shooting a Slave. We learn, upon the authority of a letter from Charles county, Maryland, received by a gentleman of this city, that a young man, named Matthews, a nephew of General Matthews, and whose father, it is believed, holds an office at Washington, killed one of the slaves upon his father's farm by shooting him. The letter states that young Matthews had been left in charge of the farm; that he gave an order to the servant, which was disobeyed, when he proceeded to the house, *obtained a gun, and, returning, shot the servant.* He immediately, the letter continues, fled to his father's residence, where he still remains unmolested.' Let it never be forgotten, that no slave-holder or overseer can be convicted of any outrage perpetrated on the person of a slave, however diabolical it may be, on the testimony of colored witnesses, whether bond of free. By the slave code, they are adjudged to be as incompetent to testify against a white man, as though they were indeed a part of the brute creation. Hence, there is no legal protection in fact, whatever there may be in form, for the slave population; and any amount of cruelty may be inflicted on them with impunity. Is it possible for the human mind to conceive of a more horrible state of society?

The effect of a religious profession on the conduct of southern masters is vividly described in the following Narrative, and shown to be any thing but salutary. In the nature of the case, it must be in the highest degree pernicious. The testimony of Mr Douglass, on this point, is sustained by a cloud of witnesses, whose veracity is unimpeachable. 'A slaveholder's profession of Christianity is a palpable imposture. He is a felon of the highest grade. He is a man-stealer. It is of no importance what you put in the other scale.'

Reader! are you with the man-stealers in sympathy and purpose, or on the side of their down-trodden victims? If with the former, then are you the foe of God and man. If with the latter, what are you prepared to do and dare in their behalf? Be faithful, be vigilant, be untiring in your efforts to break every yoke, and let the oppressed go free. Come what may – cost what it may – inscribe on the banner which you unfurl to the breeze, as your religious and political motto – 'No COMPROMISE WITH SLAVERY! NO UNION WITH SLAVEHOLDERS!.'

WM. LLOYD GARRISON
Boston, 1 May, 1845

Letter from Wendell Phillips, Esq.

Boston, 22 April 1845

MY DEAR FRIEND :

You remember the old fable of 'The Man and the Lion,' where the lion complained that he should not be so misrepresented 'when the lions wrote history.'

I am glad the time has come when the 'lions write history.' We have been left long enough to gather the character of slavery from the involuntary evidence of the masters. One might, indeed, rest sufficiently satisfied with what, it is evident, must be, in general, the results of such a relation, without seeking further to find whether they have followed in every instance. Indeed, those who stare at the half-peck of corn a week, and love to count the lashes on the slave's back, are seldom the 'stuff' out of which reformers and abolitionists are to be made. I remember that, in 1838, many were waiting for the results of the West India experiment, before they could come into our ranks. Those 'results' have come long ago; but, alas! few of that number have come with them, as converts. A man must be disposed to judge of emancipation by other tests than whether it has increased the produce of sugar – and to hate slavery for other reasons than because it starves men and whips women – before he is ready to lay the first stone of his anti-slavery life.

I was glad to learn, in your story, how early the most neglected of God's children waken to a sense of their rights, and of the injustice done them. Experience is a keen teacher; and long before you had mastered your A B C, or knew where the 'white sails' of the Chesapeake were bound, you began, I see, to gauge the wretchedness of the slave, not by his hunger and want, not by his lashes and toil, but by the cruel and blighting death which gathers over his soul.

In connection with this, there is one circumstance which makes your recollections peculiarly valuable, and renders your early insight the more remarkable. You come from that part of the country where we are told slavery appears with its fairest features. Let us hear, then, what it is at its best estate – gaze on its bright side, if it has one ; and then imagination may task her powers to add dark lines to the picture, as she travels southward to that (for the colored man) Valley of the Shadow of Death, where the Mississippi sweeps along.

Again, we have known you long, and can put the most entire confidence in your truth, candor, and sincerity. Every one who has heard you speak has felt, and, I am confident, every one who reads your book will feel, persuaded that you give them a fair specimen of the whole truth. No one-sided portrait – no wholesale complaints – but strict justice done, whenever individual kindliness has neutralized, for a moment, the deadly system with which it was strangely allied. You have been with us, too, some years, and can fairly compare the twilight of rights, which your race enjoy at the North, with that 'noon of night' under which they labor south of Mason and Dixon's line. Tell us whether, after all, the half-free colored man of Massachusetts is worse off than the pampered slave of the rice swamps !

In reading your life, no one can say that we have unfairly picked out some rare specimens of cruelty. We know that the bitter drops, which even you have drained from the cup, are no incidental aggravations, no individual ills, but such as must mingle always and necessarily in the lot of every slave. They are the essential ingredients, not the occasional results, of the system.

After all, I shall read your book with trembling for you. Some years ago, when you were beginning to tell me your real name and birthplace, you may remember I stopped you, and preferred to remain ignorant of all. With the exception of a vague description, so I continued, till the other day, when you read me your memoirs. I hardly knew, at the time, whether to thank you or not for the sight of them, when I reflected that it was still dangerous, in Massachusetts, for honest men to tell their names ! They say the fathers, in 1776, signed the Declaration of Independence with the halter about their necks. You, too, publish your declaration of freedom with danger compassing you around. In all the broad lands which the Constitution of the United States overshadows, there is no single spot – however narrow or desolate – where a fugitive slave can plant himself and say, 'I am safe.' The whole armory of Northern Law has no shield for you. I am free to say that, in your place, I should throw the MS. into the fire.

You, perhaps, may tell your story in safety, endeared as you are to so many warm hearts by rare gifts, and a still rarer devotion of them to the service of others. But it will be owing only to your labors, and the fearless efforts of those who, trampling the laws and Constitution of the country under their feet, are determined that they will 'hide the outcast,' and that their hearths shall be, spite of the law, an asylum for the oppressed, if, some time or other, the humblest may stand in our streets, and bear witness in safety against the cruelties of which he has been the victim.

Yet it is sad to think, that these very throbbing hearts which welcome your story, and form your best safeguard in telling it, are all beating contrary to the 'statute in such case made and provided.' Go on, my dear friend, till you, and those who, like you, have been saved, so as by fire, from the dark prison-house, shall stereotype these free, illegal pulses into statutes; and New England, cutting loose from a blood-stained Union, shall glory in being the house of refuge for the oppressed; till we no longer merely '*hide* the outcast,' or make a merit of standing idly by while he is hunted in our midst; but, consecrating anew the soil of the Pilgrims as an asylum for the oppressed, proclaim our *welcome* to the slave so loudly, that the tones shall reach every hut in the Carolinas, and make the broken-hearted bondman leap up at the thought of old Massachusetts.

God speed the day!
Till then, and ever,
Yours truly,
WENDELL PHILLIPS

FREDERICK DOUGLASS

Chapter 1

I WAS BORN in Tuckahoe, near Hillsborough, and about twelve miles from Easton, in Talbot County, Maryland. I have no accurate knowledge of my age, never having seen any authentic record containing it. By far the larger part of the slaves know as little of their ages as horses know of theirs, and it is the wish of most masters within my knowledge to keep their slaves thus ignorant. I do not remember to have ever met a slave who could tell of his birthday. They seldom come nearer to it than planting-time, harvest-time, cherry-time, spring-time, or fall-time. A want of information concerning my own was a source of unhappiness to me even during childhood. The white children could tell their ages. I could not tell why I ought to be deprived of the same privilege. I was not allowed to make any inquiries of my master concerning it. He deemed all such inquiries on the part of a slave improper and impertinent, and evidence of a restless spirit. The nearest estimate I can give makes me now between twenty-seven and twenty-eight years of age. I come to this, from hearing my master say, some time during 1835, I was about seventeen years old.

My mother was named Harriet Bailey. She was the daughter of Isaac and Betsey Bailey, both colored, and quite dark. My mother was of a darker complexion than either my grandmother or grandfather.

My father was a white man. He was admitted to be such by all I ever heard speak of my parentage. The opinion was also whispered that my master was my father; but of the correctness of this opinion, I know nothing; the means of knowing was withheld from me. My mother and I were separated when I was but an infant – before I knew her as my mother. It is a common custom, in the part of Maryland from which I ran away, to part children from their mothers at a very early age. Frequently, before the child has reached its twelfth month, its mother is taken from it, and the child is placed under the care of an old woman, too old for field labor. For what this separation is done, I do not know, unless it be to hinder the development of the child's affection toward its mother, and to blunt and destroy the natural affection of the mother for the child. This is the inevitable result.

I never saw my mother, to know her as such, more than four or five times in my life; and each of those times was very short in duration, and at night. She was hired by a Mr Stewart, who lived about twelve miles from my home. She made her journeys to see me in the night, travelling the whole distance on foot, after the performance of her day's work. She was a field hand, and a whipping is the penalty of not being in the field at sunrise, unless a slave has special permission from his or her master to the contrary – a permission which they seldom get, and one that gives to him that gives it the proud name of being a kind master. I do not recollect of ever seeing my mother by the light of day. She was with me in the night. She would lie down with me, and get me to sleep, but long before I waked she was gone. Very little communication ever took place between us. Death soon ended what little we could have while she lived, and with it her hardships and suffering. She died when I was about seven years old, on one of my master's farms, near Lee's Mill. I was not allowed to be present during her illness, at her death, or burial. She was gone long before I knew any thing about it. Never having enjoyed, to any considerable extent, her soothing presence, her tender and watchful care, I received the tidings of her death with much the same emotions I should have probably felt at the death of a stranger.

Called thus suddenly away, she left me without the slightest intimation of who my father was. The whisper that my master was my father, may or may not be true; and, true or false, it is of but little consequence to my purpose whilst the fact remains, in all its glaring odiousness, that slaveholders have ordained, and by law established, that the children of slave women shall in all cases follow the condition of their mothers; and this is done too obviously to administer to their own lusts, and make a gratification of their wicked desires profitable as well as pleasurable; for by this cunning arrangement, the slaveholder, in cases not a few, sustains to his slaves the double relation of master and father.

I know of such cases; and it is worthy of remark that such slaves invariably suffer greater hardships, and have more to contend with, than others. They are, in the first place, a constant offence to their mistress. She is ever disposed to find fault with them; they can seldom do any thing to please her; she is never better pleased than when she sees them under the lash, especially when she suspects her husband of showing to his mulatto children favors which he withholds from his black slaves. The master is frequently compelled to sell this class of his slaves, out of deference to the feelings of his white wife; and, cruel as the deed may strike any one to be, for a man to sell his own children to human flesh-mongers, it is often the dictate of humanity for him to do so; for, unless he does this, he must not only whip them himself, but must stand by and see one white son tie up his brother, of but few shades darker complexion than himself, and ply the gory lash to his naked back; and if he lisp one word of disapproval, it is set down to his parental partiality, and only makes a bad matter worse, both for himself and the slave whom he would protect and defend.

Every year brings with it multitudes of this class of slaves. It was doubtless in consequence of a knowledge of this fact, that one great statesman of the south predicted the downfall of slavery by the inevitable laws of population. Whether this prophecy is ever fulfilled or not, it is nevertheless plain that a very different-looking class of people are springing up at the south, and are now held in slavery, from those originally brought to this country from Africa; and if their increase will do no other good, it will do away the force of the argument, that God cursed Ham, and therefore American slavery is right. If the lineal descendants of Ham are alone to be scripturally enslaved, it is certain that slavery at the south must soon become unscriptural; for thousands are ushered into the world, annually, who, like myself, owe their existence to white fathers, and those fathers most frequently their own masters.

I have had two masters. My first master's name was Anthony. I do not remember his first name. He was generally called Captain Anthony – a title which, I presume, he acquired by sailing a craft on the Chesapeake Bay. He was not considered a rich slaveholder. He owned two or three farms, and about thirty slaves. His farms and slaves were under the care of an overseer. The overseer's name was Plummer. Mr Plummer was a miserable drunkard, a profane swearer, and a savage monster. He always went armed with a cowskin and a heavy cudgel. I have known him to cut and slash the women's heads so horribly, that even master would be enraged at his cruelty, and would threaten to whip him if he did not mind himself. Master, however, was not a humane slaveholder. It required extraordinary barbarity on the part of an overseer to affect him. He was a cruel man, hardened by a long life of slaveholding. He would at times seem to take great pleasure in whipping a slave. I have often been awakened at the dawn of day by the most heart-rending shrieks of an own aunt of mine, whom he used to tie up to a joist, and whip upon her naked back till she was literally covered with blood. No words, no tears, no prayers, from his gory victim, seemed to move his iron heart from its bloody purpose. The louder she screamed, the harder he whipped; and where the blood ran fastest, there he whipped longest. He would whip her to make her scream, and whip her to make her hush; and not until overcome by fatigue, would he cease to swing the blood-clotted cowskin. I remember the first time I ever witnessed this horrible exhibition. I was quite a child, but I well remember it. I never shall forget it whilst I remember any thing. It was the first of a long series of such outrages, of which I was doomed to be a witness and a participant. It struck me with awful force. It was the blood-stained gate, the entrance to the hell of slavery, through which I was about to pass. It was a most terrible spectacle. I wish I could commit to paper the feelings with which I beheld it.

This occurrence took place very soon after I went to live with my old master, and under the following circumstances. Aunt Hester went out one night, – where or for what I do not know, – and happened to be absent when my master desired her presence. He had ordered her not to go out evenings, and warned her that she must never let him catch her in company with a young man, who was paying attention to her belonging to Colonel Lloyd. The young man's name was Ned Roberts, generally called Lloyd's Ned. Why master was so careful of her, may be safely left to conjecture. She was a woman of noble form, and of graceful proportions, having very few equals, and fewer superiors, in personal appearance, among the colored or white women of our neighborhood.

Aunt Hester had not only disobeyed his orders in going out, but had been found in company with Lloyd's Ned; which circumstance, I found, from what he said while whipping her, was the chief offence. Had he been a man of pure morals himself, he might have been thought interested in protecting the innocence of my aunt; but those who knew him will not suspect him of any such virtue. Before he commenced whipping Aunt Hester, he took her into the kitchen, and stripped her from neck to waist, leaving her neck, shoulders, and back, entirely naked. He then told her to cross her hands, calling her at the same time a d—d b—h. After crossing her hands, he tied them with a strong rope, and led her to a stool under a large hook in the joist, put in for the purpose. He made her get upon the stool, and tied her hands to the hook. She now stood fair for his infernal purpose. Her arms were stretched up at their full length, so that she stood upon the ends of her toes. He then said to her, 'Now, you d—d b—h, I'll learn you how to disobey my orders!' and after rolling up his sleeves, he commenced to lay on the heavy cowskin, and soon the warm, red blood (amid heart-rending shrieks from her, and horrid oaths from him) came dripping to the floor. I was so terrified and horror-stricken at the sight, that I hid myself in a closet, and dared not venture out till long after the bloody transaction was over. I expected it would be my turn next. It was all new to me. I had never seen any thing like it before. I had always lived with my grandmother on the outskirts of the plantation, where she was put to raise the children of the younger women. I had therefore been, until now, out of the way of the bloody scenes that often occurred on the plantation.

Chapter 2

MY MASTER'S family consisted of two sons, Andrew and Richard; one daughter, Lucretia, and her husband, Captain Thomas Auld. They lived in one house, upon the home plantation of Colonel Edward Lloyd. My master was Colonel Lloyd's clerk and superintendent. He was what might be called the overseer of the overseers. I spent two years of childhood on this plantation in my old master's family. It was here that I witnessed the bloody transaction recorded in the first chapter; and as I received my first impressions of slavery on this plantation, I will give some description of it, and of slavery as it there existed. The plantation is about twelve miles north of Easton, in Talbot county, and is situated on the border of Miles River. The principal products raised upon it were tobacco, corn, and wheat. These were raised in great abundance; so that, with the products of this and the other farms belonging to him, he was able to keep in almost constant employment a large sloop, in carrying them to market at Baltimore. This sloop was named Sally Lloyd, in honor of one of the colonel's daughters. My master's son-in-law, Captain Auld, was master of the vessel; she was otherwise manned by the colonel's own slaves. Their names were Peter, Isaac, Rich, and Jake. These were esteemed very highly by the other slaves, and looked upon as the privileged ones of the plantation; for it was no small affair, in the eyes of the slaves, to be allowed to see Baltimore.

Colonel Lloyd kept from three to four hundred slaves on his home plantation, and owned a large number more on the neighboring farms belonging to him. The names of the farms nearest to the home plantation were Wye Town and New Design. 'Wye Town' was under the overseership of a man named Noah Willis. New Design was under the overseership of a Mr Townsend, The overseers of these, and all the rest of the farms, numbering over twenty, received advice and direction from the managers of the home plantation. This was the great business place. It was the seat of government for the whole

THE LIFE OF FREDERICK DOUGLASS

twenty farms. All disputes among the overseers were settled here. If a slave was convicted of any high misdemeanor, became unmanageable, or evinced a determination to run away, he was brought immediately here, severely whipped, put on board the sloop, carried to Baltimore, and sold to Austin Woolfolk, or some other slave-trader, as a warning to the slaves remaining.

Here, too, the slaves of all the other farms received their monthly allowance of food, and their yearly clothing. The men and women slaves received, as their monthly allowance of food, eight pounds of pork, or its equivalent in fish, and one bushel of corn meal. Their yearly clothing consisted of two coarse linen shirts, one pair of linen trousers, like the shirts, one jacket, one pair of trousers for winter, made of coarse negro cloth, one pair of stockings, and one pair of shoes; the whole of which could not have cost more than seven dollars. The allowance of the slave children was given to their mothers, or the old women having the care of them. The children unable to work in the field had neither shoes, stockings, jackets, nor trousers, given to them; their clothing consisted of two coarse linen shirts per year. When these failed them, they went naked until the next allowance-day. Children from seven to ten years old, of both sexes, almost naked, might be seen at all seasons of the year.

There were no beds given the slaves, unless one coarse blanket be considered such, and none but the men and women had these. This, however, is not considered a very great privation. They find less difficulty from the want of beds, than from the want of time to sleep; for when their day's work in the field is done, the most of them having their washing, mending, and cooking to do, and having few or none of the ordinary facilities for doing either of these, very many of their sleeping hours are consumed in preparing for the field the coming day; and when this is done, old and young, male and female, married and single, drop down side by side, on one common bed – the cold, damp floor – each covering himself or herself with their miserable blankets; and here they sleep till they are summoned to the field by the driver's horn. At the sound of this, all must rise, and be off to the field. There must be no halting; every one must be at his or her post; and woe betides them who hear not this morning summons to the field; for if they are not awakened by the sense of hearing, they are by the sense of feeling: no age nor sex finds any favor. Mr Severe, the overseer, used to stand by the door of the quarter, armed with a large hickory stick and heavy cowskin, ready to whip any one who was so unfortunate as not to hear, or, from any other cause, was prevented from being ready to start for the field at the sound of the horn.

Mr Severe was rightly named: he was a cruel man. I have seen him whip a woman, causing the blood to run half an hour at the time; and this, too, in the midst of her crying children, pleading for their mother's release. He seemed to take pleasure in manifesting his fiendish barbarity. Added to his cruelty, he was a profane swearer. It was enough to chill the blood and stiffen the hair of an ordinary man to hear him talk. Scarce a sentence escaped him but that was commenced or concluded by some horrid oath. The field was the place to witness his cruelty and profanity. His presence made it both the field of blood and of blasphemy. From the rising till the going down of the sun, he was cursing, raving, cutting, and slashing among the slaves of the field, in the most frightful manner. His career was short. He died very soon after I went to Colonel Lloyd's; and he died as he lived, uttering, with his dying groans, bitter curses and horrid oaths. His death was regarded by the slaves as the result of a merciful providence.

Mr Severe's place was filled by a Mr Hopkins. He was a very different man. He was less cruel, less profane, and made less noise, than Mr Severe. His course was characterized by no extraordinary demonstrations of cruelty. He whipped, but seemed to take no pleasure in it. He was called by the slaves a good overseer.

The home plantation of Colonel Lloyd wore the appearance of a country village. All the mechanical operations for all the farms were performed here. The shoemaking and mending, the blacksmithing, cartwrighting, coopering, weaving, and grain-grinding, were all performed by the slaves on the home plantation. The whole place wore a business-like aspect very unlike the neighboring farms. The number of houses, too, conspired to give it advantage over the neighboring farms. It was called by the slaves the *Great House Farm*. Few privileges were esteemed higher, by the slaves of the out-farms, than that of being selected to do errands at the Great House Farm. It was associated in their minds with greatness. A representative could not be prouder of his election to a seat in the American Congress, than a slave on one of the out-farms would be of his election to do errands at the Great House Farm. They regarded it as evidence of great confidence reposed in them by their overseers; and it was on this account, as well as a constant desire to be out of the field from under the driver's lash, that they esteemed it a high privilege, one worth careful living for. He was called the smartest and most trusty fellow, who had this honor conferred upon him the most frequently. The competitors for this office sought as diligently to please their overseers, as the office-seekers in the political parties seek to please and deceive the people. The same traits of character might be seen in Colonel Lloyd's slaves, as are seen in the slaves of the political parties.

The slaves selected to go to the Great House Farm, for the monthly allowance for themselves and their fellow-slaves, were peculiarly enthusiastic. While on their way, they would make the dense old woods, for miles around, reverberate with their wild songs, revealing at once the highest joy and the deepest sadness. They would compose and sing as they went along, consulting neither time nor tune. The thought that came up, came out – if not in the word, in the sound – and as frequently in the one as in the other. They would sometimes sing the most pathetic sentiment in the most rapturous tone, and the most rapturous sentiment in the most pathetic tone. Into all of their songs they would manage to weave something of the Great House Farm. Especially would they do this, when leaving home. They would then sing most exultingly the following words : –

> 'I am going away to the Great House Farm !
> O, yea ! O, yea ! O !'

This they would sing, as a chorus, to words which to many would seem unmeaning jargon, but which, nevertheless, were full of meaning to themselves. I have sometimes thought that the mere hearing of those songs would do more to impress some minds with the horrible character of slavery, than the reading of whole volumes of philosophy on the subject could do.

I did not, when a slave, understand the deep meaning of those rude and apparently incoherent songs. I was myself within the circle ; so that I neither saw nor heard as those without might see and hear. They told a tale of woe which was then altogether beyond my feeble comprehension; they were tones loud, long, and deep; they breathed the prayer and complaint of souls boiling over with the bitterest anguish. Every tone was a testimony against slavery, and a prayer to God for deliverance from chains. The hearing of those wild notes always depressed my spirit, and filled me with ineffable sadness. I have frequently found myself in tears while hearing them. The mere recurrence to those songs, even now, afflicts me; and while I am writing these lines, an expression of feeling has already found its way down my cheek. To those songs I trace my first glimmering conception of the dehumanizing character of slavery. I can never get rid of that conception. Those songs still follow me, to deepen my hatred of slavery, and quicken my sympathies for my brethren in bonds. If any one wishes to be impressed with the soul-killing effects of slavery, let him go to Colonel Lloyd's plantation, and, on allowance-day, place himself in the deep pine woods, and there let him, in silence, analyze the sounds that shall pass through the chambers of his soul, and if he is not thus impressed, it will only be because 'there is no flesh in his obdurate heart.'

I have often been utterly astonished, since I came to the north, to find persons who could speak of the singing, among slaves, as evidence of their contentment and happiness. It is impossible to conceive of a greater mistake. Slaves sing most when they are most unhappy. The songs of the slave represent the sorrows of his heart; and he is relieved by them, only as an aching heart is relieved by its tears. At least, such is my experience. I have often sung to drown my sorrow, but seldom to express my happiness. Crying for joy, and singing for joy, were alike uncommon to me while in the jaws of slavery. The singing of a man cast away upon a desolate island might be as appropriately considered as evidence of contentment and happiness, as the singing of a slave; the songs of the one and of the other are prompted by the same emotion.

Chapter 3

COLONEL LLOYD kept a large and finely cultivated garden, which afforded almost constant employment for four men, besides the chief gardener, (Mr M'Durmond.) This garden was probably the greatest attraction of the place. During the summer months, people came from far and near – from Baltimore, Easton, and Annapolis – to see it. It abounded in fruits of almost every description, from the hardy apple of the north to the delicate orange of the south. This garden was not the least source of trouble on the plantation. Its excellent fruit was quite a temptation to the hungry swarms of boys, as well as the older slaves, belonging to the colonel, few of whom had the virtue or the vice to resist it. Scarcely a day passed, during the summer, but that some slave had to take the lash for stealing fruit. The colonel had to resort to all kinds of stratagems to keep his slaves out of the garden. The last and most successful one was that of tarring his fence all around; after which, if a slave was caught with any tar upon his person, it was deemed sufficient proof that he had either been into the garden, or had tried to get in. In either case, he was severely whipped by the chief gardener. This plan worked well; the slaves became as fearful of tar as of the lash. They seemed to realize the impossibility of touching *tar* without being defiled.

The colonel also kept a splendid riding equipage. His stable and carriage-house presented the appearance of some of our large city livery establishments. His horses were of the finest form and noblest blood. His carriage-house contained three splendid coaches, three or four gigs, besides dearborns and barouches of the most fashionable style.

This establishment was under the care of two slaves – old Barney and young Barney – father and son. To attend to this establishment was their sole work. But it was by no means an easy employment; for in nothing was Colonel Lloyd more particular than in the management of his horses. The slightest inattention to these was unpardonable, and was visited upon those, under whose care they were placed, with the severest punishment; no excuse could shield them, if the colonel only suspected any want of attention to his horses – a supposition which he frequently indulged, and one which, of course, made the office of old and young Barney a very trying one. They never knew when they were safe from punishment. They were frequently whipped when least deserving, and escaped whipping when most deserving it. Every thing depended upon the looks of the horses, and the state of Colonel Lloyd's own mind when his horses were brought to him for use. If a horse did not move fast enough, or hold his head high enough, it was owing to some fault of his keepers. It was painful to stand near the stable-door, and hear the various complaints against the keepers when a horse was taken out for use. 'This horse has not had proper attention. He has not been sufficiently rubbed and curried, or he has not been properly fed; his food was too wet or too dry; he got it too soon or too late; he was too hot or too cold; he had too much hay, and not enough of grain; or he had too much grain, and not enough of hay; instead of old Barney's attending to the horse, he had very improperly left it to his son.' To all these complaints, no matter how unjust, the slave must answer never a word. Colonel Lloyd could not brook any contradiction from a slave. When he spoke, a slave must stand, listen, and tremble; and such was literally the case. I have seen Colonel Lloyd make old Barney, a man between fifty and sixty years of age, uncover his bald head, kneel down upon the cold, damp ground, and receive upon his naked and toil-worn shoulders more than thirty lashes at the time. Colonel Lloyd had three sons – Edward, Murray, and Daniel – and three sons-in-law, Mr Winder, Mr Nicholson, and Mr Lowndes. All of these lived at the Great House Farm, and enjoyed the luxury of whipping the servants when they pleased, from old Barney down to William Wilkes, the coach-driver. I have seen Winder make one of the house-servants stand off from him a suitable distance to be touched with the end of his whip, and at every stroke raise great ridges upon his back.

To describe the wealth of Colonel Lloyd would be almost equal to describing the riches of Job. He kept from ten to fifteen house-servants. He was said to own a thousand slaves, and I think this estimate quite within the truth. Colonel Lloyd owned so many that he did not know them when he saw them; nor did all the slaves of the out-farms know him. It is reported of him, that, while riding along the road one day, he met a colored man, and addressed him in the usual manner of speaking to colored people on the public highways of the south: 'Well, boy, whom do you belong to?' 'To Colonel Lloyd,' replied the slave. 'Well, does the colonel treat you well?' 'No, sir,' was the ready reply. 'What, does he work you too hard?' 'Yes, sir.' 'Well, don't he give you enough to eat?' 'Yes, sir, he gives me enough, such as it is.'

The colonel, after ascertaining where the slave belonged, rode on; the man also went on about his business, not dreaming that he had been conversing with his master. He thought, said, and heard nothing more of the matter, until two or three weeks afterwards. The poor man was then informed by his overseer that, for having found fault with his master, he was now to be sold to a Georgia trader. He was immediately chained and handcuffed; and thus, without a moment's warning, he was snatched away, and forever sundered, from his family and friends, by a hand more unrelenting than death. This is the penalty of telling the truth, of telling the simple truth, in answer to a series of plain questions.

It is partly in consequence of such facts, that slaves, when inquired of as to their condition and the character of their masters, almost universally say they are contented, and that their masters are kind. The slaveholders have been known to send in spies among their slaves, to ascertain their views and feelings in regard to their condition. The frequency of this has had the effect to establish among the slaves the maxim, that a still tongue makes a wise head. They suppress the truth rather than take the consequences of telling it, and in so doing prove themselves a part of the human family. If they have any thing to say of their masters, it is generally in their masters' favor, especially when speaking to an untried man. I have been frequently asked, when a slave, if I had a kind master, and do not remember ever to have given a negative answer; nor did I, in pursuing this course, consider myself as uttering what was absolutely false; for I always measured the kindness of my master by the standard of kindness set up among slaveholders around us. Moreover, slaves are like other people, and imbibe prejudices quite common to others. They think their own better than that of others. Many, under the influence of this prejudice, think their own masters are better than the masters of other slaves; and this, too, in some cases, when the very reverse is true. Indeed, it is not uncommon for slaves even to fall out and quarrel among themselves about the relative goodness of their masters, each contending for the superior goodness of his own over that of the others. At the very same time, they mutually execrate their masters when viewed separately. It was so on our plantation. When Colonel Lloyd's slaves mer the slaves of Jacob Jepson, they seldom parted without a quarrel about their masters; Colonel Lloyd's slaves contending that he was the richest, and Mr Jepson's slaves that he was the smartest, and most of a man. Colonel Lloyd's slaves would boast his ability to buy and sell Jacob Jepson. Mr Jepson's slaves would boast his ability to whip Colonel Lloyd. These quarrels would almost always end in a fight between the parties, and those that whipped were supposed to have gained the point at issue. They seemed to think that the greatness of their masters was transferable to themselves. It was considered as being bad enough to be a slave; but to be a poor man's slave was deemed a disgrace indeed !

Chapter 4

MR HOPKINS remained but a short time in the office of overseer. Why his career was so short, I do not know, but suppose he lacked the necessary severity to suit Colonel Lloyd. Mr Hopkins was succeeded by Mr Austin Gore, a man possessing, in an eminent degree, all those traits of character indispensable to what is called a first-rate overseer. Mr Gore had served Colonel Lloyd, in the capacity of overseer, upon one of the outfarms, and had shown himself worthy of the high station of overseer upon the home or Great House Farm.

Mr Gore was proud, ambitious, and persevering. He was artful, cruel, and obdurate. He was just the man for such a place, and it was just the place for such a man. It afforded scope for the full exercise of all his powers, and he seemed to be perfectly at home in it. He was one of those who could torture the slightest look, word, or gesture, on the part of the slave, into impudence, and would treat it accordingly. There must be no answering back to him; no explanation was allowed a slave, showing himself to have been wrongfully accused. Mr Gore acted fully up to the maxim laid down by slaveholders – 'It is better that a dozen slaves suffer under the lash, than that the overseer should be convicted, in the presence of the slaves, of having been at fault.' No matter how innocent a slave might be – it availed him nothing, when accused by Mr Gore of any misdemeanor. To be accused was to be convicted, and to be convicted was to be punished; the one always following the other with immutable certainty. To escape punishment was to escape accusation; and few slaves had the fortune to do either, under the overseership of Mr Gore. He was just proud enough to demand the most debasing homage of the slave, and quite servile enough to crouch, himself, at the feet of the master. He was ambitious enough to be contented with nothing short of the highest rank of overseers, and persevering enough to reach the height of his ambition. He was cruel enough to inflict the severest punishment, artful enough to descend to the lowest trickery, and obdurate enough to be insensible to the voice of a reproving conscience. He was, of all the overseers, the most dreaded by the slaves. His presence was painful; his eye flashed confusion; and seldom was his sharp, shrill voice heard, without producing horror and trembling in their ranks.

Mr Gore was a grave man, and, though a young man, he indulged in no jokes, said no funny words, seldom smiled. His words were in perfect keeping with his looks, and his looks were in perfect keeping with his words. Overseers will sometimes indulge in a witty word, even with the slaves; not so with Mr Gore. He spoke but to command, and commanded but to be obeyed; he dealt sparingly with his words, and bountifully with his whip, never using the former where the latter would answer as well. When he whipped, he seemed to do so from a sense of duty, and feared no consequences. He did nothing reluctantly, no matter how disagreeable; always at his post, never inconsistent. He never promised but to fulfil. He was, in a word, a man of the most inflexible firmness and stone-like coolness.

His savage barbarity was equalled only by the consummate coolness with which he committed the grossest and most savage deeds upon the slaves under his charge. Mr Gore once undertook to whip one of Colonel Lloyd's slaves, by the name of Demby. He had given Demby but few stripes, when, to get rid of the scourging, he ran and plunged himself into a creek, and stood there at the depth of his shoulders, refusing to come out. Mr Gore told him that he would give him three calls, and that, if he did not come out at the third call, he would shoot him. The first call was given. Demby made no response, but stood his ground. The second and third calls were given with the same result. Mr Gore then, without consultation or deliberation with any one, not even giving Demby an additional call, raised his musket to his face, taking deadly aim at his standing victim, and in an instant poor Demby was no more. His mangled body sank out of sight, and blood and brains marked the water where he had stood.

A thrill of horror flashed through every soul upon the plantation, excepting Mr Gore. He alone seemed cool and collected. He was asked by Colonel Lloyd and my old master, why he resorted to this extraordinary expedient. His reply was, (as well as I can remember,) that Demby had become unmanageable. He was setting a dangerous example to the other slaves, – one which, if suffered to pass without some such demonstration on his part, would finally lead to the total subversion of all rule and order upon the plantation. He argued that if one slave refused to be corrected, and escaped with his life, the other slaves would soon copy the example; the result of which would be, the freedom of the slaves, and the enslavement of the whites. Mr Gore's defence was satisfactory. He was continued in his station as overseer upon the home plantation. His fame as an overseer went abroad. His horrid crime was not even submitted to judicial investigation. It was committed in the presence of slaves, and they of course could neither institute a suit, nor testify against him; and thus the guilty perpetrator of one of the bloodiest and most foul murders goes unwhipped of justice, and uncensured by the community in which he lives. Mr Gore lived in St Michael's, Talbot county, Maryland, when I left there; and if he is still alive, he very probably lives there now; and if so, he is now, as he was then, as highly esteemed and as much respected as though his guilty soul had not been stained with his brother's blood.

I speak advisedly when I say this – that killing a slave, or any colored person, in Talbot county, Maryland, is not treated as a crime, either by the courts or the community. Mr Thomas Lanman, of St Michael's, killed two slaves, one of whom he killed with a hatchet, by knocking his brains out. He used to boast of the commission of the awful and bloody deed. I have heard him do so laughingly, saying, among other things, that he was the only benefactor of his country in the company, and that when others would do as much as he had done, we should be relieved of 'the d—d niggers.'

The wife of Mr Giles Hick [sic], living but a short distance from where I used to live, murdered my wife's cousin, a young girl between fifteen and sixteen years of age, mangling her person in the most horrible manner, breaking her nose and breastbone with a stick, so that the poor girl expired in a few hours afterward. She was immediately buried, but had not been in her untimely grave but a few hours before she was taken up and examined by the coroner, who decided that she had come to her death by severe beating. The offence for which this girl was thus murdered was this: she had been set that night to mind Mrs Hick's baby, and during the night she fell asleep, and the baby cried. She, having lost her rest for several nights previous, did not hear the crying. They were both in the room with Mrs Hicks. Mrs Hicks, finding the girl slow to move, jumped from her bed, seized an oak stick of wood by the fireplace, and with it broke the girl's nose and breastbone, and thus ended her life. I will not say that this most horrid murder produced no sensation in the community. It did produce sensation, but not enough to bring the murderess to punishment. There was a warrant issued for her arrest, but it was never served. Thus she escaped not only punishment, but even the pain of being arraigned before a court for her horrid crime.

Whilst I am detailing bloody deeds which took place during my stay on Colonel Lloyd's plantation, I will briefly narrate another, which occurred about the same time as the murder of Demby by Mr Gore.

Colonel Lloyd's slaves were in the habit of spending a part of their nights and Sundays in fishing for oysters, and in this way made up the deficiency of their scanty allowance. An old man belonging to Colonel Lloyd, while thus engaged, happened to get beyond the limits of Colonel Lloyd's, and on the premises of Mr Beal Bondly. At this trespass, Mr Bondly took offence, and with his musket came down to the shore, and blew its deadly contents into the poor old man.

Mr Bondly came over to see Colonel Lloyd the next day, whether to pay him for his property, or to justify himself in what he had done, I know not. At any rate, this whole fiendish transaction was soon hushed up. There was very little said about it at all, and nothing done. It was a common saying, even among little white boys, that it was worth a half-cent to kill a 'nigger,' and a half-cent to bury one.

Chapter 5

AS TO my own treatment while I lived on Colonel Lloyd's plantation, it was very similar to that of the other slave children. I was not old enough to work in the field, and there being little else than field work to do, I had a great deal of leisure time. The most I had to do was to drive up the cows at evening, keep the fowls out of the garden, keep the front yard clean, and run of errands for my old master's daughter, Mrs Lucretia Auld. The most of my leisure time I spent in helping Master Daniel Lloyd in finding his birds, after he had shot them. My connection with Master Daniel was of some advantage to me. He became quite attached to me, and was a sort of protector of me. He would not allow the older boys to impose upon me, and would divide his cakes with me.

I was seldom whipped by my old master, and suffered little from any thing else than hunger and cold. I suffered much from hunger, but much more from cold. In hottest summer and coldest winter, I was kept almost naked – no shoes, no stockings, no jacket, no trousers, nothing on but a coarse tow linen shirt, reaching only to my knees. I had no bed. I must have perished with cold, but that, the coldest nights, I used to steal a bag which was used for carrying corn to the mill. I would crawl into this bag, and there sleep on the cold, damp, clay floor, with my head in and feet out. My feet have been so cracked with the frost, that the pen with which I am writing might be laid in the gashes.

We were not regularly allowanced. Our food was coarse corn meal boiled. This was called *mush*. It was put into a large wooden tray or trough, and set down upon the ground. The children were then called, like so many pigs, and like so many pigs they would come and devour the mush; some with oyster-shells, others with pieces of shingle, some with naked hands, and none with spoons. He that ate fastest got most; he that was strongest secured the best place; and few left the trough satisfied.

I was probably between seven and eight years old when I left Colonel Lloyd's plantation. I left it with joy. I shall never forget the ecstasy with which I received the intelligence that my old master (Anthony) had determined to let me go to Baltimore, to live with Mr Hugh Auld, brother to my old master's son-in-law, Captain Thomas Auld. I received this information about three days before my departure. They were three of the happiest days I ever enjoyed. I spent the most part of all these three days in the creek, washing off the plantation scurf, and preparing myself for my departure.

The pride of appearance which this would indicate was not my own. I spent the time in washing, not so much because I wished to, but because Mrs Lucretia had told me I must get all the dead skin off my feet and knees before I could go to Baltimore; for the people in Baltimore were very cleanly, and would laugh at me if I looked dirty. Besides, she was going to give me a pair of trousers, which I should not put on unless I got all the dirt off me. The thought of owning a pair of trousers was great indeed! It was almost a sufficient motive, not only to make me take off what would be called by pig-drovers the mange, but the skin itself. I went at it in good earnest, working for the first time with the hope of reward.

The ties that ordinarily bind children to their homes were all suspended in my case. I found no severe trial in my departure. My home was charmless; it was not home to me; on parting from it, I could not feel that I was leaving any thing which I could have enjoyed by staying. My mother was dead, my grandmother lived far off, so that I seldom saw her. I had two sisters and one brother, that lived in the same house with me; but the early separation of us from our mother had well nigh blotted the fact of our relationship from our memories. I looked for home elsewhere, and was confident of finding none which I should relish less than the one which I was leaving. If, however, I found in my new home hardship, hunger, whipping, and nakedness, I had the consolation that I should not have escaped any one of them by staying. Having already had more than a taste of them in the house of my old master, and having endured them there, I very naturally inferred my ability to endure them elsewhere, and especially at Baltimore; for I had something of the feeling about Baltimore that is expressed in the proverb, that 'being hanged in England is preferable to dying a natural death in Ireland.' I had the strongest desire to see Baltimore. Cousin Tom, though not fluent in speech, had inspired me with that desire by his eloquent description of the place. I could never point out any thing at the Great House, no matter how beautiful or powerful, but that he had seen something at Baltimore far exceeding, both in beauty and strength, the object which I pointed out to him. Even the Great House itself, with all its pictures, was far inferior to many buildings in Baltimore. So strong was my desire, that I thought a gratification of it would fully compensate for whatever loss of comforts I should sustain by the exchange. I left without a regret, and with the highest hopes of future happiness.

We sailed out of Miles River for Baltimore on a Saturday morning. I remember only the day of the week, for at that time I had no knowledge of the days of the month, nor the months of the year. On setting sail, I walked aft, and gave to Colonel Lloyd's plantation what I hoped would be the last look. I then placed myself in the bows of the sloop, and there spent the remainder of the day in looking ahead, interesting myself in what was in the distance rather than in things near by or behind.

In the afternoon of that day, we reached Annapolis, the capital of the State. We stopped but a few moments, so that I had no time to go on shore. It was the first large town that I had ever seen, and though it would look small compared with some of our New England factory villages, I thought it a wonderful place for its size – more imposing even than the Great House Farm !

We arrived at Baltimore early on Sunday morning, landing at Smith's Wharf, not far from Bowley's Wharf. We had on board the sloop a large flock of sheep ; and after aiding in driving them to the slaughterhouse of Mr Curtis on Louden Slater's Hill, I was conducted by Rich, one of the hands belonging on board of the sloop, to my new home in Alliciana Street, near Mr Gardner's ship-yard, on Fells Point.

Mr and Mrs Auld were both at home, and met me at the door with their little son Thomas, to take care of whom I had been given. And here I saw what I had never seen before ; it was a white face beaming with the most kindly emotions ; it was the face of my new mistress, Sophia Auld. I wish I could describe the rapture that flashed through my soul as I beheld it. It was a new and strange sight to me, brightening up my pathway with the light of happiness. Little Thomas was told, there was his Freddy – and I was told to take care of little Thomas ; and thus I entered upon the duties of my new home with the most cheering prospect ahead.

I look upon my departure from Colonel Lloyd's plantation as one of the most interesting events of my life. It is possible, and even quite probable, that but for the mere circumstance of being removed from that plantation to Baltimore, I should have to-day, instead of being here seated by my own table, in the enjoyment of freedom and the happiness of home, writing this Narrative, been confined in the galling chains of slavery. Going to live at Baltimore laid the foundation, and opened the gateway, to all my subsequent prosperity. I have ever regarded it as the first plain manifestation of that kind providence which has ever since attended me, and marked my life with so many favors. I regarded the selection of myself as being somewhat remarkable. There were a number of slave children that might have been sent from the plantation to Baltimore. There were those younger, those older, and those of the same age. I was chosen from among them all, and was the first, last, and only choice.

I may be deemed superstitious, and even egotistical, in regarding this event as a special interposition of divine Providence in my favor. But I should be false to the earliest sentiments of my soul, if I suppressed the opinion. I prefer to be true to myself, even at the hazard of incurring the ridicule of others, rather than to be false, and incur my own abhorrence. From my earliest recollection, I date the entertainment of a deep conviction that slavery would not always be able to hold me within its foul embrace; and in the darkest hours of my career in slavery, this living word of faith and spirit of hope departed not from me, but remained like ministering angels to cheer me through the gloom. This good spirit was from God, and to him I offer thanksgiving and praise.

Chapter 6

MY NEW mistress proved to be all she appeared when I first met her at the door, — a woman of the kindest heart and finest feelings. She had never had a slave under her control previously to myself, and prior to her marriage she had been dependent upon her own industry for a living. She was by trade a weaver; and by constant application to her business, she had been in a good degree preserved from the blighting and dehumanizing effects of slavery. I was utterly astonished at her goodness. I scarcely knew how to behave towards her. She was entirely unlike any other white woman I had ever seen. I could not approach her as I was accustomed to approach other white ladies. My early instruction was all out of place. The crouching servility, usually so acceptable a quality in a slave, did not answer when manifested toward her. Her favor was not gained by it; she seemed to be disturbed by it. She did not deem it impudent or unmannerly for a slave to look her in the face. The meanest slave was put fully at ease in her presence, and none left without feeling better for having seen her. Her face was made of heavenly smiles, and her voice of tranquil music.

But, alas! this kind heart had but a short time to remain such. The fatal poison of irresponsible power was already in her hands, and soon commenced its infernal work. That cheerful eye, under the influence of slavery, soon became red with rage; that voice, made all of sweet accord, changed to one of harsh and horrid discord; and that angelic face gave place to that of a demon.

Very soon after I went to live with Mr and Mrs Auld, she very kindly commenced to teach me the A, B, C. After I had learned this, she assisted me in learning to spell words of three or four letters. Just at this point of my progress, Mr Auld found out what was going on, and at once forbade Mrs Auld to instruct me further, telling her, among other things, that it was unlawful, as well as unsafe, to teach a slave to read. To use his own words, further, he said, 'If you give a nigger an inch, he will take an ell. A nigger should know nothing but to obey his master – to do as he is told to do. Learning would *spoil* the best nigger in the world. Now,' said he, 'if you teach that nigger (speaking of myself) how to read, there would be no keeping him. It would forever unfit him to be a slave. He would at once become unmanageable, and of no value to his master. As to himself, it could do him no good, but a great deal of harm. It would make him discontented and unhappy.' These words sank deep into my heart, stirred up sentiments within that lay slumbering, and called into existence an entirely new train of thought. It was a new and special revelation, explaining dark and mysterious things, with which my youthful understanding had struggled, but struggled in vain. I now understood what had been to me a most perplexing difficulty – to wit, the white man's power to enslave the black man. It was a grand achievement, and I prized it highly. From that moment, I understood the pathway from slavery to freedom. It was just what I wanted, and I got it at a time when I the least expected it. Whilst I was saddened by the thought of losing the aid of my kind mistress, I was gladdened by the invaluable instruction which, by the merest accident, I had gained from my master. Though conscious of the difficulty of learning without a teacher, I set out with high hope, and a fixed purpose, at whatever cost of trouble, to learn how to read. The very decided manner with which he spoke, and strove to impress his wife with the evil consequences of giving me instruction, served to convince me that he was deeply sensible of the truths he was uttering. It gave me the best assurance that I might rely with the utmost confidence on the results which, he said, would flow from teaching me to read. What he most dreaded, that I most desired. What he most loved, that I most hated. That which to him was a great evil, to be carefully shunned, was to me a great good, to be diligently sought; and the argument which he so warmly urged, against my learning to read, only served to inspire me with a desire and determination to learn. In learning to read, I owe almost as much to the bitter opposition of my master, as to the kindly aid of my mistress. I acknowledge the benefit of both.

I had resided but a short time in Baltimore before I observed a marked difference, in the treatment of slaves, from that which I had witnessed in the country. A city slave is almost a freeman, compared with a slave on the plantation. He is much better fed and clothed, and enjoys privileges altogether unknown to the slave on the plantation. There is a vestige of decency, a sense of shame, that does much to curb and check those outbreaks of atrocious cruelty so commonly enacted upon the plantation. He is a desperate slaveholder, who will shock the humanity of his nonslaveholding neighbors with the cries of his lacerated slave. Few are willing to incur the odium attaching to the reputation of being a cruel master; and above all things, they would not be known as not giving a slave enough to eat. Every city slaveholder is anxious to have it known of him, that he feeds his slaves well; and it is due to them to say, that most of them do give their slaves enough to eat. There are, however, some painful exceptions to this rule. Directly opposite to us, on Philpot Street, lived Mr Thomas Hamilton. He owned two slaves. Their names were Henrietta and Mary. Henrietta was about twenty-two years of age, Mary was about fourteen; and of all the mangled and emaciated creatures I ever looked upon, these two were the most so. His heart must be harder than stone, that could look upon these unmoved. The head, neck, and shoulders of Mary were literally cut to pieces. I have frequently felt her head, and found it nearly covered with festering sores, caused by the lash of her cruel mistress. I do not know that her master ever whipped her, but I have been an eye-witness to the cruelty of Mrs Hamilton. I used to be in Mr Hamilton's house nearly every day. Mrs Hamilton used to sit in a large chair in the middle of the room, with a heavy cowskin always by her side, and scare an hour passed during the day but was marked by the blood of one of these slaves. The girls seldom passed her without her saying, 'Move faster, you *black gip!*' at the same time giving them a blow with the cowskin over the head or shoulders, often drawing the blood. She would then say, 'Take that, you *black gip!*' – continuing, 'If you don't move faster, I'll move you!' Added to the cruel lashings to which these slaves were subjected, they were kept nearly half-starved. They seldom knew what it was to eat a full meal. I have seen Mary contending with the pigs for the offal thrown into the street. So much was Mary kicked and cut to pieces, that she was oftener called '*pecked*' than by her name.

Chapter 7

I LIVED in Master Hugh's family about seven years. During this time, I succeeded in learning to read and write. In accomplishing this, I was compelled to resort to various stratagems. I had no regular teacher. My mistress, who had kindly commenced to instruct me, had, in compliance with the advice and direction of her husband, not only ceased to instruct, but had set her face against my being instructed by any one else. It is due, however, to my mistress to say of her, that she did not adopt this course of treatment immediately. She at first lacked the depravity indispensable to shutting me up in mental darkenss. It was at least necessary for her to have some training in the exercise of irresponsible power, to make her equal to the task of treating me as though I were a brute.

My mistress was, as I have said, a kind and tender-hearted woman ; and in the simplicity of her soul she commenced, when I first went to live with her, to treat me as she supposed one human being ought to treat another. In entering upon the duties of a slaveholder, she did not seem to perceive that I sustained to her the relation of a mere chattel, and that for her to treat me as a human being was not only wrong, but dangerously so. Slavery proved as injurious to her as it did to me. When I went there, she was a pious, warm, and tender-hearted woman. There was no sorrow or suffering for which she had not a tear. She had bread for the hungry, clothes for the naked, and comfort for every mourner that came within her reach. Slavery soon proved its ability to divest her of these heavenly qualities. Under its influence, the tender heart became stone, and the lamblike disposition gave way to one of tiger-like fierceness. The first step in her downward course was in her ceasing to instruct me. She now commenced to practise her husband's precepts. She finally became even more violent in her opposition than her husband himself. She was not satisfied with simply doing as well as he had commanded; she seemed anxious to do better. Nothing seemed to make her more angry than to see me with a newspaper. She seemed to think that here lay the danger. I have had her rush at me with a face made all up of fury, and snatch from me a newspaper, in a manner that fully revealed her apprehension. She was an apt woman; and a little experience soon demonstrated, to her satisfaction, that education and slavery were incompatible with each other.

From this time I was most narrowly watched. If I was in a separate room any considerable length of time, I was sure to be suspected of having a book, and was at once called to give an account of myself. All this, however, was too late. The first step had been taken. Mistress, in teaching me the alphabet, had given me the *inch*, and no precaution could prevent me from taking the *ell*.

The plan which I adopted, and the one by which I was most successful, was that of making friends of all the little white boys whom I met in the street. As many of these as I could, I converted into teachers. With their kindly aid, obtained at different times and in different places, I finally succeeded in learning to read. When I was sent of errands, I always took my book with me, and by going one part of my errand quickly, I found time to get a lesson before my return. I used also to carry bread with me, enough of which was always in the house, and to which I was always welcome; for I was much better off in this regard than many of the poor white children in our neighborhood. This bread I used to bestow upon the hungry little urchins, who, in return, would give me that more valuable bread of knowledge. I am strongly tempted to give the names of two or three of those little boys, as a testimonial of the gratitude and affection I bear them; but prudence forbids; — not that it would injure me, but it might embarrass them; for it is almost an unpardonable offence to teach slaves to read in this Christian country. It is enough to say of the dear little fellows, that they lived on Philpot Street, very near Durgin and Bailey's ship-yard. I used to talk this matter of slavery over with them. I would sometimes say to them, I wished I could be as free as they would be when they got to be men. 'You will be free as soon as you are twenty-one, *but I am a slave for life!* Have not I as good a right to be free as you have?' These words used to trouble them; they would express for me the liveliest sympathy, and console me with the hope that something would occur by which I might be free.

I was now about twelve years old, and the thought of being *a slave for life* began to bear heavily upon my heart. Just about this time, I got hold of a book entitled 'The Columbian Orator.' Every opportunity I got, I used to read this book. Among much of other interesting matter, I found in it a dialogue between a master and his slave. The slave was represented as having run away from his master three times. The dialogue represented the conversation which took place between them, when the slave was retaken the third time. In this dialogue, the whole argument in behalf of slavery was brought forward by the master, all of which was disposed of by the slave. The slave was made to say some very smart as well as impressive things in reply to his master – things which had the desired though unexpected effect; for the conversation resulted in the voluntary emancipation of the slave on the part of the master.

In the same book, I met with one of Sheridan's mighty speeches on behalf of Catholic emancipation. These were choice documents to me. I read them over and over again with unabated interest. They gave tongue to interesting thoughts of my own soul, which had frequently flashed through my mind, and died away for want of utterance. The moral which I gained from the dialogue was the power of truth over the conscience of even a slaveholder. What I got from Sheridan was a bold denunciation of slavery, and a powerful vindication of human rights. The reading of these documents enabled me to utter my thoughts, and to meet the arguments brought forward to sustain slavery; but while they relieved me of one difficulty, they brought on another even more painful than the one of which I was relieved. The more I read, the more I was led to abhor and detest my enslavers. I could regard them in no other light than a band of successful robbers, who had left their homes, and gone to Africa, and stolen us from our homes, and in a strange land reduced us to slavery. I loathed them as being the meanest as well as the most wicked of men. As I read and contemplated the subject, behold! that very discontentment which Master Hugh had predicted would follow my learning to read had already come, to torment and sting my soul to unutterable anguish. As I writhed under it, I would at times feel that learning to read had been a curse rather than a blessing. It had given me a view of my wretched condition, without the remedy. It opened my eyes to the horrible pit, but to no ladder upon which to get out. In moments of agony, I envied my fellow-slaves for their stupidity. I have often wished myself a beast. I preferred the condition of the meanest reptile to my own. Any thing, no matter what, to get rid of thinking! It was this everlasting thinking of my condition that tormented me. There was no getting rid of it. It was pressed upon me by every object within sight or hearing, animate or inanimate. The silver trump of freedom had roused my soul to eternal wakefulness. Freedom now appeared, to disappear no more forever. It was heard in every sound, and seen in every thing. It was ever present to torment me with a sense of my wretched condition. I saw nothing without seeing it, I heard nothing without hearing it, and felt nothing without feeling it. It looked from every star, it smiled in every calm, breathed in every wind, and moved in every storm.

I often found myself regretting my own existence, and wishing myself dead; and but for the hope of being free, I have no doubt but that I should have killed myself, or done something for which I should have been killed. While in this state of mind, I was eager to hear any one speak of slavery. I was a ready listener. Every little while, I could hear something about the abolitionists. It was some time before I found what the word meant. It was always used in such connections as to make it an interesting word to me. If a slave ran away and succeeded in getting clear, or if a slave killed his master, set fire to a barn, or did any thing very wrong in the mind of a slaveholder, it was spoken of as the fruit of *abolition*. Hearing the word in this connection very often, I set about learning what it meant. The dictionary afforded me little or no help. I found it was 'the act of abolishing;' but then I did not know what was to be abolished. Here I was perplexed. I did not dare to ask any one about its meaning, for I was satisfied that it was something they wanted me to know very little about. After a patient waiting, I got one of our city papers, containing an account of the number of petitions from the north, praying for the abolition of slavery in the District of Columbia, and of the slave trade between the States. From this time I understood the words *abolition* and *abolitionist*, and always drew near when that word was spoken, expecting to hear something of importance to myself and fellow-slaves. The light broke in upon me by degrees. I went one day down on the wharf of Mr Waters; and seeing two Irishmen unloading a scow of stone, I went, unasked, and helped them. When we had finished, one of them came to me and asked me if I were a slave. I told him I was. He asked, 'Are ye a slave for life?' I told him that I was. The good Irishman seemed to be deeply affected by the statement. He said to the other that it was a pity so fine a little fellow as myself should be a slave for life. He said it was a shame to hold me. They both advised me to run away to the north; that I should find friends there, and that I should be free. I pretended not to be interested in what they said, and treated them as if I did not understand them; for I feared they might be treacherous. White men have been known to encourage slaves to escape, and then, to get the reward, catch them and return them to their masters. I was afraid that these seemingly good men might use me so; but I nevertheless remembered their advice, and from that time I resolved to run away. I looked forward to a time at which it would be safe for me to escape. I was too young to think of doing so immediately; besides, I wished to learn how to write, as I might have occasion to write my own pass. I consoled myself with the hope that I should one day find a good chance. Meanwhile, I would learn to write.

The idea as to how I might learn to write was suggested to me by being in Durgin and Bailey's ship-yard, and frequently seeing the ship carpenters, after hewing, and getting a piece of timber ready for use, write on the timber the name of that part of the ship for which it was intended. When a piece of timber was intended for the larboard side, it would be marked thus – 'L.' When a piece was for the starboard side, it would be marked thus – 'S.' A piece for the larboard side forward, would be marked thus – 'L.F.' When a piece was for starboard side forward, it would be marked thus – 'S.F.' For larboard aft, it would be marked thus – 'L.A.' For starboard aft, it would be marked thus – 'S.A.' I soon learned the names of these letters, and for what they were intended when placed upon a piece of timber in the ship-yard. I immediately commenced copying them, and in a short time was able to make the four letters named. After that, when I met with any boy who I knew could write, I would tell him I could write as well as he. The next word would be, 'I don't believe you. Let me see you try it.' I would then make the letters which I had been so fortunate as to learn, and ask him to beat that. In this way I got a good many lessons in writing, which it is quite possible I should never have gotten in any other way. During this time, my copy-book was the board fence, brick wall, and pavement; my pen and ink was a lump of chalk. With these, I learned mainly how to write. I then commenced and continued copying the Italics in Webster's Spelling Book, until I could make them all without looking on the book. By this time, my little Master Thomas had gone to school, and learned how to write, and had written over a number of copy-books. These had been brought home, and shown to some of our near neighbors, and then laid aside. My mistress used to go to class meeting at the Wilk Street meeting-house every Monday afternoon, and leave me to take care of the house. When left thus, I used to spend the time in writing in the spaces left in Master Thomas's copy-book, copying what he had written. I continued to do this until I could write a hand very similar to that of Master Thomas. Thus, after a long, tedious effort for years, I finally succeeded in learning how to write.

Chapter 8

IN A VERY short time after I went to live at Baltimore, my old master's youngest son Richard died; and in about three years and six months after his death, my old master, Captain Anthony, died, leaving only his son, Andrew, and daughter, Lucretia, to share his estate. He died while on a visit to see his daughter at Hillsborough. Cut off thus unexpectedly, he left no will as to the disposal of his property. It was therefore necessary to have a valuation of the property, that it might be equally divided between Mrs Lucretia and Master Andrew. I was immediately sent for, to be valued with the other property. Here again my feelings rose up in detestation of slavery. I had now a new conception of my degraded condition. Prior to this, I had become, if not insensible to my lot, at least partly so. I left Baltimore with a young heart overborne with sadness, and a soul full of apprehension. I took passage with Captain Rowe, in the schooner Wild Cat, and, after a sail of about twenty-four hours, I found myself near the place of my birth. I had now been absent from it almost, if not quite, five years. I, however, remembered the place very well. I was only about five years old when I left it, to go and live with my old master on Colonel Lloyd's plantation; so that I was now between ten and eleven years old.

We were all ranked together at the valuation. Men and women, old and young, married and single, were ranked with horses, sheep, and swine. There were horses and men, cattle and women, pigs and children, all holding the same rank in the scale of being, and were all subjected to the same narrow examination. Silvery-headed age and sprightly youth, maids and matrons, had to undergo the same indelicate inspection. At this moment, I saw more clearly than ever the brutalizing effects of slavery upon both slave and slaveholder.

After the valuation, then came the division. I have no language to express the high excitement and deep anxiety which were felt among us poor slaves during this time. Our fate for life was now to be decided. We had no more voice in that decision than the brutes among whom we were ranked. A single word from the white men was enough — against all our wishes, prayers, and entreaties — to sunder forever the dearest friends, dearest kindred, and strongest ties known to human beings. In addition to the pain of separation, there was the horrid dread of falling into the hands of Master Andrew. He was known to us all as being a most cruel wretch — a common drunkard, who had, by his reckless mismanagement and profligate dissipation, already wasted a large portion of his father's property. We all felt that we might as well be sold at once to the Georgia traders, as to pass into his hands; for we knew that that would be our inevitable condition — a condition held by us all in the utmost horror and dread.

I suffered more anxiety than most of my fellow-slaves. I had known what it was to be kindly treated; they had known nothing of the kind. They had seen little or nothing of the world. They were in very deed men and women of sorrow, and acquainted with grief. Their backs had been made familiar with the bloody lash, so that they had become callous; mine was yet tender; for while at Baltimore I got few whippings, and few slaves could boast of a kinder master and mistress than myself; and the thought of passing out of their hands into those of Master Andrew — a man who, but a few days before, to give me a sample of his bloody disposition, took my little brother by the throat, threw him on the ground, and with the heel of his boot stamped upon his head till the blood gushed from his nose and ears — was well calculated to make me anxious as to my fate. After he had committed this savage outrage upon my brother, he turned to me, and said that was the way he meant to serve me one of these days — meaning, I suppose, when I came into his possession.

Thanks to a kind Providence, I fell to the portion of Mrs Lucretia, and was sent immediately back to Baltimore, to live again in the family of Master Hugh. Their joy at my return equalled their sorrow at my departure. It was a glad day to me. I had escaped a worse than lion's jaws. I was absent from Baltimore, for the purpose of valuation and division, just about one month, and it seemed to have been six.

Very soon after my return to Baltimore, my mistress, Lucretia, died, leaving her husband and one child, Amanda; and in a very short time after her death, Master Andrew died. Now all the property of my old master, slaves included, was in the hands of strangers — strangers who had had nothing to do with accumulating it. Not a slave was left free. All remained slaves, from the youngest to the oldest. If any one thing in my experience, more than another, served to deepen my conviction of the infernal character of slavery, and to fill me with unutterable loathing of slaveholders, it was their base ingratitude to my poor old grandmother. She had served my old master faithfully from youth to old age. She had been the source of all his wealth; she had peopled his plantation with slaves; she had become a great grandmother in his service. She had rocked him in infancy, atended him in childhood, served him through life, and at his death wiped from his icy brow the cold death-sweat, and closed his eyes forever. She was nevertheless left a slave – a slave for life – a slave in the hands of strangers ; and in their hands she saw her children, her grandchildren, and her great-grand-children, divided, like so many sheep, without being gratified with the small privilege of a single word, as to their or her own destiny. And, to cap the climax of their base ingratitude and fiendish barbarity, my grandmother, who was now very old, having outlived my old master and all his children, having seen the beginning and end of all of them, and her present owners finding she was of but little value, her frame already racked with the pains of old age, and complete helplessness fast stealing over her once active limbs, they took her to the woods, built her a little hut, put up a little mud-chimney, and then made her welcome to the privilege of supporting herself there in perfect loneliness ; thus virtually turning her out to die ! If my poor old grandmother now lives, she lives to suffer in utter loneliness ; she lives to remember and mourn over the loss of children, the loss of grandchildren, and the loss of great-grandchildren. They are, in the language of the slave's poet, Whittier –

> 'Gone, gone, sold and gone
> To the rice swamp dank and lone,
> Where the slave-whip ceaseless swings,
> Where the noisome insect stings,
> Where the fever-demon strews
> Poison with the falling dews,
> Where the sickly sunbeams glare
> Through the hot and misty air : –
> Gone, gone, sold and gone
> To the rice swamp dank and lone,
> From Virginia hills and waters –
> Woe is me, my stolen daughters !'

The hearth is desolate. The children, the unconscious children, who once sang and danced in her presence, are gone. She gropes her way, in the darkness of age, for a drink of water. Instead of the voices of her children, she hears by day the moans of the dove, and by night the screams of the hideous owl. All is gloom. The grave is at the door. And now, when weighed down by the pains and aches of old age, when the head inclines to the feet, when the beginning and ending of human existence meet, and helpless infancy and painful old age combine together – at this time, this most needful time, the time for the exercise of that tenderness and affection which children only can exercise towards a declining parent – my poor old grandmother, the devoted mother of twelve children, is left all alone, in yonder little hut, before a few dim embers. She stands – she sits – she staggers – she falls – she groans – she dies – and there are none of her children or grandchildren present, to wipe from her wrinkled brow the cold sweat of death, or to place beneath the sod her fallen remains. Will not a righteous God visit for these things ?

In about two years after the death of Mrs Lucretia, Master Thomas married his second wife. Her name was Rowena Hamilton. She was the eldest daughter of Mr William Hamilton. Master now lived in St Michael's. Not long after his marriage, a misunderstanding took place between himself and Master Hugh; and as a means of punishing his brother, he took me from him to live with himself at St Michael's. Here I underwent another most painful separation. It, however, was not so severe as the one I dreaded at the division of property ; for, during this interval, a great change has taken place in Master Hugh and his once kind and affectionate wife. The influence of brandy upon him, and of slavery upon her, had effected a disastrous change in the characters of both ; so that, as far as they were concerned, I thought I had little to lose by the change. But it was not to them that I was attached. It was to those little Baltimore boys that I felt the strongest attachment. I had received many good lessons from them, and was still receiving them, and the thought of leaving them was painful indeed. I was leaving, too, without the hope of ever being allowed to return. Master Thomas had said he would never let me return again. The barrier betwixt himself and brother he considered impassable.

I then had to regret that I did not at least make the attempt to carry out my resolution to run away ; for the chances of success are tenfold greater from the city than from the country.

I sailed from Baltimore for St Michael's in the sloop Amanda, Captain Edward Dodson. On my passage, I paid particular attention to the direction which the steamboats took to go to Philadelphia. I found, instead of going down, on reaching North Point they went up the bay, in a north-easterly direction. I deemed this knowledge of the utmost importance. My determination to run away was again revived. I resolved to wait only so long as the offering of a favorable opportunity. When that came, I was determined to be off.

Chapter 9

I HAVE now reached a period of my life when I can give dates. I left Baltimore, and went to live with Master Thomas Auld, at St Michael's, in March, 1832. It was now more than seven years since I lived with him in the family of my old master, on Colonel Lloyd's plantation. We of course were now almost entire strangers to each other. He was to me a new master, and I to him a new slave. I was ignorant of his temper and disposition; he was equally so of mine. A very short time, however, brought us into full acquaintance with each other. I was made acquainted with his wife not less than with himself. They were well matched, being equally mean and cruel. I was now, for the first time during a space of more than seven years, made to feel the painful gnawings of hunger – a something which I had not experienced before since I left Colonel Lloyd's plantation. It went hard enough with me then, when I could look back to no period at which I had enjoyed a sufficiency. It was tenfold harder after living in Master Hugh's family, where I had always had enough to eat, and of that which was good. I have said Master Thomas was a mean man. He was so. Not to give a slave enough to eat, is regarded as the most aggravated development of meanness even among slaveholders. The rule is, no matter how coarse the food, only let there be enough of it. This is the theory; and in the part of Maryland from which I came, it is the general practice – though there are many exceptions. Master Thomas gave us enough of neither coarse nor fine food. There were four slaves of us in the kitchen – my sister Eliza, my aunt Priscilla, Henny, and myself; and we were allowed less than a half of a bushel of corn-meal per week, and very little else, either in the shape of meat or vegetables. It was not enough for us to subsist upon. We were therefore reduced to the wretched necessity of living at the expense of our neighbors. This we did by begging and stealing, whichever came handy in the time of need, the one being considered as legitimate as the other. A great many times have we poor creatures been nearly perishing with hunger, when food in abundance lay mouldering in the safe and smoke-house, and our pious mistress was aware of the fact; and yet that mistress and her husband would kneel every morning, and pray that God would bless them in basket and store!

Bad as all slaveholders are, we seldom meet one destitute of every element of character commanding respect. My master was one of this rare sort. I do not know of one single noble act ever performed by him. The leading trait in his character was meanness; and if there were any other element in his nature, it was made subject to this. He was mean; and, like most other mean men, he lacked the ability to conceal his meanness. Captain Auld was not born a slaveholder. He had been a poor man, master only of a Bay craft. He came into possession of all his slaves by marriage; and of all men, adopted slaveholders are the worst. He was cruel, but cowardly. He commanded without firmness. In the enforcement of his rules, he was at times rigid, and at times lax. At times, he spoke to his slaves with the firmness of Napoleon and the fury of a demon; at other times, he might well be mistaken for an inquirer who had lost his way. He did nothing of himself. He might have passed for a lion, but for his ears. In all things noble which he attempted, his own meanness shone most conspicuous. His airs, words, and actions, were the airs, words, and actions of born slaveholders, and, being assumed, were awkward enough. He was not even a good imitator. He possessed all the disposition to deceive, but wanted the power. Having no resources within himself, he was compelled to be the copyist of many, and being such, he was forever the victim of inconsistency; and of consequence he was an object of contempt, and was held as such even by his slaves. The luxury of having slaves of his own to wait upon him was something new and unprepared for. He was a slaveholder without the ability to hold slaves. He found himself incapable of managing his slaves either by force, fear, or fraud. We seldom called him 'master;' we generally called him 'Captain Auld,' and were hardly disposed to title him at all. I doubt not that our conduct had much to do with making him appear awkward, and of consequence fretful. Our want of reverence for him must have perplexed him greatly. He wished to have us call him master, but lacked the firmness necessary to command us to do so. His wife used to insist upon our calling him so, but to no purpose. In August, 1832, my master attended a Methodist camp-meeting held in the Bay-side, Talbot county, and there experienced religion. I indulged a faint hope that his conversion would lead him to emancipate his slaves, and that, if he did not do this, it would, at any rate, make him more kind and humane. I was disappointed in both these respects. It neither made him to be humane to his slaves, nor to emancipate them. If it had any effect on his character, it made him more cruel and hateful in all his ways; for I believe him to have been a much worse man after his conversion than before. Prior to his conversion, he relied upon his own depravity to shield and sustain him in his savage barbarity; but after his conversion, he found religious sanction and support for his slaveholding cruelty. He made the greatest pretensions to piety. His house was the house of prayer. He prayed morning, noon, and night. He very soon distinguished himself among his brethren, and was soon made a class-leader and exhorter. His activity in revivals was great, and he proved himself an instrument in the hands of the church in converting many souls. His house was the preachers' home. They used to take great pleasure in coming there to put up; for while he starved us, he stuffed them. We have had three or four preachers there at a time. The names of those who used to come most frequently while I lived there, were Mr Storks, Mr Ewery, Mr Humphry, and Mr Hickey. I have also seen Mr George Cookman at our house. We slaves loved Mr Cookman. We believed him to be a good man. We thought him instrumental in getting Mr Samuel Harrison, a very rich slaveholder, to emancipate his slaves; and by some means got the impression that he was laboring to effect the emancipation of all the slaves. When he was at our house, we were sure to be called in to prayers. When the others were there, we were sometimes called in and sometimes not. Mr Cookman took more notice of us than either of the other ministers. He could not come among us without betraying his sympathy for us, and, stupid as we were, we had the sagacity to see it.

While I lived with my master in St Michael's, there was a

white young man, a Mr Wilson, who proposed to keep a Sabbath school for the instruction of such slaves as might be disposed to learn to read the New Testament. We met but three times, when Mr West and Mr Fairbanks, both class-leaders, with many others, came upon us with sticks and other missiles, drove us off, and forbade us to meet again. Thus ended our little Sabbath school in the pious town of St Michael's.

I have said my master found religious sanction for his cruelty. As an example, I will state one of many facts going to prove the charge. I have seen him tie up a lame young woman, and whip her with a heavy cowskin upon her naked shoulders, causing the warm red blood to drip; and, in justification of the bloody deed, he would quote this passage of Scripture – 'He that knoweth his master's will, and doeth it not, shall be beaten with many stripes.'

Master would keep this lacerated young woman tied up in this horrid situation four or five hours at a time. I have known him to tie her up early in the morning, and whip her before breakfast; leave her, go to his store, return at dinner, and whip her again, cutting her in the places already made raw with his cruel lash. The secret of master's cruelty toward 'Henny' is found in the fact of her being almost helpless. When quite a child, she fell into the fire, and burned herself horribly. Her hands were so burnt that she never got the use of them. She could do very little but bear heavy burdens. She was to master a bill of expense; and as he was a mean man, she was a constant offence to him. He seemed desirous of getting the poor girl out of existence. He gave her away once to his sister; but, being a poor gift, she was not disposed to keep her. Finally, my benevolent master, to use his own words, 'set her adrift to take care of herself.' Here was a recently-converted man, holding on upon the mother, and at the same time turning out her helpless child, to starve and die! Master Thomas was one of the many pious slaveholders who hold slaves for the very charitable purpose of taking care of them.

My master and myself had quite a number of differences. He found me unsuitable to his purpose. My city life, he said, had had a very pernicious effect upon me. It had almost ruined me for every good purpose, and fitted me for every thing which was bad. One of my greatest faults was that of letting his horse run

THE LIFE OF FREDERICK DOUGLASS

away, and go down to his father-in-law's farm, which was about
five miles from St Michael's. I would then have to go after it.
My reason for this kind of carelessness, or carefulness, was, that
I could always get something to eat when I went there. Master
William Hamilton, my master's father-in-law, always gave his
slaves enough to eat. I never left there hungry, no matter how
great the need of my speedy return. Master Thomas at length
said he would stand it no longer. I had lived with him nine
months, during which time he had given me a number of severe
whippings, all to no good purpose. He resolved to put me out,
as he said, to be broken; and, for this purpose, he let me for one
year to a man named Edward Covey. Mr Covey was a poor
man, a farm-renter. He rented the place upon which he lived, as
also the hands with which he tilled it. Mr Covey had acquired a
very high reputation for breaking young slaves, and this reputation was of immense value to him. It enabled him to get his farm
tilled with much less expense to himself than he could have had
it done without such a reputation. Some slaveholders thought it
not much loss to allow Mr Covey to have their slaves one year,
for the sake of the training to which they were subjected,
without any other compensation. He could hire young help with
great ease, in consequence of this reputation. Added to the
natural good qualities of Mr Covey, he was a professor of
religion – a pious soul – a member and a class-leader in the
Methodist church. All of this added weight to his repuation as a
'nigger-breaker.' I was aware of all the facts, having been made
acquainted with them by a young man who had lived there. I
nevertheless made the change gladly; for I was sure of getting
enough to eat, which is not the smallest consideration to a
hungry man.

Chapter 10

I LEFT Master Thomas's house, and went to live with Mr
Covey, on the 1st of January, 1833. I was now, for the first time
in my life, a field hand. In my new employment, I found myself
even more awkward than a country boy appeared to be in a

large city. I had been at my new home but one week before Mr
Covey gave me a very severe whipping, cutting my back, causing
the blood to run, and raising ridges on my flesh as large as my
little finger. The details of this affair are as follows: Mr Covey
sent me, very early in the morning of one of our coldest days in
the month of January, to the woods, to get a load of wood. He
gave me a team of unbroken oxen. He told me which was the
in-hand ox, and which the off-hand one. He then tied the end of
a large rope around the horns of the in-hand ox, and gave me
the other end of it, and told me, if the oxen started to run, that
I must hold on upon the rope. I had never driven oxen before,
and of course I was very awkward. I, however, succeeded in
getting to the edge of the woods with little difficulty; but I had
got a very few rods into the woods, when the oxen took fright,
and started full tilt, carrying the cart against trees, and over
stumps, in the most frightful manner. I expected every moment
that my brains would be dashed out against the trees. After
running thus for a considerable distance, they finally upset the
cart, dashing it with great force against a tree, and threw
themselves into a dense thicket. How I escaped death, I do not
know. There I was, entirely alone, in a thick wood, in a place
new to me. My cart was upset and shattered, my oxen were
entangled among the young trees, and there was none to help
me. After a long spell of effort, I succeeded in getting my cart
righted, my oxen disentangled, and again yoked to the cart. I
now proceeded with my team to the place where I had, the day
before, been chopping wood, and loaded my cart pretty heavily,
thinking in this way to tame my oxen. I then proceeded on my
way home. I had now consumed one half of the day. I got out
of the woods safely, and now felt out of danger. I stopped my
oxen to open the woods gate; and just as I did so, before I could
get hold of my ox-rope, the oxen again started, rushed through
the gate, catching it between the wheel and the body of the cart,
tearing it to pieces, and coming within a few inches of crushing
me against the gate-post. Thus twice, in one short day, I escaped
death by the merest chance. On my return, I told Mr Covey
what had happened, and how it happened. He ordered me to
return to the woods again immediately. I did so, and he followed
on after me. Just as I got into the woods, he came up and told
me to stop my cart, and that he would teach me how to trifle

away my time, and break gates. He then went to a large gum-tree, and with his axe cut three large switches, and, after trimming them up neatly with his pocket-knife, he ordered me to take off my clothes. I made him no answer, but stood with my clothes on. He repeated his order. I still made him no answer, nor did I move to strip myself. Upon this he rushed at me with the fierceness of a tiger, tore off my clothes, and lashed me till he had worn out his switches, cutting me so savagely as to leave the marks visible for a long time after. This whipping was the first of a number just like it, and for similar offences.

I lived with Mr Covey one year. During the first six months, of that year, scarce a week passed without his whipping me. I was seldom free from a sore back. My awkwardness was almost always his excuse for whipping me. We were worked fully up to the point of endurance. Long before day we were up, our horses fed, and by the first approach of day we were off to the field with our hoes and ploughing teams. Mr Covey gave us enough to eat, but scarce time to eat it. We were often less than five minutes taking our meals. We were often in the field from the first approach of day till its last lingering ray had left us; and at saving-fodder time, midnight often caught us in the field binding blades.

Covey would be out with us. The way he used to stand it, was this. He would spend the most of his afternoons in bed. He would then come out fresh in the evening, ready to urge us on with his words, example, and frequently with the whip. Mr Covey was one of the few slaveholders who could and did work with his hands. He was a hard-working man. He knew by himself just what a man or a boy could do. There was no deceiving him. His work went on in his absence almost as well as in his presence; and he had the faculty of making us feel that he was ever present with us. This he did by surprising us. He seldom approached the spot where we were at work openly, if he could do it secretly. He always aimed at taking us by surprise. Such was his cunning, that we used to call him, among ourselves, 'the snake.' When we were at work in the cornfield, he would sometimes crawl on his hands and knees to avoid detection, and all at once he would rise nearly in our midst, and scream out, 'Ha, ha! Come, come! Dash on, dash on!' This being his mode of attack, it was never safe to stop a single minute. His comings were like a thief in the night. He appeared to us as being ever at hand. He was under every tree, behind every stump, in every bush, and at every window, on the plantation. He would sometimes mount his horse, as if bound to St Michael's, a distance of seven miles, and in half an hour afterwards you would see him coiled up in the corner of the wood-fence, watching every motion of the slaves. He would, for this purpose, leave his horse tied up in the woods. Again, he would sometimes walk up to us, and give us orders as though he was upon the point of starting on a long journey, turn his back upon us, and make as though he was going to the house to get ready; and, before he would get halfway thither, he would turn short and crawl into a fence-corner, or behind some tree, and there watch us till the going down of the sun.

Mr Covey's *forte* consisted in his power to deceive. His life was devoted to planning and perpetrating the grossest deceptions. Every thing he possessed in the shape of learning or religion, he made conform to his disposition to deceive. He seemed to think himself equal to deceiving the Almighty. He would make a short prayer in the morning, and a long prayer at night; and, strange as it may seem, few men would at times appear more devotional than he. The exercises of his family devotions were always commenced with singing; and, as he was a very poor singer himself, the duty of raising the hymn generally came upon me. He would read his hymn, and nod at me to commence. I would at times do so; at others, I would not. My non-compliance would almost always produce much confusion. To show himself independent of me, he would start and stagger through with his hymn in the most discordant manner. In this state of mind, he prayed with more than ordinary spirit. Poor man! such was his disposition, and success at deceiving, I do verily believe that he sometimes deceived himself into the solemn belief, that he was a sincere worshipper of the most high God; and this, too, at a time when he may be said to have been guilty of compelling his woman slave to commit the sin of adultery. The facts in the case are these: Mr Covey was a poor man; he was just commencing in life; he was only able to buy one slave; and, shocking as is the fact, he bought her, as he said, for a *breeder*. This woman was named Caroline. Mr Covey bought her from Mr Thomas Lowe, about six miles from St Michael's.

She was a large, able-bodied woman, about twenty years old. She had already given birth to one child, which proved her to be just what he wanted. After buying her, he hired a married man of Mr Samuel Harrison, to live with him one year; and him he used to fasten up with her every night! The result was, that, at the end of the year, the miserable woman gave birth to twins. At this result Mr Covey seemed to be highly pleased, both with the man and the wretched woman. Such was his joy, and that of his wife, that nothing they could do for Caroline during her confinement was too good, or too hard, to be done. The children were regarded as being quite an addition to his wealth.

If at any one time of my life more than another, I was made to drink the bitterest dregs of slavery, that time was during the first six months of my stay with Mr Covey. We were worked in all weathers. It was never too hot or too cold; it could never rain, blow, hail, or snow, too hard for us to work in the field. Work, work, work, was scarcely more the order of the day than of the night. The longest days were too short for him, and the shortest nights too long for him. I was somewhat unmanageable when I first went there, but a few months of this discipline tamed me. Mr Covey succeeded in breaking me. I was broken in body, soul, and spirit. My natural elasticity was crushed, my intellect languished, the disposition to read departed, the cheerful spark that lingered about my eye died; the dark night of slavery closed in upon me; and behold a man transformed into a brute!

Sunday was my only leisure time. I spent this in a sort of beast-like stupor, between sleep and wake, under some large tree. At times I would rise up, a flash of energetic freedom would dart through my soul, accompanied with a faint beam of hope, that flickered for a moment, and then vanished. I sank down again, mourning over my wretched condition. I was sometimes prompted to take my life, and that of Covey, but was prevented by a combination of hope and fear. My sufferings on this plantation seem now like a dream rather than a stern reality.

Our house stood within a few rods of the Chesapeake Bay, whose broad bosom was ever white with sails from every quarter of the habitable globe. Those beautiful vessels, robed in purest white, so delightful to the eye of freemen, were to me so many shrouded ghosts, to terrify and torment me with thoughts of my wretched condition. I have often, in the deep stillness of a summer's Sabbath, stood all alone upon the lofty banks of that noble bay, and traced, with saddened heart and tearful eye, the countless number of sails moving off to the mighty ocean. The sight of these always affected me powerfully. My thoughts would compel utterance; and there, with no audience but the Almighty, I would pour out my soul's complaint, in my rude way, with an apostrophe to the moving multitude of ships: –

'You are loosed from your moorings, and are free; I am fast in my chains, and am a slave! You move merrily before the gentle gale, and I sadly before the bloody whip! You are freedom's swift-winged angels, that fly round the world; I am confined in bands of iron! O that I were free! O, that I were on one of your gallant decks, and under your protecting wing! Alas! betwixt me and you, the turbid waters roll. Go on, go on. O that I could also go! Could I but swim! If I could fly! O, why was I born a man, of whom to make a brute! The glad ship is gone; she hides in the dim distance. I am left in the hottest hell of unending slavery. O God, save me! God, deliver me! Let me be free! Is there any God? Why am I a slave? I will run away. I will not stand it. Get caught, or get clear, I'll try it. I had as well die with ague as the fever. I have only one life to lose. I had as well be killed running as die standing. Only think of it; one hundred miles straight north, and I am free! Try it? Yes! God helping me, I will. It cannot be that I shall live and die a slave. I will take to the water. This very bay shall bear me into freedom. The steamboats steered in a north-east course from North Point. I will do the same; and when I get to the head of the bay, I will turn my canoe adrift, and walk straight through Delaware into Pennsylvania. When I get there, I shall not be required to have a pass; I can travel without being disturbed. Let but the first opportunity offer, and, come what will, I am off. Meanwhile, I will try to bear up under the yoke. I am not the only slave in the world. Why should I fret? I can bear as much as any of them. Besides, I am but a boy, and all boys are bound to some one. It may be that my misery in slavery will only increase my happiness when I get free. There is a better day coming.'

Thus I used to think, and thus I used to speak to myself; goaded almost to madness at one moment, and at the next reconciling myself to my wretched lot.

I have already intimated that my condition was much worse, during the first six months of my stay at Mr Covey's, than in the last six. The circumstances leading to the change in Mr Covey's course toward me form an epoch in my humble history. You have seen how a man was made a slave; you shall see how a slave was made a man. On one of the hottest days of the month of August, 1833, Bill Smith, William Hughes, a slave named Eli, and myself, were engaged in fanning wheat. Hughes was clearing the fanned wheat from before the fan, Eli was turning, Smith was feeding, and I was carrying wheat to the fan. The work was simple, requiring strength rather than intellect; yet, to one entirely unused to such work, it came very hard. About three o'clock of that day, I broke down; my strength failed me; I was seized with a violent aching of the head, attended with extreme dizziness; I trembled in every limb. Finding what was coming, I nerved myself up, feeling it would never do to stop work. I stood as long as I could stagger to the hopper with grain. When I could stand no longer, I fell, and felt as if held down by an immense weight. The fan of course stopped; every one had his own work to do; and no one could do the work of the other, and have his own go on at the same time.

Mr Covey was at the house, about one hundred yards from the treading-yard where we were fanning. On hearing the fan stop, he left immediately, and came to the spot where we were. He hastily inquired what the matter was. Bill answered that I was sick, and there was no one to bring wheat to the fan. I had by this time crawled away under the side of the post and rail-fence by which the yard was enclosed, hoping to find relief by getting our of the sun. He then asked where I was. He was told by one of the hands. He came to the spot, and, after looking at me awhile, asked me what was the matter. I told him as well as I could, for I scarce had strength to speak. He then gave me a savage kick in the side, and told me to get up. I tried to do so, but fell back in the attempt. He gave me another kick, and again told me to rise. I again tried, and succeeded in gaining my feet; but, stooping to get the tub with which I was feeding the fan, I again staggered and fell. While down in this situation, Mr Covey took up the hickory slat with which Hughes had been striking off the half-bushel measure, and with it gave me a heavy blow

upon the head, making a large wound, and the blood ran freely;
and with this again told me to get up. I made no effort to
comply, having now made up my mind to let him do his worst.
In a short time after receiving this blow, my head grew better.
Mr Covey had now left me to my fate. At this moment I
resolved, for the first time, to go to my master, enter a complaint,
and ask his protection. In order to [do] this, I must that
afternoon walk seven miles; and this, under the circumstances,
was truly a severe undertaking. I was exceedingly feeble; made
so as much by the kicks and blows which I received, as by the
severe fit of sickness to which I had been subjected. I, however,
watched my chance, while Covey was looking in an opposite
direction, and started for St Michael's. I succeeded in getting a
considerable distance on my way to the woods, when Covey
discovered me, and called after me to come back, threatening
what he would do if I did not come. I disregarded both his calls
and his threats, and made my way to the woods as fast as my
feeble state would allow; and thinking I might be overhauled by
him if I kept the road, I walked through the woods, keeping far
enough from the road to avoid detection, and near enough to
prevent losing my way. I had not gone far before my little
strength again failed me. I could go no farther. I fell down, and
lay for a considerable time. The blood was yet oozing from the
wound on my head. For a time I thought I should bleed to
death; and think now that I should have done so, but that the
blood so matted my hair as to stop the wound. After lying there
about three quarters of an hour, I nerved myself up again, and
started on my way, through bogs and briers, barefooted and
bareheaded, tearing my feet sometimes at nearly every step; and
after a journey of about seven miles, occupying some five hours
to perform it, I arrived at master's store. I then presented an
appearance enough to affect any but a heart of iron. From the
crown of my head to my feet, I was covered with blood. My
hair was all clotted with dust and blood; my shirt was stiff with
blood. My legs and feet were torn in sundry places with briers
and thorns, and were also covered with blood. I suppose I
looked like a man who had escaped a den of wild beasts, and
barely escaped them. In this state I appeared before my master,
humbly entreating him to interpose his authority for my protection. I told him all the circumstances as well as I could, and it

seemed, as I spoke, at times to affect him. He would then walk the floor, and seek to justify Covey by saying he expected I deserved it. He asked me what I wanted. I told him, to let me get a new home; that as sure as I lived with Mr Covey again, I should live with but to die with him; that Covey would surely kill me; he was in a fair way for it. Master Thomas ridiculed the idea that there was any danger of Mr Covey's killing me, and said that he knew Mr Covey; that he was a good man, and that he could not think of taking me from him; that, should he do so, he would lose the whole year's wages; that I belonged to Mr Covey for one year, and that I must go back to him, come what might; and that I must not trouble him with any more stories, or that he would himself *get hold of me*. After threatening me thus, he gave me a very large dose of salts, telling me that I might remain in St Michael's that night, (it being quite late,) but that I must be off back to Mr Covey's early in the morning; and that if I did not, he would *get hold of me*, which meant that he would whip me. I remained all night, and, according to his orders, I started off to Covey's in the morning, (Saturday morning,) wearied in body and broken in spirit. I got no supper that night, or breakfast that morning. I reached Covey's about nine o'clock; and just as I was getting over the fence that divided Mrs Kemp's fields from ours, out ran Covey with his cowskin, to give me another whipping. Before he could reach me, I succeeded in getting to the cornfield; and as the corn was very high, it afforded me the means of hiding. He seemed very angry, and searched for me a long time. My behavior was altogether unaccountable. He finally gave up the chase, thinking, I suppose, that I must come home for something to eat; he would give himself no further trouble in looking for me. I spent that day mostly in the woods, having the alternative before me – to go home and be whipped to death, or stay in the woods and be starved to death. That night, I fell in with Sandy Jenkins, a slave with whom I was somewhat acquainted. Sandy had a free wife who lived about four miles from Mr Covey's; and it being Saturday, he was on his way to see her. I told him my circumstances, and he very kindly invited me to go home with him. I went home with him, and talked this whole matter over, and got his advice as to what course it was best for me to pursue. I found Sandy an old adviser. He told me, with great solemnity, I must go back to Covey; but that before I went, I must go with him into another part of the woods, where there was a certain *root*, which, if I would take some of it with me, carrying it *always on my right side*, would render it impossible for Mr Covey, or any other white man, to whip me. He said he had carried it for years; and since he had done so, he had never received a blow, and never expected to while he carried it. I at first rejected the idea, that the simple carrying of a root in my pocket would have any such effect as he had said, and was not disposed to take it; but Sandy impressed the necessity with much earnestness, telling me it could do no harm, if it did no good. To please him, I at length took the root, and, according to his direction, carried it upon my right side. This was Sunday morning. I immediately started for home; and upon entering the yard gate, out came Mr Covey on his way to meeting. He spoke to me very kindly, bade me drive the pigs from a lot near by, and passed on towards the church. Now, this singular conduct of Mr Covey really made me begin to think that there was something in the *root* which Sandy had given me; and had it been on any other day than Sunday, I could have attributed the conduct to no other cause than the influence of that root; and as it was, I was half inclined to think the *root* to be something more than I at first had taken it to be. All went well till Monday morning. On this morning, the virtue of the *root* was fully tested. Long before daylight, I was called to go and rub, curry, and feed, the horses. I obeyed, and was glad to obey. But whilst thus engaged, whilst in the act of throwing down some blades from the loft, Mr Covey entered the stable with a long rope; and just as I was half out of the loft, he caught hold of my legs, and was about tying me. As soon as I found what he was up to, I gave a sudden spring, and as I did so, he holding to my legs, I was brought sprawling on the stable floor. Mr Covey seemed now to think he had me, and could do what he pleased; but at this moment – from whence came the spirit I don't know – I resolved to fight; and, suiting my action to the resolution, I seized Covey hard by the throat; and as I did so, I rose. He held on to me, and I to him. My resistance was so entirely unexpected, that Covey seemed taken all aback. He trembled like a leaf. This gave me assurance, and I held him uneasy, causing the blood to run where I touched him with the ends of my fingers.

Mr Covey soon called out to Hughes for help. Hughes came, and, while Covey held me, attempted to tie my right hand. While he was in the act of doing so, I watched my chance, and gave him a heavy kick close under the ribs. This kick fairly sickened Hughes, so that he left me in the hands of Mr Covey. This kick had the effect of not only weakening Hughes, but Covey also. When he saw Hughes bending over with pain, his courage quailed. He asked me if I meant to persist in my resistance. I told him I did, come what might; that he had used me like a brute for six months, and that I was determined to be used so no longer. With that, he strove to drag me to a stick that was lying just out of the stable door. He meant to knock me down. But just as he was leaning over to get the stick, I seized him with both hands by his collar, and brought him by a sudden snatch to the ground. By this time, Bill came. Covey called upon him for assistance. Bill wanted to know what he could do. Covey said, 'Take hold of him, take hold of him!' Bill said his master hired him out to work, and not to help to whip me; so he left Covey and myself to fight our own battle out. We were at it for nearly two hours. Covey at length let me go, puffing and blowing at a great rate, saying that if I had not resisted, he would not have whipped me half so much. The truth was, that he had not whipped me at all. I considered him as getting entirely the worst end of the bargain; for he had drawn no blood from me, but I had from him. The whole six months afterwards, that I spent with Mr Covey, he never laid the weight of his finger upon me in anger. He would occasionally say, he didn't want to get hold of me again. 'No,' thought I, 'you need not; for you will come off worse than you did before.'

This battle with Mr Covey was the turning-point in my career as a slave. It rekindled the few expiring embers of freedom, and revived within me a sense of my own manhood. It recalled the departed self-confidence, and inspired me again with a determination to be free. The gratification afforded by the triumph was a full compensation for whatever else might follow, even death itself. He only can understand the deep satisfaction which I experienced, who has himself repelled by force the bloody arm of slavery. I felt as I never felt before. It was a glorious resurrection, from the tomb of slavery, to the heaven of freedom. My long-crushed spirit rose, cowardice departed, bold defiance took its place; and I now resolved that, however long I might remain a slave in form, the day had passed forever when I could be a slave in fact. I did not hesitate to let it be known of me, that the white man who expected to succeed in whipping, must also succeed in killing me.

From this time I was never again what might be called fairly whipped, though I remained a slave four years afterwards. I had several fights, but was never whipped.

It was for a long time a matter of surprise to me why Mr Covey did not immediately have me taken by the constable to the whipping-post, and there regularly whipped for the crime of raising my hand against a white man in defence of myself. And the only explanation I can now think of does not entirely satisfy me; but such as it is, I will give it. Mr Covey enjoyed the most unbounded reputation for being a first-rate overseer and negro-breaker. It was of considerable importance to him. That reputation was at stake; and had he sent me — a boy about sixteen years old — to the public whipping-post, his reputation would have been lost; so, to save his reputation, he suffered me to go unpunished.

My term of actual service to Mr Edward Covey ended on Christmas day, 1833. The days between Christmas and New Year's day are allowed as holidays; and, accordingly, we were not required to perform any labor, more than to feed and take care of the stock. This time we regarded as our own, by the grace of our masters; and we therefore used or abused it nearly as we pleased. Those of us who had families at a distance, were generally allowed to spend the whole six days in their society. This time, however, was spent in various ways. The staid, sober, thinking and industrious ones of our number would employ themselves in making corn-brooms, mats, horse-collars, and baskets; and another class of us would spend the time in hunting opossums, hares, and coons. But by far the larger part engaged in such sports and merriments as playing ball, wrestling, running foot-races, fiddling, dancing, and drinking whisky; and this latter mode of spending the time was by far the most agreeable to the feelings of our masters. A slave who would work during the holidays was considered by our masters as scarcely deserving them. He was regarded as one who rejected the favor of his master. It was deemed a disgrace not to get drunk at Christmas; and he was regarded as lazy indeed, who had not provided himself with the necessary means, during the year, to get whisky enough to last him through Christmas.

From what I know of the effect of these holidays upon the slave, I believe them to be among the most effective means in the hands of the slaveholder in keeping down the spirit of insurrection. Were the slaveholders at once to abandon this practice, I have not the slightest doubt it would lead to an immediate insurrection among the slaves. These holidays serve as conductors, or safety-valves, to carry off the rebellious spirit of enslaved humanity. But for these, the slave would be forced up to the wildest desperation; and woe betide the slaveholder, the day he ventures to remove or hinder the operation of those conductors! I warn him that, in such an event, a spirit will go forth in their midst, more to be dreaded than the most appalling earthquake.

The holidays are part and parcel of the gross fraud, wrong, and inhumanity of slavery. They are professedly a custom established by the benevolence of the slaveholders; but I undertake to say, it is the result of selfishness, and one of the grossest frauds committed upon the down-trodden slave. They do not give the slaves this time because they would not like to have their work during its continuance, but because they know it would be unsafe to deprive them of it. This will be seen by the fact, that the slaveholders like to have their slaves spend those days just in such a manner as to make them as glad of their ending as of their beginning. Their object seems to be, to disgust their slaves with freedom, by plunging them into the lowest depths of dissipation. For instance, the slaveholders not only like to see the slave drink of his own accord, but will adopt various plans to make him drunk. One plan is, to make bets on their slaves, as to who can drink the most whisky without getting drunk; and in this way they succeed in getting whole multitudes to drink to excess. Thus, when the slave asks for virtuous freedom, the cunning slaveholder, knowing his ignorance, cheats him with a dose of vicious dissipation, artfully labelled with the name of liberty. The most of us used to drink it down, and the result was just what might be supposed: many of us were led to think that there was little to choose between liberty and slavery. We felt, and very properly too, that we had almost as well be slaves to man as to rum. So, when the holidays ended, we staggered up from the filth of our wallowing, took a long breath, and marched to the field – feeling, upon the whole, rather glad to go, from what our master had deceived us into a belief was freedom, back to the arms of slavery.

I have said that this mode of treatment is a part of the whole system of fraud and inhumanity of slavery. It is so. The mode here adopted to disgust the slave with freedom, by allowing him to see only the abuse of it, is carried out in other things. For instance, a slave loves molasses; he steals some. His master, in many cases, goes off to town, and buys a large quantity; he returns, takes his whip, and commands the slave to eat the molasses, until the poor fellow is made sick at the very mention of it. The same mode is sometimes adopted to make the slaves refrain from asking for more food than their regular allowance. A slave runs through his allowance, and applies for more. His master is enraged at him; but, not willing to send him off without food, gives him more than is necessary, and compels him to eat it within a given time. Then, if he complains that he cannot eat it, he is said to be satisfied neither full nor fasting, and is whipped for being hard to please! I have an abundance of such illustrations of the same principle, drawn from my own observation, but think the cases I have cited sufficient. The practice is a very common one.

On the first of January, 1834, I left Mr Covey, and went to live with Mr William Freeland, who lived about three miles from St Michael's. I soon found Mr Freeland a very different man from Mr Covey. Though not rich, he was what would be called an educated southern gentleman. Mr Covey, as I have shown, was a well-trained negro-breaker and slave-driver. The former (slaveholder though he was) seemed to possess some regard for honor, some reverence for justice, and some respect for humanity. The latter seemed totally insensible to all such sentiments. Mr Freeland had many of the faults peculiar to slaveholders, such as being very passionate and fretful; but I must do him the justice to say, that he was exceedingly free from those degrading vices to which Mr Covey was constantly addicted. The one was open and frank, and we always knew where to find him. The other was a most artful deceiver, and could be understood only by such as were skilful enough to detect his cunningly-devised frauds. Another advantage I gained in my new master was, he made no pretensions to, or profession of, religion; and this, in my opinion, was truly a great advantage. I assert most unhesitatigly, that the religion of the south is a mere covering for the most appalling barbarity – a sanctifier of the most hateful frauds – and a dark shelter under, which the darkest, foulest, grossest, and most infernal deeds of slaveholders find the strongest protection. Were I to be again reduced to the chains of slavery, next to that enslavement, I should regard being the slave of a religious master the greatest calamity that could befall me. For of all slaveholders with whom I have ever met, religious slaveholders are the worst. I have ever found them the meanest and basest, the most cruel and cowardly, of all others. It was my unhappy lot not only to belong to a religious slaveholder, but to live in a community of such religionists. Very near Mr Freeland lived the Rev. Daniel Weeden, and in the same neighborhood lived the Rev. Rigby Hopkins. These were members and ministers in the Reformed Methodist Church. Mr Weeden owned, among others, a woman slave, whose name I have forgotten. This woman's back, for weeks, was kept literally raw, made so by the lash of this merciless, *religious* wretch. He used to hire hands. His maxim was, Behave well or behave ill, it is the duty of a master occasionally to whip a slave, to remind him of his master's authority. Such was his theory, and such his practice.

Mr Hopkins was even worse than Mr Weeden. His chief boast was his ability to manage slaves. The peculiar feature of his government was that of whipping slaves in advance of deserving it. He always managed to have one or more of his slaves to whip every Monday morning. He did this to alarm their fears, and strike terror into those who escaped. His plan was to whip for the smallest offences, to prevent the commission of large ones. Mr Hopkins could always find some excuse for whipping a slave. It would astonish one, unaccustomed to a slaveholding life, to see with what wonderful ease a slaveholder can find things, of which to make occasion to whip a slave. A mere look, word, or motion – a mistake, accident, or want of power – are all matters for which a slave may be whipped at any time. Does a slave look dissatisfied? It is said, he has the devil in him, and it must be whipped out. Does he speak loudly when spoken to by his master? Then he is getting high-minded, and should be taken down a button-hole lower. Does he forget to pull off his hat at the approach of a white person? Then he is wanting in reverence, and should be whipped for it. Does he ever venture to vindicate his conduct, when censured for it? Then he is guilty of impudence – one of the greatest crimes of which a slave can be guilty. Does he ever venture to suggest a different mode of doing things from that pointed out by his master? He is indeed presumptuous, and getting above himself; and nothing less than a flogging will do for him. Does he, while ploughing, break a plough – or, while hoeing, break a hoe? It is owing to his carelessness, and for it a slave must always be whipped. Mr Hopkins could always find something of this sort to justify the use of the lash, and he seldom failed to embrace such opportunities. There was not a man in the whole county, with whom the slaves who had the getting their own home, would not prefer to live, rather than with this Rev. Mr Hopkins. And yet there was not a man any where round, who made higher professions of religion, or was more active in revivals – more attentive to the class, love-feast, prayer and preaching meetings, or more devotional in his family – that prayed earlier, later, louder, and longer – than this same reverend slave-driver, Rigby Hopkins.

But to return to Mr Freeland, and to my experience while in his employment. He, like Mr Covey, gave us enough to eat; but, unlike Mr Covey, he also gave us sufficient time to take our meals. He worked us hard, but always between sunrise and sunset. He required a good deal of work to be done, but gave us good tools with which to work. His farm was large, but he employed hands enough to work it, and with ease, compared with many of his neighbors. My treatment, while in his employment, was heavenly, compared with what I experienced at the hands of Mr Edward Covey.

Mr Freeland was himself the owner of but two slaves. Their names were Henry Harris and John Harris. The rest of his hands he hired. These consisted of myself, Sandy Jenkins,* and Handy

---

* This is the same man who gave me the roots to prevent my being whipped by Mr Covey. He was 'a clever soul.' We used frequently to talk about the fight with Covey, and as often as we did so, he would claim my success as the result of the roots which he gave me. This superstition is very common among the more ignorant slaves. A slave seldom dies but that his death is attributed to trickery.

Caldwell. Henry and John were quite intelligent, and in a very little while after I went there, I succeeded in creating in them a strong desire to learn how to read. This desire soon sprang up in the others also. They very soon mustered up some old spelling-books, and nothing would do but that I must keep a Sabbath school. I agreed to do so, and accordingly devoted my Sundays to teaching these my loved fellow-slaves how to read. Neither of them knew his letters when I went there. Some of the slaves of the neighboring farms found what was going on, and also availed themselves of this little opportunity to learn to read. It was understood, among all who came, that there must be as little display about it as possible. It was necessary to keep our religious masters at St Michael's unacquainted with the fact, that, instead of spending the Sabbath in wrestling, boxing, and drinking whisky, we were trying to learn how to read the will of God; for they had much rather see us engaged in those degrading sports, than to see us behaving like intellectual, moral, and accountable beings. My blood boils as I think of the bloody manner in which Messrs. Wright Fairbanks and Garrison West, both class-leaders, in connection with many others, rushed in upon us with sticks and stones, and broke up our virtuous little Sabbath school, at St Michael's — all calling themselves Christians! humble followers of the Lord Jesus Christ! But I am again digressing.

I held my Sabbath school at the house of a free colored man, whose name I deem it imprudent to mention; for should it be known, it might embarrass him greatly, though the crime of holding the school was committed ten years ago. I had at one time over forty scholars, and those of the right sort, ardently desiring to learn. They were of all ages, though mostly men and women. I look back to those Sundays with an amount of pleasure not to be expressed. They were great days to my soul. The work of instructing my dear fellow-slaves was the sweetest engagement with which I was ever blessed. We loved each other, and to leave them at the close of the Sabbath was a severe cross indeed. When I think that these precious souls are to-day shut up in the prison-house of slavery, my feelings overcome me, and I am almost ready to ask, 'Does a righteous God govern the universe? and for what does he hold the thunders in his right hand, it not to smite the oppressor, and deliver the spoiled out of the hand of the spoiler?' These dear souls came not to Sabbath school because it was popular to do so, nor did I teach them because it was reputable to be thus engaged. Every moment they spent in that school, they were liable to be taken up, and given thirty-nine lashes. They came because they wished to learn. Their minds had been starved by their cruel masters. They had been shut up in mental darkness. I taught them, because it was the delight of my soul to be doing something that looked like bettering the condition of my race. I kept up my school nearly the whole year I lived with Mr Freeland; and, beside my Sabbath school, I devoted three evenings in the week, during the winter, to teaching the slaves at home. And I have the happiness to know, that several of those who came to Sabbath school learned how to read; and that one, at least, is now free through my agency.

The year passed off smoothly. It seemed only about half as long as the year which preceded it. I went through it without receiving a single blow. I will give Mr Freeland the credit of being the best master I ever had, *till I became my own master*. For the ease with which I passed the year, I was, however, somewhat indebted to the society of my fellow-slaves. They were noble souls; they not only possessed loving hearts, but brave ones. We were linked and interlinked with each other. I loved them with a love stronger than any thing I have experienced since. It is sometimes said that we slaves do not love and confide in each other. In answer to this assertion, I can say, I never loved any or confided in any people more than my fellow-slaves, and especially those with whom I lived at Mr Freeland's. I believe we would have died for each other. We never undertook to do any thing, of any importance, without a mutual consultation. We never moved separately. We were one; and as much so by our tempers and dispositions, as by the mutual hardships to which we were necessarily subjected by our condition as slaves.

At the close of the year 1834, Mr Freeland again hired me of my master, for the year 1835. But, by this time, I began to want to live *upon free land* as well as *with Freeland*; and I was no longer content, therefore, to live with him or any other slave-holder. I began, with the commencement of the year, to prepare myself for a final struggle, which should decide my fate one way or the other. My tendency was upward. I was fast approaching

manhood, and year after year had passed, and I was still a slave.
These thoughts roused me – I must do something. I therefore
resolved that 1835 should not pass without witnessing an
attempt, on my part, to secure my liberty. But I was not willing
to cherish this determination alone. My fellow-slaves were dear
to me. I was anxious to have them participate with me in this,
my life-giving determination. I therefore, though with great
prudence, commenced early to ascertain their views and feelings
in regard to their condition, and to imbue their minds with
thoughts of freedom. I bent myself to devising ways and means
for our escape, and meanwhile strove, on all fitting occasions,
to impress them with the gross fraud and inhumanity of slavery.
I went first to Henry, next to John, then to the others. I found,
in them all, warm hearts and noble spirits. They were ready to
hear, and ready to act when a feasible plan should be proposed.
This was what I wanted. I talked to them of our want of
manhood, if we submitted to our enslavement without at least
one noble effort to be free. We met often, and consulted
frequently, and told our hopes and fears, recounted the difficulties, real and imagined, which we should be called on to meet. At
times we were almost disposed to give up, and try to content
ourselves with our wretched lot; at others, we were firm and
unbending in our determination to go. Whenever we suggested
any plan, there was shrinking – the odds were fearful. Our path
was beset with the greatest obstacles; and if we succeeded in
gaining the end of it, our right to be free was yet questionable –
we were yet liable to be returned to bondage. We could see no
spot, this side of the ocean, where we could be free. We knew
nothing about Canada. Our knowledge of the north did not
extend farther than New York; and to go there, and be forever
harassed with the frightful liability of being returned to slavery
– with the certainty of being treated tenfold worse than before
– the thought was truly a horrible one, and one which it was
not easy to overcome. The case sometimes stood thus: At every
gate through which we were to pass, we saw a watchman – at
every ferry a guard – on every bridge a sentinel – and in every
wood a patrol. We were hemmed in upon every side. Here were
the difficulties, real or imagined – the good to be sought, and
the evil to be shunned. On the one hand, there stood slavery, a
stern reality, glaring frightfully upon us – its robes already

crimsoned with the blood of millions, and even now feasting itself greedily upon our own flesh. On the other hand, away back in the dim distance, under the flickering light of the north star, behind some craggy hill or snowcovered mountain, stood a doubtful freedom – half frozen – beckoning us to come and share its hospitality. This in itself was sometimes enough to stagger us; but when we permitted ourselves to survey the road, we were frequently appalled. Upon either side we saw grim death, assuming the most horrid shapes. Now it was starvation, causing us to eat our own flesh; – now we were contending with the waves, and were drowned; – now we were overtaken, and torn to pieces by the fangs of the terrible bloodhound. We were strung by scorpions, chased by wild beasts, bitten by snakes, and finally, after having nearly reached the desired spot – after swimming rivers, encountering wild beasts, sleeping in the woods, suffering hunger and nakedness – we were overtaken by our pursuers, and, in our resistance, we were shot dead upon the spot! I say, this picture sometimes appalled us, and made us

'rather bear those ills we had,
Than fly to others, that we knew not of.'

In coming to a fixed determination to run away, we did more than Patrick Henry, when he resolved upon liberty or death. With us it was a doubtful liberty at most, and almost certain death if we failed. For my part, I should prefer death to hopeless bondage.

Sandy, one of our number, gave up the notion, but still encouraged us. Our company then consisted of Henry Harris, John Harris, Henry Bailey, Charles Roberts, and myself. Henry Bailey was my uncle, and belonged to my master. Charles married my aunt: he belonged to my master's father-in-law, Mr William Hamilton.

The plan we finally concluded upon was, to get a large canoe belonging to Mr Hamilton, and upon the Saturday night previous to Easter holidays, paddle directly up the Chesapeake Bay. On our arrival at the head of the bay, a distance of seventy or eighty miles from where we lived, it was our purpose to turn our canoe adrift, and follow the guidance of the north star till we got beyond the limits of Maryland. Our reason for taking the water route was, that we were less liable to be suspected as runaways; we hoped to be regarded as fishermen; whereas, if we should take the land route, we should be subjected to interruptions of almost every kind. Any one having a white face, and being so disposed, could stop us, and subject us to examination.

The week before our intended start, I wrote several protections, one for each of us. As well as I can remember, they were in the following words, to wit:

> 'This is to certify that I, the undersigned, have given the bearer, my servant, full liberty to go to Baltimore, and spend the Easter holidays. Written with mine own hand, &c., 1835.
>
> 'William Hamilton,
> 'Near St Michael's, in Talbot county, Maryland.'

We were not going to Baltimore; but, in going up the bay, we went toward Baltimore, and these protections were only intended to protect us while on the bay.

As the time drew near for our departure, our anxiety became more and more intense. It was truly a matter of life and death with us. The strength of our determination was about to be fully tested. At this time, I was very active in explaining every difficulty, removing every doubt, dispelling every fear, and inspiring all with the firmness indispensable to success in our undertaking; assuring them that half was gained the instant we made the move; we had talked long enough; we were now ready to move; if not now, we never should be; and if we did not intend to move now, we had as well fold our arms, sit down, and acknowledge ourselves fit only to be slaves. This, none of us were prepared to acknowledge. Every man stood firm; and at our last meeting, we pledged ourselves afresh, in the most solemn manner, that, at the time appointed, we would certainly start in pursuit of freedom. This was in the middle of the week, at the end of which we were to be off. We went, as usual, to our several fields of labor, but with bosoms highly agitated with thoughts of our truly hazardous undertaking. We tried to conceal our feelings as much as possible; and I think we succeeded very well.

After a painful waiting, the Saturday morning, whose night was to witness our departure, came. I hailed it with joy, bring what of sadness it might. Friday night was a sleepless one for me. I probably felt more anxious than the rest, because I was, by common consent, at the head of the whole affair. The responsibility of success or failure lay heavily upon me. The glory of the one, and the confusion of the other, were alike mine. The first two hours of that morning were such as I never experienced before, and hope never to again. Early in the morning, we went, as usual, to the field. We were spreading manure; and all at once, while thus engaged, I was overwhelmed with an indescribable feeling, in the fulness of which I turned to Sandy, who was near by, and said, 'We are betrayed!' 'Well,' said he, 'that thought has this moment struck me.' We said no more. I was never more certain of any thing.

The horn was blown as usual, and we went up from the field to the house for breakfast. I went for the form, more than for want of any thing to eat that morning. Just as I got to the house, in looking out at the lane gate, I saw four white men, with two colored men. The white men were on horseback, and the colored ones were walking behind, as if tied. I watched them a few moments till they got up to our lane gate. Here they halted, and tied the colored men to the gate-post. I was not yet certain as to what the matter was. In a few moments, in rode Mr Hamilton, with a speed betokening great excitement. He came to the door, and inquired if Master William was in. He was told he was at the barn. Mr Hamilton, without dismounting, rode up to the barn with extraordinary speed. In a few moments, he and Mr Freeland returned to the house. By this time, the three constables rode up, and in great haste dismounted, tied their horses, and met Master William and Mr Hamilton returning from the barn; and after talking awhile, they all walked up to the kitchen door. There was no one in the kitchen but myself and John. Henry and Sandy were up at the barn. Mr Freeland put his head in at the door, and called me by name, saying, there were some gentlemen at the door who wished to see me. I stepped to the door, and inquired what they wanted. They at once seized me, and, without giving me any satisfaction, tied me – lashing my hands closely together. I insisted upon knowing what the matter was. They at length said, that they had learned I had been in a 'scrape,' and that I was to be examined before my master; and if their information proved false, I should not be hurt.

In a few moments, they succeeded in tying John. They then

turned to Henry, who had by this time returned, and commanded him to cross his hands. 'I won't!' said Henry, in a firm tone, indicating his readiness to meet the consequences of his refusal. 'Won't you?' said Tom Graham, the constable. 'No, I won't!' said Henry, in a still stronger tone. With this, two of the constables pulled out their shining pistols, and swore, by their Creator, that they would make him cross his hands or kill him. Each cocked his pistol, and, with fingers on the trigger, walked up to Henry, saying, at the same time, if he did not cross his hands, they would blow his damned heart out. 'Shoot me, shoot me!' said Henry; 'you can't kill me but once. Shoot, shoot, – and be damned! *I won't be tied!*' This he said in a tone of loud defiance; and at the same time, with a motion as quick as lightning, he with one single stroke dashed the pistols from the hand of each constable. As he did this, all hands fell upon him, and, after beating him some time, they finally overpowered him and got him tied.

During the scuffle, I managed, I know not how, to get my pass out, and, without being discovered, put it into the fire. We were all now tied; and just as we were to leave for Easton jail, Betsy Freeland, mother of William Freeland, came to the door with her hands full of biscuits, and divided them between Henry and John. She then delivered herself of a speech, to the following effect: – addressing herself to me, she said, '*You devil! You yellow devil!* it was you that put it into the heads of Henry and John to run away. But for you, you long-legged mulatto devil! Henry nor John would never have thought of such a thing.' I made no reply, and was immediately hurried off towards St Michael's. Just a moment previous to the scuffle with Henry, Mr Hamilton suggested the propriety of making a search for the protections which he had understood Frederick had written for himself and the rest. But, just at the moment he was about carrying his proposal into effect, his aid was needed in helping to tie Henry; and the excitement attending the scuffle caused them either to forget, or to deem it unsafe, under the circumstances, to search. So we were not yet convicted of the intention to run away.

When we got about half way to St Michael's, while the constables having us in charge were looking ahead, Henry inquired of me what he should do with his pass. I told him to eat it with his biscuit, and own nothing; and we passed the word around, 'Own nothing,' and 'Own nothing!' said we all. Our confidence in each other was unshaken. We were resolved to succeed or fail together, after the calamity had befallen us as much as before. We were now prepared for any thing. We were to be dragged that morning fifteen miles behind horses, and then to be placed in the Easton jail. When we reached St Michael's, we underwent a sort of examination. We all denied that we ever intended to run away. We did this more to bring out the evidence against us, than from any hope of getting clear of being sold; for, as I have said, we were ready for that. The fact was, we cared but little where we went, so we went together. Our greatest concern was about separation. We dreaded that more than any thing this side of death. We found the evidence against us to be the testimony of one person; our master would not tell who it was; but we came to a unanimous decision among ourselves as to who their informant was. We were sent off to the jail at Easton. When we got there, we were delivered up to the sheriff, Mr Joseph Graham, and by him placed in jail. Henry, John, and myself, were placed in one room together – Charles, and Henry Bailey, in another. Their object in separating us was to hinder concert.

We had been in jail scarcely twenty minutes, when a swarm of slave traders, and agents for slave traders, flocked into jail to look at us, and to ascertain if we were for sale. Such a set of beings I never saw before! I felt myself surrounded by so many fiends from perdition. A band of pirates never looked more like their father, the devil. They laughed and grinned over us, saying, 'Ah, my boys! we have got you, haven't we?' And after taunting us in various ways, they one by one went into an examination of us, with intent to ascertain our value. They would impudently ask us if we would not like to have them for our masters. We would make them no answer, and leave them to find out as best they could. Then they would curse and swear at us, telling us that they could take the devil out of us in a very little while, if we were only in their hands.

While in jail, we found ourselves in much more comfortable quarters than we expected when we went there. We did not get much to eat, nor that which was very good; but we had a good clean room, from the windows of which we could see what was going on in the street, which was very much better than though we had been placed in one of the dark, damp cells. Upon the whole, we got along very well, so far as the jail and its keeper were concerned. Immediately after the holidays were over, contrary to all our expectations, Mr Hamilton and Mr Freeland came up to Easton, and took Charles, the two Henrys, and John, out of jail, and carried them home, leaving me alone. I regarded this separation as a final one. It caused me more pain than any thing else in the whole transaction. I was ready for any thing rather than separation. I supposed that they had consulted together, and had decided that, as I was the whole cause of the intention of the others to run away, it was hard to make the innocent suffer with the guilty; and that they had, therefore, concluded to take the others home, and sell me, as a warning to the others that remained. It is due to the noble Henry to say, he seemed almost as reluctant at leaving the prison as at leaving home to come to the prison. But we knew we should, in all probability, be separated, if we were sold; and since he was in their hands, he concluded to go peaceably home.

I was now left to my fate. I was all alone, and within the walls of a stone prison. But a few days before, and I was full of hope. I expected to have been safe in a land of freedom; but now I was covered with gloom, sunk down to the utmost despair. I thought the possibility of freedom was gone. I was kept in this way about one week, at the end of which, Captain Auld, my master, to my surprise and utter astonishment, came up, and took me out, with the intention of sending me, with a gentleman of his acquaintance, into Alabama. But, from some cause or other, he did not send me to Alabama, but concluded to send me back to Baltimore, to live again with his brother Hugh, and to learn a trade.

Thus, after an absence of three years and one month, I was once more permitted to return to my old home at Baltimore. My master sent me away, because there existed against me a very great prejudice in the community, and he feared I might be killed.

In a few weeks after I went to Baltimore, Master Hugh hired me to Mr William Gardner, an extensive ship-builder, on Fell's Point. I was put there to learn how to calk. It, however, proved a very unfavorable place for the accomplishment of this object.

Mr Gardner was engaged that spring in building two large man-of-war brigs, professedly for the Mexican government. The vessels were to be launched in the July of that year, and in failure thereof, Mr Gardner was to lose a considerable sum; so that when I entered, all was hurry. There was no time to learn any thing. Every man had to do that which he knew how to do. In entering the shipyard, my orders from Mr Gardner were, to do whatever the carpenters commanded me to do. This was placing me at the beck and call of about seventy-five men. I was to regard all these as masters. Their word was to be my law. My situation was a most trying one. At times I needed a dozen pair of hands. I was called a dozen ways in the space of a single minute. Three or four voices would strike my ear at the same moment. It was – 'Fred., come help me to cant this timber here.' – 'Fred., come carry this timber yonder.' – 'Fred., bring that roller here.' – 'Fred., go get a fresh can of water.' – 'Fred., come help saw off the end of this timber.' – 'Fred., go quick, and get the crowbar.' – 'Fred., hold on the end of this fall.' – 'Fred., go to the blacksmith's shop, and get a new punch.' – 'Hurra, Fred. ! run and bring me a cold chisel.' – 'I say, Fred., bear a hand, and get up a fire as quick as lightning under that steam-box.' – 'Halloo, nigger ! come, turn this grindstone.' – 'Come, come ! move, move ! and *bowse* this timber forward.' – 'I say, darky, blast your eyes, why don't you heat up some pitch ?' – 'Halloo ! halloo ! halloo !' (Three voices at the same time.) 'Come here ! – Go there ! – Hold on where you are ! Damn you, if you move, I'll knock your brains out !'

This was my school for eight months; and I might have remained there longer, but for a most horrid fight I had with four of the white apprentices, in which my left eye was nearly knocked out, and I was horribly mangled in other respects. The facts in the case were these : Until a very little while after I went there, white and black ship-carpenters worked side by side, and no one seemed to see any impropriety in it. All hands seemed to be very well satisfied. Many of the black carpenters were freemen. Things seemed to be going on very well. All at once, the white carpenters knocked off, and said they would not work with free colored workmen. Their reason for this, as alleged, was, that if free colored carpenters were encouraged, they would soon take the trade into their own hands, and poor white men would be thrown out of employment. They therefore felt called upon at once to put a stop to it. And, taking advantage of Mr Gardner's necessities, they broke off, swearing they would work no longer, unless he would discharge his black carpenters. Now, though this did not extend to me in form, it did reach me in fact. My fellow-apprentices very soon began to feel it degrading to them to work with me. They began to put on airs, and talk about the 'niggers' taking the country, saying we all ought to be killed; and, being encouraged by the journeymen, they commenced making my condition as hard as they could, by hectoring me around, and sometimes striking me. I, of course, kept the vow I made after the fight with Mr Covey, and struck back again, regardless of consequences; and while I kept them from combining, I succeeded very well; for I could whip the whole of them, taking them separately. They, however, at length combined, and came upon me, armed with sticks, stones, and heavy handspikes. One came in front with a half brick. There was one at each side of me, and one behind me. While I was attending to those in front, and on either side, the one behind ran up with the handspike, and struck me a heavy blow upon the head. It stunned me. I fell, and with this they all ran upon me, and fell to beating me with their fists. I let them lay on for a while, gathering strength. In an instant, I gave a sudden surge, and rose to my hands and knees. Just as I did that, one of their number gave me, with his heavy boot, a powerful kick in the left eye. My eyeball seemed to have burst. When they saw my eye closed, and badly swollen, they left me. With this I seized the handspike, and for a time pursued them. But here the carpenters interfered, and I thought I might as well give it up. It was impossible to stand my hand against so many. All this took place in sight of not less than fifty white ship-carpenters, and not one interposed a friendly word; but some cried, 'Kill the damned nigger! Kill him! kill him! He struck a white person.' I found my only chance for life was in flight. I succeeded in getting away without an additional blow, and barely so; for to strike a white man is death by Lynch law – and that was the law in Mr Gardner's ship-yard; nor is there much of any other out of Mr Gardner's ship-yard.

I went directly home, and told the story of my wrongs to Master Hugh; and I am happy to say of him, irreligious as he was, his conduct was heavenly, compared with that of his brother Thomas under similar circumstances. He listened attentively to my narration of the circumstances leading to the savage outrage, and gave many proofs of his strong indignation at it. The heart of my once overkind mistress was again melted into pity. My puffed-out eye and blood-covered face moved her to tears. She took a chair by me, washed the blood from my face, and, with a mother's tenderness, bound up my head, covering the wounded eye with a lean piece of fresh beef. It was almost compensation for my suffering to witness, once more, a manifestation of kindness from this, my once affectionate old mistress. Master Hugh was very much enraged. He gave expression to his feelings by pouring out curses upon the heads of those who did the deed. As soon as I got a little the better of my bruises, he took me with him to Esquire Watson's, on Bond Street, to see what could be done about the matter. Mr Watson inquired who saw the assault committed. Master Hugh told him it was done in Mr Gardner's ship-yard, at midday, where there were a large company of men at work. 'As to that,' he said, 'the deed was done, and there was no question as to who did it.' His answer was, he could do nothing in the case, unless some white man would come forward and testify. He could issue no warrant on my word. If I had been killed in the presence of a thousand colored people, their testimony combined would have been insufficient to have arrested one of the murderers. Master Hugh, for once, was compelled to say this state of things was too bad. Of course, it was impossible to get any white man to volunteer his testimony in my behalf, and against the white young men. Even those who may have sympathized with me were not prepared to do this. It required a degree of courage unknown to them to do so; for just at that time, the slightest manifestation of humanity toward a colored person was denounced as abolitionism, and that name subjected its bearer to frightful liabilities. The watchwords of the bloody-minded in that region, and in those days, were, 'Damn the abolitionists!' and 'Damn the niggers!' There was nothing done, and probably nothing would have been done if I had been killed. Such was, and such remains, the state of things in the Christian city of Baltimore.

Master Hugh, finding he could get no redress, refused to let me go back again to Mr Gardner. He kept me himself, and his wife dressed my wound till I was again restored to health. He then took me into the ship-yard of which he was foreman, in the employment of Mr Walter Price. There I was immediately set to calking, and very soon learned the art of using my mallet and irons. In the course of one year from the time I left Mr Gardner's, I was able to command the highest wages given to the most experienced calkers. I was now of some importance to my master. I was bringing him from six to seven dollars per week. I sometimes brought him nine dollars per week: my wages were a dollar and a half a day. After learning how to calk, I sought my own employment, made my own contracts, and collected the money which I earned. My pathway became much more smooth than before; my condition was now much more comfortable. When I could get no calking to do, I did nothing. During these leisure times, those old notions about freedom would steal over me again. When in Mr Gardner's employment, I was kept in such a perpetual whirl of excitement, I could think of nothing, scarcely, but my life; and in thinking of my life, I almost forgot my liberty. I have observed this in my experience of slavery – that whenever my condition was improved, instead of its increasing my contentment, it only increased my desire to be free, and set me to thinking of plans to gain my freedom. I have found that, to make a contented slave, it is necessary to make a thoughtless one. It is necessary to darken his moral and mental vision, and, as far as possible, to annihilate the power of reason. He must be able to detect no inconsistencies in slavery; he must be made to feel that slavery is right; and he can be brought to that only when he ceases to be a man.

I was now getting, as I have said, one dollar and fifty cents per day. I contracted for it; I earned it; it was paid to me; it was rightfully my own; yet, upon each returning Saturday night, I was compelled to deliver every cent of that money to Master Hugh. And why? Not because he earned it – not because he had any hand in earning it – not because I owed it to him – nor because he possessed the slightest shadow of a right to it; but solely because he had the power to compel me to give it up. The right of the grim-visaged pirate upon the high seas is exactly the same.

Chapter 11

I NOW come to that part of my life during which I planned, and finally succeeded in making, my escape from slavery. But before narrating any of the peculiar circumstances, I deem it proper to make known my intention not to state all the facts connected with the transaction. My reasons for pursuing this course may be understood from the following: First, were I to give a minute statement of all the facts, it is not only possible, but quite probable, that others would thereby be involved in the most embarrassing difficulties. Secondly, such a statement would most undoubtedly induce greater vigilance on the part of slaveholders than has existed heretofore among them; which would, of course, be the means of guarding a door whereby some dear brother bondman might escape his galling chains. I deeply regret the necessity that impels me to suppress any thing of importance connected with my experience in slavery. It would afford me great pleasure indeed, as well as materially add to the interest of my narrative, were I at liberty to gratify a curiosity, which I know exists in the minds of many, by an accurate statement of all the facts pertaining to my most fortunate escape. But I must deprive myself of this pleasure, and the curious of the gratification which such a statement would afford. I would allow myself to suffer under the greatest imputations which evil-minded men might suggest, rather than exculpate myself, and thereby run the hazard of closing the slighest avenue by which a brother slave might clear himself of the chains and fetters of slavery.

I have never approved of the very public manner in which some of our western friends have conducted what they call the *underground railroad*, but which, I think, by their open declarations, has been made most emphatically the *upperground railroad*. I honor those good men and women for their noble daring, and applaud them for willingly subjecting themselves to bloody persecution, by openly avowing their participation in the escape of slaves. I, however, can see very little good resulting from such a course, either to themselves or the slaves escaping;

while, upon the other hand, I see and feel assured that those open declarations are a positive evil to the slaves remaining, who are seeking to escape. They do nothing towards enlightening the slave, whilst they do much towards enlightening the master. They stimulate him to greater watchfulness, and enhance his power to capture his slave. We owe something to the slaves south of the line as well as to those north of it; and in aiding the latter on their way to freedom, we should be careful to do nothing which would be likely to hinder the former from escaping from slavery. I would keep the merciless slaveholder profoundly ignorant of the means of flight adopted by the slave. I would leave him to imagine himself surrounded by myriads of invisible tormentors, ever ready to snatch from his infernal grasp his trembling prey. Let him be left to feel his way in the dark; let darkness commensurate with his crime hover over him; and let him feel that at every step he takes, in pursuit of the flying bondman, he is running the frightful risk of having his hot brains dashed out by an invisible agency. Let us render the tyrant no aid; let us not hold the light by which he can trace the footprints of our flying brother. But enough of this. I will now proceed to the statement of those facts, connected with my escape, for which I am alone responsible, and for which no one can be made to suffer but myself.

In the early part of the year 1838, I became quite restless. I could see no reason why I should, at the end of each week, pour the reward of my toil into the purse of my master. When I carried to him my weekly wages, he would, after counting the money, look me in the face with a robber-like fierceness, and ask, 'Is this all?' He was satisfied with nothing less than the last cent. He would, however, when I made him six dollars, sometimes give me six cents, to encourage me. It had the opposite effect. I regarded it as a sort of admission of my right to the whole. The fact that he gave me any part of my wages was proof, to my mind, that he believed me entitled to the whole of them. I always felt worse for having received any thing; for I feared that the giving me a few cents would ease his conscience, and make him feel himself to be a pretty honorable sort of robber. My discontent grew upon me. I was ever on the look-out for means to escape; and, finding no direct means, I determined to try to hire my time, with a view of getting money with which to make my escape. In the spring of 1838, when Master Thomas came to Baltimore to purchase his spring goods, I got an opportunity, and applied to him to allow me to hire my time. He unhesitatingly refused my request, and told me this was another stratagem by which to escape. He told me I could go nowhere but that he could get me; and that, in the event of my running away, he should spare no pains in his efforts to catch me. He exhorted me to content myself, and be obedient. He told me, if I would be happy, I must lay out no plans for the future. He said, if I behaved myself properly, he would take care of me. Indeed, he advised me to complete thoughtlessness of the future, and taught me to depend solely upon him for happiness. He seemed to see fully the pressing necessity of setting aside my intellectual nature, in order to contentment in slavery. But in spite of him, and even in spite of myself, I continued to think, and to think about the injustice of my enslavement, and the means of escape.

About two months after this, I applied to Master Hugh for the privilege of hiring my time. He was not acquainted with the fact that I had applied to Master Thomas, and had been refused. He too, at first, seemed disposed to refuse; but, after some reflection, he granted me the privilege, and proposed the following terms: I was to be allowed all my time, make all contracts with those for whom I worked, and find my own employment; and, in return for this liberty, I was to pay him three dollars at the end of each week; find myself in calking tools, and in board and clothing. My board was two dollars and a half per week. This, with the wear and tear of clothing and calking tools, made my regular expenses about six dollars per week. This amount I was compelled to make up, or relinquish the privilege of hiring my time. Rain or shine, work or no work, at the end of each week the money must be forthcoming, or I must give up my privilege. This arrangement, it will be perceived, was decidedly in my master's favor. It relieved him of all need of looking after me. His money was sure. He received all the benefits of slaveholding without its evils; while I endured all the evils of a slave, and suffered all the care and anxiety of a freeman. I found it a hard bargain. But, hard as it was, I thought it better than the old mode of getting along. It was a step towards freedom to be allowed to bear the responsibilities of a freeman, and I was determined to hold on upon it. I bent myself to the work of making money. I was ready to work at night as well as day, and by the most untiring perseverance and industry, I made enough to meet my expenses, and lay up a little money every week. I went on thus from May till August. Master Hugh then refused to allow me to hire my time longer. The ground for his refusal was a failure on my part, one Saturday night, to pay him for my week's time. This failure was occasioned by my attending a camp meeting about ten miles from Baltimore. During the week, I had entered into an engagement with a number of young friends to start from Baltimore to the camp ground early Saturday evening; and being detained by my employer, I was unable to get down to Master Hugh's without disappointing the company. I knew that Master Hugh was in no special need of the money that night. I therefore decided to go to camp meeting, and upon my return pay him the three dollars. I staid [sic] at the camp meeting one day longer than I intended when I left. But as soon as I returned, I called upon him to pay him what he considered his due. I found him very angry; he could scarce restrain his wrath. He said he had a great mind to give me a severe whipping. He wished to know how I dared go out of the city without asking his permission. I told him I hired my time, and while I paid him the price which he asked for it, I did not know that I was bound to ask him when and where I should go. This reply troubled him; and, after reflecting a few moments, he turned to me, and said I should hire my time no longer; that the next thing he should know of, I would be running away. Upon the same plea, he told me to bring my tools and clothing home forthwith. I did so; but instead of seeking work, as I had been accustomed to do previously to hiring my time, I spent the whole week without the performance of a single stroke of work. I did this in retaliation. Saturday night, he called upon me as usual for my week's wages. I told him I had no wages; I had done no work that week. Here we were upon the point of coming to blows. He raved, and swore his determination to get hold of me. I did not allow myself a single word; but was resolved, if he laid the weight of his hand upon me, it should be blow for blow. He did not strike me, but told me that he would find me in constant employment in future. I thought the matter over during the next day, Sunday, and finally resolved upon the third day of September, as the day upon which I would make a second attempt to secure my freedom. I now had three weeks during which to prepare for my journey. Early on Monday morning, before Master Hugh had time to make any engagement for me, I went out and got employment of Mr Butler, at his ship-yard near the draw-bridge, upon what is called the City Block, thus making it unnecessary for him to seek employment for me. At the end of the week, I brought him between eight and nine dollars. He seemed very well pleased, and asked me why I did not do the same the week before. He little knew what my plans were. My object in working steadily was to remove any suspicion he might entertain of my intent to run away; and in this I succeeded admirably. I suppose he thought I was never better satisfied with my condition than at the very time during which I was planning my escape. The second week passed, and again I carried him my full wages; and so well pleased was he, that he gave me twenty-five cents, (quite a large sum for a slaveholder to give a slave,) and bade me to make a good use of it. I told him I would.

Things went on without very smoothly indeed, but within there was trouble. It is impossible for me to describe my feelings as the time of my contemplated start drew near. I had a number of warm-hearted friends in Baltimore – friends that I loved almost as I did my life – and the thought of being separated from them forever was painful beyond expression. It is my opinion that thousands would escape from slavery, who now remain, but for the strong cords of affection that bind them to their friends. The thought of leaving my friends was decidedly the most painful thought with which I had to contend. The love of them was my tender point, and shook my decision more than all things else. Besides the pain of separation, the dread and apprehension of a failure exceeded what I had experienced at my first attempt. The appalling defeat I then sustained returned to torment me. I felt assured that, if I failed in this attempt, my case would be a hopeless one – it would seal my fate as a slave forever. I could not hope to get off with any thing less than the severest punishment, and being placed beyond the means of escape. It required no very vivid imagination to depict the most frightful scenes through which I should have to pass, in case I failed. The wretchedness of slavery, and the blessedness of freedom, were perpetually before me. It was life and death with me. But I remained firm, and, according to my resolution, on the third day of September, 1838, I left my chains, and succeeded in reaching New York without the slightest interruption of any kind. How I did so – what means I adopted – what direction I travelled, and by what mode of conveyance, – I must leave unexplained, for the reasons before mentioned.

I have been frequently asked how I felt when I found myself in a free State. I have never been able to answer the question with any satisfaction to myself. It was a moment of the highest excitement I ever experienced. I suppose I felt as one may imagine the unarmed mariner to feel when he is rescued by a friendly man-of-war from the pursuit of a pirate. In writing to a dear friend, immediately after my arrival at New York, I said I felt like one who had escaped a den of hungry lions. This state of mind, however, very soon subsided; and I was again seized with a feeling of great insecurity and loneliness. I was yet liable to be taken back, and subjected to all the tortures of slavery. This in itself was enough to damp the ardor of my enthusiasm. But the loneliness overcame me. There I was in the midst of thousands, and yet a perfect stranger; without home and without friends, in the midst of thousands of my own brethren – children of a common Father, and yet I dared not to unfold to any one of them my sad condition. I was afraid to speak to any one for fear of speaking to the wrong one, and thereby falling into the hands of money-loving kidnappers, whose business it was to lie in wait for the panting fugitive, as the ferocious beasts of the forest lie in wait for their prey. The motto which I adopted when I started from slavery was this – 'Trust no man!' I saw in every white man an enemy, and in almost every colored man cause for distrust. It was a most painful situation; and, to understand it, one must needs experience it, or imagine himself in similar circumstances. Let him be a fugitive slave in a strange land – a land given up to be the hunting-ground for slaveholders – whose inhabitants are legalized kidnappers – where he is every moment subjected to the terrible liability of being seized upon by his fellow-men, as the hideous crocodile seized upon his prey! – I say, let him place himself in my situation – without home or friends – without money or credit – wanting shelter, and no one to give it – wanting bread, and no money to buy it

– and at the same time let him feel that he is pursued by merciless men-hunters, and in total darkness as to what to do, where to go, or where to stay – perfectly helpless both as to the means of defence and means of escape – in the midst of plenty, yet suffering the terrible gnawings of hunger – in the midst of houses, yet having no home – among fellow-men, yet feeling as if in the midst of wild beasts, whose greediness to swallow up the trembling and half-famished fugitive is only equalled by that with which the monsters of the deep swallow up the helpless fish upon which they subsist – I say, let him be placed in this most trying situation – the situation in which I was placed – then, and not till then, will he fully appreciate the hardships of, and know how to sympathize with, the toil-worn and whip-scarred fugitive slave.

Thank Heaven, I remained but a short time in this distressed situation. I was relieved from it by the humane hand of Mr DAVID RUGGLES, whose vigilance, kindness, and perseverance, I shall never forget. I am glad of an opportunity to express, as far as words can, the love and gratitude I bear him. Mr Ruggles is now afflicted with blindness, and is himself in need of the same kind offices which he was once so forward in the performance of toward others. I had been in New York but a few days, when Mr Ruggles sought me out, and very kindly took me to his boarding-house at the corner of Church and Lespenard Streets. Mr Ruggles was then very deeply engaged in the memorable *Darg* case, as well as attending to a number of other fugitive slaves, devising ways and means for their successful escape; and, though watched and hemmed in on almost every side, he seemed to be more than a match for his enemies.

Very soon after I went to Mr Ruggles, he wished to know of me where I wanted to go; as he deemed it unsafe for me to remain in New York. I told him I was a calker, and should like to go where I could get work. I thought of going to Canada; but he decided against it, and in favor of my going to New Bedford, thinking I should be able to get work there at my trade. At this time, Anna,* my intended wife, came on; for I wrote to her immediately after my arrival at New York, (notwithstanding my homeless, houseless, and helpless condition,) informing her

* She was free.

of my successful flight, and wishing her to come on forthwith. In a few days after her arrival, Mr Ruggles called in the Rev. J. W. C. Pennington, who, in the presence of Mr Ruggles, Mrs Michaels, and two or three others, performed the marriage ceremony, and gave us a certificate, of which the following is an exact copy:

'THIS may certify, that I joined together in holy matrimony Frederick Johnson* and Anna Murray, as man and wife, in the presence of Mr David Ruggles and Mrs Michaels.

'JAMES W. C. PENNINGTON

'New York, Sept. 15, 1838.'

Upon receiving this certificate, and a five-dollar bill from Mr Ruggles, I shouldered one part of our baggage, and Anna took up the other, and we set out forthwith to take passage on board of the steamboat John W. Richmond for Newport, on our way to New Bedford. Mr Ruggles gave me a letter to a Mr Shaw in Newport, and told me, in case my money did not serve me to New Bedford, to stop in Newport and obtain further assistance; but upon our arrival at Newport, we were so anxious to get to a place of safety, that, notwithstanding we lacked the necessary money to pay our fare, we decided to take seats in the stage, and promise to pay when we got to New Bedford. We were encouraged to do this by two excellent gentlemen, residents of New Bedford, whose names I afterward ascertained to be Joseph Ricketson and William C. Taber. They seemed at once to understand our cirumstances, and gave us such assurance of their friendliness as put us fully at ease in their presence. It was good indeed to meet with such friends, at such a time. Upon reaching New Bedford, we were directed to the house of Mr Nathan Johnson, by whom we were kindly received, and hospitably provided for. Both Mr and Mrs Johnson took a deep and lively interest in our welfare. They proved themselves quite worthy of the name of abolitionists. When the stage-driver found us unable to pay our fare, he held on upon our baggage as security for the debt. I had but to mention the fact to Mr Johnson, and he forthwith advanced the money.

We now began to feel a degree of safety, and to prepare

---

* I had changed my name from Frederick Bailey to that of Johnson.

ourselves for the duties and responsibilities of a life of freedom. On the morning after our arrival at New Bedford, while at the breakfast-table, the question arose as to what name I should be called by. The name given me by the mother was 'Frederick Augustus Washinton Bailey.' I, however, had dispensed with the two middle names long before I left Maryland so that I was generally known by the name of 'Frederick Bailey.' I started from Baltimore bearing the name of 'Stanley.' When I got to New York, I again changed my name to 'Frederick Johnson,' and thought that would be the last change. But when I got to New Bedford, I found it necessary again to change my name. The reason of this necessity was, that there were so many Johnsons in New Bedford, it was already quite difficult to distinguish between them. I gave Mr Johnson the privilege of choosing me a name, but told him he must not take from me the name of 'Frederick.' I must hold on to that, to preserve a sense of my identity. Mr Johnson had just been reading the 'Lady of the Lake,' and at once suggested that my name be 'Douglass.' From that time until now I have been called 'Frederick Douglass;' and as I am more widely known by that name than by either of the others, I shall continue to use it as my own.

I was quite disappointed at the general appearance of things in New Bedford. The impression which I had received respecting the character and condition of the people of the north, I found to be singularly erroneous. I had very strangely supposed, while in slavery, that few of the comforts, and scarcely any of the luxuries, of life were enjoyed at the north, compared with what were enjoyed by the slaveholders of the south. I probably came to this conclusion from the fact that northern people owned no slaves. I supposed that they were about upon a level with the non-slaveholding population of the south. I knew *they* were exceedingly poor, and I had been accustomed to regard their poverty as the necessary consequence of their being non-slave-holders. I had somehow imbibed the opinion that, in the absence of slaves, three could be no wealth, and very little refinement. And upon coming to the north, I expected to meet with a rough, hard-handed, and uncultivated population, living in the most Spartan-like simplicity, knowing nothing of the ease, luxury, pomp, and grandeur of southern slaveholders. Such being my conjectures, any one acquainted with the appearance of New

Bedford may very readily infer how palpably I must have seen my mistake.

In the afternoon of the day when I reached New Bedford, I visited the wharves, to take a view of the shipping. Here I found myself surrounded with the strongest proofs of wealth. Lying at the wharves, and riding in the stream, I saw many ships of the finest model, in the best order, and of the largest size. Upon the right and left, I was walled in by granite warehouses of the widest dimensions, stowed to their utmost capacity with the necessaries and comforts of life. Added to this, almost every body seemed to be at work, but noiselessly so, compared with what I had been accustomed to in Baltimore. There were no loud songs heard from those engaged in loading and unloading ships. I heard no deep oaths or horrid curses on the laborer. I saw no whipping of men; but all seemed to go smoothly on. Every man appeared to understand his work, and went at it with a sober, yet cheerful earnestness, which betokened the deep interest which he felt in what he was doing, as well as a sense of his own dignity as a man. To me this looked exceedingly strange. From the wharves I strolled around and over the town, gazing with wonder and admiration at the splendid churches, beautiful dwellings, and finely-cultivated gardens; evincing an amount of wealth, comfort, taste, and refinement, such as I had never seen in any part of slaveholding Maryland.

Every thing looked clean, new, and beautiful. I saw few or no dilapidated houses, with poverty-stricken inmates; no half-naked children and barefooted women, such as I had been accustomed to see in Hillsborough, Easton, St Michael's, and Baltimore. The people looked more able, stronger, healthier, and happier, than those of Maryland. I was for once made glad by a view of extreme wealth, without being saddened by seeing extreme poverty. But the most astonishing as well as the most interesting thing to me was the condition of the colored people, a great many of whom, like myself, had escaped thither as a refuge from the hunters of men. I found many, who had not been seven years out of their chains, living in finer houses, and evidently enjoying more of the comforts of life, than the average of slaveholders in Maryland. I will venture to assert that my friend Mr Nathan Johnson (of whom I can say with a grateful heart, 'I was hungry, and he gave me meat; I was thirsty, and he gave me drink; I was a stranger, and he took me in') lived in a neater house; dined at a better table; took, paid for, and read, more newspapers; better understood the moral, religious, and political character of the nation, – than nine tenths of the slaveholders in Talbot county Maryland. Yet Mr Johnson was a working man. His hands were hardened by toil, and not his alone, but those also of Mrs Johnson. I found the colored people much more spirited than I had supposed they would be. I found among them a determination to protect each other from the blood-thirsty kidnapper, at all hazards. Soon after my arrival, I was told of a circumstance which illustrated their spirit. A colored man and a fugitive slave were on unfriendly terms. The former was heard to threaten the latter with informing his master of his whereabouts. Straightway a meeting was called among the colored people, under the stereotyped notice, 'Business of importance!' The betrayer was invited to attend. The people came at the appointed hour, and organized the meeting by appointing a very religious old gentleman as president, who, I believe, made a prayer, after which he addressed the meeting as follows: *'Friends, we have got him here, and I would recommend that you young men just take him outside the door, and kill him!'* With this, a number of them bolted at him; but they were intercepted by some more timid than themselves, and the betrayer escaped their vengeance, and has not been seen in New Bedford since. I believe there have been no more such threats, and should there be hereafter, I doubt not that death would be the consequence.

I found employment, the third day after my arrival, in stowing a sloop with a load of oil. It was new, dirty, and hard work for me; but I went at it with a glad heart and a willing hand. I was now my own master. It was a happy moment, the rapture of which can be understood only by those who have been slaves. It was the first work, the reward of which was to be entirely my own. There was no Master Hugh standing ready, the moment I earned the money, to rob me of it. I worked that day with a pleasure I had never before experienced. I was at work for myself and newly-married wife. It was to me the starting-point of a new existence. When I got through with that job, I went in pursuit of a job of calking; but such was the strength of prejudice against color, among the white calkers, that they refused to work with me, and of course I could get no employment.* Finding my trade of no immediate benefit, I threw off my calking habiliments, and prepared myself to do any kind of work I could get to do. Mr Johnson kindly let me have his wood-horse and saw, and I very soon found myself a plenty of work. There was no work too hard – none too dirty. I was ready to saw wood, shovel coal, carry the hod, sweep the chimney, or roll oil casks – all of which I did for nearly three years in New Bedford, before I became known to the anti-slavery world.

In about four months after I went to New Bedford, there came a young man to me, and inquired if I did not wish to take the 'Liberator.' I told him I did; but, just having made my escape from slavery, I remarked that I was unable to pay for it then. I, however, finally became a subscriber to it. The paper came, and I read it from week to week with such feelings as it would be quite idle for me to attempt to describe. The paper became my meat and my drink. My soul was set all on fire. Its sympathy for my brethren in bonds – its scathing denunciations of slaveholders – its faithful exposures of slavery – and its powerful attacks upon the upholders of the institution – sent a thrill of joy through my soul, such as I had never felt before !

I had not long been a reader of the 'Liberator,' before I got a pretty correct idea of the principles, measures and spirit of the anti-slavery reform. I took right hold of the cause. I could do but little; but what I could, I did with a joyful heart, and never felt happier than when in an anti-slavery meeting. I seldom had much to say at the meetings, because what I wanted to say was said so much better by others. But, while attending an anti-slavery convention at Nantucket, on the 11th of August, 1841, I felt strongly moved to speak, and was at the same time much urged to do so by Mr William C. Coffin, a gentleman who had heard me speak in the colored people's meeting at New Bedford. It was a severe cross, and I took it up reluctantly. The truth was, I felt myself a slave, and the idea of speaking to white people weighed me down. I spoke but a few moments, when I felt a

* I am told that colored persons can now get employment at calking in New Bedford – a result of anti-slavery effort.

degree of freedom, and said what I desired with considerable ease. From that time until now, I have been engaged in pleading the cause of my brethren – with what success, and with what devotion, I leave those acquainted with my labors to decide.

Appendix

I FIND, since reading over the foregoing Narrative that I have, in several instances, spoken in such a tone and manner, respecting religion, as may possibly lead those unacquainted with my religious views to suppose me an opponent of all religion. To remove the liability of such misapprehension, I deem it proper to append the following brief explanation. What I have said respecting and against religion, I mean strictly to apply to the *slaveholding religion* of this land, and with no possible reference to Christianity proper; for, between the Christianity of this land, and the Christianity of Christ, I recognize the widest possible difference — so wide, that to receive the one as good, pure, and holy, is of necessity to reject the other as bad, corrupt, and wicked. To be the friend of the one, is of necessity to be the enemy of the other. I love the pure, peaceable, and impartial Christianity of Christ: I therefore hate the corrupt, slaveholding, women-whipping, cradle-plundering, partial and hypocritical Christianity of this land. Indeed, I can see no reason, but the most deceitful one, for calling the religion of this land Christianity. I look upon it as the climax of all misnomers, the boldest of all frauds, and the grossest of all libels. Never was there a clearer case of 'stealing the livery of the court of heaven to serve the devil in.' I am filled with unutterable loathing when I contemplate the religious pomp and show, together with the horrible inconsistencies, which every where surround me. We have men-stealers for ministers, women-whippers for missionaries, and cradle-plunderers for church members. the man who wields the blood-clotted cowskin during the week fills the pulpit on Sunday, and claims to be a minister of the meek and lowly Jesus. The man who robs me of my earnings at the end of each week meets me as a class-leader on Sunday morning, to show me the way of life, and the path of salvation. He who sells my sister, for purposes of prostitution, stands forth as the pious advocate of purity. He who proclaims it a religious duty to read the Bible denies me the right of learning to read the name of the God who made me. He who is the religious advocate of marriage robs whole millions of its sacred influence, and leaves them to the ravages of wholesale pollution. The warm defender of the sacredness of the family relation is the same that scatters whole families – sundering husbands and wives, parents and children, sisters and brothers – leaving the hut vacant, and the hearth desolate. We see the thief preaching against theft, and the adulterer against adultery. We have men sold to build churches, women sold to support the gospel, and babes sold to purchase Bibles for the *poor heathen! all for the glory of God and the good of souls!* The slave auctioneer's bell and the church-going bell chime in with each other, and the bitter cries of the heart-broken slave are drowned in the religious shouts of his pious master. Revivals of religion and revivals in the slave-trade go hand in hand together. The slave prison and the church stand near each other. The clanking of fetters and the rattling of chains in the prison, and the pious psalm and solemn prayer in the church, may be heard at the same time. The dealers in the bodies and souls of men erect their stand in the presence of the pulpit, and they mutually help each other. The dealer gives his blood-stained gold to support the pulpit, and the pulpit, in return, covers his infernal business with the garb of Christianity. Here we have religion and robbery the allies of each other – devils dressed in angels' robes, and hell presenting the semblance of paradise.

> 'Just God! and these are they,
>   Who minister at thine altar, God of right!
> Men who their hands, with prayer and blessing, lay
>   On Israel's ark of light.
>
> 'What! preach, and kidnap men?
>   Give thanks, and rob thy own afflicted poor?
> Talk of thy glorious liberty, and then
>   Bolt hard the captive's door?
>
> 'What! servants of thy own
>   Merciful Son, who came to seek and save
> The homeless and the outcast, fettering down
>   The tasked and plundered slave!

'Pilate and Herod friends !
　　Chief priests and rulers, as of old, combine !
Just God and holy ! is that church which lends
　　Strength to the spoiler thine ?'

The Christianity of America is a Christianity, of whose votaries it may be as truly said, as it was of the ancient scribes and Pharisees, 'They bind heavy burdens, and grievous to be borne, and lay them on men's shoulders, but they themselves will not move them with one of their fingers. All their works they do for to be seen of men. They love the uppermost rooms at feasts, and the chief seats in the synagogues . . . and to be called of men, Rabbi, Rabbi. But woe unto you, scribes and Pharisees, hypocrites ! for ye shut up the kingdom of heaven against men ; for ye neither go in yourselves, neither suffer ye them that are entering to go in. Ye devour widows' houses, and for a pretence make long prayers ; therefore ye shall receive the greater damnation. Ye compass sea and land to make one proselyte, and when he is made, ye make him twofold more the child of hell than yourselves. Woe unto you, scribes and Pharisees, hypocrites ! for ye pay tithe of mint, and anise, and cumin, and have omitted the weightier matters of the law, judgment, mercy, and faith ; these ought ye to have done, and not to leave the other undone. Ye blind guides ! which strain at a gnat, and swallow a camel. Woe unto you, scribes and Pharisees, hypocrites ! for ye make clean the outside of the cup and of the platter ; but within, they are full of extortion and excess. Woe unto you, scribes and Pharisees, hypocrites ! for ye are like unto whited sepulchres, which indeed appear beautiful outward, but are within full of dead men's bones, and of all uncleanness. Even so ye also outwardly appear righteous unto men, but within ye are full of hypocrisy and iniquity.'

Dark and terrible as is this picture, I hold it to be strictly true of the overwhelming mass of professed Christians in America. They strain at a gnat, and swallow a camel. Could any thing be more true of our churches ? They would be shocked at the proposition of fellowshipping a *sheep*-stealer ; and at the same time they hug to their communion a *man*-stealer ; and brand me with being an infidel, if I find fault with them for it. They attend with Pharisaical strictness to the outward forms of religion, and at the same time neglect the weightier matters of the law, judgment, mercy, and faith. They are always ready to sacrifice, but seldom to show mercy. They are they who are represented as professing to love God whom they have not seen, whilst they hate their brother whom they have seen. They love the heathen on the other side of the globe. They can pray for him, pay money to have the Bible put into his hand, and missionaries to instruct him; while they despise and totally neglect the heathen at their own doors.

Such is, very briefly, my view of the religion of this land; and to avoid any misunderstanding, growing out of the use of general terms, I mean, by the religion of this land, that which is revealed in the words, deeds, and actions, of those bodies, north and south, calling themselves Christian churches, and yet in union with slaveholders. It is against religion, as presented by these bodies, that I have felt it my duty to testify.

I conclude these remarks by copying the following portrait of the religion of the south, (which is, by communion and fellowship, the religion of the north,) which I soberly affirm is 'true to the life,' and without caricature or the slightest exaggeration. It is said to have been drawn, several years before the present anti-slavery agitation began, by a northern Methodist preacher, who, while residing at the south, had an opportunity to see slaveholding morals, manners, and piety, with his own eyes. 'Shall I not visit for these things? saith the Lord. Shall not my soul be avenged on such a nation as this?'

'A PARODY

'Come, saints and sinners, hear me tell
How pious priests whip Jack and Nell,
And women buy and children sell,
And preach all sinners down to hell,
    And sing of heavenly union.

'They'll bleat and baa, dona like goats,
Gorge down black sheep, and strain at motes,
Array their backs in fine black coats,
Then seize their negroes by their throats,
    And choke, for heavenly union.

'They'll church you if you sip a dram,
And damn you if you steal a lamb;
Yet rob old Tony, Doll, and Sam,
Of human rights, and bread and ham;
  Kidnapper's heavenly union.

'They'll loudly talk of Christ's reward,
And bind his image with a cord,
And scold, and swing the lash abhorred,
And sell their brother in the Lord
  To handcuffed heavenly union.

'They'll read and sing a sacred song,
And make a prayer both loud and long,
And teach the right and do the wrong,
Hailing the brother, sister throng,
  With words of heavenly union.

'We wonder how such saints can sing,
Or praise the Lord upon the wing,
Who roar, and scold, and whip, and sting,
And to their slaves and mammon cling,
  In guilty conscience union.

'They'll raise tobacco, corn, and rye,
And drive, and thieve, and cheat, and lie,
And lay up treasures in the sky,
By making switch and cowskin fly,
  In hope of heavenly union.

'They'll crack old Tony on the skull,
And preach and roar like Bashan bull,
Or braying ass, of mischief full,
Then seize old Jacob by the wool,
  And pull for heavenly union.

'A roaring, ranting, sleek man-thief,
Who lived on mutton, veal, and beef,
Yet never would afford relief
To needy, sable sons of grief,
  Was big with heavenly union.

'"Love not the world," the preacher said,
And winked his eye, and shook his head;
He seized on Tom, and Dick, and Ned,

Cut short their meat, and clothes, and bread,
    Yet still loved heavenly union.

'Another preacher whining spoke
Of One whose heart for sinners broke :
He tied old Nanny to an oak,
And drew the blood at every stroke,
    And prayed for heavenly union.

'Two others oped their iron jaws,
And waved their children-stealing paws ;
There sat their children in gewgaws ;
By stinting negroes' backs and maws,
    They kept up heavenly union.

'All good from Jack another takes,
And entertains their flirts and rakes,
Who dress as sleek as glossy snakes,
And cram their mouths with sweetened cakes ;
    And this goes down for union.'

Sincerely and earnestly hoping that this little book may do something toward throwing light on the American slave system, and hastening the glad day of deliverance to the millions of my brethren in bonds – faithfully relying upon the power of truth, love, and justice, for success in my humble efforts – and solemnly pledging my self anew to the sacred cause – I subscribe myself,

FREDERICK DOUGLASS
Lynn, *Mass.*, 28 April 1845

HARRIET BEECHER STOWE AND
HER CRITICS

Harriet Beecher Stowe's *Uncle Tom's Cabin* made its first
appearance in serialised form in Dr Gamaliel Bailey's anti-
slavery weekly *The National Era*. The work's reception was
similar to contemporary reactions to Charles Dickens's novels
like *The Old Curiosity Shop* (1841) which caused thousands to
shed tears over the death of Little Nell. *Uncle Tom's Cabin*
touched a popular nerve from the beginning, appealing to people
from all walks of life.

In Britain the success of the novel could be judged by the
numerous pirate editions – so many that *Punch* felt it had to
reprimand *Uncle Bull* for *Cribbing*.[1] The reviewer for the *The
Illustrated London News* alluded to this fact in the introduction,
before going on to discuss the chief attraction of the novel, its
truthfulness:

> Her book has, in an unmistakable manner, the stamp of truth upon
> it : it is a record of facts, arranged dramatically, but thereby rendered,
> not more, but less horrible than the reality which it depicts. There is,
> indeed, shed over the narrative an evident beauty, due to the artist's
> mind which has constructed it, and which softens down the sterner
> features of the actual scenes, which it barely symbolises. We have
> here but a representative portion of an appalling whole, which, in its
> unmitigated originality, would call up sentiments of indignation too
> strong for patience. It is, in fact, the painful nature of the theme
> which has so stifled expression. Our author herself suffered under
> this influence.[2]

Interestingly, a few weeks later, readers of *The Illustrated
London News* were asked to purchase an English edition of
Richard Hildreth's (a white writer) *Archy Moore* (1836). It

patently capitalised on the success of *Uncle Tom's Cabin* and the sales of 'true' slave narratives like Frederick Douglass's :

> This work has been printed uniformly with, and as a companion volume to, *Uncle Tom's Cabin*. For this there is a good reason; indeed, an especial fitness. The present narrative comes in evidence that Uncle Tom did really give the bright side of the picture, for here we have the darker one. This book exhibits the stern reality. It is a biography which tells the incidents in a straightforward manner, without attempting a dramatic setting, which communicates artistic beauty and form to wild and uncouth materials.[3]

The reviewer for *The Illustrated London News*, in common with other Victorians, found the analogy Beecher Stowe drew between class slavery and plantation slavery unsettling, probably because it sounded too much like Karl Marx's *Communist Manifesto* (1848) :

> Here and there, too, she brings the condition of Europe into analogy : nor does England escape from the withering sarcasm of her clear-seeing and impartial judgment. The American planter, she makes one of her characters suggest, simply proceeds on the good old respectable principle of the Right of the Strongest. He, in a word, is 'only doing in another form, what the English aristocracy and capitalists are doing by the lower classes; that is, I take it, *appropriating* them, body and bone, soul and spirit, to their use and convenience. He defends both – and I think, at least *consistently*. He says that there can be no high civilisation without enslavement of the masses, either nominal or real— . . .'
>   This is the sophism which Mrs Stowe, with a woman's perception of right and wrong, would explode; in which, though there may be some questionable reasoning, there is true reliable feeling; and a sentiment which will probably survive the logic of the case, even in the world's experience. Be it as it may, we ought not to flinch from an argument, simply because it is directed against ourselves.[4]

One has to remember when reading *Uncle Tom's Cabin* that Harriet Beecher Stowe had displayed a great deal of courage in allowing the novel to go under her own name. The literary world was dominated by patriarchal figures, all too ready to belittle the efforts of women writers. The above reviewer, for example, suggests that the author is illogical. The restraint on women writers at the time is further illustrated by Harriet's tour of Britain. At a banquet in honour of Mrs H. B. Stowe, it was Harriet's husband who replied on her behalf, and it was Professor Stowe who gave a lecture on slavery – despite Harriet's obvious talent as a public speaker.

Another reviewer, this time an American, a Southerner, thought it was his duty to remind the author where her place was, backing his argument up with a quotation from the Bible:

> We know that among other novel doctrines in vogue in the land of Mrs Stowe's nativity – the pleasant land of New England – which we are old-fashioned enough to condemn, is one which would place a woman on a footing of political equality with men, and causing her to look beyond the office for which she was created – the high and holy office of maternity – would engage her in the administration of public affairs; thus handing over the State to the perilous protection of diaper diplomatists and wet-nurse politicans. Mrs Stowe, we believe, belongs to this school of Women's Rights, and on this ground she may assert her prerogative to teach us how wicked are ourselves and the Constitution under which we live. But such a claim is in direct conflict with the letter of scripture, as we find it recorded in the second chapter of the First Epistle to Timothy . . .[5]

EARLY TWENTIETH-CENTURY RESPONSES

Generally the reception of *Uncle Tom's Cabin* in the first half of this century has been critical of the novel's flaws: its racialism, sentimentality, and, in comparison to the works of other women writers, deficiencies in writing. The apogee of this anti-Stowe trend was reached in Furnas's *Goodbye to Uncle Tom* (1956) and in James Baldwin's 'Everbody's Protest Novel,' in *Notes of a Native Son*.[6] Edmund Wilson in *Patriotic Gore*[7] contributed to a re-evaluation of Harriet Beecher Stowe's writings, as did Kenneth Rexroth in an article for the *Saturday Review of Literature* in 1969.[8]

Feminists have undoubtedly made the greatest contribution to the rehabilitation of *Uncle Tom's Cabin*. Gillian Brown writes:

> To read *Uncle Tom's Cabin* as Stowe's manifesto for family integrity is, of course, no twentieth-century innovation. Ever since George Sand noted in her 1852 review that 'this book is essentially domestic

and of the family,' readers of *Uncle Tom's Cabin*, especially feminist readers, have continually noticed the novel's politicization of domesticity. In her history of literary women, Ellen Moers reinforced this reading tradition, recognizing Stowe's antislavery appeal as 'proudly and openly a woman's work' on behalf of 'domestic policy'. 'Surely no other woman writer,' Moers declared, 'has ever recorded the rattle and clutter of domestic life . . . with such confidence that upon these female matters rested the central moral issue before the nation: slavery.'[9]

A leading feminist critic, Elaine Showalter, has teased out what she considers to be the central pattern in the novel:

Uncle Tom's cabin, which Stowe first describes in the fourth chapter, is a log cabin whose facade is 'covered by a large scarlet begonia and a native multiflora rose, which entwisting and interlacing, left scarcely a vestige of the rough logs to be seen.' The title, I would suggest, is what Nancy K. Miller calls the 'internal female signature: an icon or emblem within the fiction itself that obliquely figures the symbolic and material difficulties involved in becoming a woman writer.' 'Uncle Tom's Cabin' is an allusion in the referential system of women's culture to the Log Cabin quilt which by 1850 was the most popular American pieced quilt pattern.

Radka Donnell-Vogt moreover sees the Log Cabin pattern as the most archetypal, profound, and symbolically significant of all quilt designs. It can also be found in the swaddling of infants, the wrapping of corpses, and in the inscriptions on sacred entrances. It can be read as either phallic or vaginal, depending on whether we see it as a projecting pyramid or a depression. 'It is a universal convertible bisexual pattern protecting the union of opposites in human beings, and securing safe passage from one world into the other, from day to night, from life to death. Swaddling, doors, quilts, thus mediate in the dichotomy of inside and outside, that is, in the problems of physical, psychological and social boundaries.' In its symbolic relationship to boundaries, the Log Cabin design is particularly apt for Stowe's novel of the borders between the states, the races, and the sexes.[10]

The revival of Harriet Beecher Stowe's literary stock has not been without complications. There is still resistance from Afro-American critics to her canonisation. William Braithewaite's article on Negro Literature* expresses succinctly the appeal of

Uncle Tom's Cabin to the white readership and the legacy of stereotypes it has left to black writers.

> Controversy and moral appeal gave us *Uncle Tom's Cabin* – the first conspicuous example of the Negro as a subject for literary treatment. Published in 1852, it dominated in mood and attitude the American literature of a whole generation; until the body of Reconstruction literature with its quite different attitude came into vogue. Here was sentimentalised sympathy for a down-trodden race, but one in which was projected a character, in Uncle Tom himself, which has been unequalled in its hold upon the popular imagination to this day. But the moral gain and historical effect of Uncle Tom have been an artistic loss and setback. The treatment of Negro life and character, overlaid with these forceful stereotypes, could not develop into artistically satisfactory portraiture.[11]

David S. Reynolds in *Beneath the Renaissance*[12] revisited the period covered by F. O. Mathiessen in his classic survey: *American Renaissance: Art and Expression in the Age of Emerson and Whitman* (1941).[13] Harriet Beecher Stowe, he suggests, as one amongst many nineteenth-century popular writers, had been marginalised by Mathiessen. Reynolds analyses why this was the case. He goes on to look at the problem Harriet Beecher Stowe's Christianity presents to those feminists who would like to bring her into the feminist literary canon:

> The originality of *Uncle Tom's Cabin* lay in Stowe's frank treatment of an especially wide variety of such dark themes and in her simultaneous defusing of these themes through an equally wide variety of reparative devices derived from Conventional literature. These Conventional devices (too evident to dwell upon) include the moral exemplar, the human angel, courageous endurance and heroic action, religious aestheticism, and, above all, the nurturing home. These devices are scattered liberally throughout the novel, and all of them come together in the figure of Little Eva, who is exemplar, angel, little soldier, beauty lover, and home deifier all in one.
>
> . . . Like Hawthorne, Stowe gathered under one fictional roof both dark, iconoclastic women characters and brighter ones as well. There is a crucial difference, however, between these writers' treatment of women: because Stowe mixes but does not *fuse* character types, she retains a reassuringly simple division of functions absent from Hawthorne's complex texts. She portrays the suffering inflicted on

both sexes by the slave system and gives the great optimistic message that anyone, no matter how terribly oppressed or constitutionally timid, has the capacity to be a moral exemplar. In a scene that has become an icon of American culture – the heroic crossing of the icy river by the slave girl Eliza – Stowe illustrates how the timid woman victim could be transformed into a magnificent adventure feminist.

. . . While the Conventional bestsellers of the 1850s had immense cultural significance, they are of only secondary interest from a feminist standpoint because their language was rarely gender-specific. They advanced a popularised, Christian version of the moral exemplar feminism that had been introduced by Catherine Sedgwick and Margaret Fuller. The power that women characters wield in these novels is moral and religious rather than political. The authors of Conventional novels were, by and large, conservatives with a strong distaste for public agitation for women's rights. For them woman's great power was as a redeemer of devalued males and in the case of *Uncle Tom's Cabin*, as a moral savior of a threatened social system.[14]

UNCLE TOM'S CABIN AND THE PLANTATION NOVEL

Harriet Beecher Stowe's love–hate relationship with the American South had a long history. William R. Taylor in his book *Cavalier and Yankee* looked at Southern responses to *Uncle Tom's Cabin* and the use Beecher Stowe made of the Plantation novel sub-genre:

To accomplish this purpose she adopted in *Uncle Tom* and in *Dred* many of the conventions of the plantation novel as it had developed, and even her innovations seem to be mainly extrapolations from practices already scouted out by these novelists. Certainly, she made use of the plantation setting in its classical form. Decayed old houses, kind masters and mistresses, docile and affectionate household 'servants' are placed center stage in both of these stories. While her image of Southern society was in some ways less complex and less detailed than that drawn by Southerners like Kennedy and the two Tuckers, the principal features are still there. For the most part, for example, she adopts the familial pattern for portraying the institution of slavery just as she accepts many of the Southern arguments concerning the intellectual and cultural limitations of the slave. Her exceptional slaves like Uncle Tom (whom she calls 'a moral miracle') and some of her mulattos are clearly meant to be regarded as exceptions. In no sense, moreover, is it possible to argue that either of her books is an indictment of the South to the exclusion of the North.

Some of her sharpest invective is aimed at the temporizing and hypocrisy of churchmen and politicians in the North, and as a reviewer in the *Southern Literary Messenger* noted with surprise, almost all of her villains and monsters are of Northern birth.[15]

The American critic, Philip Fisher, took another look at the sentimentality in *Uncle Tom's Cabin* which made the novel difficult for twentieth-century readers.

The objects of sentimentality were historically subject to both cruelty and neglect. Recent social historians of the family, such as Stone, have documented this thoroughly in the case of children. Certainly, the greatest achievement of sentimentality was the part that it played in creating full human reality for children. It is one of the sophisticated elements of Stowe's sentimental strategy in *Uncle Tom's Cabin* that she had both a slave and a child at the center of her novel, or rather that she interposes between the reader and the slave, a child. By doing this she is able to borrow from the nearly completed historical sentimentalization of the child, the energy to begin the more difficult and historically risky sentimentalization of the black slave.

... Sentimentality, by its experimental extension of humanity to prisoners, slaves, madmen, children, and animals, exactly reverses the process of slavery itself which has at its core the withdrawal of human status from a part of humanity. As Stowe's original subtitle put it, *Uncle Tom's Cabin* is the story of a 'man that was a thing.' Within Christianity, sentimentality, and slavery were complementary tactics, the one extending, the other contracting the circle within which every human being must find every act that is done to another to be something done to himself or that he has consented to see done. Stowe's novel is not, then, simply an example of sentimental narrative, rather it is the place where a method encounters its fated, primary subject. This occurs particularly because the slave is met within the family itself, within the realm of domestic feeling and intimacy which are the primary spheres of sentimental experience.

The slave is born, lives, grieves, gives birth, suffers, and dies within the sight of the master, his wife, and children who, in their turn, live and die within the sight of their slaves. Unlike the prisoner and the madman who are made invisible by the institutions to which they are sent so that the reality of their suffering has to be discovered by investigation and can be forgotten for the most part (a technique now used for the suffering of the old as well), the slave is a visible prisoner, confined within the family itself. The contradiction between the inevitably sentimental nature of the family and corrosive institution of slavery is the central analytic point of Stowe's novel.[16]

BIBLIOGRAPHY FOR 'HARRIET BEECHER STOWE AND HER CRITICS'

1 *Punch* Vol. XXII July–December 1852, p.135.
2 *Illustrated London News* 2 October 1852, pp.290–1.
3 *Illustrated London News* 30 October 1852, p.366.
4 *Illustrated London News* 2 October 1852, p.290.
5 From *The Southern Literary Messenger* October 1852, pp.630–38.
6 James Baldwin, 'Everybody's Protest Novel' in *Notes of a Native Son* (Boston: Beacon Press, 1955) pp.13–28.
7 *Patriotic Gore* (London: André Deutsch, 1962).
8 Kenneth Rexroth, 'Uncle Tom's Cabin' in *Saturday Review of Literature* 11 January 1969 p.71.
9 Gillian Brown, 'Getting in the Kitchen with Dinah: Domestic Politics in Uncle Tom's Cabin' in *American Quarterly* Fall 1984 No. 4 pp.506–7.
10 Elaine Showalter, 'Piercing and Writing' in Nancy K. Miller (ed.), *Poetics of Gender* (New York: Columbia University Pres, 1986) pp.234–5.
11 William Stanley Braithwaite, 'The Negro in American Literature' in Alain Locke (ed.), *The New Negro* (1925, reprint New York: Atheneum, 1969) pp.29–44.
12 David S. Reynolds, *Beneath the American Renaissance: The Subversive Imagination in the Age of Emerson and Melville* (New York: Knopf, 1988).
13 F. O. Mathiessen, *American Renaissance* (London: Oxford University Press, 1941).
14 David S. Reynolds, *Beneath the American Renaissance: The Subversive Imagination in the Age of Emerson and Melville* (New York: Knopf, 1988) pp.388–9.
15 William R. Taylor, *Cavalier and Yankee* (New York: Harper Torch Books, 1969) p.308.
16 Philip Fisher, *Hard Facts: Setting and Form in the American Novel* (New York: Oxford University Press, 1985) pp.99–100.

SUGGESTIONS FOR FURTHER READING

BIBLIOGRAPHY

Margaret Holbrook Hildreth's *Harriet Beecher Stowe: A Bibliography* (Hamden, Connecticut: Archon, 1976) is the standard and most comprehensive bibliography available. See also Jean W. Ashton, comp. *Harriet Beecher Stowe: A Reference Guide* (Boston: G. K. Hall, 1977).

BIOGRAPHIES

Early biographies include Rose Terry Cooke, 'Harriet Beecher Stowe' in *Our Famous Women*, by Elizabeth Stuart Phelps, et al., pp. 581–601 (Hartford, Connecticut: Worthington, 1884). Charles Edward Stowe (Harriet's son), *Life of Harriet Beecher Stowe: Compiled from Her Letters and Journals* (Boston: Houghton Mifflin, 1889). Annie Fields, (ed.), *Life and Letters of Harriet Beecher Stowe* (Boston: Houghton, Mifflin, 1898).

Constance Mayfield Rourke's *Trumpets of Jubilee* (New York: Harcourt Brace, 1927) has excellent biographical chapters on members of the Beecher family. Forrest Wilson, *Crusader in Crinoline: the Life of Harriet Beecher Stowe* (Philadelphia: Lippincott, 1941) is still the most scholarly biography to date. Other biographies include: Johanna Johnson's *Runaway to Heaven: The Story of Harriet Beecher Stowe and Her Era* (New York: Doubleday, 1963); Edward Wagenknecht's *Harriet Beecher Stowe: the Known and the Unknown* (New York: Oxford University Press, 1965) is a good read, but tends towards flippancy, and Noel B. Gerson, *Harriet Beecher Stowe: A Biography* (New York: Praeger, 1976).

GENERAL STUDIES

A recent study is Edward M. Holmes, *Harriet Beecher Stowe: Woman & Artist* with a foreword by Josephine Donovan (Maine: Northern

Lights, 1992). Another recent study is Theodore Hovet, *The Master Narrative: Harriet Beecher Stowe's Subversive Story of Master and Slave in 'Uncle Tom's Cabin' and 'Dred'* (Boston: University Press of America, 1989). There is a good collection of essays on Harriet Beecher Stowe's novels in Elizabeth Ammons (ed.), *Critical Essays on Harriet Beecher Stowe* (Boston: G. K. Hall, 1980). An updated and useful guide is John R. Adams *Harriet Beecher Stowe* (New York: Twayne, 1963. Rev.: London: Macmillan 1989). Alice C. Crozier, *The Novels of Harriet Beecher Stowe* (New York: Oxford University Press, 1969) marks the turning point in critical studies on Beecher Stowe. A short but entertaining study is found in Laurie Crumpacker's, 'Four Novels of Harriet Beecher Stowe: A Study in Nineteenth-Century Androgyny' in *American Novelists Revisited: Essays in Feminist Criticism*, Fritz Fleischmann (ed.), (Boston: G. K. Hall, 1982, pp.78–106).

FEMINISM AND HARRIET BEECHER STOWE

The following works help to locate Harriet Beecher Stowe in the feminist literary canon: Helen Waite Papashvily's, *All the Happy Endings: A Study of the Domestic Novel in America, the Women Who Wrote It, the Women Who Read It, in the Nineteenth Century*, (pp.70–7) (New York: Harper, 1956); Ellen Moers's, *Literary Women* (pp.55–9,129–30) (Garden City, New York: Anchor/Doubleday, 1977); Sandra M. Gilbert and Susan Gubar, *The Madwoman in the Attic: the Woman Writer and the Nineteenth-Century Imagination* (New Haven: Yale University Press, 1979), and Jane Tompkins, *Sensational Designs* (New York: Oxford University Press).

On the Cult of Domesticity read: Catherine Beecher's *Treatise*, Harriet Beecher Stowe and Catherine Beecher, *The American Woman's Home* (Watkins Glen, New York: Library of Victorian Culture, 1979); Jeanne Boydston, Mary Keley, and Anne Margolis, *The Limits of Sisterhood: The Beecher Sisters on Women's Rights and Women's Sphere* (Chapel Hill: University of North Carolina Press, 1988); Gillian Brown's *Domestic Individualism: Imaging Self in Nineteenth-Century America* (University of California Press, 1990).

For Feminism and Abolition read Jean Fagan Yellin, *Women and Sisters: The Anti-Slavery Feminists in American Culture* (New Haven and London: Yale University Press, 1989).

STUDIES OF *UNCLE TOM'S CABIN*

The best contemporary guide to *Uncle Tom's Cabin* is Josephine Donovan's *'Uncle Tom's Cabin': Evil, Affliction, and Redemptive Love* (Twayne's Masterworks series, Boston: G. K. Hall & Co., 1991). A wide-ranging collection of essays is found in Eric J. Sundquist (ed.), *New Essays on 'Uncle Tom's Cabin'* (Cambridge: Cambridge University Press, 1986). For nineteenth-century cultural background read Thomas F. Gossett's *'Uncle Tom's Cabin' and American Culture* (Dallas: South Methodist University Press, 1985). Those who desire a more general background to the novel should turn to Moira Davison Reynolds *'Uncle Tom's Cabin' and Mid-Nineteenth Century United States: Pen and Consciousness* (Jefferson, N. C. L. McFarland, 1985).

AFRICAN—AMERICAN STUDIES

Theodore Weld's *American Slavery as it is: Testimony of a Thousand Witnesses* (New York: American Anti-Slavery Society, 1839) is a fascinating read for those interested in the sources for *Uncle Tom's Cabin*.

The following books have chapters or sections on *Uncle Tom's Cabin* and Harriet Beecher Stowe's career as a reformer: George M. Frederickson, *The Black Image in the White Mind: The Debate on Afro-American Character and Destiny, 1817–1914* (New York: Harper, 1971); Jean Fagan Yellin, *The Intricate Knot: Black Figures in American Literature, 1776–1863* (New York: New York University Press, 1972); Judith Berzon, *Neither White nor Black: The Mulatto Character in American Fiction* (New York: New York University Press, 1978); William L. Van Deburg, *Slavery and Race in American Popular Culture* (Madison: University of Wisconsin Press, 1984), and Monrose C. Gwin, *Black and White Women of the Old South* (Knoxville: University of Tennessee Press, 1985).

RELIGION

Charles H. Foster, *The Rungless Ladder: Harriet Beecher Stowe and New England Puritanism* (New York: Cooper Square, 1954. Reprint 1970). Gayle Kimball, *The Religious Ideas of Harriet Beecher Stowe:*

Her Gospel of Womanhood (Lewiston, New York: The Edwin Mellen Press, 1982).

GENERAL HISTORICAL AND LITERARY SURVEYS

Lawrence Buell, *New England Literary Culture: From Revolution through Renaissance* (Cambridge: Cambridge University Press, 1986). David S. Reynolds, *Beneath the American Renaissance: The Subversive Imagination in the Age of Emerson and Melville* (New York: Knopf, 1988).

FREDERICK DOUGLASS AND HIS CRITICS

The study of autobiography has gone through many changes over the years. At the turn of this century Georg Misch, a student of Wilhelm Dilthey, approached autobiographies as source material (*document humain*) for understanding the development of the individual. Misch's definition of autobiography, though generous enough to include many literary forms, was essentially Western orientated.[1] This definition was refined by Karl Joachim Weintraub in his *The Value of the Individual* and made even more exclusive:

> This essay will take St Augustine's *Confessions* as its starting point. To begin here is not to say that 'there were no autobiographic writings prior to the *Confessions*.' There was such writing and it has received the attention of scholars. But my interest is less in all the varied forms of autobiographic writing than in that proper form of autobiography wherein a self-reflective person asks 'who am I' and 'how did I become what I am?' I search for conditions of self-conscious individuality. From this vantage point Augustine's great book has a certain claim for special consideration and the nature of classical autobiographic writing has a problematic character.[2]

St Augustine and his *Confessions* (397–401 AD) were not only representative of the age, they (the author and his book) had a paradigmatic status. What is true of the *Confessions* is true also of the critical responses to Douglass's *Narrative*. Robert F. Sayre in 'Autobiography and the Making of America' had this to say of Douglass's story:

> It is repeated in so many black autobiographies – Richard Wright's, James Baldwin's, Malcom X's – that it is truly archetypal. It also shows why autobiography has been the major kind of literature for blacks and most other oppressed Americans. The person who can

write his own story can rise from the status of the unknown and inarticulate and can thus relate that story to others and to the stories of others. The assumed accuracy and authenticity of autobiography – its historicity – give it greater authority than the fictions of novels or the theater, especially since the fictions are more likely to have been written by whites or people who have not had these experiences themselves.[3]

Because it is a canonical text both in American autobiography and in Afro-American studies, it is often used as a criterion by which to measure the literary value of later works. Here James Olney uses Douglass's *Narrative* to authenticate Richard Wright's *Black Boy*:

Just as Frederick Douglass left behind his slave identity and his name when he escaped to the North, so in his departure for Chicago Richard Wright leaves behind his black boy identity and the various names and labels the South had affixed to him.[4]

Robert B. Stepto confirms the special place Frederick Douglass's *Narrative* has in the sub-genre of Slave Narratives. He usefully schematises the different modes of narration within the slave narrative.

Phase I: basic narrative (a): 'eclectic narrative' – authenticating documents and strategies (sometimes including one by the author of the tale) *appended* to the tale

Phase II: basic narrative (b): 'integrated narrative' – authenticating documents and strategies integrated into the tale and formally becoming voices and/or characters in the tale

Phase III:

(a) 'generic narrative' – authenticating documents and strategies are totally subsumed by the tale; the slave narrative becomes an identifiable generic text e.g., autobiography, etc.

(b) 'authenticating narrative' – the tale is subsumed by the authenticating strategy: the slave narrative becomes an authenticating document for other, usually generic texts, e.g., novel, history

What we observe in the first two phases of slave narrative narration is the former slave's ultimate lack of control over his own narrative occasioned primarily by the demands of audience and authentication. This dilemma is not unique to the authors of these narratives;

indeed, many modern black writers still do not control their personal history once it assumes literary form. For this reason, Frederick Douglass's *Narrative of the Life of Frederick Douglass, An American Slave, Written by Himself* (1845) seems all the more a remarkable literary achievement. Because it contains several segregated narrative texts – a preface, a prefatory letter, the tale, an appendix – it appears to be, in terms of the narrative phases, a rather primitive slave narrative. But each of the ancillary texts seems to be drawn to the tale by some sort of extraordinary gravitational pull or magnetic attraction. There is, in short, a dynamic energy between the tale and each supporting text; the Douglass narrative is an integrated narrative of a very special order. While the integrating process does, in a small way, pursue the conventional path of creating characters out of authenticating texts (William Lloyd Garrison silently enters Douglass's tale at the very end), its new and major thrust is the creation of that aforementioned energy that binds the supporting texts to the tale while at the same time removing them from participation in the narrative's rhetorical and authenticating strategies. In short, Douglass's tale dominates the narrative and does so because it alone authenticates the narrative.[5]

Henry Louis Gates reasoned that the more popular a slave narrative was, the more it exploited and shaped the language of the genre. Since Frederick Douglass's *Narrative* was by far the most successful, one could learn about the genre by giving it a structuralist reading. Gates applies the 'classic heuristic device' (Levi-Strauss's structural model of binary opposition) to Frederick Douglass's *Narrative*:

Douglass's narrative demonstrates not only how the deprivation of the hallmarks of identity can affect the slave but also how the slaveowners' world negates and even perverts those very values on which it is built. Deprivation of a birth date, a name, a family structure and legal rights makes of the deprived a brute, a subhuman, says Douglass, until he comes to a consciousness of these relations; yet it is the human depriver who is the actual barbarian, structuring his existence on the consumption of human flesh. Just as the mulatto son is a mediation between two opposed terms, man and animal, so too has Douglass's text become the complex mediator between the world as the master would have it and the world as the slave knows it really is. Douglass has subverted the terms of the code he was meant to mediate: he has been a trickster. As with all mediations the trickster is a mediator and his mediation is a trick – only a trick; for there can be no mediation in this world. Douglass's narrative has aimed to destroy that symbolic code that created the false oppositions themselves. The oppositions, all along, were only arbitrary, not fixed.

Douglass first suggests that the symbolic code created in this text is arbitrary and not fixed, human-imposed not divinely ordained in an ironic aside on the myth of the curse of Ham, which comes in the very center of the seventh paragraph of the narrative and which is meant to be an elaboration on the ramifications of 'this class of slaves' who are fruit of the unnatural liaison between animal and man. If the justification of this order is the curse on Ham and his tribe, if Ham's tribe signified the black African, and if this prescription for enslavement is scriptural, then, Douglass argues, 'it is certain that slavery in the South must soon become unscriptural; for thousands are ushered into the world, annually, who, like myself, owe their existence to white fathers, and those fathers,' he repeats for the fourth time, are 'most frequently their own masters.'[6]

William L. Andrews in 'Poetics of Afro-American Autobiography' has questioned this special paradigmatic status accorded to Douglass's *Narrative* within the genre of Afro-American autobiography:

> Taking Douglass's 1845 *Narrative* as the master text in the history of Afro-American autobiography, Butterfield fashioned a chronicle of black American autobiography that highlights writers whose lives and styles seemed to echo Douglass's. Those who did not fit this mold were generally ignored by Butterfield, although sometimes writers who diverged from Douglass were treated didactically as examples of how black autobiographers could write about the wrong things in the wrong ways. Explicit in Butterfield's work is an ideological test for the inclusion of a black autobiography in his canon, a test based primarily on thematic, not formal, criteria – on what the autobiographies were written about, not on how they were written. Autobiographies that recount what Butterfield believed to be the paradigmatic black experience in America received careful and general celebratory study, blacks who did not lead exemplary – and I mean this in both senses of the word – lives he generally ignored. Thus Booker T. Washington, whom many have called the most influential black autobiographer between 1900 and 1960, receives little more than a couple of brief mentions in *Black Autobiography in America*, and they stress how unrepresentative

Washington's thinking was in comparison to that of his black contemporaries in autobiography. Washington's autobiography does not conform to a tradition of black autobiography that Butterfield defines as central by virtue of the prominence within it of 'the identity crisis, the alienation, the restless movement,' and a particular set of 'views on education, knowledge, and resistance' (p.155). Unfortunately, Butterfield seems to have reached this conclusion about the tradition without considering the more fundamental canon-formation question of how any historian of black autobiography should define representativeness in the genre and what significance he or she should assign to unrepresentative expression.[7]

BIBLIOGRAPHY FOR 'FREDERICK DOUGLASS AND HIS CRITICS'

1 Georg Misch, *A History of Autobiography in Antiquity*, Vol. I (Westport, Connecticut: Greenwood Press Publishers, 1973).

2 Karl Joachim Weintraub, *The Value of the Individual* (Chicago; London: The University of Chicago Press, 1978) p.1.

3 Robert F. Sayre, 'Autobiography and the Making of America' in James Olney (ed.), *Autobiography: Essays Theoretical and Critical* (Princeton, New Jersey: Princeton University Press, 1980) pp.146–68.

4 James Olney 'Some Versions of Memory: The Ontology of Autobiography': in *Autobiography: Essays Theoretical and Critical*.

5 Robert B. Stepto, 'Narration, Authentication, and Authorial Control pp.45–57 in Harold Bloom (ed.) *Narrative of the Life of Frederick Douglass*, Modern Critical Interpretations series (New York, New Haven, Philadelphia: Chelsea House Publisher, 1988).

6 Henry Louis Gates Jnr, 'Binary Oppositions in Chapter, One of the Narrative' pp.59–75 in *Narrative of the Life of Frederick Douglass*, Modern Critical Interpretations series.

7 William L. Andrews, 'Poetics of Afro-American Autobiography' in Houston A. Baker Jnr and Patricia Redmon (eds), *Afro-American Literary Study in the 1990s*. (Chicago: University of Chicago Press, 1989) pp.82–3.

SUGGESTIONS FOR FURTHER READING

BIBLIOGRAPHY AND REFERENCE

John W. Blassingame (ed.), *The Frederick Douglass Papers*. 'Series 1: The Speeches, Debates and Interviews, in four volumes' (New Haven: Yale University Press, 1979–91) is essential reading for any student of Frederick Douglass. This series is the first of a projected three; the others will cover Douglass's writings and letters. Thoroughly annotated, the series will provide the reader with valuable biographic as well as cultural information.

BIOGRAPHIES

Many early biographies have recently been reprinted, some with good bibliographies. Two early biographies are Frederic May Holland's *Frederick Douglass: the Coloured Orator* (New York: Funk and Wagnalls, 1891) and the black novelist Charles W. Chestnutt's *Frederick Douglass* (Boston: Small, Maynard & Co., 1906). The Afro-American leader Booker T. Washington wrote a pioneeering biography of Douglass in 1906, *Frederick Douglass*, (Philadelphia: George W. Jacobs & Co. Philip S. Foner's *Frederick Douglass: A Biography*. (New York: Citadel, 1964) has been superseded, but his earlier work (four volumes) *The Life and Writings of Frederick Douglass* (1950–55) (New York: International Publishers) which contains essays and letters, is invaluable, as is the handy one volume of speeches in Benjamin Quarles (ed.), *Frederick Douglass* (Washington: Associated Presses, 1968). Two other good biographies are Dickson J. Preston's *Young Frederick Douglass: The Maryland Years* (Baltimore; London: Johns Hopkins University Press, 1980) and Nathan Irvin Huggins's *Slave and Citizen: The Life of Frederick Douglass* (Boston: Little, Brown & Co., 1980). On Frederick Douglass and the American Civil War read David W. Blight, *Frederick Douglass's Civil War: Keeping Faith in Jubilee* (Louisiana State University Press, 1989). William S. McFeely, *Frederick*

Douglass (New York: W. W. Norton, 1991) is the fullest and most important biography to date.

For a treatment of the cultural milieu and race ideology read Waldo E. Martin's *The Mind of Frederick Douglass* (Chapel Hill: University of North Carolina Press, 1988).

NARRATIVE

Of recent collections of essays the two most outstanding are Harold Bloom (ed. with introduction), *Narrative of the Life of Frederick Douglass* in the Modern Critical Interpretations series (New York, New Haven, Philadelphia: Chelsea House Publishers, 1988) and Eric J. Sundquist (ed.), *Frederick Douglass: New Literary and Historical Essays* (Cambridge: Cambridge University Press, 1990).

Other articles one might want to refer to include: Nancy T. Clasby 'Frederick Douglass's *Narrative*: A Content Analysis' *CLA Journal* 14 (1971) pp.242–50; Henry Dan Piper, 'The Place of Frederick Douglass's Narrative of an American Slave in the Development of a Native American Prose Style' *The Journal of Afro-American Issues* 5 (1977) pp.183–91; Thomas De Pietro, 'Vision and Revision in the Autobiographies of Frederick Douglass' *CLA Journal* 26 (1983) pp.384–96; Donald B. Gibson, 'Reconciling Public and Private in Frederick Douglass's Narrative' *American Literature* 57 (1985) pp.549–69, and Wilson J. Moses, 'Dark Forests and Barbarian Vigor: Paradox, Conflict, and Africanity in Black Writing Before 1914' *American Literary History* 1 (1989).

FEMINISM AND FREDERICK DOUGLASS

Those interested in this field should read Philip S. Foner, *Frederick Douglass on Women's Rights* (Westport, Connecticut, 1976). There is a very good article on this subject by Stephanie A. Smith 'Heart Attacks: Frederick Douglass's Strategic Sentimentality' *Criticism* (Spring 1992) Vol. XXXIV No. 2. pp.193–216.

AUTOBIOGRAPHY

A good introduction to the study of autobiography is James Olney, (ed.), *Autobiography: Essays Theoretical and Critical* (Princeton, New

Jersey: Princeton University Press, 1980). For a book specifically on Afro-American autobiography read Stephen Butterfield's, *Black Autobiography in America*. (Amherst: University of Massachusetts Press, 1974) and William L. Andrews, *To Tell a Free Story: The First Century of Afro-American Autobiography (1760–1865)* (Urbana: University of Illinois Press, 1986).

SLAVE NARRATIVES

One should look at the many slave narratives available in print (see Chronology for surnames). Arna Bontemps, (ed.), *Great Slave Narratives* (Boston: Beacon Press, 1969) has a good selection. The following books will give the reader a sound introduction to current theories and arguments: Robert B. Stepto and Dexter Fisher (eds), *Afro-Literature: The Reconstruction of Instruction* (New York: Modern Language Association, 1978). Charles Davis and Henry Louis Gates, Jnr, *The Slave's Narrative* (New York: Oxford, 1985). Valerie Smith, *Self-Discovery and Authority in Afro-American Narrative* (Cambridge: Harvard University Press, 1987). Marion W. Starling, *The Slave Narrative: Its Place in American History* (Howard University Press, 1988). On theory itself read Henry Louis Gates, *Black Literature and Literary Theory* (New York: Methuen, 1984) and Houston A. Baker. Jnr, & Patricia Redmond (eds,), *Afro-American Literary Study in the 1990s*. (Chicago: University of Chicago Press, 1989).

On Plantation Life read John Blassingame, *The Slave Community: Plantation Life in the Antebellum South* (New York, Oxford: Oxford University Press, 1972. Rev. and enlarged 1979).

AMERICAN LITERATURE IN EVERYMAN

A SELECTION

Selected Poems
HENRY LONGFELLOW
A new selection spanning the whole of Longfellow's literary career **£7.99**

Typee
HERMAN MELVILLE
Melville's stirring debut, drawing directly on his own adventures in the South Sea **£4.99**

Billy Budd and Other Stories
HERMAN MELVILLE
The compelling parable of innocence destroyed by a fallen world **£4.99**

The Scarlet Letter
NATHANIEL HAWTHORNE
The compelling tale of an independent woman's struggle against a crushing moral code **£3.99**

The Last of The Mohicans
JAMES FENIMORE COOPER
The classic tale of old America, full of romantic adventure **£5.99**

The Red Badge of Courage
STEPHEN CRANE
A vivid portrayal of a young soldier's experience of the American Civil War **£2.99**

Essays and Poems
RALPH WALDO EMERSON
An indispensable edition celebrating one of the most influential American writers **£5.99**

The Federalist
HAMILTON, MADISON, AND JAY
Classics of political science, these essays helped to found the American Constitution **£6.99**

Leaves of Grass and Selected Prose
WALT WHITMAN
The best of Whitman in one volume **£6.99**

£5.99

£4.99

£4.99

CLASSIC NOVELS IN EVERYMAN

A SELECTION

The Way of All Flesh
SAMUEL BUTLER
A savagely funny odyssey from joyless duty to unbridled liberalism **£4.99**

Born in Exile
GEORGE GISSING
A rationalist's progress towards love and compromise in class-ridden Victorian England **£4.99**

David Copperfield
CHARLES DICKENS
One of Dickens' best-loved novels, brimming with humour **£3.99**

The Last Chronicle of Barset
ANTHONY TROLLOPE
Trollope's magnificent conclusion to his Barsetshire novels **£4.99**

He Knew He Was Right
ANTHONY TROLLOPE
Sexual jealousy, money and women's rights within marriage – a novel ahead of its time **£6.99**

Tess of the D'Urbervilles
THOMAS HARDY
The powerful, poetic classic of wronged innocence **£3.99**

Wuthering Heights and Poems
EMILY BRONTE
A powerful work of genius – one of the great masterpieces of literature **£3.50**

Tom Jones
HENRY FIELDING
The wayward adventures of one of literatures most likable heroes **£5.99**

The Master of Ballantrae and Weir of Hermiston
R. L. STEVENSON
Together in one volume, two great novels of high adventure and family conflict **£4.99**

£3.99

£2.99

£3.99

AVAILABILITY

All books are available from your local bookshop or direct from
Littlehampton Book Services Cash Sales, 14 Eldon Way, LinesideEstate, Littlehampton, West Sussex BN17 7HE. PRICES ARE SUBJECT TO CHANGE.

To order any of the books, please enclose a cheque (in £ sterling) made payable to Littlehampton Book Services, or phone your order through with credit card details (Access, Visa or Mastercard) on 0903 721596 (24 hour answering service) stating card number and expiry date. Please add £1.25 for package and postage to the total value of your order.

WOMEN'S WRITING IN EVERYMAN

A SELECTION

Female Playwrights of the Restoration
FIVE COMEDIES
Rediscovered literary treasures in a unique selection **£5.99**

The Secret Self
SHORT STORIES BY WOMEN
'A superb collection' *Guardian* **£4.99**

Short Stories
KATHERINE MANSFIELD
An excellent selection displaying the remarkable range of Mansfield's talent **£3.99**

Women Romantic Poets 1780-1830: An Anthology
Hidden talent from the Romantic era, rediscovered for the first time **£5.99**

Selected Poems
ELIZABETH BARRETT BROWNING
A major contribution to our appreciation of this inspiring and innovative poet **£5.99**

Frankenstein
MARY SHELLEY
A masterpiece of Gothic terror in its original 1818 version **£3.99**

The Life of Charlotte Brontë
MRS GASKELL
A moving and perceptive tribute by one writer to another **£4.99**

Vindication of the Rights of Woman and The Subjection of Women
MARY WOLLSTONECRAFT
AND J. S. MILL
Two pioneering works of early feminist thought **£4.99**

The Pastor's Wife
ELIZABETH VON ARNIM
A funny and accomplished novel by the author of *Elizabeth and Her German Garden* **£5.99**

£4.99

£2.99

£5.99

AVAILABILITY

All books are available from your local bookshop or direct from
Littlehampton Book Services Cash Sales, 14 Eldon Way, LinesideEstate, Littlehampton, West Sussex BN17 7HE. PRICES ARE SUBJECT TO CHANGE.

To order any of the books, please enclose a cheque (in £ sterling) made payable to Littlehampton Book Services, or phone your order through with credit card details (Access, Visa or Mastercard) on 0903 721596 (24 hour answering service) stating card number and expiry date. Please add £1.25 for package and postage to the total value of your order.

POETRY IN EVERYMAN

A SELECTION

Silver Poets of the Sixteenth Century

EDITED BY
DOUGLAS BROOKS-DAVIES
A new edition of this famous
Everyman collection **£6.99**

Complete Poems

JOHN DONNE
The father of metaphysical verse in
this highly-acclaimed edition **£4.99**

Complete English Poems, Of Education, Areopagitica

JOHN MILTON
An excellent introduction to
Milton's poetry and prose **£6.99**

Selected Poems

JOHN DRYDEN
A poet's portrait of Restoration
England **£4.99**

Selected Poems

PERCY BYSSHE SHELLEY
'The essential Shelley' in one
volume **£3.50**

Women Romantic Poets 1780-1830: An Anthology

Hidden talent from the Romantic era,
rediscovered for the first time **£5.99**

Poems in Scots and English

ROBERT BURNS
The best of Scotland's greatest lyric
poet **£4.99**

Selected Poems

D. H. LAWRENCE
A newly-edited selection spanning
the whole of Lawrence's literary
career **£4.99**

The Poems

W. B. YEATS
Ireland's greatest lyric poet
surveyed in this ground-breaking
edition **£6.50**

£5.99

£4.99

£3.50

DRAMA
IN EVERYMAN

A SELECTION

Everyman and Medieval Miracle Plays

EDITED BY A. C. CAWLEY
A selection of the most popular medieval plays **£3.99**

Complete Plays and Poems

CHRISTOPHER MARLOWE
The complete works of this fascinating Elizabethan in one volume **£5.99**

Complete Poems and Plays

ROCHESTER
The most sexually explicit – and strikingly modern – writing of the seventeenth century **£5.99**

Restoration Plays

Five comedies and two tragedies representing the best of the Restoration stage **£7.99**

Female Playwrights of the Restoration: Five Comedies

Rediscovered literary treasures in a unique selection **£5.99**

Poems and Plays

OLIVER GOLDSMITH
The most complete edition of Goldsmith available **£4.99**

Plays, Poems and Prose

J. M. SYNGE
The most complete edition of Synge available **£6.99**

Plays, Prose Writings and Poems

OSCAR WILDE
The full force of Wilde's wit in one volume **£4.99**

A Doll's House/The Lady from the Sea/The Wild Duck

HENRIK IBSEN
A popular selection of Ibsen's major plays **£3.99**

£2.99

£2.99

£2.99

AVAILABILITY

All books are available from your local bookshop or direct from
Littlehampton Book Services Cash Sales, 14 Eldon Way, LinesideEstate, Littlehampton, West Sussex BN17 7HE. PRICES ARE SUBJECT TO CHANGE.

To order any of the books, please enclose a cheque (in £ sterling) made payable to Littlehampton Book Services, or phone your order through with credit card details (Access, Visa or Mastercard) on 0903 721596 (24 hour answering service) stating card number and expiry date. Please add £1.25 for package and postage to the total value of your order.